SOLAR WINDS

CROSSROADS

BRYAN G. SHEWMAKER

Special Thanks

To my editors, particularly Cayce and Crystal of Kingsman Editing, for their many extra miles.

Act—I: Respite

CHAPTER
1A

THE YEARS OF POSTURING, of threats, false alarms, and bold statements were over. War had come to the Hourglass Galaxy. Warships of the Interstellar Combine flooded out of the galactic disc and traded fire with the surprised and outnumbered forces of the Solar Empire. Warp-driven missiles hurtled across space on firing lines light-years across. These were the opening shots of the greatest war either power, perhaps any power, had ever fought. And Robert Panzer was missing it.

His nameless ship hung in low orbit over a blue star. Doors in the ship's belly hung open, drinking the star's plasma. Deep in the ship, hydrogen was fused into heavier elements—the raw materials to fuel ongoing repairs. Like newly hatched spiders, swarms of repair drones crawled over the ship's invisible facets and dined on the buffet of work laid out for them.

Near the center of the ship, its master's remains floated in a tank of amber fluid. Shortly after his battle with the Vaar warlord, Oul'sor, Robert Panzer had died. But this was not his first death, and likely it would not be the last. The Total Trauma Tank, known as the deep-fryer to soldiers who used it, could do a lot with very little. New muscle, new sinew, new blood and cybernetics—it would manufacture them all. All while the nanites in the amber fluid preserved the brain, or what remained of it.

If the deep-fryer had a flaw, it was that it was only built to do the job correctly. Its creators didn't give thought to doing it quickly. The patient remained sedated, only awakened once they were removed. But the mind of a powerful metapsion was not so easily suppressed.

The first time Panzer's consciousness came, he had no eyes with which to see. The second time, he caught a glimpse of new cyberbones that would replace his spinal column. The third time, he saw the beginnings of new internal organs. With nothing to do but wait and float, countless questions turned over in his mind.

What the hell happened on Avalon?

The station had carried enough firepower to trade blows with a battleship. Yet not once did he see its arsenal come to life. When he fought the DOS team, he should have been tripping over legionnaires to lend aid. Yet none ever showed. So many operational failures. Too many to explain.

But all those questions yielded to another. Oul'sor had won.

Panzer saw it clearly, felt it. The instant of incredible heat as the particle cannons fired. The numbness as his body vaporized. He saw Simmonne, her body swept away in a wave of fire. For want of a better word, it was her destiny to die on that station. But he was alive. Simmonne was alive and on his ship. So few had the gift of providence, and so little of it was understood. But there was one truth to the "gift." No true provident had *ever* managed to change the outcome of a vision. Not one had ever experienced an event unfold in any way other than exactly how they had foreseen it. Was he really an exception?

There had to be another explanation.

Never make a miracle out of what perspective can explain. Eye-witness reports were science's lowest tier of evidence. He had sustained so many injuries. His brain had been baked by apollium. His body fell apart as his armor was removed.

When the wave came, everything froze except for the beams of Oul'sor's cannons. They were binary weapons, gamma rays surrounding a particle stream—both were sequenced to hit their target at the same time. The wave struck in that unfathomably minuscule gap between the firing of the particles and the gamma rays. Then he died. That answer tasted like a lie. But what else could it be? Brain trauma. He was remembering, yet he had to be remembering incorrectly.

There were only three possibilities: He had a vision and managed to change it. He somehow went back in time and tried again. Or he was not remembering things as they were.

The first was impossible. The second was preposterous. That only left the third.

"Colonel, can you hear me?"

The feminine voice was far away, but with each word, it came closer.

Andira. She would have a full recording. She could tell him what happened.

"Colonel? Robert? Please answer."

She had to know.

"Sir, can you hear me?"

"I hear you." His voice expelled from him like a dehydrated whisper. He opened his eyes slowly. Too many times he had learned the hard way. Do not open new eyes to the stupidly bright lights of the infirmary.

SYSTEM INTEGRITY CHECK—RUNNING . . .

The characters in his Neuro-Optic Display were too large, obscuring most of his vision. New flesh, new bones, new nanites inhabiting every cell. Brain trauma. He would have to reprogram his preferences. Like a small child just learning that they were a cyborg, and what to do with that information.

"Can you understand me, sir?"

With his sight adjusting, Panzer could make out the pair of cyan eyes staring into his. A mane of snow-white hair cascaded down a well-designed body clad in a Sylvanni corissè—little more than a corset with generous cutouts at the front and sides. Black fabric to contrast the hair. Andira in her peripheral body.

"Can you understand me, sir?" she repeated.

"I—" He paused and turned his head to cough out one last cup of nanite suspension from his lungs. "I understand you."

"Very well," she answered. She raised one arm clad in a long black glove, and a hologram illuminated above her palm.

Panzer let out an annoyed sigh.

"You know I have to give you a cognition test," Andira preempted his complaint. Companion AI, she'd use any excuse to fuss over him. She was not about to waste a legitimate one.

"Red triangle," Panzer answered as he viewed the hologram.

Andira nodded, and the image in her palm changed. The cycle was slow at first but hastened as Panzer continued to answer.

"Two yellow squares. Three green octagons. Seven silver cylinders. Two orange hexagons. One . . ." Panzer paused as he looked at the shifting image. "Is that a damn tesseract?"

"If I show you the same images each time, you will memorize the pattern," Andira answered. "What color is the tesseract?"

"It's the color that's pissing me off."

"And what color is pissing you off?" Andira continued without hesitation.

"Yellow."

She lowered her hand. "What is one plus one?"

"Eleven," Panzer barked. "Can we speed this up?"

"Sarcastic answers will only extend test duration. Two plus two, please."

Panzer rolled his new eyes. "Four."

"What is six hundred multiplied by the square root of nine?"

"Eighteen hundred."

Andira nodded.

"Correct. If 3X is nine-nine-nine, what is X?"

"Three thirty-three. Speed it up, Andira."

"Colonel, your math skills were significantly superior to the average Solar's. I cannot modify your nanites to properly assist without assessing your current capabilities."

Her words carried the chill of a bitter wind. If she had to make adjustments, then something had changed.

"How bad is it?"

Andira shook her head. "Please focus on the questions until test completion."

"Then. Hurry. Up," Panzer whispered loudly.

"If you multiply the ninth decimal of pi by itself and divide by two, what is the result?"

Panzer huffed, glancing at the ceiling for a moment. "If you mean the decimal to be a whole number, four-point-five."

"If you count the number of fives and nines in the first million digits of pi, and multiply those numbers by each other, what is the result?"

He contemplated for a moment, and the numbers flashed behind his eyes. His neural nanites computed the problem, and the answer arrived on his lips. "There are 100,359 fives, 100,106 nines. The product of those two numbers is 10,046,538,054."

"What is—"

"Andira!" he snapped. "My brain and my nanites are obviously working. Now tell me. How bad is it?"

She knew just how far she could push him. Slowly she peeled a pair of devices from his temples. "Bad, sir," she finally admitted what he knew. "The good news is that your brain-nanite interlinks are working correctly. But your brain is not, and your nanites are having to compensate. Your brain can no longer control the cybernetics of your respiratory system. Nearly all motor control is now being handled by your nanites as well.

"Cognition is worse. Your nanites had to solve all but the most basic problems for you. With the level of burden they are now carrying, maintenance functions will suffer. I'm sorry, Colonel, your preexisting condition has worsened."

Though prepared for it, hearing it was no easier. Panzer closed his eyes and leaned his head back on the table. "How long?"

"I can only estimate—"

"Answer the question."

"Sir. I estimate a twenty- to twenty-five-year reduction in your life expectancy. Quality of life decline will begin between five and ten."

Panzer's right fist began to clench before he forced it to relax. "Figures."

"Sir?"

He shook his head. "Nothing."

Panzer opened his eyes and stepped off the reclining table before stretching his new body. He paused to glare down at Andira. "Am I taller than I was?"

Andira turned away before offering a freshly printed set of clothes. "Colonel, counseling is recommended."

"I'm definitely taller." He laid his hand on her scalp before drawing it to his chest.

"Your skeleton required complete replacement," Andira answered. "That allowed me to restore the height lost by your incident on Menallus. You have been returned to a height of 228.06 centimeters."

"Menallus?" Panzer repeated the name. Was it brain trauma? Or had he been doing this job so long that he could no longer remember every major injury? "Great. Now I have to refit all my armor."

"I am already attending to it," Andira answered as he took the clothes. A simple vest, pants, and boots.

"Well, you're just too damned efficient."

Panzer began to dress, but as he stepped into his pants, his balanced failed. Andira's peripheral body may have had the look of a delicate strumpet, but she had no trouble halting his mass as he fell onto her. She guided him upright again and ignored his complaints as she finished dressing him.

"Colonel, counseling—"

Panzer raised his hand, and she was silent. "Not the first hit my time's taken. I have work to do."

Andira bowed her head, and his NOD flooded with data as his connection to the ship was restored.

"Damn it." He groaned as he reviewed the information. This was one of those days. Days that only came with bad news.

The moment he took a step, Andira did the same, and he turned back to her.

"You don't need to follow me. I'll be fine."

"Sir, I would prefer to keep this unit near you—"

"Not necessary," he interrupted. "But, what you can do—give me your full log of the fight with Oul'sor."

"I am sorry, sir, but I cannot comply."

"Of course not," he said as the infirmary doors parted for him. "Dare I ask why?"

"Damage to your armor destroyed most of my processing systems. I was forced to convert what survived of data storage into rapid-access rewrite to maintain my program."

Panzer closed his eyes and took a deep breath.

"What about my memory index? Was it uploaded properly?"

"The index record was uploaded, however, cranial trauma resulted in the writing of corrupted data. It is highly unlikely I will be able to recover it."

Panzer stared deep into his Neuro-Optic Display.

>>*ACCESS MEMORY INDEX*

>>*DATA INTEGRITY CHECK, DAY-185 100,0016 AN*

Red characters answered him.

ERROR—DATA CORRUPTION

UNRECOVERABLE

RECOMMEND DELETION OF SPECIFIC INDEX FILE

That was it then. He would never know exactly what happened in that fight. But there was no time to dwell on it. He knew he was needed in the CIC, but something else pulled at him. There was someone he suspected who needed his attention even more at the moment.

CHAPTER
1B

OR GENERATIONS THE TITLE of Imperial Rose had been carried by the final daughter of the reigning emperor. She was said to have a special relationship with the population, as the scion least likely to inherit the throne. The most approachable, with whom a social flub or misspoken word was least likely to offend a future sovereign. Each Imperial Rose was born into the role of goodwill ambassador of the Mandrake Dynasty. The current Imperial Rose was the twenty-seventh princess of the Solar Empire, Simmonne Mandrake. In the darkness of an unfamiliar room, she lay curled up on a giant couch. There were no more tears left for aching eyes to cry. So instead she was silent.

They were gone.

In her earliest memories, running through the corridors of the Cathedral, their faces were there. The media had long ago taken to calling them "Rose Thorns," the Imperial Rose's cadre of gamma aren bodyguards. Most gammas and betas did not have names, only serial numbers. Names were reserved for those in positions where forming personal relationships was a part of the job. Among her guards, only Isis, as their captain, had been created with a name. But as a child, Simmonne had named them all.

Amaryllis, Anemone, Angelica, Aster, Alyssum, Begonia, Browalia, Buttercup, Canna, Carnation, Catmint, Celosia, Cleome, Daffodil, Dahlia, Daisy, Delphia, Gaura, Geranium, Helconia, Holly, Hosta, Lantana, Lilac, Lily, Lotus, Lupine, Malva, Marigold, Orchid, Pentas, Peony, Rue, Vervain, and Zinnia. She recounted them all. To an aren, the emperor was the supreme authority, the source of all that was right and just. To know that a member of the Solar family had bothered to give them a name meant so much to them. Arens were so devoid of vanity or pretension, yet their names meant so much that they had them etched into their guns. Each even wore their namesake flower so others could know the names they held like a divine gift. Now they were gone. Killed by the Vaar . . . *monsters.*

Simmonne understood now why the quants called them that. She could not tear the images out of her mind. The blood flowing from Isis's mouth as she was hefted on a bayonet. Of Lilac, and her body split in two. Of Cleome lying motionless on the ground. They deserved so much better than to die those horrible deaths.

Jenna and the Twins were gone as well. Each time she thought of the Vaar carrying them away, an empty stomach tried to retch. Where were they now? What were the monsters doing to them? Were they still alive? Would she see them again? What was she supposed to do without them?

A quiet hiss preceded a blinding light, and she raised her arm. The sleeve of her dress shielded her eyes as she tried to look at the door without staring into the light pouring through it. Her eyes adjusted enough for her to see the enormous silhouette in the doorway. Him. The darkness returned as he stepped inside and the door slid shut. Heavy footfalls sounded on the metal floor, and the couch gave as he sat by her feet. Without thinking she rose and crawled into his lap. Her hands gripped his vest tightly as she pressed her cheek into him. If only she could sense him. Feel his confidence, his sympathy, something. But there was nothing, an empathic singularity from which nothing escaped.

"How are you feeling?" He finally broke the silence.

She shook her head, clinging tighter to the fabric of his vest. "They're really dead," she whispered. "Aren't they?"

"Yes," he answered, coiling his arms around her.

She sniffed, the ache in her eyes increasing as tears tried to start again. "It's my fault," she whispered.

"What?"

She took a breath. "Their leader, the one who hates you. He told us to surrender—called out to me. I was so afraid, I couldn't say anything. I couldn't tell them to surrender." The Vaar warlord's words echoed in her mind. "If I told them to surrender, they'd still be alive."

"No."

No? She raised her eyes to stare up at his chin. "What do you mean?"

"They wouldn't have surrendered, even if you told them to," he answered. "Bonded arens know that their charges might become attached to them. They'd never obey an order to hand you over to an enemy, even if it came directly from you."

"But—"

"No buts." His whisper was soft but firm. "From the day they came out of the tank, their one job was to protect you. Trust me when I tell you, they would not have obeyed. They would rather die than give you up to an enemy. Nothing you could have said would have stopped their captain from countermanding you. Be sad they're gone. Miss them. But do not blame yourself for it."

She lowered her gaze, chewing on her words. There was a question she did not want to ask, but she had to know the answer. "Where were you?"

His chest expanded as he took a breath. "I was in the Combine Embassy. Admiral Aetius called me. The Vaar changed their communications codes so we couldn't eavesdrop. I went to their embassy to get the new codes."

"Codes?" she whispered, shifting in his lap to sit up. Her arms began to tremble as her fingers coiled into fists. Her whispers soon gave way to screams. "You left us for some codes? It's your fault! You were supposed to protect us! It was your job to be there if something like this happened! And you were off stealing *codes*?"

Her fists hammered into his chest. When her left hand came down on his collarbone, she let out a shriek. The biting sting rang through her knuckles, her wrist, and up to her elbow.

"My guards are dead!" she screamed as his hands closed on her forearms. "Jenna, Julie, Jennifer. They're gone because of you! Why weren't you there? Why didn't you save them?"

"Stop hitting me." He articulated his words slowly. "My bones are bond-forged titanium. You will break your hands. I came as soon as I realized what was happening. I did everything I could."

"You let them go!" she screamed again, shaking her head and jerking against his grip. "You let the Vaar take them. Why didn't you do more? Why didn't you try harder?"

She winced as his grip on her arms tightened, and he stood before he gently set her on her feet. "I did everything I could." He spoke low and precisely. "Everything, trying to save the four of you. And for my trouble, I was shot, hit with an orbit strike, blasted, set on fire, and kicked *through* a building."

He took another deep breath, seeming to calm himself before speaking again in a whisper.

"Just how much harder do you think I could have tried?"

She sneered and tried to pull out of his grip. "Let go of me. Let go now!"

"Calm. Down," he growled, fear worming its way through her anger. "Now I am sorry about your guards. But my job was to investigate possible threats and be ready to assist if they called for it. That is what I did, and you're not going to accuse me of not trying. I did everything I could. If Oul'sor wasn't more concerned with killing me than doing his job, they'd probably have you, too."

He lowered her arms but maintained his grip.

Torn between hate and despair, all she could do was stare into his chest. Everything was cold; everything was dead. She barely noticed when he let go of one arm to take her chin and turn her head to the side. His other hand moved to her shoulder, and with a prod, he guided her with him.

A wall-mount printer was nestled in a crevice beside the couch. He stared at the device for a moment, and it let out a growl as cloth began to pour out of it into his hand. She was beyond comprehending what was happening. Her consciousness retreated inward, hiding deep behind her eyes. He led her to the end of the room. Only the dazzle of a light switched on brought her some awareness.

She was in a washroom, and he laid the fabric he had printed on the counter.

"You'll feel better after you clean up," he said, forcing her to take a step toward a glass door before releasing her arm. "I'll wait outside."

Her head turned toward him as he stepped away. "Colonel?" He stopped. "Can you rescue them?"

He shook his head. "No," he said aloud, tearing her heart down with the word. "By now, the Vaar will have taken them to their flagship. They'll be held there until a ransom can be negotiated with your father. They're civilians, and important ones at that. The Vaar won't hurt them. Give it time. A few weeks, and you'll be with them again."

"No. No, that's not good enough."

"My mission now is to get you back to the Empire safely. Then, once you're safe, I'll see what the Corps can do for them."

"But you can save them!" she protested, stepping closer to him. "You're a commando. You're the Crykeeper! Those Vaar, I sensed it. They were afraid of you, a—a deep, seething fear like I've never felt before. If you can't do it, why are they so afraid of you?"

She moved closer, grabbing his vest again, only for him to take hold of her arms and reposition them at her side.

"I'm only one man. They're on the Vaar flagship, Simmonne. There's no way I could mount a rescue operation of that scale with just my team. When we return to the Empire, I'll talk with the commandant myself. That's the best I can do right now."

She shook her head defiantly as he guided her to face the shower again.

"Clean up, we'll get you something to eat, and go from there."

He ignored her protest and closed the door.

For several minutes, she stood in silence, simply staring at the transparent door. Finally she looked down at herself in the light. Her dress was torn in many places, caked in dirt and tiny speckles of blood amid the stains. Blood, probably Isis's. Her arms began to shake as she clawed the fabric off her body, flinging the ruined garment away from her.

She hated to admit that he was right about anything. Grime covered her like the slime of her haunting memory, but what was she supposed to do? Every day of her life, Jenna had bathed her—groomed her. Royalty had servants to do those things. Status. Always status.

How useless she was. She couldn't even manage her body alone. It could not be that hard. Ordinary people took care of themselves. Soap, water, sonics—they could not be that hard to figure out. She pressed the glass door several times before realizing it was meant to swing out. Once inside she scanned the tile walls for an optical port. But she found none. How was she supposed to turn it on?

"Hot water, Majesty?" a feminine voice asked, causing her to jump.

"Yes," she answered hesitantly. "Hot."

It was the colonel's AI. A moment later, water fell from above like a planet's rain.

"Hotter," she whispered. Maybe the AI complied, but the water still felt cold on her skin. "Hotter." She shook her head in frustration, and her voice cracked when she repeated the command.

"Majesty, if I raise the water temperature any higher, it will be unsafe."

Simmonne hung her head and found the shower's corner. She sank slowly, not even feeling the tug when she sat on her hair.

"Make it a bath," she whispered.

"Yes, Majesty," the water began to pool, rising until it found her neck. Bubbles rose out of the current now passing through the water, and Simmonne pressed herself more firmly into the corner.

"Hotter."

CHAPTER
1C

ALL REALITY WAS DARKNESS. There was no concept of time, awareness, or sensation. At long intervals characters would scroll through the black with no mind to perceive them. Yet pain could exist even without awareness, and when awareness came in transitory forms, it knew the pain was there. Occasionally a flash of light pierced the darkness, but it would not last. Yet each time the light did come, the awareness it sought became stronger. What controlled the light? What did the characters moving in the darkness mean? In time, awareness progressed to the point that it could wonder despite not knowing the words to ask the question. Like a newborn realizing that it controlled its arms without knowing what they were called.

The mind of a Solar had three levels: the consciousness, the subconscious, and the digital conscious. The digital conscious existed as a result of the nanites inhabiting every cell of the body and their interface to the brain. It was through the digital conscious that perceptions such as the Neuro-Optic Display were projected into the conscious mind. Similarly it was through the digital conscious that commands given consciously to the body via the NOD would be carried to their destination.

Under ordinary circumstances, a Solar had no general awareness of their digital consciousness. No more than they did about what occurred in their subconscious mind. At most they might gain passing notice of it when falling asleep or when waking from slumber. To have an extended perception of the digital conscious—where the analog computing of the organic mind and the digital computing of the nanites met—was never a good sign. Yet each time the light returned, the consciousness came a little closer to restoration.

Who was he? Where was he? Why was everything dark? Why did he know he was in pain, yet not feel it? The mind was gaining the ability to ask questions, but it had no answers. The light returned, and it was so powerful that it merely traded the blindness of the darkness for the blindness of light. More pain came with it. Muscles clenched unnaturally, harder than they should, forced to move without the will of their body guiding them. They relaxed, the light faded, and darkness returned.

QUATERNARY REANIMATION PROTOCOL UNDERWAY . . .
EXTERNAL POWER—AVAILABLE
EXTERNAL NUTRIENTS—AVAILABLE
EXTERNAL RESOURCES—ADEQUATE

WARNING: NEUROLOGICAL DEGRADATION CATEGORY 2
MEMORY FAILURE
AUTONOMIC CONTROL IMPAIRED
NERVE RECEPTION INHIBITED
SYNAPTIC BRIDGING COMPROMISED
REANIMATION NOT ADVISED—ADDITIONAL RESOURCES REQUIRED.

The words meant something. But what? Were they telling him to wake up? Were they a warning?

INJECTION RECEIVED—MULTICOMPLEX
DOPAMINE
SEROTONIN
NOREPINEPHRINE
G.A.B.A.
ACETYLCHOLINE

The list continued for some time before the light returned briefly, as if only to remind the darkness that it was around.

ATTEMPTING NEUROLOGICAL REPAIR . . .
WARNING: UNRECOVERABLE MEMORY NODES
REPAIR FAILED. RESTRUCTURING UNRECOVERABLE NODES . . .

When the light returned again, the mind made out a shadow in its core, a shape, maybe a head and neck? There was something else, neither light nor darkness.

SENSORY RESTORATION—AUDIO
EAR STRUCTURE—REPAIRED
AUDIO-NEURO RECEPTION—REPAIRED
AUDIO-NEUROPROCESSING—RESTORATION IN PROGRESS . . .

What was this sensation called? It came and went in distinct forms. Some of it in patterns, others seemingly at random. But neurons were firing, and he was beginning to understand. The sensation came back, but not from around him. It seemed to come from within, spilling out into infinity and curving back to meet him.

He was screaming.

A switch had been flipped, and reality coalesced around him. His muscles clenched as electric shocks moved through his body. His back had arched off the table, his limbs held down by metal bands.

SELF-AWARENESS RESTORED
CONSCIOUS SIGNAL PROCESSING ACTIVE

His head whipped around as the pain continued to jolt through his body. He was in a large room, surrounded by strange aliens. The light obscured his vision of them, but a hand with two fingers and two thumbs took him by the chin. A moment later a needle pierced his neck.

The creature wore a gray uniform. Its skin was brightly colored in tones he could not name. A rigid crest rose from above its eyes in the teardrop extending above the crown of the skull. But it was the eyes he looked into.

Large and yellow. In each eye five pupils were arrayed in a pentagon around a sixth. He knew what this creature was called, but he could not find the name. The light faded, seeming to take the pain with it. His mouth shut, and he settled back into the embrace of darkness.

What was that creature called? For that matter, what was he called? He could almost think it. He could not bring it to the center of his mind from the depths of himself. Eyes—his eyes controlled the arrival and departure of the light. When he opened them this time, he saw more when he looked down at himself.

Metal bands held his wrists at his side, and a hose had been linked to each arm. One hose was clear, and fluids were spilling forth from it into his blood. The other hose was opaque, and the source of the pain that kept ripping through his muscles. But something else was wrong. The longer he stared, the weaker he became. Eventually the four-digit hand returned and pressed his head down against the table. His breathing cleared as a tight sensation eased from his neck. He had been strangling himself.

He looked toward the one holding his head down. The creature was the source of some of the noise. Talking. It was talking to the others. Why couldn't he think of their name? Another needle came to his neck, and his eyes seemed to close of their own volition.

SYNAPTIC BRIDGING COMPLETE
DAMAGED SECTORS REFORMATTED
RUNNING RECALL ALLOCATION . . .

His name. He knew it. It was almost there.

Thousands of images flashed through his mind as if life were passing him by in an instant. A home far away. Training. Faces. A battle, an injury. Death.

His name was Jonathan Clearwater, and he had died.

He drew in a deep breath and clenched his teeth as another electric charge traveled through his left arm to the rest of his body. His name was Jonathan Clearwater, Third Lieutenant of the Solar Legionnaires, and now a prisoner of war. On ND-31 the Solar Legionnaires had fought the, the . . . the Combine. That was the name of their nation. But the aliens. The ones who had killed him. Huge, angry. Vaar.

The aliens around him were shorter than the average man. They lacked a Vaar's covering of rigid plates; their only plates covered their foreheads. Their hands and feet had only four digits rather than seven. They had the eyes, the strange six-pupil eyes. They were Viss, the females of the species. If he was surrounded by Viss, then he was their prisoner.

There were stories of what the Vaar did to their prisoners. Yet another injection came to his neck, trying to push him back into darkness as his awareness reformed. The Vaar had killed him on ND-31, but now they were trying to reanimate him. He drifted again, his reality yet another blur.

They were trying to bring him back. If the things he had heard were true, it might be better if they did not succeed.

CHAPTER
1D

"FOR THOSE JUST JOINING the broadcast, we are receiving confirmed reports from the Cathedral that a member of the Solar Family has survived."

Voices, far away. Quiet but growing louder.

"We're receiving word now. There has been one survivor. First Prince Steven Mandrake is alive. I repeat, First Prince Steven Mandrake is alive. We are being told that he is being tended to by doctors aboard the Cathedral. We have no update on his condition, but we will share those as soon as we receive them."

Steven Mandrake's eyes opened as he sought out the source of the sound. At the foot of his bed, a hologram screen provided the feed from Andromeda News Network. He closed his eyes and brought his hands up to his face. His jaw had returned right where it was supposed to be at the bottom of his head. His throat was closed, and he breathed unaided. He opened his eyes again.

He recognized the white walls of a hospital room. But as he panned his head, he jumped. A figure stood next to his bed, looming over him like some form of sentry. No delta aren bodyguard.

Indorai.

"Shh," came a voice in his mind. So strange, the words speaking to him in perfect clarity. *"The others cannot see me. Cannot sense me. They'll be coming soon. Speak as I speak, give them my words, and all will be well."*

Steven nodded as he sat up in the bed. He grabbed the blanket and pulled it aside to see his new legs. Everything was where it was supposed to be.

"I told you all would be well. Keep focused now."

Steven took a breath, trying to relax as his memory of the last few days came flooding back.

"It is almost time, Steven. Follow Indorai's guidance, and you will have what is yours."

The Encephalon. The combination of countless voices speaking together, seeming to rise from the floor and slither from the walls. It had not been a dream. From deep in the Cathedral's vaults, the ancient one spoke to him.

"*I will,*" he answered.

He looked around the room for his wife, for Natalie. He expected to find her here, at his side, waiting for him to wake. But she was not here. Maybe she had stepped out for a while. Surely that was it.

They were gone. His parents, his brothers, his sisters. No one remained to take what was his. No one could deny him from taking it. It was only a matter of time now. He would go before the Senate, and they would wring their hands. They would ask questions. The nobles would make their speeches, showing everyone how they were the adults in the room. When they were finished, the senators would put on great theater, performing for their electorate. But in the end, they would hold their confirmation. He would be named emperor. Steven tried not to giggle. Thousands of nights in sleepless ambition, and now it was almost his. He would have his throne, and Natalie would have hers.

Steven turned when the door opened. Indorai's image became even thinner as the lights brightened. Two men in doctor's coats, four in fine suits. Finally two more wearing the light-blue jackets of Solar Marshals. One of the marshals sported a cybernetic for his right eye, which reflected green from an oversized lens.

"That didn't take long," Steven remarked as they approached his bed.

"Your Majesty," one of the finely dressed men began. Steven recognized Andol Seyestan, Executor of the Solar Court. A man who had spent all of Steven's life shoulder-deep in his father's anus. "We've been waiting for you to wake. I'm afraid we don't greet you with good news."

Steven sat up higher. He needed to look distressed, worried.

"Be calm. Show them an unflappable leader." Indorai did not bother to whisper. It did not matter. They could not hear him.

"Tell me," he said, taking a moment to make eye contact with each of them. He kept his eyes wide in anticipation and made the effort to tense his muscles.

"Majesty, there's no good way to say this. Your family. You're the only survivor of the attack. You and Princess Simmonne are all who remain. But we don't know where she is, or her condition."

"They're all dead?" Steven asked, still panning from one set of eyes to another. "*All* of them?" Steven nodded slowly as if in realization, then reclined in the bed.

"I'm afraid so, Majesty."

Steven looked past the foot of the bed and at the white wall. Each muscle in his face needed to react. His eyes needed to be far away. "There's more, isn't there?"

"Yes, Majesty," Seyestan continued. "While you were incapacitated, the Combine issued a formal declaration of war. They have crossed the neutral zone and invaded the Auchard region. At last report they had landed troops on more than a dozen worlds, including Avalon. Contact with the region is proving difficult to maintain. But at last report, we're losing the Hourglass."

Steven watched out of the corner of his eye as Seyestan wrung his hands.

"Majesty, until the Senate confirms you as emperor, you cannot declare war. But under the Crises and Succession Edict, as first prince, authority over military deployment falls to you. The Executor of Defense has a briefing prepared. But the Solar Marshals insist on speaking with you first."

Steven's heart began to race as Indorai confirmed what he suspected.

"Both telepaths," Indorai mused as his hollow image walked a circle around the group. *"Let them freely into your mind."*

"But—"

"They will see what I wish them to see," Indorai assured him. *"I will create a fiction for them, and they will believe what they must."*

"You are certain?"

"Absolutely."

"Majesty?" One of the marshals strengthened his inflection to regain Steven's attention. Steven recognized this one, too. Dalhee Sinj, Vice Executor of his organization.

"Do you know what happened?" Steven asked. "How the Vaar got into the Cathedral?"

"We believe so, sir," Sinj answered. "But we cannot comment on it at this time."

Of course not. Civilian police had to investigate every death as a homicide until they determined otherwise. The marshals had to assume he had committed fratricide until convinced of something else.

Steven nodded slowly. "Am I really the only one?"

Steven heard Indorai chuckle at the question. *"I suppose that works. Shock, disbelief. It may help them believe."*

"Majesty," Sinj began as he motioned to his partner with the green eye. "Agent Wyrchek is one of the agency's best telepaths. We know you've been through a lot. So if you have no objection, we will skip formal questioning, and he will gather the information we need."

"You are sure about this?" Steven asked, careful not to look directly at Indorai, who now stood behind the pair of marshals.

"Do not be afraid. I am ready."

"Fine," Steven answered as his throat went dry. "Do what you must."

"This will only take a moment, Majesty," Agent Wyrchek remarked in a voice a bit too effeminate for a grown man. "Just look into my eyes, and try to relax."

Steven drew in a deep breath and focused his gaze on Wyrchek's biologic eye. He made no effort to ward his mind. But as seconds ticked past, he felt no indication of the deep scan the man was to perform.

Wyrchek seemed to gaze through him, speaking in a high-pitched monotone. Steven kept his eyes forward but made out the image of Indorai's hands at both sides of the marshal's head.

"The Vaar attacked while they were eating breakfast. They had just sat down. His Majesty, the emperor, was giving them new assignments. The Vaar blew the doors."

The marshal took a breath, and his pupils contracted as he strained to look deeper.

"They had no warning. No intruder alert. Grenades, a small strike team. The Imperial Guard was taken by surprise. Steven, a grenade took his legs. He tried to cover Princess Brittany with his body. Pain in the neck, darkness. Sounds of fighting. Fading."

"Trust me always," Indorai said as the marshal closed his eyes and leaned away. Wyrchek turned to his superior.

"Surprise attack, no warning."

"Very well," Sinj answered before looking at Steven. "Procedure, Majesty. I hope you understand."

"Of course," Steven assured him before covering his eyes. "I'd like to be alone. Tell the defense executor to give me ten minutes."

"Of course, Majesty."

The entourage bowed to him before turning together and making for the door.

His brain was still waking up, and Steven sat up straighter when he sensed the sleeping mind behind him. Natalie? He swung his legs to the opposite side of the bed, and his smile quickly exchanged for a frown. Jasmine. Curled up on the small white couch, drooling into a tiny pillow.

He leaned back and rubbed his eyes. The executor would not give him long. Such was the life of an emperor.

CHAPTER
1E

AT THE CENTER OF the Hourglass Galaxy lay what the Vaar called the Great Anomaly, and the Solars the Void Zone. A 150-light-year radius surrounded the innermost core of the galaxy. For as long as the Vaar had known of its existence, no probe, ship, or astral body traveling beyond its horizon had ever returned. Until now. The Great Anomaly was shrinking.

Probes frozen in time for hundreds or thousands of years were moving as if no time had passed. To them, that was exactly the case. Alien ships that had tried to breach the barrier were suddenly freed, only to be destroyed by fire from Combine warships. The Time-Lost Galaxy was forever changing, and few were aware of it so far.

Oul'sor stood on the hull of the Combine's new flagship, the *Caustic Reverie*. There he saw the flashes of light as Combine ships emerged from the veil of blackness before warping out to join those pushing against the Empire. So strange to stand on the hull of the ship as he did now, his mouth exposed to space. He did not even feel the need to breathe. The moisture of his eyes did not sublimate, nor did his body expand in the vacuum.

His eyes moved back down to the hull and the dedication plaque. By long tradition, a panel on the hull of every Vaar ship bore the name of all those who had contributed to it. Designers, engineers, workers, even leaders who authorized it. His name was absent. His opinion on the ship had not changed since he had voted against it. A massive waste of time and resources. All so the fleet could boast that it was capable of making ships as large as the Empire's. But the other warlords, they wanted their symbol. How foolish, even before he knew what he did now.

"What troubles you, Oul'sor?"

His eyes turned to the alien who still gazed out into the Great Anomaly, piercing the darkness with eight tendrils branching out of his back. Somehow despite appearing as void as empty space, they seemed to cast a crimson light on everything around them. Yet no matter which of his pupils he dilated, Oul'sor could not make out the light's place in any part of the spectrum. Part of him wished he was still incapable of seeing Indorai—such a strange creature.

"That's not very nice," Indorai's said to his mind. *"Imagine how you Vaar must look to me. But surely it is not my appearance that so bothers you?"*

Oul'sor tried and failed to answer. Though his mouth moved, no sound came out. There was no air in his lungs, none to escape from his throat and carry his voice. So he gathered himself, glaring at Indorai.

"I never wanted this war, Indorai. You expect I should be happy?"

That . . . hideous face turned to him.

"I would think the news that your people have cleansed ND-31 would please you."

Oul'sor opened his mouth, baring rows of serrated teeth. *"You insult me by using the Solar's name for the sacred world?"*

Indorai's tendrils curled briefly before fanning back out. *"I am often in many places and conversations at once. Forgive me if sometimes I misplace my vernacular. You did not answer my question."*

Oul'sor turned and took a few steps to gaze down the great length of the ship, where he saw two of the canting pylons at the rear that served as its exhaust baffles. Oul'sor had to remind himself again that he could not speak out here.

"You are sure he will come?"

Indorai did not move, seeming to dissolve from one spot and materialize in another until he stood beside Oul'sor. *"You must stop thinking in moments, Oul'sor."* Indorai extended a palm toward the ship. Oul'sor shifted slightly as his vision carried through the hull to see three human women sitting around a table. His gaze seemed to halt at the sight of the pair of clones. No, not clones. What did humans call them? Twins.

"He will come," Indorai assured him. *"He has come, and he always will. To reclaim his lost property."*

"I should kill them. Greet him with their heads."

"The master does not wish it, and with all he is willing to do for you, will you defy him now?"

Oul'sor bared his teeth at Indorai again before looking back at the women. The tension in his muscles slackened even as his gut twisted. *"No. I will do what he wishes."*

One of Indorai's tendrils curled around Oul'sor's back as if to lay a hand on his shoulder. *"Of course you will. Your years begot wisdom."*

Oul'sor pulled his eyes away from the vision, tired of staring at humans.

"So what now?" he asked while plucking the tendril from his shoulder to free himself of the hideous one's grip.

"Now we must make the future happen and use him to lure her out." Indorai directed his attention toward a bulge in the ship's hull marked by transparent windows. Warlords and speakers gathered inside several. *"I knew Hahk'xess would come. Your friend is far too predictable for his own good. If the Solars truly wanted him dead, he would be. Make a suggestion to him. Tell him that he should order this ship to be placed in orbit around Origin so that the speakers may send images of it to your people, a political statement of how well the war is going."*

Oul'sor focused on his friend behind the transparency, dressed in the gold armor of the grand warlord. *"I am not certain that Hahk'xess will trust me. With what you have done, he will see you when he looks at me."*

"He will see his friend. He will worry for you, as friends do. He will hear your words. Go now. We have much to do."

CHAPTER
2A

A S HE WALKED THE corridors of his ship, Panzer was forced to admit that Andira was right. He had left the infirmary too soon. For all its magic, the deep-fryer demanded a toll. Soldiers called it a deep-fryer hangover.

Trillions of cells made up a living body. With that many parts, the whole was bound to encounter some issues. His right eye saw the world in living color but could focus no farther than the reach of his arm. The left eye saw distance perfectly but only in shades of gray. One ear heard only high frequencies; the other heard only low. His left foot had become lazy, requiring a conscious effort from him to land correctly with each step. All while his stomach turned itself inside and out in an unending series of knots.

He walked slowly, partly to keep his left foot under control. Partly because his right arm was wrapped around Simmonne. She shuffled along with him in a silent daze. Her presence was a constant reminder of the deep-fryer's most disturbing effect. A toll that only metapsions were forced to pay. As if someone had reached into his head and flipped a switch, his abilities were gone. Only with concentration could he sense her emotions. To read her mind was out of the question.

Somewhere along the line, thousands of years ago, someone with more intelligence than wisdom made a decision. They decided that grief was an inhibition to a leader. That decision led to the idea that one of a leader's qualities should be an ability to quickly process and overcome the feeling. That way they could avoid despondence and lead those who were still alive. Genetics could predispose psychology, and so it was done. The ordinary people of the Empire referred to it as *noble grief.* The trait was embedded in nearly every person of royal title. Ever the mimics, much of the nobility would adopt it as well.

Noble grief was one of many traits ancient Imperials decided to ingrain into the genetics of their progeny. When all of these great ideas proved to be far less great than anticipated, noble grief hung on. The legacy of that decision bore people who did not go through the ordinary stages and time-lines of grief. They would race through them at preternatural paces. Denial and anger were quick, if experienced at all. Few would bargain with fate and would soon overcome the loss entirely.

But humans were not machines crafted to a universal template. For some, noble grief worked flawlessly. Once the initial shock broke, they would be their old self in a day or two. Some of them skipped the process of grieving entirely. Others were condemned to a lifetime of melancholy, as they experienced no grief and obtained no closure. For others, the fate, while rare, was even worse. The loss became a tumor of the mind. It killed something within them—the essence that allowed them to form the deep connections that grief could not exist without.

Panzer held Simmonne a bit tighter to him. Even when noble grief did its job, the effect was harsh. Months, even years of grief were compacted into mere days. The buffet of sorrow became a single bitter pill to be swallowed at once. He could not predict what the effects would be. In a day, Simmonne might be back to her old self. Or she might not be so lucky. There was nothing to do but wait and see.

The twenty-meter jaunt from his quarters to the ship's command-in-control became an endurance march as every muscle in his body ached for rest. But he kept his pace and brought her along. Eventually they came to the doors of the CIC, which split to grant them entry. Buried behind the neck of the ship, the CIC extended across three decks in a large sphere. A long catwalk led to a center platform where his team waited.

Andira projected an avatar of herself atop the main console. Though translucent, she gave much the same appearance as her peripheral body. She offered up no response to his presence, having learned long ago to let him announce himself. The brothers, Kassar and Novin, stood to the right of the console, their red skin and bald heads practically glowing in the light of screens projected on the chamber's walls. Kurai were easy to separate from men at a distance, even ignoring their color. Their bodies did not expand the same way when breathing, and their posture seemed ever loath to shift. A kurai at ease was practically a statue.

Rhoxx stood on the left of the platform, dominating that side by right of immensity. He sat much like a dog by lowering his hind legs. The rest of his weight rested on forelimbs that walked on the knuckles so as not to dull the half-meter claws spanning out from each digit. The tahn'kodaz were among the largest sapient species. As a boy, Panzer had read stories that spoke of great and mighty creatures that once lived on ancient Earth. Species so ancient, they existed millions of years before the first humans. The ancients called them dinosaurs.

The ancients loved to make up stories of great beasts, and Panzer had often doubted that they ever existed. Supposedly there had once been proof in the form of fossils, all destroyed a hundred thousand years ago in the Therican War. But if these dinosaurs ever did exist, maybe they were something like the kodaz.

Three meters distanced Rhoxx's scarlet eyes from the floor beneath his knuckles. More height was needed to reach the tip of the massive humps that formed his shoulders. A broad, wedge-like jaw hung open in a quiet hiss. Unable to sweat, he regulated his body heat with his breath, exposing large, hooking teeth. The entirety of his body was covered by fine, keeled scales the color of muddy waters.

Five meters behind his jaw, his tail dangled over the side of the raised platform.

While one was enough for most, kodaz, it seemed, needed two types of bone. The first set was iron, like that of kurai, simians, and Vaar, used to support the massive body around which they were built. The second, calcium bones, were outside the body, forming a large crest over the brow, and plates to flank the spine. Rhoxx was fortunate enough to be born with bone plates that bore a natural red sheen, something apparently irresistible to the females of his species.

With nostrils larger than a man's fist, it was no surprise Rhoxx noticed them first. His head reared up, and those big nostrils flared as he took in a whiff.

"Bosss," the big kodaz greeted, turning to face him and prompting the others to do the same.

Panzer eyed Rhoxx, whose slur was back. One of life's little oddities, that for a time a traumatic brain injury had actually improved the kodaz's ability to speak Solar. Panzer guided Simmonne with him to the console. Perhaps he should have left her behind. From the looks of things, he expected very little good news. No. Being alone was the last thing she needed right now.

"So," he began as he focused on a map of the galaxy, "who wants to tell me. Why are we still in the Hourglass? And why are we behind enemy lines?"

"Needin' ssstop, makin' repairsss," Rhoxx answered quickly. "No choice but dippin' behind 'em Vaar, ssstay unssseen."

As he expected, bad news inbound. At the center console, he positioned Simmonne to his side and transferred his hand to her shoulder.

"Give me a full damage report," Panzer ordered.

"Yes sir," Andira answered. Her avatar faded away to show a schematic of his ship. Its long body was marked most prominently by a trio of crescents formed by triangular blades. The ship's neck extended back into a widening body where the largest blades formed forward-sweeping wings. The final pair of blades formed a rear-facing crescent to make up the tail. Highlights of red marred the golden wire frame, highlighting the amount of work that remained.

"The ship suffered extensive damage due to a direct hit on her hangar," Andira began. "The transpatial drive has been damaged beyond our onboard capacity to repair. We will require either shipyard repairs or the facilities of a dedicated warship of cruiser size or larger. Intergalactic travel, and point-to-point intragalactic travel are unavailable."

Panzer let out an angry sigh as he shook his head.

"I told them," he grumbled before looking at Novin. "You told them. Half the damn Corps told those assholes they were putting too much drive in too small a ship. Damn thing was going to be fragile." His tone changed to one of mocking impersonation. "Oh, just don't get shot at! That's why you have a stealth system, see?" His voice normalized. "This is what happens when the people making the equipment never have to use it."

He paused as his quickening pulse brought fresh pain to his head, and he raised his left hand to his temple. His body seemed to be punishing him, reminding him that whining was not an action fit for a leader. He shook his head and lowered his hand to the console.

"Continue," he whispered to Andira, who quickly complied.

"The compression drive has sustained damage to 46 percent of its machinery. Maximum *c*-factor has been reduced to less than seven hundred thousand. The stealth systems have been damaged. Our detection range against Combine sensors is currently ten light-years. Due to damage to the stealth system, this will increase to 207 at cruise. The rotary drive is fully functional, however, but due to counter-detection system damage, our detection radius will exceed two thousand. Due to damage to tank-array three, we are down to 60 percent fuel capacity. Communications are damaged. We can receive but cannot transmit."

Panzer closed his eyes. One downside to xenomatter fuel and its nature as a superfluid. Even with its ridiculous density, once a hole formed in the tank, the leak was difficult to seal. No doubt Andira had advised, and Rhoxx had given his blessing to purge the tank, lest they leave a trail of the stuff that no Vaar sensor officer was incompetent enough to miss.

While Andira spoke, the image of the ship had drawn out to illuminate the blue star they orbited. A short trail of stellar plasma arced out of the star into the belly of the ship. Hydrogen, raw fuel for the ship's printers to transmute for use in the ongoing repairs.

"Go on," he whispered.

"Primary weapons are online and accounted for. MIMs are online, but pulse interceptors are currently unavailable. Hull breaches on decks one through nine, compartment A—those areas are currently locked down and depressurized."

Great. Trapped behind enemy lines on a ship that might take weeks to repair itself. He opened his eyes. "Since we're all still here," he began before shifting his weight, "I'm guessing the fleet hasn't established a mininet?"

"Not yet, sir."

Of course not. Why should anything that's supposed to be happening actually be happening today? "Why not?" he asked.

"The Vaar attack coincided with a massive output of dilation waves from the Void Zone," Andira answered. "That storm is ongoing. The current wave amplitude is averaging in hours with some spikes reaching days. Due to the resulting time dilation, no ship can drop out of warp long enough to serve as a mininet anchor."

He rubbed his eyes. Time already passed slower in the Hourglass than it should, and each dilation wave—the time-stopping distortions pouring out of the galaxy's center—brought it to a standstill. He had not sensed a single one since waking, but there were so many of them, the fleet could not establish its portable astranet. He tried not to read into it. Only a provident could sense the waves, let alone maintain awareness while one passed. With his abilities suppressed, he could not expect to. Yet still it carried dark portents. If his abilities had diminished, providence would certainly be the first to go.

Worse was the mininet. Ships at warp were safe from the effect of the waves. The space-time distortion of their massless impulse drives was enough to protect them. But only while they were at warp. No mininet meant that ships behind the lines could not relay freshly printed ammo to those engaged in battle. Fuel, personnel, and other commodities could not be transferred instantly. All had to be done by ships meeting or by using transports. The Armadas were surely outnumbered already. Now they were fighting with their hands bound.

His ship was too small to sustain a mininet router, but if the mininet were online, they could at least teleport supplies to hasten the repairs.

"Show me the war. I need to know what's happened up until now."

"Yes sir." Andira pushed the display of the ship aside and brought up a map. The six-armed spiral of the Hourglass loomed before him. Andira zoomed in on the Auchard Arm, where it joined the galaxy's central disc. With the image in view, Andira moved forward with her briefing.

"The Vaar attack began concurrently with a declaration of war from Grand Warlord Hahk'xess. Shore batteries in the galactic disc opened fire on our batteries and the Auchard minefield. Our shore batteries retaliated as soon as the attack was confirmed. However it seems intelligence underestimated the strength of the Vaar batteries by a factor of three. Both sides' batteries sustained heavy damage. I do not expect them to play a significant role going forward."

Panzer's eyes widened. Everyone in the intelligence community knew the Vaar had installed more batteries, but for the estimates to miss the mark that badly? How? Worse, how did the Vaar know where all the Empire's batteries were located? Inhabited planets typically received only light batteries to protect them from landing craft. The bigger batteries meant to engage warships were *never* placed on inhabited worlds. That would only invite the massacre of the population when those weapons were inevitably targeted. It was not as if the Vaar could have infiltrated or bribed the civilian population to learn of their whereabouts. Most of the facilities weren't even manned, controlled remotely from master targeting plants.

The Empire had a mole on its hands. That or the largest security breach in living memory. No matter how many the Vaar found scouting, they would have never found them all. With the shore batteries gone, the door was open. Only an Armadas flotilla stood in the way.

"While the shore batteries were engaged, two vanguard forces of Vaar warships jumped into Imperial territory. The first force assaulted Avalon directly. The second secured the ND Star Cluster."

Of course. ND-31, the Combine's favorite pretext for pushing around the weaker nations. Now, the pretext for fighting the Empire.

"Both Avalon and ND-31 were invaded once local defenses were overcome. There has been no word from ND-31, and the colony is assumed lost. There are reports that the Vaar have secured most of Avalon. Their main force entered the battle shortly thereafter."

"Do we know how many ships they brought?"

"Intercepts from friendly vessels suggest that new forces are constantly pouring in. Total force strength at present is approximately two million currently in the Auchard Arm. Perhaps a doubling of that number in the forces poised in the other arms."

Panzer took a step back while sweeping his eyes over his team. "That's ... How? What the hell have we been doing all this time? Hahk'xess can't even order a midnight snack without us knowing how many calories. We've tapped their strategic communications. Bugged their fleet commanders. It takes months to plan an operation like this. How could the Vaar coordinate so many ships without us knowing?"

He brought his hand down on the console, closing his eyes as his headache insisted that he notice it. What the hell was happening here? How did the Vaar mobilize millions of ships, billions of troops, all without the Empire ever seeing it coming?

Andira took his silence as license to go on. "Unfortunately, after the Vaar deployed their fleet, their strategy ceased to make sense."

"Explain," he said with a grumble.

She brought the image out to bring the pair of arms flanking Auchard into view, and more red icons with them. "Consensus among intelligence has been that the Vaar would wormhole deep into Imperial territory to strike key targets in parallel."

"It would make sense," Panzer noted.

"It is *not* what the Vaar are doing." Kassar spoke in that voice that seemed to hate any sound above a whisper. With his current headache, Panzer was thankful for it.

"Beyond the vanguard forces," Andira said, "no Vaar ships made transpatial jumps into Imperial territory. Some forces took up position in the Lannax and Voder arms, but these forces have made no effort to engage the Empire. The main force of Vaar ships jumped to HG-DS-4121 in the galactic disc before distributing."

The image came focused on two sheets of red icons, one behind the other, each spanning the breadth of the galactic arm's width.

"The Vaar have formed their ships into two primary formations. Both are working their way out, sweeping through the galactic arm. The forward formation is attacking any military asset that comes within range, but it is ignoring civilian targets. It is even ignoring civilian ships that pass through the formation from behind. The second formation is targeting both military and civilian assets. However at their present c-factor, the Vaar will need at least thirty days to move through the entire galactic arm."

"Doesn't make any sense," Kassar thought aloud before transitioning to a statement as Panzer looked at him. "They're taking losses they don't have to take."

"Kassar is correct," Andira seconded, quickly regaining control of the briefing. "Aetius has taken advantage to make a fighting retreat. With their superior range, Armadas ships have been engaging the Vaar at a stand-off distance before withdrawing to avoid counterfire. Vaar interceptors are proving more effective than anticipated. Their sheer numbers are allowing high interceptor saturation. However this is still resulting in losses for the Combine."

"No sssensse." Rhoxx confirmed the sentiment.

With a lull Panzer focused on the map and the twin columns slowly working their way through the galactic arm.

"Do you know what they're doing?"

Panzer turned his gaze down to Simmonne. Her eyes were fixed on the map. For a moment he was not certain if she had actually asked the question.

"Yes," he answered as he turned back to the map. "I know what they're doing."

It was a strain that seemed to stretch his brain, interfacing his NOD to the display to take control of the image. He was a bit surprised that Andira had not figured this out, but only marginally so. She was a companion AI, not a tactical AI. Even the latter sometimes had trouble turning its attention from the perfect to the good-enough.

Panzer cleared his throat. "Your father was never willing to commit enough ships to stop a full-scale attack. So the plan has always been to evacuate the Hourglass if the Vaar invaded. The Vaar know that, so they're giving us time to do it. The front formation clears away defenses but ignores civilians. The second attacks them to make sure those ahead flee. The Vaar aren't trying to fight us; they're driving us."

He shifted the focus to the very tip of the galactic arm, where three rings of pylons popped out to be noticed.

"Most civilian ships can't make intergalactic jumps on their own. They need the gates. Ralleck Gate is useless; that galaxy will probably be next if they aren't under attack already. Stoplen and Haplen Gate lead back to the Empire. Traffic can only move one way at a time, which means it's either let civilians out, or bring reinforcements in. With both gates outbound, we're still talking billions of civilians. Those gates are about to get a lot more traffic than they can handle."

He took a breath.

"The Vaar are creating a traffic jam. That's why they didn't jump in and try to hit the gates first. They'd trap everyone here, but Aetius would scatter his fleet. The Vaar would have to hunt him down. But now, eventually the queue of civilians waiting their turn will be so big, Aetius won't have a choice. He'll have to concentrate his forces near the gates to protect them. Then the Vaar will jump in. Both columns. They'll wipe out everyone in one attack. Armadas, civilians, everyone. The forces in the other arms are there to catch anyone who tries to escape."

"Stars," Simmonne whispered. She brought her eyes up as high as she could without making eye contact. "What do we do?"

He kept his eyes on the map. "There's nothing we can do."

"But all the civilians," she whispered. "Would the Vaar really kill them?"

"Yes," he answered. "The Vaar don't play by the same rules we do. They won't go out of their way simply to kill civilians, but they consider the enemy population a legitimate target of war. If they can accomplish a military objective by attacking civilians, they'll absolutely do it."

"We have to do something."

He shook his head again. "Nothing we can do. But if I figured it out, you can bet Aetius has. What he'll do about it, I don't know, but that's his problem. We have a lot of our own right now."

CHAPTER 2B

THE FUNK THAT HAD claimed Simmonne's mind was slow to fade. All she could see were their faces. Her guards. They could be brought back. They were arens. New bodies could be grown from the same stock as the originals. Their downloaded and databased memories could be imprinted on new brains. They would live again. Except, they wouldn't.

It would not be them. Not really. They would simply be clones. Clones with another life's memories implanted as if their own. It wouldn't be them. The consciousness that saw through their eyes, heard through their ears, and controlled their bodies, that was gone and could only be imitated. What would it be like to reproduce them? Would it be an honor to their memories? A love that wanted them back in any way possible? Or would it be a disgrace to them? Would it mean reducing their existence to a product—to be used, discarded, copied, and replaced on a whim? These were questions she had never asked herself. Questions she never truly thought she would need to.

Simmonne took a breath and lowered her head. They were dead, but the three who lived needed help now. Simmonne scowled at the colonel's back while he spoke with his soldiers. He let the Vaar take them. No matter what he said, she was convinced of that fact. Of all the commandos in the Corps, she had only ever heard the names of two spoken at her family's table. Their leader, Nicolae Espada, and this man, Robert Panzer. Even those who served as vanguards for her brothers and sisters rarely had their names repeated when that task was done.

He made the decision: save royalty and sacrifice the rest. He could manipulate more than a hundred objects with his mind. He had more strength in one arm than any man was entitled to. All with the most potent arsenal the Empire could give him, and almost certainly centuries or more of experience. No matter what he said. No matter what she had seen. In her mind, it could not have been anything else. He let the Vaar take them to save her and for some ridiculous codes.

"I think this is our best bet."

His words drew her attention to the console and the map of the galaxy.

"Their formation is a bit thin here." The colonel pointed to a spot in the outer edge of the galaxy's spiral arm. "Andira, what do you think?"

"No good, sir," the AI answered. "At our current detection radius, we would never make it through."

"You're certain of that?" the colonel asked with an upward glance.

"Would you like to see my math, sir?" the AI retorted.

The colonel shook his head. "I'll take your word for it. That's it then. If we can't sneak through there, then we can't get past their lines without fixing the stealth system."

"And the compression drive."

"*And* the compression drive," the colonel repeated. "How long are we looking at to repair those systems?"

Simmonne perked up as she, too, waited for the AI's response.

"At present capabilities, twenty-nine days."

Twenty-nine days? Simmonne mouthed the words with a grimace.

"Twenty-nine days?" the colonel repeated, his tone more incredulous. "What, are they paying you by the hour now?"

"The counter-detection systems and the compression drive have to be calibrated to each other," the AI answered. "The counter-detection system will require a complete rebuild and burn-in. Given the damage to the compression drive, a rebuild will likely be more time efficient than the repair of existing systems. However this will require its own fabrication and burn-in times before the stealth system is rebuilt and the two are calibrated."

Thirty days stuck on this ship? Thirty days just *waiting*? She glared at the colonel's back with pleading eyes. There had to be another way. He shifted his weight to his right foot before rubbing his eyes. Simmonne looked back at the map and saw something. The words escaped her lips before she put full thought into them. "Can't we just go over them?" she asked. "Or under them?"

"*No!*" Simmonne took a step back in shock as the colonel, the kodaz, the two kurai, and the AI all answered her as one.

The colonel brought up a hand to silence the rest. "If we try that, they will see us." Her eyes retreated as he looked at her. "The stealth system is already damaged, and it makes us hard to detect, not impossible. It just makes it difficult for them to pick us out of all the other stuff in the galaxy. If we leave the galactic plane and enter dead space, there's no clutter. They will see us, and we will die."

When he turned away, Simmonne looked at a small icon on the map: a ship above the Vaar lines, and clearly far above the galactic plane.

"*He's* doing it," she protested, pointing to the blue icon.

The colonel shot a glance back at her before looking at the map. His chest contracted as he let out a quiet sigh. "He's in a *Rook*," the colonel said. She did not know what that meant, but she knew that tone. The one people used to answer a stupid question.

"So?" she pressed. "If he can do it, why can't we?"

The colonel stood up straight and rubbed his eyes again. "I forget, you don't know very much," he said in an annoyed tone.

What was *that* supposed to mean? Did he just insult her?

"Okay. He's in a *Rook*. He is in the fastest MID-driven ship ever. We're not. This ship is fast, but it's not *that* fast. They're not even bothering to shoot at him because they know it's pointless. If they do, he'll just open the throttle and laugh at them. If they see and shoot at us? We're going to hope like hell our interceptors can shoot them down before we die. And *then* we will die."

He turned back to the console.

"Sir," the AI said, breaking the short silence. "The *Rook* does present an opportunity."

"Which is?"

"We could use the communications package in the *Intruder* to contact the *Rook*. You could then order him to rendezvous with us. With my onboard capabilities, I could modify the *Rook*'s weapons bay with a rudimentary life-support system. It would only be enough for two, but you and Her Majesty could use the *Rook* to return to the fleet."

Simmonne perked up for a moment before that hope was dashed.

"No," the colonel answered.

No?

"Sir, it has an excellent chance of working," the AI protested.

"I don't care," he retorted. "She's my responsibility. I'm not about to put her life in the hands of some pilot I don't even know. And I damn sure am not running away and leaving the rest of you here."

This time Simmonne managed to stop the words before they escaped her mouth. He did not want to leave his team behind. She could not fault him for that. If only he had felt the same about Jenna and the Twins.

"The other alternative is to use the *Intruder* to contact the *Hurricane* and request assistance."

"We're damn sure not doing that."

"Why not?" Simmonne asked.

"Andira. Is there any way you can shave down that repair time? We don't need things factory new. Just enough to get us across."

"Why not call for help?" Simmonne asked more firmly and, again, received no answer.

"Not with onboard resources."

"Colonel?" Simmonne spoke louder, trying and failing to cut into his back and forth with the AI.

"I don't think we have that kind of time."

"Colonel!" Simmonne spiked her tone to get his full attention. "We should call for help. Call the *Hurricane*."

He angled toward her. "And how many people did you want to die coming to your rescue?"

The question hit like a closed fist, and for a moment all she could manage was a flat reply. "What?"

The colonel took a moment to collect himself. "*This* is why I told your father I didn't want anyone in the Solar Family coming here. All those jokes—stereotypes you've probably heard about arens' loyalty to the emperor? With Aetius, they're all true. By now, he's already issued standing orders to the fleet. If you or I contact them, it will be routed to him. The first thing he is going to do is ask me if I have you."

The colonel paused to take a breath and face her fully.

"If I tell him no, he's going to do the right thing. He'll say there's nothing he can do, and that we're on our own. If I say yes?" He leveled a finger at her. "You will be the only thing he sees. He will abandon everyone else in this galaxy to their fate. He will throw every ship he has at the Vaar, trying to break through and reach you. Maybe he'll succeed. Maybe he won't. Either way, a lot of people will die to save you. I will not allow that to happen. Not when we can avoid it."

Her mind raced for a solution. "But. But. The fleet, their firepower. They told me the *Hurricane* can fire over fifty thousand missiles a second, and they can hit a target a hundred thousand light-years away. Surely with that kind of firepower, they can break through?"

Fifty thousand? She watched the colonel mouth the words to himself. His expression changed as he rolled his eyes and shook his head. "Gilyard," he grumbled. "Why do they let that ass talk to civilians?"

"What?" she demanded. "Did he lie to me or something?"

"Princess," the colonel began, "Admiral Gilyard is the worst person to get your information from. Whenever he talks to civilians, he's always more concerned with impressing them than getting accurate information across. No. The *Hurricane* can't fire fifty thousand missiles per second. She can fire a maximum of ten thousand per second, each of which has five submunitions. Even then you don't just vomit them into space. You'll run out of ammo faster than you can print it. It's about well-timed, coordinated bursts."

He paused to draw in a distinctly annoyed breath. "Second, an Arc-5 can only go a hundred thousand if you fit it with aux tanks, which no one bothers to *do* since it'll take the thing days to get there at that distance. In standard configuration, the range is about fifteen thousand, and that's so the enemy can't just run from it until it's out of fuel. It's not for lobbing fire across the galaxy. So if you're thinking the fleet can just blast its way through to us, that's not going to end the way you want it to."

Simmonne was left at a loss. Why did the admiral tell her all those things if it wasn't true? It was all bluster? "But, but—"

The colonel waved his hand to cut her off. "Look, I don't have time to give you a clinic on fleet action right now."

"I'm not stupid, Colonel," she said as he returned to the console. For a minute he seemed as if he would reply but instead he shook his head. "What about your mobile router?"

"Only works in the astranet. Mininet isn't astranet. Even if it was, the fleet hasn't established its mininet." The colonel lowered his head before jerking back up. "Eyes. Andira, are there any eyes we could reach in the next day or two?"

"Two, sir," the AI answered. "Eye-11 and Eye-9."

"What are eyes?" Simmonne asked.

"Eyes are Armadas spy stations," the colonel answered. "They put them where they'll be hard to detect to monitor activity. In time of war, they're abandoned to run on automated systems. We could cannibalize one of them and expedite repair. Andira, if we go to the closest one, how much time could that shave off the repairs?"

"Approximately nine days," the AI answered.

"That's all?" The colonel seemed to balk at the response.

"The most time-consuming portions are burn-in and calibration. These steps cannot be expedited simply by adding resources. Additionally, time dilation in those regions will slow effective progress."

The colonel rapped his fingers on the console. "Eye-11—that's in the Basin," the colonel thought aloud. "I'd prefer not to go in there."

"It is extremely unlikely the Vaar would be able to find us," the AI offered.

"Yeah, and they could mass an entire fleet outside, and we wouldn't know until we tried to leave," the colonel countered. "Eye-9 should do the job. Andira, assume my supposition about the Vaar's intentions is correct. How long do you estimate before they would be in position to execute?"

"At their present speed, between twenty-five and thirty days."

"That's cutting it close," the colonel mused. "But, I don't think we have a choice."

"Colonel?" Simmonne asked. "What if you're right? I mean, about what the Vaar are doing, and we don't get out in time?"

"Then we give the Vaar a wide berth and live on this ship until the Armadas return. Andira, set a course for Eye-9. I want to get there at—"

"Sir, new passive contact," the AI interrupted. "Designated *Dodger 1*, bearing 109. Range, 209 light-years."

Simmonne's heart skipped a beat when the colonel stood upright.

"Can you identify?" he barked.

"Negative," it answered. "Signal is still too weak. *Dodger 1* is approaching, c-factor two hundred thousand."

"And you're just *now* detecting it?" The colonel's voice was incredulous.

"Yes sir."

Simmonne jumped as the colonel suddenly turned back toward her and took a step. Before she could react, his hand had closed on her arm and practically flew her to the console beside him.

"Prep the *Intruder*," he ordered. "We may have to abandon ship. I want ID on that thing now."

"Working on it, sir," the AI answered. A new screen opened above the console, and a multitude of squiggly lines began to move through it.

Tock . . . Tock . . . Tock . . .

Simmonne's head rolled as she surveyed the room. The strange tone seemed to come from all around, with no visible source.

"What's that sound?" she asked. She deigned to take a step only for the colonel's grip to keep her in place.

"Our instruments warning us we've just been swept by an active scan," he explained. "Someone is looking."

Her arms began to tremble. "Looking for us?"

The colonel did not answer. "Andira, any chance this is a friendly inbound?"

"I don't think so, sir," it replied. "Should I move to battle stations?"

"No. If they knew we were here, they'd already be shooting," the colonel replied.

"Then," Simmonne whispered, "what do we do?"

"We don't do anything to help them see us, and maybe they'll pass us by. Andira, cut the star tap, and go zero-emissions."

"Yes sir."

There was a hum in the background that Simmonne did not notice until it stopped.

"Star tap terminated. Now in zero-emissions mode," the AI reported.

The colonel took a breath. "Now we wait."

CHAPTER
2C

HIS NAME WAS JONATHAN Clearwater. He knew that much, at least. His head had become a soup of nausea, distant sounds, passing light, and incoherent memories. A man covered in flames and shot through the head. An aren brought to his knees and executed. A kurai fighting with his sword in one hand and his pistol in the other. Those images came each time his eyes tried to open, and incredible weight forced them closed.

He was moving but remained bolted to a reclining table. A brief foray into the waking world spotted a Viss walking in front of him. Clearwater turned his head briefly to make out a Vaar in full armor walking behind him in the long, tubular corridor. There was something almost skeletal about the corridor and the way support struts blended through the wall and ceiling. The strain of moving his head proved more than his neck was ready for, and the muscles gave out. His eyes closed again as he stared at the simple gray uniform he now wore.

Faces in his mind. They wouldn't go away, but he had no names for them.

When he opened his eyes again, he was blinded by bright lights. He could only make out a pair of shadows, one very large and the other small. He closed his eyes against the light. Some of his reality was settling in his mind. He was a legionnaire, a soldier of the Empire. These were Vaar. The enemy. It was clear, he was a prisoner.

He chanced opening his eyes again, letting them adjust to the light. Many chairs, large and small, filled the spherical room. The Viss's fingers danced on a data slate. Clearwater heard a series of high- and low-pitched growls as she spoke with the Vaar with her.

Both the Vaar and the Viss bowed their heads, and Clearwater noticed that they were up on a stage. Another Vaar ascended to join them. This one wore armor in brilliant, polished gold. The patterns on the armor were too intricate for his compromised mind to make out, but neither of those who bowed moved until the golden Vaar growled to them. The Vaar in the more mundane armor moved out of view, while the Viss turned to face Clearwater. She touched her slate.

Clearwater jolted as his feet dropped, and the table to which he was bound moved him upright. He was raised higher, almost to the point of being at eye level with the golden Vaar. A weak feeling of recognition made

Clearwater wonder if he knew who this Vaar was.

The Vaar was speaking to him.

VAAR LANGUAGE DETECTED—IVEX
AUTOTRANS FAILURE
LANGUAGE LIBRARY—DATA CORRUPTION
ATTEMPTING DATABASE RECONSTRUCTION . . .

The Vaar spoke to him again, his words as meaningless to Clearwater as those in his NOD. The golden Vaar took a step back and looked at the Viss. Both motioned to Clearwater as they spoke. Finally the Viss approached, took Clearwater by the chin, and clamped down several seconds before he felt it. A needle went into his neck, and it was out before Clearwater processed the sensation.

The golden Vaar stepped close to him again.

"Do you. Understand. Me. Solar?"

"Puh yeggish?" Clearwater had no more what he'd said than did the Vaar.

The golden Vaar grumbled and eyed the Viss again.

IVEX DATABASE RESTORATION IN PROGRESS.
BUFFERING . . .

"What's wrong with him?" The golden Vaar's words. "I thought Solars could understand every language."

"Grand Warlord, the fact that he is alive at all is the best we could do," the Viss answered. "He may need more time for his machines to fix him."

"Another injection?" the golden one asked.

"I don't think it will matter, Grand Warlord. It's his machines doing the work. Even if I give them more, they may not be able to work any faster."

"Give it to him."

"Yes, Grand Warlord."

The lag was shorter but still there as the Viss grabbed his chin and drove another injection into his neck.

"Do you understand me, Solar?" the golden Vaar asked again. The only answer was the drool that escaped Clearwater's mouth and dripped on his shirt. "This is disappointing. The speakers would have had great fun with him."

The golden Vaar leaned close enough for Clearwater's fuzzy vision to make out details. The Vaar's faceplate was not completely gold. The lines etched into the metal looked almost skeletal in the image of a mouth open to brandish many sharp teeth. The teeth were polished white as if actual bone had been fused to the metal. A pair of amber eyes viewed Clearwater through the gaps in retracted visors. Five pupils in each eye surrounded the larger sixth in a pentagon. They took turns dilating and contracting.

"You know, you are even smaller than I thought you would be," the Vaar commented before turning to the Viss. "Are you certain this is one of the males?"

"Yes, Grand Warlord."

Grand Warlord. Clearwater almost recognized those words. There was something significant about them.

"Grand Warlord." The Viss drew the golden Vaar's attention. "If he cannot participate, would you like me to take him to holding?"

"Not yet. He can still be useful. Wait until we are finished. Let the speakers have their images."

"Yes, Grand Warlord."

The golden Vaar turned his back, and the Viss moved out of Clearwater's vision.

ERROR IN SYNAPTIC BRIDGING.
TEMPORAL FAULT DETECTED.
REPAIR FAILED
ATTEMPTING SECONDARY REPAIR PROTOCOLS . . .

Clearwater continued to watch the words scrolling in his sight, trying in vain to divine any meaning from them as more Vaar and Viss entered the chamber. They took the chairs, and some set up equipment. A few approached the stage for close looks at Clearwater before taking their places.

When the room was full, the golden Vaar began to speak. He faced away from Clearwater, toward the crowd. His words echoed throughout the chamber. The more time that passed, the farther into the room Clearwater could see. There were hundreds of Vaar, Viss, and many with small machines. While they hung on the gold one's words, Clearwater struggled to comprehend them.

READING, 277 MILLION SYNAPTIC ERRORS
REPAIR IN PROGRESS . . .
TEMPORAL FAULT DETECTED.
REPAIR FAILED
ATTEMPTING TERTIARY REPAIR PROTOCOLS . . .

An electric jolt ripped through Clearwater's body from his spine down to the end of his left leg, which jerked against the manacle that held it. His upper body jerked a moment later, a sound like an amplified hiccup escaping his lips.

The golden Vaar paused his speech before glaring over his shoulder at Clearwater. The stare lasted for several seconds before the gilded Vaar turned back to the crowd and said something to them. The room filled with a cacophony of deep rumbles and high-pitched whines. The sound turned Clearwater's stomach, touching some primitive part of his mind that feared a predator's growl. He didn't realize that those in the chamber were laughing.

231 MILLION SYNAPTIC ERRORS CANNOT BE REPAIRED OUTSIDE OF REM.
RECOMMEND IMMEDIATE SLEEP CYCLE.
DO YOU WISH TO ENTER MEDICAL SLEEP CYCLE?
REQUEST TIMED OUT.
SLEEP CYCLE WILL BEGIN AUTOMATICALLY IN 60 MINUTES.

Clearwater's cheek twitched. Awareness was growing, enough that he felt uncomfortable by the strand of drool hanging from the corner of his mouth. Lucidity was coming slowly, but it was coming. Some words were starting to have meaning.

Grand Warlord. There was a name to come after it, an important name. A name he knew. His ears were clearing, and he began to understand the golden Vaar's words.

"Imperial technology was no match for Vaar discipline. For the training of our warriors and the worth of the cause. Some spoke openly, even seditiously. Who said we could not fight the Empire. We have proven them wrong. Origin was taken with minimal Vaar casualties. The entirety of the Solar's occupying force was put to fire. The station Avalon was taken much the same, and across the front, the Solars and their slaves are in retreat. Very soon, the Time-Lost Galaxy will be liberated."

More sounds from the many who were gathered. The golden Vaar permitted it for several seconds before raising a hand to call for their silence.

"But we cannot allow the ease of these early victories to weaken us. We face the greatest foe with whom we have ever done battle. They will learn from their mistakes. The measure of their strength is yet to be seen. Every citizen of the Combine must do their part, no matter how great or small it may seem."

The golden Vaar turned half a step as he motioned to Clearwater.

"You have all seen him behind me. The lone survivor of Origin's occupying force. A Solar. See the face of your enemy. But see him as he is now. Defeated, restrained, under our power. We face a foe intractable and powerful. But not invincible. This conflict will try us. It will give us days of great victory such as this. And, I am sure, days of regret and hardship.

"But we are the Vaar. We endure, and we survive. When we were young, Prithone attempted to paint our destruction. It failed. When we stepped into the larger universe, it greeted us with genocide. But we endured. In other galaxies, we found foes both weak and mighty. We overcame them all. For we are the Vaar. If we could not destroy ourselves, then what chance has this creature?"

Hahk'xess. The golden Vaar's name was Hahk'xess. A leader. *The* leader. Clearwater had the realization for only a moment before the mush of his brain let it go like a hand dropping a greasy object. Perhaps one out of every five words spoken, he understood, though not enough to follow the speech. Just enough to realize it was indeed a speech.

"If you will go with Ax'lel, she will now take you on a tour of the ship."

The Vaar rose to their feet, and many began to exit the room. Others, mostly Viss, came forward and up onto the stage. Some with handheld devices, and others with drones hovering by them. All stopped for a moment to examine Clearwater before following the procession.

The Viss with the data slate returned as the room emptied, and the gilded Vaar turned back to Clearwater.

"Pity he could not speak."

"Grand Warlord, Warlord Kreth'nell waits for you," another Vaar announced as he stepped onto the stage.

"He can wait," Hahk'xess answered. "Are you *certain* this one is male? He's so small."

"Yes, Grand Warlord," the Viss answered.

"Are they all this small?"

Clearwater grumbled when he heard the question.

"Yes, Grand Warlord. Some are larger, but he seems very average."

The face of the Viss seemed familiar. It was familiar. He saw this one before. When they were working to bring him back.

Hahk'xess glared. "I think you understand more than you pretend."

"Ugh, haba?" Clearwater slurred out the syllables.

"With your permission, Grand Warlord, I will incarcerate him now."

Clearwater heard a snort as the Vaar stood upright. "Very well, take him. You there, inform Kreth'nell I approach."

Clearwater was jolted again as he was reclined and lowered from his perch. One Vaar took a position behind him. Another to his side, and the cart began to move, following the Viss with her nose buried in her slate.

The lights in the room dimmed, allowing Clearwater to make out more of it. Flags and banners draped the walls of the spherical room. He could not keep his eyes on any of them long enough to know their details. In moments he was back in a round corridor, still following the Viss. The dimming light was all it took for his eyes to believe they needed to close. The awareness that seemed to resent being called upon in the first place began to slip away.

CHAPTER
2D

THE SOLAR CATHEDRAL WAS never a quiet place, much less within the Imperial Palace. The corridors were always filled with sound. Servants carried out their daily labors. Functionaries came and went. The Imperial Guard drilled for doomsday scenarios. The music of harps and pianos always carried on in the background of nearly every room. But today, the Cathedral was quiet.

The Cathedral bore the shape of a great sphere, out of which many obelisks branched like rays of light from a star. The streets of the central sphere were empty, locked down by the Imperial Guard. Flags stood at half-mast. Shops and business courts famed for never closing had shut their doors. The center of civilization had drawn a gasp.

Finally released from the hospital, Steven walked the corridors of the palace. Nearly everyone had insisted that he route to his quarters, but he refused. No one could tell him what to do now. He wanted to walk.

Deltas of the Imperial Guard surrounded Steven as he walked—an ad hoc unit hastily thrown together to replace his deceased bodyguards. Mere days ago, they had been street-level police, detectives, and other such functionaries of law, but now they made up his protective entourage. An enormous promotion, even if temporary. Arens were just machines. Machines with some biological parts. His personal guard would live again. Another day or two, and their cloning would be complete.

The quiet felt so strange. He scarcely saw a servant in the halls. It was as if the very walls of the Cathedral were in mourning.

Jasmine walked within the guards' circle with him. She had never been the clingy type of woman but was rather insistent about holding his hand now. He allowed it. She at least had the decency to keep quiet. Or at least she did verbally. Her mind had been on his siblings, on his parents. But addiction did not yield, not even to grief. She had been without for too long, and the strongest thoughts in her mind now were of her pipe. Her hand tremored.

At least Jasmine had come to see him at the hospital.

The tremors in Jasmine's hand worsened as he took his time. A good hour before he finally led the group to a router, cutting the rest of the trip short. He reached the entry corridor to his domicile to find it packed with deltas. More than two hundred lined each wall and snapped to attention in response to his presence. Typical reaction to an event: oversaturate, over-compensate. He directed those around him to join the rest in the corridor through his NOD, then led Jasmine inside.

No sooner had the doors closed than Jasmine tried to release his hand to race ahead, but he forced her to walk with him. It was amusing how the body fought the mind's control. When one needed to go, it was always hardest to hold it as one approached the rest facility. The more one needed a fix, the less they could resist when the means was near.

Of the dozens of couches in his lounge, one was indisputably hers. While two cushions had footrests, the other two held drawers beneath them. As soon as Steven released her hand, Jasmine had one of the drawers open and withdrew her favorite pipe. But her hands were shaking too hard now. As she tried to pour the vial of copper grains into it, she succeeded only in spilling most of it on the couch. She grabbed another vial, and Steven took both from her.

Carefully, and very slowly, he opened the vial and poured a filling of the drug into the fat bulb of the pipe.

"Thanks," Jasmine remarked, trying to swipe the pipe. He braced his right hand behind her head and held the pipe to her mouth. The device came alive as she inhaled, spawning the silver smoke she needed. When she tried to back off, he held her in place, forcing her to take a deeper drag.

Pure marvat. When uncut by impurities and undiluted by safety additives, it worked quickly. Jasmine exhaled through her nose and took another long puff. The tired, almost pained look in her eyes faded. Sparkles returned, and her body relaxed, nullifying the tremors in her arms.

He continued to hold the pipe in place, and her to it. By the fourth puff, she began to go limp, and Steven guided her down onto the couch. She needed three more puffs, and he did not let her detach herself from the pipe until she got them. Soon her eyes closed as her mind found another universe. Steven withdrew the pipe from her lips and laid it on the small table beside her. He deployed the footrest and let her recline.

As the drug wore off and she gained enough lucidity to realize it, she would grab the pipe and take another puff—a cycle she would repeat as long as he allowed it. She was light-years beyond helping herself and would not stop until someone made her. Such a perfect drug. She could leave this reality before inhaling enough to kill herself. Yet as the high dissipated, just another puff or two would bring it right back.

With Jasmine nullified, Steven turned his attention elsewhere. Natalie. He could hear her mind through the walls and floors. He ascended through the domicile to find her in her cosmetics room sitting in a low-backed chair with a pair of lantai servitors. The snow-white hair of the lantai pair provided an attractive contrast to Natalie's golden-red locks. One of the servitors was busy on Natalie's feet, while the other drew a brush through her long hair. A semicircle of mirrors surrounded them, and Natalie's eyes quickly picked out Steven's reflection.

"How are you feeling?" Natalie asked.

Steven considered his answer for a moment. His eyes darted to the empty glass on the table beside her. "A little confused," he said, reaching past the lantai to lay a hand on her shoulder. "I thought to see you when I woke up."

Natalie frowned, and she gazed toward the floor. "You were out for two days. Someone had to make the arrangements. For the family."

"Leave us."

The pair of lantai answered the command with a respectful bow before vacating the room. Steven brought his hands down on Natalie's shoulders and began to rub. She had always been much closer to the family than Jasmine, who had merely been tolerated. But perhaps he misjudged how close she was to them.

A Founder's Day gift from his father. Countless brunches, luncheons, and other such unimportant, but valued, moments with his sisters. The jokes Raymond would tell, funny only because of how unfunny they were. The secret fantasies she sometimes had about Zach. Girl talk with Brittany.

His parents were old. They would have died soon anyway. But only now as he reviewed her mind did Steven realize that Natalie may have been closer to the rest than he thought. It did not matter. Time would heal this wound. Those relationships had a finite lifespan. Once ascension was decided, the rest of them would have stopped putting in so much time around the Cathedral. With their interests to pursue and social circles to invest in, those get-togethers would have become increasingly sporadic. In the end they would have drifted apart anyway.

"When did you set the funeral?" Steven asked, adding a bit more pressure to her shoulders to encourage her to lean back.

"I haven't set a date yet," Natalie answered. "I just put the staff on retainer. Simmonne should be there."

Steven closed his eyes and rubbed a bit more firmly. The mention of his sister's name sent a tingle of anger through his arm. Their father's favorite from the day she was born. The new chance to raise the perfect daughter after all the rest—Brittany especially—disappointed him. It might have been hard to see her bawling over their caskets. It might have been hard until she became the thief trying to take what was his.

"That may not be possible," Steven whispered.

"Why not?" Natalie asked, finding his eyes in the mirror.

"We don't know where she is."

A single tear ran down her cheek. "We can't have the funeral without her," she protested. "It wouldn't be right."

She had a point. No matter what had happened, it wouldn't be right. The funeral would be the hardest part. Fortunately he had no nieces or nephews. Those of his siblings who wanted children were waiting until the old man made his decision. That could have been difficult, explaining to a bunch of children why their parents were gone. Only the spouses of those who were gone remained—and aunts and uncles who were passed over for ascension in favor of his father. His aunt Lylanne might attend the funeral physically. The woman was too old to have much of a mind left to take anywhere. The rest had remained distant.

"Steven?" Natalie broke the silence. "How did this happen?"

He paused his massage as he contemplated the answer. He had a rule about lying to Natalie and did his best to follow it—never tell her a lie he didn't have to. But this one, he had to. She would be empress. She deserved it. She earned it. But she could never know what it took to put her there. Her heart was too big. If she knew, she would never let herself enjoy it. So Steven let out a careful sigh as he resumed rubbing her shoulders.

"I don't know."

Natalie slipped out of his hands, rising from the chair. In a moment her arms were around him. He held her head tighter to his chest, tightening the embrace amid her quiet sobs.

STRATEGIC OPERATIONS CONTROL—MESSAGE INBOUND. PRIORITY GOLD

RESPONSE REQUIRED. RESPONSE REQUIRED. RESPONSE REQUIRED.

Steven gritted his teeth at the message in his NOD. His father once told him, *There's no rest for the wicked, and even less for an emperor.*

He could not simply answer in his NOD and send it through the astranet. SOC required a specialized terminal for the highest communications security. Steven pushed the message aside. The Executor of Defense could deal with it. He had more important matters right now.

He held Natalie tighter and began to walk her to the bedroom.

STRATEGIC OPERATIONS CONTROL—MESSAGE INBOUND. PRIORITY GOLD

RESPONSE REQUIRED. RESPONSE REQUIRED. RESPONSE REQUIRED.

Again he pushed the message away. Natalie had always slept her problems away. Whenever it got to be too much, her bed was her shelter. She was already in her nightclothes.

EOD LOWENN LODRELL: Your Majesty, your response is urgently requested by our forces in the Hourglass.

Steven pushed the Executor of Defense's message aside as he brought Natalie to their bed and set her down.

STRATEGIC OPERATIONS CONTROL—MESSAGE INBOUND. PRIORITY GOLD

RESPONSE REQUIRED. RESPONSE REQUIRED. RESPONSE REQUIRED.

Now growing angry with the message Steven swept it aside to sit beside Natalie on the bed.

EOD LOWENN LODRELL: Your Majesty, please respond. Admiral Aetius needs your response immediately.

Natalie held out her hand, and the Cathedral answered her with a glass of wine. Steven eyed the glass for a moment before letting her pull away to drink.

"You must answer, Steven."

Steven sat up straighter as the Encephalon's voice seemed to reverberate in his skull.

"I'll answer once she's asleep."

"This is the power you wanted, Steven. Your rule is just beginning. Do not undermine it with dereliction."

"I'm sorry, I have to answer a message," he said as he stood. "I'll be right back."

Natalie nodded quietly, and with a huff, Steven left to the domicile's communications closet, then stepped up onto the round platform to lay his hands on the bars flanking the simple console. With a glare, he scanned the optical port and waited.

A grainy, fuzzy hologram materialized ahead of him. Admiral Aetius stood amid the backdrop of the *Hurricane*'s admiral's bridge.

"Your Majesty," Aetius began, "allow me to express my condolences on your recent loss."

Steven waved his hand for silence, but the admiral did not seem to notice.

"We all grieve for their loss but take heart that you are well."

Of course the admiral did not react. This message was coming from the Hourglass. This was not real-time. The average time in that galaxy, for the admiral, was but a third the speed of that in the Cathedral. The message was being buffered on both ends to allow what each said to go through without odd interruptions. Only now did Aetius receive Steven's gesture and stop his verbal track.

"What is it, Admiral?" Steven asked.

Steven impatiently waited out the seconds before the admiral's answer came. "Your Majesty, have you been briefed on the situation here?"

Steven shook his head. "Not fully, Admiral. As you can probably imagine, things are a bit out of sorts here at the moment." He tapped on the bar as he waited.

"Then allow me to give you a crash briefing, Majesty. The Vaar have launched a massive attack against us. Last count is over four million ships with more arriving. I do not have sufficient forces to meet this assault. So I am asking for your permission under Edict 5 to begin strategic attacks against the Vaar."[1]

Steven's eyebrows peaked. "Are things really that bad, Admiral?"

Aetius glanced off to the side and shook his head at someone before snapping back when he heard the inquiry. "Yes, Majesty. Every tac-brain agrees. There is no scenario in which we hold the Hourglass against this assault."

"We can reinforce you, Admiral."

The admiral bowed his head but shook it slowly. "No, Majesty. To meet

---

1   Also known as the War Powers Edict, Edict 5 is the Imperial court's official policy dictating what actions flag officers may take with and without approval of the emperor.

your father's evacuation plan, I need every gateway moving civilians and our allies out. Even if I adjust that plan, we could not get enough ships here in time before the Vaar overrun us. I *must* begin strategic strikes immediately if I am to hold our position in this galaxy."

Strategic attack. The words were just a clean way to say genocide. Strategic attack meant the direct targeting of enemy worlds and the deaths of their populations. An inevitable result whether one sought it or not. Against an unshielded world, a single Arc-5 submunition was enough. When the rip-field hit the planet, it would bow around it, stripping the crust away. The energy released as byproducts while the crust was shredded would be more than enough to destroy whatever was left.

It was clearly an escalation of hostilities, even beyond open warfare. It invited the enemy to retaliate in kind. Of course, to do that, the enemy had to be able to hit the Empire's worlds. The only worlds in the Vaar's reach were unimportant. The core worlds, the meaningful worlds, were all far beyond their grasp.

"What are the projected casualties, Admiral?"

Steven watched Aetius's cheek twitch. He always had an unusually emotive face for an aren, even an alpha.

"We don't know for certain, sir. The Vaar make population figures difficult to obtain. But they have approximately four hundred worlds in this galaxy with at least a billion people. Roughly double that with populations of half a billion or less."

Around a trillion Vaar, and other Combine races then. That would not be too unbearable. Such a loss would not even register as a pinprick to the Empire or the Combine. It would almost certainly win him points among many of the quants and nakori. They might even consider it justice. Most of the Empire wouldn't even notice. The astranet was far more engrossing than a distant war.

"Deny him, Steven."

"Deny him?" Steven cocked an eyebrow. Surely the Encephalon wouldn't complain about killing a few trillion here and there to settle things. *"Why?"*

"You cannot be a hero to people who perceive no threat. Yield the Hourglass to the Vaar. Make manifest in the minds of your people the threat they pose. Create the danger from which salvation is needed. Even as you appear the one who inherited the crises you must now resolve."

"Your Majesty? Is this channel still working?" The admiral broke the phantom silence.

"I was contemplating, Admiral."

He had to look the part. He leaned side to side, gazed upward, and took a breath to show he was thinking deeply. But finally he gave the admiral his answer.

"Permission denied, Admiral."

The aren's red eyes opened wider. "Majesty, I *cannot* hold this galaxy any other way. If I begin strategic strikes, I can force the Vaar to pull their ships back."

"And kill who knows how many innocent people in the process. And escalate this war another step. No, Admiral. No strategic strikes."

"Majesty, there is no other way. At this rate, I won't even be able to get our people out before the Vaar overwhelm us."

"I said no, *Admiral*," Steven answered, raising his voice with a touch of dramatic inflection before he brought it back down. "I will not kill billions of innocent people just to hold the Hourglass. Even if they're the enemy's people. Nor will I be the one to escalate this war to that level." Steven did not bother to fully parse the admiral's response. "You have my decision, Admiral. Abide by it. Get out everyone you can and then leave. We'll retake the Hourglass on another day. Is that clear?"

Steven knew the answer when the aren bowed his head.

"Yes, Majesty."

Steven's fingers continued to tap on the rail. "Admiral, any word on my sister?"

"No, Majesty. Avalon is being overrun by the Vaar. We have had no communication with Princess Simmonne or Colonel Panzer since the attack began."

"Very well. Steven out."

The channel closed automatically as Steven stepped off the platform.

"Very good, Steven. You left him with no doubt about your reasoning."

Steven walked back to the bedroom. *"Might the Vaar see it as weakness?"*

"It is a fool who assumes his nemesis unreasonable. The Vaar will see it as you explained it to the admiral. A desire to avoid escalation. Nothing more. Were they not certain your father would mirror your answer, their attack would not have taken this form."

Steven returned to the bedroom to find Natalie lying down. Her mind was not yet asleep but rested on the same memories he had read earlier. He would need his sleep soon. Time waited for no man, and neither did politics. Tomorrow he faced the Senate. Quietly he prepared himself for bed before tucking in and pulling Natalie to him.

CHAPTER
2E

FOR THE FIRST TIME, Oul'sor set foot in the *Caustic Reverie*'s control room. It was as if the same person were responsible for every command center. The only way they seemed to know how to adapt it was to make it larger or smaller depending on the ship. A commander's chair stood where four walkways extended out to a perimeter ring. Between each walkway lay a pit where a command crew labored.

Oul'sor approached the center with Indorai behind him. Many eyes followed. Some even whispered his name as they tapped the shoulders of those nearby and directed their attention. A command center was always noisy, but Oul'sor's presence had brought a hush. The public broadcast crew was still filing out. Several of them stuttered in their step when they saw him. But all moved out of his way. None would block a warlord's path except another warlord.

"It's Oul'sor."

He turned as he heard his name, and the awed Viss from whom it had come. Even in her position down in the pit, she had bowed her head and stepped away. As if to ensure that there was no chance that even her shadow might stand in his way. But as he stared at her, he realized that she had not actually said it.

"Oul'sor. He's here."

He turned to the other side, to a young Vaar looking up at him. The eyes of hero worship, but he quickly bowed his head. Soon he heard more, whispers in both ears, and he covered his right eye. He, too, had been silent. Many young faces, all seeing him in person. Someone they had been in their youth was an example to which they should aspire.

"It will be hard to adjust." That voice, voices? That was Indorai. *"But you must learn to accept their thoughts around you,"* the hollow one said as he stepped closer. *"Feel their adulation of you as you never have. If their thoughts distract you, embrace the feelings. Let your mind be a wing and their praise your wind. Ride on it as you pass them by, and pay them no heed they do not need."*

Oul'sor took a breath. This was what the humans called telepathy. What kind of twisted creature grew up always hearing the thoughts in the heads of others. How did they ever learn as children which thoughts were their own? He took another breath and lowered his hand before forcing himself to continue walking.

The children will never believe that I saw Oul'sor.

Focus. He fixed his eyes on the three warlords on the center platform. First among them was Hahk'xess, standing tall in his golden armor. Beside him was Kreth'nell, brilliant, and who took his brilliance as leave to be . . . weird. Kreth'nell had grown his plates as infantry before finding his genius on ships. But he was still an odd one. Like any warlord, Kreth'nell had reproductive rights to any he wished. A privilege he not only exercised but did so in a way that the resulting stories of perversion made Oul'sor's skin crawl beneath his plates. But it was his favorite hobby that disturbed Oul'sor most. Kreth'nell was one of the few modern practitioners of bone-gilding. An ancient custom, but being ancient did not mean good. Were it up to Oul'sor, it would remain in the past.

Kreth'nell wore silver armor, and long bones coated in gold hung like a cape from his shoulders and back. Smaller bones in silver hung from his arms like tassel, but they were no mere ornaments. Each bone was taken from a defeated foe, preserved, and plated to serve as a trophy. Kreth'nell took his bones seriously. In his greatest victories over the nakori and the quants, he had sent boarding parties to bring back bones from enemy commanders. Gold for the most worthy—silver for the rest. A wretched practice that disrespected those who had died bravely. That was the only way Oul'sor could see it. A warrior's remains belonged to his family for them to say their goodbyes. But like him, Kreth'nell was a warlord, and none could forbid him. Or at least, none would.

When the decision was made to fight the Empire, nearly every fleet warlord had volunteered to lead the attack on the Time-Lost Galaxy. When Kreth'nell sought the task, it was decided. Kreth'nell had never lost a fleet battle in war or training.

The Warlord of the Clandestine stood with them unarmored. Dolum. Even his plates had few indicators of rank or status. If one did not already know him as a warlord, they were unlikely to assume it. Oul'sor was close enough now to overhear their conversation.

"The reports from the front are disturbing," Hahk'xess said. "Our warriors are not hearing us."

"The Council is happy that we retook Origin," Dolum answered, trying to mollify the frustration.

"Twenty thousand killed; another fifty thousand wounded," Hahk'xess returned. "To overpower a garrison of a thousand legionnaires and their machines. If we suffer those losses when we outnumber them so heavily, I tremble should they outnumber us. It must be impressed further on our warriors. They cannot simply close to melee and overwhelm the Solars. Their weapons are too deadly. And the new walkers—more than half were destroyed."

"If you fear casualties—" Kreth'nell stopped short as his head turned. The bones on his armor clacked together as his body followed. His head lowered into a bow. As the eldest member of the Council of Warlords, the only one from whom Oul'sor could not expect a bow was the grand warlord. Hahk'xess and Dolum turned to him and, as old friends so easily did, dispensed with such formalities.

"Oul'sor?" Hahk'xess said as all twelve of his pupils dilated. Hahk'xess looked him up and down. "You are not as I expected to see you. What happened to the body built for your vek'thim?"

"Destroyed," Oul'sor answered. Indorai, unseen by the others, had begun walking a circuit around the platform.

"Then how do you stand as flesh?" Hahk'xess pressed.

"Our mutual friend provided."

Hahk'xess moved his gaze until it fell on Kreth'nell. "If you will part from us, Kreth'nell." Hahk'xess spoke too low for those in the pits to hear.

"Of course," Kreth'nell answered. "I will finish the transfer to the *Pertinent Vigil*."

Oul'sor eyed him. "Leaving your command ship, Kreth'nell?"

Bones clacked as the weird one nodded. "This ship is too big a target. The Solars will prioritize it. I will route communications through it, but my command staff will be somewhere less obvious."

Kreth'nell turned to bow to Hahk'xess and then to Oul'sor before making his way out. Oul'sor allowed an utterance of disgust as the sound of the bones faded over the distance. With the odd one gone, Hahk'xess looked at Dolum before motioning for him and Oul'sor to follow. The grand warlord led them to the side of the room and through another door.

"Get out," Hahk'xess snapped to the occupant seated comfortably at his desk.

The ship's captain began to object, but one did not come to captain a ship like the *Caustic Reverie* by being a fool. The captain vacated his chair and quietly left the room to the three warlords. Indorai slipped through the door as it closed.

"I've heard some troubling things, Oul'sor," Hahk'xess began. "That you had the princess and released her to lure out the Crykeeper."

"It's true," Oul'sor answered. "I allowed my anger to interfere with the mission."

Hahk'xess's teeth sparked as he ground them together. "We *needed* her, Oul'sor." Hahk'xess growled in frustration while his fist clenched. "For the emperor's daughter, what could we have gained? We might have forced the emperor to abandon the galaxy. How many battles must we fight now, that might have been avoided?"

What has the hollow one done to you? Dolum did not voice the words. If telepathy had not brought them to Oul'sor, Dolum's expression would have. His jaw protruded forward, and his pupils took turns dilating and contracting.

"We lost many on that mission," Hahk'xess continued, "and all we have to show for it are her servants. A gruesome waste of some of our best."

"The Crykeeper cut through them like uncooked meat," Oul'sor answered. "If I were not there, you would not even have her servants."

There was an image. At first he thought it a memory. But soon Oul'sor realized it was Hahk'xess imagining the Council of Warlords, and how he would explain. A touch of shame chilled his neck. Then tension slacked from his muscles. A failure to his office Hahk'xess would be, if he did not deliver admonishment. But his first thoughts were to protect, not to punish.

"Perhaps," Hahk'xess answered.

Are you still the friend I remember? Oul'sor tried not to react to hearing the thought in Dolum's mind. He ground his teeth for a moment. Friend? Where was his friendship when Dolum tried to deny him vek'thim?

"He is quite the good little spymaster, isn't he?" Indorai projected. *"Always so suspicious. I wonder. Does he have the job because he is that way, or is he that way because he has the job?"*

"The council will have many questions," Hahk'xess continued. "I do not know if they will be satisfied with that answer. I will shield you as I am able. But I want to know what happened."

Oul'sor took a breath as he thought back to the fight. Hahk'xess had seen more than enough of his battles. He might understand.

"Most of the team was killed or wounded by the Imperial Guard. The Crykeeper took half of those left with a surprise attack. Destroyed our ship. I think with a vehicle from our embassy. Our new sensors were not effective in seeing him. He began to pick off the remains of the team. I had the princess and used her as bait to lure him out. He was lured, but my attempt to kill him failed. The team abandoned me, taking her servants with them. I stayed behind to face the Crykeeper, and perhaps recover the princess."

"And you failed," Hahk'xess added, grinding his teeth hard enough to eject a fragment with the sparks. It clattered loudly like a dropped knife upon the floor. "I will explain your reasons to the council. But you may be called to account."

"We can still have her," Oul'sor said. "I will go."

"No," Dolum interrupted. "I have already seen to it."

Oul'sor faced him.

"You are too close, Oul'sor. We cannot afford to fail again."

"You sense it, don't you? They're afraid of you." Oul'sor tried to ignore him, but Indorai continued, *"You best become accustomed to it. The more powerful you become, the greater their fear will be."*

"Oul'sor," Hahk'xess began, "you said the hollow one made you flesh again. What exactly did he do?"

"Be mindful of what you say of him," Dolum cautioned as he took a look about the room. That was followed by a long sniff. "He might be here."

"I care not an enspa's keth if he is," Hahk'xess snapped back. "He knows well what I think of him."

Only Oul'sor could hear Indorai laugh.

"What did he do to you, Oul'sor?" Hahk'xess repeated.

"He provided me a new body," Oul'sor answered. "If you wish the particulars of how, that is not in my knowledge. Does it matter? The creation of new flesh is not a technology mystic to us."

Hahk'xess and Dolum exchanged looks before the former drew himself up to his full height and stared Oul'sor down. Dolum took that moment to take a device, a poly scanner, in hand, and wave it over Oul'sor.

"Do you remember my brother, Oul'sor?" Hahk'xess asked.

For a moment the question did not make sense, but Oul'sor stood more erect when he realized its purpose.

"You wonder if I am who I appear to be," Oul'sor said. "If I really am Oul'sor."

Hahk'xess simply stared, waiting for his answer.

"You have many brothers, but I suspect you mean Don'xess," Oul'sor answered.

"What did we call him?" Hahk'xess pressed.

"I don't suppose it occurs to him that if I can put words in his mind, I can take them out," Indorai jeered.

"Don'don," Oul'sor answered. "He never triumphed in his battle with enunciation."

The grand warlord's pupils contracted. Even Hahk'xess's scent changed at the mention of the name. "Tell me about him, Oul'sor. Tell me what happened."

The severity of Hahk'xess's suspicion was confirmed, that he would wish to relive such a memory.

"Him, Dolum, and I. Inseparable. And you. The little brother who always had to do whatever his big brother was doing. We three had sworn to each other that we would all be warlords one day. So we trained, every day, before and after our studies. Trained ourselves in every way we could. And you with us."

Oul'sor smiled a bitter smile, the pain of good memories on a dark path.

"Our parents told us not to climb the Cliffs of Osena. Told us that we were not ready. So we had to prove them wrong. It was the only thing we three did that you did not want to do. You were the only one with sense enough to listen to them. But we, we teased you until you came with us."

Oul'sor's eyes moved away from Hahk'xess, to the wall and into the past.

"Dolum and I were racing to the top. You were having trouble, so Don'don lingered to encourage you. You had trouble with an outcropping. He went to help you. He slipped. You caught him. But he was too heavy. Before Dolum and I could climb down to you . . . Your grip was slipping. Don'don would not take you down with him. So he let go."

At first, Oul'sor took the intense sorrow in his flesh for his. But as he continued to speak, he realized the feelings beneath his plates belonged to Hahk'xess.

"You were so young, it was hard for you to understand death. So your parents likened it to sleep. For five days Dolum and I sat with you at his grave while you waited to dig him out if he woke up. On the fifth day, you passed out from hunger. Dolum and I carried you home. Your father thanked us for staying with you while you came to terms."

Hahk'xess nodded and took a step closer. "And what did you swear to me, Oul'sor? What was the oath you took?"

Oul'sor glanced for a moment at Dolum. "We swore then that we would be your brothers. Until you saw Don'don again."

"How touching."

Oul'sor cast a glare in Indorai's direction but quickly looked back at Hahk'xess, who turned his back and rested his fists on the desk. Dolum lowered the poly scanner.

"The hollow one can read minds," Hahk'xess said. "He could have taken this memory from yours, or even my own. But the smell of your grief is correct. I believe you are who you are. There will be many questions about your mission. I, I will do my best to shield you."

Hahk'xess turned back to him. "You're still alive, and your vek'thim is still in force. For now the council won't have an assignment for you. But Oul'sor"—Hahk'xess gave his most intense glare—"You cannot interfere with our task again. Too many have given—are giving—too much for this. Your revenge cannot hinder us."

"It won't," Oul'sor answered. "On this you have my promise."

"Perhaps you should not make promises you might not be able to keep."

"I'll have your silence, hollow one," Oul'sor thought back. *"This does not concern you."*

Indorai answered with a silent scoff.

There was so much more Oul'sor wanted to tell him. But he knew he could not. Hahk'xess would never understand, would never be able to accept it. Dolum with his pious pessimism might, but not Hahk'xess. He would rail against fate and circumstance, ready to die on principle before surrendering to inevitability. But whether they understood or not, he knew they might never forgive him. Even when Hahk'xess saw Don'don once more.

"I should go," Hahk'xess said. "I must return to Prithone—report our success personally to the council. And answer their questions."

"Of course," Oul'sor answered. "Before you go, since Kreth'nell is no longer commanding from this ship, you might order him to place it in orbit around Origin."

Hahk'xess cocked his head to the side, so Oul'sor answered the unspoken question.

"The speakers. Images of the ship and the planet could be quite valuable. To the Solars, it would be a powerful statement."

"Yes, you're right. I will do it," Hahk'xess answered before turning to Dolum. "Come back to us, and be mindful. I do not trust them."

"It is as I am to distrust," Dolum answered him. "Spare me no worry."

Hahk'xess laid a hand briefly on Oul'sor's shoulder before exiting the room. With him gone, Oul'sor cast a glare at Dolum.

"You are still angry with me," Dolum lamented.

"You voted to grant me vek'thim and then tried to deny it to me," Oul'sor answered. "Why should I not be?"

"Surely you understand my reasons."

"You explained yourself in council."

"I gave words to the council that it needed," Dolum retorted. "Surely you understand better."

"I don't care what your reasons were," Oul'sor snarled. "You had no right." He began to walk away.

"I had every right." Dolum's words brought him to a halt. "I am a warlord. As are you. Our loyalty must be to our people above all others. Even our friends and brothers. We three are the rock on which the council stands. The only parents left in a room of orphaned children. They are as we were before the cliffs. They will need us, all three of us, or surely they will fall."

Oul'sor turned back to him. "Hahk'xess said you are leaving?"

"For a time," Dolum answered. "Crossroads or no, we cannot win this war without allies. I go to make sure we have them. Perhaps, when I return, you will have found it in yourself to forgive. And if not, then to understand."

Dolum walked past him and out of the room.

"Return to us, Dolum," Oul'sor whispered. The pain crept into his bones—the feeling that before it was over, they would no longer be three.

CHAPTER
3A

*T*OCK ... *T*OCK ... *T*OCK ...

"Contact now at two-five light-years," Andira announced over the hushed chamber. "Harmonics coming into focus. Analyzing."

A new screen opened over the display, a myriad of oscillating sine waves. No two ships at warp distorted space-time in exactly the same way. If one was close enough, they could measure the superluminal disturbance, distorting space far beyond the source. Even the smallest imperfections in the drive system created fingerprints. Field sensors could identify the class and, with enough data, individual ships. Andira was chewing on that data now to learn what was out there.

Not an Echo. *Not an* Echo, Panzer mouthed as she worked. The seven waves on the screen indicated that it was almost certainly a destroyer. The Combine had a ridiculous number of active-duty destroyer classes, and Panzer knew them all. He knew their top speeds, their cruising speeds, their armament, shield strength, sensor capabilities, crew compliment. Everything. But not an *Echo*.

The Combine did not assign popular names to their equipment—only series and model numbers. Names had to be earned.[2] *Echo* was a reporting name given by Armadas Intelligence when it learned of the new class.

Tock ... Tock ... Tock ...

The new Vaar supercruisers, *Caustic Reverie* and her still-incomplete sisters, were publicity projects. They were constructs of national pride with more information available to their public than should have been. But not the *Echo*. Armadas Intelligence, Legionnaire Intelligence, Solar Intelligence—all had failed to gather more than the most basic information. Even the Corps had failed. Corps telepaths had brain-boggled Vaar into becoming

---

2   Typically in the Combine fleet, the first ship of a new class will be named by its first captain once it completes its shakedown cruise. This captain will choose a name that is usually a combination of a descriptor followed by a noun. The noun will become official for the class. The first captain of each new ship in that class will then choose a different descriptor to pair with the original noun in naming the successive ships. A new noun will only be chosen once suitable descriptors have been exhausted.

unwitting spies, silent agents, and even they failed. They simply vanished. Only a chance spotting by an Armadas' *Rook* had provided the harmonic data in Andira's archive.

Tock . . . Tock . . . Tock . . .

"Not an *Echo*." He continued his refrain.

When the intelligence services learned that the Vaar were trying to build a ship that could hide from Armadas sensors, most laughed. Panzer did not laugh. The only way the Empire could lose a war to the Combine was to underestimate the Vaar. Yet everyone seemed determined to do exactly that.

"Contact identified," Andira announced.

"Not an *Echo*."

"*Echo*-class Combine destroyer. Nine-seven percent probability."

He hung his head. Of course it was. It was stupid of him to hope it might be something else today. The sine waves faded to be replaced by a silhouette of the ship, unmistakably Vaar in its design. Yet still a departure from those that came before. The hull was shaped by a long tube, with a secondary hull of segmented compartments running the length of her spine. She retained the hammerhead of all Combine ships, but with a wide, beak-like nose extending beyond. Two-thirds down the length of her hull, three stubby sails rose out in an inverted *Y*. Each sloped back to plateau before planing back down into her body. Her tail formed an *X*, with each of the four pylons joined by a rotating ring.

Most warships had one or more sails, protrusions from the hull where powerful sensors could be isolated from sources of interference while remaining well-armored. Three primary sails on something as small as a destroyer meant an extreme emphasis on sensor capabilities. The ring on the tail was almost certainly a wake-breaker, a feature shared by his ship, albeit in different form. A dedicated stealth feature, helping to soothe the distortion of space-time so that the vessel's wake was not detectable hundreds of light-years away.

"Andira," he began, "don't give us away, but we can't waste this. Low-intensity scan—see if you can get anything useful."

"Yes sir."

Tock . . . Tock . . . Tock . . .

"Does this ship have weapons?" Simmonne's whisper prompted him to glance down at her.

"Yes," he answered, hoping his annoyed tone would discourage the inevitable follow-up.

"So!" she hissed. "Shoot them! Blow them up!"

"That is a destroyer, princess. We're in a sloop. That is *not* a fight we want to pick."

Tock . . . Tock . . . Tock . . .

She seemed to flinch in time with the sound, which grew progressively louder. If she thought that was bad, well, probably best not to tell her what the Armadas called the sound the instruments made in response to a missile's sensors.

A cone projected from each of the *Echo*'s sails. Each time one passed over them, the sound came. He should turn away. Spooling up the compression drive risked a blip for the destroyer to see. But there was probably enough distance. The Armadas needed this data, so he waited as seconds passed into minutes.

"Andira. How certain are you that they can't see us?"

"I do not have detailed data on this class's sensor capabilities," she answered. "However our sensor image at this distance is too small for an Armadas ship to detect. I am certain that a Combine warship cannot detect us."

A few years ago, that would have been some comfort. But only a decade ago, the Combine could not miniaturize disrupters for infantry use. Now only the second- and third-line troops lacked them. One of many unexplained technological leaps, and a disturbing expedience of proliferation.

The Echo was moving in a zigzag, giving a panning field of view to the sensors in its sails. In the span of a typical galaxy, time and distance were frivolities to warp sensors. Their primary limitation was the clutter they had to see through. But with a stealth ship, these things mattered. The closer it came, the smaller the chance his ship's counter-detection systems could hide them. Move and maybe be detected. Or stay, and be certain of eventual detection if the destroyer did not change course.

"Andira, break orbit. Ahead one-eighth. Come to heading zero, seven, zero. Two degrees down-point."[3]

The ship began to move, leaving the star behind before dipping its nose ever so slightly relative to the galactic plane. In moments they were on a vector to take them out of the *Echo*'s approach. He cast another glance down at Simmonne, who wrung her hands as she watched the Vaar ship with dread. His telepathy may have been out of order, but empathy was still there. Damn Vaar could have at least waited until he kicked the hangover. This would also be easier if she could get a grip on herself.

He shook his head. That wasn't fair. For such a sheltered girl who had been through what she had, she was holding up as well as could be expected. Even so, her rousing panic was distracting. He still held her by the arm and released her for a moment to wrap his arm around her.

"Andira, re-synchronize power circuit 30."

Huh? The expression came from both Kassar and Novin. Perhaps Andira knew what he was doing; perhaps she simply obeyed.

"Yes sir."

Circuit 30 handled the ship's backup lighting. Re-synchronizing the

---

3   Point refers to the mathematically-derived epicenter of the galaxy, used by cartographers to assign 3D compass directions for the purposes of navigation. A line connecting this point to the galaxy's first colony establishes the zero degree out of 360. The point itself is used as the determiner of elevation, relative to which *up* and *down* is defined.

circuits wouldn't actually do anything. But he sensed his goal accomplished in Simmonne, who relaxed slightly as he issued the command. Just a little something to make her feel that he was taking control of the situation, rather than simply waiting.

Tock . . . Tock . . . Tock . . .

"What do we do if they see us?" Simmonne asked, her voice barely audible.

"They can't hear you," he answered, raising his voice slightly. "You don't have to whisper."

In one ear, out the other. She whispered the question again.

"We run," he answered before exhaling and closing his eyes. *"Don't be afraid. This is what I do."*

That was a very bad idea. Bile welled in his throat while his stomach found new knots to tie itself into. He gripped the console and locked his knees to keep himself upright. Too soon for telepathy.

Tock . . . Tock . . . Tock . . .

"Andira," he said as the pain subsided. "Adjust power on circuit thirty. Plus five amps."

Simmonne took a breath, and he felt the tension in her back ease a tick. If the *Echo* spotted them, their only chance would be to run. The rotary drive was undamaged, and he doubted that even this new ship would be able to keep pace. But that could be little different from a thief fleeing a law enforcement officer. It did little good to outrun one if you ran headfirst into a dozen more vectored to intercept. The fact that Andira had not detected more ships on approach was his only comfort. His evidence that the *Echo* did not know what it was looking for. The distance was beginning to open while the destroyer continued on.

Andira was already busy plotting them an escape course. Of that he was certain. But he knew that such a course would almost certainly take them away from the front line, and deeper into Combine territory. Farther from a potential rendezvous with the Armadas.

Tock . . . Tock . . . Tock . . .

Panzer craned his neck as he watched the image of the Vaar ship pivot.

"The destroyer is maneuvering," Andira announced. "On intercept course with us. Distance now two-seven light-years."

What little panic he had managed to coax out of Simmonne returned.

"Andira, come to heading zero-nine-zero. Five degrees up-point."

One example did not a thesis make, and Panzer watched the *Echo* for signs of a reaction.

"Destroyer is matching our maneuvers. Now at two-one light-years."

"And you're certain they can't see us?" he quipped.

"They *cannot* see us."

"Maybe you should tell them that," he answered with a scoff.

"Do you want me to go to battle stations?"

"Not yet," he answered. "If you're right and they can't see us, let's not do anything to make it easier."

Andira dutifully continued her scans of the oncoming ship. At such low settings, they were supposed to be too weak, too randomized for Combine sensor-detectors to notice. But this was something new. He'd chanced enough. The Armadas would have to be satisfied with whatever Andira had managed to gather.

"Andira, cease your scans. Increase to one-sixth. Come to heading zero-seven-five, twenty-two degrees up-point."

This time the *Echo* gave a stronger response to their movement. A new icon appeared in the display an instant before Andira made the announcement.

"Square wave field. Missile inbound! Time to closure, one-two-five seconds."

He heard the panicked gasp from Simmonne and pulled her more firmly into him.

"Battle stations condition two. Put them on our tail, ahead flank!" he bellowed. The lights of the CIC turned red, and a shrill whine filled the air as Andira pushed the compression drive to full power. The whine was soon parsed by a rhythmic banging as the damaged drive protested the strain.

"Shields active. Field stabilizers to full. Pulse interceptors unavailable. Missile interceptors active," Andira announced. "Missile in acquisition on an intercept course."

"We have to go. Bring the rotary online," he barked.

"Time to closure, one-one-five seconds."

By turning away he bought precious seconds by forcing the missile to chase them. But his concentration was jarred when the ship lurched. He caught himself on the console, still holding Simmonne.

A new hologram sprouted from the display, mapping his ship. To switch to rotary propulsion required altering the ship's geometry. The nose and tail would extend, and their crescents would close into arrowheads The wings would fold in to do the same. But nothing was moving. Red icons flashed through the port wing, highlighting one column in an array of four.

"Failure in port interlock three," Andira reported. "Missile closure now one-zero-five seconds."

"Cut the interlock," he answered before stopping himself. "No, that will take too long."

He did not need the words. With a look to the brothers, both nodded before sprinting out of the chamber. Panzer's eyes moved to the readout of his ship.

C-FACTOR: 669,750

"Andira, more speed."

"Negative," she answered. "Drive power already at one hundred percent."

"I'm pretty sure 110 is higher than one hundred."

"Yes sir. Square wave field. Second missile inbound. Time to closure, one-two-five seconds."

Simmonne chose that moment to lose her composure. "Do something!" she screamed, fighting his grip. "Shoot them down! Shoot the ship! Do—"

Panzer brought his hand up and clamped it firmly on Simmonne's mouth.

"You stop that. Right. Now." He articulated the words carefully. Her struggles continued for a moment, and she let out a cry into his hand. Finally she growled in frustration and lowered her arms.

Panzer's attention turned back to the approaching missiles. The first moved in a zigzag before straightening itself. The second did the same. Every few seconds, each would appear to drift off course before correcting.

"Andira, switch to distortion mapping."

At his command the image shifted, clearing away the previous void of space. In its place the image seemed to take on the consistency of translucent fluid. The most visible object was the Vaar destroyer, where the fluid spiraled toward it, contracted into a sleeve around it, and gushed out in a jet behind. The next object was his ship, where the fluid flowed toward the nose before expanding into a cone behind.

Between the two were the missiles, each leaving a long trail—stones of the greatest speed falling through an ocean of unfathomable depth. The waves behind his ship took on a defined triangular shape. Those of the destroyer were smooth, spiraling curves. But those of the missiles were well-defined in their square pattern. The weapons followed the trail left by his ship, still in their zigzagging pattern. Whenever the zig brought them to the edge of the cone, they zagged back to remain inside of it.

"Wake-homers," Panzer whispered while looking at Rhoxx, who nodded his agreement.

The Vaar put a lot of their research eggs into this basket. The ability to track the disturbances left in the fluidity of space-time by a ship moving at warp. Was that how the destroyer found them? No, they were sublight in orbit of a star then. Either way that was how the missiles were tracking. But the Vaar never used just one guidance system.

"Both missiles in acquisition. Intercept in four-five seconds and six-six seconds," Andira warned.

"Ready decoys on the first missile. Prepare to agitate."

"Yes sir," Andira answered. "Primary interceptors tracking. Locking in."

Tock . . . Tock . . . Tock . . .

"Missiles still in acquisition. Closure in three-five seconds. Five-five seconds."

He felt Simmonne cringe as a new sound came from the instruments. Death's pulse.

Eeep . . . Eeep . . . Eeep . . .

"Missile 1 has acquired. Missile 1 is actively homing."

Already? he mouthed. "Launch decoys. Agitate, agitate, agitate."

Active homing; that was two guidance systems. A dull thump echoed through the deck as the decoys launched out of the ship's tail. A moment later, the hull began to flex around them, moaning as if to protest being woken. On his order, Andira short-stroked the compression drive, knotting the space around the ship. The distortion map showed many waves pouring out of the ship to form a bubble around it.

Panzer kept his eyes on the missiles and the decoys racing out to them. Together they hosed the missiles with data. The weapons reacted, and death's pulse was silenced. Like dogs drawn to meat, each missile approached a decoy. With the decoys jamming their active targeting, each missile was now passively homing on the decoys. Passive home-on-jam, three guidance methods.

"Missile 1 has lost contact. Missile 2 has lost contact. Interceptors hot on missile one. Firing."

The pulse may have faded, but the missiles were not defeated. Both sniffed at the decoys laid out for them before losing interest and moving on. The knotting of space-time by the short-stroking MID had left a zone temporarily opaque to the active sensors. But to the wake-homers, it was the same as shouting "Come and get me."

"Good lock on missile one," Andira reported. "Intercept in ten seconds."

Panzer watched the smaller icons of his interceptors move toward the missile, expecting them to merge and vanish. Instead his eyes opened wider as missile one turned sharply. A new icon lit as the Vaar missile deployed decoys.

"That's new," he muttered as the warhead swirled back toward them and slipped out of the cone of the decoys.

Eeep . . . Eeep . . . Eeep . . .

"Missile one has reacquired. Missile two has reacquired."

"Turn us into them," Panzer barked. "Fifty-five degrees down-point."

At warp or below, a fast object could only turn so quickly. He had to close the distance now, faster than the weapons could correct.

"Coming around," Andira answered.

Panzer felt another short-lived struggle from Simmonne as the ship turned toward the missiles. A bit of a squeeze put an end to it.

"Missile one closure now four-zero seconds. Missile two six-five seconds."

Panzer sighed in frustration as more icons popped off the missiles, foiling the second batch of interceptors.

Eeep . . . Eeep . . . Eeep . . .

The first missile was close enough now to resolve clearly in the display. Ninety-one meters with three segments separated by rotating bands. Decoy pods continued to dump from the midsection as the weapon mocked his interceptors. Three of the tiny missiles managed to avoid being duped. But only one successfully met the threat. The smaller warhead detonated directly in the aggressor's path. The detonation of the tiny inflation charge created a zone of death half a light-second wide. It was not enough. The missile faded out for a moment before reappearing, still hot on their scent.

"Missile one closure in three-zero seconds. Missile two, five-zero seconds."

"More decoys, on command," Panzer answered as he stared down the first weapon.

Eeep . . . Eeep . . . Eeep . . .

Death's pulse raced as the prey drew near.

"Missile one closure in one-five seconds. One-four. One-three. One-two. One-one. Ten seconds. Nine."

"Fire decoys. Ninety degrees up-point. Agitate!"

Andira sent a quartet of the distractions before pitching the ship's nose. The missiles took no notice of the decoys this time.

"Firing interceptors."

The distance was too short now. Missile one could not avoid the interceptors in time. Twenty-five of the small warheads converged on it. Missile one was wiped from the display. But missile two remained with just enough time and distance to avoid the interceptors sent for it.

"Closure in ten. Nine. Eight. Seven. Six. Five."

Eeep! Eeep! Eeep!

"Forty-five degrees down-point now!"

Too late. The missile came in, and its icon split as submunitions were deployed. The ship lurched, and the sound of grinding metal raced through the hull.

"Damn glue bombs!" Rhoxx exclaimed as he slid his feet apart to keep himself upright.

Panzer's jaw clenched. Threading charges, called glue bombs for their effect on space, altered its fluidity to behave more like an adhesive rather than a superfluid. They would do little damage to a ship's hull. But to the drive systems, to the shields, they were the equivalent of throwing metal rods into spinning machinery.

Tock . . . Tock . . . Tock . . .

Panzer closed his eyes briefly. The Vaar weren't trying to kill them; they were trying to capture them. Why? He looked down at Simmonne. Did they somehow know she was here? Did they recognize the ship and think they could capture it? Or were they still trying to figure out what they were looking at? No time to debate it.

"Square wave fields. More missiles," Andira warned. "Missile 3, closure in one-two-zero seconds. Missile 4, one-two-five."

The instruments still picked up sensor sweeps from the destroyer. Its attack sensors were still in search mode. How had the destroyer gotten close enough to send wake-homers at them if they couldn't see them? How were they feeding the missiles course corrections until they were close enough for the latter to track with their sensors? What else was going on here? Too many questions. But he did have one precious piece of information now. When the missiles came close and had all the data they were going to get, they did not go for the decoys or maneuver to see past the agitation.

However many sensors the missiles had, the wake-homer was dominant.

CHAPTER
3B

*T*OCK ... *TOCK* ... *TOCK* ... *TOCK* ...
Simmonne would have given almost anything if those sounds would just stop. The colonel's hand was still glued to her mouth, pulling her head back against his body. Her eyes were fixed on the displays, darting back and forth between the incoming missiles and the Vaar ship. The far larger vessel bore down on them as if to satisfy a desire to catch them itself.

CLASS: ECHO
TYPE: DESTROYER
RANGE: 20LY
R-BEARING: 180
C-FACTOR: 670,005
LENGTH: 71.1KM
MASS: UNKNOWN
ARMAMENT: UNKNOWN
DEFENSE: UNKNOWN
NAME: NO TRANSPONDER DETECTED, MARKER SCAN IN PROGRESS ...

"Brothers, how we doing on that interlock?" the colonel asked.

"Corridor's blocked by wreckage!" one of the kurai answered, somehow whispering and shouting at the same time. "We're digging through."

Nervous energy forced Simmonne's hands to move, to do something. Her right hand closed on something until a sharp point bit into her skin. She looked down, holding it out to see past the colonel's hand. The small golden icon of a sun, the gift from the quants.

The forlorn people raced through her mind. The captain who delivered his people's treasures, asking the Empire to safeguard them. The children in the refugee camp. What were their names? She promised them. She promised the Empire would protect them. What was happening to them now?

Something had changed in the display. She scanned it to find the difference.

NAME: *ITINERATE HUNTER*
Eeep ... Eeep ... Eeep ...

"Missile 3 has acquired," the AI warned. "Missile 3 closure in three-five seconds. Missile 4 in four-zero seconds."

"Reset interceptors for counter-intercept, and cycle on the first missile," the colonel answered far too calmly.

"Interceptors already reset," the AI said. "Cycling on missile 3."

Every few seconds the AI would call out the time again. What was it waiting for? If they had interceptors, why were they letting the missiles get so close?

Tock . . . Eeep . . . Tock . . . Eeep . . .

The maddening sounds overlapped and replayed in her ears.

"Load CASRADs,"[4] the colonel ordered. "Prepare to agitate."

"Ready."

"Launch CASRADs. Agitate!"

Simmonne winced as the banging sounds in the hull sent sonic needles into her ears as the ship rocked under her feet.

A bubble formed in the display behind their ship. Two new icons found their way into its perimeter. As the devices sprinted away from the ship, they seemed to drag the bubble, stretching it out with them.

Eeep . . .

The sound faded, and the missiles weaved and crossed over each other.

"Missiles have lost acquisition," the AI reported. "Interceptors firing."

The images of the missiles and the Vaar ship broke up as the bubble behind them continued to expand. There was a growl as the small icons poured out of their vessel, arcing around the bubble before vanishing behind it.

"Contact lost."

"Come to heading zero—" A loud blast erupted from within the ship. "Andira?"

"Critical failure in compression manifold 1," it answered him. "Drive power falling."

"More power. We can't lose speed."

"Unable to comply. Carrier circuits at maximum capacity."

The bubble that had formed behind the ship finally burst. The Vaar destroyer came back into view. Simmonne's eyes raced to find the missiles. One of them was gone. The other was pursuing one of the other devices. What did he call them? The CASRADs. The missile followed close behind it, on a path into the beyond.

"Brothers, I'm running out of tricks up here," the colonel said slowly. "How are we doing on that interlock?"

"Maintenance hatch is jammed. We're breaching now," the whisper-shouting kurai answered.

Tock . . . Tock . . . Tock . . .

"Andira, move to condition one. Load the forward tubes. Target their sails. Ready to fire on command."

Simmonne took a breath through her nose. *Finally*, he was going to fight back.

---

4   CASRAD is an acronym for Co-Agitating Short-Range Active Decoy.

"More missiles. Six in parallel—correction, twelve in parallel. Intercept in one-one-five."

True to the AI's words, a dozen of the weapons accelerated toward them. This was it. They were dead. They were going to die. Simmonne writhed in the colonel's grasp again until he squeezed her tighter.

"Brothers? About that interlock?" he asked, and Simmonne detected the faintest break in his calm tone.

"We're planting charges now," the kurai came back.

"Andira, cut power, ahead one-third."

"*What?*" The colonel's hand muffled Simmonne's scream. Why was he slowing down?

"Missile closure now eight-zero."

"Range to destroyer?" he barked.

"Nineteen and closing."

"Just a little closer," the colonel said in a taunting tone.

What are you doing? Simmonne screamed in her mind, hoping he would notice.

"Andira, charge the overdrive. I'm going to want as much power as possible."

"Acknowledged. Missile closure now seven-five seconds."

The seconds counted down to the maddening tone. *Tock . . . Tock . . . Tock . . .*

Eeep . . .

"Missiles acquired." The AI raised its volume over the shrill sounds overlapping each other. With a wave of his hand, the colonel dismissed the sound. "Closure in three-five seconds."

"Kassar? Novin?"

"Fire in the hole!" The answer came a moment before a blast ripped through the ship. Through the metal floor and into her knees, Simmonne felt the shockwave.

When she opened her eyes, the image of their ship changed. The red portion turned to amber. The crescent nose and tail closed into arrowheads.

"Engaging rotary drive," the AI said before the ship seemed to hit a bump, then a quiet, seemingly distant roar crept into the space. She looked at the display. The larger wings were merging into the hull to form a third arrowhead, while the neck seemed to lengthen.

"Rotary online," the AI announced.

"Slow to one-tenth."

Why are you slowing down?

"Missile closure, four-zero seconds."

"Come to starboard, nine-zero degrees."

Eeep . . . Eeep . . . Eeep . . .

"Closure in two-five seconds."

"Ready decoys," the colonel almost whispered as the AI continued counting down to their deaths.

"Twenty seconds."

"On command, launch decoys on bearings one-seven-five and one-eight-five, zero degrees elevation. Then alter course to one-eight-zero degrees."

"Fifteen seconds. Fourteen. Thirteen."

"Engage overdrive! Ahead flank! Launch decoys."

The previously distant roar seemed to descend on Simmonne. Was it that sound or its source causing the chamber to shake? Her hands rose to her ears as the sound intensified.

Nothing could have pried her eyes from the display. The chirping tone faded. The decoys left the ship on diagonal trajectories. The two groups of missiles bundled together more tightly, forming teams to charge at each. But to her horror, their ship turned, following the decoys behind and between.

She whined into the colonel's hand as her body coiled in on itself. Their ship was overtaking the decoys, and all the icons seemed to come together as one. Seconds never seemed so long as she waited for the result.

The multitude of icons split. The missiles missed. She stood up straighter as they sped behind their ship and raced away. But that moment of relief did not last. As if by one mind, the missiles spread from their groups, and all hooked around to chase.

Eeep! Eeep! Eeep!

"Missiles have reacquired."

"Set course for the destroyer!" the colonel shouted over the roar of the engines. "Ramming trajectory!"

Ramming trajectory?

This time a simple squeeze was not enough to stifle her struggles, and she was taken off her feet as he pulled her up to his chest.

No! No! No! Do something else! she wailed in her mind as the icons of the two ships drew closer together.

"Overdrive at capacity," the AI sounded. "We are now outpacing the missiles."

"No keep them close!" the colonel shouted.

"Sir—"

"We have to block their interceptors!"

"Destroyer is changing course," the AI advised. "Taking evasive action."

At least *someone* in this fight wasn't insane.

"Match their maneuvers," the colonel shouted back to it. "On command, launch decoys. Shoot all forward tubes. Target their sails."

"Field merger in forty seconds," the AI warned. "Destroyer's pulse cannons are targeting us."

They were all dead. This wasn't supposed to happen.

"Destroyer is shooting!"

The disrupter pulses appeared as brief streaks of light in the display. Thousands? Millions? To count their number would be futile, like counting the spray from a ruptured pipe. Simmonne let out a fresh wail as the ship lurched. A second impact followed, a third before they began to blend.

"Hull breaches in compartment A," the AI shouted. "Sealing compartment. Merger in thirty seconds."

Somewhere in the ship, something gave way. Simmonne tried to shrink away as a howl ripped through her skull.

"Hull breaches in compartment C! Sealing. Collision in twenty-five seconds. Overdrive temperature reaching critical."

The colonel said nothing to the AI, nor to answer the unspoken pleas in Simmonne's mind. At this point she could not look away or close her eyes. Only the blurring of her vision as the ship rocked interfered with the sight of impending doom.

"Merger in fifteen seconds. Fourteen. Thirteen. Twelve."

"Kassar, Novin! Brace for collision!" the colonel bellowed. To the side, the kodaz quickly spread his legs and lowered his body closer to the floor.

"Merger in ten. Nine. Eight. Seven. Six. Five."

"Fire decoys! Ninety-five-degree port turn. Shoot!"

Once more the multitude of images began to merge. Six from the nose of their ship into the destroyer, with the missiles following. But Simmonne saw it, their own ship lurching to the left, putting it and the destroyer tail to tail, and now they were racing away from each other. But they had entered the current flowing behind the destroyer. The tremors in the hull graduated to an outright quake, and Simmonne grabbed two handfuls of the colonel's clothes. It was as if the ship had struck a mountain and was careening down its slopes until, in an instant, it stopped.

Their ship moved through the flow, and Simmonne's eyes fixed on the missiles. In silent shock, she watched as they followed the path into the destroyer's wake. In one second, the missiles seemed to scatter. In the next, they came back together, turning about, then into the destroyer.

The chamber stood in utter silence as flashes lit on the display. Shock and relief formed a duet in Simmonne's mind as the missiles slammed into the destroyer from behind.

"Destroyer's traverse field is failing," the AI announced. "They're falling out of warp."

The swirling sleeve around the Vaar ship faded away—water returning to tranquility. Their ship raced away, now sheathed in a twisting sleeve of its own.

The colonel's hand finally left Simmonne's mouth to pump his fist. "Glued 'em," he growled. "Now get us out of here."

"Yes sir."

Simmonne's eyes remained on the destroyer. The three plateaus rising from her hull were now colored in red. It took another moment for her to register that the ship was slowly tumbling over its nose. She was gently lowered back to her feet and began to fall. The colonel caught her, guiding her forward, and she gripped the console until her knuckles turned white.

"Status of the destroyer?" the colonel inquired.

"They've fallen out of warp," the AI answered. "Detecting limited sensor activity. No communications activity. We are not being targeted. Would you like me to commence active scanning?"

"No. They must have had a drive blowout," the colonel mused. "Probably damage on all decks. But we can't stay. Get us two hundred light-years, then return to stealth configuration and set course for Eye-9."

Simmonne's breath came in shallow gasps. If her stomach had not been empty before, it certainly would be now. A few days ago, things were fine. Now, everyone seemed to be shooting at her. She swallowed dryly and tried to focus on breathing.

"Easy," she heard the colonel whisper as his hand came down on hers. He gently pried her fingers from the console before standing her upright. With his arm around her once again, he gently pulled her back against him. "Easy," he repeated. "Just breathe."

Her heart slowed, and the red light of the chamber returned to white. First her guards, then Jenna and the Twins. Now this. Someone had to make it stop. Movement drew her attention. The kurai had rejoined them. Both were covered in neon fluid and grime as they took their places at the console.

"Good work," the colonel acknowledged them before pointing to one of the kurai. "Get that checked out."

She noticed then that one held an arm over his chest. His sleeve was torn, and a large bloody gash ran the length of his arm. "I'll be fine, sir," the kurai answered. Not the whispering one.

"That doesn't look fine to me. Infirmary. Now."

"Yes sir," the kurai answered with a short bow before walking back out.

"Andira, how long until you can get us to Eye-9?"

"At present nondetection speed, three days, four hours."

Simmonne stood in silence. The fear remained ripe, even after the ship's wings opened and took up its new course.

"Now en route to Eye-9," the AI announced.

"Very good," the colonel answered. "I'll be in my office. Report any significant contacts."

"Yes sir."

The warmth of the colonel's arm left her before his hand closed gently on her neck from behind.

"Easy. Come on."

Easy, she repeated in her mind. *One step at a time.*

CHAPTER
3C

SLEEP CYCLE INTERRUPTED.
REPAIRS ON STANDBY.

A harsh bump brought Clearwater back to the waking world. Still far from normal, he did awaken this time with greater awareness. With that increase in lucidity came consciousness of the pain in his body. A dull ache in his chest. Sharp pains in his gut. The worst was in his head, where it seemed his skull was being sawed in two.

How bad was the damage? Could his body fix it all? Could the Vaar? Would the Vaar even care to? There was a sound, a gurgling vocalization. Clearwater needed several seconds to realize it was his pained moan.

First Lieutenant Brower. Clearwater could not make out the memory of his face. But he saw him, covered in fire before he was shot. He recalled the memory as if watching it through someone else's eyes, even as he had gunned down the Vaar responsible. Brower. That was his commander's name, wasn't it? Or was it his?

He was Third Lieutenant Jonathan Clearwater, Solar Legionnaires. More images passed through his mind as he glared up at the ceiling of the ribbed corridor: A girl, not much younger than him. Another who was several years younger. Two young boys. His children? Did he have children? Their names would not come to him. He focused on their faces until the pain in his head intensified but could not think of their names.

Another bump jarred him. The Vaar were loading him into a tram. Clearwater felt a slight push, and the view through the transparent sides became a blur.

MEDICAL SLEEP CYCLE REQUIRED FOR SYNAPTIC REPAIR.
RECOMMEND IMMEDIATE ACTION.
DO YOU WISH TO BEGIN MEDICAL SLEEP CYCLE?
REQUEST TIMED OUT.
MEDICAL SLEEP CYCLE WILL RESUME IN 30 MINUTES.

Black hair with blue streaks. Emerald eyes. She wore a lab coat. What was her name?

Clearwater dipped his chin to see the Viss in front of him. Her eyes were on her data slate as if they could not exist as separate entities. She was there when they reanimated him. He remembered the sound of his screams as she looked down at him.

The girl with the blue streaks. His mouth seemed to remember the shape needed to say her name. But it could not recall how to make the right sounds. Who was she? Where was she? Was she still alive?

He was a prisoner of the Vaar, a species known to torture prisoners of war—to execute them even for minor acts of rebellion. Each time he opened his eyes, he hoped to see another place. A place with a gaming array in the corner. A door made of real wood. A hologram on his gaming array. Another girl, blonde with a small crown. No one he knew, just something pretty to look at. A set of musical pipes in the other corner.

Each time he opened his eyes, he hoped to see these things. That he would be in that room, and the nightmare of being a Vaar prisoner would be left behind. But he saw only the Viss, her silver slate, and the dark gray walls of the tram car.

Taula.

The girl with blue streaks. Her name was Taula, and she was his. His, something. What was she?

His body slid several centimeters in its bind as the tram came to a halt. The Viss emitted a high-pitched growl, but it was too quick for him to catch what it meant. Clearwater's eyes followed as she stepped off the tram and then they were moving again.

He felt the memory of his arm raising. He saw the gold and gemstones of a Solar Cross. The face of the kurai to whom it belonged. Sergeant ahn Culan, who died in a flurry of enspa's scythes.

He recalled an aren with a face practically made of scar tissue. He died on his knees, executed.

Taula. Ears with three points. Green eyes with an inhuman luster. Why couldn't he remember what she was to him?

The tram came to a halt again. This time the two Vaar led Clearwater on his cart back into a corridor. Two more Vaar stood ahead of him on each side of a large door. Behind each a silver drone hovered with a single red eye. There was a brief cacophony of hissing, popping, and scraping metal. The door lifted into the wall, then Clearwater was pushed into the lift. Another heavy door lifted at the bottom, and he was pushed through another ribbed corridor.

Where was he? Was this a ship? A planetary base? A space station? It seemed like he remembered someone saying something about a ship, but he could not be sure. The room he entered was spherical, like every other he had seen in this place. He felt like he should have been able to tell its dimensions, but he could only understand that it was large. Cubical cells lined the walls in great stacks. The front wall of each was transparent.

They were full of people. Hundreds of people, crammed tightly into each cell. Clearwater peered into one cell as he was wheeled past it. The people inside sat on the floor, wedged together so tight, they sat practically on top of each other. Who were these people? Colonists? If so, of where?

ND-31.

The name brought back the violent images of Dolph, Brower, ahn Culan, and more. Clearwater looked for the blue streaks, fighting the pain of movement to scan each cell he passed. Finally he stopped in front of a cell on the lowest level. A loud ring moved through his table. The harness moved him upright until he faced the transparency of an empty cell, then he slid onto his feet.

His legs were not ready to bear the load. They behaved with all the strength of a gel, and Clearwater promptly fell on his face.

"Stand up!" one of the Vaar barked at him in Solar.

Clearwater tried to obey, but his body seemed to bear the weight of thousands of tons as he tried to push himself up. Impatient, the Vaar's huge hand stretched from Clearwater's shoulder to elbow as it coiled around him and he was dragged. A doorway opened in the transparency, and Clearwater was unceremoniously tossed inside.

As Clearwater rolled onto his back, the transparency merged into itself. One guard still stood with the cart. The one who had tossed him focused on a data slate.

Clearwater looked past the Vaar into the chamber. The large cells were stacked dozens tall, and recessed into the walls. In all those he could see, the scene was the same. Men, women, and children, all packed like roliams in sleep pods. He kept looking for the blue streaks, and the longer he went without finding them, the more his heart raced. An image popped into his mind, ears with three points.

"Guard!" He managed to get the word out as he struggled to sit up. "My pet!"

"What?" the Solar-speaking guard asked as he lowered his slate and glared at Clearwater.

"My pet is here. I want her."

"Pet?" the guard asked and turned to look at the other guard, who answered with a sideways tick of his head.

Clearwater struggled to stand. He managed to get a knee under himself, but when he tried to stand, vertigo sent him back down.

"I want her," Clearwater repeated. Taula. He was not even sure if she actually was his pet. He remembered her face, her eyes, her ears. He knew her, and that mattered most for now.

"Name?" the guard with the slate asked.

"Third Lieutenant Jonathan Clearwater. Solar Legionnaires. Service identity—"

"Not your name," the Vaar interrupted. "The pet's name."

"Taula," Clearwater answered. Her last name was on the tip of his tongue. Gills? Gildad? Gillen? "Gilyard," he said as it came to him. "Taula Gilyard."

Unable to keep himself upright, Clearwater began to crawl. Maybe Taula could tell him who they were to each other and what happened after the battle. Where were they? He did not even know that much. Were they on a planet? A ship? A space station? He found the wall and leaned against it.

The Vaar with the data slate turned to the other. He said something too quick for Clearwater to catch, and the second Vaar walked out of view.

"Where are we?" Clearwater asked, pain stabbing his ribs as he took in a deep breath.

The Vaar did not answer his question. Instead he turned his attention back to the data slate.

"Where am I?"

"We ask questions," the Vaar replied. "Not you."

His eyes were heavy, and Clearwater shifted to be more comfortable. There was no bed in the cell and no other furniture. Nothing took up space but what he thought was a toilet in the rear corner. After several minutes, the second Vaar returned, and Clearwater perked up when he noticed a familiar woman walking with him. Dried mud caked her clothes, her shoes were missing, and her feet were covered in filth. Clearwater did not recognize her face, but as they drew closer, he recognized the streaks in her matted hair and three-point ears.

"Is this your pet?" the Vaar with the slate asked as the two came to the transparency.

He may not have recognized her face, but Clearwater saw the light of recognition in her eyes when she saw his.

"Yes," he strained, trying to rise to his feet. But the pain through his body quickly demanded he sit back down.

The Vaar punched more commands into his slate. From her side of the cell, Taula mouthed something at him that he could not make out. Finally the door in the transparency reappeared, and both Vaar motioned Taula inside.

"Jonathan?" Taula kneeled beside him. "I thought you were dead."

Clearwater looked past her to the pair of Vaar as the one lowered his data slate. "Thank you," he said with a wheeze.

The Vaar nodded before he and the other collected the harness and walked away.

"Jonathan, are you all right?"

His eyes watered as Taula loomed over him. Packed into a tiny cell, unbathed for who knew how long, surrounded by people in the same conditions—she reeked, but she was alive.

He laid a hand on her shoulder. "Taula," he whispered. "You are Taula?"

She nodded slowly. "Yes? Jonathan, tell me what happened."

He shook his head slowly. "I died." He groaned as he strained to lean against the wall for greater comfort. "The Vaar reanimated me. But, I can't remember. I can't remember anything. How do we know each other? Are you my pet? My wife? How do I know you?"

She raised her hands and pried one of his eyes open.

TAULA: Can you read this?

He was supposed to be able to read the words, but they made no sense. She continued examining him, and he winced when her hands found a tender spot on his abdomen.

"The Vaar botched it," she pronounced. "You have reanimation sickness."

He nodded slowly. There was definitely something wrong.

"Do you remember your name? Your rank? Where you're from?"

He took a deep breath, watching her eyes. "Third Lieutenant, Jonathan Clearwater. Solar Legionnaires. I'm from . . . from . . ." He shook his head slowly. "I can't remember. I can't remember where I'm from."

"You're from Weiss," she explained, tapping his bent leg to prompt him to extend it. "It's a hive. Do you remember it?"

He tried. He tried to think of home, to think of something that he associated with the word. When he couldn't even remember the name, he shook his head. "Are you my pet?" he asked. "How do we know each other?"

"I'm *not* a pet," she answered. Even in his current state, Clearwater sensed the disdain in the remark. "I'm a scientist. We were on ND-31 together. I was your designated civilian. You were responsible for assisting me."

Designated civilian. That tasted of familiarity. He sighed as he felt a tinge of disappointment. Not a wife, not a girlfriend. Not even a pet. Just a coworker? There was something else he thought of as he thought about her. An animal—her pet maybe?

"Are all the civilians here? Have you seen any other legionnaires?" he asked as she pried the collar of his shirt away to examine his neck.

"I don't know," she answered. "Maybe all the civilians, but the cells block wireless signal so we can't get a count. You're the only soldier I've seen."

She moved to sit beside him at the wall, extending her legs before tugging on his shirt.

"Come on. You need to lie down."

She guided him over until his head found her lap, then continued examining him.

"You said you're a doctor?" he asked as he tried to make himself comfortable.

"Not that kind. My degrees are in chemistry and biophysics."

"Oh."

Well, she was a smart person who knew a lot. That was better than nothing.

"If you feel yourself wanting to sleep, don't fight it," she urged him. "Your nanites need time to fix your brain. It's easier when you're asleep."

"I keep seeing faces," he said as he curled up. "But I don't know who they are. I just know that I know them."

"Shh," Taula whispered as she shifted her position. "Just sleep. It will come to you."

His eyes had been heavy since he woke.

MEDICAL SLEEP CYCLE REQUIRED FOR SYNAPTIC REPAIR.
RECOMMEND IMMEDIATE ACTION . . .
DO YOU WISH TO BEGIN MEDICAL SLEEP CYCLE?

CHAPTER
3D

THE GREAT THRONE ROOM of the Solar Cathedral was a chamber so vast, it bent the mind to see. Gilded statues stood two hundred meters, less than a fifth the height of the ceiling. They lined walls that stretched so far that a biologic eye could not easily make out the end. Each immortalized figure cast in gold was an emperor, a general, a decorated soldier, or a figure of similar esteem.

Perhaps the most famous feature of the throne room was the Blue Floor. Every century the floor was torn up and remade. Soil was taken from every planet where the Empire's people lived. Once gathered it was mixed and melted into glass, then poured to form this great surface. In the room's northern quadrant stood the sapphire throne. Blue and gold were the colors of the Mandrake Dynasty. A sapphire had been grown and shaped into the emperor's chair. The backrest climbed many stories, and at its summit, a hologram was projected of every galaxy in the Empire's possession.

A mighty crowd had gathered, filling seats on the floor and those carved into the walls. Only the most important members of the Solar Senate had a seat here. Many had come to the Cathedral for this event, but others remained at their homes, joining in as holograms.

Steven had routed to the base of the great stairs, where people would normally stand to address the emperor directly. Thousands of eyes followed him as a hush came through the great hall. He stepped onto the waiting platform, and moments later, the platform climbed until it matched the stair just below the throne and faced out to the chamber.

He waited as the foremost members of this gathering were brought to him. The pasty, twig-like countenance of the outgoing prime speaker, Alberr Donello. The walking corpse with a foot in the grave, and another on ice, Chief Justice of the Council of Justiciars, Renno Hensherr. Lieutenant Administrator of the Department of Justice Axel Hoff, the most effeminate man Steven had ever seen. The four of them moved their platforms into an incomplete circle with his. The last member had not elected to show in person but appeared as a hologram set on his throne. The First Lord of the House of Nobles. High King Jonas von Rhinegrave IV.

Steven felt a touch on his shoulder and glanced down at the glowing tendril. Unseen and unknown, Indorai was with him. The high king was the first to speak.

"The chamber will come to order." He tapped a gavel once on his armrest. Only when he had the quiet that he sought did the high king proceed. "We gather on this day one eighty eight of our year 100,016. The matter before the Senate is to judge the competence of Solar Prince Steven Mandrake to assume the throne of his dynasty."

The high king looked at him.

"Prince Steven, all the Empire joins with you in grieving for your family."

Steven did his best not to reply with an expression. Fine words from a man who would gladly have done the deed himself if given the opportunity. Steven nodded solemnly in acknowledgment.

"That said," the high king continued, "the Empire now finds itself in a state of general war. The leadership vacuum must be filled quickly and with a man competent to discharge these sacred duties. Are there any points of order or objection before this inquest proceeds?"

"Yes," the answer came from the chief justice. The man even sounded like a corpse. "Simmonne Mandrake remains unaccounted for. It is improper to commence with these proceedings until her status has been established."

"I cannot concur," the high king answered.

"He is your ally," Indorai whispered into Steven's mind, pointing past him with one tendril at the high king. *"Even if he does not know it."*

"My ally?"

"Yes."

"Those who work only for their benefit are easily predicted." Steven shuddered as the Encephalon's voice touched his mind. **"Rely on them to act for themselves, and they can be made your ally."**

"Simmonne is twenty-seventh in line to her father's throne," the high king continued. "Barring a record from the emperor himself, there is no reason to assume her an heir of contention."

"He would rather she have the crown than you. For he sees her as a leader who can be made a puppet. But he knows he must hide his motives."

"Further we are in a state of war," the high king went on. "The default heir is alive and must now be judged. As first lord, I motion that we proceed with the matter."

"As prime speaker, I must concur," the twig seconded.

Only the corpse objected, but overridden two to one, the process moved forward.

"According to the Articles of Succession, we must establish the final fate of His Majesty Mason Mandrake, his wife Empress Marianne, and the unexpected deaths of the Mandrake siblings. To that matter, we shall call upon Lieutenant Administrator of the Department of Justice, Axel Hoff. But before the lieutenant administrator proceeds, Prince Steven, have you anything to say on the matter?"

"Be slow to give your words. Let them feel the trauma that they expect in you. Fill your hand with the unassailable shield of the victim."

Steven was silent for several seconds, and the low murmurs in the chamber were silenced. Politicians, nobles, kings, and countless common persons in their homes waited eagerly for him to answer.

"Your Excellency, I am afraid with the cranial trauma I suffered, I've little memory of the event. I can recall little more than the first shots. The Vaar pushing into the room." Steven paused and closed his eyes. With a long breath, he opened his eyes again. "And the wails of my sisters."

"Good, paint the outline for them, and allow their imaginations to color it. Ply their empathy to your purpose. Make them feel the pain they believe you carry, and bend their emotions above their reason."

The high king turned to Hoff.

"Administrator, has your department compiled its report on the incident?"

"Yes, Your Excellency."

"Then proceed."

Hoff stretched out his spindly arms to hold the rails of his platform.

"The Department of Justice investigation into the deaths of the Mandrake Family has found that agents of the Interstellar Combine did infiltrate the Solar Cathedral. There they proceeded to assault and kill the members of the Mandrake Dynasty in their dining room at approximately 06:30 interstellar coordinated time. Through means that the department cannot reveal on an open channel, we have determined that these Vaar were agents of the Combine's Deniable Operations Service. Those members of the Senate with the appropriate security clearance are being given our report to that effect now."

The high king struck his gavel as the voices in the chamber elevated, but after two more strikes, there was silence.

"Administrator," the high king began, "the Empire is home to the great fortresses. These are locations of such heavy defense that a military assault or infiltration is effectively impossible. These are Reichsylvannia, the Valhalla Shipyards, Solar Cathedral, and the core hives such as the Black Crown. You are asking us to accept an outrageous claim—that the Vaar managed to travel here from the Virgo Cluster. That they managed to infiltrate the Cathedral and assault the Solar Family. All without detection or interception. I find this claim no less outrageous than a reported contradiction to the laws of physics."

"In all the years I have existed," Indorai mused, *"I don't think I've ever heard a man with such a passionate love of his own voice."*

"You've never had to have a meal with him," Steven thought back.

"Can your department account for just how the Vaar managed to accomplish this?" The high king pressed his inquiry.

"Yes, Your Excellency, we can." The administrator touched a button on his platform's console. "This information is highly secretive. Those without the necessary clearance for this information will now be disconnected from this proceeding. Their connection will be reinstated once this information has been conveyed."

Steven's eyes moved over the chamber. Some of those attending via hologram vanished from their chairs as their link was dropped. The administrator waited several minutes until his console flashed to indicate that all without clearance had indeed been cut off.

"Every member of the Solar Family is possessed of an Astranet Emergency Recall Code. This code can be used anywhere in the astranet footprint. The individual need only reach an astranet router, and they will be transported immediately to a secure facility here in the Cathedral. This recall code is unique to every member of the Solar Family."

Where was he going with this? Steven glared at the administrator, and his mind raced. What was he about to say? Had the Encephalon betrayed him? What had he done?

"One cannot exterminate a dynasty and leave questions unanswered. Be at peace, Steven."

"I've taken care of everything," Indorai assured him.

"At 06:15 ICT, an emergency recall code was activated. Cathedral staff were summoned to answer. It is our belief that a Vaar team used this recall code to gain access to the Cathedral. They were met mostly by medical personnel and a small team of the Imperial Guard who were surprised and overwhelmed. Shortly after their arrival, the Vaar initiated some form of cyberattack on the Cathedral's security systems. This effectively blinded the internal security monitors and allowed them to invade the Imperial Palace, culminating in the deaths of the Mandrake Family.

"Memory scans were performed on the corpses of the Vaar who carried out the mission, and the information gathered tracks with this version of events."

"It seems you were busy while I slept." Steven sent the message, careful not to look over at Indorai.

"I was busy long before and shall always be."

What began as increasing murmurs soon escalated to an uproar throughout the hall. The corpse, the twig, the high king—all betrayed their surprise as they listened to the tale that was spun for them.

"We will have order," the high king said calmly, pounding his gavel again. "We will have order or employ sound cancellation. The chair has only recognized the administrator."

Steven swallowed dryly and held out a hand. The Cathedral answered with a glass of water, which he quickly drank. Once the chamber had quieted, the high king spoke again.

"Administrator, I find this difficult to believe. Has your department determined which recall code was used?"

"We have, Excellency. The recall code used to infiltrate the Cathedral." He paused, and Steven could sense it. The man who spoke the words could not believe them. "The recall code belongs to Princess Simmonne Mandrake."

The high king leaned back on his throne, a stunned look in his eyes. The corpse nearly fell off his platform. But none were more shocked than Steven. The glass slipped from his hand as he caught himself on the rails. When his glass hit the floor far below, it was the only sound in the chamber.

The high king was the first to find his voice again. "Administrator, would you repeat your findings?"

"My department has identified that the Vaar infiltrated the Cathedral, using the recall codes of Simmonne Mandrake."

"Administrator, is your department aware of any means by which the Vaar might have acquired these codes?" the high king asked.

"First Lord," he answered, "these codes are known only to the Imperial scion to whom they belong. Even the Imperial Guards assigned to those scions do not know these codes. If they are to be used, then the situation is so dire that the guards are left behind. It is the belief of my department that these codes must have been given to the Vaar by Princess Simmonne."

Steven's breath was short, and he glared at the administrator as he tried to find words. But there were none. What was he supposed to say?

"Justice," the high king asked, "is there any proof for that accusation?"

He nodded with a groan.

"Memory scans of the dead Vaar indicate that they . . ." He paused. "That they received the codes as part of a pact between the Imperial Rose and the Council of Warlords."

The high king twisted the gavel in his fingers. He panned his eyes across the chamber before speaking again. When a new uproar arose, he was slow to bang the gavel. "Under the circumstances, I believe we must call a recess to this proceeding—that the appropriate members of the Senate may review your findings. Is there an objection?"

When none was raised, he struck the gavel again.

"We will reconvene in forty-eight hours."

CHAPTER
3E

I N THE HOLLOW ONE'S company, Oul'sor stood on the human station
Avalon. The fighting here was some of the most intense along the entire
front. The Combine already controlled most of the station's surface.
But so large a station was equal to conquering a planet. As Vaar warriors
pushed to secure the station's interior, legionnaires were demolishing everything they could. Weapons, shield systems, computer networks, anything the
Combine might wish to capture.

Most of the Imperials had been corralled into the station's west arm.
The legionnaires there gave not a footspan of ground without dying for it.
All to protect the civilians that they still worked to evacuate. Though the
Vaar controlled the local space, an escape route remained. Some might have
been suspicious as to why. For now they were happy enough to use it, but
the legionnaires had already failed. Neither the station nor its population was
the target. In their hope to keep power to the station and get their people
off, they had handed over the objective.

Oul'sor and Indorai stood on the walkway of a large gantry, looking
down at the globe of one of the station's five main reactors. His people
called devices such as these *point reactors*. The Solars and their followers
called them *MAS reactors*.[5] They were the energy solution for truly immense
demands when even annihilating matter was no longer a practical solution.
The technology was not mystic to Vaar engineers, but to Oul'sor's shame
and theirs, the ability to build one as powerful as the Solars remained beyond
reach. He and his people would need it for what lay ahead.

Thousands of technicians, Vaar, Viss, quorum, and even quant collab-
orators were all toiling. Some worked to decouple the reactor from the
station. Others were planting charges for a controlled demolition to break
the station's center globe.

Oul'sor had become hollow. Like Indorai, he stood on the walkway,
unknown and unseen by those he watched. It was strange to be so close to
so many and be unseen. Yet at the same time, there was an odd comfort.
Since gaining his new gifts, it was the first time he had been in proximity to

---

5   MAS is short for Multiple Active Singularity, a reactor type that utilizes
multiple, small, synthetically manufactured black holes as power sources.

other Vaar and not been distracted by their adoration.

A few warlords had various plans for the station. Most had hoped to study its tactical systems and use them to build better weapons. Oul'sor doubted it would be of much help. He was no engineer, but in his youth, he'd taken enough courses on the subject to know that reverse engineering showed what the other had done but not how, not why. Nor did it provide the knowledge of how he built the pieces of his work. It did not provide the tools he used or the tools used to make the tools.

One had to master or examine certain fundamentals of the technology, which would be no different from trying to read a text in an unfamiliar language. The Empire was still too many years ahead of the Combine. Were it not the case, they would not be here now, working to pilfer the station's reactor. Besides, even with most of the station under their control, they'd yet to recover an intact weapon system or shield matrix. The legionnaires were thorough.

"I believe they would benefit from your assistance," Indorai said, calling his attention to the bottom floor. A pair of warriors held a human by the arms before a pair of Viss. The human wore the red uniform of a high-ranking Armadas officer. When one of the Viss asked him a question, he refused to answer. When she struck him with a cudgel to compel him, he spat in her face.

"Why don't you do it?"

He gritted his teeth as one of the hollow one's tendrils came down like an arm across his shoulders. *"You will not master the abilities I have given if you do not practice."*

He brushed the tendril off and began to walk for the undersized stairs.

"Just step off," Indorai assured him. *"Know that you will fall slowly, and you will."*

Oul'sor glared over the edge of the catwalk.

"Just step off," Indorai pressed. *"You will be fine."*

"Fall slowly," he whispered to himself and held out a leg. He went over the edge and moved so slowly that it barely qualified as falling. The hollow one descended with him, and together their feet planted on the lowest level. Oul'sor approached the small team surrounding the human. He opened his mouth, only to hear Indorai first.

"They will be quite confused to hear you but not see you."

He cursed to himself and closed his eyes. When he sensed that a worker on the reactor noticed him, he knew he was visible again. "What is the problem here?" Oul'sor asked.

The two Viss turned, one gasped, and both bowed their heads.

"Warlord Oul'sor," one began. "We did not know you were here."

"I asked what the problem is."

The senior of the two Viss raised her head. "Apologies, Warlord. The Imperials have activated some kind of security system. It has locked their computers. We cannot access the schematics for this reactor. We will need them to install it properly. This"—she pointed to the human—"is the station commander. She can override the lockout, but she will not give us the codes. We have called an inquisitor, but she is running late."

Oul'sor glared at the human, trying to kill her with his expression. Something was not quite right. The shapes were wrong. Human males were angular; females were curved. This one was an odd mashup of curves and angles. What was this thing? Female. One of the females enhanced for military service.

"You know what to do," Indorai urged.

Oul'sor had some grasp of the Solar language. Enough to read the nameplate on her uniform and know her name was Garren. He walked past the pair of Viss toward the human. The warriors holding her arms both bowed their head.

"Release her," Oul'sor directed, and the warriors complied. The human did not move as he closed his upper thumb and forefinger around her neck and the other fingers around her torso, then hefted her from the ground.

"Do not look at her," Indorai whispered. *"Look into her. Look through her eyes, through her flesh. See her mind and hear it in your own."*

She was brave. He tasted the taint of fear, but she did not show it. She hid it behind hateful eyes as Oul'sor raised her higher.

"Imagine that you already know everything in her mind. Know that all her thoughts belong to you now. She is no longer a person. Do not think of her as one. She is now an extension of you. Do not ask what the codes are. Remember them."

He tried, but no answer came.

"Solar cybernetics," Indorai explained. *"She knows she is held by the enemy. The devices in her brain have taken the knowledge from it. She can't tell you the codes because she no longer knows them."*

"Then how do I get them?" he demanded, sure that his annoyance with this game came through in his tone.

"You have been given much more than telepathy, Oul'sor. Time and space are in your perception. Know her past. Look at where she was—what she has done. What was and shall always be."

His pupils contracted as the world began to move around him. He still felt her in his grip, but he saw her lowering to the ground, returning to the arms of the warriors who had held her. They walked backward together and out through the door of the engineering bay. The farther they moved, the faster. In moments she was no longer a prisoner.

What is he doing?

For a moment he was distracted by the unspoken question of one of the Viss. He focused as the commodore exchanged fire with Vaar warriors, helping wounded subordinates escape. He felt her pain. A grenade exploded nearby, and fragments buried in her flesh from her shoulder to her ankle.

"You are close," Indorai whispered as he saw the human in her command center. *"There it is. Read her thoughts now."*

He saw her, through her, and into her sight. A screen was open, and she was . . . thinking characters into it. He knew them. He had what he needed.

"Now return to your moment. You are done with her."

He tossed the human down, surprising himself with the ring of her body striking the metal floor before she bounced. Blood flowed from her ears and nose onto the deck. He hadn't meant to kill her, but what he meant to do did not matter.

"W-Warlord," one of the Viss protested. He ignored her and walked to a nearby computer terminal. There the technicians had spliced a two-part keyboard into the device, fit for the hands of both Vaar and Viss. He took it and depressed the larger keys. A light on the terminal flashed.

"The system is open to you now," he announced.

The Viss quickly joined him at the computer, picking up a headset and looking into it to see the system as the Solars did. She lowered the headset and bowed to him again.

"Thank you, Warlord."

He turned back to the human in time to see her move. So she was still alive. Of course. He had made the same mistake that was getting the infantry killed—forgetting that Solar soldiers were as much machine as flesh. She was pushing herself up, dazed from the impact. He walked over and forced her back down with a foot on her back.

"Continue working," Oul'sor bellowed to the engineers. "Call me if you need more from this one."

She released a pained gasp as he pressed down. He wanted to feel her ribs shatter under his foot. But he knew they wouldn't. Vaar warriors had their bones and plates artificially hardened. Solars had no plates, but the soldiers had their bones replaced with advanced cybernetics. Some, their entire bodies. He could not break her bones with only his strength.

"Oh how you underestimate yourself," Indorai corrected his thoughts. *"You absolutely can. But then, the dead are not very useful, are they?"*

He turned his foot side to side, grinding her into the deck. A lot of humans would die in the time ahead. What was one more? Her arms flailed as he continued forcing the air out of her lungs. Was he really strong enough to break the bones in her body? Her head was under his toe, and he pressed so hard that, with a turn, the flesh of her cheek left a red streak on the metal.

He stopped for a moment when he felt the tendril on his shoulder again.

"I promise you will have your fill. But this one might still be useful."

Indorai was right. They might still need her. But where hate and curiosity met was a dangerous place. He continued to hold her in place and reached down to grab her left leg. One thumb and forefinger curled around her knee, and the other around her ankle. The limb was not obeying.

"Oh, I see. But you cannot simply overpower. If I gave you that much raw strength, you could not handle little Vil'na safely."

Anger flashed through Oul'sor as the hollow one said her name, and his muscles strained harder.

"You must know you are strong enough. You cannot bend it with your arms. But in accord, arm and mind can do the deed. See it in your mind, Oul'sor. Know it is happening."

He imagined the limb bending as he wished. The jar in his mind, the lid turning as the seal was broken. He heard the metal protest through her flesh, and the leg began to move. In a moment the tips of her toes touched the back of her knee.

"More trouble for her to attempt escape," Oul'sor said as he let go and took his foot off her.

When he turned back to the Viss and the warriors, he felt their fear. He wore no armor, yet even with their armor and the strength it provided, the warriors could not have done the deed.

"Isn't the taste of fear so sweet?" Indorai mused.

"Back to work," Oul'sor barked at them. The two warriors ran to reclaim the human, while the Viss moved to the terminal. Those scattered around the chamber also busied themselves. Once no eyes were on him, he rejoined Indorai in obscurity. He flicked the tendril off his shoulders.

"Do not say her name to me, Indorai."

"You mean little Vil'na? But Oul'sor, isn't that who you are doing this for?"

Oul'sor glared at him in constrained fury. *"I doubt you could ever understand."*

Indorai faded from Oul'sor's sight for a moment before reappearing on the walkway where they had once stood. *"Stop thinking like them,"* Indorai chided as Oul'sor moved for the nearby stairs. Oul'sor shook his head and walked back up to the position he had left.

The work continued for several hours, but eventually everything was in place. The timers reached zero and detonated. Thousands of charges arrayed through the station's center globe went off as one, breaking through the layers of the hull. With the hole torn, the fragments were cleared away, and a fat-belly transport waited for the precious cargo.

"Now we have the key," Indorai said. *"All that's left is to wait for the door. Little Vil'na waits at the festival. I will not trouble you there, but be ready to return as soon as it ends. Our mutual friend will be coming soon."*

CHAPTER
4A

THE DOORS OF HIS armory slid apart, and Panzer dew in a deep breath. The naturalistic smell of nano leather. The tartness of disrupter oil in the dry air. The ultraviolet light. Even the sound of the number four dehumidifier, never as quiet as its brothers. As the kurai said, home was where you kept your arsenal.

His right hand rested on the back of Simmonne's neck. She shivered as the frigid air of the room struck her. It lasted only a moment before her clothes and body adjusted. He guided her into the room past rifles and heavy weapons snug in their racks. The left rear of the room contained storage. Sidearms and melee devices divided the space on the wall bearing the sole portal.

His gaze quickly found a collection of rifles sprawled on the floor. At some point they had been knocked loose. Without thinking he held his left hand toward them. His mistake was obvious as pain washed through his skull. Daggers pierced his eyes and ears. The air was driven from his lungs, and his shoulder met the frame of the door. He released the princess before bringing his balled fist up. Lines of static washed through his NOD behind tightly clenched eyes.

When he was finally able to open his eyes, he saw Simmonne staring at him with a look of fear and shock.

"I'm fine," he whispered, trying not to wheeze as he stood upright. "Deep-fryer hangover."

He willed himself back to his center of balance and reclaimed her neck. He could navigate this room without eyes, fortunate given the blur in his vision. Mindful of his grip, he led Simmonne to the front, beside his workbench. It hurt simply to think into his NOD, but the result was achieved. A section of the floor beside the bench shimmered as it turned to fluid before rising. The fluid bowled outward to form a chair. Too much chair, it had assumed a size appropriate to him. Gritting through the pain, he directed it to shrink into something more suitable. He released Simmonne before snapping his fingers and pointing to the chair.

She obeyed, pausing to move her hair aside so she would not sit on it. For a soldier his hair was quite long, specifically so he would not look like a soldier when he did not dress like one. Her hair fell past her knees. It had to be an inconvenience from time to time. In the chair Simmonne hesitated before accepting its offer to recline.

Her blue eyes gave him an expectant look, careful not to stare directly into his. He could no longer read her mind, at least not through the 4CM field of her tiara. But it was too soon to tell. Was it a result of the hangover, or had his abilities degraded that far?

He turned to the wall-mount printer.

???: Andira, ice water and—I don't know. I remember her saying what her favorite snack was in . . . something. I can't recall. Celery. Celery and tabota ranch.

ANDIRA: Yes sir.

The printer growled before depositing the order in the large receptacle. He took it and stooped. Water and celery? Had the trauma made him stupid? What kind of comfort food was that?

???: Recycle order.

The bottom of the receptacle dropped, allowing him to return the items for disposal. He leaned a hand on the wall as he stared at the printer. Milk. He had heard she preferred milk.

???: Chilled milk and ice cream.

ANDIRA: What flavor?

???: Chocolate. Add chocolate syrup, whipped cream, and . . . and . . . Andira, what are those crunchy things called?

ANDIRA: Chocolate chips?

???: Those, too, but . . . Why can't I think of it? Small. Multicolored?

ANDIRA: Sprinkles, sir.

???: Yes, sprinkles.

ANDIRA: Would you like me to add some blue goo to help her sleep?

???: Not now.

Andira was thinking of him, not the princess. She assumed he wanted some peace and quiet, but the girl needed comfort, not drugs. From the size of the dish that came, it was clear Andira was not quite mastering the concept.

???: More. Triple—strike that. Quadruple current sample size.

The original was scrapped. The new bowl was too large for the receptacle, and he was forced to support it with one hand as the order was assembled. He took the milk first and handed it to Simmonne. She stared at the glass for a moment before drinking. For an instant, the practiced dignity of royalty ingrained in her soul from birth was gone. She tilted the glass, greedily sucking it down.

Thank you, she mouthed as he took the glass back. After a refill, he set it into a cup holder formed by the chair. Finally he offered her the bowl. Rather than take it, she shook her head.

"Have you eaten since you came aboard?"

She shook her head again, and he motioned the bowl toward her more insistently. She looked as though she were about to protest before he laid the large bowl in her lap.

"Eat," he said firmly. "I won't take no for an answer."

"I'm not hungry," she whispered, staring at the ice cream like a grim obligation.

With his balance somewhat suspect, he was careful as he lowered himself to a knee. He brought his eyes closer to hers, only for her to retreat from his glare. He took hold of the spoon embedded in the chocolate. After scraping off a lump, he waited for the syrup to drip before holding it to her lips. With some reluctance she opened her mouth, allowing him to place it on her tongue. After she swallowed, he took her hand and placed the spoon in it. She glowered at the bowl but perhaps realized he would not let it go and began to eat.

If only he could read her mind and get some grasp of what was happening behind her eyes. Bodyguards dead, handmaidens abducted. The veneer of perpetual safety into which she was born had been violently ripped away. Her eyes were moving, but the expression was far away.

He began to rise when she muttered something.

"What was that?" he asked.

"When you came, the Vaar were afraid of you. I sensed it. I've never felt that kind of fear before." She brought her eyes up, looking as close to his as she dared. She searched his face for understanding, for sympathy, for anything. "Is there really nothing you can do?"

He shook his head slowly. "No."

When she spoke again, he thought he misheard, so he asked her to repeat it. "I can pay you," she said louder. "I could give you enough to buy your own star system. Or build a hive."

Money? She was offering him money? His blood began to roil, and he took a breath to calm it. She was not *trying* to insult him. Grief. This was part of grief, trying to bargain with fate. Or with anyone she thought could change it. Unusual for someone with noble grief but not unheard of.

"Simmonne, I'm a commando, not a mercenary. I have money. If I want more, I can get it."

"Is there something else?" she asked so low, he wondered if she really wanted him to hear.

He returned to his kneeling position, and she looked away. "I would bet every troy I have that they are on the Vaar flagship," he explained. "With just my team, that's a suicide mission. If it was a suicide mission that would succeed, I'd do it. But it wouldn't. All it would do is get my team killed."

His teeth clenched. He shouldn't speak the words that were forming, but she needed to let go of the idea. He had to dispel any false hope.

"A while back, the Armadas learned that the Vaar were developing new stealth systems for their warships. Like the kind we saw on that destroyer. So they asked the Corps to look into it."

She turned her head back toward him.

"Between the Corps and the intelligence services, the Vaar were worried we'd do something like that. The test ship was a cruiser named *Polarized Aggression*. The mission was to find the ship and board it. Then capture any tech or personnel familiar with it. For this mission, nine of us showed up with our teams. The Vaar detected us coming aboard. Even with nine commandos, we lost two officers, their teams, and many more on other teams. RIDs. Reanimation Impossible Deaths."

He paused to let her fully absorb his words.

"The Vaar figured out why we were there. By the time we had control, the crew had sabotaged the equipment—wiped the data from their computers. Terminated the engineers on board so they couldn't be captured. Through sheer luck we took the bridge before they could destroy their new PACKET device. That was the only thing that kept the mission from being a complete failure."

Hope drained from her eyes, and it felt like bile in his throat.

"So, it's hopeless?" she whispered. "You can't do anything?"

"It's never hopeless," he answered. "I can't get them now. But the Vaar won't hurt them. They'll submit a ransom to your father. He might pay it. If not, the Corps *will* get them back. I'll lead the mission. I'll go to the commandant myself if I must. You will get them back. But for now, just rest. I will get you home as quickly as I can."

A tear slipped from her eye as she sat back in the chair. Panzer turned for the rear of the armory. The weapons that mocked him earlier were still strewn about in disarray. He returned each to its proper place on the wall.

As he set the last weapon in its place, fresh pain crept into his skull. He leaned forward, resting his weight on the racks. When he closed his eyes, he saw the Twins as they were carried away by the Vaar. The boiling of his blood quickened his pulse, intensifying the agony working into his skull. He needed a cigarette. He turned for the printer, and the room began to spin. A step became a stumble, the stumble became a trip, and down he went. He caught himself with one hand, tasting bile. With his other hand, he covered his mouth and looked up at Simmonne. Her eyes were still closed, and he bit into his hand as the pain intensified. He bit harder to keep silent, but the pain was winning. The strength in his arm failed, and his face met the metal of the floor as the room melted away.

Panzer regained his senses as he felt himself rolled onto his back. A large mane of hair and a feminine form loomed over him. Simmonne? No, he knew better as soon as he felt himself grappled. A moment later he was upright, and his right arm was guided over Andira's shoulder.

"Cigarette," he whispered.

Andira them to the front of the armory to the wall-mount printer. Simmonne had yet to open her eyes. Had she slept since she came aboard? His vision was clouded, and he missed the receptacle as the printer growled. After a second try, he found the pack and tore it open. With one stick in his mouth, he grabbed the self-lighting tab and pulled.

Too hard. The tab stayed in place, and the cigarette was torn in two. He growled as he spit the butt out and fumbled with the pack. Andira took it from him and held another cigarette to his lips. This time she pulled the tab, and he sucked in a breath. Panzer paused for a moment and then shook his head.

"No good." He plucked the cigarette and extinguished it on his palm. "Up the dose."

"Sir, that is the maximum safe dose."

His mouth flew open, but he slammed his jaw shut, swallowing the shout that nearly escaped. "Then give me. An unsafe. Dose."

"Sir—"

"Now!" he snarled as quietly as he could.

"Yes sir," Andira answered, and the printer growled again. When she pulled the lighting tab, he drew a hard breath, sucking the vapors into his lungs on a long drag. A light-headed sensation rose from his lungs, lifting the pain from his skull like helium lifted a balloon.

"Better," he whispered. "Set this as my default dose."

"Sir, long-term use at that dosage *will* cause brain damage your nanites cannot repair."

"Yeah," he answered mid-puff before exhaling. "And if I kick a dead guy in the head, I'll crack his skull."

Her head tilted to the side, cyan eyes blinking. "I take your point, sir."

Strength returned to his limbs. He shifted his weight to his feet before looking down at Simmonne. Dead to the world.

"Has she slept since she came on board?" he asked before taking another long drag.

"Only in short intervals," Andira answered. "I'll carry her back to your quarters."

As Andira reached for Simmonne, Panzer shot an arm forward to block her path. "Leave her," he ordered. "She shouldn't have been left alone while I was out. She doesn't need to wake up alone now."

"Yes sir," Andira answered.

She pulled out the chair of his workbench, and he sat. He snuffed out his spent cigarette before successfully lighting another. He drew it in, exhaled, then watched the vapors race to the ceiling to be expelled through the air purifier. Andira still loomed over him.

"Thank you, Andira. You can go."

"Sir, I would prefer to keep this unit near you in case you have another episode."

"Andira." He swiveled in the chair to face her. "The princess is asleep. You have me monitored at all times, and it can't take you thirty seconds to get here. I would like at least the illusion of being alone for a while."

Those cyan eyes glared back at him for a moment before she bowed. "Yes sir." She turned back toward Simmonne. "Are you certain you do not want me to return her to your quarters?"

He smiled. Could she even understand? She was a companion AI; the only feelings that ever mattered were her master's. He couldn't expect her to fully grasp that perhaps the princess was sleeping now because his presence finally made her feel safe enough to do it. He simply shook his head and waited for her to leave.

When the doors closed, he turned back to his bench and the weapon that waited for him. One of the brothers, no doubt Novin, had laid it here.

"You look like hell, Jorri," he said with a smile as he took the weapon.

Nearly the entire weapon was caked with apollium ash, as well as melted and hardened road plastic. His smile soured when he wrapped his hand around the handle. No screen opened in his NOD. No diagnostic, not even an error code. He released the handle before gripping it more firmly. Still no response.

He double-checked that no magazine was present. His hand moved to the ejection handle on the weapon's spine. The grip swiveled to the appropriate handle, but it did not move when he pulled. He tried again, turning the weapon up and bracing the butt against the table. But the handle did not move, and the ejection port did not open.

"Damn it," he whispered, reaching out to the toolbox hanging in front of him. In a moment he had the box open and a dozen implements laid out on the table. The first was a meter. Opening a flap in the weapon's side, he plugged the probes into the terminals. But when he looked at the meter, the only numbers that came into hologram view were zeros. Perhaps the internal circuit was depleted.

He opened a catch ahead of the trigger and pulled the small power cell out. Grumbling, he pulled more leads off the meter and touched them to the cell. The meter reacted with a green light. The cell had power. If the cell had power but Jorri was not answering, then something was damaged. He dropped the cell and the meter before taking Jorri back in hand. Perhaps the grip sensor was damaged. He held the pins behind the handle, pushing down to release the shroud. The handle came loose, and he held the parts close to his eyes. No obvious damage, and the meter agreed. Panzer cursed under his breath as he took more tools and began to disassemble the weapon.

The dust covers did not come off easily. The retaining pins were covered in road plastic that he had to knock loose. When he slipped the barrel shroud off and over the hypercoil, he saw a new problem. A black film, neither ash nor plastic, covered where the barrel and coil met. His hand fumbled on the table before finding an auto wrench. He slipped its metallic loop over the hypercoil, and the band closed on the cylinder. A second passed, and the device growled at him.

He held Jorri down with one hand while using the other on the wrench. He added his strength, trying to twist the cylinder off the muzzle, but it did not move. With a huff he hiked his leg up onto the table, using his heel to pin Jorri while both hands grasped the wrench. The weapon slipped under his foot, and he fell over his chair on the way to the floor.

He bolted back upright, raising the wrench overhead before stopping himself. He glared over at Simmonne, still asleep. He huffed before dropping the wrench on the table and righting the chair. Glaring at the rifle, he grabbed a long coil of metal from the wall. The bore snake lit a new screen in his NOD, and he fed the other end into the barrel. He was greeted by a sinking sensation. The hole was too big.

"Oh no," he whispered as the snake came to life, showing him inside the hypercoil. Where there should have been a tight fit, the space was wide open. The guts of the coil were gone, leaving only the tube that had enclosed them. The metal had taken on the consistency of crinkled paper. He continued to push the snake forward, approaching the seam where barrel and hypercoil met. Into the barrel he should have seen smooth metal, scored by deep grooves filled with banks of tiny electromagnets. Instead he saw more crinkling. The magnets had been plucked from the grooves and smeared into a new coating over the metal.

"No. No. No," he whispered as he continued to push. But the farther he went, the worse the sight. By the time he reached the chamber, gashes had been torn into the metal. Jagged pieces of the bolt had intertwined with more from the barrel. The bolt, the barrel, and the hypercoil's shell had all become one.

Jorri was dead.

He dropped the snake and found the chair as the strength left his legs. The apollium couldn't have done this. Nothing, *nothing* could melt Reichsylvannian steel. Most scientists agreed there was probably a temperature that could do it, but no lab had ever reached it. Panzer closed his eyes, emitting a sigh as he saw the truth. The apollium *did* cause this. It damaged the more sensitive electronics and ruined the timing. Shells were going live before leaving the barrel. Even R-steel had yielded when disrupted so many times. The magnets had been pulled from their mounts and smeared. The metal had stretched, torn, and fused to other pieces. A lesser weapon would have exploded in his arms and taken his arms with it. But not Jorri.

She kept fighting till the end.

His hands balled into fists, and he gently brought one down on the weapon.

"Damn it, Jorri," he whispered. "Did you have to leave me now?"

CHAPTER
4B

SIMMONNE HAD NOT BEEN asleep for long when the sensation of wetness forced her to wake. Heavy eyelids protested the strain of being raised, and her head rolled around her shoulders as she stirred. But soon enough she found the disturbance. The massive bowl of ice cream had melted, spilling a lake of chocolate into her lap. Still not fully awake, she acted in a haze, grabbing the bowl and setting it on the floor.

>>*ACTIVATE SELF-CLEANING*
>>*STAIN REMOVAL*

From her NOD to the dress, the fabric tingled where it met her skin as the smart fiber obeyed her command. She held the fabric away from herself, creating a path for the mass of chocolate to run down and back into the bowl.

STAIN REMOVAL COMPLETE.

Simmonne plucked the bowl from the ground and forced herself onto her feet so she could return it to the printer. Intent on returning to sleep, she scanned the room for the colonel and found him at his bench. With his elbows on the table, he sat with one hand covering his eyes. The other clutched his gun.

If he was asleep, she did not want to wake him, so she stepped lightly. He did not respond to her proximity, and leaning down, she placed a hand on his shoulder. That was a mistake.

The colonel bolted to his feet so quickly, she would have been flung away had it not been for his hand clamping down on the fabric of her dress.

"Colonel!"

The AI's voice broke through the room. Simmonne was bent backward, dangling from the colonel's grip, while his other hand was raised in a fist. The colonel's expression softened. He helped her stand upright, then lowered his raised fist until he pointed a finger at her face.

"Do not sneak up on me," he whispered loudly. "*Ever.*"

"I'm sorry," she answered as he released her dress. "I didn't mean to scare you."

He returned to his bench and looked down at his weapon. A telepath of his strength, he was either asleep, or something had him distracted for him not to simply sense her there.

"You should go back to sleep," he said as he took a tool from the wall. "The bed in my quarters would be more comfortable."

When she did not answer, he turned his head.

"I don't want to sleep," she said, not mentioning the moment of panic that now had her well-awake. "Is something wrong, Colonel?"

"It's broken." He dropped the tool he had just claimed. Before she could say anything else, he turned his back to her and walked to a cabinet on the wall. When he opened it, Simmonne saw a pair of golden cases inside. He took one of them and returned to the bench, where he opened it before laying his gun inside. After shutting the case, he took another tool from the wall before turning to Simmonne. He lifted a hand to her eyes, briefly blocking her sight. *Snap!* There was a bright flash, and the room seemed to darken as her optical nanites dimmed everything to protect her sight.

Her eyes were still adjusting when he lowered his hand and began to drag the glowing end of the tool along the seam of the case. He was sealing it shut.

"What are you doing?" she whispered as he worked.

He held up a finger in reply, drawing the tool fully around the case.

"Have you ever met a techweaver, Princess?"

"No?" Thrown a bit by the question, she ran the inquiry through her mind again. "The only kurai I've met were warrior caste."

"I'm not surprised. If you want something made, especially a weapon, they're the best. Everyone knows kurai warriors have a lot of spiritual beliefs. But so do the rest of the kurai. To the techweavers, crafting a tool is a holy task. They believe all sapient beings carry a divine spark. That we make tools is the ultimate manifestation of that spark. The divine will to reshape reality, manifested in mortal hands.

"Techweavers go total-conversion, replacing everything but their brains with cybernetics. That way they can show tools or weapons the honor of being handmade, of a sort, but without losing out on a machine's capabilities. Techweavers believe every weapon has a soul. A composite made up of those who made it and those who wielded it in battle. If a weapon is broken and can't be fixed, it can't simply be discarded. It must be laid to rest like a fallen warrior—that it might find its place in Abrogan."

Simmonne was silent as the colonel focused back on the box, carving characters into the surface.

KURAI LANGUAGE DETECTED—CU'METH.

Cu'meth was an old language. The kurai used it the same way Solars used Ancient English, or even Latin—to evoke a sense of ancient wisdom. Simmonne read the translations as they came.

GAN-SESTI RUT, KEM-SEM, URIL PASSO WAINT.

LITERAL: ONE HUNDRED YEARS AND THIRTY-SIX, OUR ROAD SPLITS.

CONTEXTUAL: AFTER ONE HUNDRED THIRTY-SIX YEARS, OUR JOURNEY TOGETHER ENDS.

EN VAIO, VET'E, VI WAAL EN KAAS BRODI.

LITERAL: YOUR SERVICE, THANK YOU, MY LIFE YOUR WORK PRESERVED.

CONTEXTUAL: THANK YOU FOR YOUR SERVICE AND YOUR WORK TO PRESERVE MY LIFE.

EN HAMAD, OOD SABAA HEIN.

LITERAL: YOUR ANCESTORS HONORED, (TO) THEIR COMPANY FLY.

CONTEXTUAL: RISE NOW TO THE HONORED COMPANY OF YOUR ANCESTORS.

KO ABROGAN, FA'AM OSHIN-KEE. VEI'EM ENU BIST.

LITERAL: IN ABROGAN, AMONG HEROES OLD. WHAT IS YOURS, TAKE.

CONTEXTUAL: IN THE REALM OF THE HONORED DEAD AND ANCIENT HEROES, TAKE THE PLACE THAT IS YOURS.

Simmonne waited until he deactivated the tool before she asked, "You can't fix it?"

The colonel shook his head. "Jormungandr went out of business years ago. This design got them sued by Titan Works over intellectual property. They lost the suit so badly, Titan Works ended up owning them. Titan Works discontinued it after a while. This was one of the few Jormungandr originals. Thanks to your father, there are no spare parts."

"My father?" She gave him a quizzical look. "What does he have to do with it?"

"Solar Edict on the Non-Proliferation of Disrupter Technology," the colonel replied before taking a breath. "Your father was worried about disrupter tech leaking to foreign governments. So now, once a model goes out of production, if the equipment isn't used on a current model, it has to be destroyed. I have spare parts, lots of them. But not a barrel or firing chamber. They're R-steel. I never figured they wouldn't outlive me."

She watched his mouth work before he spoke again.

"Can't even have them custom made. All the R-steel production back home is tied up for some secret project. I'll be dead before I can get a spot on the waiting list."

Simmonne's eyes moved from his scalp to his feet and back, taking in every detail of his posture. "Do you believe what you said, Colonel? About the weapon having a soul?"

He glanced at her for a moment before shaking his head. "No. But the techweavers who made her do."

He hefted the case from the table and walked it back to the cabinet. His shoulders had a sag, and there was a bit of a shuffle in his step. Simmonne was as subtle as she could be as she made a sweep at his feelings. Nothing. But it was in his body. For whatever reason, that gun was more than just a tool.

After placing it in the cabinet, the colonel grabbed the second case it held. This one was larger, and he brought it to the table. Simmonne spied the writing.

TITAN WORKS—O-6400

After setting the case on the bench, the colonel snapped his fingers and pointed by his feet. Simmonne moved to stand where he indicated, and he released the locks on the case.

"I acquired this some years ago to replace Jorri." He hesitated. "Never got around to it."

He drew the lid up to expose what Simmonne could only see as artillery inside. The gun was pretty, at least, though a bit boxy. The entire weapon was gilded and covered in the patterns of Nordic knot-work that Reichsylvannians were so fond of. Some parts even looked like some kind of wood, with a rich red color.

"Titan Works Hellbore," he said as he stood the weapon upright on the bench. Its length reached Simmonne's height had she stood in its place. "You might recognize it."

Something about it did look familiar, but she could not place it. Not until she saw the emblem where the ammunition went in. It would be hard to find someone in the Empire who had not at least seen that symbol— an eagle with three heads and outstretched wings perched on the hammer of an ancient god. The heagle, the icon of the Rhinegrave Dynasty. But the personal sigil of the high king included a golden hammer, with matching trim to line the eagle's red feathers. The sigil of the high king's family retained the golden hammer but lacked the trim on the feathers. This eagle had no gold trim, and the hammer was only outlined in gold with the rest of it as red as the eagle. This was the symbol of the Redguard. That was where she had seen this weapon. In the hands of some of His Excellency's bodyguards.

The high king and I do not get along.

Simmonne remembered the moment the colonel said those words to her. She had other things on her mind and had not thought much of them. But, if there was some feud between the colonel and the high king, then simply having this weapon bearing this symbol could be a provocation to a powerful enemy. The Rhinegraves took the sanctity of their icon very seriously. For one of their people simply to deface it was considered an act of sedition.

"She's a self-contained rotor cannon[6] with plasma-magnatron and integral hypercoil firing 40mm bombshell rounds."

Simmonne gave him a look as she wondered exactly what part of that sentence he thought she understood.

"She can operate in semiauto, burst, or user-selected full auto up to a hundred thousand rounds per minute. Never got around to actually using it

---

6   Rotor cannons are an evolution of the revolver cannon concept. Ammunition is fed from the magazine to a single barrel by use of a spinning rotor.
     In general, such weapons will have additional, smaller rotors that are contrarotating to cancel out any torque that may otherwise be exerted on the weapon.

much. Never even bothered to remove the gold."

He laid the weapon flat before reaching into the case again. He held out a piece of ammunition that he laid in her grasp.

"It's heavy." A metal cone painted yellow extended back into a tube cast in gold. The obese round was as long as her forearm and bore a small rib near its base.

"Eight hundred grams each," he answered as he took it back. "Each one will cost you about a hundred troys."

"Is that a lot?"

He rolled his eyes as he let out a small scoff. "Yes," he answered with the tone of someone trying to be patient with a stupid question. "For ammunition, that is a lot." He raised a finger. "In explosive configuration, it will defeat any combination of armor and personal shielding in a fifteen-meter radius. Triple that against unprotected targets. There is no known or projected combination of personal armor and shielding that can stop it. Set the cyclic to maximum, and it basically becomes a single-shot weapon. Dump a hundred-round magazine in a fraction of a second. Even tanks and warmechs will have a hard time with that."

Simmonne needed a moment for the words to sink in. When they did she blinked before staring in horror at the gun.

"And this is a *bodyguard's* weapon? Do the Redguard not care if they kill innocent people?"

Another scoff came from the colonel before his face took on a sort of superior grin. "Smart gun, smart shells. The gun knows who you consider hostile and who you don't. It can shape its blast and create exclusion zones to do things like ignore friendlies."

He collected more tools from the wall and staged them on the table, speaking as he went.

"You're too young to remember the White Mills incident," he said as he laid a hand on the weapon. "The high king was supervising a war game between his Könskreegar and the Legionnaires. Well some mental case decided to assassinate him by stealing a Legionnaires warmech. It didn't work. The Legionnaires stopped him before he could get off the base. But the Vorhan Tohl weren't happy. They decided they wanted every member to have a weapon capable of dealing with that level of threat. So Titan Works made this."

He paused, and Simmonne caught the brief frown.

"If I'd been using this, the fight with Oul'sor wouldn't have lasted very long."

Simmonne watched him carefully. One did not grow up around politicians without learning how to tell when someone was leading a conversation somewhere. She suspected—hoped—she knew where he was going. But when he said nothing more, it fell to her to press for the answer.

"So Colonel. You have your big gun. What are you going to do with it?"

He took a breath, and his head fell back. "I aim to kill some Vaar with it."

Her pulse raced as she took a step closer. "Does that mean?"

She did not move when he turned to face her. His grasp found her neck. His hand had always been too large to fit around her neck. His thumb and two fingers formed a ring, while the remaining digits rested on her chest and shoulder. She was forced to look up and divert her eyes from his.

Ever since he took her from the Rothburg, he had become very comfortable with putting his hands on her. That night, there had been something special about it. A forceful personality devoid of timidity or hesitation. But with his hand around her neck now, she wondered if perhaps she had allowed him to become *too* comfortable with it. Part of her felt compelled to say something. Yet, somehow it seemed like it was too late to try to set that kind of boundary. The idea itself somehow seemed wrong, as if she were being unreasonable. Regardless, there were more important things to be concerned about now.

"You love them, don't you?"

He did not let her move. "They're my sisters," she whispered, and he let go.

"I'll go get them."

Simmonne sucked in a deep, hopeful breath, and her eyes closed before she shot forward to wrap her arms around him. He seemed to hesitate before wrapping one arm around her.

"I know you can do it," she whispered. "I've heard Daddy and Steven talk about you. How you never lost a fight or failed a mission."

"I doubt I'm a topic of conversation in the Cathedral that often," he answered as he moved his hand to her shoulder and returned her to her previous distance.

"The Twins like you, you know. They'll be grateful."

"I'm sure," he whispered before speaking louder. "Andira, how much ammo do I have in stock?"

"Two million, sir," the machine answered.

"How many hellfires?"

"Two hundred fifty thousand."

Simmonne paid little attention to their exchange. The colonel moved for other cabinets on the wall and began ferrying things to his bench. So much had happened, but everything would be all right soon. He would fetch the Twins and bring Jenna back. Then they could leave this horrible galaxy.

"Andira." The colonel's voice caught her attention. "Inform Rhoxx and the brothers to meet me in the briefing room in one hour."

"Yes sir."

Each box he set on the bench created a small *thump* with its weight. Simmonne realized the cabinet was in fact a closet when he ducked his head and stepped into it. Several seconds later, he returned with a larger metal box that he leaned against the side of the bench. Finally he motioned her to join him.

"I need to kit this"—he motioned to the weapon—"in the meantime."

He held up a magazine with a pronounced curve and pointed to two pins holding some kind of sleeve around it.

"Pull the pins and take this off," he instructed before handing the device to her.

"What is it?" she asked as she took the weighty device in hand.

"Teleport marker. So they can send me more ammo."

"Then, shouldn't you keep it?"

"Won't be able to hit the mininet where I'm going. And I doubt the Vaar will let me use theirs."

Simmonne found the pins he was talking about—two of them on the back side. Her long nails were proving a liability as she tried to take hold of them. She felt his eyes on her and winced as her nail bent. With careful effort, she managed to secure a grip, but the pin did not move. As her frustration grew, he reached toward her.

"I can do it!" she protested, stepping back. He crossed his arms, and she continued trying to pull the first pin without success. Her frustration enflamed as she held the magazine with both hands and ground the side against the edge of the bench, trying to catch one of the pins and pull it loose. Eventually she sighed and planted the device firmly on the table.

"You're left-handed," the colonel commented.

"Yes?"

He reached down to the magazine and spun it around. "Pins come out the right."

Simmonne made a face as she reclaimed the magazine. This time she needed only a bit of pressure to turn the pin and pull it out. The second pin came loose, and she was able to pull the sleeve.

"What are you doing?" she asked as he began to disassemble the gun.

"First, I'm installing a closed-feed system. Cycles spent casings back into the magazine. Doesn't do me much good to use a stealth screen if I'm spitting out hot casings that tell the enemy where I am. Then, I'm going to install a vortex-inhibitor, so they don't detect the air disturbance when I fire."

Simmonne grabbed another magazine and paused to read the writing on the side.

Titan Works of Pommeron
Caliber: 40x150mm
Capacity: 100

Her head canted as she read the imprint, then she looked at the colonel. The shell he showed her was both longer and wider than this device.

"This holds a hundred?" she asked.

He took one of the stacked boxes and opened it to reveal five of the shells held together within a metal cage. Next he took the magazine from her and inserted it into a port on the cage's underside. There was a small sizzle in the air. The bottom shell seemed to deflate until it slid down into the magazine, followed quickly by the rest.

"Volume reduction magazine," he answered, flipping a small switch. The shells quickly came back out, returning to their original size in the cage.

He set the ammo down and handed the magazine to her.

"You can carry all this weight?" she asked as she went about pulling the pins on the new magazine.

"You'd be surprised how much a power armor can carry," he answered. A sort of smile crept across his face. "Assuming the ground under me will hold it."

Was that a funny memory of something? Whatever it was, the smile faded as he went back to work. There was nothing Simmonne wanted more than to leave this galaxy. Once he brought Jenna and the Twins back, they could do that. But what then? The four of them would go back to the Cathedral, but what about him? Would she ever see him again? Or would he just disappear into the war? No. After all of this, she could not just end up back where she started. But what was the alternative? Too much air. She needed to get him talking again. She scanned the table, looking for something to keep the conversation going. Two of the boxes were open, showing shells tipped in different colors.

"Why are some red and others yellow?" she asked as she pointed to the shells. She did not particularly care about the answer, but she had finally found something that got him to say more than a few words at a time.

"Yellow is explosive. Red is nanocendiary."

"What are those?" she asked. "Nanocendiary?"

He looked up from the gun, regarding her with narrowed eyes. "Do you just like hearing me talk, Princess?"

"W-what?" she stuttered. "I was just asking. I don't know a lot about weapons."

That *smug* tone in his voice. Like he was always so far out ahead of her. It returned as he said, "Dominion developed them back in the Eclipse. Dual-charged. First one is a vortex charge like the yellow tips. Second charge spreads nanocendiaries. The nanites are based on the same ones used to join atoms and make compounds. Only they operate in reverse. Instead of joining atoms, they rip away their electrons. It makes them a perfect oxidizer."

He paused to hold up one of the clips of red-tipped shells. Simmonne took the opportunity to make another swipe at his feelings, hoping he would not notice. As before, she sensed nothing at all.

"Everyone knows you need oxygen for fire," he began. "Except you don't. Oxygen is just a dirty little thief. When it passes other atoms, it steals their electrons. That makes them more reactive. Add a little heat to get things moving—they start recombining. Exothermic reaction results, and you have fire. But you don't actually *need* oxygen. Any good electron thief can do the job. These are the *perfect* oxidizer.

"They don't care what it is. They'll burn it. You can't put them out. Anything you put on them, they'll burn. You can't suffocate them; they're the oxidizer. They're so tiny, good luck scraping them off. These things will burn water. And I don't mean they'll laze about on top of it like oil and burn there. They'll cleave the hydrogen from the oxygen and burn the hydrogen.

Hell, these things can set *nitrogen* on fire. Each one is bond-forged titanium with its own thermal converter. The fires they start replenish their power, and they can't start a fire hot enough to destroy themselves. Until the nanites break or get the shutdown command, they don't stop burning."

He went back to his work on the gun.

"They can't burn bond-forged metals. Just discolor it a bit. But if there's even a tiny crack for them to slip through . . ."

Simmonne tried to choose her next words carefully. "Aren't these forbidden? I mean, illegal for war?"

She caught the half-grin. "Oh, so you *do* know what they are?"

She was an Imperial princess. Of course she knew her history. He didn't have to be so smug about everything.

"No, they're not illegal," he answered. "The regular services just prefer apollium. Besides we have no treaties with the Vaar. Even if we did, I'm a commando. Those kinds of rules don't apply to me. But even I don't use them unless I'm sending a message. That does answer my question, though."

Simmonne looked at him.

"You just like the sound of my voice."

If she had a smug detector, it would probably catch fire about now. "What message? Why use them now?"

His expression became more serious. "The Vaar attacked a noncombatant member of the Solar Family. They have to be punished. The Corps does . . . special things . . . to people who try that kind of stunt. Beyond that, you're happier not knowing."

"Good," Simmonne whispered as she looked down at the magazine. The final moments of her guards flashed through her mind, and she held tighter to it.

"What's that?"

Simmonne was ashamed to admit it. Even more to say it. But no matter what was in front of her eyes, all she could see were their bodies. "I want them to suffer."

"They will," he said in a reassuring tone. "I promise you that."

Simmonne nodded to herself. It was petty. It was wrong to wish harm on others. But the thought brought some comfort as she imagined dozens of Vaar flailing in a sea of fire.

She still had not found her segue. Life had to go on once everyone was home. This was her chance. She had already gotten him to say more than every other word he had spoken to her, yet the courage to turn the conversation was proving elusive. Perhaps there was another way.

In her NOD she brought up the controls to her tiara. The metal band vibrated against her scalp to acknowledge the command. The 4CM field switched off, and her mind was laid bare.

He did not react. Simmonne waited and continued pulling pins. There was no way a telepath of his strength wouldn't notice the unprotected mind a meter away. Yet he did not respond. His attention remained on the gun, his hands busy with his tools.

Please read my mind.

No reaction. She took a frustrated breath. She would have to say it. Maybe he wanted to make her.

"Colonel?" She found herself lacking in sophisticated words. "Have you ever thought about leaving the Corps?"

That got a reaction. She felt a chill as he gave her a sideways look. His head went back a moment. Perhaps he was noticing her unprotected mind. But he shrugged and went back to work.

"I've been in the Corps most of my life. Why would I leave?"

"Well, I know commandos aren't allowed to have families. Have you ever thought of having one?"

She watched his posture carefully. The dip in his chin. The slight shift of weight between his legs. Even as well as he hid it, she knew she struck a nerve. Now she had to twist. To get something out of him.

"I've thought about it," he replied with a sort of shrug. "Spend most of my time traveling. Train, practice, and wait. The mind wanders. You think about where else you could be. Or what you could be doing. Find a few brides, three or four. Buy some remote planet and terraform it to my liking. Then build a nice mansion on it."

Three or four. The Twins. After he rescued them, they might be open to the idea. At least she hoped so. There might not be anyone else. Someone who could protect the Twins from themselves. Someone she might actually like. She had to pursue this, and know if there was a meaningful potential.

She cursed under her breath. That was the wrong thing to be thinking. If he was reading her thoughts, that could discourage him. This was a mistake. She had trapped herself between trying to avoid having to say too much and wondering how much of her mind he was reading.

If you're reading my mind, please tell me.

No reaction.

"Three or four?" she asked as she grabbed a new magazine. This one was large and round. But she found pins on the back to continue working. "So, you'd have to have more than one?"

The scoff he gave that time was derisive. "Well, where you're from, I know monogamy is supposed to be something special. Where I'm from, a man with only one wife is poor. Or he's so pathetic, he's with the woman no other man wants. But that would be a far-off thing. I'd have to find one before finding more. The math doesn't quite work out any other way."

The air threatened to come back. Was he toying with her? Her tiara vibrated as she reactivated the 4CM field. If he had been reading her mind, it should have startled him if nothing else. But still, no reaction. Maybe he really was staying out of her thoughts. One wasn't supposed to go in uninvited, but how much of an invitation did he need? Maybe she shouldn't ask that question, given how many liberties he was willing to take.

"What would you look for? How would you know you found the right one?"

This time he turned more than his head and shifted around the table to face her. More open body language—that was encouraging. She switched her tiara off again.

"Well, she'd have to be something special for me to leave the Corps." She heard a change in his voice. It was slight, but there. "I'd know, because the moment I saw her, I'd know she was mine. Beautiful, yes, but more. She'd be young. Too young according to some. Still at that age where the universe is a huge, exciting place. Where she still has things to learn about it. And herself."

She flinched when he reached out. But he did not touch her. Instead he wiggled his finger, directing her to get back to work.

"Obedient," he continued. "She'd have to follow my rules."

Rules. She *knew* he was going to say that. On Reichsylvannia, when he gave her the vision, she had a taste of his kind of rules. If that was what he had in mind, he would be disappointed.

"She might even tell herself she wouldn't follow them," he said. "I'd show her otherwise."

He *had* to be reading her mind. So she tested him. *What if she isn't willing to have you dictate rules to her?*

When there was no response, she repeated the question in her mind, raising the imaginary volume of her internal monologue. Still, he did not respond to it. He was toying with her. That had to be it. He knew she was uncomfortable, so he was making her speak. It was his way of holding the power in the conversation. That or he was setting her up so he could smugly put her in her place. Maybe that was what did it for him.

"What if she doesn't want to follow your rules?"

"Then she needs to find a different man," he answered with a chill in his voice. But that chill faded when he spoke again. "That said, bringing her into compliance would be half the fun."

She cursed herself for flinching again when he reached over. She had not been able to remove the sleeve from the drum in her hands. He tapped the front to bring her attention to another pin.

"So if you found that perfect woman of yours, what would you do?"

Something was wrong. His posture shifted, and he leaned on the table with his head down. "It doesn't matter," he muttered.

"But—"

"I'm dying, Simmonne."

The drum slipped from her hand, thumping loudly on the table before hitting the floor with a metallic ring.

"Dying?" she whispered. Her eyes clouded, and she tried to blink them away. "What do you mean, you're dying?"

The colonel let out a sigh before turning to bring a leg up and sit partially on the bench. The torturous seconds passed as he collected his thoughts and lit a cigarette. "You know I hold more than two dozen records for metapsionic ability?"

Simmonne shook her head as she fell into a daze. *Dying?* He couldn't be.

"They're all from childhood," he explained, a puff of smoke leaving his mouth as he spoke. "Competency at age. The records are unofficial because my family kept them secret. But everyone assumed. I could juggle a dozen test spheres before most psions even knew that they were. Everyone just *knew*. I was stronger than any before, and maybe any who would come after. Or, I would have been.

"You asked me about these." He motioned with the cigarette. "My painkillers. Close to 150 years ago, I was exposed to a new weapon. It was made specifically to kill Solars by disrupting the bridge between the brain and its nanites. A nanoware update was all that was needed to immunize against it. But that didn't help those of us who were first exposed. I died. Not the only time, but the first is always the worst. Enough time went by between my death and reanimation, they probably should have left me."

He paused to reach up to a shelf and pull down an ashtray.

"My abilities quit growing. In fact, they got weaker. I lost some of the telepathic abilities that I had, and it takes daily practice to keep my psionics from declining. I'd hoped I might be able to grow them with practice, but no matter how much I practice, they don't improve. Instead of being the strongest ever, I doubt I'm even in the Corps' top ten. My brain is broken."

Simmonne's lip trembled as she tried to speak, and her eyes came to rest on the ember of his cigarette. "What's wrong?" She choked out the words.

"It's dying. Neurons are decaying; nanites are developing bit-rate errors. Each is trying to pick up a burden that keeps growing. So the degeneration accelerates as it goes on. No one can figure out how to stop it or how to fix it. For the last fifty years, my nanites have handled nearly all my autonomic functions because my brain can't. And the gaps in my cognitive abilities are growing. Now, it's worse."

Simmonne shook her head. This couldn't be real. He couldn't be dying on her. "Worse?" she croaked.

He nodded. "The fight with Oul'sor. He managed to douse me in apollium. The temperature was more than my armor could diffuse. Things got cooked."

"But, they, they can fix it. Can't they?"

"No." He shook his head. "They've tried everything before. Nanite replacement had no effect. Cloning and grafting new cerebral tissue didn't work either. My brain wouldn't accept the graft. Both times they tried, it nearly killed me for good. The clock is running out. No resetting it now."

Her hand balled into a fist, filling with fabric from her dress. "How long?"

He took a long puff on his cigarette. "Before the fight, a bit over forty. Now, I'll be able to keep my drool in my mouth for perhaps ten. The rest will go shortly after."

Ten years? That couldn't be all. There had to be something someone could do. They could grow entire bodies for people to transplant their brains. They did not even need the whole brain to bring a person back from death. Someone had to be able to fix it.

"So you see," he said with a sigh, "that's why even if I found that girl,

I couldn't just seize her and go start a new life. It wouldn't be fair to her, to let her love me."

A tear slipped down her cheek. "Shouldn't she have a say?"

He smiled sadly and shook his head. "No," he answered in a cold tone. "If she were mine, I wouldn't let her have a say in much. So I wouldn't let her have one on this. If you care about someone, you don't let them make bad decisions. Even if she was willing. I couldn't condemn her to thousands of years as my widow."

He took a step closer to her, and she stepped away. Her eyes darted around the armory as her mouth searched for words. But there were none. This couldn't be happening. She turned away, covering her mouth as she made for the door.

Outside the armory she waited for the doors to close, then fell against them. Her back slid down the wall until she reached the floor and drew her knees up to her chest.

CHAPTER
4C

To Jonathan Clearwater, time had almost lost meaning. The clock in his NOD had reset to zero when he died. With no local network to access, it could not synchronize. Instead the numbers simply counted forward. Thirty-seven hours since his reanimation. Most of it he had spent in sleep. When he did wake, it lasted only minutes before he was dragged back to sleep.

69,250,431 SYNAPTIC ERRORS CORRECTED.
207,749,569 SYNAPTIC ERRORS CANNOT BE CORRECTED.
IMMEDIATE MEDICAL ASSISTANCE IS REQUIRED.
NO ASTRANET CARRIER.
EMERGENCY SERVICES CANNOT BE CONTACTED.
SEEK IMMEDIATE MEDICAL ATTENTION.

This time it was a sensation that woke him. Clearwater opened his eyes as Taula was pulled away. A moment later an enormous hand clamped down on his arm and shoulder, and Taula was tossed across the floor.

"Come," a Vaar growled as Clearwater was dragged out of the cell faster than he could find his footing. He tried to turn back, to see if Taula was injured. Two Vaar were on him now, each with a grasp on his arms. His resistance was futile. Even with legionnaire augments, he would never win a wrestling match with two armored Vaar. But his struggle annoyed them. One moment Clearwater was on his feet, and the next, he was high over their heads before his face slammed down into the deck. A giant foot came down on his back and head to pin him in place. His wrists were pinned behind him and locked together. The same was done with his ankles.

Seconds later Clearwater dangled upside down as one of the warriors carried him by his ankles with a single hand. The darkness of the prison allowed him to see little as they approached the entrance. But the Vaar turned, and he was taken down the long corridor.

Doors parted ahead, and Clearwater clenched his eyes against the glaring light. The air was driven from his lungs as he was unceremoniously dropped to the floor. The two guards freed his limbs before drawing him back up to his feet.

"Stand," one growled.

His eyes had trouble adjusting to the light. Someone stood ahead of him. Much too small to be a Vaar. A Viss? Yes, this was a Viss, holding a data slate. Clearwater recognized her. He saw her when he was on the operating table. He could see clearly enough now. She was his height, perhaps a touch shorter. She wore what was obviously a uniform, but with no markings that he could see. An apron beset by many pockets covered her uniform.

Viss only had plates on their head. Clearwater tried to focus on her crest but found no markings. No rank insignia, no marks of commendation. The teardrop plate was smooth as if she had never done anything but exist.

She took a step toward him without taking her eyes from her slate. The growling words took a moment to register. "Tell me. Do you speak our language? Or are your nanites translating for you?"

Clearwater blinked and tried to answer. His mouth did not move. Human advantage would not serve here. Autotrans was offline. He could understand her, but despite his mental urging, the nanites never took over to help him speak a reply.

"I don't speak Ivex," Clearwater answered in Solar. "It's my nanites."

"Interesting."

While she made notes on her slate, Clearwater surveyed the room. Directly behind the Viss was what looked like a doctor's table, save the restraints bolted to it. Large cabinets filled the walls, but one wall held a large mirror.

"Strip and get on the table behind me," the Viss ordered, still not taking her eyes off her slate.

Strip? The muscles in Clearwater's face grew taut, and his heart raced. A room hidden from the other prisoners. Visible medical equipment. He started to realize exactly what this room was. Clearwater remained still, though not out of defiance or resolution. He froze in realization.

Her large orb-like eyes turned from the tablet to him, and their many pupils contracted. She held up a finger before deftly striking it down on her slate. Clearwater's heart skipped a beat as he waited for the consequence.

Nothing happened.

The Viss's head angled toward him and she did it again, and again. Four times she struck her tablet as if expecting something to happen. When it did not, she stepped forward and held the device closer to him. She held it at his head before slowly lowering it, and he realized she was scanning him.

"Interesting," she commented before looking at the guards. "Strip him. Put him on the table." The Viss quickly stepped to the side.

The guards did not give him a chance to resist. A sharp blow to the back of his head sent him reeling before his feet were kicked out from beneath him. His face once again became intimate with metal flooring before his arms were seized and he was dragged toward the table. By the time he recovered his senses to struggle, he was being hefted again, and his back was slammed against the upright table. A punch to his gut drove the air from his lungs. As he doubled over, one of the giant hands clamped around his head before driving it back against the table.

He tried to suck air into his lungs, but a metal manacle clamped shut around his throat, denying him the air he wished for. While one of the warriors grabbed his arm and guided it toward a manacle, another grabbed at his shirt. The fabric ripped as his right arm was bound, and his pants along with the left. Denuded, he pulled against the metal clamps before another blow to his stomach stunned him long enough for his ankles to be pinned.

No air. The ring was too tight. With him secure, the two guards stepped back, and the Viss moved in front of him.

OXYGEN INTERRUPTION—INITIATING COUNTER-SUFFO-CATION PROTOCOLS.

"You can go," the Viss said to the guards, who bowed their heads before leaving them alone.

I can't breathe! He could not get enough air to whisper the words. Either oblivious or not caring, the Viss continued typing on her tablet. He had to get a grip. He had done this in training. His soldier's lungs and his nanites could store enough oxygen and recycle enough from carbon dioxide to keep him going for half an hour. More than enough time for her to notice there was a problem.

But as minutes ticked by and she continued to type, his heart raced. She took her time. A little longer, and he might not have noticed when she spoke.

"My name is Jaegda," the Viss said, still looking at her slate. "My rank is qu'tah, equivalent to a lieutenant commander in your Armadas. You are a prisoner of war in my custody. Your name is Jonathan Clearwater, and you are a third lieutenant in your service. Is this correct?"

His mouth worked silently, lacking the air to generate a response.

"Is this correct?" She broke her gaze from the tablet. After a moment, she pressed one thumb against the tablet, his chest expanded, and he sucked down precious air as the ring around his neck loosened. "Is this correct?"

"Yes," Clearwater wheezed, gorging on air.

"Very good."

She turned, and one of the cabinets on the wall hummed. The cabinet plucked itself off the wall and moved toward her, coming to hover at her side. Jaegda set her slate on top of it before using both hands to swing the doors open. Clearwater's limbs trembled as a multitude of tools came into view. Some bore long, jagged hooks, others serrated blades, and yet others were what looked like saws.

He had been warned about this in training, the fate of a Solar captured by the enemy. Some would try to dissect him to study the technology of his body. Some might torture him for information. Others might do it for the sheer joy of it. To see a Solar, a member of the Empire's dominant race taken down, degraded, and broken. He was going to be tortured, but the service had given him a tool for this.

"There's no reason to torture me," he said, trying to sound calm. "I can't tell you anything."

"Oh but you can," Jaegda answered, reaching into the cabinet. "You can tell me so *many* things."

"I can't," he insisted. "My cybernetics know I'm a prisoner. They've taken all the classified information from my brain. I couldn't tell you even if I wanted to."

She turned back to him, holding a syringe.

"What is that?" he asked as he looked at the vial of inky fluid plugged into the device.

"I injected you with painmakers while you were on the operating table," Jaegda explained, "but now they seem to be gone. I want to know what happened to them."

She came forward, and four fingers clamped down on his chin. Her spindly arms were far stronger than they appeared as she forced his head to the right and jabbed the needle into his neck. Then with some haste, she reclaimed her slate and held it to him.

FOREIGN NANITES DETECTED—SELF-DEFENSE PROTO-COLS ACTIVE.

He groaned at the sudden heat he felt in his neck. In his carotid artery, a small battle was being fought. He did not have much time and needed to focus.

>>INITIATE ANTI-TORTURE PROTOCOLS
ANTI-TORTURE PROTOCOLS INITIATING . . .
PAIN RECEPTORS DISABLED
ANTI-TRAUMA SUBROUTINES LOADED
WAR CRIMES DATABASING IN PROGRESS . . .
PROTOCOL ACTIVE

"Fascinating," Jaegda said as she brought her eyes closer to her tablet. "Your nanites are destroying the painmakers. Is that process involuntary? Or could you disable it if you wanted to?"

He stared at the small circular light above the door to the room.

"Refusing to answer?" Jaegda asked. "I can fix that."

He peeked at her as she turned back to the cabinet and withdrew a thin metal rod. A handle lay at one end, and a silver sphere at the other. He looked back at the light as she faced him and turned the handle, which emitted several audible clicks.

"It is my understanding," she began, "that your species' genitalia are particularly sensitive to pain."

She swung the rod low, bringing it up between his legs. The soft thump of metal against flesh and a loud snap reached his ears, but neither the impact nor the electric shock registered. Jaegda twisted the handle several more turns before striking him again.

"I see!" she proclaimed, bringing the rod up to his face. "I should have foreseen this. You have a built-in anti-torture system, don't you? You don't even feel this."

She waved the rod before hitting him again as if to confirm her assumption.

"Yes, I should have foreseen this," Jaegda continued and began to twirl the rod.

"I told you," Clearwater answered, still focusing on the light. "There's no point in torturing me. I can't tell you anything, and I won't feel it."

The sound Jaegda made—there was something so unsettling about it. Like a human woman squealing in delight over a gift. But much deeper, and resonating. "Oh, I so love it when my subjects think they've beaten me."

She placed the rod back in the cabinet and held up her slate again. After she punched in several commands, she turned the screen toward him.

"Look at it," Jaegda directed before her tone softened. "Please?"

He looked at what she wanted to show him, and each muscle in his body clenched. Taula. She stood against a plain background like she had been arrested for a crime.

"You asked for this one to share your cell," Jaegda explained. "Now why would you do that?"

"She, she's my pet. I'm her owner. She should be with me. She doesn't know anything."

"No." Jaegda held up a finger and wiggled it at him before gently, almost affectionately, tapping her hand lightly against his cheek. "That might have fooled the guards. But you can't fool me. You Solars don't think very much of us, do you? But we at least go to the trouble of collecting our prisoners' names and affiliation."

Jaegda held her tablet back up to read.

"Doctor Taula Gilyard, Expeditionary Sciences Verification Agent assigned to colony ND-31." She paused. "Such an uninspired name for such an important world. She is only half lantai, and certainly not a pet with that job title." She tapped the slate. "Now why would you ask for her to share your cell? Wife? Mother of a child?"

He looked back at the light, keeping silent as his mind raced.

"Tell me, Lieutenant. If I were to bring her in here, would she have the same protections you do?"

"Y-yes." He focused on the light harder than he had ever focused on anything.

"No." Jaegda shook her head before tapping the slate again. "Voice stress analysis says that is a lie. This room is an honest room. Please keep it that way."

Jaegda positioned herself directly in front of him and took a breath.

"I did not bring you here for intelligence. You are at the bottom of the officer mountain. You could not possibly know anything special."

"Then." He hesitated, almost choking on the building dread. "Then why bring me here?"

She poked him with the slate. "Unlike your government, we do not abduct foreign citizens and experiment on them without declaring war. You are the first opportunity we've had to examine a Solar soldier for ourselves. You were captured, reanimated, and are now mostly intact. We have heard a lot of rumors about your species."

She began to walk a circle around him.

"That you can regenerate lost limbs thanks solely to your nanites. That soldiers like yourself can keep fighting after wounds that would kill one of your civilians. That even when you feel pain, you can still focus on a task. My subordinates have been dissecting the remains of your unit, but we can only learn so much from a corpse. My assignment is to find the truth. I will examine for myself how your body handles trauma and how your mental state is affected by pain. This information will be passed on to our troops, and those developing weapons."

This couldn't be happening. Was this a dream? A nightmare? It couldn't be real. No, a night terror. It had to be. Maybe he was still in his cell, with Taula, and all he needed to do was wake up.

Jaegda stopped in front of him once more. "Unfortunately, if you can turn off all pain whenever you wish, it will be hard for me to make some of those determinations." She showed him the image of Taula again. "Pain is important. It's how we know when we are injured. So I predict that you can turn off whatever you're using to avoid it. Do that, and I will focus my attention on you." She turned the image of Taula back toward herself. "Refuse, and I will bring her in here. I will ply my craft on her flesh while you watch."

Rendered mute, Clearwater could only shake his head. Jaegda seemed to ignore him. "I don't like her eyes," Jaegda said. "I think I will take them out so I don't have to look at them. Unfortunately she does not have your military enhancements, so I won't learn much from her."

He took a breath, inwardly praying that the Viss might reason herself out of what she had suggested. That tiny hope was quickly dashed.

"But I suppose it could help me familiarize myself with the anatomy of your females. It is my understanding that there are not many female soldiers, but there are some. Five or six percent of the non-aren total? She could help me study for when I get my hands on one of them."

Jaegda held out her hands in a shrug.

"Oh let's just be honest. This *is* an honest room. I will keep cutting into her until you decide to cooperate. What should I take after her eyes? Her fingers? No, then someone else will have to feed her."

The strength left him. Clearwater lowered his head and closed his eyes. "I'll do it," he whispered.

Jaegda ignored him. "Maybe her breasts. I understand it's the main thing males are attracted to, and very sensitive to pain. It would be interesting to study the psychological effects. But where to go after that?"

"I'll do it," Clearwater spoke louder.

"You know, males of my species have a psychological predisposition to protect females," Jaegda said, tapping on her slate once again. "Some of our scientists even think it's why the males evolved to be so much larger— so that we and the children could ride on their backs and be safe from the predators in Prithone's jungles. I simply assumed that males of your species would have similar attitudes. Very insensitive of me."

"I said I'll do it!" Clearwater shouted, tearing his eyes away from the light to stare into Jaegda's. "Just leave her alone."

A mix of fury and terror brought a tear to his eye as he glared into the alien's pupils. Her mouth opened in a grin of sharpened teeth. "Are you sure?" the Viss asked, resting her palm on his chest. "The pain will be quite exquisite."

"I'll do it." He nodded. "Leave her alone."

"Good," Jaegda answered before leaning closer to him. "But remember, if you turn your pain blockers back on, I'll bring her in here. I have all the medical facilities I need. I can keep her alive for weeks. Until her mind is broken and all that's left is a pile of flesh that no longer remembers a world without pain."

He turned his focus to his NOD.

>>ANTI-TORTURE PROTOCOLS
>>OVERRIDE AND DEACTIVATE

Clearwater leaned his head back, swallowing dryly as he closed his eyes. "It's done," he whispered.

He heard her rummaging in her cabinet and cringed. The first contact caused him to flinch, but there was no pain. She had attached something to his left temple before doing the same to his right. Afraid to open his eyes, he felt them buzzing while she placed several more on his body. He found the strength to open his eyes in time to see her reclaim the rod from the cabinet.

Thin metal whistled through the air and then snapped. The impact of the sphere against his groin would be agony all its own, but the sudden electrical discharge was so much more. His mouth flew open, and his lungs voided themselves in a loud wail that never echoed off the sound-dampening walls. Bile welled in his throat and he convulsed, his limbs trembling in their restraints as his body tried to escape the agony.

She did it again.

Spots formed in his vision. He had no air for another scream but soon found it and let loose. Warnings flashed in his NOD, but the pain distracted him from reading and seemed to spread like fire through his skin, up through his stomach, and into his throat.

"That was setting one," Jaegda explained before giving the handle a click. "Failure to follow my instructions at any point will result in setting two."

She returned to the slate.

"How interesting. Your nanites are trying to channel the electricity, shielding your internal organs from it. I wonder if any of the nanites at the impact site were damaged. I'll have to take a tissue sample."

Tissue sample?

"Please," he wheezed, limp in the restraints. "Please no."

"No, no, no, no, no, no," Jaegda cooed, laying a hand over his mouth. "I know, this is painful and must be humiliating. Don't make it worse for yourself by begging. We have so much more to do. I'll be taking several pieces of you before we are done today. But I promise everything I take, I'll put back. Eventually."

She tilted his chin up before tapping his cheek again.

"Not now. No sense in taking the sample while the area is numb."

His breath came in shallow gasps as the pain mutated into an ache. She returned with a marker. With her other hand, she tapped the tablet. The table split, and the clamp around his wrist forced his left arm to extend at his side. Jaegda proceeded to draw a line on his arm, just above the elbow.

"What, what are you doing?"

"I'm told your species can regenerate lost limbs if given time and nutrients," Jaegda answered. "That's what we're going to find out."

"We can!" he protested, finding the strength to pull against the bindings. "It takes weeks, but we can!"

Jaegda looked him in the eyes. "I believe you," she answered, and he took a breath. "But my job is to be thorough. So I'm afraid I can't take your word for it. I will take this arm and see what happens."

"No," he whispered. What else could he say? Why? How could this be happening? "Please, you don't have to do this."

"Yes, I'm afraid I do," she answered, holding her slate over his arm. "All of your bones have been replaced with cybernetics. It will prove problematic, but it looks like I can remove it at the elbow with the right tools. I suppose the pins I'm seeing are so the lower portion of the arm can be replaced if damaged."

She was really going to do it—cut off his arm just to see what would happen. This couldn't be happening to him.

The spinning metal and terrible wail of a saw blade assured him otherwise. His wails did not escape the honest room. He clenched his eyes as they were sprayed with his blood.

In the corridor outside, Taula and the rest of the prisoners sat in their cells unaware, doing what they could to pass the time.

CHAPTER
4D

A LATE HOUR IN THE Cathedral found Steven rising from his bed. It was nearly impossible for a royal to do something in absolute secret. No member of the family had a router in their private quarters. Officially this was so no hostile agent could enter, but this also ensured that royals could not leave without passing by their guards, who would never let them go somewhere unattended.

As he dressed, he paused to ensure he had heard a voice.

"Where are you going?"

He turned to Jasmine, who rested on her back with one eye open. Amazing. By this point in the evening, there was usually so much alcohol and marvat in her system that the Cathedral could explode without waking her.

"Go back to sleep."

As he stepped into his boots and they cinched tight, a pair of arms wrapped around him from behind.

"Are you all right?" Jasmine asked as she pressed herself into him. Steven rolled his eyes before reaching down to separate her arms.

"Go back to sleep," he repeated.

She grabbed his arm as he walked past. "Do you need to talk?"

He gave a derisive snort and a sideways glare. As if she'd be the person he'd talk to if he felt the need. He brought his arm up, and she winced as he pried her hand off.

"Go back to sleep."

"Steven—"

He did not let her finish, raising his hand in front of her face to command her silence.

"Go back. To sleep," he repeated firmly.

"Do you want me to go with you?" she whispered with some pathetic mewling expression. Something about that look sent a pulse of anger through him. His hand lowered to seize her by the neck. Both of her hands closed on his forearm as he forced her to walk backward, around the bed, and back to her side. He forced her down until she lay back in her place.

"Go. To. Sleep."

He gazed into her eyes, watching them roll back until her eyelids closed. Her hands fell away to her sides. In a few seconds, she was out, and he withdrew from her mind. Most likely she would wake later and think the encounter a dream. If not, oh well. With the annoyance subdued, he made his way out of his quarters.

In addition to his personal guard, at least two dozen deltas of the Imperial Guard—signified by their gold visors—lined the corridor. All of them snapped to attention when he joined them in the hall.

"Good evening, Majesty." The greeting came from Stokess, current captain of his guard. "To where do we accompany you?"

"To the vault," he answered.

"Yes sir."

"Personal guard only. The rest remain here."

"Sir," one of the plain visors began. In Steven's NOD, the name Nuken hovered over his helmet. "The executor ordered us to supplement your personal guard."

Steven glared at the aren, allowing several seconds to pass before answering. "The executor's orders do not trump my orders," he returned. "You will remain here."

"Sir—" Nuken hesitated, so Steven cut him off.

"If anything were to happen to Natalie or Jasmine, I would be *very* unhappy."

Nuken slowly bowed his head before turning to the rest of the plain visors.

"Back to your positions," he ordered.

"Blue team with us," Stokess barked, prompting the other half of gold visors into motion.

"Leave them here as well," Steven ordered.

"Sir—"

"I'm getting tired of explaining myself."

"Yes sir. Blue, back to positions."

Steven waited for them to comply before returning to his walk. A short jaunt to the nearest routing terminal, and he was at the entrance to the vault. The tram that led within came at his command. There was another brief argument, but settled quickly. Only he could go inside.

While the tram carried him to his destination, his mind wandered. The Senate had two days for recess to discuss among themselves. When the second day ended, they would meet to cast their votes. All the pieces seemed to be in place. Raymond, the darling prince, was dead and gone. Not even an engrammatic echo of his existence remained. He tilted his head back. Sophia, the middle sibling. She had so loved stories of intrigue, betrayal, and politicking. Were she not among the dead, she might have found some dark admiration for what he had done. Christian, the most astute of them all. Or David, he had always preferred his middle name. Even more than Raymond or Joseph, he would have been the greatest threat. The one most likely to piece together what had happened.

When one lost family, they were usually saddened by it. Was it because he killed them that he felt nothing? No remorse, no guilt, no loss. There had even been a moment of thrill. The look on Raymond's face when he had an inkling of what was happening. But that had faded quickly. No loss, but no joy. No triumph, no relief. Was it normal to feel nothing at all?

The tram began to slow as he approached it—cell 88. It came into view quickly as the tram's line ended. The large stairs, the gilded door, and the thirty vault sentries on those stairs. When the tram halted, Steven stepped out, and the deltas reacted.

"Sir. You cannot be here alone," one of their number called out to him.

Steven proceeded forward.

"Sir. You must turn back."

When he had covered half the distance to the stairs, they raised their weapons. Thirty barrels were trained on him.

"Majesty, this is your final warning. Turn back."

Steven's arm shot out toward them before he clenched his fist and drew it back. The gun arm of each aren bent quickly, forcing the muzzles of their weapons to the ceiling.

"Stand fast," he whispered. "There is no one here."

Deltas were particularly difficult to influence through telepathy. Something about this group was harder still. He heard grunts as they fought the intrusion and the psionic embrace of their bodies.

"Stand fast," he repeated. "There is no one here."

He slipped into their minds one at a time and accessed their NODs.

>>ACCESS *EVENT LOG: 4CM*

EVENT LOG ACCESS

2 EVENTS

02:30: TELEPATHIC INTRUSION

02:30: PSIONIC INTRUSION

>>*DELETE EVENT—02:30 TELEPATHIC INTRUSION*

>>*DELETE EVENT—02:30 PSIONIC INTRUSION*

ARE YOU SURE?

>>*YES*

>>*ACCESS EVENT LOG: 4CM*

EVENT LOG ACCESS

NO EVENTS IN LAST 168 HOURS. DO YOU WISH TO EXPAND LOG SEARCH?

>>*NO*

>>*CLOSE EVENT LOG*

>>*ACCESS SENSOR LOG*

SENSOR LOG ACCESS

>>*SUSPEND RECORDING—DURATION 2 HOUR*

SENSOR LOGGING SUSPENDED ON 2-HOUR TIMER

>>*CLOSE SENSOR LOG*

"Stand fast. There is no one here." He repeated the words as he cleaned the traces of his presence. The strength faded from each. One by one, he released them, and they returned to their previous stance. He opened his hand and lowered his arm.

Each delta stood in place, only their heads moving as they made constant scans of their surroundings. Not one reacted to him, the suggestion so strong in their minds that their brains did not believe their eyes. Even the icon in their sensors indicating a presence before them was ignored. With the threat removed, he walked between them, ascending the stairs to stand before the false door.

When last he was here, his father had used a key. Victor had used his badge. Steven had neither. How would he activate the router?

He looked back at the guards. They were the only ones allowed here. He closed his eyes and returned to their minds. He grimaced as he scanned their thoughts. Even by aren standards, their thoughts were so monotonous. Is anyone there? Is anything amiss? It is time for a sleep cycle? These were not DS-1 deltas, and certainly not DS-2s. They were definitely something else. A hidden model, some delta-beta hybrid. But as he jumped from mind to mind, he found what he needed. Soon two of the deltas left the formation. Each took a box from his armor and opened it.

Where there was machinery, there was maintenance. The two took their tools to the twin podiums. Just a routine test of the systems, nothing more. The hatch in the floor opened, and the router was exposed to him. He stepped in.

He did not bother to grab a halo as he stepped past the door and into the chamber. Red mist greeted him, and he heard the multitude. Many voices spoke to him, utterly devoid of inflection. With each word there were lights in the mist, like lightning deep in the clouds.

"You know that you can speak to me at any time. Yet so troubled, you felt the need to come in person."

Some part of him expected this place to be different, but it was unchanged. The pair of chairs before the raised podium, and the silver cylinder with its many cables streaming to the walls. He affixed his eyes to the cylinder.

"I want to know why," Steven answered. "You never said anything about framing Simmonne."

"A threat to power must be answered in proper measure. Her discredit secures your claim. In the minds of those who cannot think for themselves, an accusation is its own proof."

"But, was it necessary to blame her for it?"

"For the brothers and sisters now dead, you have shed no tears. What is this concern for the one who remains? Did the words not reach you when your father told you that she would inherit what was yours?"

Steven took a breath and glared down at his feet. "I didn't want to kill them all," he whispered. In his mind he saw them. Raymond, six years old and grasping for one of Steven's toys. Brittany, sitting with her tutor. Simmonne, two years old. A nightmare had left her afraid to go back to sleep. Their parents were away, so he was the one who answered when Lady Prideaux could not calm her.

"The path to power carries a terrible cost. It is one reason why the lust of so many who desire it shall never have it. In the decisive moment, you paid

the price without hesitation. Do you now regret that decision? Do you find the cost was too great?"

"It was necessary," he said. "They would have challenged my rule. They would never have stopped. Raymond, Jason—they would never have stopped looking for answers. If they had died separately, the suspicion would have been too great. Even now there is suspicion."

"The ego of most of your species compels them to wish for a destiny. I have crafted one for you. Do not hesitate now that you are on the path."

He grabbed the nearest chair and lowered himself into it. Simmonne was ten, and he had a talk with her—one that should have been carried out by their parents, but they somehow never found the time.

"The Olympian Terms are clear. If there is none among your dynasty to ascend, it passes to the high king. Are there not many in power who would turn blinded eyes? If you are the last Mandrake, even those who hate you might protect your claim. That no Rhinegrave sits on the throne."

He closed his eyes. He sat eating a late dinner. Simmonne, three years old, was asleep in his lap, holding Nela. The doll. Her treasure. The doll he gave her for a birthday days before. In a flash she was five, hanging on every word as he regaled her with stories about his battles with the Pillagers.

"Does she have to die?" He bowed his head as he awaited the answer.

"It is not by coincidence that she was absent. Do not fear for her, Steven. She has a destiny of her own. Her path is irrevocably set. She is exactly where she must be."

The tension in his shoulders relaxed and he took a breath.

"So what now?" He turned to face the astranium cylinder. "What is the price for your help? Do you want me to release you?"

"Release me?" The lightning in the mist seemed to brighten for a moment. *"Have I overestimated you? I told you, those who sought to imprison me had no concept of their futility. That to which you speak, and the entity of which it was a part. These were only ever conduits of my will."*

Steven returned slowly to his feet and approached the cylinder. "Are you telling me that all this time, you were never imprisoned here?"

"I do not and have never existed within the bounds of your reality. There is nothing from which I need be freed."

"Then what do you want? Why help me? Why give me this power?"

"That you would have what is yours. That your people would be possessed of what they need. For that I have aided you, and nothing more. But the work must continue. Ask your other questions."

Steven turned, placing a hand back on the chair.

"When I . . . When I fought my mother, she tore me apart. But then, I saw." He swept a finger around the room. "I saw this mist, and I was whole again. What happened?"

"Your people bear my gift. You bear it in greater measure."

"But," he stammered. "Metapsionics? I've never heard of anyone using them to regenerate."

"Would that you taught a child to use a weapon. Would the first you

handed them be one of mass destruction?"

Steven contemplated the answer before nodding. "I think I understand." He straightened to face the cylinder again. "So what now? You wouldn't have helped me. You wouldn't give me this power without a cost. What is it?"

"You must play the part that is yours to play. Your time grows short, and your enemies multiply. Preparations must now be made. Learn, Steven."

In an instant the chamber was as bright as the surface of a star. But the pain in his eyes was a mere suggestion. Images flashed through his sight. Worlds burned as stars blackened. A woman staggered out her door, calling out to a husband who would never answer. Another held her child tight as she faded away. In a crowded street, a little girl cried for her father who had been holding her hand and was suddenly gone. A sudden flash, and it all was gone.

New images flashed through his sight, technical schemata imprinting in his mind. Diagrams, charts, blueprints. He fell back on the chair, overwhelmed. The images kept pouring through. His head rolled back and the blinding light faded. Steven raised a hand to his eye as he straightened to his feet.

"I see," he whispered. "So that's how it has to be."

"Go now, Steven. Before you are missed."

"I have more questions."

"Seek answers in yourself before you look beyond."

Steven found himself walking for the door before he had processed the actions. He did not feel it, but another piece had been left behind.

CHAPTER
4E

THE VAAR HOME WORLD of Prithone lay 27,000 light-years from the center of its galaxy, La'fona. The Deep Sea. Prithone was a hive planet, a world that now shared its star with a hive. It was a distinction shared by many Solar worlds: Reichsylvannia, Atlantis, and many more. Few had the privilege of living on the planet itself—fewer had the privilege of a home nestled in the Nu'la'shan Mountains. From this latitude, the planet's ancient rings were always visible like a great silver band that dominated the southern horizon.

Warlord Oul'sor's home was somewhat more humble than one might expect for such a prominent citizen. Especially if that person was so esteemed as to be the Warlord of Aspiration. The one warrior chosen to serve as the ideal symbol that youth were directed to emulate. Yet Oul'sor's home was only a single story, appropriate for someone who had spent little time within its walls.

In the meditation den, Oul'sor kneeled before a bronze statue. The facsimile of a great warrior. The burning of calowa weed traced colored smoke in the evening light streaming through the windows. The weapon held by the bronze statue was one few could wield besides a Vaar. A bloodhammer. A massive mallet head began and ended with blades like great barbed spears. More blades edged the hammer's deadly scalp. When the weapon struck, the spearheads would pierce, the barbs would catch in flesh, and the hammer would drive it all through. The weapon's metal was old and blackened. The only trace of its former polish lay in the gilded streaks that striped the head.

When Oul'sor opened his eyes, his pupils took turns dilating, movement in the evening shadows. When he heard the voice, he knew for certain.

"Oul'sor. It is time for the festival."

Oul'sor ignored him. Time, it seemed, was not what it used to be. He kept his eyes on the statue.

Indorai did not abide the silence. "And who is this?" the hollow one asked aloud, coming to stand beside Oul'sor. His feet made no sound on the stone floor. "A friend of yours?"

Oul'sor's lips fought the urge to form into a sneer. "Hal'sor," he answered. "My ancestor. The most ancient warlord to whom I have a lineage."

"Ah yes," Indorai remarked. "And you Vaar believe your ancestors watch over you from the Void."

The sneer found greater purchase on Oul'sor's face as he ground his teeth in response to the dismissive tone. "Some do."

"And you, Oul'sor?"

He shook his head slowly. "I no longer know what to believe."

"That's normal," Indorai answered, still dismissive. Now that he could see Indorai, Oul'sor noted that the creature often wore his tendrils like a cloak around his body. One of those glowing tendrils unfurled to point at the hammer. "And this—Hal'sor's weapon?"

"Do not touch it!" Oul'sor bellowed, glowering at the offending appendage.

For several seconds neither of them moved. Oul'sor's eyes dilated with rage, and Indorai wore what might have been a smirk. A ripple passed through the tendril, and it was withdrawn.

"Do you intend to use it?" Indorai asked.

"No." Oul'sor turned back to the statue. "It is old. Obsolete. It would not survive impact on a Solar's armor, or a parry by one of their blades."

"If it is so useless, why do you gaze upon it?"

Oul'sor exhaled through his nose in a snort. "No concern that is yours."

This time Indorai sighed, a strange sound coming from a creature with no need to breathe. "I am trying very hard to be friendly, Oul'sor. You are making it difficult."

"We are not friends, *hollow one*," Oul'sor growled. "Especially now. Now that I know what I know. All you've done. All you will do. We will *never* be friends."

Indorai's maw opened to a wretched smile, and his tendrils fell behind him like a cape. "In time, you may think otherwise. But for now, we do have to work together. So if not friendship, perhaps civility is in order?"

Oul'sor didn't respond or acknowledge Indorai as he returned his focus to the weapon.

"What *are* you doing?" Indorai pressed.

He would not let it go. Perhaps an answer would buy a few moments of silence. "I meant to pass this weapon to Vil'sor. On my death. Or, if I lived to see it, when he became a warlord. Now he's gone. So I contemplate who should have it. Four hundred eleven sons. None of them are worthy. Three hundred who disgrace me with their lack of achievement. Another hundred who have achieved, but too little. The rest, too young. So I do not know who should have it next."

Oul'sor heard the grin in Indorai's voice. "An immortal, contemplating the passage of an heirloom. How amusing."

In a flash one of the tendrils shot out, coiled around the hammer, and plucked it from the statue's grasp.

"Put it back!" Oul'sor screamed, whipping to face Indorai. He halted, finding five tendrils pointed at him like waiting spears. Oul'sor bared his teeth, and his fists clenched in a fury that shook his arms. But he did not dare press forward. Eyes consumed by rage watched Indorai's face and the hammer before locking on the latter. A red mist seemed to flow through the weapon, end to end, before doubling back on itself.

"What are you doing to it?" Oul'sor demanded. Something was different. The hammer looked the same—and there was no change in its smell—yet he knew that it was changing before his eyes.

"The same as I did to you," Indorai explained calmly. "I give it a new start by making it more than it was. Use it now as you wish. You will find it as intractable as yourself. Make of it what you will. To break that which is foe. Or perhaps, as a receptacle for your hate."

At the tendril's urging, Oul'sor grasped the weapon with both hands. But Indorai did not let go. The new tendrils coiled around Oul'sor's mind. His eyes closed as he tried to force them out.

"What," Oul'sor strained. "What are you doing?"

"Skill and technique. Training and learning," Indorai answered. "You need much to understand your new world. So I share a portion of my understanding. It will only agonize you if you fight it."

The bulwark of Oul'sor's mind was not strong enough. The tendrils of shadow pierced, and he felt the knowledge flow into him. In the web of his consciousness, a jar formed and filled. A lid was placed upon the jar and sealed tightly, and the tendrils withdrew from his mind.

"You should be on your way to the festival. Don't want to disappoint little Vil'na."

CHAPTER
5A

THE SHIP'S CONFERENCE ROOM lay on the same deck as the control room. Panzer entered with Simmonne in tow to find his team waiting for him. Little more than a table and chairs adorned the space. Panzer led Simmonne past Rhoxx, holding her hand as she hiked a leg to step over the kodaz's large tail. She stood behind him as he took a position between the brothers.

"I don't think the four of you were properly introduced," Panzer said, breaking the air of anticipation in the room. "Princess, this is Rhoxx, my second-in-command and team heavy-weapons specialist."

"Majesssty," Rhoxx answered, bending his arms to bow his head low.

"This is Kassar, light-weapons specialist and over-qualified field medic."

Kassar answered by bringing his fists together and giving a curt bow.

"And this is Novin, my gizmologist."[7]

Novin mimicked Kassar's motion but kept his head bowed for a respectably longer period of time.

"Pleased to meet you," the princess answered in a somewhat mousy tone before looking back at Panzer.

"I've made a decision," he announced. "It will be some time before this ship is ready to cross enemy lines. In the interim, I intend to launch a rescue attempt to recover Miss Prideaux and the Katyusha Twins."

He's lost his mind. Panzer did not need telepathy for that one. All three of them had it written on their faces. Kassar's stare in particular revealed his thoughts as he threw an accusative glare at Simmonne. She responded by talking a half step behind Panzer. But none of the three protested.

"Andira. Is the *Caustic Reverie* still at ND-31?"

"Yes sir, according to fleet intercepts."

"Collate all available information on her. Cross-reference with all available data on known Combine ship design. Give me your best guess for a schematic of the ship."

After several seconds, a hologram came to life over the conference table.

---

7   Gizmologist is Imperial military jargon for a xenoengineer, an individual who is an expert in the study, cataloging, and manipulation of technologies of foreign or unknown manufacture.

It began as a simple outline before quickly filling in with tubular decks and spherical chambers. The mammoth vessels bore all the hallmarks of Vaar design, simply larger. One thousand and twenty-three kilometers from bow to stern. Longer from nose to baffles than the wingspan of a *Hurricane*-class supercruiser. But no doubt made of illstas rather than kilosteel, and only a fraction of the mass. She was a monster of a kind only a handful of civilizations could build. A thousand kilometers of Vaar pride.

The Vaar flagship looked like the misshapen, overgrown sibling of the most common destroyers. A hammerhead nose but vertical rather than horizontal. A rounded body bulged as it expanded before narrowing into a tail capped by four pylons in an *X*. Two short, hook-like wings spread at the midpoint of her body. A pair of squat sails sat near the midpoint of her back, with a larger third sail protruding from her belly. Large blisters protruded from its body where the bulk of her armament was held.

"Highlight the ship's prison," he directed. A small section of the vessel lit up in yellow. Panzer was not surprised to find it toward the nose of the ship, close to the outer hull. The Empire used a similar design philosophy. Ships were designed to keep their bow toward the enemy. Most of a vessel's non-vital systems were located toward the front and all along the outer perimeter to line the outer hull. This turned all these systems into another layer of protection for the more vital systems deeper inside.

He was about to speak when he sensed a point of curiosity from Simmonne.

"Ships this size have separate brigs for crew discipline, and prisons for prisoners," he said with a glance at her. From the look in her eyes, he estimated that he had guessed correctly. "The mission," Panzer continued as he turned back to the table, "is to infiltrate, secure the prisoners, and exfiltrate. Ideally without being detected. First question. How do we get aboard undetected? Ideas?"

Silence filled the room as Rhoxx and the brothers stared at the hologram.

"Don't everyone speak at once," Panzer prodded.

He did not blame them for their hesitation. An operation like this normally took many days to plan. Vaar ships were built like fortresses, with many defenses in the outer layers to repel boarders. The Corps had boarded Combine ships many times, and the Vaar had learned from each experience.

A mission to infiltrate a ship of this size was akin to entering an enemy's city, except that there were no civilians and no noncombatants. Every person found in that city was a hostile.

Kassar and Novin looked at Rhoxx. Panzer noted the uncomfortable feeling of the emotion detector standing just behind him. Kassar was the first to speak up.

"Sir," he began in his ever-present whisper. "I don't think this is a good idea."

Exactly the response Panzer expected. Back home, every high king had his naysmiths. Those who lived in an echo chamber had a way of losing the ability to tell their good ideas from the bad ones. The good kings always listened to what the naysmiths had to say. Their one job was to come up with reasonable and respectful arguments and counterpoints to the high king's ideas. In the tiny kingdom of this ship, Kassar fancied himself the resident naysmith. At least, when Andira wasn't trying to take the job.

"Andira?" Kassar tapped his would-be ally. "How many marines would you estimate are on that ship?"

"A ship of this size would normally carry at least a brigade," she answered. "However, Vaar flagships typically carry significant reserves to replenish forces under their command. If the *Caustic Reverie* is performing that function, that number could be in the hundreds of millions. I cannot be certain with information presently available."

Kassar's eyes returned to Panzer.

"I never said the job would be easy," Panzer answered. "Obviously we'll have to take control of the ship's transit system so they can't mass all those bodies against us. But first we have to get on board."

Still no suggestions came, and he turned his attention back to Andira's guesswork schematic. Imperial and Combine ships could both manufacture their fuel, but it was often faster to take on fuel from a tanker if one was available. Panzer raised his hand and pointed to a pair of cylinders barely rising from the hull behind the ship's dorsal sails.

"What about going in through the fuel lines?" he asked.

"No good," Rhoxx answered. "Deadyesss team already doin' it."

Panzer glared at him.

"Misssssion to t'e *Rut'less Devotion*," Rhoxx offered, attempting to jog his memory.

"Right," Panzer answered, pretending to know what Rhoxx was talking about. He would have to be careful. Temporary memory loss—another gift from the deep-fryer. "No fuel line incursion. What other options are there?"

"What'n 'bout gun port?" Rhoxx offered. "No one tryin' it yet."

"No good," Panzer returned. "This close to the front, they may be open. But with all the damage control, it will be too easy for them to lock us down if we're detected coming in."

When silence reigned, Panzer looked up. Novin wore the expression of someone begging to be called on.

"Novin?" he asked.

The shorter of the two kurai gave a nervous glance to the others before pointing at the ship's tail. "What if we went in through the exhaust baffles?"

The suggestion brought glares from Rhoxx and Kassar. It was followed by a third from Simmonne as she no doubt wondered what had provoked such a strong reaction in them.

"I don't think anyone has tried it," Novin offered. "They wouldn't expect it."

"Probably because no one would be stupid enough to try." Kassar almost broke his eternal whisper with his answer.

"I don't know," Panzer remarked. "You'd be surprised how stupid someone can be when they put their mind to it."

Kassar raised a finger before pausing. The four pupils of his eyes went up for a minute as if asking his brain to double-check the words conveyed by his ears. "Be that as it may"—Kassar found his tongue—"that is an especially bad idea."

"Why is it a bad idea?" Simmonne drew the room's eyes. "What do they do?"

Panzer held up his hand, preempting the others before he pointed to the ship's belly, where the reactors were tucked in two long banks. "Vaar reactor tech isn't as good as ours. They can't ramp up their reactors the way we can. Right now, that ship is not at warp. But if she wants to get into warp quickly, say because she comes under attack, then she has to keep generating power as if she were already at warp. But since she isn't, that's a lot of power she's producing and not using. You can't just let it linger, or eventually the heat will be a problem. So they battery what they can, and the rest"—he drew his finger to the long tail and the X that capped it—"is shunted to the baffles, and removed from the ship via giant lasers shooting X- and gamma rays out the rear. Novin is suggesting we infiltrate the ship by going through the body of one of the lasers."

"What he's not mentioning, Majesty," Kassar added, "is that if we're in there when one of those lasers fires, we'll be atomized."

Simmonne blinked at Kassar. The look on her face was one so many people had when they asked what they felt was a stupid question. "I thought a soldier's armor made them impervious to lasers."

Panzer allowed himself a short chuckle. Layperson's view of technology. Absolutes. It's on or it's off. It works, or it doesn't. Black and white. If he threw energy figures, heat capacities, and radiant opacities at her, that would just go over her head.

"To a point, yes," he explained. "Any laser you can actually pick up and hold in your hand or mount on a ground vehicle probably isn't going to do anything to our armor. But that doesn't mean it can stop a laser of *infinite* strength. Or one with an entire supercruiser behind it. Kassar is correct. Even if our armor survived, *we* wouldn't. That said . . ." Panzer turned his gaze back to Kassar. "If Kassar has a better idea of how to get aboard, I'd be happy to entertain it."

With none to offer, Kassar moved his gaze back to the schematic.

"Then we go with Novin's idea," Panzer declared. "That will put us in the tail of the ship. We will have to cross to the prison, secure the prisoners, and then get off. I don't think it'd be a good idea to try going back out the way we came in. One of the ship's hangars is probably the best bet. We're going to need a lot of controls. Andira, if we get you into their systems, how many networks do you think you could gain control over?"

"Not many, sir," Andira answered, projecting a small hologram of herself to stand by the schematic of the ship. "Every major system will be on its own independent network. With the computer capacity of a ship this size, security AIs will number approximately—"

"Short version, Andira."

"Between two and four," she answered. "But I will need much more hardware than is available in the team's armor."

Panzer rapped his fingers on the table as he contemplated. "Then we'll take a number six core with us."

"Sir," Andira answered, "it will be quite impossible for me to hide the power signature of a number six core from their security sensors. I recommend no larger than a number four."

Panzer rolled his eyes. "Okay, a number four then."

The question now was what systems to sic her on. What systems *could* they sic her on for that matter. Weapons were pointless. Control was too distributed and too redundant to cope with battle damage. Not that they'd be useful against problems inside the ship in any case. Life support was equally pointless. As was propulsion.

Priority one was to avoid detection. Priority two was to prevent the Vaar from massing if they were detected.

"Are you confident you could get control of their transit system?" he asked.

"Difficult, but possible," Andira answered.

"That's a start."

The Vaar's equivalents of astranet and mininet technologies were even further behind the Empire than their reactor tech. They could teleport from ship to ship, but the precision and power efficiency for deck-to-deck within the same ship simply was not there. As a result Vaar ships were even more compartmentalized than Imperial ships. Every crew member slept within sprinting distance of their workstation. Every team had its racks, galley, and recreation facilities. When something did need to move through the ship, it went by high-speed tram. Panzer stifled a chuckle. If only the Vaar knew how often their technological inferiority was a hindrance to their enemy.

"So, give us control of their transit system." Panzer resumed thinking aloud. "What about internal comms?"

"Very risky," Andira answered, "but possible. However with the redundancy of that system, they will quickly purge corrupted network segments and fall back to secondary systems. I have no chance to control every layer of the communications stack."

"Even just a few minutes of confusion could be enough," Panzer replied before pointing to the inner curve of the port wing. "So. We go in through the baffles. Take a tram to the prison and secure the prisoners. Then, I think, this hangar. From there we spacewalk out and leave on the *Intruder*. We'd never get this ship close enough to board, nor can we take her that close." He gestured in Simmonne's direction with his thumb. "Andira, how long will it take us to get there in the *Intruder*?"

"Approximately four days."

"That long?"

"If you want to avoid detection, yes sir."

"A lot can happen in four days," Kassar cautioned. "The ship may not be there by the time we arrive."

Panzer nodded. "Wouldn't be the first time someone did that to us. So we best not waste any time. Kassar, Novin, kit out."

The kurai bowed their heads and turned for the door.

Panzer could feel the words before they were spoken just as he felt the kodaz's eyes boring into the side of his head. He looked down at Simmonne, who continued to glare at the Vaar ship. "Would you excuse us a moment?"

She needed a minute to realize he was addressing her.

"Just wait outside," he whispered.

With some hesitation she made for the door. Once it closed behind her, Panzer turned to face Rhoxx.

"You knowin' I never quessstionin' you in front of ot'ers," Rhoxx began, "but you sssure bein' a good idea?"

"Rhoxx, how many of the things we do actually *are* good ideas?" Panzer answered. "It was my responsibility to keep her and the rest safe. I failed. Now I have to correct that failure."

"I go kit out t'en," Rhoxx answered.

"Not you," Panzer held up a hand to keep him in place "You're staying here."

Rhoxx's eyes narrowed, and his lips parted to show more of his teeth. The kodaz expressions for frustration, confusion, and anger all looked very similar.

"It bein' my resssponsssibility. Goin' where you go."

Panzer threw a thumb toward the door and spoke low. "Rhoxx, I can't leave her here alone."

"Andeera—"

"Is not good enough," Panzer interrupted before looking at her hologram, still standing on the table. "No offense."

"None taken," she answered.

Panzer looked back at Rhoxx, who still bared his teeth. "I get it. While I was under, you had to take over. Kassar has no social skills. Novin won't address someone higher than himself uninvited. And Andira doesn't care about anyone's feelings but mine. The princess just went through a traumatic experience and was then left alone for two days. I need someone who can keep her safe and be company if she needs it. That's you."

Rhoxx's lips lowered back over his teeth, and his eyes expanded to their normal diameter. "You goin' need my fi'ah'powa, you get caught."

Panzer forced a smile. "Rhoxx if we get caught in there, I don't think it's going to matter."

"But—"

Panzer shook his head and Rhoxx was silent. "Rhoxx, I need you to stay. If things go bad, you have to get her home."

Air whistled between his teeth as Rhoxx bowed his head. "As you wisssh."

"Good man," Panzer remarked, tapping the kodaz's shoulder. "Keep her safe."

He stepped away from the console.

"Time to kit out."

CHAPTER
5B

I N SILENCE SIMMONNE FOLLOWED the colonel to his armory. By the door she found a segment of wall not covered by weapons and shelving to lean against. He began gathering items from across the room.

Dying. He couldn't be. He seemed fine. He was on his feet, walking, talking, and being menacing. He seemed—well he wasn't normal, but his version of normal. Was this a trick? Did he decide he had no interest in her and made up this story about dying so he could slip away? Back into his life as a person who did not exist? No, he wouldn't do that. Would he?

It had to be a lie. A medical condition that *couldn't* be fixed? Aside from NNED, she had scarcely heard of such a thing. They could grow entire bodies from base chemicals. Pull the engramatic memory onto data banks to store until it could be put back on a repaired brain. Only a little of their brain had to be salvageable, and the rest could be made. Could he really have something the doctors and the machines could not fix?

She watched him put a cigarette in his mouth and pull the lighting tab, rousing a memory. On the balcony, in the car, in the club. He had smoked his cigarettes. He said it was to treat his condition. Was it true then?

"Andira, three retrieval suits," he said as he opened one of the cabinets to reveal a large printer. He took the outfits as they came, black bodysuits that he laid on the workbench beside the massive block of ammunition. He added four helmets afterward and went to another cabinet for some kind of metal plates. The suits were far too small for him. For Jenna and the Twins perhaps?

He held out a hand toward the tool rack. For a second he simply stood there as if expecting something to happen. When it did not, he stepped forward and took the tool he sought. Did he just try to call it to his hand and fail? He used the tool to affix the plates to the suits before opening a compartment atop the ammo block. The helmets compacted into spheres as he placed the suits inside and closed the compartment.

He opened it again.

"Andira?" he asked. "We have a personnel file on Miss Prideaux?"

"Yes sir," the AI answered.

"With what weapon does she have the highest proficiency score?"

"Shappo Ziri model 212."

Pistols. Those were the pistols Jenna carried. Simmonne remembered the funny name of the company. Again he held up his hand, this time toward one of the gun racks. Simmonne caught the sound of an annoyed huff before he walked to the rotating rack. He did it again.

"She'll need more than a sidearm," the colonel remarked as he looked down at the weapon.

"She has high marks with a CA-9600."

"I suppose an SMG will do," he answered. One of the racks spun, and he took another gun from it. He made two trips, ferrying the weapons to the block with the first. With the second he walked to some kind of dispenser and returned to the block with magazines. After shutting the compartment, he moved to another rack, where he began withdrawing what looked like metal handles.

"Hammers or maces, hammers or maces?" he muttered. "Maces."

He grabbed a fat cylinder with large flanges and screwed it onto the handle. Only when he was done did she realize it was a grenade. He crafted four of them and set them on the bench before walking to the pit at the center of the room.

"Don't move. Andira, AMAC, configuration four."[8]

"Sir, it will be quite impossible for me to hide the signature of the level four suit from the *Caustic Reverie*'s internal sensors. Given that we do not know the full capabilities of the new class, I recommend against anything heavier than configuration two."

He made a face and took a long puff on his cigarette. "We get caught in there, I'm going to need the four's firepower."

"Does that apply if you're detected before reaching the objective?"

He shook his head. "Fine, give me the pig." He held out his arms, hands level to his shoulders. His clothes cinched tighter around him. His hair began to curl from the base, while the twin braids curled around his head. In a moment his hair seemed to form a helmet as a black film rose out of the pit. The film paused at his neck. He flexed his shoulders before rolling his eyes and spitting his cigarette onto the floor. The black film moved to cover him completely. A hatch in the ceiling slid away and machines descended.

Simmonne held still as the room came to life, and the colonel's armor was assembled. A quilted suit lined with red wires came down next, but as the suit came together, she realized that this one was different from what she had seen. Metal bars adhered to him at his torso before more were added to his limbs as if to assemble a new skeleton. Coils of copper muscle covered these bones before a skin of metal plates. This armor was bulkier, with a broader chest, shoulders, arms, and heavier legs. His head looked almost comically small atop the large shoulders.

---

8   AMAC is short for All Mission Adaptive Concept. This armor suit is popular among members of the Corps due to its adaptability. Additionally, aside from its R-steel helmet and trauma plates, all other components are readily fabricated by common facilities on warships.

The helmet was the last to descend. Like the helmet she had seen previously, it had nothing to approximate eyes. Its only discerning feature was a large respirator seeming to clutch a pair of cylinders. With a hiss the helmet sealed onto his head, bringing some well-needed proportion to his silhouette. With the armor complete, he reached up to elicit another hiss as he took hold of the respirator, and he slid the faceplate of the armor up over his scalp.

He coiled his fist into a ball as a pair of barrels extended out of a ridge on his forearm. He did the same with the other arm before turning. Simmonne startled as the door beside her opened. The AI, in her faux body, joined them. She followed the colonel to his workbench.

With one armored hand, the colonel took hold of the massive block and turned to the AI. Her seemingly delicate frame had no trouble embracing the huge mass before she moved behind him. With little effort she raised it higher, and the metal rang as it clamped to his back. While he positioned more magazines over his chest like a bandolier, the AI took hold of the golden weapon and held it up to him. It compacted in his grip as he reached back to clamp it to the side of his new backpack. The grenades found purchase on his thigh. He held up a finger, as if forgetting something. The AI was on the spot, holding up an enormous pistol that soon joined the grenades on his thigh. Finally the AI handed him a rifle, tiny in comparison to the gold weapon. It folded in his grasp, and he placed it on his back beneath the box.

He took a step, and Simmonne's knees tremored when his foot met the floor. "Andira," he said, raising his foot. He brought it down, creating a pulse of thunder. "My ground pressure is way too high."

"You're carrying many tons of ordnance," the AI answered, using the projectors in the room rather than the mouth of the body standing next to him. "I recommend you wear the dispersers."[9]

He frowned and answered in an almost petulant tone. "I don't want to wear the booties."

"Wear the booties, sir," the AI prodded.

"Fine."

He returned to the pit where a large pair of metal plates descended from the ceiling. He brought the boots of his armor down on them, and they wrapped around to form a larger outer boot. He tested the new system by bringing his foot up and deliberately stomping on the floor. This time Simmonne barely heard it and felt nothing. He did it twice more before he was content.

---

9   Field disperers are used by power-armored infantry and ground vehicles. These systems utilize force-field technology to distribute the carrier's weight over a larger area, reducing ground pressure. Advanced systems can even stiffen the terrain itself allowing it to bear greater mass without allowing sinking.

"I suppose that's everything."

The war machine approached her, but inside was a dying man. He knew. He *knew* he was dying, and still he did what he did. He reached into a small cabinet and withdrew a golden box from the shelf. With his other hand, he motioned her to follow him out.

"The *Intruder* can get us into position," he said as she followed. "It will take at least three days to get there. Once we're on the ship, between five and six hours to complete the rescue. Then three days back. More if we have to evade pursuit. So it will be just you, Rhoxx, and Andira for a while."

"Doesn't she go with you?" Simmonne asked, turning back to look at the AI's body, which followed along with them.

"She writes a copy of her program to my armor when I leave, but her core program stays on the ship," he explained. "She'll keep things under control and finish repairs. Once we have your friends, we'll meet at the eye and leave when repairs are done. If there's any problem at Eye-9, Andira will reroute to Eye-11 in the Basin. So six days minimum. Will you be all right until then?"

"I'll be fine," she spat, watching for a reaction. There was none.

They walked down large stairs and through narrow corridors. He *knew* he was dying. He knew and he still took her from the *Rothburg.* He knew when he put his hands on her. He knew when she was in his lap, and he was twisting her around his finger. When he put visions in her head. He knew. The bastard knew he wasn't going to live long enough to make good on any of it!

Her jaw trembled as she glared at the back of his head. Was it nothing but amusement on his part? Was it just to toy with her? Was he just hoping to get her into bed so he could brag about it? The same aspiration as so many of the cowards who tried to flirt with her before losing their grit? That was it, wasn't it? She was nothing to him. Just some dumb little girl he could charm to amuse himself. Her hands balled into fists as she followed him into a hangar. The *Intruder* was suspended over a pit by a large claw. The ship's wings, perhaps a hundred meters spread, were folded under its diamond-like body. The colonel's team loaded equipment up a ramp protruding from its belly.

Simmonne's glare remained affixed to him. It was for nothing.

"Why?" she whispered, not fully expecting him to hear her.

But he did and turned. Perhaps he noted the tears trying to form. She wanted so much to look him in the eye and demand her answer. But even now, she couldn't meet his gaze. So she looked down at his feet as he took a step toward her.

"Why?" she repeated. "If you knew you were dying, why did you start something you knew you couldn't finish?"

Though her eyes were blurring, she saw him reach for her.

"Don't touch me!" she hissed and took a step away.

He ignored her protest, pinching the collar of her dress.

"Let go." She put her hand on his gauntlet, trying to push it away. "Let go. Let go, let go!'"

"Simmonne."

His voice was calm, and she froze as a tingle shot down her spine. The calm of his voice seemed to strangle her anger. "Put your hand down."

She hesitated but lowered her hand from his. He drew her a step closer, and his hand moved from her dress to hook a finger under her chin.

"Sometimes you see something you want, and you don't think about the consequences. Even if you should." His other hand came up, holding the box before he guided her hands around it. Her heart skipped a beat as she looked at the ornate container. Was this what she thought it could be? She took a breath. No, surely not. "Goodbye."

The word never reached her. Nothing could as she glared at the box. Her fingers hesitated when she commanded them to pry the small container open. Gold stared back at her from blue velvet. Was this what she thought it was? His badge?

"Colonel?"

Only when she looked up did she realize he had walked away, but she caught a glimpse of his back as the *Intruder*'s door sealed. The floor beneath the ship opened to a force field, and the ship was lowered through it. A second later the doors closed, and he was gone.

CHAPTER
5C

JONATHAN CLEARWATER WOULD FEEL the full measure of Jaegda's efforts. The numerous augmentations to his body to help him cope with agony were turned against him. He could turn off the pain blockers meant to keep him from feeling her efforts, but a legionnaire's hardening against agony went much further. A legionnaire distracted by pain could not do his job. Nor could a legionnaire so riddled by the pain that his mind could focus on nothing else. Even less useful was the legionnaire rendered unconscious by it. All of these measures built into him could not simply be deactivated. Enhancements that enabled him to focus despite the agony did nothing to block it. Lest the legionnaire not realize the extent of his injury.

When she cut through the flesh to reach the elbow joint, he felt every rotation of the saw blade. When the toes of his right foot were taken, he felt that, too. He remained fully aware, enough to remember her words. To assimilate the information as she calmly explained that she would see how his body prioritized multiple wounds. When teeth, his left eye, and more were taken, he remained cruelly cogent. He heard the strange song she sang to herself to block out his cries. He was still aware when she commented on her exhaustion.

If Jaegda sought the limits of just how much pain his enhancements allowed him to endure, she found it. What remained of Jonathan Clearwater had little energy. He let out quiet moans as he was jostled on the cart that now carried him. When the guards arrived at his cell, they gently removed him from the cart and laid him on the floor. Perhaps seeing what had become of him elicited some measure of compassion from them. It was just as likely Jaegda had warned them not to cause further injury that would affect her data.

"Jonathan?"

He managed only a pained moan when he heard Taula's voice.

"Stars around! What did they do?" Her hand touched his forehead, another his chest. He was barely aware of it. Too much pain for such a gentle touch to properly register. "Jonathan, can you hear me?"

Another pained moan, and his right eye opened briefly. Some lantai had a natural luminescence to their eyes. Certain chemicals built up in the blood vessels to the point that the iris cast its own glow in dim light. She had inherited the trait weakly from her mother. But as his eye opened, the faint emerald glow was all he could see.

"Jonathan, talk to me." Taula raised her voice. She shook him gently, but in his state, it was enough to draw out a loud groan.

"Taula."

His right hand reached up toward her before falling limp. The last strut upholding his mind finally gave. His eye closed as he let out a deep breath. Taula's voice was too far away now to respond to it. The mind could no longer bear the weight of consciousness.

His eye focused on the useless clock in his NOD. The numbers did nothing for him. They simply satisfied that part of the mind, ever wanting something to focus on. The rest of his mind relived the events of the past hours. The howl of saw blades, snakes of metal, the violating probes. All amid a symphony of his screams.

Exhaustion eventually took him. He did not even notice when Taula pried his eye open. The movement of her lips meant nothing. Other faces came to his mind: children, a young woman, a man in a legionnaire uniform, a woman who lied and never returned. Every face familiar, every name unknown. When he heard their voices, he had no concept of the face that matched them.

The clock continued forward.

"Johnny?"

Hours had passed when he heard the word.

"Johnny, can you hear me?"

His right eye began to open.

"Johnny?"

"Don't call me Johnny," he muttered. The words were spoken without thought, a simple reflex from a person not yet awake. But only a little bit of lucidity was needed. The moment he moved, the throbbing of his wounds quickly spirited him the rest of the way.

Clearwater let out a groan as he shifted his legs. He reached over to the left arm where his fingers ran down the sleeve of his prisoner's uniform. He found the knot and the emptiness of the sleeve beyond. It had not been a nightmare.

"Jonathan. Water."

Taula had dragged him to rest his head in her lap while she leaned back against the wall. Now she held a small cup of plastic to his face. He took it and leaned up far enough to drink. A dry throat was grateful for the moisture, and he quickly emptied the cup. Taula reclaimed it as he returned to his previous position.

"Are you hungry?" she asked, reaching over to the floor before holding something in front of him. A small cube of some kind, it looked like white chocolate, yet reeked of spoiled cheese. Clearwater shook his head slowly. "How do you feel?" Taula whispered, gently tracing her nails through his hair.

"It hurts," he whispered. "But, it's, it's mostly an ache now."

"Don't they give you implants in case you're tortured?"

"Yes." He nodded slowly. "But . . ."

"But what?" she asked when he stopped.

He almost said it. He couldn't tell her. He wouldn't tell her. What would that do to her? To see this happen to him so she wouldn't endure it. If the roles were reversed . . .

"They're not working?" Taula pressed.

"No. Must, must have been the reanimation. Nothing else is working right."

"I'm so sorry, Jonathan," Taula answered, gently hugging him. "I, I don't know. Do you want to talk about it?"

Clearwater shook his head slowly. "No. I think, I think I just want to lie here."

"I figured out where we are," she whispered. That prompted his eye to open again. "We're on a ship. I overheard the guards when they brought you back. They were talking about how we're orbiting ND-31."

"Oh," he whispered. "Is there any more water?"

"I'll have to get up to go get it."

Which was stronger? The desire for another drink, or the desire to remain still? He debated it for several seconds before thirst won.

"Okay."

His abdomen felt as if it were splitting open as he sat up. Courtesy of Jaegda's probes to take samples of his digestive system. He clenched his teeth to avoid crying out, and he rose enough for Taula to slip out from under him. The moment she was clear, he dropped to the deck to take the tension off. The impact sent a jolt of pain through his maimed arm. All he could think about was how that water better be *really* wet.

He strained his head to watch Taula fumble against the wall a few meters down. Clearwater had never understood why animals with shiny eyes could see better in the dark, but why lantai with glowing eyes were nearly blind in it. While he made out the port in the wall, she took nearly a minute to find it. In the silence, he heard the water flow, and she returned. Seated on the floor again, she grabbed for him as he began to sit up. The water was wet enough, and he quickly gulped it down. When he was finished, Taula took her previous position and guided his head down into her lap. Minutes of silence passed while Clearwater held as still as he could. Eventually Taula broke the quiet.

"Jonathan? What happened? What happened on the planet?"

Clearwater grimaced as images of the battle welled up. "I don't know," he whispered. "The Vaar, they routed in. The warp shield was up, but they routed in. Right onto the fields. No reception terminals—they just . . . materialized on the grass. A million of them. They filled the entire valley, past the horizon and into the mountains. And they had these . . . huge warmechs . . . the size of archangels. They used them to breach the wall. Then they flooded in. Too many. I think there were more than I saw. We had artillery hidden in the mountains, a hundred kilometers north. The Vaar found them almost immediately."

He paused to draw in a deep breath as another memory barged its way into his focus. His eye opened wider.

"The Ghost."

"The Ghost?" Taula repeated, leaning closer to him.

"I saw the Ghost."

"Where? What was it doing?"

"Before the attack, another Vaar ship. We shot it down, and it crashed near the pole. We went to look for survivors. We found one, dying. He kept spouting gibberish. We were bringing him back when the Vaar attacked. The Ghost took him away."

Taula hesitated, and the hand that had been stroking his hair stopped. "You're sure it was the Ghost?"

What began as an exasperated laugh became an agonizing cough that jarred every wound in his body. "Yes. I'm sure," he strained. He opened his eye again to see Taula bite her lip before her hand continued its ministrations.

"So you can remember the battle but not your family?"

Family? He knew he had one. But, the more he tried to recall them, the less certain he was. "No. I can't remember them."

"Your oldest sister, Melanie, is thirteen. Stephanie is nine. Ryan is ten, and David is six. You've been taking care of them since you lost your parents."

He was taking care of them? That didn't sound right.

"Can you find them in your memory index?" Taula asked.

"No. I can't even access it. The names, they sound familiar. I think I remember their faces, but I can't put them together."

There was something. An animal. It was furry and moved like a tiny gorilla, but it had a long pink tail. "You had a pet," Clearwater whispered. "Guile? Gills?"

"Gulliver," she corrected. "You're thinking of Gulliver."

"Gulliver." That didn't quite sound familiar, but the feeling of the name did. "Funny name. What does it mean?"

She shrugged. "I don't know."

"Where'd you get it?"

"From a ship."

"A ship?" Clearwater let out a single chuckle, but his body punished him for it.

"It's in the Imperial History Museum, right next to the *Spirit of Humanity*. I just remember the name because I thought it was funny. Gulliver was cute, so I gave it to him." Taula's eyes closed briefly. "I miss him."

Clearwater let out a breath, cringing as the obvious implications set in. "Is he?"

"I don't know." Taula shook her head. "They rushed us to the shelters so quickly, I had to leave him behind. They wouldn't let me go back for him."

"I'm sorry."

"Hey." She smiled. "He's smart. He might be able to take care of himself."

She said the words, but even Clearwater sensed the lack of confidence in them.

The weight of motionlessness took its toll, and Clearwater rolled to find another comfortable position. Every centimeter of rotation was fresh torture until he finally faced away from Taula, and his right arm beneath him helped to straighten his spine. All through the movement, he could feel her legs tense as the sounds escaped his mouth.

"It hurts bad, doesn't it?"

Clearwater nodded, afraid speaking might let more than a groan escape.

"Do you want me to let you go back to sleep?"

"Don't think I can right now."

Taula took a breath, and she shifted slightly to further recline against the wall. "Is it still hurting?"

He nodded. Silence set in for a time. He was in too much pain to do much talking. She probably had no idea what to say. But after a while, she thought of something.

"If you weren't here right now, what would you be doing?"

"Well, I don't know," Clearwater answered.

"If you were home," she specified. "Nowhere you had to go. Nothing you had to do. What would you be doing now?"

"I don't know. Probably playing *Warmetal.*"

"What kind of game is it?"

For some reason, Clearwater found the question amusing. Perhaps because someone as smart as her couldn't tell by the name. "Warmech simulator. It's actually made by the same people who make the training software."

"Is it good?"

"I like it," he answered. "Has a lot of historic campaigns. Do good enough, and it will give you alternate history."

Taula laid a hand gently on his shoulder. "Do you have a local copy?"

Confused for a moment, he panned his lone eye through his NOD.

>>*SEARCH: WARMETAL*

1 FILE FOUND.

WARMETAL 7, RONGXING CYBERSTUDIOS

The memory index contained every event of his life, but it did not survive sloppy Vaar reanimation. The memory of his home, his family, the people he knew. That did not survive. His ability to use human advantage did not survive. But the games folder in his local network—*that* survived?

"Yes," he whispered.

"Do you want to play?"

Clearwater rolled just enough that he could turn his head and look up at her eyes. "Play?"

"Play," she answered. "It would give you something to focus on besides, well, all this."

Something about the suggestion seemed so ridiculous. But as he thought on, he found few reasons to object.

"Come on, play with me," she whispered loudly. "Play with me, and pretend we're somewhere else."

>>*RUN PROGRAM. WARMETAL 7*

WARMETAL 7 INITIALIZING . . .

The dark cell faded as it was subsumed by the image of a smoking battlefield. His view panned on the burning heap of a tank before zooming out as the foot of a *Brutus*-class warmech came down it. Missiles volleyed from its boxy shoulders, while disrupters flared from its arms and bullet nose.

WARMETAL 7: ONLINE

NO ASTRANET CONNECTION AVAILABLE

LOCAL PLAY ONLY

SELECT MODE

SINGLE PLAYER

VERSUS

CO-OP

Clearwater moved his eyes.

>>*CO-OP*

INVITE LOCAL PLAYER

>>*LOCAL PLAYER / PROXIMITY*

WAITING FOR PLAYER 2 . . .

PLAYER 2 CONNECTING . . .

PLAYER "DR. RHOMBUS" IS DOWNLOADING PEER-TO-PEER . . .

From his nanites to hers, the software flowed.

"Doctor Rhombus?" Clearwater asked.

"It's a long story," Taula answered.

PLAYER 2 READY

SELECT CO-OP CAMPAIGN.

BASIC PILOTING

THE REUNIFICATION

THE PRAETHEEN WAR

THE SOLAR ECLIPSE (IMPERIAL)

THE SOLAR ECLIPSE (DOMINION)

THE STAVO INTERVENTION

THE COMBINE WAR (FICTIONAL CAMPAIGN)

THE END TIMES (FICTIONAL CAMPAIGN)

"Be patient with me," Taula warned. "I've never played before."

>>BASIC PILOTING

He'd let her figure out how to pilot her machine first. Then, maybe step on some Vaar.

CHAPTER
5D

THE TIME FOR DELIBERATION had come and gone. Once more Steven stood high above the Blue Floor to face the Solar Senate. Indorai perched behind him. If Steven focused, he could almost see him now. He could make out the inhuman lines of the creature's body and distinguish the six individual tendrils sprouting from his back. But here he was careful not to look, lest anyone wonder what he was looking at.

The sound of a gavel brought the chamber to order. Steven held his breath. In but a few moments, his destiny would be decided. Everything he had worked for, everything to which he aspired, hinged on these moments.

"Relax," Indorai whispered into his mind. *"Everything proceeds as it is meant to."*

While the roll was called, Steven glared down at the podium of his platform. Indorai had to be right. Everything had been wagered on this. What he had done to get here couldn't be for naught. Heedless for a moment of the many eyes on him, he looked back at the throne. At the chair where he would sit. The chairs where he had hoped his siblings would sit as they watched him assume his rightful place. The chair where Natalie would sit as his empress. All empty.

Three bangs of the gavel. The roll call was complete, and the proceedings began.

High King Jonas von Rhinegrave held the gavel. His hologram rose from its throne as the high king took a position at his podium. Steven took a breath as the high king began to speak.

"We assemble this day, 133 in our year 100,016. Time for deliberation has been allotted and executed to determine Solar succession. As first lord, I hereby certify that the House of Lords has completed its deliberation. Prime Speaker, has the Citizen's Congress completed its deliberation?"

A few meters away from Steven, two additional platforms hovered. On his left, Prime Speaker Alberr Donello stood upright and answered the high king.

"First Lord, as prime speaker, I certify that the Citizen's Congress has completed its deliberation."

"So noted," the high king answered before turning to gaze at the platform on Steven's right. "Lieutenant Justice, has the Council of Justiciars completed its deliberation?"

There was a bitter taste, shame from Lieutenant Justice Alhi, as he looked at the high king. "First Lord, as lieutenant justice, I certify that the Council of Justiciars has completed its deliberation."

The lieutenant justice had equipped himself with an unusually strong 4CM system today. But all the same, Steven caught the thought as the justice gave him a sideways glance.

You really did it, didn't you? You killed them.

Steven shifted uncomfortably. The thought came in so clear, at first he thought that the justice had sent it to him deliberately. But Alhi was not a telepath. He did not know his thoughts were being read, let alone with such ease.

The high king laid his gavel on his podium. "Given the testimony of the Solar Marshals, and the many unknowns of this occasion, I cannot in good conscience call for the votes of the Senate at this time."

Steven cast a glare at the high king. His mouth began to open until he felt Indorai's tendril on his shoulder.

"Just wait," Indorai whispered. *"Allow your ally to play his part."*

Steven closed his mouth, and the high king reclaimed his gavel, striking it soundly to quiet the murmurs rising in the chamber. The high king did not wait for the sounds to fully subside before he continued.

"I find troubling the sheer amount of circumstantial evidence, and the many unknowns preceding this occasion. Princess Simmonne is still unaccounted for and cannot be subjected to questioning or telepathic inquisition. I find suspect the idea that access to the Cathedral and the Solar Family could have been so easily accomplished, even by those means outlined by the marshals. With no will presented or found naming a specific successor, I do not believe it is appropriate to determine succession at this time. I call for a vote of no-decision, pending further investigation into the death of Emperor Mason Mandrake."

That was it. That was what Indorai meant. Of course, he should have seen it coming. A vote of no-decision would force the Senate to wait until Simmonne was found before proceeding. Meanwhile he as high king would temporarily gain the powers of emperor until she could be found, interrogated, and a new vote held. How foolishly optimistic for a man so well-known for his shrewd politicking.

"Prime Speaker?" The high king turned to him. "What say you?"

Steven tried not to stare daggers at the man as the prime speaker returned the high king's gaze. "I decline the motion, First Lord."

Steven didn't let himself smile and turned his gaze to the platform of the lieutenant justice. The branch of the justiciars was made up of lawyers. As one might expect from any occasion when a group of lawyers had control of something, their policies often made little sense. While the chief justice decided the policies of the group, it fell on the lieutenant justice to cast the votes in functions of the combined Senate.

"Lieutenant Justice, what say you?" the high king asked.

An uncomfortable silence fell over the Blue Floor. Steven caught the lieutenant justice regarding him.

Your own family. You killed them, and you framed the Vaar. And somehow, the one sister you didn't get. I should have known. I should have known when you called me to your chambers. It wasn't your siblings you were worried about.

"Lieutenant Justice, what say you?" the high king repeated.

You killed them all. Mason, Marianne. All of them. Does the throne really mean that much to you?

"Lieutenant Justice?"

Alhi raised his head to look at the high king. "First Lord, I ask for a recess."

More murmurs in the hall were quickly silenced by the high king's gavel. "I'm sorry, Lieutenant Justice," the high king answered, "but the rules of order do not allow a recess during the vote of such a motion. I ask again, what say you?"

Steven continued to eavesdrop in Alhi's mind. *You are one of three votes needed. No, you won't. That big house of yours? Those universities you're paying for your children to attend? I don't know if she will think you're so charming when you're no longer wealthy.* Alhi's eyes lowered back to his podium as he spoke to himself. *Get the kids out of school. You'll pay for this, Steven. One way or another, you will answer for what you have done.*

"Anytime you're ready, Lieutenant Justice," the high king remarked, visibly irritated as he leaned an arm on his podium.

The faces of his grandchildren filled his mind as the chief justice once more looked back at the high king. "I . . ." He paused, and his voice seemed to crack. "I decline the motion, First Lord."

"Behold the ruin of justice," Indorai taunted.

"Very well. The motion fails to carry," the high king answered, his expression betraying his utter lack of surprise. "I call for the votes. Prime Speaker, how does the Citizen's Congress vote?"

"First Lord, by a margin of ninety-eight percent, the Citizen's Congress finds His Majesty Solar Prince Steven Mandrake competent to discharge the office of emperor."

"So noted," the high king answered. "Lieutenant Justice, how do the justiciars vote?"

The shame was thick as Alhi gave his answer. "First Lord, by a margin of seventy-five percent, the Council of Justiciars finds His Majesty Solar Prince Steven Mandrake competent to discharge the office of emperor."

The high king turned his gaze toward Steven and stood a bit straighter. "Solar Prince Steven Mandrake, the House of Lords votes with sixty-four percent majority that you are competent to discharge the duties before you. With the affirmative votes of the Citizen's Congress and the Council of Justiciars, I recognize you as Emperor of the Solar Empire. Your coronation is to be carried out at the time and date of your choosing. All rise!"

All those in physical attendance rose to their feet and bowed. The high king was not expected to bow, nor would he. But as Steven scanned the chamber, he found one more who had not. Lieutenant Justice Alhi. The justice lowered his eyes when they met Steven's and sighed. With reluctance he lowered his head, only now giving Steven the bow he was due.

"This proceeding is closed," the high king pronounced. "The next meeting of the Senate is to occur per its standard schedule."

Three bangs on the gavel, and it was done.

"So how does it feel to be emperor?" Indorai asked.

Steven rested his arms on his podium and gazed out over the chamber. The high king's hologram faded away. The platforms that held the prime speaker and the lieutenant justice descended to the floor. Steven turned his gaze on Alhi as he stepped off his platform and approached a routing terminal.

Damn that man. By taking so long to answer, he had just birthed a hundred conspiracy theories. Those silent promises the justice made, Steven's suspicions had been right. He was going to be a problem. Perhaps it would have been better to let him go that night. Or to not have invited him at all.

"If you had done that, he would have certainly voted with the high king," Indorai remarked.

"How do you know that?"

A second tendril came down on his shoulder as if to hug him. *"I know this may be hard to imagine, Steven, but some people just don't like you. It's always easiest to think the worst of those we don't like."*

Steven scoffed. *"Can't say I was ever fond of him either."*

Alhi stepped onto the routing terminal and was gone. It would take hours for all of those who had chosen to come in person to empty the chamber. For now Steven watched as lines formed in some areas to use the routers. Small pockets of senators and nobility gathered to discuss their newest and latest scheme.

"He's going to be a problem," Steven said.

"No. He won't," Indorai assured him. *"He authored his doom long ago."*

Steven shook his head. *"With the performance he put on today, it will look very suspicious if he dies."*

As Indorai laughed, there was an instant where his four voices seemed to merge into one before splitting apart again. *"Only if the circumstances of his death are suspicious. Do you know how the lieutenant justice began his career as a judge?"*

"Criminal court, in the Elysian Commonwealth."

Indorai emitted a disturbing chuckle. *"No. Justice Alhi was one of those men who took a long time to find his niche. Yes, before Imperial law, he was a criminal judge. But before that, he was a civil judge."*

Steven turned back for a moment to look at Indorai, and he could almost make out a mouth. A mouth he was certain was full of sharp teeth. *"How does that help me?"*

"Early in his career, he oversaw the divorce of a man named Royman Socorro. Judge Alhi awarded his departing wife, Enella, custody of their children. Even though he was warned she was unfit. Less than a year, she drowned both of the children. Poor Socorro was never the same after that. What might happen if he found himself in the same room as the judge who doomed his children?"

Steven fidgeted as he looked back at the chamber and weighed the scenario in his mind. An angry father avenging the death of his children? That could work, but the timing. If Alhi died too quickly, even that perfect motive would not be enough to dissuade suspicion. Justice Alhi was already an elder. That case would have had to be at least ten centuries ago, probably more.

"What is that human saying?" Indorai asked. *"Something about how revenge is served? Mr. Socorro is in prison for the murder of his former wife. Such a long sentence. Prison is now the only life he knows. The justice's grandchildren will finish their schooling in three years. But Mr. Socorro will be released in one."*

For all his knowledge of the law, Alhi was still a fool by Steven's reckoning. Imperial judges were paid extremely well. Just how big a fool did one have to be to get themselves into financial peril even with such generous pay? That was what bothered him most. Fools could be hard to predict.

When you've got people by the balls, they start to get desperate. And desperate people are prone to doing stupid things.

Admiral Yun's warning. Steven found himself wishing he had paid it greater heed when it was given. Alhi's grandchildren were the only real leverage. Two attended Olympus Mons, with the rest of his grandchildren already deployed into their adult lives. Perhaps he needed to get a better grasp on them.

"Do not overextend," Indorai cautioned. *"You would not want the justice to feel his back in a corner. Now come. The media waits to fawn on you."*

CHAPTER
5E

E VERY SPECIES HAD SPECIAL days in their year, and the Vaar were no different. Sometimes these days were shared by all. At other times, they were regional, planetary, or even continental. Vil'sor had made his home on Dalleton. On this world the Festival of Dreams was a sacred day. Many years ago, a fable-weaver had spun a story about a young Viss. She committed all her hopes and all her wishes to paper. She lay them in a basket and sent them into the sky, hoping the spirits of her ancestors in the Void would grant her wish. The story gained such repute that the festival was born. Nearly all families with ties to this world would come here on this night so that their children could send a basket to the sky.

The fleet even played a part in the ceremony. High in orbit, a small vessel, normally used for tending the larger warships, was waiting. As the baskets climbed higher, the ship would send out small drones to collect them. The children would see the light of the baskets vanishing in the sky and believe that those in the Void had taken them.

Oul'sor did his best to follow the hollow one's advice and not pay attention to each person who noticed him. In most years, there was an air of love and revelry, but as Oul'sor strode through the crowds, he could not ignore what a somber occasion it had become. The Combine had gathered many forces for the assault on the Hourglass. As many as they could possibly gather without alerting the Empire as to what was coming. But now the war was in the open, and more were being called. The first conscripts to bolster the ranks had already been summoned to training. For many here tonight, it would likely be the last moment they spent with their families. Even the planet seemed to know this, chilling them with air too cold for its season.

Oul'sor looked behind him. The hollow one had promised not to disturb him this time. For now he seemed to keep his promise. In the center of the grassy field, a great stage had been arrayed, and the night's performance would soon begin. He could sense her in the crowd and made his way closer.

Vil'na stood with two of her aunts. They held the basket, and Vil'na held parchment, scribbling every hope she could think of onto the paper. As he approached, her head reared up, and she sniffed the air before turning to him.

"Yuja!"

He dropped to a knee to catch her before rising with her tight in his arms.

"Yuja?" she said, pushing far enough away to look at him. "You're you again!"

"Yes," he answered. "Have you told the spirits everything you want?"

"Not yet," she answered, hugging him tighter.

"Well then we must finish."

He carried her over to her aunts and the basket before setting her down. She quickly reclaimed the parchment and resumed her scribbles. A gong echoed over the plains; it was almost time. A choir had gathered on the stage and stood in the dark. Even the town on the horizon had shut down so that nothing would challenge the lights in the sky.

Oul'sor kneeled beside her as she continued listing her youthful wants. But soon a hush came over the crowd as the choir began, and he looked up at the stage. A young Viss, at most a year Vil'na's senior, offered her melody. The choir joined, and he held Vil'na tight.

War has come
and the horns are blowing now.
I don't know what awaits us ahead.
Father says
be good and tend your books.
And one day
you can build your own dreams.
I raise my hand, and I wave goodbye.
Bless him with speed and aim
until he can come home again.
Whether he wins or fails,
bring him home.
Mother's wheeze,
though she tries that I not hear,
she'll be strong
as she waits for all news.
Brother stands,
ready to give himself.
He is too young to go,
but his time is coming.
Let it be over.
There's no rhyme to who lives and dies.
Gentle fate has turned away.
Now we must stand this day
all as one
until the end.
Father's gone,
and I'm still standing at the door.
I should really go inside.
I can't turn away.
He's still with me.
I'll just wait here awhile, until I see him again.

He'll be back.
I must believe.
War has come,
and the horns are blowing now.
I won't know what is ahead,
but I will wait.
I will stand.
I will wait.

As the words were sung, Vil'na put the last of the paper in the basket. One of the event workers presented Oul'sor with a small disc. With a smile, he attached the cables dangling from it to the basket. A button at the center awaited Vil'na's touch. With a grin, she pushed it, and the disc came to life. From its edges, the disc began to glow, shifting colors every few seconds. Vil'na released the basket and he opened his hand. The disc rose, carrying the basket with it. Oul'sor took Vil'na back in his arms and held her as they watched the basket climb.

"Wait!" Vil'na blurted out, reaching for the basket.

Oul'sor seized it and pulled it back down. Vil'na quickly reached inside to sort through the papers. Near the bottom she found the one she wanted. He saw the words she had written.

Please give Father and Yuja back to me.

With quill in hand, she marked out "Yuja," and beneath the plea wrote a new phrase.

Thank you.

He smiled as she placed the parchment back, and he released the basket to the sky. It joined thousands more to climb toward the stars. A hush came over the plain. In orbit the tender decided the time was right and dispatched the drones. Young Vaar and Viss all exclaimed as they watched the glow of their baskets streak upward and vanish into space.

Oul'sor used his new gift to peek into Vil'na's mind, sharing her imagination as some ghostly Vaar reached out a great hand and swept the baskets into one of his before fading away. He held her until the last light had ascended, and the hush over the crowd melted away.

While Vil'na continued to stare into the sky and imagine, Oul'sor looked down at Oul'da, Vil'na's aunt and one of his many, many disappointing children. Oul'da had made such a wreck of her life that she had given up trying to do anything with it. But at least she had learned to recognize the fool in the mirror and do what she was told. That and the fact that she had no children of her own were the only reasons Oul'sor had allowed Oul'da to take Vil'na.

"Oul'da," he said, and waited until she looked at him. "After tonight, I want you to take Vil'na to Ner'thess, and wait there until the war is over."

"Ner'thess?" she asked. "But, that is on the rim. There is nothing there."

"Nothing," he agreed. "And no reason for it to ever be a target. Take her there, and wait until I tell you that you can leave."

Oul'da nodded before joining Vil'na to continue gazing upward.

Oul'sor peered down at Vil'na. She had not even asked if he had succeeded in avenging her father. Her confidence in him was so great that she took his presence as all the answer she needed. He wanted to tell her that he had failed. But she would never understand. She couldn't understand how much had changed—was changing. Better for now to let her assume. And let her assume that he would be commanding forces from here on out, far from the battlefield. Such a young mind, she deserved better than to be wondering constantly who she would lose next.

He held her until she and her aunts were the last in the field with him.

Act—II: The Burning Dream

CHAPTER
6A

IN THE COCKPIT OF the *Intruder*, all was quiet. In the center seat, the chairs to Panzer's sides were empty. Kassar and Novin were asleep on the padded shelves that passed for bunks. Opposite them was the slab that would have been occupied by Rhoxx. Despite predictions, six days had passed. The seemingly endless column of reinforcements still flowed toward the front. As the numbers bloomed, Andira was forced to plot an ever-widening course.

Panzer looked down at the can in his hand. He twisted a small knob at the can's top, and it chirped to indicate that it had begun cooking. A moment later, it chirped again, and he peeled the lid away to release the steam. Between his fingers, the lid formed into a fork. Hengzu pork, thrice seasoned and peppered. He took a bite, part of a futile battle to avoid too much thinking.

This was his life. Whether it was on his ship or in this shuttle. Every shot fired, grenade thrown, bomb planted, prisoner interrogated, or plot executed. All came after many hours of waiting to get there. So many hours. Some species would live their entire lives in fewer hours than he had spent doing what he was doing now.

He was on his fourth bite when he realized he had forgotten his drink. He eyed the pack that hung above his bunk. Without thinking he held out his hand and called a can of Overclock to his grasp. He had opened the can before it dawned on him. He called it successfully. He took a quick drink before setting the can aside and holding out his hand again. There was pain this time, a quick jolt, but a second can of pork came to his grasp. His psionics were back.

Panzer held the can level with his shoulder before releasing it while trying to call it back before it hit the deck. The can was more than halfway down before it shot back up to his fingers. He did it again, feeling a stab behind his eye as he brought it back. They were back but definitely diminished. It was still too soon to run a measurement, but part of his mind was gone. It wouldn't return at full strength.

He turned his attention back to the first can. Somewhere in the process, he found himself looking at the picture on the side. Happy Stars brand. Happy Stars' target market was the image on the can: a man and his children around a fire on a starry night—rich men taking their children hunting or camping on wilderness worlds. Lest they have to take a printer and eat printed food like ordinary people for a while.

Panzer resumed eating. He had his chance at that life. Instead, he got the hours. It would not be long now. He would pass and few would notice. On Acheron his file would be opened, he would be marked as dead, and his security clearance would be revoked. His ship would be scrapped. The commandant would breathe a sigh of relief and recruit his replacement. The emperor would lament the loss of his errand boy. The empress would remark on how sad it was. She might even light a candle for him on the anniversary of his death, sentimentalist that she was. Steven would spend an hour, maybe even two, lamenting the death of an old friend. The only people who would truly mourn his passing were his team and his mother back home. Perhaps the only real tragedy would be that his team's stories would never be known. The day they followed him, they became unpersons.

A twinge in his hips prompted him to rise. The chair showed some reluctance to let go. Panzer turned and looked down at it. His first week in the Corps, he had ripped the *Intruder*'s central chair out and installed one larger. But large enough simply would not fit. It seemed only small people were allowed to design the *Intruder*. Not that there were many men of his size. He was a giant, like all men of his family, and so few understood why it was engineered into them to stand head and shoulders above most other men.

Every generation would know its own suffering. Some of those generations would even need heroes. His family did not leave their existence to chance. It believed in a duty to manufacture heroes and keep them at hand. Like the pistol at the bedside, ready to meet a threat in the night. The symbolism was there for those who would see it. He could no more hide among a crowd of other men than could a mountain among trees. Because of the primitive instinct to look to the biggest, most fearsome member of the pack for protection when a threat loomed, all eyes were drawn to him. No matter where he went.

Panzer returned to the chair. He spent his life in shadows and obscurity, where such symbols had no value. It had even been a hindrance. He could wear whatever uniform he liked to blend in, but people tended to remember the giant man they'd never met before.

The second can was ready, and he looked at the image once more. One other person would miss him.

Simmonne. The girl had become far more attached to him than he might have imagined. The way she excused herself to cry when he told her he was dying, the feelings behind her eyes when she saw him off—a person didn't develop attachments that strong so quickly. But there was no time to explore it. He could not blame her for being upset. He should have never had anything more than a professional relationship with the princess. Should never have painted something on the canvas of her life that he could not finish. Even if he wanted a life like that of the child and father on the can, it wasn't his to have.

How might that child be engineered if he had one, he wondered. His size or smaller? Above the Krojer Threshold or below it?[10] How many children? Keep with Sylvanni custom, or embrace his status as an exile and disregard it? His eyes, or hers?

He turned the can so that the family faced away. These thoughts were not productive. Even if he survived this mission, he'd be dead long before any of these things mattered. He probably shouldn't have given her his badge. She might draw the wrong conclusion. But in time she would put it away. Years later she might take it out or stumble across it while looking for something else. For a moment she would pause, thinking back to an interesting character she once knew. She would smile, then put it away. The token would be an echo of a memory.

It would do more for Rhoxx. If he did not come back from this one, Rhoxx might read something into it. Might think he had a new obligation and a way out of the future to which he was otherwise condemned. At least Panzer hoped that was the message he would receive. Actions could speak louder than words, but words were easier to understand.

A tone sounded over the bunks and roused the brothers from their slumber. Only a few hours now. Panzer watched warrior caste discipline in action. Within thirty seconds of waking, both were on their feet. Within five minutes, both had expelled and hit the tiny sonic shower. Within ten, they had their cans open. Within twenty minutes, they sat cross-legged on the small floor. They would remain in this state of battle meditation until it was time to kit out, and they focused only on the mission ahead. They would each contemplate their tasks and the plan. They would do their best to envision everything that could possibly go wrong, and how they would react. On another mission, Panzer might join them but found no desire to meditate today.

Panzer crushed the empty can. Work was approaching. In his NOD Andira laid out the sensor feed for the surrounding area. Vaar destroyers were on patrol, twelve of them. Together they formed concentric rings, each a light-year apart, all focused on ND-31's star system. Andira had carefully pierced each ring, drawing them closer. Thus far, undetected.

Panzer pried himself out of the chair again and squeezed past the brothers. He squeezed himself again to descend the tiny stairway to the second level. He had donned his armor before departing simply to walk it to the *Intruder*, and now he had to put it on again. With lesser facilities, the process took longer. By the time he was back in his suit, Kassar and Novin were on their way down to don their own.

---

10   Named for Dr. Alec Krojer, the Krojer Threshold represents a particular threshold of high intelligence where demonstrable negative effects on a person's ability to socialize become increasingly likely. Whether to opt for a child likely to be above or below this limit is one of many decisions parents must make when determining the genetic engineering for their children.

Habit compelled him to look for Jorri. Instead the Hellbore waited for him. He took it in hand, frowning for a moment before composing himself. It was not the Hellbore's fault that it was not Jorri. The Hellbore had three magazine terminals, the primary magwell on the underside, and shallow wells on each side of the receiver. Panzer withdrew the ammo hose from the armor's backpack and inserted it into the lower well. The drum magazine went to the right. Auto-diagnostics for the weapon ran in his NOD. Everything was as it should be.

With somewhat simpler armor, Kassar and Novin were dressed more quickly. Panzer took note of Kassar's choice of weapon. He had brought his AS-20. Kassar was proud of that weapon, and he had every right to be. The monks of Andos Shyna didn't sell their weapons to everyone. Perhaps ten members of the warrior caste received one each year. Kassar was not yet an adult when he earned his. A compact but tall weapon, it housed three 15mm barrels on each side of its wedge-like stock. On the kurai's back, a pair of wire frames reminiscent of wings held four spheres.

After a quick inspection, Kassar turned to assist Novin in saddling the computer core. The device looked more like a beer keg than the high-tech piece it was. But beneath its unassuming form were literal tons of hardware. The muscle Andira would need to fight the *Caustic Reverie*'s AIs. Once Kassar had hoisted it onto Novin's back, the latter shifted his weight. Novin then raised his arms, shadowboxing for a few seconds as he acclimated to his new balance.

"Sir," Andira caught his attention.

"Yes?"

"I'm noticing something strange."

"Go on."

"There are no abnormalities on ND-31."

Panzer held out a hand. "Meaning?"

"With a ship the size of the *Caustic Reverie* in such close orbit, I should be reading many. Massive tectonic disturbances, volcanism, aberrant weather patterns. But I'm not reading any."

"Nothing? What about tides?"

"Maintaining stealth limits me to optical observation. However I see no signs of major tidal shifts either."

"Show me."

A screen opened in his NOD, and at first he could not even see the planet. Andira quickly tightened the focus, blowing up the blue marble until it was comfortably in sight. The *Caustic Reverie* shared the image. The black-hulled ship appeared to move in an equatorial orbit, seeming to be barely beyond the planet's atmosphere.

"Well, obviously the ship is there," Panzer remarked. "I don't know. There's been a lot of reports about weird stuff on that planet."

You must go there.

He shuddered as he recalled the Encephalon's words but pushed them away. This was not about the Encephalon, and his mission was the ship, not the planet.

As time passed, Andira made her approach, ducking behind the star to keep it between them and the ship. The more mass she could put between them, the lower their odds of being detected. But soon the critical juncture came. They were barely above light speed now.

"ETA, ten minutes," Andira announced.

She had moved the *Intruder* into the same orbital plane as the planet. The ship accelerated opposite the planet's orbit, using its speed to hasten the journey.

"Any sign they've detected us?" Panzer asked.

"No sir. No reaction."

That much was good. Though the thought of the *Itinerant Hunter* tracking them popped briefly into his thoughts. No point in stopping now. Timidity accomplished nothing. The planet and the ship continued to grow in the sensors. Andira caught the planet's orbit from the opposite side of the enormous warship. Only a few years ago, the Vaar couldn't have built a ship of that size.

"Plotting orbital intercept. Five minutes."

Panzer turned to the brothers, both of whom answered the unspoken question with raised thumbs.

"Novin?"

"Yes sir?"

"That's more mass than you're used to carrying. Make sure you compensate."

"Yes sir," the kurai answered as he fastened his helmet, prompting Kassar to do the same.

The image in his NOD had become a blue glow of the planetary horizon. There was something beautiful about that kind of view. The kind of thing one did not notice often enough. In minutes the upright hammerhead of the *Caustic Reverie* peeked over the blue. No matter how huge something was, a little distance could hide its scope.

"Ready to deploy in two minutes."

"Depressurize," Panzer ordered. The stairway to the lower deck rose from it, allowing doors to seal. A gentle hiss followed as the atmosphere was removed from the lower bay. The brothers followed him to the front of the bay to the deployment doors. The ship continued to grow larger as Andira made fine adjustments. Every few seconds, there was a flash from the ship's tail as the lasers fired to shed the excess energy.

"One minute."

"Kassar, Novin?" He glanced back at them. "I haven't said this to you as much as I should. It's been an honor to have you at my side."

Both slung their weapons to clasp their hands together and bow.

"Opening hatch," Andira announced.

The square panel in the floor slid back, lighting the deck in the planet's blue light. That glow faded as they passed over the *Caustic Reverie*.

"Ready to deploy," Andira said. "Good luck to us."

Panzer led the way, diving down through the hatch. Kassar followed, and Novin brought up the rear. Andira's copy on the *Intruder* led it away. No sense in dallying and giving the warship more time to realize someone was sharing its orbit. Panzer's thrusters guided him as the three came down on the ship. Its hull was jet black, save for the many gray blisters that lightened its exterior.

Andira could only drop them so close to the ship's baffles, lest the periodic discharges risk giving them away. That left ten kilometers they would have to cover on foot just to reach the tail. Panzer gave his thrusters another kick as he swiveled to align his feet with the hull. His armor could hide from the sensors in the ship's skin, but no reason to make that job harder with a rough landing.

The three met the hull of the ship, and together they began the run to carry them the rest of the way. Each step, even each breath, was carried out in unison. The kurai called it *shou-hera*, the hunter's run. If Panzer leaped over an obstruction, the others would land in his footprints. If his head turned, so did theirs, so that all would see the same thing.

On such an enormous ship, the outer hull was landscape. The many blisters were hills, flanking the plain they crossed. One rose like a giant dune, its cap peaked by the batteries of an interceptor array. The ship would need them. Sooner or later, the Armadas would destroy this ship. They passed several of the great dunes on their path to the baffles. It would be quicker to fly, but that was even more likely to result in detection.

Panzer's blood chilled. He fell to a knee, and his momentum carried him into a slide as he drew the Hellbore from his back. Someone was watching them.

Atop one of the blisters, he noticed a humanoid figure. He drew down on it, optical sighting only as he thumbed the safety. Fifty meters up by one of the gun ports.

No one was there.

He scanned the blister, looking between the gun turrets. He was certain he saw it, a figure standing beneath one of the guns. Their arms crossed as they looked down at the trio. But still he saw nothing. An active scan would confirm, but the risk was too high. He zoomed in with the optics, scanning the guns. Nothing.

Panzer glanced back at Kassar and Novin, who kneeled behind him with their weapons drawn. Both looked at the blister. He waved his hand to get their attention before holding up his fingers in a knife-hand. He bent at the wrist, bringing his fingers perpendicular to his forearm before straightening. Kassar was the first to answer, taking a hand off his weapon to make a zero with his fingers. Novin mimicked the motion a second later. Neither had seen.

Jitters? No. Someone *was* standing there. At least, he thought so. His eyes moved in his NOD, and a small screen opened. He rewound his short-term memory and paused the image. Nothing was there. No soldier, no worker, nothing but the silent guns of the blister. A trick of the light? Intersecting shadows from the gun barrels to form a specter? Whatever it was, he'd been mistaken.

He returned the Hellbore to his back and motioned the brothers to follow. Soon they reached the baffles. From this vantage point, only two of the tail's pylons were in view, canting away from each other. The shortest laser was the best bet, so he led them up the slope of the port tail.

It was a bit of an odd sensation. With most of the ship behind them, its substantial gravity seemed more interested in pulling them off the tail rather than down the slope. The trip took time, forty-five kilometers up a forty-five-degree slope. Two hours carried them to the top of the tail, and then another five kilometers along its flat roof.

Kassar and Novin moved to Panzer's sides as he peered over the edge. His biologic eyes could not see it, but his sensors and his nanites saw the intense blasts of X- and gamma rays spilling out of the ports on the tail's leading surface.

"Andira, do you have the interval?" he asked as the nearest of the lasers released one of its awesome blasts, utterly silent in the vacuum.

"Yes sir," she answered. "Each is firing an average of once every thirty-seven seconds."

"Calculate. Can we make it through?"

"The safety margin is very low," she answered. "It is 720 meters to the aperture of the nearest laser. It is 1.7 kilometers to the focusing apparatus."

"Can you confirm the presence of an access hatch?"

"Negative. Too much material in the way."

Panzer looked at Novin. He was already prepared, holding up a metal disc. The small automatech quickly came to life. Its metal skin flowed like water as it morphed four pods out of its body to serve as thrusters. Novin waited for the laser to fire again before the tiny drone flung itself out of his hand. The machine made a hard turn, diving toward the aperture before disappearing inside.

Panzer connected to the feed, seeing through the drone's sensors as it moved through the tube. A silver ring glowed in red incandescence—the emitter for the laser, building up until it discharged again.

"I don't see a hatch," Novin said as he impelled the drone to move faster.

"Twenty seconds," Andira cautioned.

The red glow steadily brightened as the laser drew nearer and continued to build power.

"There," Kassar sounded. "Directly above the aperture."

Panzer found it in his view. A small hatch, likely meant for a quorum rather than a Vaar. Novin guided the drone to it. "Looks like a fairly standard seal," Novin said. "It will have a trip sensor to alert if it's opened, but I'm not seeing any other security."

"Ten seconds," Andira cautioned a bit louder.

"Can you crack it without security knowing?"

"Easily," Novin answered as he spun the drone and set it on a return course. "Would only take a few seconds."

Novin took a metal cylinder from his belt.

"Open the hatch, spray the foam. If anyone even notices, it will look like a glitch, sir."

"Andira, do we have enough time to get to that hatch and get it open between discharges?"

As she answered, Andira created a wireframe simulation in his NOD, showing their movement as glowing lines on the necessary course. "Safety margin is low, and you are each carrying a lot of mass. It will take you approximately eleven seconds to reach the aperture, make the turn, cover the distance, and decelerate to acceptable impact. This leaves only twenty-six seconds to open the hatch, ingress, and close it."

Panzer forced a chuckle as the laser fired again. "Twenty-six? Sounds like plenty of time." His tone became more serious as he turned to Novin. "Be sure to give yourself enough room to maneuver."

"Yes sir."

ANDIRA: Sir, perhaps I should control your armor for the maneuver.

???: I can handle it.

ANDIRA: Respectfully, sir, your cognitive processing is impaired and likely your reflexes as well. Please allow me control of your armor.

He sighed.

???: Fine.

ANDIRA: Thank you.

"We ready?" he asked aloud.

The brothers nodded their affirmation.

"We go in three blasts."

"Yes sir," Kassar, Novin, and Andira answered together.

The laser fired again.

"One."

A second blast.

"Two."

The third blast came, and his thrusters were lit before he got the word out.

"Three."

As if some giant hand had grabbed hold of him and spiked him like a ball, he shot downward in a dive. The aperture approached quickly, a twenty-meter hole in the metal of the ship, and his body lurched as he turned in to it. Kassar and Novin were just behind. Panzer saw a spark and turned his head to the disaster unfolding.

In compensating for his added mass, Novin had overdone it. Upon the turn, his shoulder clipped the edge of the hole, and he careened. Like a stone hurtled into a pipe, he bounced from one side to the other, desperately trying to regain control.

"Kassar, get that hatch open!" Panzer shouted as he took manual control.

"Sir!" Kassar began to protest.

"Do it!"

Panzer turned over, bringing his feet toward the base of the pipe. In one motion he separated the Hellbore and the magazine before kicking his thrusters to full.

"Sir," Andira began as he overcame his inertia to accelerate toward Novin.

"No."

"Twenty-eight seconds," she warned.

Panzer closed in, focusing on the kurai's waist rather than his flailing arms. He spread his arms, ready to catch him in a bear hug.

He missed.

"Twenty-five seconds."

In his efforts to regain control, Novin overcompensated again, slamming back into the wall and out of Panzer's reach. Panzer flipped again as he reached the aperture, briefly leaving the pipe until his thrust plunged him back in.

"Twenty seconds."

Panzer held out a single hand this time as he focused on the bouncing kurai. Razor blades seemed to drag through his scalp as he tightened his focus on Novin's waist. The kurai's spin began to slow.

"Kassar, door?"

"Working on it!"

"Novin! Cut thrust!"

"Fifteen seconds."

The two met with jarring impact, and Panzer powered ahead. He dove on Kassar, who kneeled over the hatch, racing to open the releases.

Panzer and Novin flipped in time, both thrusting to slow themselves before reaching the hull. As Panzer's feet hit, his teeth clapped together, and a loud ring sounded through his armor.

"Twelve seconds."

"Move!" Novin screeched, practically throwing Kassar out of his way. From his belt he pulled a tool for each hand and set upon the small hatch.

"Ten seconds. Nine."

Panzer scanned around him, but he did not see the backpack or the Hellbore. The focusing apparatus rose on a column ten meters above them. He fired his thrusters again and clapped his hand on the missing articles.

"Six. Five."

"Inside!"

"Four."

He looked down as both kurai motioned him to be the first through the hatch. He thrust again. His shoulder clipped the frame this time, and he cartwheeled before colliding with the inner door.

"Three."

Kassar was inside. Bolting upright Panzer shot his arm through the hatch, grabbing Novin by the helm and dragging him through.

"One."

All three of them grabbed the hatch. With the longest arms, Panzer found it first and pulled it shut. The tiny airlock thundered, the walls shaking around them as the titanic laser let out another blast.

Panzer took a breath and leaned back against the wall.

"That was exciting," he said with a scoff.

"Damn it, sir." Kassar rose to his feet and leveled a finger. "You have *no* right to risk your life for one of us."

Panzer turned to him. Kassar dropped his arm, offering no resistance as Panzer's hand closed around the kurai's gorget. Panzer lifted Kassar above the deck.

"Your lives belong to me," Panzer answered. "*I* decide what it is worth risking to save them."

"Yes sir," Kassar answered. Panzer set him down.

No real venom in the words from either, but Kassar was remiss if he did not object. Panzer was remiss if he did not reestablish dominance after such an outburst. It was far from the first time they'd had this exchange. But as Panzer looked at the now-bowing kurai, he realized that it may be the last.

ANDIRA: If Rhoxx saw you risk yourself that way, he'd be very upset.

???: That's why we won't tell him.

Perhaps it was for the best that Rhoxx was not here. There was no way he'd be able to squeeze through that hatch. Panzer turned to Novin.

"You all right?"

"Sir." He seemed to hesitate. "Kassar is right. You—"

"Novin."

"Yes sir?"

"How's the core?"

Novin took a knee, dropping the keg-like device to the deck. He spun it once in a visual before pulling a cord from his armor and plugging it into the side.

"Minor damage," Novin answered. "Still mission-capable."

"Good. Let's get out of this airlock."

CHAPTER
6B

SIMMONNE HAD NOT LEFT the colonel's quarters since he departed the ship. She'd spent much of the time asleep or deep in thought. She lay curled up on a couch of ridiculous size meant for a man of ridiculous size. What kind of savage had such an enormous couch with no pillows, she did not know, so she had printed several, one of many things she did to distract herself and stop doing what she was doing now. By her head she held his badge and could not take her eyes from it.

As a Solar Princess, she was a keeper of the Empire's traditions and knew something about its symbolism. The design of the Commando Corps' icon had not meaningfully changed over the eras. The layout had been drawn from some ancient group known as Masons. The skull of a Therican sat in the center with four mandibles and a wreath of horns. There were three eye sockets, with the largest centered on the forehead. A sword pierced through the skull from top to bottom. Above the skull two more swords met at their pommels before angling down and away from each other to flank the skull. Beneath the skull lay a scroll bearing the words *Semper Vigilo* in the Latin tongue. Everything was backgrounded by a four-point shield. The badge was gold, a trait normally reserved for flag officers.

Simmonne traced the edge of the badge. This couldn't be what she thought it was. He had to have given it to her for another reason, but only one reason came to her mind.

Dominion women wore pahri or corissè, with dresses being reserved for the very young, very old, or specific occasions. In all cases, the attire would include some manner of collar. When a man of aristocracy took a bride, he would present her with an individualized charm from his house. She would then wear it on the collar, showing exactly who she belonged to. He was a commando. He had no family, no house. Except for the Corps.

He *couldn't* be asking her to marry him. They barely knew each other. She did not know him at all. Why would he even be so eager to marry her? Men were not like that. She was being stupid. This had to be something else. But what else was it supposed to be? Why else would he give her his badge?

The question of why did not stop gnawing at her. The image she had of him, had it been wrong? Instead of the grand, imperious warrior, was he just a frightened, drowning man reaching out to her? Or, if this really was a proposal, was it his way of saying he did not have much time left but was willing to share it despite his verbal claim to the contrary?

Simmonne sat up slowly. She had to say no. Hopefully he would understand. She stroked the badge with her finger again. That night on Reichsylvannia, she'd have done anything for him. He knew it; he had to. He might have thought she would pounce on this.

She sighed quietly. What if she said no, and he died? Would she spend the rest of her life wondering what she missed? Simmonne caught herself pacing and sat back down on the couch. Simmonne wanted to be angry with him. To be furious that he would push this on her. But instead she fought the tears trying to creep out of her eyes.

For a moment she saw Isis and the rest of her guards. If only they were here. When she could not talk to Jenna or the Twins, she could always depend on Isis for an objective opinion. But Isis wasn't here, and she never would be. A tear fell on the badge, and she brought a hand up to wipe her cheek.

Maybe if she knew a little more about him. These were his quarters. Perhaps something here could tell her more. She returned to her feet but took only half a step. She shouldn't go snooping, but she was going to. With the badge back in her pocket, she took a breath. If he was going to be so insufferably closed, she would find a door to open.

She turned to the wall behind the bed and waved a hand. A small drawer slid out of the wall in response. A thick metal security binder lay inside. She found it heavy in her hands but unlocked. She opened it to find sheets of gold. Imperial treasury bonds—bearer bonds more specifically. He had more than a few. Denominations of thousands, and tens of thousands, even some in hundreds of thousands. Why would he have these? One generally had to be aristocracy just to buy them. Then again, he was a commando. Maybe those rules did not apply to him either. As she continued to thumb through the binder, the contents eventually changed. She found new sheets, some in gold, some in other colors. All bore the names of corporations. Many of them she had at least heard of. Dominion corporate notes.[11] His guns he kept sealed away in a vault-like armory, but all this money just sat in a drawer by his bed? Then again, who would rob him on this ship?

She placed the binder back where it belonged and looked at the second drawer. It was empty. There was nothing in the third drawer either.

"Are you looking for something, Majesty?" the AI asked.

---

11   Dominion corporate notes are an end run around Imperial laws that forbid the individual nations from issuing their own currencies. These notes function almost identically to bearer bonds but are issued by Dominion corporations. These notes are backed by dividend-paying stock in that company. They are freely liquid and in many areas accepted as freely as troys. The nation allows only the wealthiest and most established corporations to issue notes of this kind. Not coincidentally, the Rhinegrave Dynasty has at least partial owner-ship in most of these corporations.

Of course! His AI. She might know everything about him.

"Adria," Simmonne began, "may I ask you about the colonel?"

"My name is *Andira*, Majesty."

Simmonne nodded. "Andira, may I ask?"

"That depends on the nature of your inquiry."

Her heart raced. She recognized the solution right in front of her. Everything that she needed to know. "Andira, how old is Colonel Panzer?"

Simmonne's expression soured when the AI answered, "All records pertaining to Corps personnel are classified absolute secret. I do not have a record of you possessing any security clearance above secret."

"You can't even tell me how old he is?" Simmonne said before jumping, startling herself with how much she had raised her voice.

"Corps records are absolute secret."

Simmonne huffed. "So there is nothing you can tell me?"

"Nothing beyond what you already know."

Simmonne threw out her hands. "Then—" She stopped herself. "Surely there is *something*."

"All information pertaining to the identities of Corps personnel are absolute secret."

Simmonne huffed as she scowled angrily at the ceiling. Fine. She would do it the hard way. Simmonne moved to the next well where the metal bulged out to form a dresser. A collection of models stood on the surface. Most of them looked very much the same, save for their differences in size. Armadas warships that almost looked handmade. Some of them had unique appearances. While the Armadas ships were painted in the blue and gold of that service, the more shapely were red and gold. Two ships sat together in the center. One was *H.M.S. Hurricane*. But beside the *Hurricane* sat a larger model. Was it not to scale with the rest? This model was red and gold, shaped like a great wedge with wings and a high-sloping top. A small plaque was attached to the base.

"*Prince of Mars*—Artist's Concept," she read aloud.

She examined the model at length. The ship itself did not interest her. Her eyes sought imperfections. Any she might find in seams or where different colors of paint met. She found none, and that told her nothing. If her impression of him was correct, these would have no flaws. He would not consider them finished until they were flawless.

Simmonne pursed her lips. Did she even know him well enough to make that summation? She returned the model to its place. She opened the first drawer in the dresser. Inside she found a metal case. This could be something.

"Your Majesty," the AI addressed her in an admonishing tone, "I do not think Colonel Panzer would appreciate you snooping through his things."

Simmonne's lips worked, mockingly repeating the AI's words. Maybe he wouldn't. But if he was going to do this to her, then she was going to find out more about him. One way or another.

"Majesty," the AI spoke louder.

"I heard you," Simmonne answered, moving a hand over the lid of the case.

"Majesty."

"His soldiers put me here," Simmonne shot back. "He never told me I couldn't look. Neither did they. Did he tell you I wasn't allowed?"

"No," the AI answered. "However—"

"Then I'm looking."

Simmonne slid the latch that sealed the case, and its roof split to reveal the contents. A chill crept out of the box, and Simmonne beheld food. *Real*, organic food. Garesenny caviar, pork bacon from Sanghu. Reichsylvannian rock lobster, Pommeron avedas liver. Atlanean beef. Cheese, a *lot* of cheese. Some cheeses with names she had heard of; others she had not. These were not just organic novelty foods. Many of these were prized for some unique element of their taste that printers could not easily mimic. She slid the heavy drawer out farther, finding bottles of alcohol behind the food. She had at least seen each label once before.

These were the kinds of things royalty and nobility ate. Most of them could not even get Reichsylvannian lobster. The Dominion refused to export it. When her mother wanted it for her birthday, her father had contacted the high king personally to make sure it arrived. Her eyes moved from the lobster to the pork. People always talked about bacon like it was some kind of magic food. Sanghu in particular. There was probably more than her weight in food in this larder. He wouldn't notice if she tried a little.

No. She was a vegetarian, and she would not steal from him. She was already certain the AI would tattle on her for snooping. She closed the lid and pushed the drawer back into place so she could continue rummaging through his things. A drawer of clothes, and a lot of them vests. Did the man even own a shirt? Most people wore printed clothes and simply discarded them after. Aristocrats kept wardrobes with name-brand clothes that were as much art as clothing. She found labels to be sure, and each was name brand. Simmonne looked briefly back to the drawer with the food. He had the tastes of aristocracy if not the title.

Simmonne flinched when she opened the next drawer. Apparently he did not feel there were enough weapons in his armory. Guns and knives lay in this drawer, each inside a fancy case. She quickly closed it and moved on to the top drawer in the right-hand column.

There was only one thing in this drawer, a golden case. Simmonne found it heavy when she picked it up. The case did not respond when she waved a hand over it. There was no optical port for a NOD to interface, and she did not see any other mechanism to open it.

"Your Majesty." The AI's tone bordered on hostile and caused Simmonne to jump. "I can assure you that if you tamper with that, Colonel Panzer will be angry."

Simmonne perked up and glanced at the ceiling. "What is it?"

"None of your business."

Well that was rather rude for an AI. Simmonne looked back at the case.

She had to know. This might even be the secret to who he was. He would already be annoyed that she went through his things. It was probably better not to make him angry. But if it could tell her more about him, she had to know.

"Majesty," the AI seemed to growl at her. "Put the case back in the drawer, or I will take it away from you."

Why was the AI being so defensive about it?

"Majesty!" it snapped.

"Fine," Simmonne whispered and set it back in the drawer. She would know what was in it, but perhaps not now.

That was it for this cabinet, so she moved on to the next. In the long end, she found his uniforms. Another box sat on a shelf, and this one was not sealed. She carried the box to the table. Medals, most of which she did not recognize. More importantly, she had found something that could speak to her. One by one she laid them out on the table. Thirty-two in total. She paused as she took one in hand. Beneath a blue ribbon, polished copper formed the numbers 150, and above the numbers an etched scroll read *The Emperor's Thanks*.

He received this for 150 years of service. She did not find a two hundred-year medal. At least now she had some idea of how old he was. Fourteen was the youngest one could join the services. But he was an officer, so he most likely had an education. Simmonne knew he was young for a colonel, but not *that* young. Every colonel she had ever met was two thousand at least. Was his rank part of being a commando?

Simmonne set the numbered medal aside, finding what she had originally been seeking. Two Solar Crosses, one with a large pin in the center of the ribbon. He wore this one when they met. She showed it the respect it was due as she carefully took it from the box. Her eyes moved in her NOD. Steven had taught her this trick. Every medal had a tiny chip in it. One could hold it and see a record of who it belonged to, and why it had been awarded to them.

ACCESSING . . .

YOU ARE NOT THE AUTHORIZED RECIPIENT OF THIS MEDAL.

BE ADVISED THAT THE SOLAR CROSS IS PROTECTED BY SOLAR EDICT #17. UNAUTHORIZED POSSESSION, WEARING, DUPLICATION, AND FALSE CLAIMS TO THIS AWARD ARE PUNISHABLE BY A 5 PERCENT PRISON SENTENCE.[12]

ACCESSING COMMENDATION . . .

<>ACCESS DENIED<>

---

12 Due to the sometimes-vastly different lifespans of species in the Empire, prison sentences are generally set as a percentage of the average life expectancy for the offender's species.

THIS COMMENDATION CERTIFICATE IS CLASSIFIED. THOSE WITH PROPER AUTHORIZATION SHOULD CONTACT THE DEPARTMENT OF COMMENDATION, CASE #113217264289347

"I'm a member of the Solar Family!" Simmonne protested to the inanimate object. Its only response was to keep the message in her NOD. As she regained her composure, she gently returned the first cross to the box and took hold of the second. A different case number, but the same rejection.

Out of everything here, nothing actually helped her. She returned the medals to their case and the case to its spot. She was running out of places to snoop and still knew next to nothing. There had to be something that could tell her the answer she sought. The AI wouldn't help, and nothing here did. She could ask Daddy. Steven knew him. They even seemed to be friends. But she needed to know something sooner.

Maybe one of his soldiers could tell her something. The kurai were gone. Besides, one of them, Kassar, did not seem to like her very much. But the kodaz, Rhoxx, was still here. If the AI refused to tell her anything, though, he probably wouldn't either.

Simmonne looked back at the one drawer. Whatever was in that sealed case, she was sure it would tell her exactly what she needed to know. But Andira was quite clear that he would be angry. She wrung her hands before shaking her head. She didn't know how to open it anyway.

"Andira?"

"Yes, Majesty?"

"Where is Rhoxx?"

"He is in his quarters, Majesty."

"Where are they?"

Simmonne accepted the signal that came to her NOD, which offered a path to the destination.

"Majesty?"

Simmonne rolled her eyes and let out an annoyed sigh. "Yes?"

"You wished to be notified when we arrived at the eye."

"Oh," Simmonne answered, relaxing her posture. "May I see it?"

The navigation path was minimized, and a new screen opened to show her a map. A red ring surrounded the black sphere. A far wider blue ring was drawn around it, highlighting a thick belt of asteroids. The image shifted to focus on one of the larger asteroids in the belt.

"No," Simmonne answered. "I mean, may I see the black hole?"

The map faded away, and a field of stars entered her NOD. A red ring drew her gaze to the black hole, where a single span of blackness broke the field of distant stars. Simmonne was not sure what she'd expected to see, but there may as well have been nothing. This black hole took its name seriously. There was no band of plasma, no geysers of light sprinting from its poles— just a dark spot she would not have noticed if she wasn't looking for it.

"Show me the base please."

The image shifted again until her eyes fell on an asteroid, brown with tinges of red. Were it not for the many craters on its surface, it would almost be a perfect sphere. A small graph flanked the asteroid, announcing its radius as fifty-seven kilometers.

"That's it?" Simmonne asked.

"The facility is concealed within the asteroid," the AI explained.

It did not look like much, but then, it was a spy station. That was probably the point.

"We will dock in fifteen minutes."

Simmonne did not answer. Instead she shrank the visual display while returning the navigation display to the center of her sight. She had questions, and it was time to find answers.

CHAPTER
6C

CLEARWATER'S WOUNDS HAD FINALLY stopped hurting, for now. The combination of Taula's company with games to play had helped to keep his mind occupied. But once it was quiet and she had to find sleep, Clearwater was left with his thoughts. The gnawing in his gut would not go away. Even when his mind had been distracted, it was still there. On the pause menu, on loading screens—each moment of pause, it reasserted itself.

His tongue traced the gaps in his teeth, and he flinched when a rogue pain stabbed at his left arm. He looked down at the stump, confused by the pain he felt in a forearm that was no longer there. This would not be it. Jaegda would do more. It was only a matter of time until the guards came, and he was taken back to the honest room.

Clearwater's gaze turned on Taula, lying against him with her head on his chest. He ground his remaining teeth together as one memory unburied itself. She was in his lap, screaming. Just another in his long list of failures. Some man he was. He finally found a pretty girl willing to give him the time of day, and what did he do? He broke her ribs.

In the deepest fog of reanimation, he thought she was his pet. It made sense. It would be so much simpler if she were. Simply buy her, sign his HOELO agreement, and take her home.[13] No worry that she would lose interest or think he wasn't good enough. No father to prove himself to or bride price to pay. He wouldn't rate a woman like her any other way back home. Even then, a pet like her would probably cost more than he could afford. He wanted to squeeze her a bit tighter to him, but he did not. With his luck, he would probably crush her.

Clearwater turned toward the transparent front of the cell. The nameless faces floated through his mind again. The sight of them filled with many things, but foremost among them was shame. He did not know why. He

---

13 HOELO is an acronym for High Ordinance for Ethical Lantai Ownership. All lantai and lontil are legally the property of the Rhinegrave Dynasty. All common persons who own lantai or lontil slaves are partaking in an indefinite lease. This lease stipulates minimum standards of accommodation, healthcare, housing, and treatment that can revoke possession if violated.

could not even name the faces. But the feeling was there.

The damage to his memory seemed to be centered on the long-term. He still remembered names and faces from his unit. Each time he looked out of the cell, he found himself seeking them. But he knew they were not there. He was the only one.

Why did the faces make him feel this way? Taula said they were his brothers and sisters. He knew he had siblings, but so much of it didn't make sense. His father was decorated—that was why he had more brothers than sisters. Was he ashamed of them for something? Or were they ashamed of him?

His father, he was dead, and his eldest brother. His mother? She was not at home with them. She left, something about new clothes. Did Dad have only one wife? Why was Dad gone? How did it happen?

The swelling between his legs forced him to shift constantly. He did his best to keep quiet and to move as slow as possible. Taula remained in her slumber. If he were honest with himself, the thought that she might want to move if awakened bothered him more than the thought of waking her.

He closed his eyes, but he could not sleep. He knew that as soon as he did, the guards would come. Until exhaustion overpowered his resolve, he would remain awake. The waiting was just as bad as what had already happened. At least, that was how he felt until he saw them.

Jaegda, flanked by two of her guards, came into view on a line to his cell. The Viss held the slate that seemed like a fifth appendage. Clearwater said nothing. He did not move at all, even when they stopped directly before the cell.

For several minutes, Jaegda did not even look inside. Her eyes were down on her slate as she typed. Clearwater began the slow process of disentangling himself from Taula. They were here for him. No need to wake her. He paused when Taula let out a quiet moan, protesting any disruption in her sleep. Jaegda finally looked up at him. Her orb-like eyes reflected the dim light of the prison like some nocturnal predator.

"Stand in front of me."

With a quiet sigh, Clearwater pushed his back against the wall, using his legs to rise. When he reached the transparency, Jaegda held out her slate toward him before moving it up and down several times over his body.

"You have not been eating," Jaegda remarked. "Why not?"

Clearwater glared at her, momentarily taken back by the inanity of the question. "I haven't had much of an appetite," he answered.

"Starving yourself will hinder your regeneration and corrupt my data," Jaegda replied with a hiss in her tone. "You will have to be punished for that."

Clearwater hung his head. As if she needed an excuse for more torture.

"Bring them both," Jaegda directed one of the guards.

Clearwater's eyes lit up, and his posture straightened as the doorway opened in the transparency. "You said you'd leave her alone!"

Jaegda did not look up from her slate. "I changed my mind," she answered. "It would be a useful study of psychology to see how she reacts to viewing our sessions. And if you should forget our agreement, she will be near."

Clearwater's lip formed a snarl as he glared at Jaegda and the transparency slid up to open the cell. "You—"

He began to spring at the Viss, but the guards were ready for him. A long rod jammed into his side. The electric shock seemed to petrify his body, tensing his muscles into stone. Something broke off the staff, remaining embedded in his flesh. Clearwater fell face-first as ripples of electricity pulsed through his flesh.

"That's enough," Jaegda commented.

The guard upended his shock stick and flipped a switch on the base. The electrical pulses stopped. But before Clearwater could move, the second guard's foot came down on his back. With several tons of Vaar bearing down on him, he could not move. A metal ring closed around his neck. The foot on his back moved away as his right arm was drawn up high on his back, and his wrist was chained to his neck.

The electric convulsions had awoken every pain that had finally slept. Clearwater could barely muster the strength to turn his head.

"Leave, leave her alone," he tried to shout but could only manage a gasping whisper.

The guard who had stuck him had Taula now. The Vaar simply opened his massive hand and closed it on her, pinning her arms to her sides as he carried her out of the cell. She only briefly revealed a look of shock and horror. The Vaar who had chained him grabbed his ankles, and Clearwater found himself once more being dragged.

The lights in the honest room were as blinding as before. Clearwater's wrist was unbound from his neck, but before he could do much of anything with it, a Vaar foot pinned his arm to the deck.

"Leave him alone!" he heard Taula shout as his prisoner's uniform was removed. As his eyes adjusted, Clearwater made out the same table that held him last time. It waited but a few meters away. Beside it, a second table had been prepared.

He was hefted off his feet and hurtled into the first table. He moved slowly from the impact, but the guard handling him interpreted it as a struggle and drove a fist into Clearwater's gut. The blow forced the air out of his lungs, and the Vaar secured him to the table.

In a moment, Jaegda stood in front of him, scanning once more with her slate.

"Unacceptable," the Viss commented. "Very unacceptable."

"Leave—" Clearwater gasped for air. "Leave her alone. You promised—"

Jaegda covered his mouth while gazing into her slate. "No, this cannot be allowed. We will have to feed you." Jaegda turned to the guard still holding Taula and motioned downward. The Vaar obeyed, setting Taula on her feet. "Strip and get on the table," Jaegda directed her.

Much as Clearwater had in her place, Taula froze. Jaegda's hand clamped down tighter on Clearwater's mouth, reducing his protests to little more than a muffled howl. Clearwater shook his head, tried to speak, but could do nothing. Taula did not have his enhancements. The way the Vaar handled him was injuring, but to her it could be murderous.

Jaegda's hand left his mouth, and a moment later, it was filled with her rod. The familiar whistle and pop sounded in the chamber. Clearwater heaved in his restraints as the electric charge assailed his flesh.

"When one of you disobeys, I will punish the other," Jaegda warned, facing Taula. "Strip and get on the table."

In such pain his body trembled, and he turned his head from Taula, only seeing her from the corner of his eye.

Clearwater sighed in defeat as Taula drew her arm into her shirt. A moment later she had stripped. Her face was a cowl of anger and humiliation as she awaited the next instruction. Taula followed the silent direction as Jaegda pointed to the table. The same Vaar who had carried her in bound her limbs in place.

"Eating is a social activity among humans, isn't it?" Jaegda asked.

Clearwater could not answer. Taula chose not to. Jaegda struck a button on her slate, and a whir of machinery sounded in the room. A metal cylinder descended from the ceiling, stopping level to Jaegda's eyes between Clearwater and Taula. Clearwater's mouth was freed as the Viss turned her attention to the cylinder.

"Leave her alone." Clearwater panted, trying to block out the pain.

The two tables rotated until Clearwater and Taula faced each other, on opposite sides of the cylinder. Jaegda paid him no mind as she opened a compartment and removed a pair of transparent bags filled with some inky substance. She plugged them into terminals on the cylinder. Her hands moved under the cylinder, and she withdrew a thin but long black hose before the Viss faced him. The needle at the end of the hose jammed into his right arm.

"Liquid nutrition," Jaegda said as she turned back to the cylinder and withdrew a separate hose. The Viss turned to Taula, and Clearwater winced at the sound of her cry as the needle was stabbed into her arm.

Jaegda turned back to Clearwater.

"I'll give you two some time to dine and then we will work."

CHAPTER
6E

I**N THE CORRIDORS OF** the *Caustic Reverie*, Oul'sor approached the quarters
that had been appointed to him. Had he not transferred his command
to another vessel, Kreth'nell would have used them. For now, it was the
largest ship of the Deep Fleet, but its title would be short-lived. He had been
on the losing side in both votes. The Council voted for this ship and had
already voted to begin the construction of larger vessels.

To his relief, Oul'sor had initially found the corridor empty. It seemed he
could hear the thoughts of those around him. But worse was being forced to
feel what they felt. He had plenty of his own feelings and had no desire to
feel theirs. He had the warrior's discipline to keep his own feelings in check.
But these new feelings from outside—he was not prepared to manage them.

Soon. Soon he would have the confrontation he desired. He knew not
exactly when. But something whispered portents of things to come. It did
not feel immediate, but it carried the anticipation of a day drawing close.

His focus within was being forced outward. There were sensations in
this hall. There were thoughts and feelings. Someone else was here. He
found them as he rounded the curve in the corridor.

A young Viss sat by his door. In front of her lay what, compared to
her, seemed to be an enormous platter. The average Viss was barely half the
average Vaar's height and less than an eighth the mass. The enormous steak
beneath the transparent lid was obviously not for her.

Oul'sor sensed the surprise when she realized he was there. The platter
and its lid clattered as she quickly seized them in hand and bolted to her
feet. The young Viss steadied the platter and met him with her head bowed.

At first Oul'sor said nothing as he loomed over her. He tried, and failed,
not to hear her thoughts.

*Warlord, I wish you to exercise your privilege. No. Wrong. Warlord, will you honor
me with your privilege? No, that sounds as a child. Warlord, I wish a child—will your
privilege be mine? That sounds terrible. You have to say something.*

Oul'sor gave her more than enough time to decide exactly what she
wanted to say. When she kept repeating and rejecting the same lines in her
head, he spoke the first words.

"How long have you sat at my door?"

"Not long, Warlord," she answered.

Oul'sor flinched. Lies tasted so . . . *vile*. He could only liken it to the
mouthfuls of rotten meat eaten in survival training. If such a simple lie

tasted to awful, how much worse was one more severe? Telepathy was bad enough. But feeling the sensations of others? This was not meant to be.

Oul'sor composed himself and looked down at the platter. A sor'ket steak, dressed in shavings of fried renta. By the scent, the gravy covering the steak was velmess. A difficult meal for even an experienced chef.

"Warlord. I—"

"I know why you are here," Oul'sor interrupted. "Think you the first, or even hundredth, to wait at my door?"

She did not answer. Her nervous arms brought a fresh rattle to the platter as she raised it higher.

As Oul'sor drew in the powerful aroma, his pupils dilated. He had not eaten since Indorai revived him. He had not even felt the need. Days had passed without a single pang of hunger or thirst—without any whispers of the need to close his eyes. Did he even need to do those things anymore? He could exist in a vacuum without breath. Did any of the old ways to sustain himself still matter?

The young Viss remained silent as Oul'sor returned his gaze to her. Out of uniform, she had done her best to make herself inviting. A mostly sheer outfit showed off her young form. He looked again to the plate. Copulation gifts were common enough but also quite illegal despite their ubiquity. Perhaps she felt a well-prepared meal was the best way to walk the center— offer him something made with care to satisfy any expectation. At the same time, offer something that could be argued as something else if he turned out to be intractable on such rules.

Her unease grew as she waited for an answer. He did not care to delve into her mind any further.

"I decline," Oul'sor answered, controlling the wince as he had no choice but to experience the sting of rejection. It was at that moment that he recognized her. She worked on the ship's bridge—she was one of those who had watched him with awe when he entered.

"Please? Warlord?" She held the steak closer to him.

"No," Oul'sor answered. "You should try Kreth'nell. I have never heard of him declining an offer. His esteem will be even greater after this battle's victory."

"Warlord Kreth'nell is a great Vaar," she answered. "But he is not you, Warlord."

Kreth'nell is not Warlord of Aspiration—that was what she really meant.

"Have I not made myself inviting, Warlord?"

Oul'sor's upper lip curled. "Would you ask the Sovari?"

She took a moment, deciding whether she really wished for the answer. "Yes, Warlord," she replied with a nod.

"You come to my door quite inviting," he assured her, "but I am still mourning my son. I have no spirit now for Von'tu's endeavor."

The young Viss bowed slowly. "Forgive me, Warlord," she answered. "I meant you no discomfort."

"What is your name, child?"

"Nel'va. Warlord," she answered as she bowed her head further.

"Nel'va," he repeated. She fidgeted as he reached down with one hand. Between his right and left thumbs, he took her chin. Her eyes were a bright shade of violet, blending into faint shades of ultraviolet. They remained on him as he guided her head from side to side, examining her face more closely.

"Your face wears few years. Perhaps too few to be seeking a mother's burden."

"I may not survive the war, Warlord," she answered as he released her. "I thought it imprudent to wait."

Oul'sor ground his teeth. If not for the enormity of this conflict, she would still be in military school. But the Council had voted, over his objection, to shorten the duration by more than a year. Now those like her, mere children, were swelling the ranks.

His status of mourning aside, this was a bit impudent of her. So young, with no accomplishments to her name, to approach a warlord for the task. Perhaps she thought her appearance was enough. When he was younger, it likely would have been. Could he even reproduce with this new body? A pointless question. His days of children were behind him.

"When Hahk'xess is here again, entreat him," Oul'sor instructed her. "Tell him I sent you."

Her large eyes flicked toward him for a moment. "Yes, Warlord." She bowed once again and began to turn. But she stopped, turned back, and held the steak toward him.

Oul'sor raised his hand.

"Please, Warlord?" she asked. "I spent much time on it. It should not be wasted."

Briefly Oul'sor saw visions in her mind. A small kitchen brought to ruin by a cook attempting a task above her measure. Oul'sor took the platter, warm to the touch as it kept the meal ready for consumption.

With a final bow, she turned and retreated down the corridor. Nel'va. He would remember her name. It was impudent of her to approach him but also bold. Where other Viss would not, because he was in mourning, she went to the well when there would be little competition. If she kept that boldness and reined in the impudence, she would amount to something.

Once certain she was gone, Oul'sor entered the quarters. There was no hint of hunger in his stomach, even as he took in the aroma of meat. He found the trash receptacle in the wall, pulled it open, then prepared to commit the steak to it. But a growl escaped his teeth, and he closed the receptacle. Too much had gone into this meal to simply throw it away.

He cast the lid aside and took the steak in hand. It tasted as good as it should, better than he had expected after seeing the images of its preparation. Young Nel'va had slaved over the endeavor until she got it right. But she obviously knew quite little about feeding a Vaar. To her, the steak seemed enormous, but to Oul'sor it was the quantity of an appetizer at best. In four bites, he had devoured the steak and sent the platter to the receptacle.

Nel'va. Oul'sor shuddered as a sense of unease came over him. A fear that something was imminent. Did she mean him harm? That was not it. Yet still, there was something. A strange sense he could only call doom as he thought on her.

These quarters were needlessly lavish, he noticed. A separate entryway, bedroom, dining room, office, and meditation chamber. These quarters were meant for a warlord. But too often, warlords forgot their duty to exemplify moderation rather than cast it aside. In the computer room, Oul'sor took a seat in front of the computer console.

"Device, I require the personnel record of one Nel'va. Bridge officer on this ship."

Oul'sor waited as the hologram screen came to life and spilled the data he required. Daughter of Nel'ken, a ship architect. Her mother, Ru'va, was a marine, currently serving as a training officer on Tu'fon. The young Viss had little in the way of service accolades, with less than a year's half on duty. Despite her accelerated training, her test scores had placed her in the seventh percentile.

Oul'sor's teeth ground firmly together as the sense of creeping doom worked its way through his bones.

"Device, draft a letter."

Oul'sor chose to type rather than dictate.

TO: JOOR'TONN—CAPTAIN, CAUSTIC REVERIE
FROM: OUL'SOR—WARLORD OF ASPIRATION

REEN'VUL NEL'VA, SERVICE# 70432579412387966812, CURRENTLY ASSIGNED AS A SENSOR SPECIALIST ON THE CAUSTIC REVERIE, IS TO BE IMMEDIATELY REASSIGNED TO ANOTHER DUTY STATION. THIS TRANSFER, TO OCCUR IMMEDIATELY, IS TO BE TO ANOTHER POST OF SIMILAR RESPONSIBILITY. THE REASONS FOR THIS TRANSFER ARE UNDISCLOSED AS FOR NOW. REASONS AND INITIATOR ARE NOT TO BE SHARED WITH THE REEN'VUL AT THIS TIME. NO REPRIMAND IS INHERENT IN THIS TRANSFER.

OUL'SOR
WARLORD OF ASPIRATION

Oul'sor hesitated briefly before sending the message. The ship's master would not appreciate someone outside of the appropriate department meddling so directly in matters of his personnel. Not that there was anything he could do about it. Nor was there any great likelihood he would argue the matter over such a junior officer. But the impending feeling when Oul'sor thought of her—it was enough to compel his hand.

"Nothing has been taken from you, Oul'sor."

Oul'sor spun so fast, the chair broke from its mounting in the floor, and he landed on his feet with his fists raised. Before him, by the door, Indorai stood with his back against the walls, his tendrils coiled about him. The four voices continued.

"You have only been given. So why turn down pleasure?"

"You solicit payment on debts not owed to you," Oul'sor growled. He walked past Indorai to the entryway. There his bloodhammer waited on a pedestal. He took the weapon in hand and moved himself into a measured stance. Excellence was not a threshold but a habit, and of late, he had practiced too little.

At first Oul'sor hoped that ignoring the irritant would be enough for it to go away. He was wrong.

Ko'funn's Dance was one of the most basic movement patterns taught to novices of the bloodhammer. Too many who used such a weapon abandoned the form as soon as they learned more advanced techniques. But fundamentals were the mother of mastery. Thus Oul'sor went through the movements.

His practice was interrupted by the sense of an impending threat. He spun on his heel, raising the head of the hammer in an upward arc. With a brilliant flash, the hammer met a glowing tendril, and to his surprise, Oul'sor saw it deflect away.

"Good," Indorai commented as Oul'sor faced him. The creature recalled the offending limb. "You sensed the intent of the attack and foresaw its value."

Before Oul'sor could reply, he was forced to move again, deflecting a strike at the knee with the hammer's haft.

"Good," Indorai repeated. "You sensed the intent of the attack. The knowledge has seeped into your instincts. But without conscious mastery, you are hobbled."

Oul'sor drew himself up to his full height. "If you test me, Indorai, you may not like the answers."

The four voices let out a hideous, mocking tone of laughs.

"Precious child. Let not ego in new power lead you astray."

A sudden rage welled up within, and Oul'sor snarled as he bounded forward. The hammer rose over his head before descending with a whistle. Indorai did not so much as move. As if he were an empty hologram, the hammer passed through him from above. Oul'sor barely managed to stop the hammer before it made a hole in the deck.

A gargle escaped Oul'sor's lips as one of the tendrils looped around his throat. One hand held the hammer, and with the other, he grasped at the strangling appendage. It was no use. His fingers simply passed through it until his fingertips dragged on his plates.

"You have taken to psionics like an enspa to breeding," Indorai said as the illusion ahead of him vanished. "But you have an idiot's grasp of telepathy. You guard neither your thoughts nor your feelings."

The tendril took Oul'sor off his feet, dragging him even as he tried to return to his upright stance.

"Perhaps you are simply too . . . Vaar. And something served so well by subtlety cannot integrate itself into your nature. Be thankful you fought your nemesis while he was weak."

Oul'sor managed to roll over onto his fists, one still grasping the bloodhammer. The tendril released him. Intent on taking the creature by surprise, Oul'sor reached for Indorai's leg. But just as the hammer had, his hand passed through Indorai while finding no substance. Indorai's image evaporated.

"It seems your reflexes command better than your intent." Indorai's voice came from behind. "Your strength cannot touch me. Only your mind."

Oul'sor saw red as he stood and turned to see Indorai not six steps away. He took one step to charge before letting out a gasp. He never saw the tendril coming. To his eyes, it seemed to have simply teleported into his chest. Now, blood weeped down his black plates.

"Do you think that is your rage you feel, Oul'sor?" Indorai asked.

The strength was leaving his body. Oul'sor could feel only the fresh pulses of pain in his wound as he fell to his knees.

"Your disdain for me makes you easy to manipulate," Indorai taunted him. "I need only magnify it to slay your reason with rage."

Oul'sor grasped at the tendril, but it had no substance.

"I told you, your strength cannot touch me." Indorai extended another tendril to twitch side to side in front of Oul'sor's face. "You must know that your hand will feel the sensation. You must know it before your hand touches. You must imagine your hand seizing it and pulling it out."

Oul'sor grabbed at the tendril again, to no effect. His eyes narrowed, and he concentrated before trying again. The tendril pulsed in reply, and Oul'sor emitted a howl of fresh agony.

"Do not think you will grab it. Imagine, and *know*. Your will must be immutable."

Oul'sor's hand closed on the tendril.

"You have already pulled it from your flesh," Indorai continued as Oul'sor used the hammer to push himself onto his feet. "You must know you are impervious. No blade may cut you. No projectile may pierce you—in this place, where time is broken and reality malleable. If you cannot do it here, you are worthless and cannot do it anywhere."

A gurgling hiss escaped his mouth as Oul'sor exposed his teeth and pulled at the tendril. The pain intensified like thousands of flaming needles in the flesh of his chest. Oul'sor imagined the tendril leaving his wound, and in moments, his hand moved away, pulling the tendril with it.

Oul'sor stared only briefly. With a howl of anger, he pulled. His intention was to pull Indorai toward him, but the tendril merely contracted in his grasp and slipped away. Oul'sor raised his hammer anew, taking a step to charge.

The air pulsed around him. He was thrown back and struggled to remain upright as his feet slid across the metal floor.

"Your wound, Oul'sor."

Oul'sor looked down.

There was no wound. He touched the place where it had been. He had always been fast to regenerate, but no one regenerated *that* quickly. Even the pierced plates had regrown.

"You have taken well to the gift," Indorai said as his tendrils returned to their coiled position around his body.

Oul'sor closed his eyes, forcing himself to relax. Forcing his arteries to constrict more slowly. Forcing the tension from his muscles. Rage and anger were brothers oft mistaken for one another. Though he managed to shed the rage from his plates, anger remained laced within them.

"I was promised satisfaction, Indorai." Oul'sor spoke slowly. Equally slowly, he opened his eyes to look at the creature. "And it was denied me."

"Neither I, nor our master, promised you any such thing," Indorai rebutted. "Salvation for your people is all you have been promised. If that is not enough for you, then you are unworthy of the station."

Anger's brother tried to return, and Oul'sor was forced to breathe deep to keep him out of the door.

"I know your master's desire," Oul'sor growled, "but I cannot carry this task without satisfaction."

"*Our* master," Indorai said sternly. "Twice now you have died at your foes' hands. You live now only by our master's will. Your people will live only by your usefulness. I believe he should have left you dead—and discarded to oblivion your entire, misbegotten people. Find satisfaction if you can, but remember your purpose. You have found some purchase upon the gift. But it is useless if you do not think the correct thoughts."

Oul'sor lowered his hammer to the floor as he managed to lock the mental door, and the unwelcome brother was barred entry.

"Our mutual friend comes soon. But you are not yet ready."

He had no time to react to them. Oul'sor winced before his entire body went stiff, and the tendrils entered his mind.

CHAPTER
7A

ATOP THE TRAM, PANZER nodded to the brothers as their destination approached. The tram could not stop at the prison. An unexpected stop at such a secured area would attract attention. A kilometer short of their destination, the three jumped off the tram. Their thrusters carried them down gently to land without a sound. The remainder of the trip was made on foot.

The ship's prison was exactly what its name implied and contained its tenants behind multiple layers of security. The entrance existed as a small, unassuming loading dock with a large security door. Behind the door, an elevator shaft would descend in a large spiral. If the prisoners got out of hand, the elevator would be locked down. Anyone attempting to reach the outer door would face a treacherous climb. More security would lie beyond, but one step at a time.

Two guards posted on the prison's loading dock usually had little worth—warriors with the distinction of having the lowest aptitude scores, worst disciplinary records, or some other trait. The guards who were actually worth their functioning organs would be deeper inside. Soon Panzer and the brothers stood beneath them, pressed against the wall of the tram's channel.

"*On my signal.*"

Panzer hissed, trying not to double over as pain arced between his ears. Telepathy was still too much. He turned to see Kassar's hand on his shoulder. He shook his head and switched to point-to-point.

"On my signal. Andira, ready?"

"Ready, sir."

None of them were strangers to the task. The Vaar had done everything they realistically could to harden themselves against the intrusions they had been subjected to so many times before. First it was equipping their personnel with 4CM systems. Next it was to build deadman's alarms into the armor of the guards, and their robots. Each millisecond they sent a broadcast to the ship's computers. Any disruption in that signal or major changes in the biologic's vital signs, and a notice would be sent to nearby security. Credit to the Combine for trying, but this was an issue Andira already knew how to handle.

There was only one obstacle to overcome here. Andira needed to hear them speak to mimic them properly. The ship's internal time was approaching the top of the hour. The check-in came with nothing to report from the sentries. Now they were ready.

Panzer motioned to the brothers, who began to climb onto the loading dock. They moved in unison but painfully slow, taking no chances that the Vaar or their drones might notice them. The ship's designers had done them a small favor by having this tram channel double as a massive conduit for air recycling through the ship. The tiny but nonstop motion of air in the tunnel helped to hide the air displaced by the brothers' bodies.

While they were positioning themselves, Panzer slowly raised an arm until his hand extended above the floor. He froze when he heard pings in his helmet. The brothers did the same. The drones had noticed something and were scanning for any cause for concern. A minute passed before the pings stopped and the drones returned to idle.

The brothers continued while Panzer pulled the RA-117 from the small of his back and uncoiled the weapon. If any of them screwed up, shots would be fired. Then their only hope to avoid alerting the ship would be for Andira to intercept and override the sentries' comms, then try to convince security that the fire had been a negligent discharge. Not a bet he would prefer to make.

The brothers were now behind the warriors and their drones. Sloppy, undisciplined rejects. All Vaar warriors were taught that when performing sentry duty, always try to stand with something solid at their back if they could. All to prevent exactly the kind of thing that was about to happen to them. Kassar and Novin stood ready with their verrirs drawn, awaiting Panzer's command.

"Ready, Andira?" Panzer asked.

"All four signals have been captured. Ready to assume."

"Take 'em."

The two kurai sprang forward. Both swung their blades up, filling the air with sparks as the drones were sliced in two. The sentries startled at the sudden noise and turned. The brothers had enough time for their toes to reach the dock and spring again, driving their blades upward. The air filled with a loud crack as the tips of their blades penetrated the visors of the warriors' helmets. Both convulsed, falling to their knees before they were driven onto their backs.

Panzer climbed onto the dock while both warriors held their swords, moving them in widening circles to open the wounds and ensure they did not leave enough intact brain matter for regeneration. Once on his feet, Panzer took a small disc from his forearm and plastered it on the wall. From it Andira would continue broadcasting her false signals to convince the ship that the sentries and their bots were unmolested.

The security door was the next challenge, a metal plate of solid illstas more than a meter thick. The door's weight was half of its security. Even if revolting prisoners somehow made it to the door, they could never lift it. The door had no hinges or gears. It could only be moved by a network of rails, and powerful electromagnet sensors in the door's elevation channel would watch for unauthorized movement, or any attempt to bypass it by cutting through the wall.

The brothers were working on the problem. Kassar braced his hands on the door to keep himself stable. Novin climbed onto Kassar's shoulders, then struck his toolbox against the wall where it adhered.

"Sir," Novin called before tossing Panzer a device.

Panzer caught and positioned it on the center of the platform. Andira did the work of programming it, and a second later, it projected the hologram. Now if anyone passed by in a tram, they would catch a glimpse of the sentries and their drones standing their boring vigil. Panzer leaned against the wall and waited.

Novin had a lengthy task ahead of him. Panzer tried and failed to keep his mind from wandering in the interim. He thought of Simmonne in his quarters, waiting for him to return with her handmaidens. There was no way Andira could contact her core program on the ship, but if she could, she would probably report that the princess was snooping through his things by now.

There was something between them. He knew he had made an impression on the girl. But it was not until he told her the truth that he realized how much of an impression it had been. A person did not react that way for just anyone. For a moment there was a fantasy, of the two of them. Alone in some home far away. She was in his lap, asleep in his grasp, smiling as she enjoyed the blissful dreams he put in her mind. Perhaps if things had been different.

No. No self-pity. Most useless and insipid of all feelings. He glanced up when he heard Novin's voice.

"Andira, check hearing—clear."

"Confirm hearing clear," she answered.

Novin had cut a hole into the wall above the door with a torch. After a warning to Kassar, he let the cutout hit the dock and echo through the tunnel.

"Deploying spider," Novin announced as he snatched another tool from his kit. The small automatech stood on his palm astride eight limbs. He guided the small machine to the hole, and it quickly crawled inside. Panzer joined their datalink to see through the machine's eyes as it stood atop the door inside of the wall. The machine was glaring at the metal rails designed to lift the door, observing circular pods between them. Pressure plates.

"This is a lot of security for a prison door," Novin remarked.

"Can you handle it?" Panzer asked.

Novin took his time before speaking again, guiding the drone to fully examine the shaft. "Whoever built this door was expecting something like us."

"Can you handle it?" Panzer repeated.

"Twelve pressure sensors. Six current sensors," Novin thought aloud as he guided the automatech to begin climbing one of the rails, carefully avoiding the pressure plates. "I'm not finding a power tap. I have to keep going."

Novin continued his examination for several more minutes.

"I found the power tap. This will take longer than I thought."

"We have . . ." Panzer paused to glance at his chronometer. "Five hours before the shift change. We have to be off the ship by then. How long?"

"I have to remove all the sensors. Then cut off the main power to the door, close the circuit so they don't see a fault, disassemble the current sensors—"

"I don't need every detail," Panzer interrupted. "How long?"

"Between thirty and ninety minutes."

"Do it."

More time for his mind to wander. Maybe it was brain trauma, but his discipline was lacking. He thought of their night on Reichsylvannia. How desperate she had been to sense him. He didn't acknowledge it, but he heard the silent plea in her mind when they left the bar that he do anything but take her back to her life. If only.

He huffed. No self-pity. Nothing good came of it.

"I'm working as fast as I can, sir," Novin spoke, thinking that the annoyed exhale was for him.

"You're doing fine," Panzer answered. "Don't mind me."

Fresh pain began to well up through his neck, and thin tendrils extended out toward his ears. He switched his transceiver so only Andira would hear.

"Andira, more meds."

"Colonel, if I go any higher, side-effects risk—"

"Do. It. Now." Needles throughout his armor pierced his skin, and a moment later, the pain began to subside.

In the Dominion, women kept themselves chaste until marriage. Marriage was a contract. Exclusive sexual access was part of what the husband gained from any wife he took. The more sexual partners a woman had, the worse her ability to pair-bond. But outsiders lived in some kind of a sexual free-for-all. Most never even married. When they did, the marriages rarely lasted. Most women spent their youth sleeping around, ignorant that even a thousand-year youth was fleeting. All the benefits their youthful beauty brought them would fade. Only later did they consider settling down. By then, their youthful beauty and personality were gone. The men they would want a relationship with no longer wanted them. Only the masses of pathetic men who based their self-worth on female approval sought their hearts.

But it was too late. Their primary bait for catching men had slipped away. They would keep searching for emotional fulfillment they could no longer achieve, filling the void with yet more meaningless liaisons. Then they would take to the astranet to spew hate at men. To complain that it was somehow unfair that after wasting their best years, no man would give them theirs.

He had simply assumed Simmonne would be the same, despite the Mandrakes' best efforts to craft their image. Despite the remaining importance of marriage for those of title. Some of her sisters had reputations. For pretty much any nobleman, athlete, or other celebrity, the clothes came off quickly. The princes had their reputations, but they at least took the time to learn the names of those they invited into their bed. He might have been forgiven for assuming that she was like her sisters. Had he known better, he might have kept his distance and avoided the position he had put her in.

That was not true. After having to be there for the emperor's little chat with the Encephalon, he was not in full control of himself. Maybe if he was, things could have been different.

Excuses. The hill on which those who could not accept responsibility were fated to die. Even a good excuse was still an excuse. He had done it, and thanks to him, she would pay the emotional price.

He was brought out of his circling thoughts by Novin fifty-seven minutes later.

"Almost ready, sir."

Panzer looked up as Novin took the final steps. From his tool kit, he withdrew a black cylinder, a fusion battery, and slapped it to stick on the wall. There he connected some cables to it before reclaiming the kit and dropping off Kassar's shoulders.

Panzer nodded and took the RA-117 back into his hands. At his signal Novin sent the command to the battery. There was a scraping of metal, and the door began to rise. Both kurai deployed metal rods. With a hiss the rods extended, becoming braces that wedged under the door.

With the door secured, they began to police the area, grabbing the pieces of the destroyed drones. Each took one of the dead sentries by the leg and dragged the bodies into the elevator shaft.

Andira mutated the hologram on the loading dock, offering the image that the door remained closed behind the phantom guards.

The three tested their boots to ensure they adhered to the metal, and then they descended the spiraling shaft. Soon they came to the elevator, and Novin cut their access through its roof. Now came the portion where they were most likely to be caught. With a bit of strain, Panzer could barely make out the minds of the guards beyond the door. When he pushed his mind further, he drew in a gasp. Minds, far more minds than he expected, and they were not Vaar.

If this ship's prison was like that on other large warships, there would be a booth on the left with two guards on duty. Unlike the pair tasked with spending their day staring at a wall, these guards would at least be capable of walking and breathing the same time. Beyond them would be a rec room where the remaining guards spent their time trying not to die of boredom. No less than six total for every ten-hour shift. A lot to try to neutralize without causing an alarm. Even if Andira could hijack their signals to prevent a deadman's alert, all it took was one yelling the right phrase to trigger a ship-wide alert.

Once again the brothers went to work. Novin was already placing an array of devices around the elevator door. Sound prisons used to keep noise from leaving one medium and transferring to another such as from metal to air. Panzer smiled sadly to himself—using sound prisons to infiltrate a prison. There was a joke in there somewhere.

After he had placed all of the sound prisons, Novin repeated his previous task. He climbed up and out of the elevator. At the wall he began disabling the security that would detect their unauthorized entry into the secure area. By the time he was ready, three hours remained until the shift change and unavoidable discovery.

"We're set," Novin announced as he climbed back into the elevator.

"Door," Panzer ordered.

Novin took a metal rod from his kit and smacked it against his hand. The device extended for a meter before forming into a pronounced wedge. He tested the device, twisting the handle to ensure that the wedge properly split into two and came back together. He braced himself, focusing before jamming the rod under the door. He turned the handle a single click, prying it up a centimeter's height.

With the tiny opening, Andira could scan beyond the door without raising an alarm.

"Sir," she began. "Many life signs. Twenty-four thousand humans. One hundred sixteen lantai. Four kodaz. Eight thousand roliams."

Over thirty thousand? Panzer's mouth hung open until he realized the answer. Twilight. The Vaar had put the colonists from ND-31 on this ship. "Andira, can you confirm the presence of Jenna Prideaux and the Katyusha Twins?"

"Yes sir."

Her images filled his vision. The prison was laid out much as he expected. The corridor from the elevator bore the booths for the guards. Beyond lay a great spherical chamber. Cells lined the walls, stacked atop one another up through many layers. Between the main holding room and the guards' booth, another corridor split off into an interrogation chamber. Andira highlighted their objectives, a lone cell on the highest levels of the main chamber.

"Can you signal capture all of the guards?"

"Yes sir."

She highlighted their positions. Two were less than four meters away, in the security booth. Two more were walking laps in the main chamber. Only four? The standard compliment for the on-duty guards was six. Where were the other two? His eyes moved to the second corridor and the interrogation chamber. If they were in there, someone was being interrogated. They had to be there, with a closed door hiding them from low-powered scans.

Panzer nodded to Novin, who withdrew one last tool from his kit, a second holoprojector. He placed it on the floor before switching it on. The device projected an image of the door over the door itself, but a shade thicker. As the door was raised, the sound prisons would keep it quiet, and the false image would hopefully prevent the guards in the booth from noticing.

Novin stowed his tool, and both kurai took their blades in hand. Panzer held the RA-117 at the ready. At his signal Novin sent the command to the second battery, and the door began to rise. The brothers were in first, keeping so low as to require a free hand on the floor so they would not tip over. Panzer followed them in a duck-walk, and together they moved toward the booth. Behind a transparent pane, both warriors were seated. One complained that his son did not give proper attention to his studies. The other nodded and listened.

They moved in single file, each with a shoulder to the wall, ducking under the transparent pane. Kassar in front with Novin in the middle. Directly ahead, through the corridor, Panzer could already see the cells, and one of the two guards marched their endless circle. There was no actual door to the booth, simply an open cutout in the wall.

"Signals captured," Andira reported. The guards had their drones in their charging racks. One fewer step. Kassar entered first with Novin behind. Two distinct thumps announced the guards being dispatched. The brothers moved back out into the corridor, and as one they proceeded forward. At the side corridor, Kassar stopped. He held up his hands with his fingers together, pointing to the ceiling. A single rotation of his wrist indicated a closed door. They would leave it for now.

They proceeded to the central chamber. Five hundred meters separated the inner walls of the great sphere. The prisoners were kept in cubical cells with transparent walls. These cells ringed the deck level with more stacked above, as if to turn the entire room into some sort of despondent stadium. There was pain in this room, of people with poorly tended injuries. There was discomfort. Fatigue. But worst of all, despondence. Panzer turned from it for now to focus on their task.

Two Vaar guards walked with their drones. They would occasionally stop before peeking into the cells. Panzer glanced up toward the highest row of cells, where their objectives waited, and motioned the brothers on. Kassar went right and Novin went left. Panzer continued toward the middle of the room. The brothers stalked their prey from behind, waiting for the opportune moment. Directly opposite the room's entrance lay a recess in the wall, a lift for the cells. If a prisoner happened to look out and see one of the guards fall, it could cause an uproar.

The chamber was dim, and the cells were dark. The only illumination came from a narrow band of lights ringing the ceiling. Standard Vaar incarceration methods—keep the prisoners in the dark. Do not feed them enough to have the strength to fight. Maintain a frigid temperature so they huddle together for warmth. Give them no entertainment or distraction to pass their time, so that it may be used to incentivize them.

But in the darkness, something warm drew his attention. To his side in one of the lower cells. Two children sat together in a corner. They were playing a game. They spoke in whispers so as not to wake the sleeping adults. A sad smile crept onto his face when he sensed one of them giggle.

The sensation was overpowered by the spike of pain and fear from a Vaar having his skull gouged, followed almost immediately by that same sensation repeating. The light of their beings was quenched in the darkness.

A moment later the brothers had returned to his side. Panzer continued to stare for a moment at the children in the cell before spurring himself back to action.

He tapped Kassar on the shoulder before pointing at the entrance. He would keep watch in case the missing pair of guards showed themselves.

"Let's go," he said, switching his thrusters to minimum power. Novin followed as they climbed to the uppermost row and the cell Andira designated in his display. This cell was clear enough on its own. The uppermost cell was more than twice the size of those it was stacked atop. Its walls were opaque metal. A modicum of privacy served as a privilege extended to the VIPs contained within.

Novin scanned the cell. "We have a problem."

It was about time. This was all going far too well. "What is the issue?"

"The entire cell is sealed with multiple electromagnetic circuits," Novin explained as he kneeled and continued scanning. "I can't open the door without breaking them. Unauthorized circuit break is certain to cause alarm."

"Can you bypass?"

"Not without opening the door. I'll have to bypass the connection to the cell. If it's accessible."

Novin rose before climbing to the top of the cell and remained silent for several minutes.

"I've found the power input. It's covered in sensing nanites. I can spoof them, but this conduit is heavily shrouded. I can't cut through it undetected, sir."

He meant the other prisoners would see the glow as he cut through the shroud. Panzer turned his back to the cell and glared down into the chamber, at the other cells. So many people. How many were hoping for the rescue that their objectives were about to receive? A sickening sensation worked through his stomach as he contemplated these people's future.

"No choice," Panzer said with a sigh. "If we stay invisible, they won't know what's going on. Do what you have to do."

"Yes sir."

Moments later he heard a loud snap, followed by a quiet growl. Even the tiny amount of blue light flashed brightly in the dark chamber. Panzer sensed the surprise, then the curiosity as those in their cells saw the glow. He felt their attention drawing toward him, dozens, then hundreds all wondering what they were seeing. Confusion. He took a breath and withdrew his mind.

At least the room was dark enough that when Novin was finished, they would not be able to see.

Separated from them only by the cell's wall, Panzer could pick out the minds of Jenna and the Twins. Faint traces. His weakened telepathy left him unable to be positive, but he was fairly sure they were asleep. He turned back to the cell and laid a hand on it. There was no pain wrapped in their sleep. A good sign. He kept his eye on the chronometer while Novin worked and their window shrank.

Twenty minutes later, Novin's work was done. He rejoined Panzer at the door and had it open in moments. With the Hellbore at the ready, Panzer moved into the dark cell.

DARKNESS CANCELLATION—ACTIVE

His sensors quickly brought illumination to the room. Compared to the others, it was much larger, extending to the prison wall. Cubicles at the rear indicated private rest and bathing facilities. A kitchen occupied the right rear corner. A table lay in the center with two couches to the table's right. But it was the most prominent feature of the room that surprised him. It was what covered the beds and couches, stacked against the walls so thick that it barely left room to walk on the floor. Toys, countless toys—more specifically, stuffed animals.

Panzer found the objectives. The three beds had been brought together on the table's left. The Twins lay where two beds had been pushed together. The third ran along the foot of the previous two, where Miss Prideaux slept. He approached the beds, crushing stuffed animals beneath his feet until he loomed over them.

The Twins faced each other, each clutching a stuffed animal. Such an innocent picture. The fact that both looked so pretty, even in these conditions, was a good sign. It indicated that they had at least not been mistreated. He slung the Hellbore as he moved to stand over Miss Prideaux. She had no stuffed companion, and her teeth clenched behind a tense jaw. Quietly he lowered a hand and closed it on her arm.

Her hand fell on his before she opened her eyes and gasped.

"Who are you?" she demanded in a low whisper.

Panzer laid a palm on his faceplate and raised it over his brow. There was a faint glow in her eyes as her nanites ran through the spectrum to settle on infrared.

"You," she muttered with a distinct lack of excitement. "Took you long enough."

She sat up quickly and was on her feet even quicker.

"Get them up," Panzer directed. "We need to move."

"How many are you?" Miss Prideaux demanded.

"Just my team."

"That's all?" Her voice rose high enough that Panzer was surprised it did not wake the Twins.

"Best I could do on short notice."

???: We need light in here. Close the door.

Novin obeyed, closing the door of the cell moments before Miss Prideaux triggered a light switch on the wall. Both of the Twins remained undisturbed by the sudden illumination.

"Girls, wake up," Miss Prideaux said.

Both muttered before simultaneously grabbing at their blankets and pulling them over their heads. Miss Prideaux huffed, grabbing the blankets and throwing them off the bed.

"Get up!" Miss Prideaux barked, grabbing both by an arm and shaking.

"What?" they protested in unison, slowly opening their eyes.

"We're leaving. Get up!" Miss Prideaux urged, still shaking them.

Panzer tapped her on the shoulder before pointing his thumb at his backpack. He took a knee to grant easier access. "Top compartment."

Miss Prideaux followed his instructions and found the retrieval suits.

"Colonel!" The Twins sat up. One flung herself into his arms, and the other looped around the beds to do the same. Surprised for a moment, he stood slowly. That was a somewhat warmer greeting than he had expected.

"Are we leaving?" one of them, Jennifer, asked.

"Yes," Miss Prideaux answered for him, grabbing the Twin by the wrist to pull her off him before doing the same to the other. "Come on, we need to put these on."

All three wore baggy sleepwear, and Miss Prideaux quickly turned hateful eyes toward Panzer. "Turn around."

He turned his back to them and crossed his arms. While Miss Prideaux dressed them, he eyed the countless animals in the chamber. He reached down to grab one, a rabbit with oversized eyes and whiskers. He pulled it up by the ears.

"Is there some story behind these?" he asked as he held the bunny out to the side.

"Vaar hospitality," Miss Prideaux answered. "Apparently, all women love stuffed animals."

He dropped the rabbit back into the pile.

"Compress your hair!" Miss Prideaux barked at one of them. A moment later he heard the snap-hiss as the helmet was fitted to one of the suits.

???: Miss Prideaux, how are they doing mentally?

VI-BARONESS JENNA PRIDEAUX: What do you think?

He sighed.

???: Can you keep them under control or are they going to be a problem?

VI-BARONESS JENNA PRIDEAUX: I'll handle them. Just don't start any firefights.

???: I can't make that guarantee.

VI-BARONESS JENNA PRIDEAUX: You better. If anything happens to either of them, the emperor will know you're responsible.

Temptation. But it might make for an awkward conversation with the emperor if he simply left her behind.

One of the Twins released a pained yelp before Miss Prideaux barked at her. "Compress your hair! Colonel, what's our escape plan?"

"I have a shuttle waiting to pick us up."

Another pained yelp from one of the Twins, and another bark from Miss Prideaux. "What did I just say about hair?"

After several seconds he heard two snap-hisses as helmets sealed to the suits. After several more seconds, Miss Prideaux spoke again. "Colonel, I need a weapon."

Panzer faced them again. Both Twins were encapsulated in the suits, and the plates were fitted. Miss Prideaux held her helmet under her arm. With the way she glared at him, part of him was unsettled with the prospect of handing her a weapon. But if it did come to that, she would probably keep her fire directed at the Vaar. He withdrew the CA-9600 and handed it to her with magazines. An amateur practiced until they got something right. A professional practiced until it was so ingrained into them that they couldn't do it wrong. She inspected, loaded, and charged with professional hands.

"Let's go," he said, turning back toward the door.

Novin opened, and Panzer led them through the door to the edge of the platform.

"Twins. Stand on my feet."

They carefully obeyed. Both were nervous, but the tension dropped sharply as he wrapped his arms around them. For them the embrace meant the comfort of simply being held in a time of fear. For him the sharp shift in feelings was a distraction he did not have time to further examine.

>>OBJECTIVE STEALTH SCREENS—ENGAGE

The retrieval suits obeyed the command, masking the three as his cloak came back online.

"Hold tight," he said before stepping over the edge. As he floated down on his thrusters, he glanced back up to Novin and Miss Prideaux. Novin dipped his shoulder, offering her the opportunity to climb on his back. Instead she snubbed him, stepping off the edge and plummeting to the deck. Her legs bowed when she hit, and she went down on her hands but quickly rose back to her feet. With a shrug Novin floated his way down.

Miss Prideaux pulled the Twins off Panzer before Novin's feet hit the floor. Panzer was about to give the command to move when something new caught his attention.

An empathic scan.

He turned to the cell behind him. A child stood at the transparency with her hand pressed against it. She was the source. She had sensed the presences beyond the transparency. He should have looked away, but instead he took a step closer to the cell. She had turned her back on a circle of other children, siblings perhaps. Without thinking Panzer took a knee and touched the glass.

"Sir?" Kassar asked.

His equipment detected the signal from the girl, and he opened the screen in his NOD.

KINDERGUARD BROADCAST CODE IDENTIFIED.
DECRYPTING . . .
NAME: EMESSA SARDONN
AGE: 6
PLACE OF BIRTH: CITY OF ANNPORT
PLANET: CRYSTAL RIVERS
NATION: ELYSIAN COMMONWEALTH
CURRENT RESIDENCE: COLONY OF TWILIGHT
PLANET: ND-31
GALAXY: HOURGLASS

LEGAL GUARDIANS: AVIE SARDONN—FATHER / JUNETTE SARDONN—MOTHER

EMERGENCY CONTACT: AVIE SARDONN—FATHER

ASTRANET CONTACT CODE: 5154-2387-9514-7638-8528-2101-5984

He stared through the characters at the girl and her curious expression. His hand moved to meet hers at the glass. He read the Kinderguard output. More Kinderguard nodes indicated that the children she had been set with were her siblings. An unusually large family for Elysians. He found another node with them.

Panzer knew he needed to lead the rest out, but he could not look away from the cell. People slept on top of each other, crammed into a space suitable for less than half their number. He tried to see the events that brought them here. There was nothing. Providence did not answer his request.

"Sir, we need to move," Kassar urged.

Panzer continued to scan the cell until his eyes came back to little Emessa. With a quiet sigh, he let out a whisper.

"To this end."

He lowered his hand and stood, turning back to his team, Miss Prideaux, and the Twins.

"We can't leave these people."

Kassar had rejoined them in the chamber's center. He and Novin quickly exchanged looks with each other.

"Sir. This isn't our mission," Kassar replied, painfully careful in his tone. "If—"

"We leave them here," Panzer cut them off, "they're going to end up in a Vaar internment camp. We've seen those camps, Kassar. And that's if they don't die when the Armadas destroy this ship."

"Wait," one of the Twins, Jennifer, said. "They'd destroy this ship with these people on it?"

"We can't let the Vaar hide behind sapient shields," Panzer answered. "If we do, they'll use them at every opportunity."

Kassar hung his head before speaking. "Andira? How many of these people are there?"

"Sensors show approximately 32,120. This is short of the total number of ND-31 colonists. It is likely the rest were killed in the invasion."

Kassar looked directly at Panzer. "Sir, we can't fit all these people on our ship. We definitely can't fit them on the *Intruder*. Even if we only tried to take the children. We can't get them out."

Panzer turned back to the cell. Kassar was right. Neither his ship nor the *Intruder* had the space or life support for so many people. The commando in him said this was a fool's idea: impossible, unworkable, and pointless. That part urged him to listen to Kassar. But another part of him gnawed. To every problem there was a solution. What was the solution here?

The *Caustic Reverie*'s shuttles were no doubt legion. Could they use them? No that was a stupid idea. There was no way they would get them all past

Vaar lines without being recaptured or shot down. They would be lucky to get them off the ship before it opened fire on the unauthorized departures.

He took a step back and scanned the prison. These were the same pods the Vaar generally used for prisoners. They were designed to stack and store, but more importantly to move. The cells could be moved via tram or other means through or off the ship, obviating the need to let the prisoners out. How did that help him?

"Sir."

Panzer ignored Kassar's verbal poke. Mininet. His eyes opened wider as the idea filtered through.

"Andira? How close are we to the ship's nearest routing hub?"

"Eleven-point-six kilometers, sir," she answered as he deployed a screen in his NOD, showing the facility nestled beside a hangar and a cargo bay on the ship's port. Panzer turned his head to regard Novin, who had moved beside him.

"This ship is the Vaar supercruiser," Panzer said, thinking aloud more than communicating. "It probably has the routing capacity to move them."

"Move them where, sir?" Novin asked the obvious question.

"Sir," Kassar interjected again. "This is—"

"Kassar," Novin interrupted and turned to him. "He has made his decision."

Kassar's posture shifted as he readied his argument. But the resolve for it drained, and his posture sagged. Without another word, Kassar nodded.

"Colonel," Miss Prideaux said, grabbing the Twins and pulling them to her side. "They are the priority here."

"I will decide the mission priority, Miss Prideaux." Panzer turned back to the cell, ignoring the hate radiating from her. "The *Hurricane*," Panzer mused. "Novin, do you think you could establish a routing link between this ship and the *Hurricane*?"

Novin took his time answering, likely reviewing data on his screens. "Probably, sir."

"Probably?" Miss Prideaux hissed.

"If they're using the same basic architecture," Novin continued, "I can probably establish a link. But holding it open will be another matter. And how do we get the *Hurricane* to accept the linkage? If the fleet still hasn't established their mininet, they'll have to drop out of warp to accept the transmission."

"I'll use my ident codes. The moment my codes are recognized, it will make its way back to Aetius. Andira, can you get ahold of enough cargo trams to move these people without raising an alarm?"

"Possibly," she answered. "Chances of success are approximately 60 percent. But the Vaar will be aware that something is going on."

"If that's the best we can do," he answered.

"Sir," Kassar began, "even if we start routing people out, all they'll have to do is raise the shields or go to warp, and we'll be stuck."

Panzer contemplated that problem until he shook his head. "They can't do enough of either to stop us without shredding the planet. That would give us some time while they make the distance. If they do?" Panzer shrugged. "We get as many out as we can."

This plan was insane. Panzer knew it. Kassar knew it. They all knew it.

"You can save them?" Julie whispered.

Panzer looked at the Twins. "I can try."

With a deep breath, Panzer turned back to the cell and dropped his cloak.

Little Emessa quickly took a step back from the transparency as the huge, armored man appeared before her. Shock, surprise, and curiosity quickly spread through the chamber as more and more people took notice. Murmurs arose, and Panzer silenced them.

"My callsign is Crykeeper." He projected his voice. "I am a colonel in the Solar Commandos."

"A commando?"

"Commando?"

The word was repeated many times over, spreading like a rumor through the prison.

"Kids, come look. A commando!"

"Thank the emperor!"

"Are you here to save us?" a voice called out.

He raised his arms and motioned for silence. "I'm going to try to get you out of here. Everyone remain calm, remain quiet. Parents, keep your children under control. Whatever happens, stay calm."

The shot had been fired and could no longer be called back.

"Sir," Andira said, "records show a single legionnaire among the prisoners. He is not in this chamber. I believe he is in the interrogation room. Third Lieutenant Jonathan Clearwater. He was part of ND-31's garrison."

"Andira, do what you need to do. Novin, remain here. Kassar, with me."

Panzer turned back to Emessa, now with both hands on the glass as she glared up at him. He closed an eye to concentrate.

"Be patient. I will get you out."

It was easier to speak than listen, easier to project thoughts than hear them. Panzer knew that much had worked when he saw the girl's subdued smile. He turned and motioned for Novin to follow.

CHAPTER 7B

S IMMONNE HAD FOLLOWED THE waypoint to her destination and now stood outside a door large enough for a kodaz. She scanned the optical port and activated the door chime. But as seconds became a minute, there was no answer. She toggled the chime again.

"Adri—" Simmonne caught herself. "Andira? Is Rhoxx in his quarters?"

"Yes, Majesty."

Simmonne thought to toggle the chime again when the door opened. A wave of heat and humidity flooded out. Simmonne squinted into the darkness within. She waited, but no one came.

"Mr. Rhoxx?" she called. Still with no answer, she stepped a toe into the door. "Mr. Rhoxx?"

DARKNESS CANCELLATION ACTIVE.

INFRARED ILLUMINATION DETECTED.

TRANSLATING . . .

As Simmonne stepped inside, the room brightened enough for her to see. Of course, the room wasn't completely dark. The kodaz saw best in infrared, so of course that was how he lit his quarters. This room was huge, fit for a huge alien. The half of the room she stood in now was quite spartan. Some kind of large wedge stood upright from the floor. It was only when she looked at it more closely that she realized it was a chair appropriate for a kodaz.

"Mr. Rhoxx?" she called a bit louder, turning to the second half of the room, which was dominated by a large pool and bordered by an encircling walkway. The water was not the crystal-clear she would expect but seemed almost muddy. Was Rhoxx in the pool? Where else could he be? A kodaz was a bit too gigantic to hide in plain sight.

In her NOD she tried to remember the command to artificially enhance the light levels, but the sound of scraping metal stole her attention. On the far end of the room, on the opposite side of the pool, a cage in the wall had opened. A big fat animal stepped out. Its body was pink, with a big nose that reminded her of the mask on the colonel's helmet.

An animal? On this ship? Simmonne began to tiptoe toward the door when she heard the creature make a noise. She had heard that noise on the net. Oh, what was this creature? Bacon was made out of them. A *pig*! That's what it was called.

Simmonne froze. Were pigs dangerous? She looked back at the door, and then again at the pig. If the creature noticed her, it seemed to ignore her. When it reached the edge of the walkway, it brought its snout down to the water. Why did Rhoxx have a pig in his quarters? She was about to call out to him again, but her call became a startled cry when the water exploded.

The pig let out a terrified squeal cut short as jaws slammed around it, and bones audibly shattered. Rhoxx's forelimbs rested on the walkway, and his head reared back. Simmonne saw only the rump and hind legs. There was a snap, then a crackle. Rhoxx's jaw opened wider, and the pig vanished into his gullet. Simmonne did not move as the kodaz turned toward her.

Rhoxx finished his climb out of the pool. Barely able to fit on the walkway, his weight created an audible ring with each step on the metal floor. Simmonne lowered her hands from her mouth as the kodaz drew near.

"You . . ." she stammered. "You just ate that pig alive!"

"It not be tasstin' asss good. Eatin' bacon what killed already," the big kodaz answered, stopping in front of her. "But. You prob'ly accussstom, kodaz eatin' wit' utensssil and courtly manner. I sssorry I be offendin' you."

"N-no," Simmonne answered, dropping her hands and adjusting her posture. "I . . . just wasn't expecting it."

No matter how revolted she was, she was not about to criticize him for how he ate in his quarters.

"Sssso. What brin' you, me, Majesssty?" As he spoke, a thick metal ring around his neck moved. The ring thinned as the material flowed outward, forming into a pair of cyberlimbs. Humanity's gift to the kodaz, dexterity. For many kodaz, cyberlimbs were often status symbols as much as they were tools. But the black metal of his limbs and the collar they branched from was a simple black. She found no ornamentation on him as he reached into his mouth.

"I . . . was wanting to . . . talk." Simmonne tried not to cringe as he plucked a hoof from between his teeth before tossing it back into his mouth and swallowing. "To you."

He said something in reply, but she did not catch it.

"Come again please?"

Simmonne listened carefully to each syllable out of his mouth. The kodaz had a great deal of trouble with the Solar language. Their brains processed language in fundamentally different ways from humans or most species. Their language had no real concept of tense. Most syllables they pronounced in their throats with little help from their mouths. Some sounds they simply couldn't duplicate. So she listened intently to pick out his words. Some thought them plodding and slow. From what she understood, being able to speak Solar at all showed how intelligent they actually were. Most kodaz she had met used cybernetics to smooth out their speech. For whatever reason, he apparently did not.

"I be ssssayin', what we talkin' 'bout?"

She regained her composure, ignored the smell of blood on his breath, and focused on the matter at hand. "I was hoping to talk to you about the colonel."

Rhoxx dipped his snout, and the pair of high-set, widely spaced eyes swiveled so that both stared down at her. That meant something. Kodaz put much more emphasis on body language. Was that look suspicious? Or was it dismissive? Alien emotions were harder to read than human. Kodaz were particularly tough, perhaps even more so than deltas. His knuckles were flat on the floor, but the tip of his tail traced side to side. Suspicious.

"You wantin' know what?" he asked.

"Well. Anything you can tell me," she answered. "I don't even know for sure how old he is. The colonel, I mean. I know he's a commando, so he doesn't have any family. But, that's really it. That and he likes cheese. Did he have a family before? Or, did he just crawl out of a pile of guns somewhere?"

Rhoxx's jaw parted slowly, exposing more big conical teeth. The tips of his tongue barely protruded past the top lip. That one was easy. That was confusion.

"You not knowin' who him be?"

The question took her by surprise, and Simmonne shook her head. "Should I?"

Rhoxx blinked slowly. One eye remained on her while the other drifted away. She was not certain what that meant, so she tried to focus on his feelings. Whatever he felt, it might not have had a direct human analog.

"How you not know?" There was a faint hiss in his question.

"Know what?" She took a step forward. "What is it I'm supposed to know?"

Rhoxx shifted his knuckles closer to his body and more of his weight onto his back legs. The tip of his enormous tail created a sloshing sound as it dipped in and out of the dark water.

"I not able tellin' you, what him not choosin' ssshare."

"Please?" Simmonne pressed.

"Sssorry. Absssolute Sssecret. Not able tellin' you."

"Absolute secret," Simmonne repeated. "I'm a member of the Solar Family. Isn't that enough?"

"Classssified ain't just about you bein' able keep a sssecret," Rhoxx answered. "It about you needin' know. If you not already knowin', you not needin' know."

She needed to control her body language. Confidence. She stood up as straight as she could and glared directly into the red eye looking down at her. "I *need* to know," she answered. She retained eye contact as she reached into her dress and produced the badge. The kodaz's pupils zeroed in on the piece of metal in her hand.

"Why you havin' it?" She didn't need body language or empathy to pick out that accusatory tone.

Soften up. Don't be confrontational. She relaxed her posture and lowered her volume. "He gave it to me."

Rhoxx bent at his elbows, bringing his head down as he turned his snout toward the door. Now he glared at her with one large eye brought down to her level.

"He givin' it?"

Simmonne nodded. "Just before he left."

Each of his teeth was longer than her hand, and the air whistled through them as he took a breath. "Givin' it?"

Again she nodded.

He returned to his previous posture and glanced upward as he entered deep thought. He was feeling a lot of something, but she could not make out what it was.

Rhoxx finally looked back down at her.

"Why him give it?"

Simmonne shook her head. "He . . . didn't actually say it." She hesitated. "But, I think we both know why."

The air whistled between his teeth again, and he shook his head. "Not matterin'. If him not choosin' tell, not bein' my part to tell."

"Please, Rhoxx?" she whispered. "Please? I need to know."

His jaw worked, his teeth scraping as he ground them together. "No, Majesssty," he answered. "I not able tellin' you."

She was about to protest when he cut her off. Unfortunately she missed his answer.

"I'm sorry?"

"I sssayin', maybe Rhoxx tell you a sssstory. Pass t'e time."

A story? She closed her eyes. She really was stupid. At first she felt that he was condescending to her. Only after a second did it dawn on her. So she opened her eyes and smiled. "I would like that."

The big kodaz motioned her toward the corner where the large wedge sat. She walked toward it with him.

"Rhoxx," the AI interjected, "I must remind you that all information about Corps personnel is classified absolute secret. Further I—"

"Andeera?" Rhoxx interrupted.

"Yes?"

"Hussssssssh."

Simmonne smiled as Rhoxx turned one eye to her.

"Bein' her no mind. Not always agree, what bein' right our boy."

His cyberlimbs gripped the wedge, opening a panel on the side. A moment later a chair rose out of the metal of the floor, and Rhoxx motioned for her to sit. Simmonne did, crossing her legs as the kodaz mounted the wedge, leaving his chin resting on top. Simmonne was forced to look up at him for only a second until her chair began to raise. A moment later she was eye to eye with the kodaz.

"Andeera. Be give me. Ar-tic-u-late-or."

A wall-mounted printer to his side churned, and Rhoxx faced it. His long tongue snaked out of his mouth, groping at the receptacle. Simmonne spied a small cylinder clasped in the fork of his tongue before it retreated into his mouth.

"Maybe now you able understand me," Rhoxx remarked, facing her.

Simmonne smiled and shook her head. "I was not going to complain."

"Hmm. Yes. Royal manners. You probably also used to kodaz talk more normal. With articulator implants. But, we only able to have sso many. Our immune ssystem never really learn ignore them. So I never able to ssspare one for this."

She had never heard that before, and unsure what to say, she simply nodded.

"Ssso. Ssstory time." He rose off his seat for a moment, possibly deciding where he should begin. "You know who be the Vorhan Tohl?"

"The Redguard? Of course. They're the high king's bodyguards."

"Yesss. Only kodaz, kurai, and sssimians. My people being first. Vorhan Tohl. Even be our language. Meaning royal protector." He exposed many teeth when he smiled. "Well, there once a young kodaz born. Him be what we calling a soga. Exceptional child, born to ordinary parents. Him parents good people, but plain people. Yet they see this young kodaz being special. They ask the Vorhan Tohl to examine him. They agree, the boy a soga. So they take him, train him be Vorhan Tohl."

Simmonne's eyes widened slightly. No. This couldn't be going where she thought it was.

"The boy receive him first gift from the high king. Him first pair of cyber-limbs. They tell him, 'Take this gift from the high king. That your dexterity be as great as your potential.' Most Vorhan Tohl, generational. Being best among the best, not enough. Loyalty matter just as much. Firsst-generation asspirants, no legacy of loyalty.

"They receiving the best nourishment and education. But also training. Much training. No day without training. Able quit anytime. But if quit, never coming back. Of the assspirants, only one, ten thousand go on become firsst-generation Vorhan Tohl."

Now the story was making sense. He grew up training to be Redguard. But at some point, he must have washed out. Not that becoming a commando auxiliary was anything to disrespect.

"Well this kodaz. Him grow up be big, strong, and very good-looking." He paused to flash her another big, toothy grin. Simmonne returned the smile. The ruby-red bone that formed his crest was like a giant, gorgeous gemstone to her, but from what she heard, a naturally red crest was irresistible to the ketha.

"When it come time, of the ten thousand, the good-looking kodaz be the one."

Then he *was* Vorhan Tohl. Simmonne thought back to the colonel's gun and the heagle emblazoned on it. That could explain why he had that. But, how did Rhoxx end up going from Vorhan Tohl to this?

"Him becoming first-generation Vorhan Tohl. Assigned to the Fourth Contingent, spend him days guarding the Rothburg. You meet the high king. What you thinking of him?"

Simmonne stopped herself from answering that question. She had not spent enough time with the man to form much of an opinion. Most of that time she'd spent trying to hide her discomfort with the feelings of an elder who was obviously imagining her in his bed. "He seems very sure of himself, as a high king should."

Rhoxx's eyes narrowed a bit. "Him wanting everyone think he a tough, but fair and generous man." Rhoxx waved his snout slowly in a long shake of his head. "But him a tyrant, that one. Always been. Never learning. No one *always* get them way. Not even a high king. Well. The kodaz spend many year patrolling the Rothburg. But finally, old Jonass deciding have him first son.

"Whenever a new Rhinegrave born, a great competition held in the Vorhan Tohl. Determine who be the captain and lieutenants of their personal guard. That good-looking kodaz enter the competition. Him win. Chosen as captain. The first, first-generation captain in thousands of years. Him parents, very proud of him."

"I'm sure they were," Simmonne answered.

Pride. That was one of the few near-universal emotions. She picked it up clearly enough. But now, they were back. The story was on a course she could not accept. Her feet dangled well off the floor, and one arm grabbed at the chair as she leaned in closer to him.

"Two kurai winning the lieutenant ssspots. The senior, 103rd-generation Vorhan Tohl. A paragon of the warrior caste. The other, a caste-jumper, originally techweaver caste. Him earn the junior lieutenant place. First time in long, long time, two of the three be first generation."

Kassar and Novin? One kodaz, two kurai. The math worked. But this was insane. Too insane. How did all three of them go from being the guardians of a prince to commando auxiliaries? Her free hand found the quant medallion at her neck. Either this story was insane, or it did not have a happy ending.

"Jonass having him son and name him Victor. The three standing together, and while him still a baby in him mother's arms, they taking an oath to him. Protect him. Guard all him own, all him love, and him personal honor. This for all them days. And if somehow they outliving him, spend the rest of their days guarding him grave."

Unconsciously Simmonne shook her head. Prince Victor died over a hundred years ago. He died in the Outlands War. She had seen the anniversary of his memorial on the astranet. But, Steven called him Victor. *Twice.*

"Prince Victor not quite a soga," Rhoxx continued. "A soga come from ordinary parents. But him something very special. An incredible psion. Not cry much as a baby. When him hungry, already able send him mother him hunger so she feed him. Telepathy come so natural, hard getting him actually talk."

Empathic projection as an *infant?* Telepathy before he could talk? Metapsionics didn't manifest that young. Most never had hints until adolescence started. She was considered an early bloomer, able to sense emotions at eight. Was Rhoxx toying with her? She thought back to the armory and what the colonel said. Dozens of records. Competence at age. This couldn't be real. Why didn't anyone tell her?

"Break most of him toys, trying play with them with him mind," Rhoxx continued. "And them not strong enough for it. By four, already able crush servitor automatech with him mind."

Psionics at four? That was beyond impossible. But, she had watched him juggle a hundred chairs and tables, plus Jenna. All like it was nothing. The Rhinegraves were the first metapsions, and they were strong. But, that young?

"They must have been very proud of him," Simmonne remarked, still trying to process it.

"Oh yes," Rhoxx answered, something in his feelings shifting. "Sso proud, not seeing the danger."

"Danger?"

Rhoxx nodded. "All that power in the mind of a child. The Vorhan Tohl trying warn him parents how dangerous it be. But they too proud to be listening. Until too late."

Simmonne leaned forward again. "What happened?"

"The young Victor be a . . . difficult child. Never like being told what do. One day him mother get frustrated. She slap him. He get angry. Throw her againsst wall so hard, shatter her spine."

"He shattered her *spine*?" Simmonne exclaimed.

Rhoxx nodded. "Bad time that. Him sorry after. Hard getting him use him abilities after. But a decision made. Every son of the high king be going through the Eightfold Gauntlet. Spend years of him youth, be living among the Eight. Learning our ways. So if him be king one day, be our king, too. Most be going at eight. They sending him at six. But being a problem. Always a shepherd for the boy. One of the Vorhan Tohl, but not among him guards. Go with him, be a mentor, in charge of him studies."

Simmonne leaned back into the chair. "I suppose after what happened with his mother, no one was eager to volunteer?"

Rhoxx raised an arm, extending a long claw. "Only one. Nuset ahn Kalonen. Kah'lennka Grand Master, 109th-generation Vorhan Tohl. Him volunteer, be the shepherd. And so under Nuset guidance, the prince go. From kodaz, kurai, and simian. Him learn violence. How to do it, why do it, and when. Art and music from the buun. Technology and industry from the techla. Finance from the avarirs. Craftsmanship, the thouse."

An image formed in Simmonne's mind, forcing her to suppress a giggle. The thought of the colonel standing tall and holding a serving tray. "What did he learn from the lantai?"

One of Rhoxx's eyes moved upward in thought before he answered, "Mostly what doing, teenage hormones." Rhoxx showed some of his teeth before his expression became more serious. "But, most important lesssons, him learn from Nuset. Teaching him self-discipline. Having to teach him, both hands sssometimes. But teaching him. If the prince ever speaking of him father, him not talking the high king."

Unsure of what to say, Simmonne simply nodded.

"When him complete the gauntlet, return home. Attend RAAMS. There him meet you brother, Sssteven."

Simmonne perked up. "I did know that they knew each other. So they went to school together?"

Rhoxx nodded. "Be Sssteven second time there, no longer active duty. There study politics of war. Readying himself be emperor."

It made a little more sense now. Steven was 260, the colonel 187 if she understood Rhoxx correctly. "So that's how they became friends," Simmonne remarked more to herself than to Rhoxx.

"Not at first," Rhoxx answered. "Hate telling you this, but you brother be a bit a bully in them days."

Steven a bully? Well, it was a long time ago, and he was young then. She doubted it, but it wasn't unbelievable.

"Him try that on the prince. Not going too well for him," Rhoxx mused.

"Yes, I don't imagine him allowing someone to treat him that way. Did they fight?"

"Not first." Rhoxx shook his head. "Mostly verbal. Each using other, sharpen him claws. Not until a student banquet. Then, they fight."

"What happened?"

"It a bit of a rule. Sssssylvanni men not liking men from outside, talking, flirting with them women. Sssylvanni women, typically not liking outsider men either. But Steven a prince, and a bit girl crazy. None the other student willing tell him stop, being Imperial prince and all. But the high prince, he tell him stop. At the banquet, Ssteven getting many hands on serving girl. Prince tell him stop, and they fight."

Simmonne leaned forward until she had to catch herself to stay in the chair. "Who won?"

Rhoxx paused. "Hard saying. Both guards break them up pretty quick. But the red prince smash a gravy boat on blue prince head. So, got hardest shot in. Steven having to go out, treat for pieces and gravy burns."

Simmonne wasn't sure how to feel about that. Steven knew how to fight. But, growing up trained by the kodaz, kurai, and simians—it was probably a good thing the guards broke them up. As much faith as she had in Steven, that fight was probably out of his league.

"But, a respect each other form," Rhoxx went on. "And where respect be sown, friendship can grow. Two have much in common. Especially there. Difficult times."

"Difficult?" Simmonne asked before looking at the printer on the wall. She found an optical port.

>>*ICE WATER*

The machine growled, and Rhoxx glanced over at it. He gently grasped the glass with two claws and handed it to her. There was something almost comical about seeing the small glass in his huge talons as she took it from him.

"Thank you," she said before taking a drink. "What was so difficult for them?"

Rhoxx took his time before answering. He even raised one claw, scratching gently at the keeled scales on the bridge of his snout.

"The more we be given, the more be expected of us. As high prince, he given much. What consider exceptional other, only consider adequate for him. He a Rhinegrave, sssupposed be better. But it also breed resentment. Graduate firssst him class. Him earn it. But all whisper behind him that he not, sssaying it only because him Rhinegrave. That sssituation, a common ground him and Sssteven have. Sssadly, things begin to bad for the prince after."

"Why?"

Rhoxx let out a sigh, and Simmonne shifted in her seat. Another universal emotion bloomed within him.

"In school. Him meet a girl name Elsa. She working voice bar."

Voice bar? Simmonne had to think on that one a moment. But it came to her. Entertainer was one of the few jobs a woman in the Dominion could have with no one looking down their noses at them. But a lot more wanted it than could have it. Many of them started out at voice bars. They worked primarily as servers, ostensibly trying to get to know potential fans and build an audience between performances. Not many succeeded from what she knew.

"What was she like?" Simmonne asked.

"Elsa? She a pretty little thing. Very friendly. Never meeting a stranger. When he come in the bar, she be starstruck. Just stand there staring at him. So he get up, take her by arm, and sit her in him lap while he eat, listen to performances. When it her turn, he tell her stay put, sing where she be. She belong him after that."

Simmonne was silent for a time, thinking back to when she was in his lap on Reichsylvannia. She shook her head to clear it. "So what happened next?"

"The prince deciding after a bit to marry her."

"He has a *wife*?" Simmonne couldn't stop the question from slipping out. She realized how stupid it was even as she said it. He was a commando. Commandos did not have family.

Rhoxx shook his head. "And it where problems begin. You see, old Jonas already picking out a wife for him boy. Pretty girl name Aleela Andrepont. Orion girl, formalize alliance between the houses. But the prince, him refuse."

"Why?" she asked. "Most Reichsylvannians have several wives. Did he just not like her?"

That or perhaps he did not think an Ori girl would be the submissive kitten he would no doubt prefer.

"Terms of alliance," Rhoxx answered. "Andrepont family wanting them daughter be high queen when the prince's time. But him refuse. Him insist Elsa being him high queen."

Her confusion played on her face as she tried to choose the right words. "But, why? Does it really matter who is high queen? She has no power."

Rhoxx's eyes narrowed. "It matter," Rhoxx answered, a bit of a hiss in his words. "High queen no power maybe. But sssuposed be example, all

Dominion women. It matter more than little."

"So what happened next?"

The air whistled through Rhoxx's teeth again as he drew in a long breath and let out an equally long sigh. "Many arguments. Until the patience break. The high king give the prince one last chance. Do what him told, and preserve the alliance. When him refuse, the high king disown him. Exile him from the Dominion."

"Exile?" Simmonne whispered. "His son?"

"I tell you, old Jonas be a tyrant," Rhoxx answered. "Him thinking a little time without him status, on him own, humble the prince. Make him come back, ask for forgiveness, and behave."

Rhoxx snorted and shook his head again.

"If'n the old king ever bother get to know him own son, him know that never work. So the prince leave. Him thralls, the good-looking kodaz, the two kurai, and Elsa going with him."

"You." Simmonne stopped herself. "That kodaz—and the kurai. They went with him even once he was exiled?"

Rhoxx stared into her. "They be taking many oaths as Vorhan Tohl. But the highest being to the prince. *Not* him father."

That explained why he was not at home being a prince. But how did he end up in the Corps? He still had a family. Did this story get worse? "What did he do after he left?"

"Him no longer Rhinegrave in name. No identity. Join Legionnaires, assume identity as Rolan Speer. His identity be the big secret everyone know. But, the high king not done. Flex him muscle, get him assigned far away. Superiors trying keep him away from dangerous zones. But then, you father ordered Steven, destroy the Pillagers."

The Pillagers. Simmonne actually knew a bit about that conflict. Steven took charge of Imperial forces and hunted them down.

"Sssteven flex him own muscle, get the prince assigned to himself. Them working together on the project. The prince helping Steven formulate the plans to hunt them down."

"So they were more than just friends," Simmonne whispered. "They were war buddies. He helped him fight the Pillagers."

The shift in Rhoxx's feelings drew her attention back to him. "Help, one way putting it."

Simmonne sat up straighter. "What is that supposed to mean?"

"It mean Steven take a lot of credit. Work not his."

Simmonne shook her head. No, no conquering the Pillagers was Steven's accomplishment. He did that. No one could take that from him. She opened her mouth, ready to argue, but Rhoxx beat her to the words.

"Sssteven a mind for logistics and politics. Both be important to war. But him not be a tactician. That where the prince coming in. And Steven taking credit."

Simmonne tried to speak again, only for Rhoxx to press his statement forward.

"Him not sssteal credit. Not understanding. The prince encourage him take credit. Knowing Steven wanting be emperor. Knowing him needing that claw in him hand, taking down Pillagers. When the campaign over, Sssteven's blessing enough for the prince be promoted to captain. Him request garrison duty, and get it."

Rhoxx paused before looking straight into her eyes.

"On Miner-9."

A chill crept down her neck and out through her arms. Simmonne knew that name. The first world to come under attack in the Outlands War.

"No," she whispered.

Rhoxx nodded. He opened his mouth wide as he repositioned the articulator grasped by his tongue. Simmonne knew this story. But she remained quiet as Rhoxx relived it.

"Him commanding garrison," Rhoxx said, and his jaw shifted. "The Outlanders panic when Empire learn they be helping Pillagers. They attack, try to siege the planet. Six time they trying breach shield and land. Ssix time, the prince and him legionnaires repelling them. Him earn him Sssolar Crosses for the battle. Some sssoldiers having more. But him only sssoldier, earning two for distinct acts, same battle. But it not be enough. The Outlanders growing desperate. Managed breach planetary shield again, and rain bombs down on it. Made kill Solars. Kill lantai, too. Other bombs fall, break open buildings to let it in."

Rhoxx took a breath. Simmonne sensed the bitter taste in the room. The kodaz variation on a familiar feeling.

"The two kurai be away when it all begin. Sacred holiday. But the kodaz be there. Anoxelyne not kill kodaz. Just put him to sleep. He awake in a broken home. Dig through. Him find him prince, over Elsa's body. The thralls dying with her. Him wounded, but make it to her. Him visor open. Breathed the gas. Died with her. That kodaz wonder sometime if him open it because already dying? Or because of how him find her? But the kodaz find them, both gone."

A long snort sounded through his nose, and his mouth worked side to side for several seconds.

"The colony be broken. No power. So the kodaz carry them both into the mountains. Bury them bodies in the snow. Try preserve them until help come."

Rhoxx sighed, closing his eyes.

"Waiting long time. Gilyard finally show up on *Yamato*, and breaking the siege. Bodies recovered. But for Elsa, too late. Not having him cybernetics be preserving her. Nothing they able do."

Simmonne reached into her pocket and clutched the badge. Everything. He lost everything. That was how he ended up in the Corps.

"The kodaz thinking about that day," Rhoxx said, his eyes looking past Simmonne to the far wall. "When the kurai return, they offer commit hadoko, contrition, not being there. The prince say no."

"Well of course he did," Simmonne offered, not sure if Rhoxx heard her.

"It being the oath. Guard him, and all that belong to him. And they fail."

"I . . ." Simmonne hesitated, trying to draw his eyes back. "I am certain he does not blame his loyal bodyguards."

"Sssympathy neither sought, nor wanted, Princess," Rhoxx answered as his eyes came back to her. "We all got weight be carrying."

Simmonne pulled the badge out of her pocket and held it in her lap. "So that's how he ended up in the Corps."

"The commandant be there. When him reanimated," Rhoxx answered. "Name him Crykeeper."

"Why?" Simmonne looked up at him. "What does it mean?"

"Rhinegrave man *never* be crying. *Ever.*"

"But. Not even then?"

"Ever," Rhoxx repeated. "It impressed on them, from birth. Never cry. Cry a way to signal distress. Ask for help. Ask for mercy. Not for them. They be the ones others beg for mercy. They be the ones people asking for help. Never the ones be crying. I thinking the commandant be unsettled by it. So name him Crykeeper."

"That's horrible! Why give him a name that reminds him of such a painful event?"

Rhoxx snorted quietly. "If it be making you feeling better, rest of the Corps be calling him something else."

"Well, what do the rest call him?"

"Overkill."

Her thoughts flashed back, and for a moment she was in the armory again. There she watched the colonel tinkering with his big gun. The thought of the enormous shell in her hand brought the faintest smile. "I can see that," she answered before looking back down to the badge. "He's a Rhinegrave. And no one told me. Not even Steven."

Rhoxx extricated himself from his chair, and Simmonne's seat lowered until her heels met the floor. She stood as the kodaz did the same.

"Maybe them thinking you not needing know," Rhoxx answered.

"Well. Thank *you* for telling me," Simmonne replied, still staring at the badge.

"Being a reason Rhoxx be telling you." He waited for her to make eye contact again. "Some people thinking Rhoxx not very smart, because him big and him talk funny. Maybe him smart. Maybe him not. But you knowing what he be?"

"Very handsome?" Simmonne replied with a small grin.

"Well that much be obvious," he returned. "But Rhoxx, be obssservant. Him noticing everything go on around him. Including how people ssscent be changing, when them around each other."

He drew a bit closer, once more focusing on her with one eye.

"How them be looking at each other. Especially when the other not be looking." He drew back away from her. "Rhoxx knew a boy once. Saw the universe as something to conquer. Not simply pass through on the way to the end. Him pray every day, Maiden of Fate to see that boy again. But maybe Rhoxx not being the one who can find him."

Maiden of Fate? Simmonne mouthed the words before looking back at Rhoxx.

"Oh. So you're a pious man?"

"It making you lose respect for me, Majesty?"

Simmonne quickly shook her head. "Not at all. I think everyone needs something to believe in."

"It okay," he answered with another toothy smile. "You not needing believe in Who Is Many and One. He believe in us."

Simmonne looked back at the badge, quietly reflecting on what she had just learned.

"Well," Rhoxx spoke up again, "thinking I might still be hungry. If Your Majesty be excusing me."

Simmonne's eyes widened. Not wanting to watch him dine, she quickly nodded. "Thank you, Rhoxx."

"As you going," he said just before a link dropped into her NOD. The door closed behind her, and she opened the file. An image of a bright day and a clear sky. In the center of the frame, Rhoxx sat in his gold armor and red cape. He was not wearing his helmet. Three kurai were with him. They seemed to be at some kind of racetrack. Two kurai wore similar armor. Their faces were concealed by their helmets. The third kurai, was that Nuset? His face was exposed.

But Simmonne's eyes were drawn to the center. On Rhoxx's neck sat a small boy wearing a red cape and a small crown. His hands rested on Rhoxx's crest as he looked over the crowd.

CHAPTER
7C

THE WAIT FOR JAEGDA to return was a torture all its own. Directly across from Clearwater, Taula lay bolted to her table. Both had been stripped. Clearwater tried not to look directly at her, but he saw the look in her eyes, the tears trying to form as she contemplated what came next.

Jaegda. Somehow, Clearwater was going to find a way to kill her. He wanted to tell Taula it would be okay, that no one would hurt her, but it wasn't true, and he had no tongue. All he could do was take the pain and hope Jaegda would keep her word. But either way, Taula would see it.

Clearwater turned his head as he heard the side door open, and Jaegda emerged. As always her eyes were glued to her slate. Clearwater's eyes tracked her as she approached.

"Please don't do this."

Taula's voice did not draw Jaegda's gaze. Instead the Viss's rod snapped the length and landed between Clearwater's legs. He tried to hold it in, but the scream escaped as the pain ripped through him. His head jerked side to side, his body in so much agony that he saw it without registering what he saw. The entry door to the chamber opened and closed.

"You are here to watch, not speak," Jaegda said to Taula, pointing at her with the rod. The Viss turned back to face him. "Now we will begin—"

Clearwater was as shocked as Jaegda when her slate suddenly flew out of her hands. The Viss's mouth opened, and a word became a wheeze that became silence. The rod flew out of her hand next. Jaegda's throat seemed to contort, and the Viss suddenly seemed to levitate. She clawed at her throat, and her legs kicked beneath her.

"What's happening?" Taula exclaimed.

Unsure, Clearwater simply watched Jaegda writhe. A stealth screen faded, and he saw the hand first. An enormous figure in black armor, highlighted by red, appeared before them. Huge, but humanoid, it held Jaegda's neck level with its shoulders.

A second figure came into view behind. The smaller figure's face was masked by his helmet, but he wore khalak. A kurai with a painted pattern on his helmet. The skull of a kazonak, with its toothy maw and scythe-like tusks. On the forehead of the skull was the mark of Iden, black ax and spear crossed over a red delta.

The larger figure took a step back, with Jaegda still dangling from his grip.

"Who are you?" Clearwater asked, eyes dancing between Jaegda and the black figure.

"I'm a colonel with the Corps. That should be sufficient for now," the enormous figure answered.

The Corps? Clearwater was speechless as he stared at the commando. The kurai stepped up to Clearwater, using a knife to break the restraints at his wrists. When he tried to rise, he was pushed back against the table.

"He's in pretty bad shape," the kurai remarked before turning back to the colonel. "Needs more than I can do."

"Do what you can," the tall figure answered.

The kurai turned back to Clearwater before brandishing a mediron. "This will hurt."

Clearwater almost laughed at the warning. Compared to what had already happened, how painful could a shot from a mediron be? He barely felt the needle enter his leg.

THIRD-PARTY NANITES DETECTED.
MEDICAL NANITES
SUPPLEMENTARY NANITES
DO YOU WISH TO ENABLE ACCESS?
>>YES

What might have otherwise been a painful burn was little more than a sudden warmth. The tiny machines raced through him, patching wounds as they could. But when Clearwater looked at his left arm, there was no change. Fingers and toes, but not limbs. The larger cyberbones were more than the machines could regenerate.

"Give it to him," the colonel directed.

The kurai removed a metal tube from his back with a large white medical cross on its surface.

"This will hurt more," the kurai warned as he opened the tube. He took hold of Clearwater's arm and poured a silvery fluid from the tube onto the stump. This time Clearwater most certainly felt the pain.

"Don't touch it." The kurai intercepted Clearwater's hand when he reached for the stump. The silver fluid seemed to congeal at the end of the stump, and he shuddered as he felt it moving beneath his skin. In the opposite direction, the fluid sprouted outward, and moments later, a metal hand had formed at the end of a solid bar. A final zap caused him to twitch as the emergency prosthesis fully integrated with his nerves.

"Breathe deep."

The kurai shoved an inhaler into Clearwater's mouth.

"Deeper."

Clearwater expanded his chest, drawing the gas as deep into his lungs as it would go.

MULTIPLE STIMULANTS DETECTED.
MEDICAL APPLICATION VERIFIED.
AUTHORIZE SYSTEM ENTRY?
>>YES

"Exhale through your nose. Keep inhaling."

Clearwater began to feel light-headed when the inhaler was finally pulled from his mouth. By the time it came out, he once more had the blessing of stereoscopic vision. He glared up at Jaegda, still dangling in the colonel's grip. Her face was taking on a violet shade. Her hands scratched at her captor's hand, and her feet were still kicking. The kurai in front of Clearwater redrew his knife, and a moment later, he was free as the restraints at his ankles were cut. Ahead of him the kurai broke Taula's restraints before handing her clothes to her.

Clearwater let out a growl. The kurai returned to examine him more and found the probes still embedded in his side from the guard's shock stick. They were promptly pulled out. A second later the kurai stuffed the prison uniform into his hands. While Clearwater dressed, Taula crossed her arms over her chest, watching Jaegda squirm in the commando's grip.

"We're here to get everyone out," the commando said as Clearwater pulled his shirt on. "Stick with us and do as you're told. Understand?"

"Yes sir," Clearwater answered while Taula nodded.

"What about her?" Taula locked eyes on Jaegda.

The colonel faced Clearwater. He used the same hand with which he was strangling the Viss to motion toward Clearwater. "She do this to you?" The colonel shook Jaegda like a doll.

"Yes sir," Clearwater answered.

"We can't take her with us. She'll give us away any chance she gets, and we can't leave her behind to create an alert." The colonel held out his hand, and the kurai who had cut Clearwater loose proceeded to hand over one of his knives. The colonel offered it to Clearwater. When Clearwater hesitated, the colonel jiggled the blade. "Come on, Lieutenant."

How did the colonel know he was a lieutenant? Stupid question. Commando, that's how he knew. Jaegda reached for the blade, but her arms were too short. Clearwater took the weapon.

"Make it quick," the colonel directed.

Clearwater looked over the blade. A kurai long-knife. A sharp, straight edge on the front contrasted the deep serrations on the rear, and a pronounced gut-hook made up the tip. A vicious weapon designed to stab deep, hook tissues, and rip them out. The pommel was a solid sphere, capped in small spikes. Its black blade bore a luster as gold veins spread through the metal. His blood pumped as he looked up at Jaegda, and the colonel lowered her until her feet were just off the ground.

His fingers clenched as he held the blade forward. The sounds of his screaming. The saw and the song she sang while she violated him. All of her pupils were dilated, and her mouth worked silently. He thought of the look in Taula's eyes as she lay on the table, waiting for this Viss to return.

Something snapped inside.

Clearwater let off a shout as he drew his arm back. Rather than drive the blade into her, he struck her face with the spiked pommel, tearing flesh to expose the iron bone of her cheek. Clearwater drew back as Jaegda raised an arm to protect her face. Clearwater used his new metal hand to grab Jaegda's wrist and pull her arm straight. The long-knife passed effortlessly through her elbow. Her mouth flew open, but she had no air to scream. Clearwater threw the severed limb away, grabbed her uniform, and drove the pommel into her face again.

Three hits, four hits, five, and more. Fluids squirted onto his face as the pommel slammed into her left eye. Ten strikes, eleven, and twelve, Clearwater shouted again as he pressed the assault. Fifteen hits, twenty-five, and thirty. Finally he stopped, readying the blade for her skull.

Jaegda hung limply in the commando's grasp. Phosphorescent blood squirted from her arm each time the arteries contracted to pump it, but the sphincters within had finally sealed to halt the flow. Her remaining arm hung at her side while her legs twitched. The assault had collapsed her six nostrils into one. Bone was exposed where the flesh had been torn away at her cheeks.

"Finish it, Lieutenant," the colonel prodded.

It did not seem he had much to finish. Clearwater drew the knife back, but his arm did not seem to want to move. He found himself glaring at the blade. There was something almost pretty about the glowing orange blood coating the handle.

"If you don't finish her, she will revive as soon as I let go. Lieutenant."

Clearwater looked at the colonel and the faceless, featureless faceplate of his helmet. He let out a sigh. "I can't, sir," he whispered as he lowered the blade. "I can't kill a helpless person." He flinched when he felt a hand on his shoulder.

"It's okay, Jonathan," Taula whispered.

Clearwater gazed into her green eyes.

"It's okay," Taula repeated, touching his wrist with her other hand. He did not fight as she slipped the blade out of his grasp. "I can." Taula took a step before swinging the knife with both hands, driving the blade through Jaegda's remaining eye.

"That works too," the colonel remarked.

Clearwater glared at Taula as he processed what had just happened. Her hands strained on the blade. He realized she was trying to twist it but did not have the strength to rotate it through the Viss's iron skull. Finally the kurai who had supplied the weapon came forward.

"I'll take this back now," he said in a digitized whisper. Taula lowered her hands, allowing him to reclaim the weapon. The kurai gave the desired twist before withdrawing the blade.

"Good enough." The colonel tossed Jaegda's corpse like a bag of refuse. "Now listen carefully. We have a plan to get everyone out. We're going to use the ship's tram system to reach the nearest routing point. We'll bounce a signal to the nearest Armadas ship and then transmit everyone out."

Clearwater did not protest, but his mouth hung open. The entire prison? That would never work, would it? The colonel motioned for them to follow and led them to the door. The kurai took point, brandishing his six-barrel gun. As soon as the door opened, Clearwater spotted a pair of guards lying dead beside it. His arm and Taula's quickly found each other as they walked back to the prison.

The colonel and the kurai led them to the entrance corridor, where four more figures waited. One of them wore black khalak, another kurai. Clearwater did a double take at the symbols on the second kurai's helmet. The mark of Iden, but it was imposed over another symbol. A compass rose, but rather than cardinal directions, each of its arms pointed to the symbol of an element. The mark of the technical caste.

The markings on the kurai's helmet were a curiosity. He couldn't believe who else walked in the room. Through the clear visors of their helmets, he saw their faces. Clearwater turned to Taula to find a look on her face no less shocked than his. Vi-Baroness Jenna Prideaux and the Katyusha Twins. What were they doing here?

"Here's the plan," the colonel began as their groups came together. "We're going to go topside to the loading dock. Novin is going to stay here to operate the loading equipment. Andira will summon the trams. Once all the pods are loaded on the tram, Novin will join us up top, and we'll get out of here."

Lady Prideaux embarked on a short bickering session with the colonel, but Clearwater paid it little heed. Two adopted daughters of the emperor and a princess's handmaiden. How did this happen? Was the Imperial Rose here? No matter how many questions he had, he kept silent as the argument ended.

"Let's go," the colonel barked.

CHAPTER
8A

THE *CAUSTIC REVERIE* WAS a new ship, of a new design. One that had been rushed into service before proper star trials could be completed. As things began to go haywire, Panzer hoped that their actions would seem like bugs and malfunctions rather than hostile intrusion. For the moment it seemed to be working.

Cargo trams had been gathered across the ship. Andira had created the illusion of thousands of kilometers of track going offline. Trams and their transponders no longer reported back to central control. Doors across the ship seemed to open and close of their volition. Even power outages had been created in various compartments. All to aid in the illusion of ongoing cascade failure.

Andira moved through the networks like an unseen assassin. Already she had killed more than thirty security AIs and replaced them with her programming. A small error by the Vaar had produced a windfall. One of the ship's engineers had broken protocol. His personal data device was connected to multiple secure networks at once. With this bridge over an otherwise impassable river, Andira's progress was multiplied. But even with this great fortune, time was running short.

Panzer stood on the loading dock for the ship's prison. Each cargo car could hold four cells, stacking them in vertical pairs. The train stretched more than a kilometer through the corridor now. Kassar was perched on the rearmost cell, moving to maintain his position as more were added.

Miss Prideaux and the Twins stood behind Panzer. Novin remained down in the prison, operating the equipment to move the cells. Each cell was moved into a lift where it ascended to a diagonal ramp before sliding out onto the dock where a thin-armed crane waited to load it.

Panzer's mouth worked as it wished for a cigarette, but it was not an option. Andira did not need anything to distract her. So he looked at his NOD, manipulating the armor's systems himself. A pair of needles in the armor jabbed his legs, and he let out a contented sigh as more painkillers entered his system.

ANDIRA: Sir, your levels are becoming toxic.

???: Focus on your work.

Despite all Andira's success, this was taking too long. Less than two hours remained until the shift change. At that point there would be no hiding what was going on.

"Sir," Andira said, "the Vaar are starting to become suspicious about the missing trams. Four maintenance teams have reported their failure to locate. Security teams are being tapped to assist in the search."

"Any indication that they know where they are?" he asked.

"Not yet, sir."

"Novin, how much longer?"

"Sir. Fifteen more cells. Twenty more minutes."

Panzer frowned. "What can I do to help speed it up?"

"One-body job, sir."

For a moment that turned the frown into a faint smile. Novin's respectful way of saying to stay out of his way. Panzer glanced back over his shoulder. The Twins held hands while Miss Prideaux loomed behind them. Lieutenant Clearwater sat on the floor beside the trio. The lieutenant's real hand clung to his metal replacement. Battle was one thing, torture another. That kid had a long road ahead. The hutai scientist sat with him, her arm interlaced with his.[14] The Digital Face Analysis knew it the moment it saw her with the lieutenant. Admiral Gilyard's daughter. Another VIP to get out of here.

He brought his attention back to the Twins. Miss Prideaux watched the loading ramp, tapping her foot as she waited for the work to finish. But the Twins, their eyes were on him. He tasted their feelings. A lot of fear. But also hope. Hope that this was almost over. The minutes passed, and the final cell was loaded. The last car attached to the train was a passenger car, which backed up to become the front of the train.

Once Novin had joined them on the dock, Panzer guided Miss Prideaux and the Twins toward the forward car. He slid the door back and waited until all three had climbed in and sat on the high benches. The lieutenant had trouble finding his feet, even with the help of Gilyard's daughter. Panzer moved to them quickly, pushing her aside and taking the lieutenant's arm.

"Come on, Lieutenant," he said in a low voice. "On your feet."

"Yes sir," Clearwater answered while Panzer did most of the work to draw him up. Once he had that pair situated in the lead car, Panzer panned his vision over all of them.

"Stay here. Stay quiet. If any shooting starts, put yourself flat on the floor."

Both of the Twins nodded, as did Gilyard's daughter. Lieutenant Clearwater offered no real response, while Miss Prideaux clutched her weapon tighter. Panzer slid the door closed before ascending to the top of the car. Kassar had taken his position at the rear, and Novin ascended to the middle. When all were in place, he gave the order.

"Andira, move us out."

"Yes sir."

---

14 The child of a man and lantai is referred to as a hutai, while the far more rare offspring of a woman and a lorim is referred to as a lanen.

With an electrical thump, the train began to move. Panzer lowered himself to a knee as they accelerated. Fifty kilometers to the routing point. Now that the train was moving, Andira had no choice but to step up the failures on the ship. At random she dropped and raised security cordons, emergency partitions, and tram access nodes to disguise her deliberate effort to ensure that no other tram could join them on their route.

Panzer took a breath as a chill ran down his spine. Five kilometers ahead, something was about to go wrong. He forced himself to exhale. Things had gone ridiculously well. Did he have jitters as a result? Or was some fragment of remaining providence trying to warn him?

The train turned in to a new corridor and began to climb. As the hull leveled out, they crossed a four-line bridge running above a massive cargo bay. For kilometers in every direction below, great cubicles, loaded with supplies, filled the space.

Two kilometers onto the bridge, the train stopped. Panzer's boots remained anchored in place, but he fell to his hand as the train decelerated.

"Andira, what happened?" Panzer asked as he pushed himself back to a kneeling position.

"Engineering has initiated a ship-wide shutdown of the tram system."

Panzer shot a look over his shoulder. Kassar and Novin returned his look as they waited for directions.

"Is it part of their troubleshooting or do they suspect we're here?" Panzer asked.

"Stand by."

"Colonel, what's happening?" Miss Prideaux called up as the passenger car door slid open.

"Debugging, sir," Andira answered, allowing Panzer a short breath of relief. "No intruder alert has been posted."

The relief was short-lived. Security was already sweeping to help find the missing trams, and Vaar engineers were painstakingly thorough. In Panzer's mind, the odds of the engineers restarting the system before security stumbled on them were zero. Even less were the odds that they would finish before the shift change at the prison. If the Vaar found them here on the bridge, it was hard to think of a worse place to fight.

"We have to get this thing moving—now."

"Unable to comply. No power to line circuits."

"Damn it," he whispered before looking ahead. "How far to the routing point?"

"Eleven-point-seven-six kilometers."

Too far. His team and Miss Prideaux could make that run in no time. But the wounded lieutenant and the fleshies would never keep up. Worse, once the civilians were out of their cells, anything that caused a panic would make that many impossible to corral.

"We have to get this thing moving," he thought aloud as he looked around the wide-open bay.

"Sir, if we manage to move the train while the grid is offline, it will alert the Vaar to our activity," Andira warned.

"Yeah, and we're fried if we wait for them to find us. Can you restore power?"

"Negative. Manual overrides in place."

Panzer turned toward the rear of the train. "Novin, any ideas?"

"Sir," Andira interrupted, "if they have cut power to the transit system, it is certain that they have cut power to routing terminals."

"We'll eat that meal when we get to it," he shot back. "Novin?"

"The security cars are self-powered," Novin answered. "We need one."

"Andira, can you get one?"

"Negative. Security cars are not controlled by the central network."

Panzer grimaced as he took another look around the vast chamber. Vaar security teams were full squads of fourteen warriors. Neutralize fourteen warriors and skip off with their tram all without being detected? They might get four or five quietly. But never fourteen. Not with only three on his team.

"Andira, who is the captain of this ship?" Panzer asked.

"Shako Joor'tonn, sir."

"Do we have a visual record of him?"

"Yes sir," she answered as an image of the Vaar captain popped into his NOD.

"Do we have any logs of his voice?"

"Stand by." A progress bar popped into his NOD as Andira raided the ship's communications archives to find what he sought. "Voice sampling complete."

"Who is the ship's engineer?"

"Shako-nep Yon'baah."

"Can you connect me to him, and make it look like it came from the bridge?"

"Yes sir."

He nodded. "Do it."

After a pause, a screen opened in his NOD, showing a Vaar at his console. Both eyes had been replaced with cybernetics beneath a crest that bore the level of commendation one would expect for the chief engineer of the Combine's new flagship. Two voices answered Panzer's call, that of the Vaar and Andira's translation.

"Yon'baah reporting."

"Yon'baah," Panzer began, placing special emphasis on the contraction of the Vaar's name. "What is the status of the transit system?"

"Offline, sir," the Vaar answered. If Andira's translation of inflection was correct, the answer was confused. "We are still troubleshooting."

"Reactivate the transit system immediately."

Definite confusion entered the Vaar's voice. "Captain, we cannot complete debugging without disabling the system."

Panzer gritted his teeth. The easiest way to gauge Vaar expression was by paying attention to their eyes. But the engineer's cybernetics betrayed nothing. Was he confused or suspicious? Was he suspicious of the inquiry?

Did he find a fault in Andira's translation or the image she was providing of the captain? No. If anyone made a mistake here, it wasn't her.

"I understand that," Panzer answered in his most authoritative tone, "but you're not the only one on this ship with something to do. Reactivate the transit system immediately. You can take it offline again in two hours."

Yon'baah reached down out of view, and his arm moved as he typed something into a console.

"Did you hear me, under-captain?"

Yon'baah's head shot back up. "Yes, Captain. I will reactivate the transit system immediately."

Panzer nodded before killing the channel.

"Think he fell for it, sir?" Kassar asked.

"I have no idea."

Three blasts of a horn echoed across the ship. Two short, one long. He had his answer.

"Well, it was worth a try," Panzer muttered. "We have to get moving now! Novin?"

He turned in time to see Novin drop off the train and sprint toward the train's rear.

"Sir, all ship's security has been put on alert," Andira announced. "Security is locking down all transit points. Security AIs now on high alert. Detection of my intrusion is imminent."

"What's going on?" Miss Prideaux called from within the passenger car.

"Andira, close all security partitions and all emergency bulkheads except for those between us and our destination. Lock every door on this ship that you can."

"Yes sir."

It may reveal their location to the Vaar, but the priority now was to keep them from flooding the area with marines. Panzer looked behind him to the corridor they used to reach the bridge. The thick partition descended to seal the path.

"What's going on?" Miss Prideaux demanded as she climbed out of the car and poked her head over the roof. He briefly dropped his cloak.

"The Vaar know we're here," he answered.

"Colonel, you have to get us out of here!"

"Working on it, Miss Prideaux," he shot back before dropping off the car.

"Get down!" Miss Prideaux barked at the Twins, practically throwing them to the floor.

Panzer turned to Lieutenant Clearwater. "Lieutenant, can you fight?"

The lieutenant sat up slowly from Gilyard's lap, holding one arm to his ribs. "I need a weapon, sir," Clearwater answered, breathing heavily.

Panzer plucked the RA-117 from his armor and handed it to the lieutenant. He handed the magazines over next, and with no armor to clamp them to, the lieutenant stuffed them into the waistband of his pants.

"Stay here with Miss Prideaux," Panzer directed. "Watch her back.

Twins, stay on the floor."

They nodded, covering their heads with their hands.

"Novin?" Panzer barked as he turned to find him.

A hundred meters behind the tram, Novin was kneeling. His left hand banged down on his knife, and the right guided as he cut into the track.

"Kassar, stay put!" Panzer ordered as he sprinted to join Novin. With a hole cut, Novin was pulling cabling out of the track's innards before slicing it as well. Now with a mass of frayed cabling, Novin took a magazine from his armor before forcing it to belch its power cells onto the floor.

"How long?" Panzer asked.

Novin paused. "Twenty minutes. Maybe thirty."

"How can I help?"

"Splice the cells while I build the adapter." Novin tossed him a wenger rod.

Panzer kneeled and grabbed a handful of power cells. His eyes turned briefly to the dropped security cordon behind them.

"Andira, have the Vaar figured out where we are?"

"Stand by."

The first shots of the coming fight were already being exchanged. In the electric realm, Andira was one against an army.

CHAPTER
8B

SIMMONNE'S MIND WAS A mere step above a trance as she walked back to the colonel's quarters. He was a *Rhinegrave*. And no one told her. Daddy did not tell her. Mom did not tell her. Even Steven did not tell her. Steven had even called him by his true name, yet no one said a thing. He was a Rhinegrave, and Daddy still trusted him to be her vanguard. He had trusted him to be his own vanguard, at least twice that she knew of, and even for Steven.

It all made so much sense now. That was why he was so tall. That was why he had red hair. Dominion parents didn't give their sons red hair—that was a trademark of their ruling family. That rasp in his voice—modification so it would not be recognized. The same with his face and why he did not look like images she had seen. But it was all there. Maybe that was why no one told her. Maybe they all assumed she would realize it for herself.

Back in the quarters, she sat on the couch and withdrew the badge. The decision had been made before he offered. In all the Empire's years, the Mandrakes and the Rhinegraves had never intermarried. Perhaps through extended and distant relations, but never through the line of the rulers. Even when the families had been on friendly terms, it had not been done. To many in the Empire, the Rhinegraves were the only check on the Mandrakes' power. The only people who kept them bound to the Olympian Covenant. To others, the power of the Mandrakes was all they saw to keep the Rhinegraves from trying to dominate everyone and everything. A Rhinegrave prince and a Mandrake princess? The rest of the Empire—the royal families especially—would lose their minds.

Simmonne gently dragged her finger down the front of the badge. Would they really? She would never be a reigning empress. Daddy certainly wasn't going to name her his successor. It would be Steven or Raymond. Soon after, any claim she had to the throne would be gone forever. The line of succession was strictly linear. Neither the empress nor a reigning empress's spouse could inherit the throne unless they had no children of adult age. Steven or Raymond—neither had children yet. But as soon as they did, the linear succession was complete. Her sisters would take the names of their spouses. Her brothers would change their surnames to publicly acknowledge their claim was no more. They would continue to carry the titles of prince or princess, but their actual rank and authority would be reduced to the countships they had cultivated. Or whatever other status they had earned.

The Master was a Rhinegrave, but he was disowned and disinherited. He would never be high king, and no path through her could put him on the throne. Maybe it would not be the crisis she first thought it could be. But if that were the case, then she still had a decision to make.

There was something else she had not considered, and for a moment, she was angry at herself that she had not. The colonel was a provident. Did he know the answer already? According to Daddy and Mom, providence was random, unreliable, and mostly involuntary. Many visions brought random and useless information. But even the good ones brought portents of things that couldn't be changed.

If he did foresee her answer, what did that mean? What would be the point of asking if he knew she would say no? How would that not create something he could not change? All he had to do was not offer. So did that mean she was simply fated to say yes? Simmonne shook her head. She could not let that influence her. She did not even know if he had foreseen any of it.

Simmonne took a breath and stood. She had been in the same dress for too long. There was a large wall-mount printer by the couch and she moved to it. At the optical port, she brought up a spectrum of clothing. It felt almost scandalous to be considering clothes from a printer. Aristocracy wore designer clothes or outfits hand-tailored by their servants. Printed, disposable clothes were for ordinary people. But that was what was available, so she went through the list.

The more she browsed, the more she was drawn to Dominion fashion. After a few minutes, she found what she wanted, and the printer growled. Moments later she held the orange pahri in her hands. A minuscule top and even more minuscule bottoms with a narrow tail-veil. She thumbed the heart pattern on the front of the bottoms. This was what he based her disguise on during their night out. If she said yes, this was how she would dress for a very long time.

She held the outfit tighter, recalling the vision as the night ended. If she took it at face value, even this napkin of fabric would be more than he would permit. Simmonne shuddered before turning and tossing the pieces of the pahri on the bed. With her eyes back on the optical port, she found herself scrolling through dresses. Bigger, heavier, more fabric. More.

The printer required several minutes to fabricate her next order. After enough time to grow impatient, she held the Delseah dress.[15] Padded shoulders capped numerous layers of brightly colored ruffles alternating between

---

15 Bretay Delseah was a woman of the Orion Estate who enjoyed a wildly successful acting career in the Empire's 97th millennium. She was partly known for her elaborate attire that she later developed into a popular fashion line. By the time of her death, her numerous fashion-related companies had made her one of the ten wealthiest women in Imperial history.

blue and pink. She carried the heavy dress to the bed and laid it out, then returned to print one more item. A corissè. Little more than a corset with generous cutouts. Stars forbid the belly or sides be covered. Simmonne laid it on the bed as well.

Simmonne stared at the pieces. The first rule Daddy taught her about negotiation was always to open with an unreasonable request so that the real request would be more palatable. Maybe she could negotiate to something acceptable. To spend the rest of her life nude was unacceptable, but she could stomach a corissè. *Maybe* a pahri, if she had to.

She frowned as she looked down at the outfits. This was stupid. He was Sylvanni—negotiating with a woman was beneath his dignity. Even more when she was a wife. Somehow she doubted being a former prince would make him any more reasonable in this regard. But she wasn't Sylvanni. He knew that. Surely he was prepared to offer some wiggle room.

Willing to follow all my rules.

Simmonne pouted as she glared at the items. None of this mattered. She could spend all day rationalizing, planning, and pre-negotiating. But none of it mattered. This was not just about her or her feelings. Jennifer and Julie had given her their entire lives as her handmaidens. The only reason she had ever sought a Reichsylvannian husband was for them. They lived the way they did because of her. She owed it to them to find something better. To find a life when the days at the royal court were done. To ensure they continued to live as well as she did. Her feelings didn't matter. He was going to die soon. She could not do that to them.

She focused on the Delseah. He would find this least appealing. Best to wear it when she gave him the answer.

A blast of noise filled the room. Simmonne shrieked and jumped, nearly tripping on her high heels. The blast came again. An alarm was ringing through the ship.

"Andira?" Simmonne shouted as the alarm ceased. "Andira, what is happening?"

"Stand by," the AI answered.

A second later, the door opened, and the AI entered in the same body she wore when Simmonne came aboard. The machine practically teleported, rounding the bed in an instant to take Simmonne by the arm.

"Come with me," Andira directed. Whether Simmonne intended to or not was irrelevant, and she barely moved her feet in time to avoid being dragged as the machine led her out of the room.

"Wait! What's going on?" Simmonne demanded, trying to twist her arm out of the machine's impervious grip.

An icon was flashing in her NOD, begging for her attention. Simmonne focused on it, and a screen opened to show the map of the black hole's system. A red icon moved toward them. A moment later, an image of Rhoxx opened.

"Andeera, be reportin'."

"The *Itinerant Hunter* has found us," the AI answered. "They hid behind the singularity to mask their approach."

"Can we be runnin'?" Rhoxx asked as Andira led Simmonne back to the colonel's armory, then shuffled her to the corner.

"Negative," Andira replied. "Both drives are offline for repair. They will be on us before they can be restored. The *Itinerant Hunter*'s forward shields are down. High probability she is preparing to dispense boarding craft. Bringing station defenses online."

A cold sweat broke out on Simmonne's brow as she glared at the icon. It was between the station and the singularity now, making a path directly for them.

"Distortion from the singularity is hindering passive targeting," Andira warned. "Calculating firing solution."

Simmonne fumbled for something to hold until she grasped the quant medallion still around her neck.

"Torc-6s are coming online," Andira announced. "*Itinerant Hunter* is scanning our location."

"Shoot them," Simmonne whispered before her voice steadily rose into a shout. "Shoot them. Shoot them!"

"*Itinerant Hunter* is raising shields," Andira answered. "*Itinerant Hunter* is firing!"

Simmonne cried out in fright and frustration, bringing her free hand to her temple. There were brief flashes on the screen before spheres of distortion expanded from the asteroid currently hosting the ship. Her hand shot out to brace against the wall as she felt the ship—and through it, the station—rock with the impact.

"Firing solution computing. Target velocity, point-one *c*. Range, four hundred light-seconds."

"Shoot them!" Simmonne squealed as the ship rocked again.

"Torpedoes away."

Simmonne watched as six of the asteroids in the belt suddenly lit up. The great rocks had shattered to reveal the torpedoes buried within. The *Itinerant Hunter* never stood a chance. With less than a light-year to cross, the ship's interceptors simply lacked the time. Two of the weapons were struck while accelerating. The remaining four made contact. The four blasts merged into one, creating a single expanding sphere on Simmonne's screen. When the spheres faded, Simmonne beheld only a field of splinters where the destroyer had been.

"*Itinerant Hunter* has been destroyed," Andira announced.

Simmonne started to heave a sigh of relief—until Rhoxx spoke.

"She gettin' off assssault shipss?" the kodaz asked.

"Scanning," Andira returned. "Sensor distortion is high. Scanning."

The question was answered as the assault ships announced themselves by firing on the station.

"Contacts! Four type IV assault ships, range point-one-one light-seconds."

"Can you intersssept?"

"Negative. Assault ships are too close, we are within the blast radius."

"Kittin' now," Rhoxx answered. "Prepare, repel boarderss."

"Acknowledged," Andira replied. "Energizing exterior hull. Sentry drones booting. Kilowire traps online."

"What do we do?" Simmonne screeched. "What do we do? What do we do?"

Andira spun to face her, and Simmonne winced as the machine locked a painful grip on her arms.

"Hysterics will not improve our situation, Majesty." The machine spoke slowly and clearly. "Please remain calm."

The machine's grip loosened as it guided her back into the corner.

"Please remain still," it said, briefly letting go. "I require this."

The machine's hand darted up to Simmonne's scalp to grab her tiara, and she tugged it away so rapidly that the fibers holding it into her hair snapped.

"Ow!" Simmonne screeched, raising her hands to her scalp. "What are you doing?"

The AI did not answer. Instead it moved in a blur across the armory. Its hands went into and out of cabinets, swiping tools and placing them back.

"Assault ships have reached our shield perimeter," Andira said while she worked. "They are attempting to phase-cancel our field."

"Can you ssstop 'em?" Rhoxx asked.

"Negative. Shield projectors were damaged by threading charges," Andira returned. "Assault ships have penetrated our shield perimeter. Expected opposition, nine-seven. Repeat, expect nine-seven boarders."

Ninety-seven boarders? What were they supposed to do against that many? Andira returned, startling Simmonne as it brought its face directly to hers.

"I have constructed a stealth screen from Colonel Panzer's spare parts," the AI explained, returning Simmonne's crown to its previous position. "Please do not deactivate it until instructed."

As the AI turned away, Simmonne looked down at her hands, half expecting to see through them. But everything appeared as it always did.

"It—is it on?"

"Yes, Majesty," the AI answered before its tone shifted. "Transports are reaching deployment."

Through Andira's feed, Simmonne watched as the image shifted to an optical view of one of the assault ships. The long craft bore a pronounced chin, with three backward canting pylons at its tail. Simmonne spotted the doors opening in its side before armored figures began pouring out. There were many, some much larger than the others. Vaar and Viss. The video followed them down until they reached the rusty, cratered surface of the asteroid. Soon they were bounding in the microgravity, riding their thrusters to cross large tracts with each jump.

The ship lurched, and where she would have fallen, Simmonne was caught by Andira's quick reflexes.

"Docking doors have been destroyed," Andira announced. "Atmosphere emergency containment activated automatically."

Simmonne could not take her eyes off the feed. The image switched to another sensor. The docking doors were down in a large crater. One of those camouflaged doors now sported a large, obvious hole. From the angle on some hill, she could barely make out the nose of their ship. The Vaar were descending in the crater from four directions.

The feed switched again. Now she saw from inside the hangar, under the ship. Bright flashes suddenly filled the view. The Vaar were throwing grenades through the breach in the doors.

Seconds later the first wave came in, four at a time. The quartet of one Vaar and three Viss entered in a circle, and their formation became a wedge as they engaged with the artificial gravity of the hangar floor. A second quartet, this one of four Viss, immediately followed.

Why wasn't the AI shooting them? Did the ship not have guns for this? Or were those offline, too? The first group boosted up out of view, but Simmonne could guess where they were—on the ship. The feed switched to another angle. She was right. Several Vaar were on the spine of the ship, converging on a large hatch.

"Rhoxx," Andira called, "it appears they will make entry through the dorsal cargo hatch."

Simmonne clutched her medallion so hard, the metal bit into her hand. Two Vaar carried a large object to the center of the hatch on the ship's spine. The device had the appearance of a large cross, and the pair positioned it before motioning to others. Four Viss deployed cylindrical pods, planting each a few meters from the cross's arms.

"Rhoxx, another team is preparing to make entry at the ventral cargo hatch."

"Underssssstood."

Simmonne's back met the corner, and she slowly slid down the wall.

"Rhoxx?" Simmonne whispered.

"Yess, Majessty?"

"Can you stop them?"

She watched the kodaz's face in the subscreen as his eyes swiveled forward.

"You pretty head not for worry. You jusst lettin' Rhoxx and Andeera be handlin' t'is."

She wanted to take comfort in his words. But against ninety-seven, what could the two of them do? She tried but could not stop her thoughts from flashing back to Avalon. Her guards dying around her. Gunshots, bayonets, and blood. Isis's scream. Lilac rent in two. A tear streamed down her cheek.

Simmonne was jerked back to the moment by Andira's grip, and the machine's cyan eyes stared into hers.

"Your Majesty, the Vaar will reach this room quickly. I need you—"

"No," Simmonne interrupted. "No! No! No! You have to stop them. You have to stop them. You have to do something—"

The machine gave her a firm shake. "You are a member of the Solar Family." Andira spoke sternly. "Please act like it, Majesty."

Act like what? She was not a soldier. She did not kill people for a living. She did not know how to shoot guns or throw grenades. What did the machine want from her? Isis, Lilac, and the others—all dead. All dead thanks to the monsters trying to enter the ship.

"Majesty, stay here and do not move until I tell you. Do you understand?"

For a moment, Simmonne simply stared into the machine's eyes.

"Do you understand, Majesty?"

Her lip trembled as Simmonne nodded.

Andira turned her back. A new image opened in Simmonne's NOD. She could see a corridor now, and the walls were moving. Gaps were exposed and metal racks slid out, each bearing a number of metallic cubes. Cube by cube was dropped to the floor, then the arms retracted. As the walls closed, the cubes began to move. Each of them transformed, brandishing arms and legs. In moments, a collection of boxy automatech stood in the corridor, their arms made of guns now pointing ahead.

Simmonne slowly returned to her feet. Her heart was beating so rapidly, she felt light-headed. Her fingers twitched as she struggled to control her breath. The device the Vaar had placed on the ship's hatch was doing its work. The metal was rippling and bowing inward to form a crater. It would not be long now.

Finally she saw the device fall through, and the warped metal poured into the ship in taffy-like strands. As soon as the gap appeared, the marines on the hull threw objects inside. The feed on the left side of Simmonne's vision, showing the waiting automatech, went blank as the grenades detonated. A second later, the floor vibrated.

"Vaar have entered the ship," Andira's voice warned over the speakers. "Sentry bots are engaging."

Simmonne could still see the Vaar through the external sensor. More grenades, then several of the Viss backed away from the hole as they fired their rifles into it. The automatech were shooting back. Simmonne winced when one Viss's head split in a shower of sparks. The marine's lifeless body fell and slid off the ship.

While the marines continued throwing grenades through the hatch, Simmonne watched another group come into view. These Viss wore much bulkier armor, and they carried heavy shields. Simmonne recognized those shields—similar to what she had seen the Vaar use against her guards. Those Viss advanced in pairs, twelve that Simmonne could see, and began dropping into the hole.

"What do we do?" Simmonne whispered. "Andira? What do we do?"

"Stay where you are, Majesty."

"Andeera," Rhoxx's voice sounded. "I be in posssition. Lower decks."

"Acknowledged."

Simmonne could not hear the sound of gunfire yet, but she could see clearly as more and more of the Vaar poured in from the hull. Her panic spiked when that external view blacked out as well.

"The Vaar have reached the primary cargo lift," Andira reported. "They are advancing into the inner hull."

"Andira?" Simmonne whispered. "Can you fight them?"

"We are in the process of fighting them, Majesty."

That was not what she meant. Simmonne looked at the armory's big, heavy doors. If the Vaar could get through the hull, they could probably get through those, too. What happened when they got in? The colonel had an entire library of guns, knives, and bombs in this room, but Andira had yet to grab one.

"Vaar are moving through the lift shafts, entering all decks."

"I engagin'!" Rhoxx's voice came over the sound of a roar—big guns if Simmonne guessed correctly.

Andira turned to Simmonne and took hold of her.

"Get down, Majesty."

Simmonne was forced to her knees and then farther until she lay on the metal floor.

"The Vaar are approaching the armory," Andira explained. "Do not move. Do not make a sound until I direct you, Majesty. Do you understand?"

Simmonne fumbled with her words.

"Do you understand, Majesty?"

Simmonne nodded.

Andira stood erect and pulled her hair back. Her ears seemed to ripple, and her white hair turned to an almost glowing blue. When the rippling stopped, Simmonne noticed three points now on each ear. A lantai? With her transformation complete, Andira walked away, positioning herself at the center of the armory to face the doors.

ANDIRA: I REPEAT. STAY IN YOUR SPOT, AND DO NOT MOVE. DO YOU UNDERSTAND, MAJESTY?

SIMMONNE: YES.

Simmonne could feel it in the floor—heavy footsteps approaching the door.

"Rhoxx, the Vaar are attempting to access my main core. Prepare for communications loss. Preparing for total lockdown."

"Understandin'!" Rhoxx shouted back.

Simmonne could sense them clearly now, out in the main corridor. At least fourteen minds, all guarded by powerful 4CM systems. Her eyes could not stay still and moved to Andira, the door, then back. What was about to happen? She heard new noises. Something was happening outside.

The doors slid open.

A pair of Viss raced through, their weapons at the ready, and immediately aimed at Andira.

"Please don't hurt me!" Andira shouted, throwing her arms up.

Each of the Viss side-stepped, clearing the way for a Vaar to step in. Two more Viss entered behind him, while more passed the door to continue through the corridor.

"Down!" the Vaar shouted. Andira quickly lowered to her knees.

ANDIRA: STAND BY.

Stand by? Simmonne mouthed the words in her NOD. She froze as the Viss scanned the room, and for a moment, she swore that one stared directly at her. Then she remembered what Andira did to her tiara, and she fought to remain silent.

"Take her." The Vaar gestured to Andira. Another pair of Viss stepped forward to obey. "Who are you?"

"Please!" Andira begged, conjuring tears as she was seized. "I'm just a pet! Please don't hurt me!"

As she was drawn to her feet, Andira's arms were pulled behind her back, and the pair of marines affixed manacles to her wrists.

"Pet," the Vaar mused and then grumbled. "Lantai. Where is your master? Where is the princess?"

"She's dead." Andira sobbed. "My master took her body."

"Where?" the Vaar shouted, stepping closer. Vaar were huge. The creature's waist was as far from the floor as Andira's scalp. His massive hand wrapped around her torso and lifted her off the floor. "Where did he take her?"

"I—I—I don't know. He didn't tell me!" Andira wailed, kicking her legs as she dangled in the alien's grasp.

The Vaar threw Andira down on her side, and a loud ring echoed in the room.

ANDIRA: BE READY.

Simmonne's eyes traded between the Vaar and Andira as she was drawn back to her feet by the Viss that had bound her. The Vaar, meanwhile, took a device from his thigh and held it in front of him.

She watched the Vaar sweep the device side to side, never taking his eyes off of it.

"These readings don't make sense," the Vaar said. "She might still be here. Take this one outside, Sol'ga. Guard her. The rest, continue searching."

Simmonne watched but only caught glimpses of what happened next. One of the Viss nudged Andira with her weapon. Andira took a step forward, and her hands seemed to liquefy. Simmonne watched as the manacles around Andira's wrists fell through her liquid hands. In the time it took for the bindings to fall, Andira spun and grabbed the Viss's weapon by its barrel. The Viss had no time to react as Andira used one hand to force the carbine up into the marine's chin. With her left hand, Andira struck the Viss's right hand, forcing a pull of the trigger.

Blood and electric arcs sprayed on the ceiling. The manacles struck the floor as Andira spun again. Still holding the Viss's corpse, she hurtled it at the lone Vaar's head. Andira retained the weapon as the corpse flew and put a burst of fire through the next Viss's helmet.

Simmonne covered her eyes and pressed her forehead to the floor as the fight continued. The sounds of screaming and gunfire resounded around her. She kept her eyes closed and moved her hands to her ears to try to block it all out. She rolled on her side, curling up into a ball.

No! No! No!

For a moment she was on Avalon again, watching her guards as they died. She was forced to open her eyes to a loud crash less than a meter away. The Vaar warrior had landed on his back, with Andira astride his chest. The warrior's helmet was off, and Andira bore down on him with her pilfered rifle. Simmonne turned her head away just before she heard the gunshot. A second later, she felt a hard grip on her arm.

"Come on," Andira beckoned.

Simmonne began to rise before covering her mouth to silence a gasp. There was a hole large enough that she could have stuck her fist through it. Simmonne could see the back wall of the armory through Andira's forehead.

"Are you all right?" Simmonne asked as she was dragged onto her feet.

"I am functional, Majesty," Andira answered. "Let's go."

Andira did not wait and dragged Simmonne toward the door. Simmonne kept one hand over her mouth as she stepped through the orange blood pooling on the floor. Six dead Viss, one dead Vaar. Andira had more holes in her torso, arrayed in a diagonal from her left shoulder to right hip.

"Where are we going?"

"Rhoxx and I will trap the Vaar on the ship and eliminate them," Andira answered, peering both ways into the outside hall before dragging Simmonne to follow. "You will wait on the station while we neutralize the threat."

In the corridor, Simmonne could hear distant gunshots. Big weapons. They were punctuated by Vaar shouting and many pained screams.

"The ship is now in lockdown. Stay with me."

Andira dragged her down the corridor to the lift. The machine released her briefly to pry the door open. The lift was not there waiting for them.

"Climb down," Andira ordered before grabbing Simmonne by the arms. The machine picked her up and quickly positioned her on a small ladder. "Go."

Simmonne began to descend. Andira stepped onto the first rung and pulled the door closed, then she jumped. The AI fell six levels before hitting the bottom of the shaft. Andira looked up at Simmonne.

"Majesty, please accelerate your locomotion."

"I'm trying!" Simmonne shouted back.

High heels and ladders were never meant to live in harmony with one another. But Andira was unsatisfied with her progress. She squatted before leaping. When she met the wall, she kicked off of it to climb higher, repeating the action until landing on the ladder beneath Simmonne. A second later, Simmonne felt Andira's arm wrap around her.

"Let go."

Simmonne did as she was told, and Andira slid them down the ladder. A moment later, Simmonne was back on her feet as Andira set her down on the roof of the lift.

"There are Vaar on this deck. Stay behind me." Andira threw open a hatch. This time, she whisked the princess up, dropped to the left, then set Simmonne down again.

Andira offered the Viss's rifle. "Hold this."

Simmonne cringed and kept the weapon out and away from her body. Andira used both hands to open the lift's door and then the outer door to the corridor before reclaiming the gun. Once again, Simmonne was pulled forward.

They raced toward a four-way intersection. The path directly ahead had been blocked by a descending bulkhead. But as they neared it, Simmonne could see the circular ripples in the center. There were Vaar on the other side, and they were about to come through. Green lights glowed over the side corridors. As they approached, the rippling metal flowed out, and a Viss jumped through the new hole as they rounded the corner.

With no choice but to follow Andira's grip, Simmonne looked back as the light to the corridor turned red. Something was moving down the halls. The Viss was following them. Simmonne watched the marine round the corner as she raised her weapon but then she stopped. Simmonne let out a cry of shock and disgust when the Viss's body collapsed into segments amid a spray of blood.

"What happened to her?" Simmonne shrieked as they rounded another corner.

"Kilowire trap, Majesty."[16]

They rounded another corner and made a final turn before Andira stopped at a small airlock.

"Here."

Simmonne was pushed into the airlock as the first set of doors opened.

"Wait!" she protested. "What am I supposed to do? Where do I go?"

"We have the Vaar contained on the ship, Majesty," Andira answered. "Find a place on the station to hide while we neutralize them. Rhoxx or I will come and get you when we are finished."

There was little chance to argue, but Simmonne thought to try until she heard more gunshots. Andira staggered as disrupter pulses ripped through her side. Simmonne let out a gasp, covering her mouth as Andira's body fell to pieces.

ANDIRA: GO, MAJESTY!

Simmonne turned as the outer doors opened. The drop-off ahead of her was not a short one. But the closing inner doors behind her reaffirmed her lack of choice in the matter. When the door shut, muffling the sounds of the firefight on the other side, Simmonne peered over the edge. She had fallen farther on Avalon, and it had hurt.

To minimize the drop, she began to climb down and soon found herself

---

16   Kilowire refers to kilosteel filaments generally around one nanometer in
      diameter.

hanging from the airlock. Her hands slipped before she was ready. When her feet hit the hangar deck, she crumpled and let out a cry. She tried to curl up, but pain shot from her feet to her chest, and she hissed. She wrapped her arms around herself, waiting for the pain to fade.

With a deep breath, she rolled onto her back and sat up. There she froze.

Directly in front of her, a Vaar stood near the bottom hatch they had used to enter the ship. Did he hear her? It seemed he did not. His eyes were focused on a scanning device in his hand. For a moment, she forgot she was cloaked and held still, hoping not to attract his attention.

On her hands, she crawled away, then she sensed it. A sensation of curiosity from the Vaar. His head rose, and he snorted a long breath. His head turned briefly to the left and then he turned to her. Simmonne froze again as the blue visors of his helmet turned red.

The warrior made a sound almost like a growl. Simmonne began moving faster, trying to get on her feet before tripping on her dress. Crawling now, she continued to add distance between herself and the Vaar. His hand rose to his helmet. Simmonne allowed herself a single breath when the Vaar turned back toward the hatch.

On her feet, she turned to view the hangar, looking for anything that could be a hiding spot. But aside from the ship, the hangar was empty. She saw a door a hundred meters away. She hiked up her dress and dashed to it. In her panic, she did not think the next step through. It was only after the door opened that she realized her mistake and turned back.

The Vaar beneath the ship spun toward her and the open door. The warrior reached over his shoulder and drew the rifle from his back. Simmonne flinched when she saw the bayonet spring to attention beneath the barrel.

The Vaar walked toward her.

Simmonne flew down the corridor and took the first corner she found. There she stopped, and with her back against the wall, she panted for breath. Her eyes closed as she searched for the Vaar's mind and found that he was coming fast. She held her breath, sensing him stop in the doorway she had gone through.

When she heard his heavy footsteps in the corridor, Simmonne turned and ran.

CHAPTER
8C

THE ALARM HAD STOPPED. By now, every Vaar on the ship was alerted. Clearwater remained in the forward car while the colonel and his team worked. Clearwater sighed nervously as he held tighter to the RA-117. One magazine in the rifle, three more in his waistband. Forty-core magazines, fifty shots per core. Eight thousand rounds. His heart was pumping. No armor, no jamming to foil smart-targeting. No protection against shrapnel or blast waves. His odds of making it through a firefight weren't very good.

Clearwater looked around the car, open in the center with its benches on the walls. Taula sat to his side, nervously rocking back and forth with her hands clasped. Lady Prideaux had thrown the side door open and was panning from the rear of the train to the front with her rifle. Clearwater's eyes moved down to the Twins, who were prone on the floor. They still covered their heads with one hand, gripping each other with the other. Three Solar handmaidens, two of them adopted children of the emperor. Where were the Rose Thorns? He still could not fathom how they ended up here, but some part of him was happy they were here. It was surely the only reason a commando had shown up.

Clearwater took a breath. He was a legionnaire. Whatever happened in the next few minutes, he had a duty—to ensure that the handmaidens left this ship alive.

Clearwater looked at Lady Prideaux. "I'll be back."

He mouthed the words again to Taula when she looked at him, then he stepped out of the car. Few parts of his body did not hurt as he moved toward the colonel and his auxiliary behind the train. He could not even manage a jog but forced himself into a brisk walk.

As Clearwater approached, the colonel's head turned toward him.

"Lieutenant, I thought I told you to remain in the passenger car."

"Yes sir," he answered. "I have no coms. I just wanted to ask if we knew how long."

"Ten more minutes." The answer came from the kneeling kurai. He worked feverishly as he constructed some box-like device that he had hooked into cabling from the tracks.

"Andira, patch Lieutenant Clearwater into our network," the colonel ordered.

Who was Andira? He received his answer quickly as a connection request lit in his NOD. The image that opened stole his breath: a diagram of the ship that zoomed in on their position. From the side and rear, a multitude of angry red icons were approaching.

"Back to the car, Lieutenant," the colonel said.

"Yes sir." Clearwater turned and began the painful trek back, but his attention remained on the screen. Hundreds? No, that was definitely thousands of Vaar closing in. The only thing inhibiting them was the multitude of closed doors and emergency partitions. Nothing that would keep the Vaar away for long.

Scenes of ND-31 flashed through his mind. Brower covered in flame. Sergeant ahn Culan flailing and fighting as enspa tore him apart. Sergeant Dolph the moment he was executed. His brisk pace halted as he fell against the train. The platoon had thousands of automatech—it had tanks, warmechs, artillery. All that, and the Vaar overwhelmed them. Here, they had only five people who could fight. Four and a half, more realistically.

The prosthetic rattled with his trembling body. Not again. No matter what happened, he would not go back to being a prisoner. With Jaegda dead, he shuddered to think of what the next inquisitor might do.

"Colonel," the AI said over the shared com, "at the current rate of progress, we will not restore the locomotion before the Vaar breach this area."

Clearwater heard the colonel's real voice as he answered. A deep, rasping tone, almost a bass-shifted simulacrum of what a human voice should be. "What's their most likely entry point?"

"It appears they will make entry on the lower levels of this cargo bay first." The view of the ship zoomed in and highlighted a small door on the bay's lowest level. There the red icons were massing, halted only by a pair of doors farther out. "Next breach will come from behind." The image shifted to the large partition blocking entry onto the bridge. "It appears the majority of Vaar forces intend to approach from the rear. Based on bay-access records, I believe they may be staging armored units."

"Great," Clearwater muttered. To be overcome by a tsunami of marines was bad enough. Now the Vaar intended to roll over them with tanks.

A loud voice washed over the tracks. "Solar Commandos. This is Captain Joor'tonn. Do you hear me?"

The colonel held up a hand to Clearwater. The kurai on the floor continued working.

"Go ahead, I can I hear you," the colonel answered, his voice digitized again.

"I admire the audacity of your efforts," the Vaar returned. "But you have failed. The entire ship is locked down. My marines converge on you. Surrender, and I promise fair treatment for all members of your party."

Fair treatment? Clearwater looked down at his metal arm. The same kind of fair treatment he was given?

"Your Solar is very good, Captain," the colonel replied, "but your bluff needs a bit more work."

A large spark in the kurai's work area drew Clearwater's attention.

"I wish to avoid any unnecessary losses, Commando. Also I do not wish the prisoners you are attempting to rescue be harmed without purpose. For their sake, surrender."

They were done. The escape had failed. Clearwater turned his rifle over and pulled the bolt back just enough to confirm he had a power core chambered.

"More likely you don't want your entire marine force wiped out trying to subdue a commando team. This is a very nice ship, Captain. It would be a tragedy if it were destroyed before it ever saw battle."

Clearwater cringed at the colonel's answer. Why would he taunt them at a time like this? The captain's Solar was good, and his tone carried incredulity like a native speaker.

"Truly your audacity is remarkable. But it will not serve you here. I do not know how many marines it will take to subdue you, but I know how many I have. You have my offer. Surrender, or be destroyed."

Sweat beaded on Clearwater's brow. He thought of the interior of his cell. His artificial limb let out a tiny shriek of metal scraping on metal as he gripped the rifle. There had to be a solution. He had to get out. He began looking around, seeking nothing in particular. Panicked eyes would always search for some escape.

"Oh, Captain, if it were just me, that *might* be enough."

There was a pause before the Vaar answered. "Explain."

"Do you really think I'd be stupid enough to come on this ship alone? You have no idea how many of us are here. But I'll make you a counteroffer. Withdraw your marines, and I won't detonate the fifty-seven inflation charges my team planted throughout this ship's power network."

Clearwater heard a long breath on the other end. Seconds ticked slowly before the Vaar said, "We all must die sometime."

The captain closed the channel.

"Well he called my bluff," the colonel answered. "Get ready."

Lady Prideaux had come to stand beside Clearwater, and the colonel's head turned to scan the cargo bay.

"All right," the colonel said. "We don't have long before they break in here. Most of them are going to come from behind. Kassar and I will backtrack and take a position to delay them. Lieutenant, Miss Prideaux, stay near the train. You have an elevated position and clear line of sight to their only entry points—"

"We shouldn't divide," Lady Prideaux interrupted.

"Fighting them on the bridge would be stupid," the colonel shot back before pointing at the train. "Those pods aren't armored. We fight them up here, any rounds that miss us go right past, hit the train, and kill civilians."

The colonel reached down to his thigh to pluck the quartet of grenades fixed there.

"I've got to start carrying more of these," the colonel muttered before handing them to Clearwater. "That's all I have. Make them count. Plan on buying Novin about ten minutes. It's mostly cargo bays ahead of us, so if we can get moving, we shouldn't have insurmountable opposition."

"And then what?" Lady Prideaux spat. "What are we supposed to do once we get the train moving?"

Clearwater's eyes darted between them. She had a very good point, but she was a lot braver than he was to address a commando in *that* tone.

"We can worry how we'll jump off that bridge when we get there," the colonel answered before raising his voice. "Novin! Miss Prideaux and the lieutenant will do what they can, but you might have to defend yourself. Kassar! Leave two of your drones here and follow me."

The kurai stood upright, and the wireframe wings on his back extended. Two of the spheres in the frames dropped free before moving to hover overhead. The skin of each seemed to liquefy as the two morphed from spheres to triangular forms, each with a long barrel projecting from its nose.

Clearwater turned from the pair of automatech to realize the colonel was staring directly at him.

"Keep them off the bridge."

Keep them off the bridge? With what? Four grenades and a pair of rifles against a supercruiser's marine contingent? But Clearwater did not ask the questions. Instead he nodded. "Yes sir."

With a motion of his hand, the colonel directed the kurai on the train to drop down and follow. Both sprinted to the end of the bridge where the partition had begun to rise. They dropped and rolled beneath it, and it was closed again.

Clearwater turned to the remaining kurai, Novin, still working on his project.

"I'll take the front," Lady Prideaux said before motioning Clearwater to follow her to the edge of the bridge. She pointed down and across the cavernous chamber below. "It looks like they'll be coming through near the center of that wall. We can put them into a crossfire."

Clearwater listened as she laid out her plan. He could not help but wonder just how much combat training she had. He doubted life in the emperor's court involved many force-on-force exercises.

"What if they try to come from the other side?" Clearwater asked, using his nanites to zoom in on the door she had indicated.

"Check the schematic," Lady Prideaux answered in an annoyed tone. "We're against the hull. No one is going to come from that direction. None of those doors are large enough for a vehicle, so it will just be infantry."

Clearwater rolled his eyes. Fine legionnaire he was not to have realized that already. "Okay," he answered. "How much ammo do you have?"

"Five mags," she answered.

Think. He had to think. He had been given some training in boarding operations. "They'll try to slip through and set up barrier fields so they can mass inside," he said. "Prioritize the generators. If they get enough setup to block our fire, we're done."

"Right." Lady Prideaux nodded. "We don't have much time. I'll be at the front. Good luck, Lieutenant."

"You, too, Lady."

She sprinted for the front of the train and found some relief. It had not occurred to him how long it would take to move on foot from the front to the rear for an ordinary person. She was obviously enhanced, running much faster than any fleshie was capable of. Perhaps she was more than just one of the Imperial Rose's servants.

No jamming, no shields, no armor. Any Vaar who got a good look at him was likely to land a hit. Or many. Meanwhile he had only his eyes and the sensor built into the rifle. One shot from an RA-117 was unlikely to get through a Vaar warrior's defenses. Two might but would not likely be fatal. He set the burst counter in the weapon to five rounds. Now he had to worry about not dying.

Almost every part of his body protested as he went prone near the edge of the bridge. If he could see them, they could see him. So he scooted back until the door below was no longer in view. Instead he used the rifle, looking through his NOD and through the sensor as he edged the muzzle over the side.

He took one more look toward Novin, still working on his device. Either the colonel had a lot of faith in his technician, or a lot of faith in Lady Prideaux. When Clearwater looked back, she had made it to the front of the train. He had seen her, the Katyusha Twins, and Novin decloak in the prison. Her suit obviously had the ability, why wasn't she using it? Did she figure it would be a waste against the number of sensors they were about to face? Or did she not know how to use it?

Back home whenever the Imperial Rose was in the news, they often went out of their way not to mention Lady Prideaux. Most Dominion women wouldn't even touch a weapon unless someone made them. Like handling physical currency or wearing heavy clothing, it just wasn't done. Masculine behavior. Dad had always figured she was a Rhinegrave spy, planted to watch the Mandrakes. Spy or not, he was about to see if she actually knew how to fight.

The red icons in his NOD were coming closer, and Clearwater refocused. By his estimate it was 1,412 meters from the edge of the bridge to cross a diagonal line to the door on the lower level. The RA-117 had a smart muzzle; he just had to remember how to access it. A nervous tremor brought a rattle to his temporary arm.

Visions of ND-31 raced through his mind. The colossi breaching the shield and bringing down the wall. Sergeant ahn Culan, Lieutenant Brower, Sarge. If only they were here now.

"Breach imminent," Andira warned.

With a blink Clearwater focused back on the door and the rifle. He triggered the smart muzzle in his NOD. He highlighted the doorframe, indicating to the weapon that anything that came through was a target. As he zoomed in through his NOD, he saw the edges of the door running like condensation on a cold mug.

His pulse raced, and his hands were sweating, but it all fell away. His breath was heavy in his ears. He did not even feel the recoil as the door fell and he pulled the trigger. His NCP was still working, overclocking his mind as the battle began. The RA-117 let out its distinct sound, like hundreds of strands of fabric tearing with each shot. Nine hundred rounds per minute, but in battle-mind, the weapon's pace seemed lazy.

Lady Prideaux had opened fire as well. Together they welcomed those attempting to come through the door. Clearwater spotted the amber glow as their pulses struck shielding. A pair of Viss in heavy armor led the way. Their bulky power armor gave them the appearance of turtles walking upright. Each of the two held half of a metal frame that formed a dome around them. A third turtle Viss walked behind them, bearing a broad cylinder integrated into the frame by a pair of cables.

Clearwater focused his fire on the generator. The pulses were stopped, and the trio of Viss marched through the twin streams of fire coming down from the bridge. He switched to full auto and let the rifle loose. It did not work. The power shield was too strong.

VI-BARONESS JENNA PRIDEAUX: Boom them! Boom them! Boom them!!!

As soon as he saw the message, Clearwater laid the rifle down and rolled on his side. His right hand plucked one of the grenades from his boot and twisted the handle. A fully cyberized legionnaire recruit had to be able to throw a grenade five hundred meters into a five-meter radius. This was nearly three times the distance. He tried to twist the handle, but it did not move. He twisted with greater force, and the handle grunted at him but did not move.

He had already twisted it.

With a quick shake of his head, Clearwater rose to a knee and extended his metal hand forward while drawing the grenade behind him. He windmilled his entire body into the throw so hard that he fell forward as the weapon left his grasp.

"Boomer out!" he shouted.

The weapon tumbled end over end as it flew out and down. The throw was good but too late. As the Viss moved forward, the shield around them ballooned out. The field rejected the grenade, which bounced. The flanges separated from the grenade's head, each letting off their blast before the main charge detonated. The entirety of the shield bubble seemed to wobble as the vortex charge distorted it. But the weapon detonated above, leaving no open path for Lady Prideaux to shoot through.

VI-BARONESS JENNA PRIDEAUX: Hit them again! Again! Now! Now! Now!

Clearwater cursed as he grabbed a second grenade. On his knee again, he twisted the handle and held out his arm.

"Boomer out!"

While Clearwater drew the grenade back, a Vaar warrior joined the Viss in the shield bubble and raised his rifle. His aim was good. The disrupter pulse barely missed Clearwater's neck, taking instead a piece of the muscle atop his left shoulder. The twin punch of flesh torn away and free static ripping through his muscles caused him to fall on his face. His throw was bad, and the grenade detonated many hundreds of meters from the Vaar.

Still growling obscenities, Clearwater held his wounded shoulder. A trench had been carved through the muscle, three fingers wide and down to the bone. He pushed away the warnings in his NOD. Blood flowed down his back and chest. But nothing vital was hit. His nanites would stop the bleeding.

VI-BARONESS JENNA PRIDEAUX: AGAIN! HURRY!

Two grenades left. Clearwater grabbed for one. His left arm was less helpful now as he twisted the handle and scooted farther from the edge. Once more he drew back.

"Boomer out!"

Clearwater had managed to scoot far enough back that the sharpshooter below had no line of sight to him. But he could not hide the grenade. The Vaar's first shot split the handle from the head. The second shot destroyed the main charge in flight.

LIEUTENANT JONATHAN CLEARWATER: Last one.

VI-BARONESS JENNA PRIDEAUX: Save it! Too much shield now. You won't get through!

Clearwater grabbed for his rifle and used it to peer over the side. She was right. Six more of the turtle Viss had come through the door and set up additional generators. The bubble was more than a hundred meters across now. Vaar and Viss moved in, their weapons trained on the bridge.

Clearwater withdrew the rifle from the edge. If he let it linger too long, the sharpshooter was liable to shoot it, then he would have no weapon. The Vaar had made entry. Now they would progressively lengthen the shield and work their way forward.

Clearwater glanced over his shoulders at the pair of drones the other kurai had left behind. Thus far, they had contributed nothing to the fight. Both merely hung over the train. Their weapons pointed at the Vaar, but no shots were fired. They knew their guns couldn't penetrate the barrier. It would be a waste of ammunition.

When his eyes returned to the Vaar, Clearwater saw more moving into the bubble. Turtle Viss arrayed generators in two columns. With no heavy weapons facing them, they had all the time in the world. Yet more were carrying rods. At the edge of the bubble, they inserted the rods into sockets in the frame. They were building a shielded tunnel. They'd lay it until it reached the bridge, then they'd come up from below. Neither Clearwater nor Lady Prideaux would have a line of sight to shoot until they had made it up.

"What do we do now?"

CHAPTER
9A

ANDIRA HAD CLOSED THE partition that Panzer and Kassar moved to take their positions. The tram corridor ahead continued for just under a kilometer before descending to a deeper layer. There was little for cover here, but the ramp would at least limit how many could muster a line of sight at once. Two maintenance hatches faced each other on opposite sides at the ramp's top. Some would attempt to come through there.

Panzer withdrew the Hellbore from his back and coaxed it to full size. The Vaar were approaching the train from behind. But that would not last. If Novin took too long, they'd circle through other corridors to surround them. If that happened, it was over.

Kassar worked beside Panzer. Long cable coiled many times over his shoulder and across his chest. Kassar drew lengths of the cable before snapping them off and tossing them to the deck. On impact each cable moved, articulating itself to rise into an upright frame. The barriers were completed as each snapped to life to create a freestanding power shield. Four in all for them to shelter behind.

One of Kassar's drones hovered behind him. The other was sent to the bottom of the ramp ahead, where it kept watch over the closed partition. When Panzer linked to the drone to see through its sensors, the partition appeared to be sweating. It was not condensation. The Vaar were using phase resonators to liquefy the partition. Not long now.

Panzer watched the partition shift in its frame. The partition's lean became more pronounced, and finally it gave. The heavy plate of metal fell into the corridor with a thunderclap. The tremor ripped through the deck, registering in Panzer's nerves more than a kilometer away.

The image from the drone turned grainy, and lines of static moved through it from top to bottom. A lot of Vaar and a lot of jamming had been exposed by the door's fall. But he could still see. There was only a handful of armored Viss at the fallen partition, and they scrambled to gather their equipment and clear out. Beyond them, everything was dark. The jamming was too strong for the drone to see through. With more sensor power, he could pierce the darkness but also give away the drone. He refrained.

HELLBORE MASTER CONTROL
MASTER ARM—ON
>>PRE-GUIDANCE

AUTO-PLOTTING . . .

A yellow line projected in his vision, leading from the muzzle of the Hellbore to the ceiling of the ramp ahead. Panzer bent that line in his mind, guiding it to follow the ramp's descent. The data was transmitted to the observing drone. Through its sight, he made fine touches to hook the line parallel to the deck of the lower corridor.

In the darkness something moved, and then it came forward. Silver wheels, segmented, with tubular sensor pods jutting out from the side. Seeker drones. They raced toward the ramp, intent on finding a target, rolling to it, and exploding.

Panzer had to make a decision. He doubted the drones would see him or Kassar, but they would see the barricades Kassar had erected. That would be enough for the Vaar to realize something awaited them.

Panzer fired.

Three rounds from the Hellbore were enough. A cyborg's eyes could register the glint at the top of the ramp. There each shell made a hard turn to travel down the ramp before engaging their MIDs at the bottom. At such speed and distance, they may as well have teleported. The three shells arrived as a team. Forty-five meters of detonation radius was enough. The seeker drones were simply unmade. The violent burst of the shells ripped them into clouds of metal dust. Most of the shrapnel thrown by the blasts came from the floor.

The Vaar knew they were here now, waiting for them at the top of the ramp. They responded with more seekers. The quarter-meter machines raced up the corridor, dozens at a time. Kassar held his fire while Panzer slung one shell at a time. Each detonation wiped a score of seekers out of sight.

Panzer switched feeds to one of the drones that Kassar had left with the train. Lieutenant Clearwater and Lady Prideaux had a much more significant fight on their hands. Should he send Kassar back to help? With the Hellbore, he could keep this confined space locked down for some time. Panzer continued firing in semiauto, smiting the seekers as they came. Kassar's drone at the base of the ramp held its fire, keeping its presence discreet.

This was way too cautious for the Vaar. They favored storm tactics to quickly overwhelm the foe with numbers and firepower. Was this a change in strategy? Or were they just trying to keep him busy so they could surround the train?

Panzer's lapse in concentration allowed a seeker to slip through. The rolling disc hit the ramp at such speed that it bounced a meter on its way up. Kassar covered the lapse. The multi-barrel disrupter in the nose of his drone came to life, shredding the suicide wheel as it reached the top of the ramp. A moment later the Vaar gave a more serious response.

Massive blasts ripped through the corridor as vortex charges tore the maintenance hatches apart. With the hatches permanently open, grenades were hurtled into the corridor. Kassar and his drone handled that. Cybernetic reflexes and drone speed operated together as both Kassar and his drone shot the weapons, catching them as they rolled and bounced. None survived long enough to detonate.

Panzer split the yellow line in his sight, directing each of the new leads to the open hatches. One round for each. The blasts shook the corridor anew. A Viss's arm twirled in the fragments of debris and armor that blew out of the hatches into the corridor.

No more from the hatches. Why didn't his screens show them coming? At current sensor power, he wouldn't see them through the walls. But Andira had a feed on all the ship's personnel beacons. Of course. The Vaar knew there was an intruder in their system. That group had turned their personal beacons off. But with that realization came another question: was the sea of beacons farther down the corridor legitimate?

"Hurry, Novin," Panzer whispered. "They're up to something."

More seekers came, many more. Panzer switched to automatic to ensure that none passed. There was more movement in the shadow zone. Something much larger than seeker drones. Panzer didn't need to see them to know. Juggernauts. Their lives were expendable, so the Vaar would send them to soak the fire in the corridor. As the shadow zone grew, so did the jamming.

???: Andira?

. . . SYSTEM BUSY . . . REQUEST QUEUED . . .

Kassar and his second drone fired again. Small missiles had raced out of the shadows and up the ramp. But as with the grenades, none made it through. Panzer shifted and lay prone behind one of Kassar's barricades. This response was too gentle. The Vaar weren't throwing punches; they were poking at them.

"Kassar. I have things under control here. Go back and help the others."

"Sir—"

"Don't argue. Just do it. Give me one drone."

"Yes sir."

Kassar didn't hide his displeasure, but he obeyed. The drone at the bottom of the ramp remained, transferred to Panzer's control. The other followed Kassar as he sprinted back toward the partition. Andira was too occupied to raise the bulkhead for him, so Kassar drew his blade to cut through the nearby maintenance hatch.

The Vaar had not moved. While Panzer tried to figure out their plan, the Vaar were acting on it. In a pair of maintenance shafts beneath his perch, technicians had gone off-grid. Beneath him they had planted phase resonators. Panzer's first indication of the plan came when the deck vibrated beneath him. His feet sank into the floor.

Panzer tapped his thrusters an instant before the resonators switched off. The floor remembered that it was metal and solidified, catching the tip of his boot and creating a loud screech as he pulled free.

With his feet clinging to the ceiling, Panzer glared down at the floor.

"Clever," he muttered as he looked at Kassar's barricades. Each was half-submerged in the floor. The shield generated bright light that turned the corridor orange, each wasting power as it tried to repel the floor in which it was now embedded.

Simultaneous with the phase resonators, the Vaar had sent another wave of seekers. But behind them, a more significant threat approached. The juggernauts he expected were marching out of the shadow zone. His NOD tagged their markings. The Fourteenth Juggernaut Cadre, the worst of the worst among the criminals condemned to serving as jugs. Each was painted solid black and carried a rotary weapon in each hand.

Panzer ignored the seekers approaching the ramp. They would not see him, but the juggernauts housed powerful sensors in the cobra-like hoods of their helmets. The self-propelled grenades mounted in their pauldrons could be another issue. The jugs came out of the darkness in rows, twelve across.

Confident in the Hellbore, Panzer began setting targeting markers in his NOD. While the seekers spilled over the top of the ramp, Panzer arrayed his targets to blanket the juggernaut formation. The boomers did not see him. While he clung to the ceiling ten meters up, they rolled beneath him. Several stopped to examine the submerged barricades before resuming their search.

Four meters tall and more metal than flesh, the march of the jugs sent a tremor through the ceiling with each step they took. Seventy-two of them had emerged from the shadow zone. Panzer moved his targeting markers with them, waiting to see just how many he was being fed. As they came closer to the ramp, Panzer withdrew the drone halfway up. He fired.

The Hellbore barked twenty shells in a fraction of a second. They skipped at the ramp and plunged down. The detonation of twenty shells created a rolling storm of lightning that flashed both ways through the corridor. Beneath Panzer, the seekers spun like coins, searching for the source of the attack. Panzer was about to send his drone back down when the seekers showed him their newest upgrade.

Twenty of the devices sprang upward, and at the ceiling, they detonated as one. Panzer let out a growl as he was caught in the overlap of three blasts. His feet clung to the ceiling, but it mattered little as the ceiling crumbled. In the time between his fall and impact with the floor, the Vaar sent more missiles up the ramp. They struck the spot where he had been, and he was buried in yet more rubble as the ceiling came apart. The corridor was black now, the overhead lights obliterated by the blasts.

"Sir, are you all right?" Kassar's voice. "I'm coming back."

"Negative," Panzer answered, letting out a groan as he pushed himself up from the floor. "Situation under control. Follow your previous orders."

A heavy electrical cable thunked against Panzer's helmet from above as he pushed himself out of the rubble. Smoke and wreckage clogged the corridor. The seekers that did not jump had retreated to the ramp, silhouetted by the light behind them. There they remained. Kassar's drone had returned to its previous position. Panzer looked through its sensors.

The burst from the Hellbore had devastated the jugs. Not one had kept its head as the rounds detonated above them. But a more resolute target was behind. Now he knew why the Vaar had taken so long to bring real force against him. They needed time to load tanks on a tram and bring them forward. Three of the machines emerged from the shadow zone.

These were not little urban bubble tanks. This was heavy metal. Each of the vehicles hovered out of the shadow zone before setting down on armored wheels. Even in a controlled landing, they rang the corridor like a bell. A pair of small turrets with twin guns perched over the aggressive chin between the forward wheels. Behind them the hull rose with enough armor to form a casemate around a much larger gun. The tank in the middle traded this weapon for a sensor pod.

Panzer reached behind him to grab a heavy chunk of debris and toss it away. Several of the seekers reacted to the motion by swiveling and laying their sight on his position. The three tanks advanced up the ramp, forcing Kassar's drone to press against the wall to avoid their path. While the tanks rolled over the broken bodies of the first juggernaut wave, more moved out of the shadows to follow them.

Now was as good a time as any. Panzer toggled the ammunition feed to the second mag well on the Hellbore, the drum magazine. Two hundred fifty rounds. Twenty-five per tank, two for the seekers at the top of the ramp. For the rest, he set the target markers on the jugs and drew a blanket of detonations into the shadow zone. The tanks would make effective obstructions, so Panzer allowed them to climb half the distance up the ramp.

HELLBORE MASTER CONTROL
MASTER ARM—ON
>>CYCLIC CONTROL
>>MAXIMUM

The Hellbore let out a single sharp pulse, 250 rounds gone in thousandths of a second. The seekers went first, becoming a powder sprinkled into a cloud of fire. The rounds set on the tanks needled through them. The blasts pierced their noses and exited the rear. Jets of flame squirted out the back of each machine.

The shells fired into the zone crippled the jamming source, and the shadows in the drone's sight faded away. Panzer's eyes went wide as he saw just how many Vaar were staged there. Hundreds in formation with their power shields. A barrier field had been erected ahead of the formation. It did not hold as the shells slammed into it, and the Vaar scrambled to escape the hell unleashed on them.

The nanocendiary rounds detonated within microseconds of each other. All light in the corridor turned red. Panzer watched a broken juggernaut take a few steps. It had been torn open, and a gout of flame poured out of its body. It fell against the wall of the corridor and slid to the floor. More fire shot like a geyser out of the center tank as its hatch flew open. A Viss tried to climb out, surrounded by a blanket of flame. The fire reduced her to ash before her legs made it out of the hatch. Even her iron bones burned like dry wood.

Behind the tanks Panzer spotted one Vaar, who had been at the edge of one of the blasts. His shields were gone, but he did not yet realize that he had been killed in the attack. The visors of his helmet were cracked. The warrior threw his helmet off and opened his mouth to scream. He was silent when only fire came out of his mouth.

"That should hold them awhile," Panzer muttered as he stood. He moved to eject the empty drum before stopping himself. It was just a magazine, but it was still Hellbore tech. No reason to leave it for the Vaar to find later.

The flames grew in the corridor. The machines knew where he was but did not approach. The fire expanded the other way, moving with a mind of its own as it sought more to consume. Fire-suppressant gas poured out of the walls and ceiling. It had all the usefulness of oil poured on an open flame. A concussive blast ripped through the hall. Panzer turned his head away as shrapnel peppered his perch.

In seconds the only color was red, and the only sound was the billowing fire. On reflex Panzer raised the Hellbore again to a loud noise. Slowly he lowered it back down as metal fell from the roof of the ramp. He glanced down at the Hellbore.

"Not bad."

CHAPTER
9B

I N THE CORRIDORS OF the unfamiliar station, Simmonne took corners at random. She had to find somewhere, someplace to hide—at least until Rhoxx and Andira could fight them off. Or remain hidden once it was over. A panicked mind did not have the wherewithal to even read the signs on the walls until she was deep inside. The same Vaar was still behind her; she could sense him. He was having *fun*. He was still some distance away but drew closer.

At a three-way intersection, she was forced to stop and make a choice. The sign to the right indicated a cafeteria. To the left, an entertainment room. She went right. A large room might be enough to keep her from being cornered. But still, hopefully it had places to hide. The door rose to give her entry, and she quickly scanned the room.

More than a dozen tables, each with four chairs. At the rear, a terminal of food printers. But no other exits. That was bad. Only one way out. She turned, but the Vaar was coming closer to the intersection she had just passed. The way was already blocked. She retreated deeper into the cafeteria.

Her eyes moved to the printer island. Too obvious. She ran to the rear of the room by one of the tables. There she squatted down and held fast to one of the chairs. The cafeteria door opened again with a hiss.

The Vaar stood in the doorway, both hands on his gun as he surveyed the room. There was a momentary flash before lights projected from the eyepieces of the warrior's helmet. The light cast the image of some sort of grid on the floor and the walls. His head swiveled as he scanned the room.

Simmonne covered her mouth. The AI said the cloak hid sound, but how well? She did not want him to hear her breathing. The Vaar's head began to turn toward her, and she held her breath as the light engulfed her. Mercifully it moved on quickly, then the light vanished, and the Vaar stepped farther into the room. The tall reach of his crest made a scraping sound against the ceiling as the door closed behind him.

"I know you're here, little one."

His voice crawled over her skin. So inhuman. He seemed to growl and hiss at the same time.

"You cannot hide from me," he continued as he slowly approached one of the tables. "Please, come out. My orders are to take you back to our flagship. You'll be reunited with your friends. We won't hurt you. You'll be treated as our guest until we have some dealings with your father. I'm sure your friends miss you. Surely you would like to be there, to comfort them?"

Simmonne watched him take one hand from his gun to pinch a nearby table between his fingers. He turned it onto its side and slid his foot into the space beneath. When he was finished, he grabbed one of the chairs. What was he doing?

The door opened as he stepped back toward it and placed one of the chairs within its frame to block her path. She bit her lip so hard, she flinched. She had trapped herself in this room, but she had to remain calm. Maybe if she could just evade him long enough, he would grow convinced she was not here.

Once he had positioned four chairs in the doorway, he moved to the next table.

"Your people's stealth technology is impressive. But your cloak is imperfect. I will find you."

He moved on to the next table, repeating his actions.

"We Vaar are Prithone's apex predators. Do you know anything about our world, little princess? It is not a place your people would like. Prithone is the land of predators. The small are eaten by the large, and them by the larger. Not even the greatest are safe, devoured by massive swarms of the tiny. Even the plants want your flesh. But to us, it was home. Hunt and devour, be hunted, and be devoured. Your people's stealth technology is impressive. But not enough."

He lied. She did not sense it, but he had to be lying. If he knew where she was, he'd be on her. She heard a series of tiny clicks and saw colored lenses moving over the visors of his helmet.

"Our eyes can see the spectrum. From radio waves to gamma rays. But I cannot see you."

He moved suddenly, flipping a table to crash against the wall before his hand seized at the air beneath. When he found nothing, he continued his taunting.

"Our tongues can sense the magnetic field of a living body at hundreds of paces."

Two hatches opened in the face of his helmet, allowing a large tongue with broad forks to protrude from it. He retracted his tongue, and the small port sealed.

"I cannot taste you."

She tore her eyes away from him to look around. She was going to run out of tables. She did not know if having an obstruction between them helped, but she would rather have it than not. The printer station was the only other place to go.

"Our brains can cross-reference our senses—impose them over one another. We can 'see' sound, 'hear' light. These are not helping. But so many species, so dependent on their eyes and ears. They forget the other senses."

She heard what sounded like a long puff of air—a little louder, and it would be wind.

"I *smell* you."

She emitted a quiet whimper behind her hand and subconsciously slid a bit farther from him.

"I can smell your . . . what is the word?"

Fear. He wanted to say fear.

"Perfume." He nodded to himself. "Yes, I smell your perfume. Your species must have quite the weak sense of smell, if such an overpowering odor is needed. I can't seem to pinpoint it. But I know you are in this room. You are very close. I will find you soon."

She wanted to run. She had to get away. But where would she go? She would never get through the doorway without moving the chairs. Then he would know exactly where she was. Either way she had to move, now. She crawled toward the printer island.

"You're moving."

His words brought her to a stop, and she heard the gust again.

"I must tell you, the Crykeeper will not be coming to save you."

She forced herself to keep going, rounding the island until she was kneeling behind it. She peered around the edge at him. He took several steps, side to side, sniffing the air with each.

"We know he's coming," the Vaar said, a smile evident in his voice. "We knew when we failed to capture you that he would come to rescue your servants. He is walking into a trap."

"No," she whispered, covering her mouth again to quiet herself.

"There are millions of infantry on that ship. They know he is coming. I wanted to be there, you know. He caused us many problems. I hope he dies well. I hope he dies. If they manage to capture him alive,"—the Vaar shook his head—"they will take him back to Prithone and dissect him alive. Sew him back together to heal, so they can study him some more. I have seen the results. I would not wish that on any warrior."

She shook her head quietly. They couldn't kill him, they couldn't. He was, maybe not invincible, but something. But still, millions of Vaar. What could he do against so many?

"Surrender to me," the Vaar said. His arm extended and his tone changed, almost conciliatory. "Surrender to me, and I will tell my superiors that you surrendered in exchange for sparing him. They won't like it. They will be angry with me. But they will feel compelled to honor the terms we have negotiated."

She rose slowly to her feet but continued clinging to the island. The Vaar flipped the table that had been her previous shelter.

Millions. Even he could not fight so many.

"But you must do it soon," the Vaar prodded as he tipped the final table. "If we wait too long, we will not have time to return before it is too late."

Maybe, maybe if they were all captured. Maybe he could figure out some way for them to escape. Or, maybe they would stay until Daddy paid a ransom. But they would all be alive.

She leaned around the island. "How do I know you'll keep your word?"

She was not sure if her voice would leave the cloak, but she was soon answered when his head turned toward her. She backed away slowly as he came to the island and rested one of his giant hands on it.

"Our people are not so different," he answered before sniffing the air again. "We both war, and we fight to win. We use deception and trickery to gain an advantage. But when we give our word, it is good. To ignore the terms of a surrender is a crime against civilization."

He motioned with two fingers, trying to draw her closer.

"Come now. We might be able to save the two still fighting my warriors. Turn off the cloak. Let us negotiate face to face."

Like hell she was doing that. Then he certainly would have her. She took another step away from him. What should she do?

"Surely you don't want him to die," the Vaar pressed. "After he saved you so valiantly from us, on Avalon."

Simmonne froze, only able to whisper, "You?"

"Oul'sor, the old fool ruined everything with his tantrum. His lust for revenge. But he is not here now to bend victory to defeat."

"You were there?" she asked, regaining enough composure to tiptoe to the side.

His head went in the wrong direction. He could not pinpoint her sound, at least not exactly. The Vaar nodded his enormous head. "Yes. One of your guards stabbed me in the knee. It still hurts, even though it has healed. A lesson that even a small thing can still bite."

A tear welled in her eyes as she recalled it. Lilac—she had stabbed with her bayonet a moment before this monster cut her in two.

"I lost many friends on that mission. Warriors who had fought at my side on countless worlds. Some I trained with as a child. How many more must the two of us lose over this? Please, come with me. The warlords will negotiate with your father, and then you will go home. Far from the war, neither of us will lose more in this chase."

"I'm not going anywhere with you," she whispered, shaking her head and backing away until her back met the wall. She could no longer see him in the present. Only the memory of him looming over Lilac as his bayonet violated her flesh.

"Please, let's end this."

"Somehow, I'm going to watch you die." She did not know if he heard her, but he kept his hand out. Waiting for her to come to him.

"Please," he repeated.

She looked back at the door and thought of an idea. Simmonne slid against the wall, trying to move far enough to escape his peripheral vision. She was circling behind him as he lowered his arm, realizing she wouldn't accept his offer. From behind him she took hold of a chair and turned toward the door. She took a step, then hurtled the chair with all of her strength.

Her dress was too long. Without the height of her heels, she stepped on it, tripping and falling to the floor. But the chair crashed into those in the doorway. On her stomach she turned her head to see the Vaar whip around and face the door. He came forward and she froze. His metal-clad foot landed, catching the sleeve of her dress and pulling it taut.

She could not stop herself from curling up into a ball as his other foot passed over her. The heavy footfalls sent tremors through the deck, registering in her bones as he barreled to the door. He stood at the door now, glaring into the hallway and sniffing the air again. She had hoped he would go farther, but he didn't. This was her only chance. With all of that armor on, maybe he would not feel it if she slipped by him.

She rose onto her hands and began to crawl toward him from behind. Her hands trembled. He was as wide as the door; there was no room to go around. She had no choice but to crawl beneath him. She could only pray he would remain still.

She moved closer before drawing herself into as small a form as possible. Between his ankles she heard him sniffing the air more intently. Just a few more steps. His visors turned down to face her. His hand came down, and she threw herself forward.

Her foot came within the circle of his hand, slipping out an instant before it closed. She hit the floor and slid. Paralyzed by fear she could only look back at him.

"Very clever, little one."

He turned. *He turned!* His back was to her, now looking back into the cafeteria. He thought she retreated in. Or was this a trick? She allowed herself a breath when he took one of the chairs and placed it back at the door. He thought she was inside, but it would not last.

She rose to her feet.

Run, stupid! She forced her feet to move. With his sense of smell, he would realize his error soon. She turned her back to him and hoisted her dress as she made for the intersection. She had to find somewhere to hide. Somewhere his nose would not help. But where? Where could she go?

CHAPTER
9C

C LEARWATER REMAINED PRONE ON the bridge where he watched his doom come inexorably closer. The marines were rapidly constructing their shield tunnel that stretched through the cargo bay. Already it was close enough that Clearwater could not see its end without raising his head, exposing it to the sharpshooter below.

The tunnel the marines were erecting was tall enough for a Vaar. There was enough width for up to four Vaar or twelve Viss to cross through it. With each segment added, additional generators were installed in the foot-hold bubble. The bubble in turn had widened as more and more marines staged themselves at the mouth of the tunnel. Vaar and Viss both. The new Viss were equipped in much more agile armor than the turtle-like suits of those installing the tunnel.

Clearwater nudged the barrel of the RA-117 over the edge. The sharp-shooter saw it. Clearwater heard the loud snap and felt the tremor in the metal beneath him as the pulse struck the place where his weapon had been. Hot debris came down on the back of his neck. He barely noticed.

The construction brigade had at best another hundred meters. Then they would be under the bridge. Clearwater reached down to the final grenade tucked in his boot and transferred it to his waistband. He could pick the right time and drop it on them as they massed below. For all the good it would do. With so many marines, it would do nothing to stop them. He had a better use for it.

He would not let them take him alive. They would not put him back in that cell, back in the torture chamber. If it came to that, the grenade was his deliverance. They wouldn't even be able to reanimate him this time.

If he had his AICES, he could make a roadblock in their tunnel for a little while, but all he had was his rifle. Even if he survived the fall down there, he would not last for very long.

Just a few more minutes now. The Vaar would come up from below and try to swarm them. Clearwater scooted back from the edge, and once sure he still had concealment from below, he shifted to his knee. He turned in time to see Novin take on a hunched stance, holding his jury-rigged box with cables pilfered from the tram line snaking out of it. The kurai strode forward, keeping the train between himself and the Vaar's edge of the bridge.

Clearwater could not keep up. His body pulsed with every step he took. While the kurai sprinted, Clearwater could only manage a slow jog. The intense pain seemed determined to convince what little remained in his stomach that it wanted to come out, each footfall a new strumming on the harp of agony.

By the time Clearwater made it to the front of the train, Novin was at work again. The kurai lay half in and half out of the lead car. His head was under the console as he worked to wire his box into it. Clearwater never caught the kurai's rank, so he just used the name.

"Novin?" he wheezed. "How long?"

"Ten minutes," the kurai answered. "Maybe twelve."

"Jonathan?" He turned at the sound of Taula's voice to find an expression of barely subdued fear. "Are we going to make it?"

He wanted to say yes. To give her that hope. But he did not have the strength to tell a good lie. Instead he shook his head. "I don't know. Stay on the floor. Don't get up."

Taula nodded slowly before sliding out of her seat and down to the floor. She kept her eyes on Clearwater for a moment before lying flat by the Twins. Clearwater was not sure which Twin it was, but she reached out to take Taula's hand.

Clearwater limped toward the nose of the train, scanning for Lady Prideaux. He found her hunched down and leaning against the nose of the car. Clearwater had to look twice as he moved around to see her face. A faraway look filled her eyes, her mouth hung open, and her skin was as pale as bleached fabric.

He began to reach for her, but his hand seemed to stop of its own volition. Sylvanni upbringing. One did not touch someone higher in the peerage uninvited. It took a conscious effort to force his hand forward to her shoulder.

"Lady Prideaux?" he asked. "Are you all right? Are you hit?"

Her lips moved slowly, and her vacant expression remained as she whispered, "They're afraid. They know something is about to happen. I can't keep them calm. There's too many. I can't . . . suppress it all." Her breath became more rapid, and her tone more urgent. "I can't keep them subdued. The children, I can't—"

"Lady Prideaux?" Clearwater shook her gently. "They're coming. I need your help."

Her eyes closed, and she drew in a deep breath. The color slowly returned to her cheeks. When she opened her eyes, her expression quickly became one of disdain as she looked at the hand on her shoulder. Her gaze quickly moved to Clearwater's eyes. He withdrew his hand.

"Are you okay, Lady Prideaux?" he asked.

"I'm fine, Lieutenant," she barked. "I don't need to be coddled."

Clearwater took a step back. She raised her weapon overhead with both hands, briefly using it to peek over the edge of the bridge.

"You should head back to the rear," Lady Prideaux remarked as she shifted farther back, ready to use the forward car as cover.

Clearwater gazed toward the train before looking back at her. "I don't think that's a good idea."

"We could put the Vaar in a crossfire," Lady Prideaux rebutted.

"Yeah, but we'll also be shooting at each other," Clearwater protested, pointing toward the end of the train.

Lady Prideaux turned back toward him as if to argue before she saw what he meant. "Fine. Watch my back." She moved farther behind the nose of the car. Suddenly her head went up, and she cocked it to listen. "They're coming."

Clearwater raised his rifle. She was right. A long tunnel of Vaar and Viss flowed out of the door and through the shield tunnel.

"Novin. Company is coming."

"Twins! Don't move!" Lady Prideaux growled. "Whatever happens, stay down!"

"Taula, stay with them," Clearwater added. He took a breath. He had a duty. He'd defend them as long as he could, but he was not going back.

"Here they come," Lady Prideaux whispered.

From beneath the bridge, a dull roar traveled through the air. Thrusters.

The first shots came from Kassar's drones. Clearwater had forgotten they were there until he heard what sounded like the buzzing wings of thousands of insects. They had cloaked themselves, but their presence was felt as Vaar drones raced up over the edge of the bridge. The silver spheres shattered and fell, swept from the air by twin streams of fire.

Stun grenades came over the edges with the drones, and a handful slipped through. Clearwater winced at the blinding flash as the weapons detonated at no less than six points along the train. On the edge of one blast, he recoiled from the electric current that danced on his skin.

Lady Prideaux was the next to fire. She rotated, and Clearwater did his best to dodge when she fired on a target behind him. The waste heat of her disrupter pelted his face as the sizzle in the air announced the pulses racing past his head. Clearwater spun to face her target.

Two Vaar and two Viss. They had landed together ahead of the train, not five meters away. The Vaar were in front, each with a raised power shield in one hand and a rifle in the other. The Viss were behind. Clearwater brought his rifle up and added his fire to Lady Prideaux's. Together the automatic volley broke through the power shield. A Vaar let out a gargle as the pulses ripped through his body and he fell onto the bridge.

Clearwater had wondered how intent the Vaar were on recapturing him alive. He had his answer as the pair of Viss stepped out and fired their weapons. Clearwater turned his head, flinching as a torrent of fluid collided with his chest and neck. The Empire called it *suppression foam*—whatever the Vaar called it, it worked the same.

The fluid hardened, and the arm Clearwater had raised to shield his eyes was now locked in place. When he tried to move it, an electrical shock ripped through his muscles. The more he forced it, the stronger the shock became. The electrical current alone could not stop a military-grade cyborg. But the hardening of the foam did the rest. He fell to a knee as his eyes sought Lady

Prideaux. Her situation was just as dire. The Viss targeting her had effectively glued her to the nose of the lead car, with most of her body already encased in the hardening foam.

No! No! No!

The foam had covered his mouth, so he could not scream the words. His left arm could still move, and he reached for the grenade. His access was denied; the foam had already formed a solid shell around it. The pressure of the torrent on his back grew as the pair of Viss stepped closer, continuing to hose them down.

Disrupter pulses ripped out of the foam and into the distance as he squeezed the trigger. He couldn't aim and hit the walls and ceiling. *No! I won't go back!* His muffled scream escaped the foam as he tried to force his arms together. If it was like Imperial foam, he was strong enough to break it. He had to concentrate.

A temporary deliverance came as the twin streams of foam elevated. The one targeting Lady Prideaux sprayed onto the roof of the lead car. The one aimed at Clearwater arced over him to the deck meters ahead. To his side he saw Lady Prideaux, with little more than her eyes and forehead still exposed. Her eyes were rolled back into her head, her eyelids twitching. Psionics. She was doing it. Time—she bought time.

As the electric currents intensified, he ignored the warnings in his NOD. The muscles in his right arm and chest drew so tautly, he was sure they would rip apart. He could not keep up the intense pressure for long, but he heard the loud pop in the foam, and with a fresh roar, he forced his arms together. The foam around his torso crackled and fell away. With his knee still glued to the deck, Clearwater pivoted at the waist, extending the rifle with one hand.

The RA-117 barked. The head of the Viss closest to him split like a large fruit thrown against the ground. Her body fell, then Clearwater swept past the lone Vaar to the second Viss, who still wrestled with her rebelling weapon. Shots meant for her head instead found her neck, separating her head from her body.

The entire time, the lone Vaar still standing was firing his disrupter. His attempt to strike the invisible drones filled the air with the sound of their fire. But now with a free disrupter in his face, the Vaar turned to Clearwater.

Someone beat them both to the shot. To protect his head, the Vaar had raised his power shield high. The shots had targeted the warrior's exposed feet. The Vaar howled as his left foot was shredded, and he fell to the deck. The warrior's limbs flailed, and for a moment, his shield did not obstruct his head. The warrior's reward was an automatic burst through his skull.

Clearwater turned back to the lead car. He could no longer see Novin. Was he the one who fired? Lady Prideaux!

Clearwater faced her, still glued in place, her mouth and nose covered. He placed both hands on the deck. He grunted, his face twisting with strain as he pressed against the deck. The foam popped, and he was free. He rammed the butt of the rifle into Lady Prideaux's foam. He slammed the weapon into it again and again before the hardened shell finally crumbled.

Lady Prideaux fell forward, and Clearwater grabbed her arms and quickly sat her upright against the car. Her head rolled around her shoulders, and she struggled to focus on him.

"Lady, are you all right?"

"Yes—4CM," she whispered. "I'm fine. Keep fighting!"

Clearwater nodded and reclaimed his weapon before aiming down the bridge. What he saw was pandemonium. At least fifty Vaar and as many Viss rocketed up the left side of the bridge. The Viss retreated with their less-lethal weapons, leaping over the side while the Vaar fired like crazed men, desperate to hit the invisible drones that were thinning their numbers. Each time one fell, they all moved together, shooting a new patch of open air. Dozens of bodies already littered the deck. Those standing seemed almost to dance, constantly shuffling their feet. All they could do with minimal cover to make difficult targets of themselves.

Shots beside him drew his attention. Miss Prideaux had reclaimed her SMG and was firing down the right side of the train. Clearwater tucked himself further into the cover offered by the car. Novin had been on this side, and now Clearwater couldn't see him. He held the rifle away from his chest, aimed through the gun cam, and fired.

The nearest Vaar was ten meters away. The first three pulses broke through his shields. The fourth round tore from his armpits to his thighs and left him on his hands and knees. At first the Vaar were so preoccupied with the drones that no return fire came. So he switched to full auto, held the trigger, and swept the barrel. That garnered return fire.

"Reloading!" Lady Prideaux bellowed as she withdrew behind the car. With one hand she ejected the magazine. But when she reached for the next, she found it still glued by foam to her gut. Clearwater winced as she let out an ear-piercing shriek and tore it free. Within moments, she was back to firing.

A bright flash of sparks erupted over the train's tail. The Vaar had found one of the drones, and Clearwater caught a glimpse of it as it fell onto the train.

"Novin, you've got to hurry," Clearwater murmured before letting off another stream of fire.

Clearwater flinched and recoiled as sparks and electric arcs sprayed in front of him with return fire. One of the incoming bolts struck his artificial arm, bisecting it at the wrist. He leaned back behind the car, staring at the glowing tip of metal.

"Shit," he whispered as he clenched his right hand. He had flinched and dropped the rifle. Now it lay more than a meter away, too far to reach for it without exposing himself to the fire still coming in. Disrupter pulses continued to fly past. Some struck the wall far ahead, and others struck the deck beside him. Certainly some were suppressing him, while others were advancing toward. He had no choice. Clearwater raised his right hand, hesitating before leaning out for the rifle. It was a mistake, and he paid for it.

The first pulse tore a fist-sized hole through his shoulder. The second bored a hole above his waist. The third was content to take the top halves of his ring and little fingers. The only sound he could manage was a gargle as his face slammed to the deck. His head whipped around as a pair of hands jerked him behind the car.

"Lieutenant?"

CRITICAL INJURIES DETECTED—LUNG TRAUMA

CRITICAL INJURIES DETECTED—RIGHT KIDNEY

CRITICAL INJURIES DETECTED—INTESTINES

LUNG TRAUMA—REPAIR IMPOSSIBLE. SEALING RIGHT LUNG . . .

RIGHT KIDNEY DESTROYED—REPAIR IMPOSSIBLE. SEALING BLOOD VESSELS . . .

INTESTINAL TRAUMA—SEALING WOUNDS . . .

Clearwater was not sure which hurt more. The large holes torn in his flesh, the heat and electric discharge, or the new burning as his nanites tried to control the wounds. Yet more pain for a body that already bore too heavy a load.

"Lieutenant!"

Lady Prideaux was practically in his lap, glaring into his eyes.

"Lieutenant, can you fight?"

Clearwater glared down at his right hand. Even as foaming blood leaked from the corners of his mouth, he nodded. His brain and his trigger finger were still talking. It curled on command.

"*Rifle*," he managed to wheeze, testing his trigger finger again.

Lady Prideaux looked at the weapon and raised her hand. The gun snapped from the deck to her grasp. Psion. Stupid, he knew she was a psion. Why didn't he just ask her to get it for him? Because he was stupid, that's why. She pressed the rifle to him.

His right shoulder was useless. He no longer had a left hand. His right arm bent at the elbow and he took the handle. Lady Prideaux leaned forward, wrapping her arm around him and firing her weapon down his lane.

"If you can still fight, you better do it now," she said before returning to her side.

His shoulder was useless. He raised his left arm, using the bar of metal to brace his right wrist and bring it up. How was this going to work? How could he aim out without exposing enough of himself to catch more shots?

"What is going on?"

Disrupter fire still filled the air, but none of it came their way. Unable to do much else, Clearwater flopped his right arm out until the rifle lay on the deck, pointing downrange. Every one of the Vaar he could see had their backs to him, and their weapons alight. Through the wall of bodies obstructing his vision, he caught sight of the black figure in bladed armor.

There was something awesome and terrifying in the kurai's speed. He came on too fast to simply run. Instead he bounded from one foot to the other in a zigzagging motion. He came in uncloaked to draw their fire, and indeed he did. At least fifty Vaar fired at him. So very few hits, so few pulses to illuminate his shielding. Despite FTL weapons, the plurality of their volleys missed. His body moved faster than their arms could zero their aim.

No one moved *that* fast. Even legged automatech didn't run that quickly. But the kurai, Kassar did. Kassar's torso moved like an auto-aiming turret when he stopped. Six barrels in his flakker, six explosive-tipped rounds for each target. Each shot produced a thunderclap that echoed across the bridge and turned his target into a mist of splinters and phosphorescent gore.

Clearwater watched an engine of death turning its wheels. In those moments he understood why the Corps was so feared. Why people spoke of it in whispers and rumor. Kassar was back to his bounding sprint in less than a second. The Vaar in Clearwater's lane backpedaled as they sprayed with their weapons. As Kassar closed in, he fell into a slide. Under the aim of their barrels, he fired six rounds so rapidly that the average ear would only hear one. His shots neither haphazard nor misguided, each found its mark and pulped the target.

Against the seventh Vaar, the kurai hurtled his weapon ahead. Betrayed by his reflexes, the Vaar raised his rifle to deflect the mass coming for his head. It was all the time Kassar needed to explode off the deck and drive a blade into the warrior's skull. Kassar had reclaimed his weapon before the Vaar hit the deck, and in the same motion, he reloaded and bounded for the train. The kurai's foot met the top of one of the cells as he leaped over to share his slaughter with the Vaar in Lady Prideaux's lane.

"Holy hell," Clearwater wheezed an instant before the kurai was back on his side, letting his flakker speak for him. The tide of Vaar rising to the bridge was slowing. A group of four Viss rocketed up onto the bridge. Two landed ahead of him, and two landed behind. The two in front were dead before their feet found the floor. The two behind opened fire.

As the rounds slammed into his back, Kassar turned and hurtled a knife. He threw it too hard. The blade had so much velocity, it deflected on the shielding of the Viss he targeted. Undaunted the kurai charged the pair, who shuffled away as they continued to fire. Clearwater saw the puff in Kassar's torso—the kurai had been hit. Kassar did not seem to care. In almost no time, Kassar had closed on them, flipping his weapon to hold by the barrels. He used the handle like a hook, dragging one Viss's feet out from under her. In almost the same motion, he spun on one heel, raising the other to strike the Viss still standing.

While the second Viss staggered, Kassar drew the first onto her feet and rammed his shoulder into her. Clearwater heard the scream as the blades of the kurai's armor pierced hers and sank into her flesh. Kassar used both hands to force her weapon toward the second, then that Viss died to forced friendly fire. Kassar hurtled the Viss off the bridge. He kicked his weapon back up to his hands, reloaded, and took her head for good measure as she fell.

Kassar performed his turret impersonation once more, clearing the remainder of the Vaar on Clearwater's side.

???: I'm going down. Stay here.

Clearwater did not know what else to do, except try his best to raise his thumb in acknowledgment.

That wasn't power armor he was wearing; that was a warbody. It had to be. As Clearwater thought it, Kassar flung himself over the side of the bridge. In seconds he heard gunfire and screams coming from the marines below. Clearwater almost felt sorry for them. Almost.

CHAPTER
10A

PANZER WATCHED THE SEA of fire he created. The Vaar grew desperate in their efforts to combat the flames. Holes the firefight had torn in the floor allowed the nanites to spread through cabling, temperature insulation, and more to create fires in the walls and beneath the floor.

A few of the Vaar's attempts to quell the flames had verged on comical. Their first solution was to release suppressant gas. Rather than smother the flames, the result had been a fuel air bomb. When that did not work, the Vaar took their normal brute-force approach. *More* fire-suppressant gas. As one might have expected, the result was an even larger blast to rip through the corridor.

When that did not work, the Vaar tried depressurizing the entire chamber. That was a bit concerning. The nanites did not need oxygen from their environment. But if the Vaar could depressurize this chamber as quickly as they did, it meant they were successfully wresting control of this area away from Andira. The effort had not been completely futile, and some of the tiny machines had been sucked away as the air was pumped out of the area.

In truth it was the Vaar's fear of the unknown fire that held them back. If they were to set their shields to high opacity, most would probably get through safely. But the Vaar did not know that. A little over a kilometer down the corridor, they had set up new equipment. They had deduced the source of the flames and were broadcasting directed EMPs.

"Come on, Novin," Panzer mumbled. They had to have a significant fight going on behind him. If Kassar had arrived and found everything under control, he would have come right back. Another EMP registered in his NOD. The effort was as futile as the fire suppressant—and a sign of desperation. The nanites were too small. Even if they hadn't been hardened against such hazards, they were simply too small to absorb enough of the pulse to be damaged by it. The Vaar would have better luck throwing vortex grenades into the flames to gradually disrupt the machines.

All the same, the flames began to ebb. They could not burn the bond-forged metal of the floor and walls. Everything that could be burned, had been burned. The machines could only reignite and reburn ashes so many times.

"Come on, Novin."

Perhaps he should go back. Maybe things were worse in that room than he expected. He looked back at the flames. It was too late to do that now.

The flames would not last much longer. His indecision had cost him the opportunity.

"Sir."

Panzer let out a calming exhale when he heard Andira's voice. "Welcome back."

"Sir, the Vaar have purged me from the life-support systems."

Panzer nodded. "Yes, the lack of air was somewhat of a hint," he quipped as another EMP flooded through the chamber.

"Sir, at the rate the Vaar are purging me from their systems, I will not be able to hold the transit system much longer."

Panzer's lips twisted into a frown, and another EMP registered in his sensors. "How are the others doing?"

Panzer noticed the lag of several seconds before she answered. "Jennifer and Julie Katyusha are uninjured. Taula Gilyard is uninjured. Vi-Baroness Prideaux has sustained minor injuries. Lieutenant Clearwater has sustained critical injuries. Kassar has sustained minor injuries, fighting at ninety-four percent of his usual efficiency. Novin is uninjured. Kassar currently has the Vaar bottlenecked—"

"Sir, we're online," Novin interrupted. "Ready to go."

"Understood," Panzer answered while rising to his feet. "Andira, prepare to bring the *Intruder* in."

"Yes sir. Already moving it into position."

Panzer turned as something caught his mind. At first it seemed no more than a stray thought. One of many, too fleeting to pay much heed, too insignificant to remember. But it was there. He focused on the feed from the loyal automatech that remained at the bottom of the ramp. There he could see the fire dancing in the hall. The sensor revealed nothing else, but it was in his mind. Someone was standing in the fire.

"Sir?" Andira tried to get his attention. "Is everything all right?"

Panzer took control of the drone, panning its view, zooming in and out. It could not see. But the harder he looked, the more his gut seemed to sink. There *was* something there. He kept low as he crept toward the descending ramp and looked over it to see the drone.

"Sir, the Vaar are continuing to breach the ship. If we don't go now, they will get ahead of us."

Andira's warning was just, but Panzer did not hear it. The nanocendiary flames could never decide if they favored red or blue, but there was more red here than there should have been. His right arm trembled, but he did not notice. While the higher, reasonable mind sought answers, the primitive mind knew something was near, and it was afraid. He stepped off the floor and onto the inactive tram rail to slide down the ramp. The presence seemed to grow stronger.

"Sir, what are you doing?" Andira's words were far away.

At the bottom of the ramp, the drone hovered at his side. As he looked at the corridor ahead, he saw what the drone could not. Less than a hundred meters away, it stood in chest-high tongues of fire. Too short to be a Vaar, too tall to be a man. Amid the backdrop of red and blue, he saw black. Eight long tendrils branched out of the creature's back, flowing and dancing like the fire all around. It had no form, only an outline where the light seemed to bend around it.

"Andira. What is that?"

"Please specify."

Panzer highlighted the silhouette in his NOD, drawing a square around it. "That."

"Flames, sir, from the nanocendiaries."

Panzer shook his head slowly. "*That* is not fire."

The image seemed to shift, and in a corridor of flame, Panzer felt a deep chill. He could not see any eyes, but all the same, he felt the gaze on him.

"I see you, and you see me. Don't you?"

A voice in his mind, flanging, resonating, echoing. Between the first and last syllables, Panzer's eyes began to roll back in his head, stopping only when the sentence ended. His knees were weak, and he staggered back a step as his mind grappled with the words. That telepathy. Not even the commandant's voice was that strong.

"Sir, we have to go, now!"

"Sir, we can't stay here. We have to move."

Novin's and Andira's voices were distant whispers in a crowd.

"Yes. You hear my words, and I need not soften them for your mind to survive."

Panzer clenched his eyelids together, his teeth gritting painfully as he tried to shake it out of his head. Even with his eyes closed, he saw red. The mist—metapsionic static.

"Andira to Kassar, something is wrong with the colonel. Report to his location immediately."

"You see me. You endure my words. How many voices do you hear?"

Only in the presence of the Encephalon had he seen the static before. What monster haunted this place? Panzer's lips parted to suck a deep breath through his teeth. He did not know what it was. He did not know why it was here. He only knew the best answer.

"I'm on my way," he broadcast before opening his eyes. He raised the Hellbore to his shoulder, cyclic to nine hundred rounds per minute. Panzer pulled the trigger and sent the torrent of 40mm shells on their way. The first blast erupted, and more followed fractions of a second behind. The floor beneath the entity cratered. The flames twisted, sputtered, and died—even the nanites couldn't escape the swirling blasts. But the presence remained, its tendrils whipping about in the blasts like streamers in a strong gale.

Panzer kept the trigger depressed. A hundred rounds. Two hundred. Thirty seconds and 450 rounds passed and detonated before he let off the trigger. In a fifty-meter circle, the flames were gone, and now there was only red. The mist that surrounded the entity, unharmed by the torrent of violence unleashed upon it.

Run.

Panzer turned and his thrusters fired as he rocketed up the ramp. At the back of his mind, he knew. It was following him. It saw through his cloak, and it was following.

At the top of the ramp, he glanced back. The tendrils clawed at the walls and the roof of the tunnel ramp. Panzer pushed forward on his thrusters as he hovered, accelerating toward the large partition. He forgot to call the drone back with him, and its signal was dark. He did not cut thrust until he reached the maintenance hatch Kassar had used to move past it. He overshot the mark, cutting thrust too late and slamming firmly into the partition. With a grunt he returned to his feet and backtracked for the door.

Panzer spotted it at the top of the ramp as his right leg went through the hatch. He raised the Hellbore again and released a burst of fire. The mist had followed it up the ramp, and once more, its tendrils danced in the blast, but even as the walls and floor around it ripped apart, it remained unbroken.

"Yes. You definitely see me."

Panzer threw himself through the hatch, following the narrow tunnel around the partition where he emerged onto the bridge. A massacre of Vaar and Viss lay on both sides of the train hovering in place. Panzer rode his thrusters to it and up onto the tail car.

"I'm here. Where's Kassar?"

"Here," Kassar answered as he boosted over the bridge from below, landing on the tail car with him.

"You all right?" Panzer asked, noting a trio of holes in the kurai's armor.

"Nothing I couldn't handle, sir."

"Novin, go!" Panzer barked as he turned back to the partition.

Slowly Panzer's jaw opened until his helmet stopped it. The black tendrils had slid beneath the illstas partition And lifted. The entity came back into his view as the train began to accelerate. Panzer reached back to Kassar, finding his helmet. Panzer pointed toward the being with his Hellbore.

"Kassar, what do you see?"

"The partition is rising, sir."

Panzer nodded as they sped away. "Do you see the person opening it?"

"No sir." The confused tone almost mirrored Panzer's disbelief.

He was cracking up. His brain was in worse shape than he thought, and he was cracking up. Why now? He should have had a few years before he reached this point. Even so, there was something more comforting about it. Insanity was a shade better than meeting something that could survive hundreds of Hellbore rounds. He was all set to begin taking comfort in that notion until he heard it.

"It is impossible to outrun me. I will not hinder your errand, but I will decide when you leave this ship."

Panzer closed his eyes. *"What the hell are you?"*

No answer came to his call, and as the next partition closed behind them, Panzer glimpsed marines rocketing up onto the bridge. Approximately every half kilometer, another partition closed behind them. They had reached the forward quarter of the ship, mostly cargo bays, hangars, and other storage. They just had to make it to one with a suitable routing terminal.

Panzer's momentum tried to hurtle him forward, but his boots clung to the pod beneath him. He threw his arms out to his side to keep his balance as he slid and the train came to a stop.

"Novin?" Panzer barked, turning toward the front of the train. He saw the problem before an answer could come.

"Partition is closed."

While Kassar reoriented himself, Panzer engaged his thrusters, lifting off to race toward the front of the train.

"Andira?" he asked.

"I am losing access to transit control," she answered as his feet came down on the lead car. "Attempting to reestablish control."

Panzer glared at the partition. Regardless of whatever he saw, there were a lot of Vaar just behind. "Andira, how thick is that partition?"

"Four-point-six-three meters, sir."

Panzer shouldered the Hellbore. Even braking so hard, Novin had brought the nose to a halt less than six meters from the barrier.

"Novin, can you back us up?"

The train lurched again, and Panzer with it as it was kicked into reverse. "That's far enough."

With a hundred meters stand-off, Panzer aimed the weapon.

HELLBORE MASTER CONTROL
MASTER ARM—ON
>>SHELL CONTROL/MANUAL CONFIGURATION
MANUAL CONFIGURATION SET
>>SET EXCLUSION TARGET
READY

He focused on the track, following it with his eyes to where it ran through a slot in the bottom of the partition. An amber glow surrounded the track in his NOD.

HELLBORE MASTER CONTROL
MASTER ARM—ON
EXCLUSION TARGET SET
>>CYCLIC CONTROL—750 RPM

Panzer drew the muzzle up, aiming a meter above the track before loosing the Hellbore into the partition. Electric arcs sizzled in the air with a visible corona. Debris rained down on his head, his shoulders, and on the train like metal hail. His back was getting lighter, and he watched the ammo counter for the backpack plunging in his NOD as he carved through the partition. Panzer worked the muzzle in circles, enlarging the forming hole. Finally he left off the trigger with a path exposed.

"That should do it. Take us forward. Easy." A second later Panzer rocked as the train lurched forward again. "I said easy, Novin."

"Sorry, sir. This isn't like driving a conveyor."

The train pushed scraps of debris out of its path as it inched through the hole. Panzer was forced to take a knee. "Kassar, watch your head."

"We're almost there," Novin called back.

The train took a wide turn before straightening out, passing through a thick tunnel with many partitions on their way out of the citadel of the ship and into its outer hull. Panzer saw the obstruction before Novin called out, and the train began to brake. An inactive cargo tram lay directly ahead. The ammo counter plunged further in his NOD as he let the Hellbore loose on it. Novin pushed through the wreckage to approach the end of the line.

To Panzer's left, three armored doors faced a loading dock. From the door to the edge of the dock ran a cargo trench ten centimeters deep. The train lurched to a stop before creeping forward again as Kassar did his best to align the second, third, and fourth cars to the trenches.

"Kassar get up here," Panzer ordered, hopping down to the dock.

After grabbing the door to the lead car, Panzer slid it open before peering inside. Miss Prideaux remained looming over the Twins, still on the floor. Lieutenant Clearwater sat on the floor ahead of Miss Prideaux. His hand covered the disrupter wound through his chest and shoulder, and he drew breath in short gasps.

"Miss Prideaux," Panzer spoke, "keep them in place." As Kassar joined them, Panzer pointed to Clearwater. "Tend to him."

Novin was already out of his chair, and Panzer turned to let him pass.

Kassar kneeled in front of Lieutenant Clearwater, brandishing his mediron. "This will hurt," the kurai said before jamming the needle into the lieutenant's flesh, directly below the wound in his chest. Panzer winced as the lieutenant spasmed and brought his right hand up to bite down on his knuckle. Panzer knew that pain well. Critical Trauma Nanites healed quickly, but painfully. Panzer watched the lieutenant, tough kid, only letting out a growl. The four women, particularly the hutai he was sweet on, might have something to do with that. He'd seen and heard plenty of soldiers screaming bloody murder while the CTNs did their work.

Panzer looked back at the loading dock, where Novin was already squatting in front of one of the three doors, working to get it open.

"Andira, can you get those doors open?"

"Negative, sir. I do not currently have control over automated doors. I am attempting to reclaim."

"You wouldn't have a spare, would you?"

The lieutenant's question brought Panzer's attention back to the train, where Clearwater was holding his damaged cyberlimb up to Kassar.

"No sir," Kassar answered. "Just that one."

Panzer looked at the tactical display. As far as the Vaar still on network, many were coming. Andira locking the partitions would dam the river, but not for long. More units spilled into other tram ways, corridors, and maintenance tunnels, all intent on bypassing him and his people before circling back around to come at them from farther ahead.

"Lieutenant?" Panzer drew his attention. "Can you fight?"

The lieutenant's expression sank, but he found his inner legionnaire and nodded while Kassar helped him to his feet.

"Yes sir. I can. I can fight."

The sound of doors opening drew Panzer's attention to the dock. Novin had the doors rising, revealing the chamber beyond. A large chamber half a kilometer long and just as wide. The Vaar called these monstrosities of chaos *logistics bays*. A single room to handle the movement of personnel and cargo from trams, routers, and shuttles. The three trenches from the loading dock ran to the center of the room before meeting at a ring and branching out to other portions of the bay. A single routing pad sat within the circle at the room's center, recessing into the deck. Novin had already sprinted through the center trench to the routing terminal.

Novin was there for only a minute before running back.

"Lieutenant." Novin pointed to Clearwater. "I need your help."

Novin led the lieutenant to the front of the car before pointing down at the control console.

"Someone needs to reposition the train," Novin explained. "The controls are useless. I had to bypass them. So control with this box. Flip this switch here, you move forward. Flip it down, you go backward. Rotate the switch—right is more throttle, left is less. Understand?"

"I got it."

A sense of relief came over the lieutenant's face as he slumped down into the smaller of the two frontal chairs. Novin bolted back out of the car, making for the router while Panzer and Kassar followed.

Panzer kept his eyes on the tactical display as Novin drew his knife and began ripping into the routing terminal. Andira had done everything she could, closing the partitions and maintenance hatches. Then she had deleted the software controlling those systems before causing electrical shorts to blow control circuits. It was the best she could do while being forced out of their systems. The Vaar had no choice now but to breach or blast through each one. They brought forward more tanks to blast through each partition in their path.

"Sir, we have a problem."

"What is it?"

"Vaar engineering," Novin answered. "This thing is going to require a huge amount of power."

Panzer glanced at his ammunition counter. "Ammo's reaching a premium, Novin. How much are you going to need?"

Novin shook his head. "It would take me way too long to build that kind of adapter with my field kit." Novin glanced up at Panzer before pointing. "Your suit, sir. I think I can run it off your reactor."

"Any other options?"

"No sir."

Panzer looked between Novin and the routing terminal before dropping his chin and shaking his head. He turned his back to Novin before pointing down with his thumb at his back.

AMAC CONTROL
AC PANELS OPEN
>TAP 1

>TAP 2

Panzer dismissed the notices as Novin inserted cables to wire his suit to the terminal.

"Starting draw."

An electrical thump resonated through his armor, and the helmet display darkened as power was diverted.

EXTERNAL FEED INTERRUPTED

"Not enough," Novin warned. "Sir, I need you to authorize more."

>>DISABLE OFFBOARD AC GOVERNOR

ARE YOU SURE?

>>YES

The lights in his display dimmed further, and Panzer felt the suit settling around him. With so much power leaving the armor, it had disabled the locomotive systems until he decided to move. He brought up his back-mounted sensor to see the twin cables extending out of his back and down to a panel by the routing terminal. Novin had his suit hooked in via a cable in his armor's forearm.

"I have power," Novin announced. "It's going to take some time to bypass their system's lockdown."

"Andira, can you help him out?"

"Negative. I no longer have access to routing functions of the transit system."

"I can do it, sir," Novin assured him. "I'll have to break the router's connection to their network—recycle it through my own to spoof the command signals. Then—"

"Novin?" Panzer interrupted.

"As long as we have local power, I can get it online."

"How long?"

"Ten to fifteen, sir."

Panzer grimaced. "Andira, how long until we're swimming in marines?" Marines, and whatever that *thing* was.

"At the rate they are breaching partitions, approximately nineteen minutes."

Less than twenty minutes to offload every pod. That would never be enough. "Novin, can you get the loading equipment online?"

"Yes sir."

The sound of large circuits coming online created an echoing thump through the chamber. The previously dim glow of emergency lighting was replaced by overheads as the bay came to life. At the loading dock, pylons extended from the terminus of each trench. They engaged with the second, third, and fourth cars of the train. The loading system did the rest, drawing the pods two at a time in their stacks off the forward cars and pulling them into the trench. There the six pods formed a line and moved until they reached the circle around the terminal.

Panzer timed the pods as they made the trip. Thirty-one-point-two-three seconds. One hundred four pods, three pods per thirty-two effective seconds. Allowing for time to reposition the train to continue offloading, more than an hour to transmit the entire load.

Panzer turned his gaze. He had given this order before. Each time, he hoped he would not have to again.

"Kassar?" he asked. "How are you on ammo?"

The kurai glanced down at his weapon. "Two and a half mags, sir. Full load on sidearm."

Panzer motioned him closer before switching his coms point-to-point. "Kassar."

"Sir?"

Panzer's suit had the strongest reactor. He had to stay and play battery. So he said it. "If we don't throw something in their way, the Vaar are going to be on top of us before we get these people out. I—"

"Abrogan rejects the timid," Kassar interrupted. "I'll do what I can to slow them down."

"Kassar." Panzer grabbed Kassar's arm as he began to move away. "You keep an exit path."

"Yes sir."

Panzer released him before offering up the Hellbore.

"I'll stick with this." Kassar raised his weapon. "But I will take a magazine."

The statement did not fully compute, but Panzer plucked one of the magazines off his chest and handed it over.

"Novin, spare a wengner?" Kassar asked before Novin tossed him the tool in response.

"Good luck," Novin added.

With a nod, Kassar jogged to the train, turned, and broke into a sprint.

Panzer muted his transceiver. "Abrogan. Not today."

"Andira, it's time." Novin's statement brought Panzer back. "Is the *Intruder* in position?"

"Affirmative."

Grenades. Kassar was going to improvise grenades out of the rounds he had taken.

"Ready for signal bounce," Novin announced. "Sir, I need you to input your codes."

Panzer complied, entering the long cipher into his NOD.

"*Intruder* has received signal," Andira reported. "Scanning for valid recipient."

Panzer's foot tapped while Andira worked, scanning for any Armadas ship that could serve as the next bounce.

"A *Rook* has received our signal," Andira announced. "Stand by."

Panzer held his breath. The pilot would initially be confused at seeing the routing signal. He would be even more confused about where it was coming from. But he would see the priority flag added by the command code. From there he would route it to the nearest warship, where the blue-girls would examine it. The gammas would show it to their captain, who would bounce it further up the chain. All until it reached someone who could identify the code. Until it reached Aetius.

But as the seconds ticked by, Panzer's foot kept tapping. "Come on," he whispered. "Show it to Aetius."

Panzer opened the connection window in his NOD. A mixture of Solar and Vaar characters—translated into the former—filled his view.

CARRIER SIGNAL SENT
AWAITING RESPONSE . . .
AWAITING RESPONSE . . .
AWAITING RESPONSE . . .

Panzer gritted his teeth.

"It's black priority. Show it to Aetius."

AWAITING RESPONSE . . .
REQUEST EXPIRED

By the time Panzer got the order out of his mouth, Novin had already closed and reopened the channel.

ROUTING CLIENT CONNECTING TO DESTINATION SERVER . . .
CONNECTION ESTABLISHING . . .
AWAITING RESPONSE . . .
AWAITING RESPONSE . . .

"Show it to Aetius," Panzer whispered more loudly before his voice rose. "Show it to Aetius, idiots!"

AWAITING RESPONSE . . .
AWAITING RESPONSE . . .
RESPONSE RECEIVED
ESTABLISHING CONNECTION . . .
CONNECTION ESTABLISHED—H.M.S. HURRICANE
GATEWAY ESTABLISHED, ROUTING TERMINAL 713

"We're in!" Novin proclaimed with a pump of his fist.

"Go! Go now!" Panzer bellowed, clapping Novin on the shoulder. Panzer moved as far as the cables would allow him to give the ten-meter pod room to slide into place. The twin-stacked pods moved into the center of the terminal, and a metal safety sleeve rose out of the floor to obstruct the view of the pods.

TRANSPATIAL CONNECTION ESTABLISHED . . . H.M.S. HURRICANE
TRANSMITTING IN 3 . . . 2 . . . 1 . . .

A flash of green light pulsed out of the sleeve and into the room. The safety sleeve dropped back to the floor, and the pods were gone.

TRANSMISSION COMPLETE . . .
DESTINATION CONFIRMS RECEPTION . . .
MAKE ANOTHER TRANSMISSION?

Panzer heaved a breath of relief before nodding down at Novin.

"Colonel!"

The sudden bark drew his attention as Miss Prideaux approached, leading the Twins by their arms toward the routing platform.

"Colonel, I demand you transmit the Twins and me next," Miss Prideaux barked again as she moved to stand in front of him.

Panzer glared down at her. "We depart by Courteon protocols, Miss Prideaux."[17]

"Damn the protocols!" Miss Prideaux screeched back. "I want them off the ship now!"

Panzer lowered the Hellbore and stood it upright on the stock by his foot before taking an at-ease position. He looked over the woman too short to be as far into his face as she wished to be.

"Colonel!"

Panzer was completely prepared to tune her out and simply listen to the sound of the next batch of pods approaching. But then he heard the demure voice that said, "We can wait."

Panzer glared down at the Twin who spoke. Miss Prideaux grappled with her and hissed like a rabid snake. "Be quiet! You're going *now!*" Miss Prideaux turned back to him. "Isn't that right, *Colonel?*"

Both of the Twins cringed from the reprimand. They could not see it, but behind his faceplate, Panzer smiled. Sheltered, fawned over, pampered, and not true aristocracy. But while their guardian zealously demanded violation of the protocol, they were willing to wait. Even after what they had been through, and to find escape so close. Panzer chuckled to himself, neither to be derisive nor condescending.

It knew not species, nor class. It knew not station, gender, age, nor rank. Courage came in all forms.

"Novin. Courteon protocols."

"Yes sir."

---

17 Courteon protocols are the Imperial custom dictating evacuation order from stricken ships, space stations, and similar situations. These protocols require that the people are evacuated in the order of children, civilian women, civilian men, noblewomen, noblemen, non-crew military personnel, and finally crew.

CHAPTER
10B

Simmonne was running out of station and had not found a place to hide. Everything was so clean and sterile—nothing had strong odors. She bounded down a stairway and took the sharp turn to continue descending. The Vaar still tracked her at a jog. When she exited the stairway, she found herself in a long corridor. She was on the station's lowest level, and there were only five doors ahead.

At the far end of the wide hall stood the doors to what was obviously a cargo lift. Her eyes moved to the signs hanging from the ceiling. The more distant pair of doors were cargo bays, probably empty. But the other two. To the left, waste processing. To the right, water recycling. Chemicals.

She moved quickly to the water room, and the doors slid open. In the center lay a pool, perhaps ten meters square. The walls were lined with large metal drums, stacked five to a column to touch the ceiling. Emergency stores. But there was no strong scent in the air, nothing that would hide her. Her eyes moved to the pool. Maybe she could wash the perfume off.

She did not have that kind of time. The Vaar's mind drew closer. He would be at the stairwell soon. The low ceiling over the stairs would slow him but not for long. She turned back and ran to waste processing. When the doors opened, the air seemed to ball itself into a fist and drive into her sinuses.

Machinery filled the room. Metal consoles lined the walls. Some made periodic noises, but most offered only a quiet hum. More machinery stood out on the floor in three rows across the breadth of the room. This was her spot, if she could handle it. But at the door, she realized the problem. The scent was *so* overpowering, it would be the obvious hiding place. She could hide here, but she needed to send the Vaar elsewhere.

She glanced back into the corridor. The Vaar had reached the stairs. She heard the metallic pounding as he slowly wedged his way down. She did not have long. She sprinted to the lift. The doors opened and she peered inside. She had to do something—convince the Vaar that she had taken it up to another floor.

The pounding on the stairs grew louder. Hastily she hiked up her dress and stripped off her stockings. After inserting one into another, she tied them into a knot. She rubbed the fabric against her neck, her face, her hair, and under her arms. Anywhere it might pick up more of the perfume. She looked up. She had hoped that maybe she could put it atop the lift. Through a maintenance hatch or something. But she saw none. She was running out of time.

Her search brought her to a small maintenance panel in the wall, beneath the call buttons. She gritted her teeth against the pain in her fingers as she wedged her nails under the panel to force it open. Wires and terminal ports greeted her. She wadded the stockings into a ball and stuffed them into the panel before slamming it shut. That would have to do. She hit the button to send the lift up and felt the tremor in the deck as she turned. The Vaar had reached the other end of the corridor.

She froze, now fully within his sight. His head cocked as the lift's doors closed and it began to climb. If she could just get back to waste processing. With any luck the elevator would lead him to believe she had made it to another floor. He began to walk toward her.

If she went through one of the doors now, he would know she was there when her NOD sent it the command to open. She had to be calm. She forced her focus away from him and into her NOD, moving through the options.

>>*DISABLE DOOR AUTO-OPEN*

Her NOD would not open the door, but the Vaar's body would trip the proximity sensor. She still had to get into her spot before he realized she was still here. The hairs on her neck tried to pull her back as she walked toward him. Her eyes darted between him and the doors to waste disposal. He stopped for a moment, sniffing the air before continuing forward. His steps were so large, he was going to make it to the doors before her.

As the distance between them shortened, she pressed her back against the wall. Almost there. Her hand was on the edge of the door, the Vaar not two meters away. The proximity sensor triggered the door. The lights!

>>*DISABLE AUTO-ILLUMINATION*

She raced into the dark room. So close to the Vaar, the tremor of his steps reverberated in her feet. She continued forward to the last row of machinery. She sank to the floor, leaning her back against the metal. When she tried to catch her breath, she covered her mouth. Was it supposed to smell *this* bad? The sulfuric odor watered her eyes and seemed to claw at her throat. She focused on small breaths, trying not to retch.

Her eyes closed as she tried to focus on the Vaar. She had hoped at least to find frustration. Instead she found a tinge of hunger but mostly annoyance. He stopped at the end of the hall. A moment later she heard a gentle rumble in the walls. The lift was descending.

Just go up! That was all he had to do. Go up and try to determine to which floor she had gone. Her heart skipped a beat as the lift began to ascend. Had he taken the bait?

No. He was still on this floor, and he was coming closer. Her heart skipped when she heard the doors open. She cringed and rose on her hands to peek over the machinery at him. The Vaar stood in the doorway with his gun in one hand. The other drew back and hurtled something into the room.

She drew in a panicked gasp, but it was no grenade. Something hit the wall and slid to the floor. She turned to it. The wadded-up ball of her stockings.

"Nice try, little one," the Vaar taunted her. "Clever to try to hide here from my nose."

She turned back to him in time to see him tap the faceplate of his helmet.

"Nasal filters. I still smell you."

The sound he made—was it laughter? She sank as she turned back to stare at the wall. What was she supposed to do now?

"It's time to end this game, little one."

She peered over the machine again. He was fiddling with his gun. She counted two barrels, one larger beneath a smaller. He took something from a compartment in his armor and stuffed it into the larger barrel.

"If I have to use force to locate you, you might be injured. Come out."

Too frightened to move, she could only stare at him until he raised the weapon. Her hands moved to cover her head, and she cringed as the weapon fired. A loud ring issued as something struck the wall, and an explosion of light filled the room. Long strands of glowing fiber whistled through the air. They stuck to the walls, the ceiling, the floor, and the machinery, emitting an amber glow.

"They are made to use against your commandos," the Vaar explained as he loaded another round. "They are meant to grab and hold a soldier in armor. You will not enjoy their touch."

He fired a second time, to the opposite corner of the room. One of the filaments passed so close that she felt the wind on her face before it struck the wall.

"If they touch your flesh, you'll tear your skin to pull them off."

She darted up to her feet and spied him as he shouldered the weapon to fire again. More falling than climbing, she went over the machinery, trying to put it between her and the wall behind. She stumbled, her chin smacking the floor as he fired again.

Get out! Get out!

He was blocking the door. She had no choice. She had to go through him again.

Simmonne crawled for the edge of the room before her dress tightened and she was pulled back. Her head whipped around, and she saw the glowing strand. The tip of the filament curled over the top and clung to the hem of her dress.

"No." She grabbed hold of the fabric and pulled. The filament did not release her. Her hands twisted and jerked, trying to rip the fabric and free herself. But the smart fiber was far too strong for her fingers to tear. She sat with her feet against the console and pushed with her legs, pulling at the same time with her hands.

"Please." She emitted the strained words as her legs burned, and her hands slipped free of the cloth. She sucked in a deep breath, grabbed it again, and gave a final push. Every ounce of strength in her body converged on the task. An audible rip broke through the air, followed by a dull thump as her head slammed into the opposite console. Dazed, she sat up slowly. The Vaar loomed over her.

His head turned to the filament and the small piece of her dress it still held. She climbed to her feet dizzily as the Vaar came forward. His fingers brushed the floor, but Simmonne flung herself over the middle row, flipping and landing hard on her back.

She clawed to her feet. One row left. She drew herself over it and sent the command to the doors. She tried so hard to spring into a run that she lost her balance and fell into the doorway. It was only when she regained balance and broke into a run that she realized she had lost.

She looked back at the Vaar, his eyes now on the open doorway. In one motion he brought his gun up and brushed a switch on the side before he held tight and fired. The projectile whistled past her before bursting into the hallway ahead. In a flash of silver rather than amber, fibers stretched from ceiling to floor and wall to wall. She could not stop herself before she barreled into them.

"No!"

The mesh of wires gave as she plowed into it, each plucking audibly like the strings of a guitar. A moment later they separated from their anchors, and the net engulfed her. These strings did not cling to her, but to each other. The impact with the floor knocked the wind from her lungs, and the net began to contract. Sparks danced through her vision as the stealth screen failed. But she had greater problems.

The pressure of the net pushed down on her spine, as if trying to jam her head down into her shoulders. Her arms were pinned against her body, and her legs began to bend. The net contracted, forcing her into a ball.

She could not breathe. The net was squeezing so tight, her chest could not expand. She could not free herself. Soon the Vaar towered over her once again.

"Course the prey long enough, it makes a mistake."

While he was gloating, she was suffocating. Blurry vision was turning dark. Sharp pains streamed through her cheek. Bright flashes mocked what little sight remained. Then the distant sound of a terrible collision. She could not turn her head, only her eyes as two shadow figures moved against one another, and the hall shook around her. One of them rose, and the other seemed to fly away. The one that remained bore down on her.

The strands of the net shrieked as they were sliced apart. Her body unfurled, and her mouth flew open to draw in a long gasp.

"Stayin' 'hind me, prinsssess."

Her vision began to return, and she recognized the kodaz standing above her.

"Quickly now." His giant hand prodded at her. "Be gettin' up, 'hind."

Still gasping, she nodded and grabbed his hand as he guided her up to her feet. Rhoxx stepped forward enough to push her against the wall so she could hold herself up. She looked down the corridor. The Vaar rose from the ground.

"Shoot him," Simmonne wheezed, probably inaudibly. But she was silent as she took stock of the kodaz. The massive guns on his back were gone—only broken mounts remained. His armor was covered in burns, scratches, and holes. Nearly his entire helmet was destroyed, save for a small piece of the left side. But he was alive.

The Vaar raised his weapon, but it did not fire. The warrior glanced at it for a moment. Several long gashes had cut into the weapon, and the Vaar dropped it on the floor.

CHAPTER
10C

THE FORWARD CAR OF the train had two conductor seats. The first intended for a Vaar was set low in the floor. The second seat intended for a Viss was mounted higher. Clearwater fell into the second seat with his legs over the side as he leaned back against the canopy. The pain of the medical nanites' repairs was fading, leaving a dull throb deep in his torso as they continued to work.

Through the other side of the canopy, he watched the next set of pods go through the router. Lady Prideaux shouted loud enough for Clearwater to hear her two hundred meters away. Unconsciously he sneered as he heard the conversation. One of the only times nobility were ever expected to wait for *anything*, and still she had to go first. Clearwater closed his eyes and tested his body, taking a deep breath.

The car rocked as the second batch of pods was withdrawn from the three cars mated to the loading dock. As a child, he and a friend had once argued about who was the greatest, the LEF, the SARC, or the Corps. Something in his childhood had compelled him to argue for the LEF. After today, he might have to change his vote. Clearwater opened his eyes to see a flash from the bay. The second transmission of pods was complete.

"All right, Lieutenant," Novin called out, "I'm going to withdraw the loading sleds, and I need you to move the train forward."

Clearwater sat up straight and faced the controls. The main console was dead, bypassed by the kurai's wire work. The box Novin had assembled earlier was now wired into the train, little more than a box of metal framing, cables, and wire from Clearwater's perspective.

"Flip the switch forward and turn it. Turn it easy."

The switch was on the left side of the box, and Clearwater reached for it until the metal limb reminded him that he no longer had a left hand. The right came up and he flicked the switch forward. His fingers found the metal ring at the base of the toggle, and he turned it to the right.

Clearwater's head was thrown back as the train lurched forward, and he quickly turned the dial back. He went too far and was thrown forward against the console. Hissing through his teeth, Clearwater glanced back at Taula, now sitting up from her bench. He cringed, hoping he had not just killed half of the colonists in the pods.

"Turn it *easy*, Lieutenant," Novin scolded.

"Sorry." He carefully turned the ring forward again.

"That's enough. Stop. Stop. *Stop!*"

Clearwater switched the ring back to its original place.

"Good enough," Novin sounded. "Extending sleds."

The metallic clanging echoed through the metal as the loading dock mated to the train once again, and the next batch of pods was withdrawn.

Clearwater was still patched into the network with the colonel's team. He sorted through the screens to find the remote view and pulled up the feed to Kassar. An explosion caused Clearwater to jump in the chair.

Clearwater saw through the kurai's eyes in his NOD. Kassar was holding an ordnance shell. He heard Kassar grunt as he stripped the shell out of its casing, and with haste he inserted a wengner rod into the shell's base and gave it a turn. The image shifted as the kurai peered out of a hatch and tossed the shell before withdrawing. Another explosion sounded.

"All right, Lieutenant," Novin cut in. "Move it up."

Clearwater lowered the screen to focus on the switch again. He gave it as gentle a turn as he could until told to stop. The next set of pods was on their way.

Back in the remote view, Clearwater jumped again at the sudden appearance of a Vaar face. That face vanished in a cloud of pulp. A juggernaut was charging, and the gun was firing. Each shot caused the jug to stumble. The warrior had no arms. By the fifth shot, it was on the ground with no legs. On the sixth, it had no head.

Kassar dropped the weapon to his sling, took another shell, de-cased it, primed it with the rod, and threw. This time Clearwater caught a glimpse of downrange. A hole had opened in one of the large partitions. Clearwater caught only a glimpse of Vaar firing from the other side as Kassar tossed his improvised grenade.

"Lieutenant, are you dead?" Novin's voice broke loudly in his ears.

"Moving now!" Clearwater answered, toggling the switch to move the train again.

A lull came to Kassar's battle. The kurai frantically pulled shells from the magazine and primed them with the rod. At one point, as Kassar looked down, Clearwater caught sight of his leg. There was a hole in the armor, and meat hung out from a wound. Kassar did not seem to care and continued priming his stash of shells.

The show continued with Clearwater acting on the periodic prompts to move the train. Most people would live their entire lives without ever seeing Solar Commandos. They would hear about them in stories and the latest fiction. Some would question if they actually existed. So many of the stories he had heard seemed ridiculous. Too far-fetched for even well-crafted fiction. But here he was, living part of a commando's story and vicariously experiencing another chapter.

As the rhythm of the train continued, Clearwater kept watching. Kassar did not stay put for too long. After a minute or two, he would go down through maintenance corridors. Sometimes he found a Vaar or drone to shoot; other times he moved unopposed. He went from one tram tunnel to the next. Once there, he would move through them under a cloak, letting off shots and throwing grenades to sow confusion. Then he would move to the next. One warrior covering three different tunnels the Vaar were attempting to use so that they could cut off and surround the train. Clearwater was not sure if the kurai still had any of his drones. But even if he did, what he watched defied belief.

"Just a few more, Lieutenant," Novin called. "Move it up."

"Got it." He toggled the switch again.

It occurred to him as the cargo sleds extended that this was one of those events. It was a Corps mission. He would never be allowed to talk about it. But it did not matter. No one would believe him anyway.

Kassar was doing the work of a section. The Vaar probably thought they were facing that many. When Kassar ran out of rounds for his rifle, he used grenades and a pistol. When he ran out of rounds for the pistol, he took the weapon of a dead marine and continued. For seventy-four minutes, the kurai did this, and for seventy-four minutes, Clearwater remained in awe.

"Last one, Lieutenant."

"Once the train is in position, get up here, Lieutenant," the colonel added.

"Yes sir!" Clearwater gave the switch a final toggle. He closed out the feed to Kassar and grabbed his rifle. The pods were ahead of him as he stepped out onto the loading dock and made his way into the bay. Freedom's taste was on the tip of his tongue as he approached the routing point. There the colonel, Novin, Lady Prideaux, and the Katyusha Twins all waited.

"Here, sir!" Clearwater announced as he moved to stand beside Lady Prideaux and the Twins.

His NCP had triggered to battle-mind in time for him to see the shockwave rippling through the air. On the outer edge of the bay, an explosion had breached the hangar doors. Heat on his skin made him stagger. Marines flooded through the hole by the time he recovered.

"Get down!" Lady Prideaux shouted as she grabbed the Twins and dragged them to the deck.

Clearwater locked gazes with the red visor of a Viss who had poured through the breach, simultaneously selecting the other as a target. Clearwater's trigger work was hundredths of a second faster. A five-round burst met the marine's helmet. At least one round pierced the eyepiece to divide her skull. The Viss was dead, but the electrical spasms in her body were enough to pull the trigger.

Every muscle in Clearwater's body locked up as it was flooded with the current. He fell.

LETHAL INJURIES DETECTED
PRESERVATION PROTOCOL BOOTED TO STANDBY
MEDICAL ASSISTANCE REQUIRED!!!
MEDICAL ASSISTANCE REQUIRED!!!
MEDICAL ASSISTANCE REQUIRED!!!

The first thing Clearwater saw was his leg. His right foot and shin were smoking where they had been severed from the rest of his leg. Six rounds had walked across his body. One through his pectoral—almost in the same spot as the previous injury—one below the ribs, one through the hip, and the remainder into his leg.

By the time Clearwater recovered from the shock and raised his weapon again, the fight was over. The colonel had ended it by sending rounds from his assault cannon through the breach.

"*Jenna!*"

The shrill, stereo wail drew his dimming vision. The Twins were kneeling over Lady Prideaux. Her blood spread toward Clearwater's.

AUTOREPAIR ERROR

INJURY STATUS UPGRADED TO FATAL

INITIATING PRIMARY PRESERVATION PROTOCOL . . .

ERROR, NO CARRIER

"Oh no," Clearwater whispered, spurting blood on his breath. "Not again."

He saw the colonel. The cables that had linked him to the router dangled like tassels from his armor as the commando joined the Twins. Clearwater reached out toward them. Novin clasped his hand, but Clearwater did not feel it as everything darkened.

CHAPTER
11A

PANZER GLARED AT THE hole that had been opened in the hangar doors. With Kassar effectively roadblocking them, the Vaar had thought outside the hull. A contingent of marines boarded an assault ship, left one hangar, and came to this bay. While pods were transmitting, they were using phase resonators to bore through the doors. When barely a centimeter remained, they used vortex charges to blast through and flood in. With most of his armor's power going to the router, it had taken eleven seconds for Panzer to bring the locomotive systems online and respond to the breach. Eleven seconds. It may as well have been eleven minutes.

The Hellbore quickly ended the matter, and for good measure he had sent rounds through the breach. They passed through the breaching collar and detonated inside the transport, now venting to space. It would take hours for a bay this size to depressurize. If they were still here by then, they would have larger problems.

Panzer looked down where he was kneeling over Miss Prideaux. She should have just stayed down and let him and Novin handle it. Instead she popped back up to join the fight and grabbed the attention of three marines. Their combined fire had put two rounds through her suit. The first had passed through her chest, obliterating her heart. The second pierced her visor and her jaw. She was dead, and a few centimeters higher on the second round would have been enough to make it permanent.

"Please. Please, you have to help her," one Twin whined at his side. "Please do something."

The brain was all that mattered. Panzer sighed and took his hand off his knife. A head was easier to carry than a body, but watching him decapitate her and carry her bodiless head around was the last thing they needed to see. Panzer laid a hand on each of their arms and drew them up to their feet.

"Come on."

"Wait!" Jennifer protested as he walked them around the router. "Stop, please, you've got to help her!"

"I will," Panzer answered. "But you need to wait here."

The router's safety sleeve was still up, and he positioned the pair on the opposite side of Miss Prideaux's body.

"Stay," he directed before returning to Miss Prideaux. As he kneeled once again, he pulled the medkit from his armor. The hole in Miss Prideaux's helmet was too small for his needs, so he carefully removed it. He pulled the cable from the medkit and deployed the needle. Miss Prideaux no longer had a jaw, and her neck was not in much better shape. He drove the needle into the flesh just behind her ear.

MEDKIT SCANNING . . .
THIS PATIENT IS DEAD.
SELECT COURSE OF ACTION
REPAIR & RESUSCITATE
PRESERVATION ASSISTANCE
>>PRESERVATION ASSISTANCE
ACKNOWLEDGED, ETNs CONFIGURED FOR PRESERVATION.
DISPENSING ETNs . . .

While the medkit pumped the nanites into her, Panzer where Novin and Dr. Gilyard kneeled over Lieutenant Clearwater.

"How is he, Novin?"

"Dead."

No shields. No armor. No jamming. Kid didn't stand a chance.

"Preservable?"

"I think so," Novin answered, flashing the medkit in his hand. "Getting some weird readings. Something's wrong with his head."

"The Vaar," Dr. Gilyard spoke up. "He died on ND-31, and they botched the reanimation."

Death while already suffering reanimation sickness, not good. Panzer turned his attention back to Miss Prideaux. He held the medkit with one hand and her helmet with the other, carefully threading the medkit through the hole in the visor. He put the helmet back on to conceal as much of the gore as he could.

"Sir," Andira said, "additional Vaar ships en route to this position. Earliest ETA, approximately eleven minutes."

"Damn," Panzer whispered before facing the router. Holes filled the safety sleeve, and looking through one, he saw more on the floor of the device. Whether the marines had been shooting to disable it or not, that was what they had done. Now the *Intruder* was the only way out.

"Andira, how many?"

"Reading six destroyers. Possibly more."

The *Intruder* could hide from one ship, maybe two, but if enough came in close with overlaying sensors, someone would see something. The *Intruder*, however, had to make it past the same concentric ring of escorts they passed on the way in.

"Kassar, what is your situation?"

"Situation difficult and unstable," Kassar answered, speaking up over the pained howl of a Vaar. Difficult and unstable was Kassar-speak for overrun, out of ammo, and likely fighting hand to hand.

"Prepare to withdraw. We're leaving."

"Yes sir!"

The moment he pulled Kassar out of the road, the Vaar would be on them. The timing had to be flawless. "Andira, bring the *Intruder* in."

"Yes sir. Sir, I will not be able to dock undetected."

"That's why you're not going to dock," he answered. "We'll fly out to you."

Panzer rose from Miss Prideaux before returning to the Twins, who tried to hug each other past their hysterics.

"Listen," he barked to get their attention. "My shuttle is coming to pick us up. We'll have to float out to it. Understand?"

Both nodded.

"It will take a couple of days to make the trip," Panzer continued. "The *Intruder* isn't really designed for this many people, so we're going to put you to sleep once you get aboard. Understand?"

They nodded again.

"All right, come on." He motioned for them to follow as he returned to Miss Prideaux.

"ETA Vaar destroyers, now ten minutes."

"Kassar, you ready?"

There was a pause before the answer came back. "I think you might have to leave without me, sir."

Panzer stood up straighter, turning to face the train. "What's the problem?"

While he waited for the answer, he checked the Hellbore's ammo counter. The backpack was nearly empty.

"Suit compromised," Kassar answered. "Legs are injured—cut off. You better go, sir. I can't reach you."

"Andira, show me his location."

The screen opened in his NOD, showing a three-way intersection of tram terminals. Kassar had overachieved, pushing more than a kilometer through the advancing Vaar. He had forced those closest to the bay to double back and try to help reopen the routes rather than proceed to interfere with the escape. Hostile icons filled the intersection, while the marker for Kassar rested in a ventilation chamber above. The Vaar did not know where he was, but they were looking.

"Stand by, Kassar. I'm coming back."

"Sir!" Novin and Kassar began.

"No arguments," Panzer countered before facing Novin. "Get them on the *Intruder*."

"Sir."

"The mission comes first. Follow my orders."

Novin bowed his head slowly. "Yes sir."

"Coming in," Andira announced. "Be advised I cannot maintain position long without being detected."

"Twins, come here!" Panzer shouted as he bent down to Miss Prideaux. He dragged her corpse to Lieutenant Clearwater's and piled her onto him before hefting both up and handing them to Novin. Panzer turned to Gilyard's daughter.

"Dr. Gilyard, I don't have any more suits. You're going to be exposed to a vacuum."

Her face paled as if she were already dead, but she nodded slowly. "I understand, Colonel. Exhale, hold tight, and hope."

"It won't be long," he assured her, taking her by the arm and guiding her behind Novin. "Hold tight."

He gave her a boost so that she could wrap her arms around Novin's neck, and Panzer quickly turned to the Twins, guiding them to the sides.

"Stand on his foot. Wrap your arms around his." He guided them into position. "Andira, can you get these doors open?"

"Negative. There is a manual switch. There." Panzer found it highlighted in his NOD on the far side of the room. "I will attempt to restrain the containment field until they are clear."

"Be ready," Panzer directed before sprinting toward the switch. The metal cabinet containing the levers was locked, and his knife was the key. Two levers waited inside the cabinet, and Panzer grabbed the first. "Dr. Gilyard, exhale. Opening in three. Two. One."

Panzer threw the lever. The sounds of gears and hydraulics thundered in the bay. Of the two doors, the marines had bored through one to make entry. That door moved slowly as it dragged the attached assault shuttle with it. The right door moved much more quickly, and the air of the room obeyed its lust to rush out. The blue light of ND-31 spilled into the bay. With his boots adhering to the deck, Panzer remained stout against the sudden wind. Novin used his ankle thrusters to levitate from the deck and follow the air outside.

Panzer switched to a private channel as he raised the lever, bidding the doors to close.

"Andira. ETA on destroyers?"

"ETA now eight minutes."

"Back the *Intruder* off so this ship won't see you, and wait to pick us up. If we don't make it out before the two-minute mark, send the *Intruder* back without us."

"Sir—"

"Follow my orders, Andira. If it comes to that, Kassar and I will find our own way off."

"Sir, the odds of successful escape without the *Intruder* are approximately zero."

Panzer shrugged as he nodded. "My orders stand."

"Yes sir."

"Kassar, on my way to you."

With the Hellbore in hand, Panzer boosted through the bay, turning at the tram and continuing through the corridor.

"Sir," Kassar called, his whisper quieter than normal, "you have no right to risk your life for me."

"Your life belongs to me, Kassar. I decide what to risk for it. Andira, show me the best ways out of the hull from his position."

Kassar had already found it, as evidenced by the highlight Andira had placed on the shaft where he was hiding. But he was blocked by closed partitions. Too many to cut through in a timely manner. Panzer touched down on the deck.

"That vent shaft is part of the fire control system." Panzer aimed for the partition. "It proceeds fifty meters before merging with an expulsion shaft, which leads directly out of the hull."

"Yes sir," Kassar answered. "Partitions are closed. I can't get through."

"I'm going to open them. When I do, go through and get out. Andira will pick you up."

"Sir, you won't fit through this duct."

"I know. I'll double back to the hangar." The Hellbore opened the way, and he thrust to the next corridor. "Andira, can you open the partitions?"

"Negative. I have no access to the fire control system. It will be no more than ten minutes before I am purged from the ship's systems completely."

Outside of the ship's citadel, decompression gas was the primary method of fire control. But now he needed a lot of fire, and he didn't have any more nanocendiaries. Two more partitions kept him from Kassar, as did a lot of hostile Vaar.

"Andira, highlight the nearest fire sensor."

A device in the ceiling was outlined in his NOD, a small cube with an even smaller cylinder protruding down.

>>*AMAC CONTROL*
AMAC CONTROL—ALL SYSTEMS NOMINAL
>>*EJECT POWER CELL #4*
CELL EJECTING . . .

After a slight vibration in his armor, a red cylinder landed with a thud before Panzer turned to grab it. The red metal was etched with symbols warning of flammable contents: 209-octium, useful as a fusion fuel but harder to ignite than virgin hydrogen.[18] He held the cylinder while pulling his knife with a free hand, and he drew the blade around one of the end caps to expose the silvery substance inside. With the seal broken, the octium began to sublimate into the air with a slow whine at first before the gas began venting so quickly, the cell tried to rocket out of his grasp with a loud roar.

Panzer ran under the fire sensor and placed the cell on the deck before backing off. He raised his arm and deployed the twin-linked RA-117s. The weapons pulsed as he sprayed fire around the cylinder. The gas continued to leak but didn't react. Panzer brought his left arm up, firing with both weapons.

"Come on. Come on. Come on," he mumbled as he slowly dug pits into the deck.

Finally the octium consented. The electric arcs of the impacting

---

18   209-octium is a synthetic hydrogen isotope with seven neutrons that have been impregnated with synthetic particles both to be stored as a solid and to reduce radioactivity.

disrupters provided the spark, and the octium ignited. A jet of fire rocketed upward like a tiny volcano and engulfed the fire sensor.

The fire alarm blared through the corridor as the flames poured from the cylinder. Panzer heaved a sigh of relief as the partition ahead began to elevate.

"The partitions are opening!" Kassar called.

"Then go. Now!"

"Yes sir. Movin—whoa!" Kassar was cut off. For a kilometer and a half forward and back, the partitions had opened, and the decompression vents with them. Millions of cubic meters of air rushed through those vents to steal oxygen from the flames. Panzer watched in his NOD as Kassar's icon flew through the vent into the decompression shaft and was hurtled out of the ship.

A second later, the feed was replaced by a camera on the *Intruder*. Aided by his thrusters, Kassar rocketed toward the shuttle.

"I've got him, sir," Andira announced.

"On my way out," Panzer answered.

When he closed the screen, he startled and quickly drew the Hellbore. The Vaar were a kilometer away, but that thing was already here. Without the partition between them, the empty image stood directly ahead of him, black tendrils flowing in the air.

"Hello."

Panzer winced with the telepathic touch. "Goodbye." He spun on his heel and opened his thrusters.

He had a straight shot to the loading bay now. He made the trip in seconds, touching down on the deck ahead of the door release.

"Sir, destroyers imminent," Andira warned.

"Almost there." Panzer grabbed the handle and pulled it down. The containment field activated, and the functional door began to slide open again. He did not wait for it to finish. He thrust down the length of the door, ready to turn through the field and leave the ship behind. He started to make the turn when an ebony limb shot across his chest, wrapping over his shoulder and back. Panzer's head, arms, and legs went forward as his body was yanked backward with incredible force. His thrusters sputtered as he was hurtled through the bay. His shoulder clipped the deck, and he skipped off the loading dock, past the train, and finally impacted the wall of the tram corridor.

"Ugh." He groaned as he climbed to his feet. "What the hell—" Panzer froze. On the edge of the loading dock, the empty silhouette looked at him, and with it, the red mist.

"It is quite impossible to outrun me." The telepathic voice felt like claws descending from his scalp down his face and neck. *"I do not simply move through space, but time as well."*

"Colonel, destroyers are here. Sensor thresholds approaching critical mass."

Panzer sought the containment field of the now-distant doorway, obscured by red. "Andira," Panzer said with a sigh, "send the *Intruder* back. I'll find my own way off."

"*Sir!* We will not leave you behind!" Novin screeched into their coms.

"Kassar. Novin. Get the princess and the Twins home."

"No sir!" Kassar shouted. "I'm coming back!"

"Andira, get them out of here."

"Sir," Andira started.

"Stop. Questioning. My. Orders," Panzer growled. "Andira, send them back. *Now.*"

"Yes sir."

Kassar and Novin's protests continued until Panzer closed the channel.

"I'm sorry," he whispered before looking up at the hollow image.

CHAPTER
11B

SIMMONNE REGAINED HER BREATH, and her senses came with it. She backed away behind Rhoxx as the kodaz moved to better position himself between her and the Vaar. Simmonne sensed it. Across any species, gender, or other barrier, she knew that feeling. Tightly controlled, smothered, but still there. The monster was afraid.

Rhoxx had no guns left. Gone as well were the cyberlimbs that belonged on the armor's belly. He was alive. But could he fight?

"If you are here," the Vaar called to Rhoxx, "I take it the rest of my warriors are dead?"

"Ssstandin' back." Rhoxx glanced back at Simmonne. "T'at right. All dead."

"I suppose then you'll expect me to surrender."

That was anger, deep in Rhoxx, but swelling out. The kodaz shook his head. "You tryin' take what belon' my lord. Only him able ssspare you now." Rhoxx parted his lips to bear his teeth. "And him not here."

"It's a duel then," the Vaar answered.

The warrior produced a pair of metal cylinders. He raised them as high as his shoulders before striking them together. The sound of shifting metal filled the corridor as each cylinder bloomed. She knew what those weapons were called—what was the name? Tonfa. The cylinders became a pair of tonfa. But unlike the human weapons, each bore a long scythe-like blade at the long end. On the short end, a triangular spike. Fully deployed, each of the blades emitted a mournful wail. The Vaar brought his arms ahead to point the blades at Rhoxx.

Rhoxx answered by rising on his legs. Armor slid away from his hands to brandish his claws, deadly natural weapons bond-forged and cyberized into modern killing tools. He smacked one set against the other, sending a metallic ring through the corridor.

"I am Gor'vett," the Vaar said. "Might I know your name, warrior?"

Simmonne backed away. Rhoxx's tail stopped flicking. The kodaz shifted his weight forward onto his knuckles and parted his legs. His tail rose to point straight behind him. "No."

Rhoxx's mouth opened, sucking in a long breath before he sent it back out. Simmonne fell against the wall, her eyes shutting as she covered her ears. Rhoxx's roar was unlike anything she had heard before; it shook something primitive within her. She opened her eyes as the sound abated to see the kodaz launch forward.

She felt each step the kodaz took in her bones. For all his bulk, he seemed to move so fast. With a dozen tons of enraged kodaz barreling toward him, the Vaar took a step back. But the warrior had height and reach. He drove his arm forward, punching with the long spike of his tonfa. Rhoxx turned his head, catching the spike with the fragment of his helmet that remained. The kodaz answered with a broad sweep of his right arm.

Rhoxx's claws created a flash of sparks as they were intercepted by the weapon in the Vaar's left hand. The warrior was slammed into the wall so hard that the corridor shook. Rhoxx's claws drew five long gashes through the wall where the Vaar was a second before.

The smart thing to do would be to run. Run and put some distance between her and them. But Simmonne only moved as far as the door. She saw Lilac, split in two by this monster's bayonet.

At the corridor's end, the Vaar had come to terms. This was not an alien he could simply overpower. He moved quickly now, stepping in to strike before stepping back out. Each swing of his tonfa turned the gentle wail into an air-piercing scream. Each strike aimed for Rhoxx's exposed head. But with one attack, he kept his offense going for too long. Rhoxx's teeth slammed shut on the Vaar's forearm with a loud crunch.

He could not bite through the Vaar's armor, but neither could the Vaar free his arm from the crushing force. The Vaar twirled the tonfa, gripping it as he aimed for Rhoxx's head. Rhoxx hooked the Vaar's legs with his claws and took him down.

"Get him," Simmonne whispered before shouting, "Kill him!"

With the kodaz's back to her, she could not see exactly what was transpiring. But she felt the blast of hot air. The Vaar ignited the thrusters in his armor, and both combatants were swept down the hall. When the Vaar cut the flow, Rhoxx flew over him. The big kodaz lost his grip, and the Vaar lost one of his tonfas. Rhoxx crashed into the stairs, and both scrambled to their feet.

The two charged each other again—the Vaar intent on reclaiming his weapon, and Rhoxx barreling down to stop him. The Vaar won, snatching the weapon from the ground before holding both up to shield his face. Rhoxx's blow sent the Vaar reeling, and the kodaz pursued.

So fixated on their fight, Simmonne did not fully comprehend that they were speeding toward her until she was forced to flee the door. The Vaar's back met the doorway as Rhoxx slammed into him. One swipe of the kodaz's claws batted the protection of the tonfas away. A second strike let out a wail of metal at the Vaar's neck. Rhoxx threw an uppercut that took the Vaar off his feet, and his helmet clattered on the floor.

Simmonne scampered for one of the towers of stacked drums. Rhoxx seemed to be winning, but he could lose. She should use the opportunity to hide, but this was Lilac's killer. For Lilac, for all her guards. If she could not avenge them, she had to watch as Rhoxx did it in her stead.

A blood-curdling roar brought her back to the fight. Rhoxx had gone in for the killing blow, but the Vaar swung to meet it. The blade of his tonfa found one of the holes in Rhoxx's armor, cleaving his arm at the elbow.

"Rhoxx," she whispered, her eyes darting between him and the lost appendage. Blood flowing from the stump was quickly halted as Rhoxx backed away, and his armor cinched around the wound. Now on defense, Rhoxx flung his left arm side to side, using his remaining claws against the Vaar's renewed assault.

She had to do something. She had to help. But what could she do? She didn't have a gun. If she came too close, one of the giant aliens would squish her like a bug.

Rhoxx batted one of the Vaar's blows aside before turning. The kodaz lunged, throwing his hip into the Vaar. The warrior was taken off his feet again and collided with drums. Water sprayed across the room as the tower collapsed on him and the drums burst. Rhoxx paused to examine his arm.

The Vaar did not stay down for long, rising out of the drums with an angry roar. He scanned for a missing tonfa, but with Rhoxx bearing down on him again, he did not have time to find it. Instead he grabbed one of the nearby drums and hurtled it. The drum exploded in Rhoxx's face, shattering the beautiful crest of bone on his brow. Dazed by the hit, Rhoxx's blocks were slower, and the Vaar pushed him back.

When the Vaar came in for a blow from above, Rhoxx tried to catch him with another hip-check. He missed. Twisting on his heel, the Vaar maneuvered around him and struck. The blade found a gap in the abdominal plates of Rhoxx's armor. Rhoxx's pained roar became a gargle as the blade sank into his organs. With his open hand, the Vaar grabbed Rhoxx by the shoulder, driving the blade deeper into the kodaz's guts.

Rhoxx's mouth opened, and fluids poured out onto the deck. The Vaar took another step, withdrawing the blade and pushing Rhoxx to the ground.

"Rhoxx." Simmonne covered her mouth. He wasn't moving. His eyes were closed. No, not dead. He couldn't be dead. She focused her mind on him, his agony. Alive, but dying?

Her fixation was broken when the Vaar turned to her. His mouth hung open to show broken teeth, and blood wept from his nostrils. All twelve pupils of his eyes locked on her. She backed away and he followed. Between the stacks of drums, her back met the wall and the Vaar came to her.

"It's over, little one." He growled. "Come here."

She could not see Rhoxx with the Vaar in the way. She couldn't even sense him with the mass of barely contained rage looming over her. How would she tell the colonel he was dead? That he died trying to protect her? Her guards, Rhoxx. Not again. How many were going to die for her?

"Come here. *Now!*" the Vaar shouted.

She flinched as he grabbed one of the drums and slammed it into the ground so hard that it split into a blast of water. It was over. With a resigned nod, she stepped forward. Then she heard the roar.

She saw the gleam of teeth as the Vaar turned, and Rhoxx's jaws slammed together. The Vaar let out a wail of agony as the long teeth pierced his unprotected eyes and trapped his head. The Vaar flailed, knocking drums out of the towers. Simmonne pressed her back to the wall and brought her arms up to shield herself as the towers collapsed, but she kept her eyes ahead.

Wrenched by the unrelenting grip, the Vaar moved with the kodaz. Rhoxx's long tail extended back, then curled over the edge of the pool. The Vaar's foot slipped on one of the rolling drums while flailing blindly at Rhoxx with his tonfa. With a great pull, Rhoxx drew the Vaar off his feet and plunged them both into the pool.

The splashing continued under the surface like a broken fountain spewing endless streams of bubbles, and the warrior's agonized screams vanished beneath the water. The floor shook as the two continued to pound each other. Slowly, the rattles began to ebb, the splashes ceased, and the bubbles stopped. Still trembling, Simmonne had to peel herself off the wall. She stepped over and around the heavy drums as she approached the pool. At the edge she crouched and peered over the side.

"Rhoxx?"

The water was too deep. She could only make out a single silhouette at the bottom. She could not read beyond her own fear to grasp the number of minds beneath her.

"Rhoxx!" she shouted.

Seconds became minutes, and she continued to stare. He could breathe underwater, but she could not make out any movement. What if he was too injured? She couldn't focus enough to scan for him. She had to calm down.

The large silhouette broke into two. "Rhoxx!"

The surface of the water exploded as Rhoxx hurtled out, belly-flopping onto the deck. She was on him in an instant, wrapping her arms around his scaly neck.

"I thought you were dead," she whispered, hugging him tightly. "I thought you weren't coming up."

"Havin' ssstay," Rhoxx answered with a wheeze. "Not make him missstake."

He paused to hack up a mass of fluid. Simmonne looked at the pool.

"So, he *is* dead?"

"Waterlogged."

She released him to look at his severed arm. "We have to get you back to the ship. Can you walk?"

He took a deep breath before letting out a sigh. "I t'inkin' maybe I jusss' lie down here a minute." His mouth opened wider to let out a gargle that made Simmonne cringe. "Don't you be worry. Notin' deep-fryer not fixin'. All 'em Vaar dead. Go get Andeera. Ssshe comin' get me wit' a cargo raft."

"Okay," Simmonne answered, rising to her feet. "I'll go get her. Just, just wait right there."

Rhoxx swiveled one eye to her. "I not goin' anywhere."

She nodded and made for the door, pausing a second to look back. "Thank you, Rhoxx."

"Jusss, doin' what I do. Prinssesss."

CHAPTER
11D

EVER SINCE THE CONSTRUCTION of the Solar Cathedral, every emperor began his reign by ascending the two thousand stairs. Each emperor made the climb alone. Each stair was meant to be taken in contemplation of every step they had taken to reach this point. Every word they would speak while on the throne. Every nation, every race, every person in the Empire. All were meant to be in their thoughts as they climbed.

The entire ascent was broadcasted, of course. Few would watch it in its entirety. Steven stood in a small lift, which ferried him up to the beginning of the stairs. The lift corrected itself to bring him up at the appropriate second. Steven had arrived early, prolonging the trip.

He was in his greatest finery. A pristine white shirt, five thousand threads of Dalkotta silk. A silk made only for the clothes of emperors and kings. Pants and coat in blue were made of the same fibers. Over his right shoulder, he wore a heavy baldric lined in quantum stars. Synthetic gemstones required such great time and care to make, only the most elite of society could afford it. Along the baldric he wore the commendations awarded him for his time in the Armadas. He looked down at the baldric and wished he had spent more time in the service. More commendations would have looked more impressive. At least one award for valor would have eased his self-consciousness. A Solar scion was never intentionally allowed into a situation where such a commendation could be earned.

Steven thumbed the baldric. A part of him had always expected to be elated at this moment. That he would strain to maintain his composure. He had always expected that his mother would be here in the lift with him to send him up the stairs. That his father would be waiting for him at the top. That he would step onto the throne pedestal and see the eyes of his siblings. That he would see their efforts to be dignified, even going so far as to pretend to be happy for him. All while they seethed inside. It was an experience he would never have now.

He thought of Simmonne. Their father wanted her to be here, to make the climb. His lips moved into a sneer. Why? Why would he choose her? Why would he even think she wanted it? This wasn't what she wanted out of life. Not that he would ever know that. Steven could never understand how a man could read minds and see the future yet understand so little about his children.

His mouth became dry as he contemplated the words he had to speak.

What he had done, what he had to do. It was the way of things. There would always be a need for power and a need for someone to wield that power. Many a ruler had to do great and terrible things to be that person. He was not the first, and he would not be the last. The time was fast approaching. He toggled his NOD to access Galaxy News. Four people sat around a table, each taking turns talking to keep their audience entertained as the moment approached.

"In a little over two minutes, Prince Steven will enter the corridor."

"You have to wonder what's going through his mind about now."

"I can't imagine what he must be feeling now. His entire family gone, a major war, and everything else. Few emperors have ever come to power in such turmoil."

The lift let out a chime. One minute warning.

Steven left the talking heads in the background. He stood as straight as possible. Shoulders back, but not so far back that it looked forced. Careful steps from heel to toe. His face had to say grief and resolve with every expression. He needed to retain a thousand-meter stare. The lift chimed again—thirty seconds. Steven stared at the door. Thirty seconds to destiny.

The talking heads fell silent. The lift slowed to a stop, and the door slid down.

A narrow corridor greeted him and led to the base of the stairs. The walls and floor were all cast in gold. A pair of deltas snapped to attention as he stepped between them. A dozen spherical automatech hovered silently along the walls, each providing a feed for the media outlets fixated on this moment. Beyond them, to the right of the stairs, was Indorai.

Steven still could not see him fully, but it seemed that even Indorai had adorned himself for the occasion. He wore his tendrils about him like a cloak, their silver color now replaced with gold. Steven did his best to show no reaction to his presence and did not look at him directly. His hand clenched slowly, popping his knuckles. He proceeded forward.

"Are you planning on accompanying me?" Steven sent the thought as he kept his sight focused on the stairs.

"The emperor must make the climb alone," Indorai answered as he bowed. *"I will meet you above."*

Steven paused before the first step and peered up at the long way ahead. If only it could have come another way. He inhaled a deep breath through his nose and let it out through his mouth. He took the first step.

"The climb has begun." One of the talking heads broke their silence. "The ascension of Steven the First. We will continue our coverage through the climb and the coronation."

The small drones followed from a respectful distance as Steven took the next step on the gilded stairs. Many alcoves lined the walls, each bearing the statue of someone important. Many called this Emperor's Boulevard, and to have a statue on it was one of the Empire's greatest honors. The first two statues went back to the beginning: Emperor Christopher I and High King Manfred. Steven paused to face Christopher. He tried to find some semblance of himself in the first emperor's face, but there was none. Too many generations apart, maybe, for a likeness to be shared.

"Prince Steven, looking now at the image of Emperor Christopher I. It really is a testament to the Mandrakes. A hundred thousand years and counting. Most civilizations do not last as long as they have held the throne."

Steven knew that voice. Hallex Valken, "the most trusted man in media." A bag that never ran out of hot air as far as Steven was concerned. He continued up the stairs, leaving the talkers to talk. Natalie waited for him at the top. After all these years, he would finally keep the promise. Just a little longer.

"Prince Steven stopping now at the statue of Donetter Keems. Truly a hero. For viewers who may be rusty on their history, Donetter Keems served in the Legionnaires during the Eclipse. He remains the most decorated soldier in Imperial history, and the only four-time recipient of the Solar Cross. Truly someone worthy of his position on Emperor's Boulevard."

Steven did not stop there simply for appearances. Donetter Keems was a hero of his. As a child he had planned on giving his mandatory service to the Legionnaires. It was only when he was mature enough to realize how far he'd be kept from danger that he decided on the Armadas. He could not tarry too long. For the audience Steven raised his arm and returned the statue's eternal salute.

Valken continued to narrate every stop he made, informing the ignorant on the identity of each statue. There were only two thousand steps and four thousand alcoves. As time went on, the dwindling number of slots forced incredible scrutiny on any candidate to hold a position here. If the Encephalon was right about the war to come, it would almost certainly add a few statues to the Boulevard.

Steven had allotted himself ninety minutes to climb the steps and make the respectful stops he needed to make. The time passed quickly. He had not allotted himself enough to make every stop he planned. But that was fine; it was his coronation. He could make people wait.

As he approached the end of the great stairway, the sounds of the chamber bled from above. Few in it spoke above whispers, but their sheer number created a cacophony to beckon the way. That multitudinous din was silenced by a single booming voice.

"All rise for His Solar Majesty Prince Steven Mandrake."

That silence came as quickly as though every soul in the chamber had died as one. Steven stepped onto the final stair and out onto the Blue Floor with his back to the crowd. Ahead lay the star dais, the towering platform with yet more stairs, but atop which his throne stood. The hatch to the two thousand stairs slid shut, and he wasted no time beginning the final climb. With the first step, he brought the news back into his NOD.

"Prince Steven ascending the star dais now," Valken said, "the last time he will do so as a prince. I am sure he will have much to say at the top."

In other circumstances, Steven would not have been alone in this final stage. Those he had chosen to be the officers of his court would stand on the stairs of the star dais. As he ascended, he would stop to touch each on the shoulder, a small but public confirmation of his endorsement. But in the haste of his coronation, there was no time to formally select such persons.

The sapphire throne was in view, and he resisted the urge to hasten. No sense risking a trip on the stairs and an embarrassing start to his reign. He almost forgot to pause as he came to the final stair near the seats that had belonged to his brothers and sisters. All empty now. He bowed his head briefly before at last completing the climb.

Dressed in their finery, Natalie and Jasmine waited. Jasmine greeted him with a restrained smile, while Natalie simply acknowledged his presence with her gaze. Two others stood on this high level, bearing the objects of the ceremony. Steven turned so his right side faced the crowd.

Not since the last coronation had so many gathered in person on the Blue Floor. Every senator with enough clout to gain a seat had come, more of the nobility than would ever be gathered for any other occasion. The entirety of the Senate's justiciars. The archdukes of many nations, even many of the isolationist species who so rarely ventured beyond their home stars. Alien species Steven had rarely, if ever, beheld with his eyes. But at the forefront of them all, with seats closest to the foot of the star dais, the kings and queens of the pillar nations watched him.

Franseo Andretti, known as the Jolly King to the people of Del Tierr, had made his body an obese caricature of itself to bolster that image. Szymon Novak II of the Orion Estate was a man so pretty he would have made a fine woman. He was the youngest of the royals by far. Queen Sera Stofferson of the Republic of Andromeda had a mind ravaged by NNED. She likely had no idea where she was, let alone why she was there. Yet still she wore a crown. The only people as useless as her idiot sons were her idiot daughters.

Most formidable of those at the floor was King Banū Yao. Neither his height nor build contributed to his presence. He was somewhat scrawny and showed all of his 2,500 years. As a younger man, he might have been prettier than Szymon Novak. All of his imperious aura was in his face, an expression that seemed always to be scheming, and eyes that spoke of a mind with the vision to carry out its plans. A perfect example of what the Yuani people called "the face of a king."

Last among them was the mother to a nation of needy children. Queen Alana Mae wore the outward mask of the kindly old matron, but behind that mask, she wore the face of a vindictive shrew, needing only the flimsiest of pretexts to destroy a person, their family, and every enterprise they had touched. Her days as queen of the Elysian Commonwealth were numbered, and her replacement, Duchess Helga Faulk, sat a few seats behind her.

Only one monarch was absent from the front row. High King Jonas von Rhinegrave IV, who sat neither with the other monarchs nor at his chair as first lord. Steven turned to face him now. With the previous emperor and empress deceased, it fell to the high king to perform the crowning. A pair of lantai servitors stood beside him, each holding a blue pillow that bore a crown.

Steven beheld the crowd in his peripherals and kept his eyes straight ahead on the high king. His red hair and beard, always worn in braids, were now bound by so much gold that his hair might have appeared to be made of the metal from a distance. His great coat and cape of red and gold seemed to add to the immensity of the man who wore it. Something about it had always been funny to Steven, the Rhinegrave obsession with their height and build. The size did not make the man any more than the crown made the king.

The high king broke the silence with a booming voice. Steven did not turn his gaze as the high king spoke, and Indorai materialized behind him.

"We are gathered here on this day 135 of our year 100,016 for the coronation of our new emperor. Steven Mandrake, are you prepared?"

Steven raised his chin slightly. "I am, High King."

The high king gave a nod, and Steven raised his right hand.

"Prince Steven, do you swear to uphold the safety and prosperity of all nations?"

"I do," he answered.

"Do you swear to uphold the Olympian Terms, the covenant of nations, and to the best of your ability, respect the sovereign dominion of those nations?"

"I do."

"Do you swear to preserve and protect the continued existence of all sapient species who bear their loyalty to the Solar Empire?"

"I do."

"Do you accept this sacred task and the powers of this office, of your own free will, unbeholden to any but your loyalty to the Empire and its people?"

Steven nodded slowly. "I do."

"Then as High King of the Dominion, First Lord of the House of Nobles, and on behalf of the Senate in its entirety, I recognize you as Emperor Steven Mandrake the First."

The high king turned to the first of the servitors and took the Solar Halo from the pillow. It was designed to hover about the emperor's brow. Solid gold had been taken from Earth from similar crowns of ancient royalty. A quantum star the size of a fist was set at the center. Its size could break the light that entered it and cast rainbows on any wall and floor close enough to the wearer. Latin words of wisdom in blue enamel lined its primary ring. Golden posts evoked the cardinal directions, each capped in its own gem.

Steven did not need to bow his head as the towering king brought the halo down. No human head could comfortably bear such weight, and in place, the great crown hovered about his brow. It was finally where it belonged.

The high king turned again, this time taking the pillow from the second servitor. On it lay the aquanna, the most ornate and formal of the crowns reserved for the empress. The high king held the pillow and looked at Steven expectantly.

When Steven married for the second time, it had created much talk, rumor, and gossip, most of it in anticipation of this moment. Emperors generally did not marry more than one wife, and thus no official protocol existed to determine which one owned this crown. Only Steven's whim. But there was never any question in his mind.

Steven beckoned her forward. Jasmine already knew and cast her gaze down, and Natalie stepped forward to meet him. Steven took the aquanna from the pillow and held it high before bringing it down. Its beauty seemed to fit so perfectly with the red-gold fibers of her hair.

Natalie did not smile. At first she did not react at all. Then she let out a sniffle. A single tear slipped from her eye to roll down her cheek.

"This has to be an emotional time for Natalie and Jasmine as well." Valken's voice wormed back into Steven's NOD. "All the talk in the media so far has been how recent events affect His Majesty. But the rest of the Mandrakes were their family, too. To lose them all so suddenly, I don't know that anyone can simply parse that kind of tragedy."

With an annoyed tweak in his cheek, Steven dismissed the news again.

A second tear joined the first. As Natalie reached toward her eye, Steven reeled her in. She sobbed a bit louder and returned his embrace. The 4CM of her new crown was nothing to him now. Her thoughts were many. Tea with Emily, hard liquor with Eliza. A Founding Day gift from his parents. Perhaps she had been closer to some of them than even she realized.

Steven turned his gaze as Jasmine joined the embrace. Natalie took another breath, composing herself before gently pushing away. With a solemn nod, Steven held out his hands, motioning Natalie to the seat that was now hers, and Jasmine to the one that had been added for her. Once they sat, he turned toward the podium, beside which Indorai now stood.

"Your public awaits."

In his NOD Steven brought his speech to the forefront of his sight. Directly ahead of the throne, a podium rose, and Indorai stood beside it. Steven laid his hands on the podium and remained silent.

Don't speak immediately. Always wait a moment at the podium. Let them focus their attention and anticipate what you have to say.

He was only seven when his father spoke those words to him. Whatever mistakes he made in the final years of his life, he had been a good man. Steven's moment of reverie was soon broken.

"Now you must give the words of leadership. The only true freedom most seek is from responsibility. You must give them that freedom, with direction and conviction."

"Five days ago, I woke up and had breakfast with my family. Four days ago, I woke up and became an orphan." He paused to allow those words to sink into the minds of all who listened.

"I long suspected that I would be the one to succeed my father. I expected to stand just behind where I am now and listen to him give his departing speech to those he served for so long. I expected that he would be the one to set the crown on my brow. That I would come to this podium and give an uplifting speech. That I would leave this podium and celebrate the accomplishment of a lifetime ambition."

A scripted pause. He closed his eyes and counted to twenty so that all who watched could see and believe he was holding back his tears. That he carried a burden of mourning that even noble grief struggled to process. All to make him look stronger by pushing through it.

"Instead, I come to the throne as the son of murdered parents. The brother of murdered siblings. I come to the throne not in a time of peace but in a time of war against a wicked enterprise."

Another scripted pause, he stood up straighter and looked around the hall.

"For years now, the Interstellar Combine has tried to paint itself as some kind of victim. This, this is nothing new. Those who victimize others often try to wrap themselves in a blanket of victimhood, as part of some means to justify their actions. Perhaps a life spent in politics has desensitized me, but I am not surprised by this. What does surprise me, what disappoints me, is how many of you have allowed yourselves to fall for this lie.

"Let us not forget that when we entered the Hourglass Galaxy, we found the Combine pursuing wars of aggression against not one, or two, but three other civilizations. Civilizations whose only crime was needing to expand to new worlds so as to build better lives for their people.

"My father recognized the Combine's naked lust for conquest for what it was. He did not intervene to protect trade or other interests. There is literally nothing the quants, the evulta, or the nakori have that we need. There is nothing they have that we do not—and do not have better incarnations of. He did it because he saw a great evil being enacted, and he would not be the man who did nothing. He did it because it was the right thing to do."

He paused again to spread his gaze throughout the chamber. Some looked directly ahead at him. Others had their heads down. But all hung on his words.

"It is the founding mission of the Empire to unite all sapient species under one banner. I can think of no nation whose conduct better exemplifies this need than the Combine. Its history and that of the Vaar is one of constant bloodshed. Their behavior, indeed their national identity, is that of a bully. One that uses force and intimidation against anyone and everyone weaker than itself. And that, until now, has never faced anyone strong enough to stand up to it."

He held out a hand, allowing the Cathedral to bring him a glass of water. He drank slowly, making the audience wait.

"Over the last few days, I have tried to separate my feelings from my reason. As I have asked myself how to respond to the Combine's aggression, I feel I have done as well as any man could be asked. To make a decision rooted in reason rather than emotion. To implement a task forward-thinking, rather than reactionary. Yet I find myself coming to the same conclusion.

"As emperor, I am issuing a formal declaration of war against the Interstellar Combine. When one begins a war, he must have a clear objective in mind. He must also have in mind a clear understanding of when it will be time for the war to end. My study of the Combine's actions and its history leads me to only one conclusion. That not even the unconditional surrender of our enemy will be a sufficient end."

Murmurs rose through the hall. Steven answered them with a glare that called for silence, and it was respected.

"The aim of this conflict shall be nothing less than debellation, the destruction of the Interstellar Combine as a state entity. If this is not done, the Combine will use the peace that proceeds this conflict to rebuild its strength. And then to menace us or others once again. I will not allow that to happen.

"I would not blame the Combine for believing that we would run from this conflict. That we would simply abandon our allies, and our holdings, and take the easy temptation of peace at the expense of others. It has been so long since the Empire has faced a major conflict, an existential threat. I would not blame them for thinking we lack the resolve to see this through. But every generation must face its own tribulations. It must fight its own battles and endure its own suffering. It must find its own path to triumph. I know we are equal to this task."

He consciously reshaped his face to an expression of determination.

"By my authority as emperor, I am ordering all assets of the Solar Armed Forces be brought to active duty. All reserve forces are to be activated. Not even the Combine may stand against the full might of the Empire. But make no mistake. The Combine is an intergalactic civilization, whose majority enterprise for the sum of its existence has been war. Victory will not come quickly. The Empire will be required to project its might on a scale never seen before.

"To this end I am using my power of edict to nullify the Supercruiser Act.[19] I task the kings and the archdukes to enhance their forces. That they may be ready to maintain the order of their territories as the forces of the throne carry out the task ahead. I speak to every resident of the Empire, and I ask you to join me in this endeavor. This is the trial that has been handed to us, and I ask you to help ensure that it is ours alone. That we raise an armament so great that we do not allow this to become a generational burden. But instead for it to begin and end with us. That our children will know of this conflict but not be asked to fight it. The recruiters of the Solar Armed

---

19   The Supercruiser Act is most well-known by the general public for its prohibition that forbids the individual nations from building and operating their own supercruisers. The act in its entirety is the primary law of the Empire restricting the size and capabilities of the royal and noble guard forces as a whole. Its many provisions extend beyond supercruisers to the total number of warships, capabilities, and individual soldiers a nation may have at any given time.

Forces wait to receive you."

Steven let out a long sigh, scripted but no less in earnest. His pause brought utter silence to the chamber.

"You must complete the task, Steven."

He ground his teeth as he tried to summon the words.

"Anger is the most powerful of emotions. Its capacity to originate action is unmatched. For your family's death, there is great anger. Power uncontrolled and unguided begets only ruin."

Behind closed eyelids, he saw Simmonne, four years old, asleep in his lap.

"Is there any other way?"

"None."

"The final matter I would address today," he said to his audience, "is my sister. By now everyone knows how the Vaar entered the Cathedral. The specter of betrayal from within the family. I do not think enough time has passed for me to truly process this. I know only what the evidence suggests. Even her whereabouts at this moment are unknown. I will not leap to conclusions or pronounce premature judgments. However, by my authority as emperor, I am ordering Princess Simmonne's immediate arrest by any police or military force in a position to do so. Once this arrest is executed, she is to be brought immediately to the Cathedral to answer either for betrayal or the gross negligence that allowed this tragedy to occur."

He took a step back from the podium and turned. A hum of applause filled the chamber. Not of sensation and fanfare. Slow, some out of obligation to do so as the speech ended, and others out of solidarity.

"That was not the plan, Steven."

"It was enough. The suspicion has been cast."

With his head high, Steven turned to his seat. In a move he had practiced countless times before, he sat at last on the sapphire throne. The next speech was to be given by the Executor of Defense, and Steven leaned back in his chair.

"My attention must now be divided elsewhere." Indorai's voice slipped into his mind. *"If I am needed, call me, and I will answer."*

Steven did not answer. He looked at Natalie and reached over the great arm of the throne to find her hand.

CHAPTER
12A

KASSAR, NOVIN, RHOXX. THEY would never forgive him. That feeling had lingered in the back of his mind as a tingle in his spine since the armory had come to the front. The red mist permeated the chamber now. There was a roar as the fire control ceased, and air pumped back into the chamber.

"What the hell are you?" Panzer called out to the creature on the loading dock. The creature's black tendrils seemed to have no defined length. While the upper pair coiled about its body, the rest flicked about behind it.

"You can see me," it answered. *"You can endure my voice unfiltered. You must tell me. How many voices do you hear?"*

How many voices? What kind of question was that? How many was he supposed to hear? Even though he could not see it, he could sense the smile on its face. Something wicked, beyond alien in its guise.

"You only hear one, don't you?" it asked as one of its tendrils pointed at him like an accusing finger. *"The rest hear four. Their minds cannot handle it, a voice that speaks to them outside of time. That speaks to them from past, present, and beyond. It creates a resonance in their consciousness, a fourth note, and so they hear four voices. But you only hear one."*

Panzer glanced again at the containment field and the open door across the bay. He looked down the corridor, where thousands of marines should have been barreling down on him now. But instead, when he looked at the tactical map, he saw the icons moving away.

"Andira, why are the Vaar retreating?"

"Sir, I—" Andira's voice cracked as the empty visage raised an arm toward him. Panzer heard something pop in his helmet, and then nothing.

"Andira?" he whispered. "Andira?"

"Your little friend will not help you here," the creature remarked as it lowered its arm. *"We need some privacy. I would prefer she not record me."*

"Andira?"

>>ACCESS COMPANION

ACCESSING . . .

ERROR—NO COMPANION INSTALLED

"Andira?" Panzer whispered as he glared at the message.

"We went to a great deal of trouble to bring you here," the hollow image said. *"I imagine you will be quite the legend for this rescue. The colonists will tell stories of you to any who will listen. The commando who came into the jaws of the beast to rescue them."*

Panzer's gaze turned as a second hollow image formed beside the first. This one was taller, broader, but less defined. He made the mistake next of reaching out with his mind.

His breath caught in his throat and he gagged. Panzer doubled over, laying a hand on his helmet. Capillaries burst in his face as blood trickled out of his mouth and nose. In an attempt to scan them both, he touched the mind behind the tendrils. The sensation of frostbite tickled his nerves as he fell against the wall. Like a hand that had grabbed frozen metal and could not let go, he could not withdraw.

"Even the most gifted child is but a child. Be mindful of your fumbling."

The grip on his mind withdrew, and Panzer wheezed as he sucked in a deep breath.

"This must be strange for you," the empty vessel said mockingly, *"to know wherever you go that you are the strongest. Now to feel so small."*

"What?" Panzer wheezed, still fighting for breath. "Who are you?"

"The longer we exist, the more identities we gather. I am old and many. I am the augury of rebirth, precursor of change, and omen of ruin. I am that which providence portends, mastery of movement. The old nemesis."

Unsure of what to say, Panzer said nothing. He sensed a powerful mind in this creature. It taunted his senses like static on his skin. Even the commandant wasn't this strong. Not even close.

"You see my presence but not the details." Panzer sensed a strange air of disappointment. *"Perhaps that was expecting too much. Very well. I will show you."*

There was a thunderclap in his mind, and Panzer held an arm to shield his helmet. Lightning ravaged the mist as it condensed around the hollow image. Long tongues of voltage danced across the bay, sparking on the floor, the ceiling, the train, and the containment field. The second image did not move.

"No," Panzer whispered as the creature took shape. He knew this visage. From family history, Corps archives, and ancient records. Two and a half meters tall with a scalp crowned by a wreath of small horns. A mouth with four mandibles, two within that opened like a man's, two larger beyond that opened horizontally. More tiny horns rimmed its jawline. It wore a carapace of plates much like a Vaar but in the color of fresh blood. Two toes on each foot brandished broad claws. Its hands seemed too wide for its arms, each with vicious serrated claws.

Two eyes seemed to glow like pools of molten metal. The third eye was the largest, set in the center of the forehead. It opened to reveal a silver disc, barely visible in the sea of gold.

In disbelief Panzer stared. He had never heard of its kind having the black tendrils that sprouted from its body. But the rest of its form was unmistakable. He did not even hear his whisper as he beheld the ancient foe.

"Therican."

"Yes," it answered, its mouth unmoving. *"The first Therican, and the last, as it were."*

The only thing unchanged was the creature's tendrils, impossibly black save for edges that produced a silver glow. They contracted and came together to form a cloak around the Therican.

Panzer worked to find his breath and managed to stand straight. "You're the one who's been helping the Vaar with their tech. The one telling them about us."

"Oh, I've done much more than that," the Therican answered. *"I was preparing for this day thousands of years before you were born. My name is Indorai."*

It was no longer invisible, no longer hollow. What about its defenses? Panzer's hand moved for the Hellbore's handle before he stopped. He needed information. So many of the answers seemed to have fallen into his lap. Where the Vaar were learning scientific and technological secrets. How they knew to build 4CM systems before ever contacting humanity. The answers and the information were here.

"I'm flattered," Panzer answered. "Why are we talking?"

"So many are born believing they are special. Yet we are born as nothing, and so few possess the capacity to become more. The weight of mediocrity and futility builds as years pass over them. They wither, and the fire of arrogance is extinguished as they realize they are nothing, were nothing, and nothing is all they shall ever be. They assign meaning to things without it. To the life that has none. To children that shall never matter. To beauty that is fleeting, work unrewarding, and wealth insubstantial.

"You were brought here by purpose, but not the purpose you believed. The process of growth is often painful and rarely voluntary."

The Therican glanced aside at the second hollow image, but the silver disc in its third eye remained on Panzer. After several seconds, it looked back at him.

"You must come with me now."

???: Andira, are you there?

No answer came.

"Go with you?" Panzer answered with a scoff. "Why would I do that?"

"I know things your people could never learn on their own. I know the truth of what transpires here. Do you think this tiny feud between your Empire and the Combine has meaning? That any of your feuds and politicking mean anything?" The Therican's head shook slowly. *"It does not matter. It never did."* He extended his arm, offering one of his clawed hands. *"This is your invitation to relevance. I offer you my hand in friendship."*

Panzer's eyes narrowed, and his arm edged a bit higher. "Friendship? From a Therican?" He let out an audible scoff. "You said you were the first. Were you alive when your people were trying to destroy mine?"

"Oh yes," the Therican answered. *"I was there. I remember your ancestor, Manfred."*

Panzer held his breath. It knew who he was. Could it read his mind? How did it know?

"I existed long before him," the Therican finally spoke with its mouth, its organic voice no less unsettling. Each movement of its jaw brandished many large, sharp teeth. "But I remember him. There is some resemblance, even after all these generations. He was not so large and hated long hair on men, but you have his posture. Despite all that genetic work, some of him remains in you."

Panzer's heart pumped quickly, and his muscles bulged beneath the skin. "Then you were there. When your people were killing trillions of women and girls with disease. While they were bombing men to death from orbit. You were there while countless more starved and died. Why are you really here now? Some kind of revenge? Is that why you're helping the Vaar? Payback for your people? Or for your old master?"

The third eye blinked. "Old master? There is only one, and only one there will ever be." The Therican's foot slid forward until the claws of its toes slipped over the edge of the dock. It leaned toward Panzer. "I know he told you to come here." The Therican, Indorai, pointed back toward the view of ND-31 through the open bay door.

How did he know that? Was the Encephalon somehow in communication with this thing? Panzer cursed himself. If this thing was somehow able to read his mind, he had just given something away.

The Therican laughed. *"You're probably wondering if I can read your mind. If I know what you have in your secret vaults. No. Your mind is not open to me. The immunity of your mind is a sovereign privilege bestowed on you. Even I cannot see through it."*

If that were true, how did he know? How much did he know?

"Come with me, and I will answer all your questions," Indorai said, offering his arm again. "Refuse, and I will no longer be friendly."

Panzer's hand moved for the Hellbore.

"It did not work the first time," Indorai chided. "Or the second. How many times must you try?"

Panzer's eyes flicked back and forth between the Therican and the second image. "The answer is no," Panzer said. "Enemy of my forefathers, you are no friend of mine."

Indorai lowered his hand slowly. "I knew you would say no, but I wanted you to remember that I *did* ask." The hideous mouth moved as the outer mandibles parted, and the inner jaw seemed to grin. "I invited a friend of yours to join us."

The Therican turned to the second image as it materialized. The first thing that came into view was the bloodhammer. It hung from the hand of a Vaar, tall even by his species' standards. His enormous crest fanned out at its apex to be broader than the shoulders beneath. Panzer sensed the new mind as the warrior came into full view. The hate radiating from the Vaar told him what the face did not.

"Oul'sor," Panzer whispered.

"I leave it to you now, Oul'sor," Indorai announced before turning back to Panzer. "Accomplish your task."

Cracks ripped through the Therican's body like breaking ice. As the body disintegrated, the hollow image was left in its place. To the side Oul'sor hefted the bloodhammer. When Panzer looked back at the hollow image, it was gone. Only a slurry of matter remained where it had stood. Panzer turned his focus back to Oul'sor.

"How many times am I going to have to kill you, Oul'sor?"

The Vaar rotated the bloodhammer in his grasp. "At least once more."

Oul'sor took a step off the ledge to join Panzer in the trench.

"Think maybe you should go put some armor on?" Panzer nodded toward him.

Oul'sor did not answer.

"Suit yourself."

Panzer's hand shot over his shoulder to seize the Hellbore. The weapon extended in his grasp, and he took aim.

Everything stopped.

Panzer's arms, legs, and even his eyes were paralyzed. A dilation wave? Now? He had not sensed one since he came out of the deep-fryer. But he was sensing one now?

That was not the case, Panzer realized, because Oul'sor was moving.

The Vaar approached with his hammer resting on one shoulder. Panzer could not even strain his body to move. As with the time stop of a dilation wave, his body did not even seem to exist. Yet Oul'sor walked toward him, almost leisurely. The Vaar stopped before him, planted his feet, and held the hammer with both hands. His body twisted, winding up the swing.

Panzer sent the command to his armor to engage his thrusters. But there was no answer. Oul'sor let the swing loose, stepping in to deliver the blow. Sensation returned, and Panzer felt the g-forces of his thrusters opening to full. The bloodhammer missed by centimeters. With a terrible wail of metal, the weapon carved a channel through the wall where Panzer had been.

Panzer cut thrust, spinning to face Oul'sor again and beholding the damage his hammer had done. The deep channel caught his attention—more like the cut of a massive blade than a hammer. Carved through a wall of solid illstas. *That* was no ordinary bloodhammer. When his feet met the trench, Panzer brought the Hellbore back to his shoulder.

The world froze again. Yet Oul'sor still moved.

The Vaar came toward him faster this time, holding the hammer with one hand near the end of its long handle. He came forward, skidding on his feet into the wind-up. When the hammer came in, Panzer was once more able to move. But it was too late for him to dodge the swing.

The hammer came in with such speed that it engaged Panzer's shielding, piercing through in a brilliant flash. Panzer let out a grunt, drowned out by the shrill sound of compressing metal as the armor of his right arm was compacted. His arm slammed into his torso, and the force hurtled him to the side. His ankle struck the top of the trench, then he tumbled over the deck. He only stopped when he collided with the still-raised safety sleeve of the routing terminal.

PRIMARY SHIELD PROJECTORS—OFFLINE

CONCUSSION FIELD—OFFLINE

SECONDARY SHIELD PROJECTORS—ENGAGED

Panzer was clambering to his feet when Oul'sor hopped onto the deck with him. The Vaar pointed the hammer toward him.

"Do you remember what you said to me, Crykeeper?" Oul'sor spoke in a strangely calm voice. "Do you remember what you said? About how my son died?"

Panzer glanced at the Hellbore. Undamaged. The same could not be said for his right arm, where armor paneling was flaking off onto the deck.

Panzer seized on Oul'sor's pause, raising the Hellbore again. This time he managed to fire a shot before everything froze. All had stopped as the first round left the barrel, in the fraction of a second before the shell's tiny MID came online. Just beyond the muzzle, the yellow-tip round froze like everything else.

Oul'sor came toward him again, walking as if he had all the time in the universe. He stooped to examine the Hellbore. His gaze eventually moved to the single round that had escaped the muzzle. After rising, Oul'sor positioned himself again, wound up the hammer, and stepped forward.

When he could move, Panzer's thrusters were open to full, but it was too late. The added thrust augmented his momentum when the hammer slammed into his right side again. Panzer could not stop the impact, not before he slammed into the wall. With the concussion field offline, his body took the full brunt of the hit. His head slammed against the side of his helmet. Combat instinct took over as the conscious mind was dazed. He turned his back into the wall to push himself up, but his body gave out. He slid down until he was seated.

Oul'sor was on him with impossible speed. The Vaar's foot came down on his chest, the large toes covering his faceplate and binding as his helmet was pressed against the wall. Barely conscious, Panzer choked on the blood that ran down from his eyes, nose, and scalp.

Lucidity raced back when he felt a foreign grip on the Hellbore, then a pull extended his arm. The Vaar's toes cleared his faceplate, and a fist came in. Panzer's head was still recoiling from the first blow when the second landed. The third came even quicker. Panzer could not ask himself what happened as his helmet was driven into the wall. Questions like how Oul'sor could pack such strength. How could he punch an R-steel plate so hard without shattering his own bones? The hits kept coming, dribbling his head into the wall until Panzer went limp.

He was too dim to feel the pressure mounting on his arm. Blurry vision yielded three Oul'sors looming over him. The Vaar's second hand clamped down on Panzer's forearm. Suddenly the pressure was released, and Panzer sagged against the wall.

CRANIAL REPAIR COULD NOT BE COMPLETED.
SEEK IMMEDIATE MEDICAL ASSISTANCE.

Cognizance returned as he read the words. Still he saw three Oul'sors, each holding and examining a Hellbore. Something else as well.

Panzer glared down at his right arm, and for a second, he could only stare. What he saw made no sense. The metal had been twisted until it sheared. Even the barrels of the weapons mounted in the forearm had been destroyed. Bond-forged titanium, plated in bond-forged chromium, plated again in microkil—all twisted like taffy until pulled apart. His right hand and most of his forearm were gone, still clutching the Hellbore. Panzer started to register the pain as his suit worked to seal the wound.

He looked up in time to see the three Oul'sors merging back into one. The Vaar threw his arm out, and the Hellbore cartwheeled through the air. Panzer's left arm came up as he tried to seize the weapon in his mind. As if it slipped through his physical fingers, his mind failed to arrest its movement. The weapon passed through the containment field and spun off into space.

Panzer's remaining hand found the deck as he leaned forward, ready to return to his feet. The bloodhammer was in front of him, resting on its head. He began to reach for it when the weapon rocketed away, finding Oul'sor's grasp with an audible report.

Panzer blinked. Did he just use psionics?

The Vaar pointed the weapon at him again.

"You told me he died like a coward. I don't believe you. But since you slander him, you're going to show me, Crykeeper. You're going to show me the *right* way to die."

Panzer reached across himself to his right thigh, but he found no pistol. He looked at his other leg but did not find it. It was gone, knocked loose at some point. He found it lying behind Oul'sor, by the routing terminal.

Panzer held out his hand to the pistol. The weapon responded, but Oul'sor's hammer intercepted it. The pistol exploded as the two weapons met. The ruptured fusion cells ignited the octium, and the explosion ripped through the chamber. Panzer scrambled to his feet.

When the flames cleared, Oul'sor stood unharmed, both hands holding his hammer. Panzer reached across himself again, farther this time. His knife was still there, and he brought it up to assume a fighting stance. Only three weapons left now.

Whatever the Vaar was doing, it seemed to be straining him. His head and shoulders had begun to droop, and he did not hold the hammer as high.

Time seemed to behave this time as Oul'sor gathered himself and charged.

Panzer held the knife at the ready. As Oul'sor closed in, Panzer dropped his fist. The twin-linked disrupters in his left arm snapped out and fired. He heard the impacts, the sizzle, and he saw the sparks. But no holes opened. Oul'sor charged through a stream of fire that should have cut him into pieces, and Panzer was forced to thrust away as the hammer tore through the bulkhead.

Still on his thrusters, he spun, keeping the fire on Oul'sor until everything stopped again.

The disrupters were silent. The Vaar ran to him this time, ducking out of the line of fire. When Panzer could move again, the hammer came down on his forearm, crumpling the armor, and the twin barrels burst open. The impact sent Panzer's arm down with such force, his body followed, but he never made it to the deck.

A large foot came up with a kick, the hammer followed, and Panzer took the impact to his chest. The spearpoint on the hammer pierced until it met the R-steel trauma plate. The force concussed his chest, punching the air out of Panzer's lungs as he was once again sent tumbling.

He regained consciousness on the other side of the bay, his NOD filling with urgent warnings he could not read. Oul'sor still stood where he had delivered the blow. Panzer's armor creaked like a hinged door as he forced himself back to his feet. Somewhere inside he heard fragments breaking away.

"Andira," he whispered. "If you're there, I could use some help."

SPINAL TRAUMA . . .

INTENSTINAL TRAUMA . . .

LIVER COMPROMISED . . .

KIDNEY TRAUMA . . .

RIB FRACTURES . . .

Panzer cleared the warnings away. There was pain in every nerve. Blood on each breath. His left eye had become a new paint on the inside of the helmet. His left arm was heavy as he raised the knife. But he could still stand. If he could still stand, he could still fight.

The world seemed to stutter this time. It paused once as Oul'sor raised his weapon. It paused again as he adjusted his grip. Oul'sor's eyes were on Panzer's blade. But Panzer had something else in mind. He concentrated on the air between them, forcing it into the grasp of his mind as his enemy drew nearer. Time finally froze, and Oul'sor charged.

When the universe decided to progress again, a sonic boom ripped through the chamber. Panzer had imagined the concussive blast giving Oul'sor a turn at being hurtled away. It did not. The blast should have sent him careening. It should have hit hard enough to break iron bones, split muscles, and strip the plates of his carapace. But the impact merely forced Oul'sor to stagger a step back.

An opening was still an opening. Panzer seized it, springing forward and twisting the blade in his grip until the edge pointed up. He did not know if it would cut what disrupter pulses did not. He had his answer when the tip met Oul'sor's gut. Panzer felt resistance and heard the cry of pain when the blade sank through to its hilt. With all the strength his left arm could give him, Panzer drove the blade up, cutting into Oul'sor's ribs and gut. As he came to the end of his reach, he yanked the blade free before bringing it down. The motion helped him duck the fist that came in for his helmet. But this time the blade did not cut; it merely glided across the plates of Oul'sor's thigh.

Before Panzer could ready another attack, the Vaar's giant hand clamped down on his helmet. Panzer's feet were dangling as he was hefted from the deck. He chose to take the free hit, driving the blade into Oul'sor's forearm. The hand let go, and rather than allow gravity to take his feet back to the deck, Panzer tapped his thrusters. It gave him the altitude, and he stabbed his knife into Oul'sor's neck.

He did not get the chance to draw the blade further. Oul'sor's knee came up, then his fist delivered the second blow. Panzer went over the edge and back into the tram trench before his momentum stopped.

He managed to clamber up and peer over the edge. Oul'sor stood with one hand at his neck. His hammer lay by his feet. Vaar blood was phosphorescent, luminous. Yet something like the ink of a squid was on the ground by the Vaar's feet, spilling out of his neck, and coating Panzer's blade.

Somewhere in the fight, Panzer's neck had broken. The heavy gorget of his armor was all that kept his head in an upright position. For the moment, Oul'sor seemed to be in even worse shape. But his head reared back, and his mouth opened. The wind drew through the room, but Panzer sensed something more than the rush of air. There was something metapsionic, like a telepathic hand trying to touch everything around it.

Panzer climbed back onto the deck as Oul'sor stood taller. His jaw fell open as he watched the Vaar. The blood flowing from his neck stopped and reversed itself. The enormous gash cut into the Vaar's torso drew the blood back in as the wound closed. There was a temperature spike in Panzer's sensors, briefly bursting to thousands of degrees before dropping back off. It came again as Oul'sor lowered his hand from his throat, and the wound was closed.

"What. The. Hell?" Panzer whispered before glancing at his knife. Vaar could regenerate, but no Vaar regenerated anywhere near that fast. What was that air current? The temperature spike? The blade had pierced him the first time, yet somehow the R-steel glanced off in a cut. What the hell was going on here?

With his wounds healed, Oul'sor called the hammer back to his hand. Panzer was shaky on his feet as the Vaar looked back at him. Panzer did not have to understand what he saw to know he saw it. That little feat of regeneration took several seconds, which gave him two solutions: wound the Vaar faster than he could heal or go for the head and shut it all down.

His left leg tried to give out when Panzer took a step forward. He had taken too many blows already. Each hit of the hammer struck like the kick that had sent him through an office building. Synthetic organs were ruptured. Cracks had formed in every bone.

First he felt the ripple, as if time was about to slow again. But it did not happen. Oul'sor raised a hand to his head as if beset by a sudden spell. Panzer had to take the opening and fired his thrusters. Whatever had taken him, Oul'sor shook it off in time to raise his hammer. The haft caught Panzer in his chest, bringing him to a halt. In turn, Panzer brought his blade down, driving it into the Vaar's shoulder. But Oul'sor still had two hands to work with. One of them seized Panzer's head, and he gained new momentum as he was spun before he was slung at the wall. He lay still in a pool of himself.

SKULL FRACTURES . . .

TEMPORAL LOBE TRAUMA . . .

The list went on, but Panzer did not read it. The parts of his brain needed for such a task had been bludgeoned away. A searing heat radiated through his body as his nanites tried in vain to heal injuries. Even with the support of his armor, they were piling up faster than they could be addressed.

It wasn't going to work. Too much was broken.

"Get up, Crykeeper," Oul'sor called to him. "You're not dead. Get up!"

When Panzer hit the wall, he was inverted and slid down onto his head and shoulders. The lower half of his body was doubled over, with his toes touching the deck past his head. Slowly he rolled out of the indignant position until he lay on his side.

The hand grabbed his head before he was plucked up and hurtled back into the wall. A fist smashed into his torso. Another followed it. Punches came in so fast that their impacts kept him pinned in place even after the Vaar let go of his head. Panzer gagged as he choked on teeth that dislodged from his gums. He could hear nothing over his armor shrieking with every hit. Finally Oul'sor's hand clamped on his helmet again and pulled him up.

"No, no, no," Oul'sor whispered. "You can't die yet. Please don't die yet. I have not heard your pain. I will. I *will*. I will hear you cry out!"

Panzer was tossed, and he slid to a halt at the router's safety sleeve, the new pain not registering.

What the hell am I supposed to do? Disrupters don't hurt him. He heals when I cut him. He's beating me to death through my armor.

???: ANDIRA?

There was no answer.

Perhaps this is how it ends.

The eye Panzer still had blinked. Looking back at him was the open door of the cargo bay, the containment field, and the blue oceans of ND-31. Perhaps there was a solution. He had lost his grip on the knife and reached out to it as Oul'sor came toward him. The Vaar swung his hammer as Panzer tried to grasp the knife. His mental hand could only put a finger on it, sliding it on the deck where it followed Oul'sor like a lost pet.

Oul'sor grabbed his helmet again, drawing Panzer onto his knees.

"Get up!" Oul'sor growled before shouting, "*Get up, Crykeeper!*"

Panzer did get up. As his knife drew closer, he gave it a jerk. The blade found his hand, then Panzer wrapped his arm around Oul'sor and drove the blade into the small of the Vaar's back. With that anchor, Panzer hit his thrusters, flinging both of them up to the ceiling. Oul'sor let out a gargle as his cranium met the metal and Panzer cut thrust. When they hit the deck, Panzer rolled atop the Vaar and hit his thrusters again. Oul'sor's mouth opened in a furious growl as Panzer rode him like a sled through the containment field, out of the ship, and into space.

Face to face with the Vaar, Panzer watched for any sign. Any sign that the decompression was killing Oul'sor. But the pupils of the Vaar's hate-filled eyes simply contracted. Panzer's thoughts were scrambled again as the hammer slammed into the side of his helmet. A hard punch separated them from each other.

With his thrusters, Panzer quickly regained control and turned back. He hoped to see Oul'sor clawing at his throat, twisting his body as vacuum and suffocation took him. Instead the Vaar reoriented himself to face him.

When he tried to sigh, Panzer coughed up blood. He glimpsed the local star retreating behind the planet. A large landmass of green rested between the sparkling oceans. It was actually a pretty sight. Panzer turned back to see Oul'sor raise his hand in a taunt. Panzer's eyes moved down to his knife at bits of his reflection where the black blood did not cover the blade. The faceless mask stared back at him, its features made up of cracks covering the plate.

His thrusters carried him forward. The Vaar made no effort to dodge, attempting instead to intercept him with the hammer. With a thrust to the side, Panzer dodged the swing before turning to slam into Oul'sor. He wrapped his arm around the Vaar again and set a course for the planet.

The blows rained on his head, each one seeming to punch a new warning into his NOD. His jaw broke loose from his skull. Overburdened muscles finally tore. Two centuries of combat instincts were all that remained as Panzer's mind and body began to diverge, his thoughts now independent of his body's actions.

Knew this was a one-way trip.

The flesh beneath his left eye split to follow the new crack in his skull.

There are worse deaths.

Oul'sor's right arm was over Panzer's shoulder. The left was grabbing at his helmet, trying to pry him off.

To some stripling with a lucky shot.

Panzer shifted, driving his shoulder higher into the pit of Oul'sor's arm.

Untested and unworthy.

The acceleration was closing the distance, and the first flickers of red entered his sight.

To an accident. Random and meaningless. Withered and empty. An object of pity in the prison of a broken mind.

Oul'sor writhed as the plasma of atmospheric entry engulfed them both.

We're both warriors. We gave our lives to something that will never love us back.

Another elbow strike created an overpressure that burst his eardrums. Oul'sor's plates were blended with the plasma, scalding red. But they did not flake away. They did not burn. They simply radiated the heat.

Whatever you've become . . .

Oul'sor's mouth opened in a quiet scream as the Vaar threw another elbow.

I make no apologies. I've always done what I had to, to win. But if this is how I die, I'm glad it's to someone like you.

A final blow, and the two were separated. Panzer's thrusters went silent, and the two plummeted down through the blue sky.

I hope it gives you some peace.

CHAPTER
12E

THE PLUNGE THROUGH THE atmosphere meant little to Oul'sor. The scalding plasma had heated his plates but little else. The new flesh he commanded seemed more annoyed than damaged by the violent treatment. While he and the Crykeeper continued in a free fall through Origin's twilight sky, on the hull of the *Caustic Reverie*, Oul'sor knew Indorai was watching. More than watching—his unwanted coaching was inescapable.

"Manipulation of one's own body through psionics is difficult, Oul'sor." The incessant voice rang in his thoughts. *"Just as judgment is the path of ease against self-reflection. The mind is built to analyze beyond, not within. You must concentrate."*

Oul'sor heard his growl as the thickening atmosphere brought him the sound. His eyes closed as he concentrated on his body. The air was thick enough now to hear it rushing past his ears as he rotated. But Oul'sor did not hear it.

I don't understand why I'm not hitting the target.

The memory of a child's voice shattered his concentration, and his eyes flew open to reacquire the Crykeeper. The two were drifting apart as they fell on different trajectories. Oul'sor let out a fresh growl, flailing his limbs to reorient himself.

Are you ever afraid? When you're in battle?

Not always. But, often. Fear is not weakness. It is only weakness to be a slave to it.

With thickening air to breathe, he was doing so faster as the memory filled his mind.

But how do you overcome it?

Focus and confidence. Like armor, fear can protect you by dissuading you from unnecessary risk. But like too much armor, it will weigh you down if you let it take control. Focus on the importance of your task. Confidence in your skill. This is how you make armor of fear.

Do you think I can be a warrior one day?

"Hatred is a powerful thing, Oul'sor." Indorai's voice inserted itself. *"Hatred can keep you warm at night. But like any power, you must control it and shape it. Or it will control you. Focus."*

His eyes closed again. He could not simply grip his body with his mind as he could the hammer. He had to feel himself moving and know that he already was.

"Focus, Oul'sor."

The shifting flow of the air told him the tale as his feet approached the clouds. With eyes open again, Oul'sor found the Crykeeper, more distant now, falling headfirst. Playing dead again? With ruthless focus, Oul'sor reached out with his mind. He did not care what was in the Crykeeper's thoughts, only whether or not he was still thinking. Yet there was nothing there. As if he did not exist.

"He has his privileges, and you have yours. Focus, and do what you must."

An infinite weight seemed to come down on his skull. The strain of breaking from the flow was becoming harder to bear. His fall, and the Crykeeper's, began to slow.

"Focus with intelligence, Oul'sor. With no time, the particles between him and you become a barrier impassible."

His teeth ground together at the advice he kept forgetting.

"In this place, time is broken. The pieces are easy to manipulate. Do so with intelligence and focus. Become the singularity."

His eyes squinted but did not close. The world continued to slow, but his momentum continued unimpeded.

"All things flow through time, and through time, all are connected. Bring them all under your mind."

Oul'sor imagined the bubble and defined it as his time. All that lay within it were subject to his definition of now. Nails seemed to sink through the flesh of his skull as he was forced to divide his focus. One half to moderate the flow, the other to drive his body forward. The perimeter of his reality moved with him. The air in his path granted him passage before rejoining the rest in its suspension. He was in a dive now and readied his hammer. The moment the Crykeeper was engulfed in his perimeter, his time would flow. Oul'sor did not intend to permit him enough to react.

For Oul'sor it took moments. To the rest of the universe, his movement was instantaneous. As the perimeter crossed his body, the Crykeeper reacted. The knife came up, striking at Oul'sor's finger on the hammer's haft. The blow was too strong to be blocked, and the Solar was driven into a spin even as the hammer was deflected. The moment the Crykeeper twirled out of the perimeter, he was frozen again, and Oul'sor fell past him.

So you are still alive. Or are you?

His focus arrested his fall. Gravity was only a suggestion now. An insistent suggestion but nothing more. Oul'sor readied the hammer again as he moved back toward his foe.

Were you ever actually alive? I tear your limbs, but you don't cry out. I break your bones, but still you fight. What monstrous confection of organic and machine are you? Are you nothing but an engine of death? Still trying to turn so long as any gear still moves?

Oul'sor swung the hammer in an uppercut, trying to time the impact to the exact moment the perimeter engulfed his nemesis. No less than a finger's length separated the hammer from its target when Oul'sor felt the blast of heat, and the Crykeeper's thrusters launched him out of the perimeter. Oul'sor followed through on the swing of the hammer, finding himself above his foe. There he allowed gravity to whisper the suggestion to him.

What am I supposed to say to her?

Viss aren't mystic. Just talk to her and tell her what you want.

Oul'sor slid his hands up the haft, choking up his grip for faster strikes.

I failed admission. I'm sorry.

There is no shame in failing at a mighty endeavor. Only in giving up. Try again, until the urutagh see your value.

Oul'sor retained the hammer with one hand, reaching out with the other as the perimeter crossed again. The curved blade came for his eye, and Oul'sor caught the fist that held it. Oul'sor was jerked forward as the Crykeeper fired his thrusters again, trying to break the grapple. When that did not work, his foot came up, aiming for Oul'sor's head. The haft served as an effective block, and Oul'sor drove the head of the hammer forward. The black helmet snapped back as his weapon struck.

The Solar was stunned, so Oul'sor seized the opportunity, flicking his arm and sending the Crykeeper into another twirl. With both hands free now, Oul'sor gripped the hammer. The knife could not cut him. He over-committed to throwing all his strength behind his next swing. The hammer found its target. Shards of metal sprayed across Oul'sor's face and chest as armor fragmented under the blow.

When the Crykeeper was hurtled away, he did not stop upon leaving the perimeter. Instead he merely drifted, leaving a wake of metal fragments. Oul'sor's grip was slipping. The burden was too heavy. He could only slow his time now; he could not stop it.

Cry out! Let me hear your pain. Let me have some satisfaction when I wound you!

Black clouds below lit up with blue as lighting pierced their shroud. It would not matter if he did cry out. His cries of agony would bring no satisfaction. Oul'sor looked down at his bloodhammer. He was going to win. There was no question. But it would not be his victory. It would be hollow. This strength, this toughness, this might. It was given to him. It was not earned through trial and pain.

All things move through time, and through time all things are connected.

"*Focus, Oul'sor.*"

Oul'sor ignored Indorai as he turned back to the Crykeeper. Strength without direction was nothing. His victory had to come from the one part of him that was truly his. *Control the power.* Oul'sor followed him down, into the storm, never looking away.

He's not coming back, is he, Yuja?

Oul'sor raised his hammer as if to strike, but his eyes closed. The weapon felt like part of his body. The power he now wielded was given to him. The strength was not earned. All that was here was his hate.

Memories flooded through him. Of lessons taught. Of punishments that afflicted the giver more than the receiver. Of hopes and dreams and a young Viss now in a faraway place. So be it. If his hate was all that he brought to this fight, then it would be his hate that ended it.

Of all the seeds I planted, you took the only flower.

The hammer's black metal began to glow, its visage becoming that of magma, but its hardness intensified.

You took him from me.

Rain fell as the summer air shed its warmth for winter's bite. Only the air around Oul'sor was spared, growing hotter as the energy of Origin flowed into him. The hammer turned white with heat.

You took him from Vil'na.

The temperature in the air plummeted, and the moisture became a rain of sharp ice. But around Oul'sor, a glowing sphere had formed, obscured by the steam of the ice that flash-boiled in his wake. The hammer flashed to blue before its radiation revealed ultraviolet.

I know I should not hate you. You were both warriors doing your duty.

Oul'sor's plates glowed with heat as the vortex of ionized air swirled around him. His eyes opened, finding the Crykeeper still in his fall, now below the clouds.

But we all choose our deaths.

He raised the hammer over his head.

When you killed him, you chose yours.

With a raised knee, Oul'sor forced his foot down. The hammer would be his lexicon of malice, and he leveraged his entire body as he hurtled it. The glowing trail of plasmafied air that followed the hammer overtook and vaporized the ice in its path.

The Crykeeper tried to react. But it was in vain—even the energy in his armor had been pulled away. Oul'sor felt the psionic pulse—the weak, desperate attempt to turn the hammer aside. It was too little, and the hammer struck its target. Oul'sor let out a roar.

Too much power. When the hammer hit, it did not annihilate the foe in a blast of unequaled fury. Instead the head punched through the Crykeeper like a bullet through paper, and the spinning handle cut like a blade, severing what remained of his right arm.

The mountain became a volcano as the hammer plowed through the stone, melting rock like wax. The face of the mountain split to belch black ash into the sky, clearing a path for the molten rock that flowed out of it.

As the two fell through the rising clouds of ash, Origin protested.

Time stopped, but it was not Oul'sor's hand that guided it. Even his eyes felt pain as a new sun seemed to rise on the disassembling landscape. His gaze briefly left the Crykeeper as golden arcs of light spilled like lightning from the sides of the broken mountain. Together they pierced the veil of Origin's night, bringing unnatural daylight to the landscape. The arcs flashed through the sky, chasing the shockwave of the hammer's impact. They rapidly gained ground on the supersonic flow.

"Focus, Oul'sor."

Unwanted though his counsel was, Indorai was right. Oul'sor set his sights on the Crykeeper falling lifelessly through the imploding cloud of ash. The magma was flowing up the mountain as Oul'sor threw himself into another dive. Oul'sor intercepted his quarry with a hand clamped down on the Crykeeper's leg. His scream echoed through the mountains as Oul'sor threw himself into a spin. The supersonic rotation created a howling drone to echo off the rock faces as the mountain completed the task of reassembling itself. Night returned, and Oul'sor let go.

Hurtled down to the mended face of the mountain, the rocks yielded like water when the Crykeeper's body made impact and slammed through layers of rock. When his momentum stopped, his body continued to move. He rolled out of the crater and began to tumble down the mountain until coming to rest on a ridge.

The ridge shuddered as Oul'sor's feet came down on it. His body contracted, forcing him into a squat as rock gave beneath him. But the fall did nothing to him.

Oul'sor stood upright and walked slowly toward the Crykeeper, who lay on his face amid the stone outcrop. Blood pooled around him. The enormous hole his hammer created went through his gut and out of his back. His legs were splayed far apart as organs tried to escape through the bisecting cut left by the handle. The Solar did not move. Oul'sor extended a foot, hooking his toes under the Crykeeper's neck so he could flip him onto his back.

Movement. The Crykeeper still held the knife. His arm trembled as it rose.

"You're still alive?" Oul'sor whispered. "You still want to fight? Were you born a monster? Or were you made one?"

Oul'sor's foot came down on the Crykeeper's chest as he grabbed at the arm that held the blade. His mind was weary; the manipulation of time had taken a heavy toll. But he focused on the arm. He knew within him that the metal was shearing, and the flesh was tearing. The shrieking metal confirmed his bias, and the arm ripped free from its shoulder. Oul'sor tossed it over the ridge.

"Not this time, Crykeeper," Oul'sor whispered, shifting his posture. "This time, you die."

Oul'sor closed his eyes and coiled his fingers into a tight fist. His mouth opened as he drew a torrent of air into himself. He felt all the energy of Origin. Even brighter than when he plunged through the atmosphere, his plates began to glow. As he bent, Oul'sor drew his fist back.

A final cry left his lips and echoed through the mountains as Oul'sor's fist came down. The R-steel plates that formed the Crykeeper's helmet held against the strike, but nothing below was so fortunate. The layers of granite beneath them shattered into gravel. The Crykeeper's body convulsed. The shockwave ripped through his body, liquefying tissue. A shockwave traveled down his spine, separating vertebrae, and continuing until the toes snapped off of his feet.

The mountainside collapsed, and the ridge gave beneath them. Oul'sor fell freely while the pieces of the Crykeeper's body fell with the tumbling rocks. With what little strength remained in his mind, Oul'sor took hold of his body, guiding himself away.

He saw the glow.

Was the mountain about to reassemble itself? Oul'sor watched for the Crykeeper, searching amid the falling rocks, but he couldn't see it.

It was gone.

For a second, he noticed a smaller glow. But he saw no head, no body, no limbs. His head snapped to the side. He felt as though someone had brushed against him. But there was no one. Oul'sor had no choice but to draw himself away from the mountain, lest he be buried in the landslide.

A black tendril entered his sight from behind and curled over his chest. The landscape shifted around him, and he felt solid rock beneath his feet. Now in the distance, the mountain continued to shed rock toward its base. Indorai stood beside him and released his tendril's grip.

"What happened?" Oul'sor demanded. "Where is his body?"

Indorai offered a second tendril, which grasped Oul'sor's hammer. Quickly he seized the weapon back before demanding his answer again.

"What happened, Indorai? Tell me!"

The creature seemed to sigh as it glared toward the mountain. The collapsing rock filled the air with a sound like a distant, poorly led orchestra of drums.

"You deviated from your orders, Oul'sor," Indorai chided. "You were told to leave his head intact."

"*Where. Is. His. Body?*" Oul'sor yelled.

"Fortunately for you, your disobedience was expected," Indorai said. "But it would be unfortunate for you, and all Vaar, if you made a habit of it."

Rage began to take over. Oul'sor drew back his hammer and began to swing, but one of Indorai's tendrils coiled around it again, and Oul'sor was held in place.

"You've done enough for now, Oul'sor." Indorai pushed the hammer firmly against Oul'sor's chest before releasing. "Our friend has involved themselves. You've done your part. Now, I must do mine."

"Indorai!" Oul'sor growled as the Therican faded away.

Indorai was gone, and Oul'sor screamed toward the stars. Even the broken mountain seemed to adopt an intimidated silence at the sound of the Vaar's rage-filled cries.

Act—III: A New Destiny

CHAPTER
13A

I N ROBERT PANZER'S MIND, the first sensation was that of his body face-down on a hard surface. Yet when his eyes opened, he seemed to be gazing into deep space. A multitude of stars and galaxies filled his sight. His hands found something solid, and he pushed himself up off the invisible floor.

Hands. His arms were back. He looked down at himself to see that he was wrapped in his dress uniform. Every commendation was burnished to a high luster. How did this happen? The invisible floor accepted his feet and he stood. All he could see ahead was the void of space.

"Where am I?"

"You are dead, Crykeeper."

He spun on his heel when he heard the response. A Vaar shared the floor with him, some meters away. On instinct Panzer's hand moved for a weapon. When he didn't find one, he brought his hands up and squared his feet into a fighting stance. The Vaar answered by raising his hands with his palms outward.

"I bring no fight," the Vaar said, spreading his fingers to emphasize his empty hands. "Would you destroy that you sought?"

Panzer's eyes narrowed as he studied the Vaar. He wore no armor, but his body was covered in markings. His tall crest was filled with markings carved into the plates. But his NOD did not respond and did not provide any translation to them. Yet in some he found recognition. The striped shield that indicated a bodyguard to someone of great status. The staff that crossed over that shield. The pinwheel symbolized enlightenment but was cast in silver to denote him as a follower. Many more such runes were carved across his plates, on his chest, his arms, even his thighs.

He needed to know what these markings meant. His NOD gave no answer. His eyes worked, but no screens opened. As if half of his essence were gone, nothing digital responded to his commands.

"Who are you?" Panzer asked, lowering his hands slightly.

"My name is Ullenk."

"Ullenk?" Panzer repeated the name. "Prime bodyguard to the Sovari Soma?"

The Vaar gave a single long nod.

Panzer did his best to blank his mind. Thought prisons were a purely digital space, so fully blended into the subject's consciousness that they could not distinguish it from reality. It was supposed to be impossible to subject a Solar to one without their assistance, but with what he had just experienced, he was not ready to let anything stand on assumption.

Ullenk said nothing more, perhaps giving him time. He took that time to consider what he would say next. If this was a thought prison, then every thought in his head was being recorded. Without his NOD he could not check his CIAD implant. But information on the Sovari Soma was classified priority secret. If he even knew what the words meant, then the implant was not regulating his memories. Without his NOD, he could not activate it manually.

If this was a thought prison, whoever was running it wasn't doing a very good job for an interrogation. The easiest way to get information was to convince the subject that they were in a debriefing. The last thing an interrogator wanted to do was create a strange scenario like this and put the subject on guard. He was still suspicious, but he needed more information. So he asked the question. The one he suspected that a Vaar running a thought prison would hope he could answer for them.

"If you are here, where is the Sovari Soma?"

Ullenk shook his head slowly. "He is dead, Crykeeper. Killed by Indorai."

Indorai? Killed by the Therican?

"I am Kubari Soma now," Ullenk continued before hesitating. "A . . . contingency vessel . . . for the Soma symbiote."

Ullenk raised his chin, and somehow Panzer was able to see into the Vaar. Through his plates, through his flesh, he saw Ullenk's spine, and the silver creature within. It laced through his ribs, coiled tightly about his spine like a constricting snake. The pass-through vision faded as Ullenk lowered his head to resume his previous posture.

"When did he die?"

"At Yuros," Ullenk answered. "We were on the planet waiting for you when the urutagh came."

Ullenk pointed out to the side, and Panzer followed the indication. At first he saw only darkness before a light at the end of a tunnel. He heard shouting in a Vaar language. Panzer did not speak this language. Without his NOD, without his nanites, he should have been unable to understand it. Yet the more he listened, the more he understood.

"Sol'nus reports Oul'sor has taken the bait. They're following."

"Hurry, Master. Now is our chance!"

Panzer seemed to be watching through another's eyes. He could make out a pair of Vaar now, stumbling toward the light. Both were dressed in elaborate armor, with layers on the helmet that overlapped like petals on a flower. One was wounded, holding an arm tight to his ribs.

The eyes through which he saw turned, and he saw what could only be the Sovari Soma. A very old Vaar. His jet-black plates had faded to a gray. The plates themselves were withered and cracked with age. His vision lowered for a moment. A Vaar hand took the old one's arm to usher him more quickly. Was this Ullenk's sight?

The sight moved back to the two Vaar in the lead. The pair stumbled through the exit. Ullenk followed with the old one. The exit brought them onto a large rock outcropping where a transport lay with its boarding ramp open. The sight turned back to five more Vaar who followed.

"Bring it down!" Ullenk barked.

As the Vaar made it onto the ledge, they turned back, and each hurtled a grenade to collapse the cave that had been their avenue. Ullenk's sight returned to the transport where the wounded Vaar ascended the ramp.

The wounded Vaar's body thudded against the ramp as he fell to the tendril coiled tightly about his ankle. The warrior screamed, the tendril snapped, and the hapless Vaar was hurtled off the mountain. Ullenk's weapon came into view as he raised it, only for the weapon to spark as it was cut in two. The sight glared down at the glowing tendril now embedded in his chest.

A hand shot out to grab the tendril, and the ancient one tore it out. But the old Vaar had no time to save the others. As Ullenk's vision panned, Panzer saw and heard a cry of agony unlike any other, quickly cut short. The other Vaar, their armor, even their weapons crumbled into dust that blew away on billowing winds.

The first Vaar up the ramp had passed by Indorai without knowing he was there. As Ullenk staggered the Therican came into view. Each of his tendrils reared up and back like a snake ready to strike. The sight became blurry and Ullenk fell.

"How sad." That was Indorai's voice. Mocking, taunting, and sadistic. "The last in a line of failure and futility. You should never have tried to flee. Then at least you could die where you lived."

The vision blurred and faded. As Ullenk fought for consciousness, Panzer saw only glimpses of what had transpired. The death of the Sovari Soma was not a quiet one. A single tendril shot out. The Sovari Soma raised his hand, and the tendril deflected. As it if had struck an invisible wall, the piercing point skipped aside. Another followed.

Psionics? Was the Sovari Soma using psionics? Could that even be possible? Only humans had psionic abilities.

The vision cleared briefly. The Sovari Soma moved his arm in an arch. Boulders ripped away from the ledge to smash into Indorai. On his body they shattered, but the Therican was not moved.

If the Sovari had psionic abilities, that could explain so much. Why the Vaar knew what they were. Why they had 4CM technology before the Empire even arrived. But how did they keep something like that a secret? How did no one in the Empire find out about it?

Panzer frowned as the vision came and went. Even if Ullenk had not told him how it ended, he could see it coming. He watched the Sovari land blows with his fist, with stones, and none had an effect. As if the Therican were letting him attack just to delight in the futility of his efforts. And then came darkness.

When Ullenk's eyes opened again, the Sovari Soma was on a knee. His mouth hung open. His teeth were gone, and blood drained from his mouth. Indorai loomed over him, his tendrils spread like great open wings.

"You pathetic creature." Indorai's voice seemed almost sympathetic. "Servant of a false savior. I don't suppose oblivion will be much of a change for you. Die now."

The Sovari Soma's crest was broken, and the plates of his face fell away. The Therican's tendrils expanded, the head of each pointing inward. As the tendrils came together, the Sovari Soma emitted a defiant shout. His left hand shot up and coiled tightly. The tendrils were suddenly bound together, stopping mere centimeters from the Vaar's face.

Panzer took a step back as new color invaded the image. A mist, like that of the Encephalon, or Indorai himself, but colored in a vibrant orange. The Sovari Soma shouted again. As his shout ended, the Vaar drove his fist forward. He struck only air, but it rippled in a shockwave, the rocks crumbled, and the sound of an explosion erupted. The tendrils faded away, and Indorai flew back before also fading away.

The Sovari Soma gazed down at the hand that had delivered the punch. That hand soon came undone, turning to dust. The Sovari Soma fell.

Panzer heard a cry of pain as Ullenk rolled onto his front and crawled toward the fallen Sovari Soma. With one hand he grabbed at the elder and dragged him toward the ship.

"Ship, auto-navigate." Panzer saw a mist of blood on Ullenk's breath. "Dey'kon II. Now!"

The ramp closed, and the sound of whining engines filled the air. Ullenk continued to drag the Sovari Soma into the cargo bay before he was able to sit up.

"Ullenk." Most of the plates of the Sovari Soma's face were gone. Those that remained were crumbling as if something were still eating away at them. His exposed flesh began to do the same.

"Master?" Ullenk whispered. "Forgive us, Master. We have failed you."

The elder Vaar's eyes were glazing over, and he struggled to form words. "Ullenk. You. You must take the symbiote."

"No, Master. Save your strength. You can survive this."

The elder Vaar shook his head. "I am already dead, Ullenk. Don't let it die with me."

"But Master," Ullenk whispered. "I am not worthy."

The Sovari Soma's eyes squinted as he fought for each breath. "Then you must *become* worthy. Our people are not ready for me to be the last Sovari. I must not be the final." The Sovari Soma's body convulsed, and his back arched as his eyes shut. "Do it. Now."

The image moved down as Ullenk placed his mouth over the Sovari Soma's. A sickening sound of tearing flesh filled the air, and in the corner of Ullenk's eyes, Panzer saw the Sovari's limbs trembling. The sound of ripping flesh gave way to gagging. Ullenk's head reared back, and a silver snake wriggled at the base of his sight. The symbiote made its way into the new host. The scene moved as Ullenk fell back. The final length of the symbiote slipped out of sight. Ullenk looked back as the elder's body collapsed into dust. Then the sight was gone.

Panzer let out a long sigh.

"I'm sorry, Ullenk," he said. "We made way to you as soon as we received your message."

"I do not blame you, Crykeeper," the Ullenk in front of him answered. "Afterward I gathered the rest of the vunata and came here. We tried to jump in close enough to make it through the atmosphere before your legionnaires' orbital defenses could respond. We failed. I was the only survivor of the crash. But, our creator was able to fix the rest of us."

"Your creator?" Panzer asked, cocking his head slightly. "What do you mean?"

"I was asked to speak to you first, a friendly face as you would say."

Ullenk bowed his head and turned. A bright light erupted beside him. The golden light was so intense that it washed out everything else. The black of space, the distant stars—all had faded away.

CHAPTER
13B

SIMMONNE LAY QUIETLY ON a medical table in the ship's infirmary. The room was much less open now. A large hatch in the floor had opened to bring up a bed large enough for Rhoxx. Once he was on it, the machinery had assembled a large cylindrical tank around him. The massive deep-fryer hummed quietly beside her as Rhoxx recovered.

As soon as they were aboard, Andira had brought the engines online. They were underway now, heading to a new hiding spot. Time passed slower in this galaxy. It passed even slower when they were as close to a black hole as they had been. Simmonne did not understand exactly how that worked; she merely knew that it did.

As if the universe were spying on her thoughts, the clock raced forward in her NOD by several seconds.

"Andira?" Her query was as much to break the silence as it was to acquire information.

"Yes, Majesty?"

"Time passes slower in this galaxy, does it not?"

"Yes, Majesty."

"And those . . . waves . . . that come out of the center. They make it stop awhile. Correct?"

"Technically it does not stop," Andira corrected, "but it does dilate time significantly."

Simmonne sat up, using her NOD to raise the back of the table so that she did not recline so far. She tested it once before sitting up straight and bringing the chair into compliance.

"Then why does my clock race forward when a wave hits?"

"Because the clock in your NOD is programmed to synchronize with a Department of Standards timekeeping source. In this case, the ship. Separate clocks on this ship track both Hourglass Integrated Time and Interstellar Coordinated Time. My clocks are immunized against the effect. If your NOD is set to ICT, it will race forward when it re-synchronizes with the clocks on the ship."

Simmonne tried to avoid crossing her eyes at the answer. "So . . . because I lost several seconds of ICT, my clock sped up to get me back on track?"

"Yes, Majesty."

"Oh."

Simmonne focused on the clock on her NOD.

>>CHANGE TIME REFERENCE
SPECIFY TIME ZONE.
>>HOURGLASS INTEGRATED TIME

At her command, the clock switched from 08:30 to 16:24. She was not sure what world served as the official timekeeper for this galaxy—Avalon perhaps—but this was the time she was experiencing, not the ICT as stipulated by the Cathedral.

>>SHOW SECONDS

The time expanded to 16:24:33. But as Simmonne watched, she realized the seconds were ticking by too quickly.

"Andira?" she asked. "I think something is wrong with my NOD. The seconds are going too fast."

"We are currently in a zone of significant time dilation, Majesty," Andira answered. "More severe than the Hourglass standard. My clocks set to Hourglass time are accounting for it."

Simmonne shook her head. The idea that time could move at different rates in different places had never made real sense to her. Even when she had experienced it herself. She slipped her hand into her pocket and withdrew the badge.

"Andira, how long have the colonel and his team been gone?"

"In Hourglass Standard or ICT, Majesty?"

"I'm experiencing Hourglass Integrated, right?"

"Yes, Majesty."

"Hourglass then."

"They have been gone for ten days, thirteen hours, Majesty."

Ten days? Simmonne mouthed the words. It did not feel that long to her. Only three sleep cycles. The black hole. It was the time they spent near the black hole.

Simmonne took a breath. "That is longer than they expected. Could something have gone wrong?"

"Delays of this kind are typical, Majesty," Andira answered. "It is likely my program on the *Intruder* was forced to re-plot its course several times to avoid detection. Given the vessel's limited speed, that could add days to the trip."

Simmonne sighed, looking down at the badge and stroking it with her thumb. Andira had said it would take Rhoxx a day to come out of the tank.

"Your Majesty," Andira said as Simmonne adjusted the table again. "You would be more comfortable in Colonel Panzer's quarters."

Simmonne did not answer. There was nothing she could do to help Rhoxx recover more quickly. After what he did, it did not seem right to leave while he was still healing. She reclined the table again and laid the badge on her chest, then stared at the ceiling.

"Andira, can you dim the lights?"

"Yes, Majesty."

Simmonne had not meant for Andira to dim them as far as she did, but it was not worth complaining about. No longer blinded by the light, she let her gaze drift. If only her guards had been here. With more help, Andira might not have lost her body. Rhoxx might not have been so gravely wounded. Simmonne blinked as a single tear slipped down her cheek.

They were gone. They gave their lives for her. It was why they were born. Still, it didn't make their sacrifices easy to accept. She could not bring them back. She could mourn and honor their memory. That was all. She would have new guards, but they would not be replacements.

Rhoxx was Redguard. She turned toward the deep-fryer. What was it Rhoxx said to the Vaar leader? He was trying to take what *belonged* to his lord? So she was not crazy. She was not reading too much into the badge. It was exactly what she thought it was.

Her finger came up to the neckline of her dress, pulling at it in the hope that some of the heat would escape. She had put on another Delseah, and it weighed a ton. She contemplated changing into something else, but she had to keep it on. It might be easier for the colonel if he did not like the way she looked when she gave him her answer.

Simmonne knew it would not work, but she tried once again to open an astranet connection.

NETWORK INACCESSIBLE.

She had a public address where citizens and subjects could send her messages. An AI answered most of them, but sometimes when she had nothing to do but wait, she would look through the inbox herself. The number of messages in there may as well have been infinite. Messages from little girls wanting encouragement, lonely men trying to get her attention, people hoping to draw her to their pet charity cases. AIs screened the most vulgar messages. Jenna and Daddy had taken greater care to keep those inaccessible to her over other things the astranet could provide.

But there was no astranet here, and this slayer of boredom would not heed her call. She had never bothered to install any games, movies, or even music on her nanites. It had never occurred to her to do it. The astranet was always there.

As she moved her finger in her collar, she snagged the chain of her medallion and drew it out. The gift from the quants. A small golden sun. She grimaced when she saw that it was bent. Without thinking, she laid the colonel's badge back on her chest and tried to bend the medallion back into shape.

The device emitted a tiny *ping!* Now she had two pieces in her hand.

"Oh." She groaned, looking down at it. It must have happened when that Vaar caught her in his net. Or when Rhoxx cut her out of it perhaps. Either way, it was broken. She removed the chain from her neck and was about to slip it into an inner pocket when she noticed something. Beneath the metal, she saw what looked like a tiny piece of circuitry. It, too, was broken. When she examined the other half of the medallion, she found the broken circuitry there as well.

"I wonder what that was," she muttered to herself.

"Majesty?"

"Nothing," she answered before frowning. The poor quants. This medallion probably meant something to them. Now it was broken. She would see about fixing it later. With both pieces in hand, she reached into her dress and slid them into a hidden pocket.

"Andira, tell me about this place we're going to."

"Actually, Majesty, we entered the Basin two hours ago. This region consists of sixty-four black holes. These range in size from 917 million to 0.0038 standard stellar masses. It is believed that all of these originated from the center of another galaxy devoured by the Hourglass."

Simmonne huffed quietly. Big numbers and dry space terms.

"Why are we here? Specifically?"

"The numerous overlapping warp fields from so many singularities in close proximity will help to confuse Vaar sensors, Majesty. If the Vaar found a means to track us, it is highly unlikely they could do so here."

Simmonne sat up a bit. "But the colonel and his team will be able to find us, right?"

"Yes, Majesty. Colonel Panzer specified the coordinates in the Basin for this scenario. The team will redirect here when they do not find us at Eye-7."

Perhaps that was why it was taking so long. Simmonne closed her eyes and turned her attention back to the colonel's badge. She had to say no. She had realized long ago she would never have a classical relationship: meet someone, get to know them, fall in love. For royalty, for celebrities and aristocracy, things rarely worked that way. But all the same, she had to say no to this. No matter how she felt, she had to do better for the Twins. The thought of them weeping over his casket was too much.

It was probably for the best. She doubted she could be the person he wanted her to be.

"Ship detected."

Andira's words caused Simmonne to bolt upright. The rapid rise sent the badge catapulting off her chest. It let out a loud ring as it struck the floor. Simmonne was on her feet in a second, bringing it back to her grasp.

"Is it the Vaar?" She stuffed the badge into her pocket.

"Range, thirty thousand kilometers and closing."

"Is it the Vaar?" Simmonne repeated louder.

"It's the *Intruder*, Majesty."

The petrification seeped out of her muscles. But her stomach sank. Now she had to face him and give back the badge. Simmonne held the badge in front of her one more time, and she caught herself in a sniffle. Simmonne closed her eyes and returned it to her pocket.

"Andira, can you guide me to the docking bay?"

"You may wish to wait, Majesty," Andira cautioned. "I believe they have wounded."

"Wounded?" she whispered. "Guide me to the docking bay."

"Majesty—"

"Now!"

The waypoint came into her NOD, and Simmonne was out of the room.

A brisk walk became a high-heeled run as she raced back to the landing bay. When she arrived, the *Intruder* was ascending through the force field where it was grasped by the docking claw.

"No," she whispered.

If charity work had taught her one thing, it was the feeling of despair, and she felt it like a thick fog shrouding the bay.

She rushed down to the landing bay as the *Intruder*'s forward ramp lowered. With a view into the cargo hold, she paused. On her left she saw five silver sacks, trauma bags. Her high heels caught a gap at the top of the ramp, causing her to stumble, but she remained upright as she dashed for the bags.

A transparency rested over the face of each occupant. At the first bag, Simmonne glared down to see a man's face. It was not the colonel. He was too young, more boy than man, lying in the bag with his mouth open.

"Majesty?"

Simmonne ignored the whispered voice and looked into the second bag. She did not know this person either—some woman with black hair bearing blue streaks. But Simmonne froze when she looked at the third and fourth bags and saw the identical faces.

"No," she murmured, falling on her knees. "No. No."

An optical strip lay above the transparency, and Simmonne glared at it.

PATIENT: JULIE KATYUSHA
CONDITION: ALIVE
STATUS: CLASS-I STASIS

Simmonne looked at the second bag.

PATIENT: JENNIFER KATYUSHA
CONDITION: ALIVE
STATUS: CLASS-I STASIS

"Jenna!" Simmonne shrieked when she saw the broken face in the next bag and the blood pooled inside.

PATIENT: JENNA PRIDEAUX (VI-BARONESS)
CONDITION: DECEASED
STATUS: CLASS-IV STASIS

"Jenna!" Simmonne wailed again, clutching at the bag.

A pair of arms took hold of her shoulders, pulling her back but keeping her upright. Simmonne spun, expecting to see the colonel. Instead she saw Kassar's face.

"Colonel. Where is the colonel?" Simmonne demanded.

The kurai's four pupils sought the floor as he continued to guide her away from the bags. Briefly Simmonne noted that neither were in their armor, wearing a simple khaki shirt and pants instead.

"What happened? Why are the Twins in those bags? Where is the colonel? Tell me what happened!"

Neither kurai answered her as Kassar continued to back her away.

"Let go of me!" Simmonne screamed. "Colonel? Where are you? What happened?"

"He's not here, Majesty," Kassar whispered.

Kassar led her to the opposite wall. Movement caught her eye, and Simmonne turned to see a hovering slab of metal ascend the ramp into the cargo bay.

"Where is he?" Simmonne demanded. "Tell me what happened!"

Held to the wall by Kassar, Simmonne watched as Novin scooped Jenna's bag into his arms before lying her on the cargo raft. Simmonne began to babble as he added the Twins and then the strangers.

Simmonne glared at Kassar's downcast eyes.

"What happened to Jenna? And the Twins? Why are the Twins in those bags?"

"The *Intruder's* life support is not meant for this many people, Majesty," Kassar answered. "We had to put the ladies Katyusha and Dr. Gilyard into the bags for the trip."

Now with all five loaded on the cargo raft, Novin swiped his hand to send the device in motion.

"And Jenna?" Simmonne asked. "What happened to her?"

Kassar shook his head. "She was killed in the escape, Majesty."

She covered her mouth as tears formed at the corners of her eyes. Despite having read it, to hear it out loud felt as though a hand had grabbed hold of her guts and begun to twist.

"Can—can she be revived?" Simmonne whispered, lowering her hand.

"We'll know soon," Kassar answered. He motioned with one arm for her to follow the cargo raft.

"Where is the colonel?"

Kassar was silent again.

"Where is he?" Simmonne shouted. But still Kassar did not answer.

Useless. As soon as Kassar released her, she raced to catch up to the raft. It moved quickly. Kassar and Novin trailed behind as the device led them to the infirmary. The room was abuzz with activity as more tables flowed up and out of the floor to receive the new patients.

The two kurai hefted Jenna's body and laid it on the first of the empty tables. She paused to see both kurai hold a hand to their heads. They glanced at Simmonne, then stepped away from Jenna. More machinery came from the floor and the ceiling, forming a new deep-fryer tank around Jenna's body.

"Initiating scan," Andira announced. "Anomaly detected."

Anomaly? What did that mean?

"Foreign object detected," Andira continued.

A hologram screen jumped out at Simmonne. A skeletal image formed in front of her, revealing a small disc in the left of the chest.

"Majesty, do you know what this is?" Andira asked.

Simmonne stared blankly.

"Majesty?"

Snapped out of her trance, Simmonne answered, "I don't know what the object is. Jenna has a cyber pouch in her left breast and armpit. I know she sometimes keeps a weapon there, but it's supposed to be undetectable."

"Not to *my* sensors, Majesty," Andira replied. "I will extract it."

"Can you revive her?" Simmonne asked, looking up at the ceiling. "*Please. Please*," she chanted under her breath in the short time until Andira answered.

"Yes."

Simmonne let out a sigh, and a chill swept through her body.

"There has been significant brain trauma. The process will take time."

"How long?" Simmonne asked. "What about her memory?"

"I can keep memory loss to a minimum, but that will slow her convalescence. At least thirty-six hours will be required."

"But she'll be all right? Right? She'll still be Jenna?"

"Yes, Majesty," Andira assured her. "Please do not worry. This infirmary has dealt with more severe trauma than this."

Simmonne's hand found her chest as she leaned against the tank. She stood there for a time, letting her heart slow before turning her attention elsewhere. Kassar and Novin had transferred the remaining patients to the other tables. Another deep-fryer was being constructed around the boy. The Twins and the strange woman were on their own tables between Jenna and the boy's tank.

Reluctantly Simmonne took her hand off Jenna's tank and turned to the other tables while Kassar and Novin unwrapped the Twins.

"What's wrong? Why aren't they waking up?" Simmonne asked as the bags were removed.

"Relax, Majesty," Kassar answered in his soft tone. "We will wake them now."

Kassar paused to look around.

"Andira, how long until your new body is ready?"

New body? How did he know Andira's body had been destroyed? Stupid. Networking. She probably told them both what had happened as soon as they were aboard.

"One hour."

"I'll do it myself," Kassar answered. He left the table briefly to take a small case from a shelf. When he returned, he moved to one Twin and motioned Simmonne over. Then he laid the small case on the table and opened it. Now that her panic was subsiding, she was sensing more from the two kurai. There was more than despair. There was . . . shame. Intense shame behind both of their eyes.

Kassar took a metal strip from the tool kit and gently adhered it to Jennifer's forehead.

"Majesty, please take her hand."

Simmonne complied. With her other hand, she brushed a lock of hair from Jennifer's face. She knew this much from the astranet. People some-times panicked when first brought out of stasis. Something in the brain thought they were dying. It helped to see a friendly face, to realize more quickly that they were safe.

Kassar jabbed an auto-syringe gently into Jennifer's neck. "It will require a minute."

Simmonne nodded while looking down at Jennifer. She was wearing one of the suits the colonel had packed. But her face and hair were clean. Hopefully that meant the Vaar had treated them well.

Simmonne smiled when Jennifer drew in a breath. Her eyes opened briefly before closing again. Jennifer's legs twitched, and Simmonne held tight as her arm did the same. The eyes opened again amid a deep gasp, and Simmonne felt the flicker of consciousness coming back. She smiled. The Twins had switched where they parted their hair. This wasn't Jennifer. This was Julie.

The panic never came. Instead Julie's eyes opened slowly. Her eyes rolled around for several seconds before finding a place to focus.

"Simmonne," Julie whispered.

"It's all right," Simmonne whispered back. "You're safe now."

Weakly, Julie turned her head, finding Jennifer on the next table. "Is she?"

"We will wake her next," Kassar answered. "Don't try to move. Your motor control will be impaired for a few minutes."

Simmonne felt the sense of urgency as Julie's eyes opened wider.

"Colonel Panzer," she whispered, looking to Kassar. "Is he still on the ship?"

Still on the ship with the Vaar? Simmonne's gaze landed on the kurai as well.

"Just rest," he answered before eyeing Simmonne. He motioned her to follow as he turned his attention to Jennifer.

"You left him?" Simmonne moved to Jennifer. "How could you leave him?"

"Majesty." Kassar looked up from Jennifer to her. "Please? Take her hand."

Simmonne did as he asked but still glared at him. He was still on the ship? How? Why? He was . . . *him*. Surely he was all right. But, why would they leave him?

"What happened?" Simmonne whispered while Kassar worked to revive Jennifer. Still he did not answer. "Kassar, tell me what happened."

"I can't, Majesty," he replied. "Corps missions are—"

"If you say the words 'absolute secret' to me, I'm going to scream!" she warned, nearly crossing that threshold already.

Kassar chose to say nothing and gave Jennifer the injection. Simmonne's focus was thus forced to shift as Jennifer drew in a quiet gasp. Her eyes flut-tered open and quickly found Simmonne.

"Simmonne?"

"You're safe," she answered. "Don't try to get up. Give yourself a few minutes."

Jennifer nodded slowly before her eyes went wide and moved to Kassar.

"The colonel," Jennifer whispered before coughing. "Is he . . . still on the ship?"

"Just rest, Lady," he answered her.

Simmonne watched him walk away to a print terminal, the repeated question and worry making the thump in her chest harder to ignore. He returned with three glasses of water and placed one in the hand of each Twin. The third, he set down.

"Use the straw," he directed before turning to the strange woman Simmonne had seen. "Majesty?"

"I don't know her," Simmonne protested, still holding Jennifer's hand. "Who are these people?"

"This is Dr. Taula Gilyard." Kassar pointed to the strange woman. "The legionnaire is Jonathan Clearwater. If you please, Majesty?"

"But, I don't know her." What did he expect her to do?

"No, but she knows who you are."

He had a point. With a frown, Simmonne looked down at Jennifer. "I'll be right back."

Simmonne stood by Kassar but did not take the woman's hand. What did Kassar say her name was? Gilyard? That sounded familiar.

Kassar did his work and administered the injection. The calm awakening of the Twins had lured Simmonne into a false sense of security. Dr. Gilyard's eyes opened slowly and blinked a single time. Her mouth opened, and out came the most piercing shriek Simmonne had ever heard. She jumped back as Dr. Gilyard bolted upright and tried to leave the table. But her legs were not ready to bear weight. She began to fall only for Kassar to come over the table and easily heft her back on

"Majesty?" Kassar whispered, turning to her.

Simmonne swallowed before stepping forward. Kassar held the doctor down through a fresh scream.

"Dr. Gilyard?" Unheard, Simmonne raised her volume. "Dr. Gilyard!"

The woman's panicked eyes darted in a circle before resting on Simmonne. She saw the look of recognition as the woman took in a deep breath before exhaling. Simmonne nearly choked on the sense of panic blasting out of the doctor like a supernova. But mercifully it ended quickly, and confusion swept the fear aside as it came to dominate the woman's face.

"You're all right, Doctor." Simmonne laid a hand on her shoulder. "You're safe."

The doctor blinked. "Imperial Rose?" she whispered, turning her head to see the Twins. "The last thing I remember . . . is . . ." The doctor trailed off before looking at Kassar. "Did I die?"

"No," Kassar assured her, gently crossing her left arm over her waist before inserting the third glass into her right hand. "You passed out from vacuum exposure. Since we had to do it anyway, I put you in a trauma bag once we had you breathing again."

Vacuum exposure? Simmonne's eyes darted to the kurai. What the hell happened?

"Jonathan?" Dr. Gilyard began to sit up again only for Kassar to push her back down.

"Stay put." Kassar's voice almost broke a whisper. "You need to stay immobile for at least an hour."

"Where's Jonathan?" Dr. Gilyard looked up at Kassar before scanning the infirmary. Kassar turned his head, using his sharp chin to direct her attention to the deep-fryer at her right. "Will he be all right?"

"Andira?" Kassar queried, passing the question.

"Lieutenant Clearwater has extensive neurological damage. Dr. Gilyard, do you know the source of this?"

"Who are you?" she returned, looking up to the ceiling.

"My name is Andira, Doctor. I am the ship's AI. Do you know what happened to Lieutenant Clearwater?"

"Neurological damage," the doctor whispered to herself. Her body was still trembling—not all of her terror had faded. "Yes. He died on ND-31. The Vaar reanimated him, but they screwed up. Can you help him?"

"Scans suggest that some permanent memory loss will be unavoidable," Andira explained. "This will complicate his recovery. But I should be able to reanimate him successfully."

Dr. Gilyard heaved a sigh of relief. There was something odd in her feelings. It made more sense when she finally noticed the points in the doctor's ears. Lantai? No, the points were too faint. Hutai, or maybe even lannen.

"We'll be right back," Simmonne said, taking hold of Kassar's arm. He let her lead them to the door. "I want to know where the colonel is, and I want to know *now*."

Shame—the sensation made her want to vomit. She raised a hand to her mouth as a tremor shot through her body.

"He's dead, Majesty," Kassar whispered, staring at the floor.

Simmonne turned her head away from him, slowly lowering her hand. "Dead?" The word was almost silent past her lips. "What do you mean dead? He can't be dead. Where is he?"

Kassar turned back toward the infirmary.

"Don't walk away from me!" Simmonne shouted, grabbing his arm again. But with the cyborg in motion, she was not strong enough to hold him back. The impulse caused her to lurch forward, and Kassar caught her on her way down to the floor. He stood her upright again.

"Andira?" Kassar broke his silence. "How long until Rhoxx can come out of his tank?"

"I have accelerated his convalescence and will bring him out shortly," she answered. "I will apprise him of your mission report. The rapid regeneration will result in chemical imbalances. This will affect his mood."

"Understood."

"Kassar?" Simmonne demanded, grabbing his arm again. "What

happened? Where is he?"

When he did not answer, Simmonne scanned the infirmary for Novin. She found him near Rhoxx's deep-fryer. The kurai had found a spot on the floor where the wall and a cabinet formed a corner. There he sat with his head in his hands. Despair covered him like a blanket. The acrid sensation radiated from him like smoke from a smoldering fire.

"Novin? Tell me what happened. Where is he?"

"He's dead, Majesty," Kassar answered her again. "All that's left now is to recover his body. If we can."

"No." She shook her head. "I don't believe it. What happened? Did you see him die?" She grabbed Kassar with both hands, trying to shake him, but he was too stout. "Did you see him die?" she screamed. "Tell me!"

The sound of banging metal drew her attention. Rhoxx's tank was disassembling itself, leaving pieces to retreat into the floor and ceiling. The oversized table supporting the kodaz on his belly slowly descended to place him on his feet. On unsteady feet, Rhoxx opened his eyes and rotated them in opposite directions before they stopped to look down the length of his snout.

"Rhoxx?" Simmonne whispered.

The metal floor rang with his steps as Rhoxx approached her and Kassar. With claws extended, his right hand came up, and he inserted long talons between the two of them. One eye remained on Simmonne as he gently, but firmly, forced her to step away. His other eye remained squarely on Kassar. Rhoxx pushed Simmonne more than a meter away before both of his eyes locked on the kurai.

In a flash Rhoxx reared up on his hind legs, and both of his forward limbs clamped down on Kassar so hard, Simmonne was certain the kurai must be dead. Rhoxx's roar bellowed above her gasp and forced her to shield her ears as the kodaz slammed Kassar into the wall. The entire room seemed to jump.

"You *leavin'* him!" Rhoxx screamed. "*How you be leavin' him!*"

Rhoxx drew back before slamming Kassar into the wall again, then again, and again.

"How? How? *How you be leavin' him?*"

"Rhoxx," Simmonne whispered. She took a step closer before Rhoxx's glare turned briefly on her. The avalanche of fury she felt froze her in her tracks. Rhoxx turned back to Kassar whose head rolled about his shoulders.

"He ordered us to go," Kassar answered. Blood from reopened wounds stained his shirt while more dribbled out from the left leg of his pants.

"*You! No! Ssssupossin' leave. Him!*" Rhoxx continued to scream, slamming Kassar into the wall four times more.

"Rhoxx, you're going to kill him!" Simmonne protested.

"Ssstayin' out t'is, Majesssty," Rhoxx answered, his enormous head twitching toward her. "Not bein' you bussssiness."

Rhoxx turned suddenly, smashing Kassar into the floor with such force that the kurai's body skipped before rolling to the opposite side of the room. He crashed into a pair of rolling cabinets that promptly emptied their contents onto him.

"He ordered Andira to bring the *Intruder* back." Novin spoke up from his spot on the floor.

Rhoxx emitted a growl as his head swiveled to the other kurai. The kodaz's heavy steps carried him forward until he loomed over Novin who still sat with his head in his hands.

"Andira not able disssobey," Rhoxx growled. "Her obedienssse her progammin'. *You* able. You breakin' her computer core so sshe not able obey? You jumpin' out t'e ssshuttle sso you not taken wit'? No. You two *leavin'* him! You leave him to t'e enemy!"

Novin lowered his arms before looking up at Rhoxx.

"We can't disobey him any more than you can," Novin answered. "He told us to bring them back."

"*I* may be lettin' him out my sssight, but *I never* leavin' him to t'e enemy!"

Simmonne found the ability to move and crossed the room, stepping over Rhoxx's tail on her way to Kassar. Still covered in the contents of the cabinets, he had sat up and was staring at the floor. She offered her hand. He did not take it, but he stood on his own.

"We have to recover his body," Novin said.

"Ussin' you brain techssson," Rhoxx snapped at him. "By now him body halfway to Prit'own."

"Did either of you actually see him die?" Simmonne set the query once more.

"Wit'out *Intrudah*, no escape possible," Rhoxx answered. He seemed to be calming down and backed off of Novin. "Him not lettin' Vaar take him alive. Takin' t'e ssssilensse if him havin' to."

"Silence?" Simmonne asked. "What is that?"

"It's a suicide cocktail, Majesty," Kassar answered. "We all have it in our armor for . . . situations."

Simmonne took a step back from him, rapidly shaking her head. "No. No, he wouldn't do that."

Simmonne's arm crossed her stomach as she felt bile welling in her throat. It couldn't be true. He couldn't be dead. Not like this. Not after all that happened.

"Andeera. Bein' how lon', till able leave?"

"Not for several more days," she answered. "The Vaar incursion into the ship set my repair schedule back significantly."

Rhoxx's upper lip rose briefly in a sneer.

"Will somebody *please* tell me." Simmonne waited for Kassar, Rhoxx, and Novin to look at her. "Did anyone *see* him die?"

"No, Majesty," Kassar answered. "But—"

"Then he's alive!" Simmonne interrupted. "He's still alive."

One of Rhoxx's eyes turned toward her.

"Maybe him be," Rhoxx answered. Simmonne was not sure what the feeling was that she sensed from him.

"So what do we do?" she asked. "How do we get him back?"

"If him bein' live. Him essscape. Come to uss. If not, followin' orderss when ssship be ready."

"Orders? What orders?"

Rhoxx turned for the infirmary door and began to walk.

"What orders, Rhoxx?" Simmonne pursued him, racing to get between him and the door. "What orders?"

"Takin' you home."

"We can't just leave him!" Simmonne protested.

Rhoxx was silent for a few moments.

"We wait assss lon' as we able."

CHAPTER
14A

I N THE BORDERLESS REALM, Panzer glared at the show of rippling lights slowly drawing inward. It was so bright. His optical nanites should be blackening his eyes, protecting them from the light that could boil his retinas. He should be discomforted by the intensity, yet he felt no need to avert his gaze or even raise his hand. Nor did his NOD answer when he tried to query the wavelengths he was seeing.

Like a star dying to supernova, the sphere of light collapsed on itself in a final brilliant flare. A silhouette now stood before him. The thing had a feminine shape but was certainly no woman. Now that Panzer could see without being blinded, he noticed Ullenk. The Vaar had brought his hands together as a human might in prayer, then bowed his head.

The new creature had chosen a woman's shape but not features. Skin glowed like molten metal sheathed in golden robes. Formless, featureless orbs of silver stared back at him where the eyes should be. Some facsimile of hair danced like flickering fire. The imitation of fabric it wore never stopped moving, as if beheld to a wind only it could perceive.

The entity seemed to float rather than walk, and Panzer's right foot slid back as the thing drew closer to him. When he moved his left foot back to join the right, it ceased its advance.

"Hello."

The voice was perhaps the most accurate part of its female impression but far from perfect. The single word sounded more girlish than womanly. More than a little unsettling given its source.

"Who, and what, are you?" Panzer asked.

"The colonists who were here called me Ghost. My name is Anagram." Ullenk maintained his bowed stance, unmoving, like a statue or dedicated follower as it spoke.

The Ghost of ND-31? No. Superstitious garbage from overworked technicians.

"Anagram?" Panzer repeated with a cocked eyebrow.

A ripple of silver moved briefly over the golden skin of the creature's face.

"I wonder what the sounds of your name might mean, in other tongues," she answered.

Panzer kept his face like stone, but she did have a point. In Errdir, the ro-bert was a boogeyman. In the dead language of the kodaz, a vyk'tor was a multi-tool. There were only so many sounds organic mouths could make.

"That answers the who. Not the what," Panzer said as he looked the creature over. "What are you?"

"I am a wave entity."

It was harder to keep an expressionless face when he heard the words. "Wave entity? What is that?"

He feigned ignorance, at least of the concept. He had heard the term in the speculations where science bled into pseudoscience—where scientists traded their mantle of reason for that of clergy, preaching concepts in which they had faith but no actual proof. If this thing claimed to be something so outrageous, he would give it the opportunity to explain its nature.

"I am a quantum sapience, composed of wavestrings organizing and organized by repeating patterns in space-time."

"Fair enough," Panzer answered. "Why am I here?"

"You're not." The silver orbs that were its eyes grew larger, as if to mimic a wide-open glare.

That was enough to peak one of his eyebrows. Panzer pressed his right hand several times against his chest, then dragged it down his left arm. He rubbed both hands together as they met. For a dead man he certainly had a lot of substance and sensation.

"You could have fooled me," he quipped.

"You are dead," the entity assured him. "Did Ullenk not tell you this?"

With a small scoff, Panzer glanced at the Vaar, still with his head bowed. "He did mention that. But since Solar is not his native tongue, I tried to assume he meant something else."

"The Vaar have an engineered talent for language," the entity returned. "I assure you that Ullenk knows the words he uses."

Ullenk still had not moved out of his bowed posture, and his eyes remained closed. Panzer still could not sense him, nor the entity that had joined them. How could he not sense them? If this were not a thought prison, what other explanation could there be? An Imperial interrogator would know how to fool a telepathic brain in a thought prison. They would know how to simulate the necessary input. A Vaar inquisitor likely would not.

"That raises a lot of questions," Panzer said as he returned his attention to the entity. "Like how we're communicating, or how I am perceiving any of this. If this is the afterlife, I'll have to insist on a refund of my admission fee."

The entity, Anagram, raised its arm to point a single golden finger. Panzer did not immediately turn, not about to show his back to either of them. Instead he angled toward Ullenk and this Anagram before walking backward. Once he had added enough distance to keep them in his peripheral vision, he looked toward what the entity wanted him to see.

A large cylinder stood on the invisible floor. As Panzer glared at it, the walls of the device seemed to become transparent, then when he realized what he was looking at, it took on an entirely new view.

As he looked down he saw himself, lying in the cylinder.

The damaged plates of his armor, and the hole punched by the bloodhammer, were all where he remembered them. The arms that had been torn away rested beside his torso. Then there was the gruel that had been his head. His helmet lay beside the lumpy red puddle, but there was simply nothing left of his skull, nor the vertebrae that should have been connected to it.

"That's raising a lot more questions than it answers."

"You are dead," Anagram assured him. "Everything you are perceiving is a simulation. Even you are simply a simulation based on data gathered while scanning the remains of your brain."

Imperial technology could not restore a brain that badly damaged. Even trying to pull memories postmortem would be an exercise in futility. Among the lumps that remained, he doubted there was one the diameter of his thumb.

"It was necessary for us to communicate in this manner," the entity continued. "Even through telepathy, when combined with the time required to restore your body, it would give Indorai the opportunity to catch me. This cannot be allowed. When the repair of your body is complete, the events of this simulation will be incorporated into your memory so that you recall it as if you had experienced it."

Mention of the Therican narrowed Panzer's eyes, and he turned back toward Anagram.

"The Therican?" Panzer asked. "What is your relationship to him?"

"Therican?" Anagram hesitated. "Yes. Indorai's creations. Made in his own image. Or rather, the twisted image he made of himself in his teacher's service."

"He created them? What was he before? What is he?" Panzer took a step closer to her. If the ancient enemy was returning . . . "Tell me."

A ripple seemed to pass over her eyes.

"He was one of us—once—an outcast in our society for whom we could never find a place."

Panzer's head swiveled as the star field around him was overwritten. The floor disappeared, replaced with solid rock, and a rocky valley expanded before him. Rain fell down mountains into the valley to form a river. But he saw no plants or animals to drink it. There was only gray stone and a yellow sun on the horizon.

"You must understand how rare sapient life is in this universe," Anagram continued. "We do not know if we were truly the first. But we were the first to reach the stars."

The first sapient species? Panzer tried not to let his incredulity show at such a bold claim. Shades of blue and red began to fill the scenery as alien plants and mosses swept over the valley. Eons passed like seconds as he watched movement below the surface of the river. The sounds of animals whispered deep in the vegetation. His eyes were drawn to the sky where streaks of light rose from the land to the deep sky as years and years continued to pass.

"Like your people, we thought to find others in the universe, but there were none to find. Before Earth, or its star, had formed, we were the undisputed masters of this universe. And we were alone."

Panzer tried not to roll his eyes.

"Then why are we speaking?" Panzer asked. "I've never bothered trying to converse with a bacterium."

"Bacteria does not have sapience," Anagram answered. "You do. And it is your people who are rapidly inheriting our sins. Hold your questions now, and listen."

This time Panzer did not move away when Anagram drew closer.

"The universe was a different place in our time. By the understanding of your science, even the word *universe* might be somewhat of a misnomer. Like your people, we were explorers at heart."

The valley faded away, returning to the view of the stars. Though he could not see it, Panzer felt the ripple expanding out through the cosmos.

"Over many ages, we spread to all corners of reality. We sought to understand everything. In a breadth of time beyond your reason, that time came. There was nowhere left to explore. We had completed our understanding of physics, and there was nothing left to learn. But the nature of exploration remained within us, so we looked beyond."

An image formed in front of Panzer—swirling clouds of pink and gold, the plasma circling and revealing the presence of a black hole. Tiny ships— too small for him to make out their features—moved amid the plasma. As the image changed, he understood. At first it seemed as if they were clearing the plasma away, but they were helping to draw it in, force-feeding the matter to the singularity. In time it had grown, and all the gas was gone.

More ships entered the image, forming a cloud around the black hole. For a moment Panzer's stone face was lost. Somehow, the black hole itself seemed to shrink. Metal segments of lustrous silver began to form around the shrinking singularity. The monster was being placed in a cage.

In minutes the singularity had been bound. A nearly perfect sphere of silver was now its prison.

"Our universe is particularly difficult to access or depart," Anagram continued. "In our lust for more to explore, we looked to move beyond it. This was our answer. In your language, it would be called the Crossroads, a transpatial hub powerful enough to punch through reality and open the door beyond."

Panzer turned toward Anagram slowly, an eyebrow raised. "Other universes?"

"Is the idea so foreign to you?" Anagram asked as her silver eyes briefly increased in luminosity. "Did your own Empire not attempt it with the *Amarego*?"

The throat he didn't have felt dry. How did she know about the *Amarego*? In the years before the Eclipse, the Armadas commissioned a ship to conduct an experiment in multiverse transit. Its maiden voyage was its last—neither the ship nor its wreckage were ever found. How did Anagram know about it?

For that matter, how did *he* know about the *Amarego*? Panzer cursed himself. That kind of secret was not stored in his brain, but on his NCP. Had it somehow survived the damage to his head? Was any of this real? Or was he succumbing to a thought prison?

"Your people were and remain far from the comprehension necessary to do what you attempted. Fortunately for you, you failed. But sadly, a reach that extends grasp is a common failing among explorers."

Anagram raised her arm, moving until she seemed to hold the silver sphere.

"The Crossroads was our attempt, and far more successful. It was a time of great contentment for us, but also of arrogance and hubris. We began to call ourselves the Ascendant, for we were breaking free from the bonds of our reality. But we were naive in our superiority. We did not realize that the inaccessibility of our universe was a precious gift that we were squandering."

Panzer's eyes moved between Anagram and the Crossroads.

"You opened the door to something you couldn't handle."

Anagram gave a single nod. A ripple passed through the colors of her skin.

"At first, there was no threat. The doors must be opened from within. We believed that if we found a threat, we could simply close our door. The first universe we found had no sapience. But our lust for discovery was ripened. New laws of physics, treasures to find, and mysteries to unravel.

"Once out of our universe, it proved almost painfully easy to travel to others. In other universes, all we required was technology little different from your transpatial drives. We traveled to and between them as easily as your Empire crosses galaxies. And it was our fevered exploration that caught the eye of our doom, the one you know as the Encephalon."

Their eyes met at the name. Knowing about the *Amarego* was one thing. But how did she know about the Encephalon? Had she cracked his NCP? Had she taken the secrets locked within him? Had he just become the greatest security breach of all time?

"You still don't believe, do you?" Anagram asked. "You do not trust."

"You've given me no reason to," Panzer answered before motioning with his arm. "There was a time I could present illusions no one could see through. And there's nothing you're doing here that I couldn't do in the dark room of my ship."

Anagram broke eye contact to turn her silver gaze to the sphere above her palm.

"This is why you are here," she said a bit more forcefully. "This is why your Empire and the Combine find themselves at war. Why it is *now* and not another time. When we made contact with him, he called himself Teacher. It is what he always does to any species with which he chooses to commune. He selects a name that hints at depthless intellect and unknown wisdom. That is how he inserts himself into their affairs. He feeds their hunger for knowledge and the power it brings. That hunger blinds them to the cost. So it was with us. So it has been with you."

Anagram's eyes seemed to dim, and even the luster of her golden skin seemed to dull with it.

"The Teacher knew things, even about our universe, that we did not. He knew what no one else could, for no one else was there to see it for themselves. To see, not only the birth and death of stars, but the universes in which they form. We believed we had found a fountain from which all knowledge could flow. And greedily, we drank from it."

Anagram took a step back as her light seemed to dim further.

"Indorai became his emissary. And we were all happy for him. The outcast for whom we could never find a place or purpose at last had one. We saw the Teacher as a great benevolence for choosing the least of us to be his agent. At the time, we lived in bodies of machinery, and our only prospect to grow was to find a manner to build better machines. It was the Teacher's guidance, delivered through Indorai, that we learned to take this form. Nigh indestructible and impervious to the ravages of time."

Panzer returned his attention to the sphere. Something about it nagged at his perception, demanding his attention like a neglected child.

"So what went wrong?"

If nothing else, she was telling an amusing story and giving him time to reason. If this were a thought prison, whoever was running it was either a fool or a genius. One tried to provide comfort and familiarity in a thought prison. Throwing strange and esoteric information at the subject simply put them on guard, negating the point entirely.

"As we followed the Teacher," Anagram continued, "we began to change. It was slow at first, and few noticed. One of our deepest desires had always been to find another sapient species. It was that desire more than any other that led to the Crossroads and breaching the walls of our universe. To some degree, the Teacher had satisfied that desire. But he was a species of one. As we continued to explore under his guidance, eventually we found another."

Anagram held one arm ahead. A spiral galaxy swirled into existence above her palm. Strangely it was mostly red, not blue, stars that swirled through the galaxy's arms, and the core was a strange hue of green. A galaxy in another universe? Perhaps that was why it did not look like a spiral should, with young, blue stars dominating much of its arms.

"When we found them, the result was not triumph, wonder, or satisfaction. For so many, it was a deafening apathy. In one universe, our explorers found an entire galaxy, with more than a hundred sapient species within. They did not even bother to contact them."

For a moment Anagram's imitation voice sounded as if it were about to cry, and she were having to force herself to go on.

"The fact was reported with no more joy than the cataloging of a new type of star. It was then that I, and others, realized we were no longer the people we once were. We, who were Ascendant, had become Fallen, and we did not even realize it."

Panzer began to walk a circle around the image of the sphere, still unable to look away from it. He took several seconds to compose his words. He was receiving a lot of information, and it needed to stay that way.

"You tell an interesting story, Anagram, but I fail to see what it has to do with me, the Empire, or the Combine."

"It has everything to do with you," she answered, interposing herself in his path so that he came to a stop. "You have inherited our war. Those of us who realized what had happened to our people came together. In council we decided that we had to go our own way. In our naivete, we thought the Teacher and the Fallen would simply let us go." Anagram's molten eyes narrowed. "We were wrong."

Her molten skin seemed to cool until it barely glowed, and the intangible wind ruffling her clothes seemed to ebb. Even her voice changed, as if maturing in seconds from girl to woman.

"While we were contemplating what to do, the Fallen were acting. At first it seemed innocent. They modified the Crossroads to be better suited to the new forms the Teacher had given us—to make it respond to the telepathy we now possessed. But they were doing more, using the door to break down the wall. They were modifying the Crossroads into a space-time sink to force our universe and another to merge." Anagram met his gaze.

"Merging universes?" Panzer asked, raising one eyebrow and allowing fresh incredulity into his voice. "Can you understand why I might be a little skeptical of that?"

"Our universe is difficult to enter or leave," Anagram continued, ignoring his question. "By merging it with another, that protection could be permanently stripped away. There would be no way to escape the Teacher then. Those of us who remained Ascendant had to close the door before it was too late. When we realized what the Fallen were doing, we tried to destroy the Crossroads."

Anagram returned her eyes to the silver sphere.

"Indorai led the Fallen against us through cannibalism, devouring our waveforms. For none were allowed to reject the Teacher or his teachings."

Anagram extended her arm again, returning the Crossroads to her palm.

"We failed. We were unable to destroy the Crossroads. We merely knocked it askew on the proper axis of time. The result was what you call the Void Zone."

Now that was useful information, assuming it was true. With the sphere no longer monopolizing his gaze, Panzer looked into Anagram's eyes once again. "And the dilation waves?"

Anagram shook her head. "The door was closed but not shut. The merger of this space-time with another was arrested but not stopped. It continues now as the Crossroads attempts to return to its proper position. Each time it moves, the space-time of the other universe leaks into this one. But it does not mix as it should. The two space-times flow over one another like oil and water. That is why time slows as the waves pass—it is the interference of two different times. The higher consciousness of your provident mind enables you to remain aware by perceiving both space-times at once. Even though you could only act in one."

"Providence." Panzer's eyes lit up, and he looked away as the realization worked its way through his mind. "It makes sense. That's what it is. A counter-time, flowing opposite our own. A strong metapsion perceives it. And as the alien time flows backward, it shows us the future. But, there has to be more to it."

Panzer's eyes moved briefly to Ullenk. He remained silent, even now, still in his praying posture. Anagram gave him a moment to process before speaking again.

"Metapsionics, the gift and taint of our Teacher—your Encephalon. None develop these abilities naturally. It is the fingerprint of his hand upon your species."

Panzer took a breath. If this was a thought prison, when was he captured? Was it on the *Caustic Reverie*? The fight with Oul'sor, his death on ND-31—those could all be false memories. But how would those memories be implanted without his NCP detecting them? It took a high-level telepath to accomplish that kind of memory forgery. The Vaar had no metapsions, except perhaps Oul'sor. Panzer had seen it. He had sensed when the Vaar used psionics to pull his hammer to him. But if Oul'sor were implanting these memories, how did he become telepathic? When did he find the many years it took to develop that level of skill? If the Vaar had him in a thought prison, and somehow found a way to influence him telepathically, why allow him to remember that Oul'sor had gained those abilities?

They wouldn't. Vaar didn't think that way. The Vaar were always trying to deceive the enemy, even to the point of a deception costing more than it was worth. If Oul'sor had developed telepathy strong enough to alter memories to foil a Neuro-Cortical Processor, he would never let that knowledge remain. And how would Oul'sor affect his mind? No telepath had ever been able to do that. No one could touch his mind unless he enabled them.

But if this wasn't a thought prison, then it was worse. He took another breath. He had no choice. He needed more information, and he was not going to get it without giving some up.

"I wouldn't be too worried about your old Teacher," Panzer said, watching Anagram closely for any reaction.

"How like we were, you are," Anagram answered. "The childish arrogance. To believe that victory in the battle has won the war. I know what is in your emperor's vault."

Her silver eyes narrowed. Panzer simply stared her down as he waited for her to finish.

"It is not the Encephalon."

Not the Encephalon? Then what was it? If the thing in the vault was not the Encephalon, then he was not contained. That could not be the case. Anagram's gaze turned to where the silver sphere had been.

"When the Crossroads was sent askew, those on board were trapped and doomed to die." The inflection of her voice changed. Possibly lament? "All except Indorai. He managed to break free and reemerge in this universe. I suspect that he devoured the waveforms of all Ascendant and Fallen on the station to endure.

"Those of us who remained, knew that the Crossroads, and perhaps he, too, would return one day. But we could not agree on a solution. Most went into hiding somewhere the Encephalon could never find. But some of us tried to prepare and exploit his one weakness."

Simulation or not, he felt a chill. The Encephalon, free? It could not be real. Even the cruelty of the universe had limits. But if the Encephalon was free, in some alternate universe, what the hell was in the vault?

"What weakness?" Panzer pressed.

"His sheer abhorrence for waste," Anagram answered. "The Encephalon will evaluate every sapient species he encounters and decide their fate. With worlds like this one, we sought to flood this universe with life—to create so many sapients that he would be forced to change his methods. And perhaps we could expose another weakness to exploit."

Panzer's gaze moved again to Ullenk.

"So it's true," he whispered. "We were right. The Vaar are an engineered species."

"Yes," Anagram answered, motioning with one arm for Ullenk to come closer. The Vaar finally left his praying posture and moved to stand beside her. "The Vaar are but one of thousands of species created on origin worlds such as this one. Created from its native life and, when ready, sent to a home world to develop into a civilization. Most of the sapient species in your Empire were created on this very world."

The feeling of incredulity returned as Panzer faced Anagram once again.

"You're not about to tell me you created humanity, are you?"

Anagram shook her head. "No. You are not one of my creations. But most are. The M'gah, the Elrua, all of the Rhinegrave Eight but the tahn'kodaz. The ingridi, the seru, the quants, the evulta, the nakori, and many more."

Panzer's eyes narrowed. That was a long list of bold claims. But all the eight except the kodaz?

"The lantai?" he asked. He tried again to reach out with his mind, but there was nothing there to reach out with—an arm trying to grasp with no hand.

Anagram nodded before looking at him as if anticipating what was coming next.

"You made them as servile as they are," Panzer said. "You made them from humans, didn't you?"

Anagram turned, floating a few steps away from him. "Stars have died in less time than Indorai required to escape the Crossroads. But when you are immortal, you have the time. He emerged to find a sea of life I, and those who helped me, had created. His first step was to create what your people called the Common Control Organism, and that you think is the Encephalon. A mouth that could whisper through the crack of the door to his master on the other side."

If Panzer had a pulse, it was racing, and the fingers of his left hand began to coil into a fist. "The lantai?"

Anagram raised her hand, still facing away from him. "The Teacher commanded him to create the Thericans. We had hoped to force the Teacher to adapt. He did, in the worst way possible. Once Indorai had created an army for him, they set about to purge all the species we had created. As well as any others deemed unfit. Any who had yet to achieve space travel were spared for later judgment."

The image at the center twisted again, and Panzer recognized a map of the local universe. There he saw the red line that began in the Hourglass. That line spread to the next galaxy, bouncing from it to another, and another. All until crossing the gulf to the Solar Group. The line landed in Andromeda, turning the galaxy red. From there it moved to the Solar Galaxy.

"The lantai?" Panzer asked again.

Anagram darkened at the question. "I saw what they did to your people and thousands of others. I cannot tell you how sorry I am."

"Not sorry enough to do something about it!" Panzer snapped. As he took a step toward Anagram, Ullenk stepped toward Panzer. The Vaar stopped when Anagram held up her hand to him.

"What would you have had me do?" Anagram asked. "There is nothing I could have done that would have mattered. My survival, and that of all Ascendant, depends on not being found. You do not appreciate the terrible risk I take simply to commune with you. Nor the fury many of my people will have for my decision."

Her light faded further, and Anagram became translucent before Panzer's eyes.

"I cannot tell you how I wept for you. Your people were everything we once sought, the gold of the universe for which we so fervently mined. Another sapient species not of our creation. You are what we went to other universes to find, and we could not help you. I did not expect you to survive the Thericans' assault, and I could not protect you from it. But I could not bear for you to become nothing."

"You did make them out of humans." Panzer's voice became a rasping growl, and his right hand joined the left in making a fist.

"No." Anagram raised her finger. "I examined dead humans, killed by EVE-V and famine. I used their genes as the template to create the lantai."

"How is that not making them out of humans?" Panzer demanded. "How—"

"Please calm yourself, Crykeeper." Ullenk had broken his silence. Panzer's eyes fell on him. "Please, Anagram has a reason for everything," Ullenk whispered.

Panzer turned back to Anagram, using his expression to demand his answers.

"I used human genetics as a model," Anagram explained, "as you might begin with someone else's blueprint to craft your own weapon. I examined how the human genome functioned and used it as a starting point to assemble one for the lantai with the modifications I deemed appropriate. I created them in your image, but not from you."

Panzer made a deliberate effort to uncoil his fists and slow his racing thoughts. "Why did you make them so servile? Why do you make them so dependent on their own slavery that they kill themselves without it?"

Anagram's form seemed to solidify. A dull heat returned to her colors and she turned. She held a red apple that she raised for him to see. When his eyes moved to the apple, she answered.

"Your species consumes more of this fruit than any other. Is this an error? This is how the apple tree reproduces. Does the fact that your species likes to eat this fruit mean that it is an evolutionary mistake on the part of the apple tree?"

Panzer's pulse was slowing. His posture relaxed as he allowed reason to reassert itself and contemplate the question. "No."

"No indeed," Anagram agreed. "Because your species so loves this fruit, you have expended your time and energy to ensure its survival. When you left Earth, you loved so much to exploit the apple tree that you took it with you. The apple tree could have never left Earth on its own. But because it was useful to you, you spread it. Earth is gone, but the apple tree endures thanks to you. Such was my design with the lantai. To be spared the Thericans, they had to pose no threat to anyone. But that left them vulnerable. By ensuring their servility, I ensured that another species would preserve them. And through them, some . . . image . . . of your species would survive if you did not.

"When I realized that your people had survived the Thericans, I watched. I sent the lantai to your family, whom I knew would accept them for who they were. I left them for your ancestor, Jonas II, to find. Now alive under your family, they are as safe and protected as they can be. They may yet outlive humanity."

She knew who he was. That shouldn't be a surprise. That was not the kind of information the NCP would have concerned itself with protecting.

"I never expected humanity's victory over the Thericans," Anagram went on, "but you only won a single battle in a war. When the servants of the emperor recovered a piece of the Common Control Organism, they believed they had imprisoned the Teacher, who introduced himself to you as Encephalon. But all they did was take a piece of a communications device. They gave him a seat to whisper into the ears of your rulers."

Panzer looked away. That couldn't be true. How could it be? All this time, the Encephalon was free? Simply looking on them and laughing? But he had felt the creature's mind. He had interposed himself between it and the emperor. None knew better the power on the other side.

"I knew the Crossroads would return one day." Anagram brought his attention back. "But I failed to understand when. I created the Vaar in the hopes that when that day came, they would be the soldiers who defended this universe from the doom that would follow. But they have failed, and the Crossroads returns more than a million years before I expected it."

Ullenk lowered his head, returning to his bowed posture as he faced

Anagram. "We beg your forgiveness, Anagram," Ullenk offered. "The children—"

"I do not fault you, Ullenk," Anagram answered, silencing him. "The flaw in the Vaar is a flaw in my design. I sent the Sovari to them, to correct their errors and guide them toward the proper path. To live free and proud, but with the strength and resolve to face any foe. Races so often are like individuals. In their adolescence, the Vaar turned from the counsel of their foster parents.

"I never wished the Vaar to worship me and tried to guide them through the Sovari. But when the Vaar turned from their counsel, they were vulnerable. I could not intervene when Indorai set upon them."

"The Council of Warlords loves nothing more than its own power," Ullenk interjected, grinding his teeth as he said the words. "The Sovari were never meant to rule the Vaar, and never tried. But Indorai convinced the warlords that the Sovari were planning to overthrow them. That was enough to turn the Council against them, though it was Indorai himself who killed most of them. All in preparation for this day. We came here in the hopes of using the tools on this world to finally escape."

"What tools?" Panzer pressed. "Tell me."

"This world contains a minor hub of our spatial network," Anagram answered for Ullenk.

"Spatial network?" Panzer asked. "Like the astranet?"

"In the same way a campfire is analogous to a nuclear device, perhaps."

Panzer tried not to reply with a hostile expression. That seemed unnecessarily condescending.

"That is how the Vaar took this planet from the colonists," Anagram explained. "By tapping into that network to bypass your legionnaires' shielding."

With a frown, Panzer looked past the two of them into the open field of stars. He needed information and had to move the conversation past this digression.

"So Indorai killed the Sovari. Sounds like I need to kill Indorai."

"You couldn't begin to harm Indorai." Anagram's tone was biting, and the color that had faded from her suddenly returned to a near-blinding level. The never-ending motion of her clothes increased, as if the intangible breeze around her had become a violent wind.

"Indorai has the same gifts as you but in greater measure. He has had eons to master his abilities, and to wield powers you would never live long enough to discover. Even time bends to his gift. You cannot face him. Just the small measure of himself he left with Oul'sor was too much for you."

"Then why am I here?" Panzer raised his voice. "What do you want?"

Anagram extended her left hand. The silver sphere seemed to inflate from nothing, visible once more.

"How long has it been since you felt a dilation wave?"

Thrown off by the question, Panzer had to contemplate it before answering. "I haven't perceived any since I fought Oul'sor on Avalon. But

I—" Panzer fell silent as implications clicked in his head. In his weakened state, he might not have perceived them. But he never told Andira not to warn him when they were coming. She had not issued any warnings since Avalon.

"You slept through the storm," Anagram explained. "Now the waves are scant, as the Crossroads is nearly back in position. It returns soon. Everything is because of the Crossroads. It was because of this that the Encephalon incited war between you and the Combine. If neither of you was faced with the threat of the other, you would take your time to study it. But now you are at war. The Vaar are terrified and desperate. They know they cannot defeat you in open war. Indorai has convinced them that it is their weapon against you. Now fear motivates them. Rather than study it, they race to take control and reactivate it to use against you. Billions of their infantry now wait in transports for the moment the Void Zone falls."

Panzer held a hand to his forehead as the realization swept over him.

"That's why they didn't flood us with marines on the *Caustic Reverie*," he said. "They were out of stock. The marines we saw were all they had."

Anagram nodded. "And Indorai readied Oul'sor to face you, hoping I would do exactly as I have done. To intervene on your behalf. Even now he scours this planet for me."

"What happens if he finds you?" Panzer asked.

Anagram's golden lips moved into a smile. "He will not. This is not the first time he has attempted to entrap me. But you must be concerned with your own task. The Crossroads must be destroyed."

Panzer drew to his full height and smiled at her. "I think the fleet can manage that. If I can get ahold of Aetius—"

"Your fleet will not be able," Anagram interrupted.

Panzer shot her an annoyed glare. "Not to sound like an arrogant child, but do you understand how much firepower an Armadas' fleet has? One Arc-5 will ruin any unshielded planet. A whole fleet can sterilize a galaxy in short order if so motivated."

"The Crossroads is not a galaxy," Anagram countered. "It is the construct of a species that was traveling to other universes billions of years before your own existed. Remember that. With time it could be done, but you have no such time."

Anagram raised her hand, and the silver sphere enlarged. Panzer could barely make out features on its surface. Pyramids covered most of its landscape.

"The Vaar will land soon," Anagram pressed. "They will fortify their positions, but the Crossroads is offline, and they cannot initiate its reactors. That was why they attacked your station, Avalon—to steal one of its generators. You have eleven days before they can complete their work. If you do not stop them by then, the Crossroads will come back online. The merger of realities will resume."

The merger of realities still seemed a bit far-fetched, and Panzer flexed his jaw as he thought on it.

"Even at warp velocities, it would take a long time to merge two universes."

"Indeed," Anagram answered, "but the more the merger progresses, the faster it will occur. We will reach a point of no return long before the work is complete. The Fallen were on the cusp of it when we managed to stop them. If the Vaar bring the station online, it may be only a matter of days. More importantly, it will open this universe to the Encephalon directly. If that happens, there is no hope."

"What will happen?" Panzer stared into the silver globes she called eyes.

"The death of destiny. Lack of access is the only defense. The slaughters wrought by the Thericans will be as nothing. Your people, all peoples, will be broken, and if any survive, it will be only as his slaves. Entities far worse than the Thericans await his command."

Panzer flinched as new imagery entered his mind. In a realm where space was not black, he saw a field of red and many objects within. Glowing spheres, trillions of them. For the first time since awakening, he felt a metapsionic sensation, a malevolent heat burning in the sea of red. There was no thought. There was no reason. There was only hate.

The image left him, and Anagram and Ullenk returned to his sight. The lungs he lacked seemed to be fighting for breath. Panzer glanced down and saw that his left arm was trembling.

"If the fleet can't destroy the Crossroads, what do you expect me to do?" Panzer asked.

"Marshal all the forces you can and go to the surface. I will place in your mind the full schematics of the Crossroads and knowledge of its control systems. The Crossroads will see you as one of us with 'administrator privileges.' I suspect you will know what to do. But you must not share knowledge of this purpose with your allies."

"Excuse me?" Panzer asked, pointing at Anagram. "You want me to plan a major operation and not tell anyone why I'm doing it?"

"The Encephalon's grasp holds many without their knowledge," Anagram answered. "You endanger those you tell. Invent what reason you must, but conceal the truth. Your sovereign mind makes you the one person who can keep secret what you know."

Panzer turned back to the Crossroads. What choice did he really have? Most had never even heard of the Encephalon. What proof could he even offer of such outrageous claims?

"Bring your closest allies here," Anagram pressed. "I cannot send them to the ground in the Crossroads' current state, but I can place them in orbit. I trust you could handle it from there."

"You still haven't explained how I'm supposed to destroy it if the fleet can't," Panzer shot back. "What, do you expect me to rip it apart with my bare hands?"

Anagram shook her head, seemingly out of annoyance. "You will have full knowledge of the Crossroads. I suspect you will find a solution. But if not, you will have to finish what we started, and self-destruct the station.

You will understand. It was to be our last solution if we found danger on the other side. And what we hoped to trigger had the Fallen not stopped us."

A self-destruct? It would be best to capture the station. But if it was the only option . . .

"What about Indorai?" Panzer asked. "Or even Oul'sor? Oul'sor saw through my cloak—ripped my armor like paper. Shooting him didn't work. Cutting him didn't work. And how the hell does he stop time?"

Anagram smiled. Her silver eyes briefly faded and her head shook slowly. "Oul'sor has changed." Her glowing gaze returned. "He is now a creation of Indorai, piloted by the personality that was Oul'sor. Your provident mind allowed you to perceive him as he moved in ways you could not."

"Providence?" She referenced it before. What did she know of providence? If it was more than him, he had to know what she knew. But the answer did not taste real, and Panzer turned his eyes to the Crossroads. "I have not experienced anything provident since Oul'sor and I fought on Avalon."

"You have," Anagram corrected. "You lost the strength to sense the waves of the Crossroads, but you were able to sense Indorai clearly enough in front of you. No human has lived long enough, whole in mind and body, to truly master metapsionics. Oul'sor was given a shortcut by Indorai. But your provident mind could see it."

Panzer crossed his arms and listened in silence. He thought Oul'sor might have simply pinned him in place with overwhelming psionics. But if he did that, why would he have let go before he could strike? No. The sensation was too close to what dilation waves felt like. In some manner, time had been skewed and twisted. Anagram floated closer as if she were about to embrace him, but instead she guided herself directly in front of him.

"I can restore the damage to your mind. Oul'sor is powerful now"—Anagram's eyes seemed to glow brighter—"but the power is not his own, and his proficiency is borrowed. You have skill and experience he does not."

Panzer's arms dropped to his sides. "You can repair the damage?"

Her eyes flared. Like tiny supernovae, they seemed to explode before returning to their previous, silvery glow.

"Yes, and more. While most of my people are content to hide, some of us have wanted to fight. I can place a measure of our technology within you. You had the potential to be the most powerful metapsion of your species, yet the damage to your mind makes you but a fraction of who you were. Even that was limited by the technology the Encephalon gave your species. I can fix this, but I will also be forced to limit your growth."

Panzer narrowed his eyes and stooped further to bring his face closer to hers. "You want me to do this, and you're going to tie my hands?"

A ripple passed through her as if she were a body of fluid touched by a pebble.

"Even you do not realize how strong you will be. You are not ready for it. Were I to restore you all at once, you would be a danger to everyone around you. Including yourself. But I think you will find yourself able to face

Oul'sor. When he steps off the line, you need only do the same."

"Step off the line?" Panzer barely edged the question out before a gargle escaped his lips. His head shot up as he felt something sapping his strength. His body convulsed. Anagram floated back, and Panzer fell to his hands and knees. Agony began to course through his veins, but he heard Anagram clearly.

"We've no time to slay your demons, nor put at ease the hungers within you. There are many among us. They believe it is folly for me to help you. That I do no more than unleash a monster from its cage."

Panzer coughed before a pained growl ripped its way out of his throat. The world around him began to spin, yet Anagram's voice remained clear.

"So be it. If you are to be a monster, better you be your own monster than his."

His mouth opened in a shout, and his eyes opened to blackness. Panzer's fists flew out at his sides, slamming into hard metal. But it was the punch of his mind that broke the walls of the cylinder, exploding it out in a shower of shrapnel.

A red mist crept from the corner of his sight, swirling about him as if he were the eye of a storm. A fresh shout echoed around him as the mist seemed to crackle in sheets of lightning. His empty lungs forced him to draw air in a gasp, and he fell on his hands once more. The storming mist subsided, and he was left panting on the floor.

For several minutes, Panzer did no more than draw breath. But when his eyes opened, he saw a Vaar standing before him. His legs opened into a fighting stance as his fists rose, but the familiar face brought him to ease.

"Ullenk."

The Vaar nodded.

Panzer's head swiveled as he took stock of his surroundings. A small chamber deep underground. Walls, ceiling, and floor of solid rock, yet a dim light with a source he could not find.

Panzer looked down at himself. He was in his dress uniform. His head shot up to look toward the ceiling.

"Crykeeper?" Ullenk asked.

"I—" Panzer paused, shaking his head at what did not make sense. "I sense them."

"What do you sense?"

Panzer looked at the Vaar, his pupils dilated.

"The animals," Panzer whispered. "The creatures on the surface. I can sense them. A small creature, like a rodent. It's afraid, hiding from a predator."

Panzer began to turn, surveying the rocky walls around him.

"A deer, or something like one. It's rutting. It smells a female. It knows there are predators about, but it does not care. It must find the female. Something like a primate—it's . . . thinking. It found a nut to eat but cannot pierce its shell. It looks for a rock. And—and . . ."

Panzer's face coiled into a sneer.

"Vaar marines. I can hear their thoughts. Bored. Resentful. They're tearing down the Twilight colony, angry that they are not on the front lines."

Panzer took a breath as his eyes stilled on the ceiling.

"We're kilometers underground," he whispered. "How can I sense them from this far?"

Ullenk took a step closer. "How do you feel?"

Panzer glared at him, having missed the question.

"How do you feel?" Ullenk repeated.

Panzer glanced down at his open hands, slowly coiling his fingers into fists. He could not keep his eyes open when he began to laugh.

"Crykeeper?"

Panzer opened his eyes again, still laughing as he beheld his hands. He had little breath by the time he managed to arrest his laugh. "I was dead for so long, I forgot how it felt to be alive." Panzer looked to Ullenk. "I sense . . . so much. Including . . ."

Panzer stared into the Vaar. Not one, but two minds were looking back at him. Two entities, two souls, he might call it—they occupied the same vessel.

"The Soma," Ullenk finished the sentence.

The Crossroads came to Panzer's mind, and the knowledge was a waterfall. Floor plans, system diagrams, equipment specifications. Maps. It was all there, as if the knowledge had always been a part of him. But there was more, and even his mind could not process it all at once. They washed through him like a flood, threatening to sweep him away if he looked too long into them. Ullenk's movement demanded his attention as the Vaar raised his arms. Panzer's eyes lit up as he saw the Hellbore in the Vaar's hands. Ullenk surrendered the weapon.

HELLBORE MK-II MASTER CONTROL

SYSTEMS CHECK . . .

ALL SYSTEMS ONLINE

Mark-II? Panzer mouthed the words.

"It's time for you to go," Ullenk said while Panzer struggled to take his eyes off the Hellbore.

"Non-localized astranet," Panzer whispered. "Incredible."

Teleportation was easy, at least within the astranet. But organics were fragile. They required routing. But non-localized routing? The ability to use any massive body, a planet or a large ship? Even the Empire had never been able to get it right.

Focus. Now was not the time to get lost in possibilities.

"Come with me, Ullenk," Panzer urged. "I can grant you asylum."

Very slowly, Ullenk shook his head before bowing. "I must follow the path Anagram has set for me." The Vaar's head jerked and he glared behind himself. "Indorai approaches."

Panzer quickly readied the Hellbore.

"Anagram wishes you to take this as well." Ullenk held out his hand as if about to drop something from it.

With the Hellbore in his right hand, Panzer offered his left. Ullenk's fingers opened and deposited something in Panzer's palm. Soft, furry, and alive. Panzer drew his hand out from under the Vaar's enormous appendage and saw a creature there. Like a kodaz it walked on the knuckles of its forelimbs. A long, naked tail protruded from the tuft of fur at its rear. Its mouth had the appearance of a rat.

The creature looked up at him and bared its teeth. The tiny animal took a step back in his palm, hissing and spitting. Then, without further warning, the creature sank its teeth into his thumb. Panzer flinched with surprise. The rodent's incisors could not pierce his skin, and instead of pain, he felt only an annoying pinch. Despite its inability to get through, the creature was giving its best effort.

"Stop that," Panzer growled as he eyed the creature. He blinked as the animal's red eyes turned up at him. Its small mouth released his thumb. There was a spark behind its eyes. Panzer was about to project on the creature—to instill a crippling fear of biting him again—but there was no need thanks to that tiny spark. The animal knew what his words meant. It was not the conditioning of a trained animal but an understanding of the definitions. With the creature now quietly growling, Panzer looked up into Ullenk's eyes.

"What the hell am I supposed to do with this?"

"A guest here was fond of it," Ullenk answered. "Do not worry. This problem will solve itself."

"*I sense you.*"

Indorai's voice in their minds caused both Ullenk and Panzer to stagger.

"Go." Ullenk raised his voice. "I have my own path."

Ullenk raised his arms high. His hands faced forward and opened. Panzer's world was engulfed in blue light, and the rocky chamber faded away.

CHAPTER 14B

THE HOURS WERE PASSING slowly. Jenna and the young lieutenant remained in a deep-fryer. As soon as the Twins and Dr. Gilyard were ambulatory, Simmonne led them toward the colonel's quarters. The Twins had obviously been well cared for, but the doctor carried the stench of a long-unwashed body. Thus Simmonne led her to the one place on the ship that she knew held a working shower.

"Through there." Simmonne pointed to the door.

"Thank you, Majesty," Dr. Gilyard answered with a bow.

Simmonne quickly seized on the doctor's feelings of relief and anticipation. She clung to the good feeling like found treasure, a small thing. People were always so nervous around royalty, and she was already full on negative emotions. The doctor made a detour to the wall-mount printer.

"Andira?" the doctor asked. "Could you print me a Telkera suit?"

Telkera? Simmonne stuck up her nose. She thought a professional woman would have better taste. Then again, they were limited by what was in the ship's printers.

"Yes, Doctor."

"I'll also need—"

"There is a toiletries printer in the shower, Doctor," Andira interrupted.

"Thank you."

With that Dr. Gilyard retreated into the washroom, and Simmonne led the Twins to the printer. She was not going to inflict a Delseah on them, but they needed something other than prison clothes. A pair of Latche dresses, simple but elegant, in the light blue the pair often favored. With both dresses and ensemble, she offered them to the Twins.

"*Printed* clothes?" Jennifer asked, turning her nose up at the offering.

Subject people, or *residents*, as they preferred to be called, wore printed clothes. People of high status wore art, and art required a person to craft it. Simmonne did not blame Jennifer for her reluctance, but there weren't many options.

"It's all we have right now," Simmonne whispered.

Julie may not have vocalized her complaint, but she seemed even less enthused by the prospect. She took the clothes, yet held her arms out as if disgusted to have the fabric near her body.

"I think I'll wait until after I can use the shower," Julie commented.

If the circumstances were different, Simmonne might have smiled. The thought of wearing printed clothes was so beneath them that they were in no hurry to depart what the Vaar had forced on them. The three of them may have been a bit spoiled.

Simmonne wanted to smile. But she didn't. Without saying anything, she walked past them and sat at the table. The Twins joined her as she withdrew the badge and set it down. Quietly she grazed her nail over it.

"What's that?" Julie asked, pushing the printed clothes aside.

"It's his badge," Simmonne whispered. "He gave it to me."

"He gave it to you?" the pair asked in unison, both leaning over the table.

Simmonne nodded as her eyes became cloudy.

"He *gave* it to you?" Julie pressed.

Simmonne could feel an odd mix of confusion and excitement. She pushed both feelings away. One in particular was inappropriate now.

"Was he—" Jennifer hesitated. "Was he asking . . ."

"I think so." Simmonne nodded. She closed her eyes and took a breath.

"What did you say?" Julie was practically coming across the table now. "What did you say?"

"You didn't say yes, did you?" Jennifer asked, joining in on the interrogation. "Or did you?"

At least she wasn't crazy for thinking it. If they thought the same thing, then she was not overthinking it.

"I didn't say anything," Simmonne answered. "He left when he gave it to me."

Julie's face crinkled with exasperation. "What were you going to say?" The Twins pulled chairs around the table to sit beside her.

"It doesn't matter now." One of the tears she had been fighting slipped out. "Now he's dead, and it's my fault."

Instantly there was a gentle hand on each shoulder.

"It's not your fault—"

"Yes it is," Simmonne interrupted Jennifer. "He went because I wanted him to."

Both of them said something, but Simmonne was not listening. How could he be dead? She thought back to him in the armory tinkering with his gun. She thought of Avalon as she watched from Oul'sor's grip as he systematically took the Vaar special forces apart. How could anyone kill someone like that?

But what was he supposed to do without his shuttle? Even if he stole a Vaar ship, if the Vaar had enough to push the Armadas back, how would he get one through? How would he avoid leading the Vaar straight to this ship if he did? Part of her wanted to feel some of Rhoxx's anger at Kassar and Novin for leaving him behind. But she could not muster it. Only a sense of cold as she looked down at the badge.

Dr. Gilyard left in her tacky suit. Julie stayed with Simmonne while Jennifer carried her dress to the washroom, holding the garment at arm's length like a piece of filth.

"Did you want to say yes?"

"I don't know," she answered. Did he do this just to torture her? Did it matter now? "You two should clean up." She nodded in the direction Jennifer left. "I'll be fine."

Time passed in relative silence until Jennifer emerged from the washroom wearing the printed dress like she did it as a reluctant favor. Jennifer replaced Julie at the table, and Simmonne felt an arm around her as a tear slipped out of her eye.

They also sat in silence until Julie returned.

"I suppose we only have printed food," Julie said as she returned to the table.

Food? Simmonne stopped herself from screaming the word at her. They were thinking of food now?

Simmonne took a breath. That was not fair. Who knew what the Vaar had been feeding them. After what they went through, it was probably a good sign that they were hungry.

Simmonne choked back a feeling of shame at the thought, doubting she would cope so well if she had been in their place. She thought of the colonel's larder hidden in the nearby dresser but did not say anything. None of them knew how to cook real food anyway. So Simmonne was silent as Julie printed meals at the wall.

Julie returned with the first plate and set it in front of her sister. She returned a second time with her own plate. On her third trip, Julie gently grasped Simmonne's hand, sliding it and the badge to her lap before laying a plate of sliced fruit in front of her.

Simmonne took a slice of a cinnamon-slathered apple. Just enough to signal to them that it was all right for them to eat. She did not wish to be rude but did not engage when they tried to get her to speak.

Something in the room changed. Simmonne looked up but saw only the couch across the room. Her scalp was tingling, and there was a sense of something she could not explain.

"Your Majesty?"

Simmonne looked up at the sound of Andira's voice.

"Yes?"

"Please report to the infirmary."

"What's wrong?" she asked, clutching the badge as she stood.

"It will be easier to explain at your destination."

With a dry swallow, Simmonne made for the door, and the Twins followed. Though she began slow, she found herself moving quicker with each step. A sense of calm was setting in. Her brisk walk slowed as she came within sight of the infirmary. The door was open.

Simmonne's breath left her as she walked right into his gaze and came to a halt. Her mouth worked, but no air moved through it. Her mind and body were paralyzed until he looked away.

She felt the Twins' hands on her as she caught herself on the doorway.

"Colonel?" Julie asked.

Simmonne made sure she did not stare directly into his eyes again. Kassar and Novin were in the room, on either side of the door. Rhoxx stood behind the center table where the colonel sat. In her new body, Andira loomed by him, holding a scanning device in each hand.

"What? But . . . you . . . how?" Simmonne had trouble forming the words and could only stare at him. The air in the room was not helping. A sense of alien jubilation from Rhoxx blanketed her in one sensation. Raw confusion from Novin was powerful enough to prove disorienting. A mix of confusion and even suspicion from Rhoxx clouded her senses even further.

The colonel sat in his black uniform and white jacket, the version of the attire that bore colored badges rather than the full medals. There was something different about him. Even though it had stared her in the face, it took Simmonne a second to recognize it. His eyes. The black irises that had made it nearly impossible to tell iris from pupil were gone. His eyes were nearly as blue as her own.

"What is that, sir?" Kassar asked.

Simmonne's eyes moved to the colonel's hand where he held some kind of creature. Whatever it was, she did not recognize it. A small furry body, a long pink tail, and bright red eyes. Simmonne tried to find the name in her mind. It looked almost like a rat. Or was it a mouse? A mouse. Why did he have a mouse?

"What's going on?" Dr. Gilyard asked from the hall. "Excuse me, ladies."

Simmonne could not move. But the Twins moved into the infirmary to allow the doctor a path. As soon as she stepped inside, a new sound filled the air.

"Eeeeeeeeee!"

The small rodent reared up on its hind legs, flailing its forelimbs.

"Eee! Eee! Eee!"

"Oh my . . ." Dr. Gilyard managed to get the words out before losing her voice. Simmonne was hit by another emotional punch of confusion and joy as the doctor raced toward the colonel.

"*Eeep!*"

The animal leaped from the colonel's hands and into the doctor's arms.

"Gulliver!" the doctor exclaimed, bringing the animal up to nuzzle her cheek. "What? How?"

"Well, that explains that," the colonel muttered.

His voice. Simmonne looked at him again. His voice was different. It was as deep as before, but the gravelly rasp that haunted every word was gone.

The small critter was still making excited sounds as Dr. Gilyard cradled it in her arms. She had always heard of mice and rats as filthy creatures carrying disease and malady. Surely that's not what that thing was. Simmonne could not help but look at the animal. Emotions were always more difficult across species lines. Animal emotions were another thing entirely. But she knew joy when she sensed it.

Also a sense of longing. The Twins remained utterly focused on the colonel.

"Sir?" Kassar's inquiry brought Simmonne's attention back to the colonel. "What happened? How did you get here?"

Simmonne heard him sigh, and he slid one palm against his pant leg as if to draw sweat from it.

"I'm not sure I believe it myself," he said after another sigh. "I ran into something. It looked, and claimed, it was a Therican."

A Therican? Simmonne blinked. That was impossible. They were dead, all of them, a hundred thousand years ago.

"I had another encounter with Oul'sor," the colonel continued. "The fight didn't quite go my way. We ended up on ND-31."

Simmonne tried to listen as the colonel related the events. The Twins were enraptured. But Simmonne's mind pulled her in a different direction. Ancient aliens, a weird planet, but the man telling the story held her attention.

Along with his voice and eyes, his cheekbones had changed, too. They were a bit higher, more pronounced. His jaw was even more square than it had been. His entire visage, she could see now what she could not before. The lineage of a Rhinegrave. But all that mattered was that he was alive. He was alive, and now she had been thrown back into the net of uncertainty he trapped her in when he left.

Simmonne wanted him to look at her. But as he told the tale, he watched Andira, who used her peripheral body to run a number of scanning devices over him.

"Then I was here," the colonel finished.

"How do you feel?" Andira asked as she set one device down to pick up another.

He took a deep breath before looking up to the ceiling. "Alive," he answered in a whisper. "It's hard to describe. But, I actually *see* the colors. I don't just know they're there. I can feel the air in my lungs. The temperature of the room. And . . . I understand things now."

Andira paused to stare at him. "What do you understand?"

"So many things," he answered with a grin. "Metapsionics. How they work. Why we could never quite figure it out. We did. We just . . . couldn't prove it. Couldn't manipulate it. The nanites don't cause it—they're just devices. They're like—"

The colonel paused as he seemed to search for the words.

"We don't have words for them," he said. "It's like a baby in its crib, looking at its arm. It doesn't know the words *arm* or *control*. But it knows it can control that arm. I—I'll have to invent words for them. For the technologies we could make with this knowledge."

The colonel leaned back and took a breath.

"Some of them were right. It all works on such tiny scales. We could never observe it—why psionics don't push back on you. You're not applying force directly. You're starting a reaction. Like pouring oil in a forest and striking a match. You didn't put in all the energy released when it all burns. You're just starting a reaction to release what's there. And the nanites. They work on constants we didn't even know exist. Didn't know how or what to look for."

The colonel caught himself and paused to pull out of the spell that had been taking him.

"It could take me years to fully comprehend it all." He smiled. "But it's there."

"It appears you will have them. There is no sign of your preexisting condition." Andira paused as the colonel looked at her, and Simmonne held her breath. "Your brain has completely regenerated."

Simmonne saw a faint smile as he nodded.

"I know," he answered, looking down at his hand as it slowly coiled into a fist. "It's why I feel so different. Like I could rip kilosteel apart with my bare hands."

He *laughed*. Simmonne was not certain she had ever heard him laugh before. To another person's ears, the deep, resonating tone might have sounded wicked. But she smiled as she heard it.

"I was dead for so long, I forgot how it felt to be alive."

Andira took up yet another device and ran it in a slow circle about his head.

"What about your metapsionics?"

The colonel continued staring at his hand, slowly coiling and uncoiling his fingers. "I haven't had any visions since Avalon. Or sensed any dilation waves. But I'm stronger. Anagram said it would take time for my abilities to fully restore, but I'm already stronger. I'm not even trying. I can hear Rhoxx thanking Avun-Adra that I'm back."

Simmonne and Andira both looked at the kodaz standing behind the colonel. He nodded.

"I see the Twins trying to imagine Anagram. You're mostly there, but her colors were brighter."

The Twins glanced at each other. Simmonne held tighter to his badge, waiting for him to say something about her.

"I'm not the strongest," he said, clenching his fist once again. "But I have the potential once again."

"Sir." Andira brought his attention back to her. "Your nanites have changed."

The colonel said nothing, and Andira answered the silence by projecting a hologram in front of him, a pair of images. Simmonne recognized one as a dermal nanite. It looked almost like an urchin inside the red field of a skin cell. Its many spines extended through the cell, some reaching out of the membrane toward others. The second image was very different. Simmonne saw a cutaway with a solid sphere in the center, and another beyond, encapsulating the cell. As the image zoomed in, the new nanite revealed its tiny spines—silver threads connecting the inner and outer spheres through the cell.

"This is not a known model of human nanite," Andira said in an almost accusatory tone. "Were you aware of this?"

"Yes," he answered, and Simmonne saw another, larger, smile. "Everyone else is walking around with the old stuff. I have the next gen now."

"Have you noticed any changes to your internal network?"

The smile remained as he shook his head. "All of my programs are still installed. They all check out. I'm showing a lot more storage space now."

"How much more?"

"Around 250,000 percent."

"That seems likely to be an error," the AI offered.

The colonel's smile faded slowly and he shook his head. "It's no error."

The AI folded her hands and glared at him. "It is not only your dermal nanites. All the nanites in your body are a different model."

He simply nodded. "So. What's my life expectancy now?"

Simmonne perked up as she prepared herself for the answer.

"Impossible to say. There is no trace of your preexisting condition. But given the changes in your anatomy, I do not have enough information to provide an acceptable answer."

He nodded slowly. "I think I'm going to live a very long time. If no one manages to kill me."

For now the AI said nothing else and resumed scanning him.

He was cured. Was this real? Part of her wanted to jump, squeal, and giggle. But another part was afraid that, any second now, Andira would say she found something. That he was still on the short path.

Simmonne slowly walked backward, out of the infirmary, and rounded the doorjamb until her back met the wall. She withdrew the badge she'd put back in her pocket. He was going to live. Despite her excitement, part of her felt shame as she looked down at the badge in her hand.

She was going to say no. For the Twins' sake, she was going to say no. To save them from becoming emotionally attached, only for him to die so soon. But what did she say now? Could she even say yes now? What if he read her mind and knew? Would he still want her? Surely if he did read her mind, he'd realize what she wanted to say. She kept her eyes on the badge as she walked back to his quarters, never looking up until she was standing in front of the printer. At the optical port, she placed the order. A small choker and an even smaller ribbon. Her nails made it a frustrating task, but she looped the ribbon through the badge and tied it to the choker.

On Reichsylvannia, when their evening together ended, she had silent pleaded in her mind for him not to take her back. Now he had given her that choice. Say yes and go with him, or say no and go home. There was only one choice.

She buttoned the choker around her neck, allowing the heavy badge to rest on her chest. As she turned back for the door, she saw the pahri and corissè still lying where she had left them before. He would definitely prefer she wore the pahri. If anything at all. She shook her head and gathered both items before feeding them into the printer to be recycled. There had to be some limits, and he would just have to respect that.

With each step back to the infirmary, her heart beat a little faster. If he read her thoughts . . . No, there was no *if.* When he read her thoughts—he would sooner or later—what if he changed his mind? The Vaar that terrorized her days ago had nothing on the fear slipping ice into her veins. She needed to be calm. So she took a breath before stepping through the infirmary door.

"Simmonne."

She jumped when she heard his voice in her mind. She looked at him, but he did not look back. His eyes were still on Andira as she drew another blood sample from his left arm.

"Come here."

She slowly walked toward him. Her heart could not beat any faster than it already was. Andira had stepped aside to claim another tool, and Simmonne took her spot. Quickly she averted her eyes when he looked at her. *Was* he looking at her? Or the badge? His fingers gently pinched her thumb and guided her hand away from the badge and down to her side.

With her hand out of the way, he moved more abruptly. His fingers slid down through the neck of her dress to pull her forward. He continued to pull until she was between his legs, and her thighs pressed against the edge of the table. Still he did not say anything, and Simmonne knew he was in her mind.

She had always expected to feel something when she knew a telepath was in her mind. Most would do something, a courtesy, that let their target sense their presence. But he did not. She had to look away as he pressed his thumb against her chin and tilted her head up. With all her focus, she tried to breathe calmly and hold a single thought in her mind.

Yes.

"Excuse me, Majesty."

Simmonne turned to Andira, who held a new device. Without thinking, Simmonne tried to step away, but the hand holding her dress did not let her move.

"No," the colonel whispered. "She stays where she is."

"Sir—"

"Work around her," the colonel answered with much more volume.

"Yes sir."

Andira went about her work, and Simmonne waited for the man to say something. Anything at all. Any time would be good. What was he doing in her head? Was he probing her psyche to see if she was genuine? Was he taking the memories of what happened while he was away? Or was he putting things in? Like he had on Reichsylvannia. Both of them remained silent while Andira worked. Simmonne's lip trembled as she struggled to hold her previous thought and found herself practically screaming at him in her head to say something.

The left side of his mouth curled into a grin. Nervously she smiled back.

Say something. Please?

Her hands found his chest, and he pulled her closer to him. For a second he looked away, toward Andira. When his eyes came back, Simmonne felt his accusatory glare. Andira just tattled, didn't she? Told him that she went through his things while he was gone. For a moment, Simmonne wondered if Andira had shared the little detail about having to hide from a Vaar officer.

"Sir," Andira spoke up. "I cannot find anything wrong with you. However, I must recommend that you be quarantined for at least seventy-two hours."

"Quarantined?" he said with a scoff. "I don't think so."

"Sir, you've been affected by an alien intelligence with unknown ramifications."

Simmonne's hand closed tighter on his shirt.

"If Anagram meant me ill, I don't think she would have shared all this information with me."

"Even so, sir, we do not understand the full ramifications of these changes."

"I do," he answered.

"Can you explain it?" Andira countered.

"Not yet."

"Then do you really understand it?"

He glared. "Andira. Enough."

"Yes sir."

The colonel's head gave a small tick. "Andira, I'm assembling a lot of Anagram's data in my NOD and will upload it to you. Analyze and collate all of it. Top priority. Even over ship repairs if necessary."

"Yes sir."

The colonel waved his free hand at Andira. She bowed her head and stepped away. He drew Simmonne up to the tips of her toes and closer to his face. Her thoughts were racing too fast for even her to know what they were. Then they were brought to a halt.

"Go to my quarters and wait for me."

His telepathic voice was stronger than before. Its sheer strength blurred her vision and created a short ring in her ears. The tension in his arm relaxed, allowing her to set her heels down. But when she tried to turn, he gave another tug on the dress.

"Take them with you."

She realized he was looking past her, and she turned her head. The Twins were still standing at the door, watching them. Simmonne turned back to the colonel and offered her best hurt expression. He saw through it so easily, she could feel it. Finally he released her and she stepped away. She shot a glance over her shoulder as she walked to the Twins. Without a word, she took each by the hand and led them out of the infirmary.

CHAPTER
14C

S USPENDED IN THE DEEP-FRYER, Clearwater's limbs gave the occasional spasm as the machine performed its work. The brute-force reanimation by the Vaar, and a second death soon after, had left plenty of work to do. The cleanup of impaired motor control and damaged synapses was rather simple for the machine. More complicated were its efforts to fill the holes in his memory. Without access to a backnet log, a complex process had to be carried out.

The process bore some similarities to pulling data off a demolished computer. Defects found in his hippocampus, neocortex, amygdala, prefrontal cortex, and neural nanites had all been identified. The device had to scan those regions in depth, translating what it could of the corrupted information into its own programming language. From there an AI had to reverse engineer the data. Any information it could not recover was filled in with the AI's best guess. Once this was done and the physical damage was repaired, the fixed memory had to be overwritten. In his unconscious state, Clearwater experienced something beyond a dream while the deep-fryer did its work.

He was eleven, and twelve was approaching. The long deck he stood on served as the entryway to the family home. Light snow fell beyond the deck's overhang. Black walnut trees stood in two rows beyond and, between them, the house router. Ryan was on his left, with David on the right. Both were trying not to cry. Froggy was not Froggy yet, simply Stephanie. The woman behind him held a new child. Zach was still alive. Their elder brother stood with their mother. He was already the tallest member of the family.

Dad was in his uniform, the insignia of a first lieutenant glinting on his shoulder. A strap was tight over his chest, supporting the long can of personal effects on his back. Sleepless nights wore on his face.

"But you promised," Clearwater protested. "You said this year we would finally go."

"I know," Dad answered. His eyes were the same color as his uniform, while his mouth wore a frown. "Orders are orders. I'm sorry it won't be for your birthday, but I promise we'll go when I come back."

"Too bad you never keep your promises," Clearwater muttered.

Dad took a step forward, glaring down with the look that quieted so many youthful insurrections. But it did not work this time.

"I said you never keep your promises!" Clearwater shouted. "You promised me last year. And the year before that. And the year before that! What good are your promises?"

There was a wounded look in Dad's eyes before he closed them. He took one breath, then opened his eyes again. "Jon, you're too old to act this way. Do you think I want to go? You want to be a legionnaire someday? This is how it is. They call—I go. I'm not leaving because I want to."

Clearwater turned away, pushing between Zach and Mom on his way back into the house.

"Jon!"

Dad called for him, and he ignored him. He went to his room in the corner of the house on the second floor. He slammed the door and sat at his desk. There it lay, and he grabbed the plastic card, reading the words printed on the device that served as a keepsake as much as an admission token.

GLADIATOR GAMES—BATTLE OF CHAMPIONS
WILL THE STREAK END?

His fist balled around the plastic, which tried to cut into his hand. Last year Dad waited too long, and the tickets sold out. The year before, he was deployed and came back too late. The year before that, he saw the price and decided his son needed a lecture on the value of a troy more than he needed a ticket. Burrel Kaymore and his warmech *Blackfire* had never lost. For his one hundredth match, he faced "the most violent player in the game," Lu Sin, in his machine *Ion*. Kaymore's streak was going to end before Clearwater ever got to see him fight in person.

In the opening contest, Rels ahn Veka forced Tega Du to tap out in the non-cybernetics hand-to-hand. Ryko Totz beat Gorman Watu in the ten-round quickdraw. In the cyborg box, Stellan Jugas won his first title, ripping the arms off To Shar. The Villous Hawks beat the Bears of Pommeron in the five-man close quarters gunfight. It was the greatest upset the five-man CQB Championship had seen. Tragedy struck in the main event. Lu Sin dealt Burrel Kaymore his first loss. Rather than the float of shame, Kaymore died when his ejection system malfunctioned.

Clearwater had watched the show from home. Mother couldn't be bothered, so Froggy was in his arms. Her right hand clung to his right thumb, and her left hand to his index finger. She only let go when he fed her, and she cried if he tried to take his hand away. Even when she slept, he could not reclaim his hand without waking her and having to give it back.

Clearwater's heel slammed into the bottom of the tank as the restored memory was seared into his mind. The next memory was the last the machine had to restore.

Two legionnaires were standing on the porch when his mother opened the door. The brown uniforms in the corner of his eye had snatched his attention. Clearwater was on his feet in an instant, ready to run to the door to greet his father.

"Are you Leha Clearwater?" The legionnaire wore a major's insignia.

Clearwater's heart fell to his feet.

"May we come inside?"

He was too stunned to move. His mother took his arm and moved him away from the couch to clear the guests' path. His mother sat on the chair by the couch, and Clearwater found a seat on the floor. Even the walk to the chair on the other side of the couch was too much in that moment.

"On behalf of His Majesty, and the Solar Legionnaires, we regret to inform you . . ."

He tried not to cry.

"We have confirmed that he was killed in action. Unfortunately, his body could not be recovered."

He tried not to cry.

"The specifics have been classified."

He cried anyway. There was so little he remembered of that day, but he remembered his mother's face. The tears she never cried. The dry, matter-of-fact way she asked about the death benefits. The way she told him to act like an adult when he sobbed too loudly. He had never gone into his memory index to relive that day, but he relived it now. Unconscious in the tank the restored memory lingered in his mind, like the memory of an unwelcome dream.

His legs jerked as the reconstructed memory was finalized.

CHAPTER
15A

THE CORRIDORS OF THE ship had become quiet to the ears, but not to the mind. Every thought on the ship was there for Panzer to know. Through the walls and floors, near and far, all were there. Lieutenant Clearwater dreamed in the deep-fryer. Miss Prideaux faded in and out of consciousness as her metapsionic mind refused to be fully suppressed.

In his quarters, Rhoxx prayed to Avun, thanking the many faces of his god that his lord had returned. Novin, exhausted and spent, was fast asleep, dreaming about nude kuress. Kassar remained awake, though he felt just as tired. He watched his combat recording from the *Caustic Reverie*, taking diligent notes on anything and everything he could have done better. But the thoughts that called to Panzer were ahead.

Girls, don't ruin this.

We don't even know him!

You're the one he likes.

This is crazy.

Panzer smiled as he tasted the substance of the Twins' thoughts. They were far less shaken than he might have expected. But they were having a little trouble coping with what Simmonne was laying out for them. She might have given them a little more time, given what they had been through.

Panzer stopped outside his door. "Andira?"

"Sir?"

"How long will Miss Prideaux need to recover?"

"The disrupter wound to her skull caused considerable depolarization in her neurons. At least thirty more hours will be required to repair the damage."

Panzer nodded. A fair amount of time. But not enough. "Keep her in suspension until I order otherwise."

"Yes sir."

The door almost seemed to stare back at him. He should go in there, let Simmonne down easy, and give the Twins a reprieve. He should tell them that now was not the time to start something. A Therican among the Vaar. The new Oul'sor. The Crossroads. The weight of the universe seemed to be crawling onto his shoulders now.

If he walked through that door, he'd have to be a different man when he walked out. His days with the Corps would be over. Did that bother him? But more than that, he'd have to be someone he had not been in a very long time. Could he still be that person? How long could one wear one identity before they became that identity? What would Elsa say if she were here?

Panzer shook his head. Stupid question. She'd want to know why he wasn't already in there.

He knew when he gave Simmonne the badge that she might interpret it as a proposal. But he did not actually expect it. That was foolish. The girl had attended her studies on the Sylvanni. So what he meant to be a keep-sake, had become an engagement gift. The fact that she accepted should surprise him, but it didn't, and it was strange that it didn't. Was it because of how inexperienced she was? So desperate to keep what she'd found that no suggestion seemed unreasonable? That wasn't it. He did not fully under-stand what was here, only that it was here.

But where did they go from here? He had prepared himself to die, not to live. He had money, but this was his only home. He would have to buy one. Where? What kind? He was not the kind of man to buy dinner without a plan. But this, he was going to have to work some of it out as he went.

A storm was coming. Anxiety never solved anything, but it did a fantas-tic job of blinding people to opportunities. Panzer closed his eyes, drawing one of his favorite quotes of the Patriarch from his mind.

A leader must ever be the well from which hope is drawn. To go on living when all others surrender to despondence. By your example, to show through all tribulations that life goes on. This is the acme of leadership.

He could go stew in a dark corner and worry about things that he currently could do nothing about. Or he could take the opportunity waiting beyond the door. Timidity did not change one's life—only boldness did. Panzer chose to open the door and step inside.

The room fell quiet as the three pairs of eyes within turned to him. They rose to their feet. In his NOD Panzer toggled the door and the lock. There would be no disruptions tonight, no interruptions. In the Basin they would not be found, and no one on this ship would interfere.

He pointed to the floor in front of him. Only Simmonne obeyed, despite a glance into the Twins' minds proving they knew he meant all three. He would deal with that in a moment. Simmonne approached, her eyes down, and her hand playing with the badge at her neck. The Twins kept silent for now, simply watching.

The sense of nervousness, even fear hovered in the air. Sweet was the sensation; he could almost smell it. It would be nice to enjoy it for a while and savor the innocent tension. But the time for waiting was over. There were better things to savor. He refocused his attention on Simmonne. She had stolen a glance at him but quickly cast her eyes back down to avoid his. Even now, she could not bring herself to look him in the eye.

In the same way a hand might sneak under a skirt, Panzer brought a mental hand up to the back of each of their necks. A telepathic grasp on their minds would do more than keep him apprised of every thought. A gentle grasp to ensure their minds were wholly in these moments. No thoughts of recent loss or fear. Only his presence, thus far silent.

Silence was a powerful tool too often discarded by those so enthralled with talking. His silence made them more anxious. He drew a breath through his nose and touched Simmonne's mind. Their night on Reichsylvannia was in her thoughts, focused most intently on the vision he gave when they parted. That night he had to let her go. But she knew tonight there was no escape. She had crossed the point of no return. Where there had been disdain, there was now anticipation. He noticed the ember of rebellion waiting to catch fire. That was good. More satisfying that way.

Panzer took a step to put her within reach, positioning himself between her and the light over the door. In his shadow she would feel all the smaller. Perhaps one should not use the same techniques here that he used on prisoners of war. But fear was fear. There might come a time when she was no longer unable to decide whether he awed or terrified her. When fear no longer tickled her with excitement. But it was not tonight.

She flinched when he reached out, pinching the fabric of the layered dress over her breast. She couldn't abide the silence, and the words slipped out.

"So what do we call you? Robert?" She hesitated. "Or Victor?"

For a moment Rhoxx popped into her mind. That was why she seemed even more intimidated by him than before. He could only imagine the stories her family had fed her. The Mandrakes with their constant, craven fears. Always looking for Rhinegraves in the shadows, always afraid that they were never more than a day away from losing their precious throne. But the question needed an answer.

"What makes you think you're allowed to call me either?" He said the words in a loud whisper, meant to carry just a hint of menace. "I told you before. You only have one word for me."

Master. She did not say it aloud, yet. He pinched her dress more firmly, pulling her a bit closer.

He hates it. You hate it, don't you? Please, don't be reading my mind. Focus, Simmonne. Keep your composure or he won't listen.

How adorable. She thought she had this all planned out in her little head. Some kind of negotiation. She just couldn't find the path to seize the initiative. He would show her exactly how he negotiated.

"Why are you wearing an onion?" he asked, watching her shrink a bit at the question.

"You don't like it?"

The temerity of this girl, to ask him that question with a straight face.

"No. I don't."

"I could—" She stopped herself, taking a breath and standing as tall as she could. "I would be willing to wear a corissè, if you prefer."

He answered her with his coldest stare and felt the sensation as she recoiled.

"Or, a pahri?" Her posture sank as soon as she said it. She folded too quickly and knew it. Not that she ever had a chance of winning.

Panzer released the dress to seize the fabric at her shoulders. He gave her just enough time to realize what he was doing, and she let out a tiny gasp. The many layers ripped at the front and back as he pulled his hands apart. Stunned for a moment, she simply stood there as he brought the two halves together and tore them again. But the moment she moved, he dropped the pieces to seize her wrists, bringing them over her head to hold in one hand.

With such a horrific dress, Panzer should not have been surprised to find such unflattering undergarments beneath. Two quick tugs elicited a tiny yelp as he tore them away as well. He held them up to her face, forcing her to confront the misdeed before dropping them to join the destroyed dress. None too gently he cupped a hand behind her leg, drawing her even closer as he forced her knee up to strip her shoe and stocking off together. He did the same to her other leg, leaving her utterly naked.

He was not finished.

She pulled weakly at his grip as he took hold of his badge. With his thumb and forefinger, he split the small choker from her neck. How *badly* she wanted it back. But at the moment, she could not have spoken if her life depended on it.

With the badge in his pocket, he plucked her tiara from her brow. Simmonne's eyes followed it, and her mouth worked wordlessly as his hand compressed around it. The only sound in the room was the tiny shriek of metal as the small crown collapsed in his grip. Her eyes widened. Finally he opened his hand, tossing the fragments aside to clatter loudly on the floor.

Her thoughts raced as fast as her heart. All her thoughts of negotiation, ground rules, and compromise were now in even more sundered pieces than her clothes. Panzer brought her shattered thoughts to a halt by speaking.

"You will be naked."

With a deep breath, she brought her eyes closer to his. A nervous swallow before she spoke. "*All* the time?"

"All. The. Time," he answered, using one finger to flick her bangs with each word. "*Never* clothe yourself without my permission. But. *If* you are good, I might permit you a pahri out in public."

The helpless expression on her face began to fade. The ember was catching fire. "I, I just can't . . . be naked. All the time."

There was a hint of conviction in the protest. Panzer leaned down closer to her and answered calmly, "Yes. You can."

The ember flickered, and she tugged against his grip. Her eyes narrowed, and she stood up straight. "Well, I *won't.*"

The inflection in her tone. She almost believed what she was saying. He leaned even closer until she had to turn her head to avoid his eyes. "Yes. You will."

Panzer grinned as he felt the ember fighting for survival. Good that she had some rebellion in her. Obedience without submission carried little satisfaction. Simmonne flinched when his right hand touched her, and he dragged the back of his fingers gently down her side. She tested his grip on her wrists, letting out a quiet whimper. Such an adorable blush on her face.

Some negotiator you are.

The girl was so hard on herself. He needed to take her mind elsewhere. She had the familiar dichotomy he expected from a girl so sheltered. A certain shyness about her body, fighting a burning desire for it to be appreciated. So he gave her some appreciation and let her feast on the attention as he continued tracing her skin.

She was all Mandrake. For all the grief her family gave his about their standard, the Mandrakes were a family very much with their beauty standard, and they followed it diligently. Bright hair and eyes. Skin that had never known a freckle, mole, body hair, imperfection, or mark. Perhaps a bit more chest than a girl her size was entitled to. Tens of thousands of man-hours had gone into writing his own genetic code. He doubted any less went into hers. He turned her from side to side, making a point of inspecting her, letting her feel that he was taking in everything. So vulnerable in his grip but titillated, still too nervous to say anything.

But Panzer could not become fixated. They were not alone. As he moved her to face him once again, he turned his gaze on the Twins. They could not have been quieter if they were dead. Their eyes were fixed like lasers on him and Simmonne. She may have been nervous, but their condition was much more delicate. Both flinched when he did no more than point at them.

"Come here."

They looked at each other, then back at him. Neither moved.

Please, please don't throw this away.

"Be silent." He glanced down at Simmonne, and she nodded.

When the Twins did not move, Panzer narrowed his eyes briefly. Their ears did not actually hear anything. But all the same, the Twins raised their hands to protect themselves. What could only be understood as a blistering static ripped through their perceptions before fading as quickly as it had come.

"I can make you come to me," Panzer said. Moments later he realized he had put much more menace into the words than he meant them to have.

Fearful of another static blast, both shuffled toward him until standing just beyond Simmonne. He had to handle these two differently. So much had been sprung on them so quickly. They were not ready mentally or emotionally. But there was little time to court before this opportunity might be lost.

"The rules apply to the two of you as well."

What do we do? The thought came in stereo, and he had to stop himself from laughing. He knew their reputations in the Solar Court as shameless teases before even meeting them. On the handful of occasions they had been in the same room, they did all they could to get his attention. Now that they had it, neither was sure what to do with it. So much about their behavior made so much sense.

"Don't keep me waiting."

Once again the sound of his own voice carried more force than he intended. But it was enough to spur both to action. Their hands fumbled and they took their time, as if hoping he would tell them they could stop. Both deigned to keep their undergarments, looking at him for that permission.

When his look told them it was denied, they finished the job. He held out his empty hand, and it took them a moment to realize what he wanted. Both handed their bundled clothes to him.

Unwilling to release Simmonne, he used his mind. The sound of shearing fabric once more filled the room as he turned their clothes into a confetti of scrap cloth on the floor.

"*What?*" they protested together.

It was not enough to simply denude them. The option to put clothes back on had to be removed as well, leaving them feeling yet more vulnerable.

"If I decide to permit you clothing, *I* will pick something appropriate," he answered them.

This was too much for them, coming at them too quickly. They tried to cover themselves with their arms. The emotion in both threatened to boil over. But that was the plan. He could have charmed them into surrendering their flesh at any time, but that would never be enough. Their hearts, their minds, he would own those as well.

He forced Simmonne to walk backward as he corralled the pair and led the three to the couch. He stared at the couch for a moment. It figured. Leave a woman alone with a couch, and the couch would accumulate pillows.

"Grab the pillows."

The Twins obeyed before following the next instruction to lay them on the floor. The two drew strength from each other, so he needed to separate them. He guided Simmonne to kneel on the center pillow. He did not touch either of the Twins and instead pointed down. Both obeyed reluctantly, kneeling where he directed but keeping eyes on him.

"Stay."

He walked first to the cabinet by his bed and removed the security binder. One could not simply print adornments for a princess and her handmaidens. Under the circumstances, this would have to do to provide some troy gold. He removed a collection of the bonds from the binder before venturing to the printer.

What is he doing? Three naked women at his feet, and he seemed to be ignoring them. In the Twins' minds, it did not compute. Panzer fed the bonds into the printer, instructing it to use the troy gold in the process, and began placing orders. As the items came, he tossed them on the couch for the three to see. The Twins' fear started to build as they saw the forming collection. The final orders included four glasses of wine, and he summoned an end table from the floor to receive them. Finally he sat on the couch to face them.

The first item he held was the golden collar with Simmonne's name etched on it. She sucked in a breath when he took hold of her hair. It became a quiet exhale when he closed the metal band around her neck, and it locked in place with an audible *click*. The instant he took his badge from his pocket, her eyes followed it. He kept a firm grip on her, but she relaxed a little when he affixed the badge to her collar.

There was something coming, and Panzer was ready for it. He clamped down harder on Simmonne's mind, seeing himself through her NOD and the image that came to life. An image of a silhouette with a band around the neck labeled in red.

WARNING. THIS DEVICE IS ATTEMPTING TO GAIN ACCESS TO BODILY SYSTEMS, INCLUDING YOUR CENTRAL NANITE NETWORK AND CENTRAL NERVOUS SYSTEM. IT IS NOT RECOMMENDED THAT YOU AUTHORIZE THIS.

DO YOU WISH TO AUTHORIZE?

YES

NO

MORE INFORMATION

From his mind through hers, and into her NOD. All with ease that led Panzer to surprise himself.

>>YES / PERMANENT

The device was engaged now. A little bit of pressure on her mind kept the memory out. As far as Simmonne knew, she never saw the message.

As he reached for the second collar, he paused. Both minds were on the precipice. But which one? Of the two of them, one did seem ever so slightly more demure than the other. Julie cringed when she saw the name on the collar. To leave a path of escape, he did not take hold of her. Instead he tilted her chin up with one hand. That was enough.

"I can't do this!" she exclaimed, darting to her feet. She began to back away from him. "I, I want to leave."

Now he would take custody of her heart.

He pulled his shoulders back, making himself as large as possible as he stood. No words. Instead he pointed deftly at her vacated cushion. She simply stood there with her arms crossed, a pathetic look on her face as she shook her head.

"I want to leave," she repeated.

Julie, please don't do this.

"Be silent." He eyed Simmonne briefly before turning back to Julie.

Jennifer had proceeded to full-blown panic, afraid to even rise off her cushion. So he approached Julie, who retreated farther from him. He held out a hand, and she let out a whimper, feeling the pressure on her hips. Her feet skidded on the metal floor as he drew her to him, and his hand closed on her arm.

"Let go."

"Hush," he cut her off. "I don't think you understand your situation. You're mine now."

"I want to go. Please, let me go," she whispered, looking up at him with the most pathetic expression he had ever seen.

"No." He pulled her a bit closer. "I'm a mind reader, Julie. You can't hide things from me."

An emotional mind was easiest to read—no control over what it thought. So many loose ends, begging to be pulled. Simply reminding her that he could read her mind gave him all he needed. The floodgates opened, and out spilled every thought she hoped he did not know.

"You put me in your dream regulator," he said in a whisper. "You thought Simmonne was being a prude when she told you of the vision I gave her. You were so *angry* at her for it. You spent the next several nights fantasizing. About me snatching you out of your bed and doing far more to you. But then, that was always your favorite fantasy, wasn't it?"

She shuddered helplessly as he took the intimate secrets out of her mind.

"The fantasy you were so embarrassed by that you only ever told Jennifer. The man who came in the night and kidnapped you away. Who took you somewhere far off to have his way with you. Who recaptured you when you tried to escape and punished you for it. You spent so many hours finding similar stories on the astranet to read or dream, each night programming your dream regulator with it. Then we met, and you decided to give the stranger my face.

"One night on the *Hurricane*, you awoke. You weren't sure if you were still dreaming or awake. So you lay there, trembling, afraid. But begging deep inside that I was actually there, that I had come for you. When you realized I wasn't there, you cried. Even when the Vaar took you, you dreamed of me coming. But not to rescue—to take you for myself. And you *dare* try to leave when I offer you *exactly* what you want?"

People were wont to behave as they were treated.

"You don't care about us!" she shouted at him, beginning to cry.

He kept his voice calm. He who was in control was calm. "How dare you say that to me."

The tears intensified as Julie glared at Simmonne. "You didn't take us from the *Rothburg*. You took *her*. You ignored us. You didn't care. You still don't. We're the ones who liked you. We were the ones trying to get your attention. But you took her. Now? We're just some kind of bonus now that you have what you really want."

He squeezed her arm tighter. She tensed up so he squeezed tighter still until she let out a tiny cry.

"You weren't within my reach at the *Rothburg*. You are now."

She blinked several times, trying to see through her tears. "And what about tomorrow? Will you go back to ignoring me?"

Me. He almost asked her to repeat it. That may have been the first time he had ever heard either of them use that word. In person, on the astranet. Always we, never me. The Twins' persona was so cultivated, practiced, and baked into them. He did not allow himself to smile.

"Am I ignoring you now?"

"What about—"

"Love?" he finished for her. "Julie, love is like anything valuable. It does not come to us simply because we wish for it. It is something people have to build between each other. And you will never find it if you hide from it."

He held her by both arms before pulling her into him.

"Do you think I don't know what you really want? You've lived your entire life in someone's shadow. Never able to be yourself. A distance not of your own making, between you and everyone else. You loved her like a sister, but part of you carries such resentment. That she always received the attention you craved. You worked so hard to hide it from her. To swallow it so deep that she would never know. You tried to push her to be more adventurous so you could have some for yourself. So much cruelty in such a short life."

Out of the corner of his eye, he glanced at the others. Jennifer was in tears as well but hung on every word as if they were spoken directly to her. Simmonne was so hurt by what she was hearing. But not all tears were bad. This had to come out lest it poison the future they were building.

Julie offered no resistance as he led her back to the couch and took her pillow without being told. He returned to the couch and held her collar for her to see.

"I'm only one kind of person. If you're part of my life, then I am your master. I take care of what belongs to me. This is my own design, and only I can remove it. It has an uplink to my NOD. You put it on, I'll always know where you are and what you are doing. I'll know how you feel even if you're far away. If you are happy, stressed, depressed, and more."

He waited for her to look at him.

"You'll never be invisible again."

He allowed her to take it, and she wiped the tears out of her eyes as she examined it.

"Do you want to wear it or throw it away?"

Simmonne may have been smarter than they were, but they were definitely more mature. She knew exactly what he was saying, and every implication raced through her mind. But his work was done. Every objection she raised, she also slew with the same words.

Never invisible again.

She sniffed, drying the last tears as her hands pried at the metal. He took it from her and opened it before closing it around her neck. She never saw the message generated in her NOD either. One more left.

"You promise?" Jennifer asked as he took her by the hair. "Promise we're in this too?"

He closed the final collar on her neck and handled the pop-up. "You are now."

"I'm sorry, Julie." Simmonne was crying now as she embraced her friend, her sister. Soon all three were in tears again. But not all tears were bad, so he gave them a moment before speaking sternly.

"Stop crying." He looked at each of them. "The life you had is over. Time for a new one."

He collected the wine and handed each a glass.

"Together we form a new house. So let's drink to that. Our new house."

All three raised their glasses.

"Our new house."

The Twins drank greedily, while Simmonne thought she would escape with only a sip. He disabused her of that notion, tilting the glass with one finger and forcing her to drink it all. When all three had finished, he took the next item from the couch, a pair of metal bands matching the collars. Simmonne figured it out immediately and offered her arms. He allowed himself a smile as he closed them around her wrists.

Only after they had locked did she notice the golden band connecting them. With a quizzical look, she drew her hands behind her back and watched the illusory band pass through her without impeding her movement. She shrugged, realizing she would find out how they worked soon enough.

Chains would look better.

He answered the thought with a dial in his NOD, and her eyes reacted as the fiber changed to a thick chain of gold. She bit her lip in a grin as he handed her the second pair, and she closed them on her ankles. Once he had done the same with the Twins, he took the final item, an actual golden chain in the shape of a *T*.

"Something to attach a leash to," Simmonne said with a knowing grin. He returned the expression before affixing the center clip to her collar. He added the Twins' before attaching the longest end to his belt. With a sigh he took a moment to admire them. As pretty a picture as he had hoped it would be. He gave them a bit of time to mentally prepare.

"Well?" Jennifer asked, signaling that she was ready.

"Well . . ." he led her.

"Well, *Master?*"

He shrugged at her. "Well what?"

"Well, we're naked," Julie added.

"And we can't get away," Simmonne finished, tugging at the chain.

"No, you can't."

He took hold of the leash and pulled, drawing all three higher on their knees.

"Now I have my way with you."

He'd have to be careful not to overdo it. But he *was* a telepath. There was really no excuse for this to be anything but a mind-blowing experience for them.

CHAPTER
15B

Simmonne's body was even more taut than the chain she clung to as she looked up at him. This was really happening. The Twins—she knew he would be able to handle them. This, her life, it was all going to change. She hoped she was ready.

She could not help but think back to Reichsylvannia. The images he put in her mind. She had tried to resist, but everything she told herself had been in vain. He conquered her mind before she knew there was a fight for it.

"Look at me."

His voice in her mind always brought a shudder. Every thought was so strong that it seemed to wash her away. Meekly she peered up at him.

"Look me in the eye."

She couldn't. He knew she couldn't.

"Look me in the eye."

She forced her eyes up and once more was paralyzed by his glare.

"Little princess, I have not begun to conquer you."

She gasped as she looked away, and his hands descended to her. To him she had no mass as he slid her forward on the pillow until she was kneeling between his ankles. It did not take her long to figure out what he was positioning her for. With a snap of his fingers, he directed the Twins to join him on the couch. They pulled the leash tighter, drawing her even closer to him. For a moment they exchanged glances, both Twins nodding at something unspoken. But soon like a pair of curious cats, they were perched with their hands on his thighs, eager to watch.

He ran a hand across the body of each, almost as if petting them before turning his attention back to her. One hand tangled into her hair, and the other closed on her breast. She tried so hard not to tremble, even as the pressure on her flesh mounted. After she let out a little squeal, he took his hand to his pants. Soon the veined organ was staring back at her, centimeters from her face.

For a moment she grimaced. Of course. He *was* a Rhinegrave. So obviously his geneticist had determined that he couldn't be the manliest of the manly men unless it terrified any woman expected to do something with it. She closed her eyes; she needed to concentrate. She had watched astranet videos in her few private moments. But this was the real thing. She couldn't do this. She was going to mess it up. Why did she have to go first? She began to shake until he tugged at her hair. He traced it over her face, her nose, her eyes, and lips.

"Stick out your tongue."

His grip tightened until she complied. Opening wide she stretched her jaw, and he pushed past her lips. She brought her hands up until there was a sharp bite on her wrists. The illusory chain suddenly became very real, metal flowing from one wrist to the next as they were drawn behind her back and locked together.

"You do it, you do it right. No hands."

No hands? How was she supposed to . . .

"Use your mouth. Obviously."

That was certainly easy for him to say with that smug tone. She grumbled as well as a full mouth would allow. But she had to focus. The taste, the feeling of utter helplessness, him. Anything. Nothing would matter nearly so much if he would just let her sense what he was feeling. The only thing she was certain of from her . . . studies . . . was that the tongue was queen. So she tried to put it to work.

"That's right."

Soon his hand in her hair became her guide, and she relaxed slightly. She could do this. He knew what he wanted. If he took control, she could do it. Self-conscious as a bit of drool leaked down her chin, she tried to wipe it away. But the harder she pulled, the tighter the manacles coiled around her wrists. At first she was barely taking any of him, but soon he became less gentle. He pushed a bit deeper, and she gagged. Almost as if there were some mercy in him, he pulled back, but he gave her only a second to breathe before sealing her throat again. He did this several times, toying with her. Her jaw was aching, eyes watering, and in her stomach, bile brewed.

No!

She clenched her eyelids together. She would not ruin the moment. Her body began to shake from the lack of air and the strain in her gut. Maybe she'd pass out first. Every ounce of willpower converged as she tried to control herself. But he just kept going deeper.

Sweet oxygen raced into her lungs as he finally pulled back and out of her mouth. She doubled over, coughing loudly.

"Pathetic."

The sheer contempt in his tone. Pathetic? She was trying! She had never done this before. She wasn't an expert. What did he take her for? She was not some whore supplementing her stipend with sexual favors! She trembled with anger more than fear. For a moment, she thought of biting as she glared at his face.

"Do it, little girl. I dare you."

Just that easily he ripped the anger out of her grasp and she panicked again. How did he push her buttons so easily? Meekly she moved to take him back in her mouth before he pulled her head away.

"No. You don't deserve it."

She wanted to cry. The fact that she knew he was in her mind, manipulating her feelings, didn't help. "I'll try harder," she whispered.

Like a twinkling star in the darkness, something was there. She felt it, a tiny taste of satisfaction. She quickly took him when he brought her closer but started choking again. Her newfound resolve faded when he didn't stop. He just kept going, determined to make it into her throat.

No more! I can't! No more!

"Make her take it all." The voice barely registered in her ears. She felt a new pair of hands on her head, roughly pulling her forward. Her eyes flew open, and she tried to glare through blurred sight. Jennifer's hands were on her head. A wicked sensation from her, but Simmonne sensed more. Jennifer enjoyed watching her choke. Oh. She was going to pay for that!

"You'll get your chance."

She couldn't do it. Her legs were trembling, and the colors of her sight were dimming. The world around her started to fade.

She came to, pain in her scalp as her limp body dangled from his grip on her hair. She let out a whine to see he was still rigid. He was not finished. She wasn't doing a very good job.

"Oh don't worry." His voice in her mind was smug once again. *"I'll make sure you get more than enough practice to master it."*

"Hooray," she answered with more wheeze than the intended sarcasm.

He let go. Was he done with her? She could do it. She just needed more time.

"Don't be greedy."

How did he do that? In that moment she would have given anything to have the torment back. But she could only watch as he seized Jennifer by the hair, and her body went rigid.

"Since you're so excited."

Simmonne watched him force Jennifer down. She seemed to have far less trouble, going slow before feeding herself more and more of him. After a moment he drew her back up, turning her head to him.

"You've done this before, haven't you?"

"No, Master," she answered with a grin.

"We . . ." Julie hesitated, looking down in an expression to match the air of embarrassment. "We practiced on fruit."

Simmonne did not need empathy to read his reaction. His entire body stiffened, and he brought his empty hand to his mouth as he tried not to let the laugh escape.

"What? Don't laugh at us," Julie mewed.

"Oh I'm laughing," he answered. "If I couldn't read your mind, I'd say you were lying. What possessed you to do that?"

"Well," Jennifer answered, blushing, "when I found a man, I wanted to keep him."

"Smart girls."

He pushed Jennifer back down, shaking his head and still grinning.

Simmonne felt the tension binding her wrists slacken. The chain had become illusory again. She quickly wiped her mouth while glaring at Jennifer. That little bitch, showing her up. Payback time. Simmonne rose high on her knees, grabbed two handfuls of Jennifer's hair, and forced her down as hard as she could. Time to see how she liked having Master crammed down her throat until she passed out.

When Jennifer began to struggle, Simmonne surprised herself by pushing harder. The sudden gagging sounds only served as encouragement. A tiny part of her, always buried so deep, decided it had been ignored long enough. After so many nights kept awake by their pornographic dreams. So many times distracted by their constant, lurid thoughts every . . . single . . . day. After she did so much to find someone for them. If they wanted a man so damn bad, now they had one. And they were going to take everything he gave them!

"Let her up."

She didn't want to. She wanted to watch Jennifer go limp in his lap. But she obeyed, dropping her hands to her sides and grinning while Jennifer gasped for air. Simmonne sat back on her ankles and watched quietly as Julie was directed to take her turn.

She watched Master's face and smiled at the satisfaction she saw there. Of course he was happy. He had three women servicing him. Any idiot could guess how he felt. But she needed more, to more than simply know it was there. So she pushed at him, grasping for anything.

When he allowed Julie to rise off him, Simmonne's eyes moved to the available flesh. Pathetic? Master was not going to think her pathetic. She started this, and she would finish it. And damn it, she *would* sense him! She laced her fingers behind her back and attacked. But her new enthusiasm counted for little. Soon her jaw and throat were aflame once more, and her gut was in full rebellion. She tried to pull away only for his iron grip on her hair to pull her back.

She sensed him! For just a moment, but there. That possessive, commanding feeling that she was going to stay exactly where he wanted her. The sense of aggression. She tried to draw some strength from it and force herself forward. She could not take it all, but she would take what she could. He was close, and she felt him tighten. He drew back until only the tip was in her mouth. He wanted to be sure she tasted it. She knew she was supposed to swallow and did her best to comply.

Satisfaction. Sweet satisfaction. Hers or his? It didn't matter. She held still, pressing her lips on him as firmly as she could. She had already surmised that he would decide when it came out.

"Good girl."

The compliment made her shudder. He sat still for a moment, her precious time to actually see the star. But finally he placed his hand on her forehead. She whined as he pushed her off him, and it was gone. Wanting to feel his body, she put a hand on his knee, intent on climbing into his lap. But he drew a yelp when he pulled her hair to force her back down on the pillow. Was he going to make her do it again?

"That was the easy one."

Easy for who exactly? But she nodded, mindful of his grip.

Her eyes moved to the Twins. He had certainly lit a fire in them. A moment ago both were teary wrecks. Now they were quiet, but there was no doubt what was on their mind. She licked her lips, cleaning away the film. So that was fellatio.

"You know you enjoyed it."

She blushed as he released her. Only because he enjoyed it so much.

"Liar."

She couldn't hide anything from him. Yes she enjoyed it. The way he toyed with her. Finally a man, a *real* man, taking what he wanted. No asking, no babbling, no cowardly flirting. Not acting like he was going to do something just to lose his nerve. Just a man taking what he wanted. Was that too much to ask?

"Be careful what you wish for. You might get it."

She gave him her best, most fearsome glare. *Bring it on, big man.*

He sat quietly for a while, fondling the Twins. But soon enough he closed his pants and rose to his feet. Simmonne let out another yelp as he used her hair to pull her to her feet. She tried to move away, wanting him to pull her hair again. She was not disappointed and let out a little cry as she was pulled into his body. But it worked for a moment. It amused him.

He tugged at the leash, urging the Twins to come along as he led all three toward the bed. It was time. This was not the place she had imagined. Or the circumstance. But it would do.

"It will do? We'll see about that."

He unclipped the leash from his belt before attaching it to the headrail. Simmonne followed his arm, not that she had a choice, as he guided her up onto the bed, sitting between the Twins. Her heart thumped as he began to undress. He was so calculated in everything he did. One arm withdrew into his shirt before he pulled it over his head. Boots and socks quickly and deliberately removed, and finally pants as well.

Her body contracted as she began to curl up. Her bout of confidence scampered away when she needed it most. With a huge naked man looming over her, she suddenly felt far less confident. Was she really ready for this?

Be gentle.

She flinched as his finger came to her chin.

Then she felt it. Desire. She knew what she needed. The animal instinct to exert his dominance—she focused on it harder than she had ever focused on anything. His hand moved to her forehead, and with a deft push, he left her on her back. Soon the Twins were lying beside her, watching every second. She never expected to have an audience for this moment, but this was Master's show. The time was now, and she would be first.

The sheer intensity of what radiated from him was both exciting and frightening. That kind of aggression was so strong but tightly focused. The *desire*. How did anyone control themselves while feeling that? How did he seem so calm and gathered?

His hands started at her ankles and glided up her body. She crossed her arms over her chest, trying not to panic. What a child he had to think she was.

Please, please be gentle.

"*Of course I'll be gentle. If I wasn't, I'd rip you apart like wet paper. But I won't be as gentle as I could be.*"

That's not comforting!

With what she sensed, Simmonne kept expecting him to pounce on her like a hungry predator. Instead he leaned down, kissed her belly, and worked his way up. His hands left her hips to clamp firmly around her forearms, and he pinned her wrists over her head. She felt tiny in his grasp. His lips closed on her breast, flooding her with a tormenting sensation. The more of it she felt, the more desperately she needed it.

He took his time, and she realized the cruel man was teasing her.

"The secret is in the teasing," he whispered. "If you're not ready to beg for it, then you're not ready."

She looked to his face. "Do you want me to beg, Master?" She wasn't sure whether she wanted him to say yes.

He grinned. "You will before the night is over. But it won't do you any good."

It was decided. She was *not* going to beg.

"*Yes. You will.*"

No I won't!

So cruel. She broadened her mind to the sensations around her. The Twins were so eager to drink in every detail. So anxious about what came next. But she also felt their jealousy over her going first. Too bad.

As the sensations grew stronger, her pulse raced with them, and Master had her full attention. His body was huge, and without trying, he forced her legs wide apart. He drew her ankles to his chest, then took a moment to adjust himself. He filled his empty hand with her breast, then began to push.

The air hissed between her teeth as she felt herself stretching. Tears formed as he pushed deeper, and she pulled pointlessly against his grip. By all stars, was it supposed to hurt *this* bad? She let out a sigh of relief when he pulled back, but the reprieve was short-lived.

He emitted a cruel chuckle as he moved in a slow but insistent rhythm. A little more with each push. She began to relax as her body adjusted to him, but apparently that was what he was waiting for, and with a firm thrust, he gave her more.

Simmonne squealed. Mercifully, he was motionless after. Maybe he was giving her time to recover—maybe just enjoying the feeling of her quivering under him. Probably the latter. Men cared so much about the size of their weapon, it probably made him happy to know it hurt her. Part of her was ready to beg if it was for him to stop. The shock of the pain had nearly broken her grip on his feelings. By mental fingernails, she still clung to them. If she could cling to what he felt, she could go on. She could draw the strength from him and tell herself that pleasure would follow.

The pause gave her time to open her eyes. There she saw Master's hand on Jennifer's back while she whispered into his ear. He answered with an amused grin and a nod. Both of the Twins shifted, moving to their knees by

Simmonne's head. As Master's hand left her wrists, their hands replaced it to keep her pinned. If they needed to be his little helpers so they would not feel left out, fine. Both of his hands were at her breasts as he stood straight and began to move once again.

It still hurt, but to her surprise, the pain felt . . . good. It was supposed to feel good eventually, wasn't it? Her back arched as she let out another whine. But there was something new. Maybe not so much a pain, but an odd, yet strangely stimulating ache that she had started to let her body move toward. As if it were a pleasure confused about its identity, yet it felt as if she could chase it.

He stopped.

"No," she whined, rolling her hips in an effort to feel the building pressure once more. He couldn't make her endure what he did just to stop as soon as she felt something else.

His laugh taunted her. She was not going to beg. Not for pleasure. But she let out a sigh as he resumed. The confused ache seemed to expand through her as he worked into a rhythm. Her breath came in short gasps, and the links of the leash jingled in her ears. Both grew louder as he picked up his pace, seeming to increase in intensity each time she thought she might be able to accommodate it. It was as if he was determined to make this difficult for her, and maybe he was. There was obviously a hint of sadist in him.

"Sadist?"

He drew back before forcing himself forward, and she screamed. Too hard, too deep, too much!

"Be thankful that I'm not."

If she nodded any harder, her neck would break. She blinked at tears, more than a little grateful that he waited before doing any more. He waited long enough for her to wonder when he would resume before he did. The confused ache returned. The prodding feeling seemed to be figuring itself out, drawing a tingle through her and a gasp from her lips.

He stopped again, ignoring her inarticulate cry of frustration.

Above her the Twins leaned toward each other. Both hesitated, looking uncomfortable. They looked at him until he met their gazes, then they kissed each other. It did not last long, and both looked even more uncomfortable after. Those bitches! They were trying to steal his attention now? They were that desperate for it? Master released her for a moment to drag his hands down their backs. Something unsaid passed between him and the Twins. He shook his head and both nodded. Soon enough he returned to her.

He reclaimed her breast with one hand. The other he placed on the bed to support himself. Her rump was lifted as he leaned forward, his chest pushing her legs toward her body. The confused ache grew from there, and she heard the first moan before she realized that she had made it. Her shoulders lifted as her head reared back. For moments she floated in a sea of simple fascination with the responses of her own body. He was having his way now, pumping her body like he owned it. Then again, he was Master. As far as he was concerned, he did.

"As far as you're concerned as well, little girl."

She could not formulate a reply, verbal or mental. None of her studies or late-night fantasies had prepared her for what she felt. The air fled her lungs, and what started as a moan became a scream. Briefly she overpowered the Twins, bringing her arms up as she tried to latch onto Master. But Jennifer and Julie bore down, pinning her arms back in place.

"Listen to her go!" one of the Twins exclaimed while the other giggled as Simmonne vocalized again.

The experience couldn't be real, yet she did not have the imagination for such a thing. Soon she was reduced to panting as the tension begged to be let out, almost making her body feel desperate and on edge. The newest sensation came as a sense of urgency, building rapidly within.

"Ready to beg?"

"N-no!" She barely got the words out. She was already catering to his every whim. She would not beg for the privilege. That was too much, but so was this feeling—as if something needed to be let out, and it needed out now.

"You will."

No I won't!

The imperious presence looming over her only seemed to grow more powerful each second. The more she focused on him, the more she felt within herself. As that presence grew, it seemed to subsume the entirety of her universe. She was light-headed. Each time she tried to catch her breath, a powerful moan emptied her lungs and forced her to fight for air again. Meanwhile his pillaging of her body could only go on for so long. The urgency was growing; it had to be soon.

"Only when I allow it."

That was beyond unfair. She wasn't sure she could bear it.

"I am your master. I decide what is fair."

She would not beg. No matter what he said or did to her body. No matter how deep in her mind he burrowed. Briefly she thought of him ripping the dress off her, and the pieces of her tiara on the floor. It was too late for them. But this one, tiny scrap of dignity, she wanted to keep.

"Beg for it."

No!

"Beg for it." The Twins seemed to have vanished from her universe, only to return as Julie leaned down to whisper in her ear.

"Beg for it," Jennifer echoed in the other ear. "Maybe he'll reward you."

"I have your mind, little girl. I can keep you like this as long as I wish. I can finish and come back to you later without ever letting you come down. Suspended in this state, until it becomes a madness and consumes your every thought."

The thought somehow intrigued her, but at the same time, it sounded like the ultimate torture. She shook her head furiously until the need for air forced her to stop. What was her resolve against something so overwhelming? Her body was not enough. He had to have her soul, her self-control, her dignity—everything surrendered to him. Perhaps she did, too. If he was

Master, then he had to crush any rebellion she could offer.

"Please."

She whispered it so softly, she only knew she heard it when she felt his smugness. It caused her to shudder anew.

"I thought you weren't going to beg."

It wasn't enough for him to win. He had to bite her with that humiliation, too.

"Please . . . Master?" She panted the words, fighting for the air to do it.

"I told you that you'd beg and that it would do you no good."

She was so close, yet he had control. He truly wasn't going to let her go. "Please?"

He did not answer. The sensations that were already so overpowering grew a little stronger as they were bolstered by fear. That he might actually do it—take what he wanted and leave her like this, cruelly suspended on the edge.

"Please, Master?"

He shook his head now, too far gone to taunt her more.

"Pleeease?"

"Yes."

Sweet release. Her voice seemed far away as her entire body was given to catharsis. Her eyes clenched shut, her body and mind both in his grasp. Her mind could not take any more, but he made his final motion and let out a loud groan. She had heard words like *bliss* and *ecstacy* before, but only now did she understand them, cascading in waves through her flesh.

Simmonne's body was mush when she opened her eyes to find her head still swimming. She had passed out. Yet even now, ripples of pleasure flowed, aftershocks of something she could never have believed or described. To feel not only herself, but him as well—the feelings he kept locked away so jealously were so clear now. She clung to them within her like a treasured prize. Never to be surrendered. Her arms were free, and she brought them down to embrace herself, floating in afterglow. Brittany told her once never to bother with a man unless he was a telepath. Now she knew why. Parts of her still ached, yet there was so much more.

As some measure of meaningful awareness returned to her, she realized Master was no longer looming over her. She wanted to sit up and find him, but her body refused. There was no energy left even to raise her head. When he returned to her field of view, he had a can of Overclock in one hand and used the other to clean himself with a towel.

He eyed her as he lowered the can.

"And you thought you wouldn't beg."

She could only answer the taunt with a shy smile.

"What?" Julie whimpered. "What about us?"

Simmonne snickered as she tasted disappointment. They need not worry. His feelings, finally, were clear to her. He would have his way with all three. To do any less would be a treason against himself. He swallowed the last of the drink before crushing the can. His other hand seized Julie's lead of the leash so that he could draw her up high on her knees.

"You're next."

He wanted all three of them, and he had all three of them. Eventually enough energy returned to her body for Simmonne to roll on her side and observe as he took the Twins in turn. It had never occurred to her that she would actually enjoy watching it. She surprised herself when she urged him not to be so gentle with them. To make them squeal. She did not fully understand everything she felt as the night went on, but there was time. He was going to live, and they had their lives to explore it all.

By night's end, he had changed the sheets and lay on his back with them. Simmonne found her spot on top of him with her head on his chest.

"Master, can we . . ." She hesitated, averting her eyes when he looked at her.

"Yes?"

"I always thought it would be romantic . . ." She moved up to nuzzle his cheek. "To share our dreams."

He smiled, and the wall-mount printer growled a minute before he drew out four devices.

"What should we dream about?" she asked as he placed the first device on her head.

"I'll program the dream." He planted a device on each Twin before fiddling with his. "I have memories of a few good places."

With a happy sigh, she laid her head back down. Four minds of contentment. She carried them with her over the veil and into his dream. Her eyes closed and the night was silent.

CHAPTER
15C

THERE WAS AN OLD proverb from a time before the Empire. *Fear makes the wolf bigger than he is.* When Clearwater opened his eyes, the room was dim. He was lying on a medical table and heard the gentle hum of machinery. He might have simply closed his eyes and returned to sleep. But what had awakened him was still there, on his chest, staring him in the face.

A rat!

Clearwater bolted upright, launching the critter off him in the process. The small animal sailed over his feet before catching itself on the bottom edge of the table. Clearwater raised his foot, ready to deliver a kick, when he heard the angry noise.

"Nep!"

He froze, his leg ready and bent.

"G-Gulliver?" Clearwater whispered. As his adrenaline faded, the giant rodent was gone, and only little Gulliver remained as he climbed back onto the table.

"Gulliver?" Clearwater repeated. He held out his hand. "But, how?"

It looked like him: the knuckle-walking arms in place of a normal mouse's forelimbs, the wider head, hips, and shoulders. The small fur ball chattered at the hand he offered. All doubt in the creature's identity disappeared when Gulliver climbed into his hand and attacked his fingernail.

"Ugh." Clearwater groaned as he heard the clicking sound of the nail being trimmed. "Come on."

Gulliver had seized his thumb, and Clearwater tried to wiggle it away. In response, Gulliver wrapped both arms around the digit. Clearwater grabbed the rodent, but Gulliver held his thumb like his life depended on it.

"You're lucky I like your owner," Clearwater whispered, pulling more and more firmly until his thumb slipped from Gulliver's grasp.

"Bek!" the small creature spat at him.

"How are you here?" Clearwater asked, holding Gulliver closely to his face. The big red eyes stared into his own amid the chittering sound.

With his fingernails safe, Clearwater turned his head, looking for Taula. To the right of his table was a deep-fryer, obviously occupied. The white tank hummed just loud enough to be noticed while it tended its patient. It seemed, for the moment, that it was only him and Gulliver as he noticed nothing more than tables, cabinets, and a few chairs, all stark white.

He realized he was not alone when someone stepped out from behind the deep-fryer. He did not recognize her, dressed in a black corissè with snow-white hair that seemed out of place for a young face. Clearwater checked that his blanket was positioned to keep him modest as the woman moved in front of him. Before Clearwater formulated an introduction, she reached out, taking him by the chin as she bent to inspect his face.

Clearwater said the first thing that came to mind. "I, uh, don't think we've met."

"My name is Andira," she answered. "I am the ship's AI. This unit is one of my peripherals."

Clearwater gave her a curious stare. If she was a machine, that explained something about the odd shade of her eyes. But mimicking automatech were supposed to have a mark. It had to be something obvious on their face that told organics that they were talking to a machine. But she had no mark. Was she a companion?

"Oh," Clearwater whispered before clearing his throat. "Where is Taula? Is she all right? Is she in the tank?" He pointed with his thumb.

"Dr. Gilyard is present and healthy," Andira answered, bringing her face closer to his while looking into his eyes. "I asked her to excuse us while I evaluate you."

"Oh. Good." Clearwater turned his gaze to Gulliver, who had begun squirming. He set him down, and Gulliver jumped off the table to amuse himself elsewhere.

"So, who's in there?" He motioned to the deep-fryer again.

"Vi-Baroness Jenna Prideaux," Andira answered. "She will be fine."

The vi-baroness. Clearwater took a breath. He was certain something had happened to her when he went down.

"How do you feel?" Andira asked, using her surprisingly strong grip on his face to turn his head to the side.

"Tired," he answered. "I—"

"Please do not move your head," Andira interrupted when he fidgeted.

"So, are you my doctor for now?"

"For now," she answered.

"Well, am I going to make it, Doc?" Clearwater asked, forcing a single laugh.

"Negative. You'll be dead within the hour."

Clearwater froze, staring directly into her cyan eyes. Dead? What was wrong now? Then why was he out of the deep-fryer?

"Apologies," Andira said. "I sometimes have trouble with humor and sarcasm."

His hands had latched onto the edge of the table, and Clearwater had to force them to let go.

"So, I *am* okay?"

"You will live," she answered, holding up her right hand to show her palm. A red triangle illuminated over her gloved hand. "Please identify the shapes, their number, and their colors."

The test began with red triangles, blue circles, and yellow squares. The test was simple enough to let his mind wander. Memories that had been out of reach began to rise to the surface of his thoughts.

An argument between Zach and Melanie about how Zach was not Dad, and Dad or not, Melanie was too young to go out in a pahri. He could hear their voices now. He could even remember their faces as they shouted at each other.

Another argument, also involving Melanie. Social school had determined that Froggy was developmentally immature for her age.[20] The report blamed it on a lack of appropriate parental figures. But how mature was someone that age supposed to be?

Clearwater smiled briefly, recalling the faces of Ryan and David as he gave them a through-the-eyes view of a monitor's cockpit. Froggy, in his arms before she was Froggy. The smile faded. He was feeding her while the rest of them tried to figure out where Mom went. That memory turned into another, then the last things he said to his father.

I'm sorry, Dad. I just wanted to spend time with you.

"Test complete," Andira announced as she banished the holograms.

"How'd I do?"

"You passed. However, you did have significant neurological trauma due to—"

"Bad reanimation," Clearwater answered. "But I think you fixed my memory."

"I was able to re-partition your memory index and use it to repair the damaged memory in your brain. However, there may be some variance."

"Variance?" Clearwater asked. "What kind of variance? Can I trust my memory?"

Andira briefly disappeared behind the deep-fryer. "Most humans do not have perfect memory. Your memory index does and was used to restore your organic memory. Thus you may remember a few things differently. The changes should be minor—things such as colors, times, or exact words. It is unlikely you will notice."

She returned to him with a cup of water. Now confronted by his thirst, he quickly took the cup and drank it in a single gulp.

"Oh," he remarked as he lowered the cup from his mouth. "So where am I?"

"You are on a ship belonging to an officer of the Solar Commando Corps."

---

20 Given the ease with which information can be electronically transcribed to the brain, especially in young children, primary school education for Solars places greater emphasis on teaching children to socialize with their peers and operate in groups than it does on skills such as writing and arithmetic. As a result, non-telepathic children between the ages of three and twelve attend schools referred to as *social school*.

"I remember," Clearwater whispered. "The commando, his team. The Katyusha Twins. Did everyone make it back?"

"Yes." Andira gave a single nod. "The colonel, the Katyusha Twins, and Princess Simmonne are currently in each other's company. Vi-Baroness Prideaux is behind you. The other prisoners were successfully transmitted to Imperial custody."

Clearwater gave Andira a double take.

"Imperial Rose is here?" Clearwater sat up straighter. Not just Imperial handmaidens—the actual princess was *here*?

"Yes," Andira answered simply.

"How did she end up here?"

"I'm sorry, Lieutenant, that information is above your security clearance."

Clearwater shifted on the table. That made its own kind of sense. Surely something had to go wrong—really horribly wrong—for her to end up here.

"I don't suppose I could see her?" Clearwater asked.

To meet a member of the Solar Family, not many people could say they did that. Maybe, just maybe, he could even get a picture with her.

"Princess Simmonne is currently occupied with official duties." Andira dashed the hope. "But I will pass on your request at an appropriate time."

Clearwater raised his hands, shaking them as he shook his head. "No. No, that's all right. I wouldn't want to bother her."

"Very well."

Stupid question anyway. Who was he to ask to meet someone in the Solar Family? Maybe he would be lucky enough to see her around the ship. That would be enough.

"You appear to be in order," Andira announced after running some kind of device around his head. "However, you may experience residual disorientation. I recommend you spend the next few hours resting and avoid standing."

"I think I can manage that," Clearwater answered as Andira stepped away. She vanished behind the deep-fryer again before returning with an arm full of freshly printed clothes, the same brown shirt and shorts the Legionnaires issued as sleepwear.

Andira warned him not thirty seconds ago. With the clothes in hand, he stood and raised a foot to put on the shorts. No sooner had he done so than disorientation proceeded to uppercut his sense of balance. He fell straight into Andira. He might as well have impacted a kilosteel bulkhead when she caught him. Her seemingly lithe figure did not budge, and with both hands, she stood him upright.

Once he had dressed, she promptly placed him back on the table like a parent seating their child at the dinner table. Andira had nothing else to say, and Clearwater watched her walk away. There was a tall hatch in the wall that slid open to reveal a compartment. She stepped into the small alcove, closed the hatch, and he was alone.

Clearwater took a deep breath. He was tired but did not think he could go back to sleep. Now that his head was working again, dozens of games installed on his NOD were accessible. Many of them whined that they had not been updated since he arrived in this galaxy, but none of them sounded appealing at the moment. Part of his brain wanted to explore the ship. The other part sided with his body to veto the idea. But he had to do something. He could already feel his mind being drawn. Drawn somewhere he did not want it to go.

The time in his NOD was 11:30. Rest likely made better sense anyway.

To his side, the infirmary door opened, and Clearwater squinted as the brighter light from the corridor flooded in. In the doorway, a woman dragged a brush through long hair.

"Eeen!"

Clearwater flinched as he felt the scurrying at his feet. Taula quickly bent to catch the ball of fur that leaped at her.

"Hey there, big guy."

"Hey," Clearwater answered.

"Eeep!"

Clearwater made a face when he realized that Taula might not have been talking to him. In the same thought, he looked down, double-checking that he had, in fact, dressed.

"How are you?" Clearwater asked.

"I'm good." Taula held Gulliver with one hand while continuing to brush her hair with the other.

"How did Gulliver get here?"

"Colonel Panzer brought him," she answered.

Panzer? Was that the commando's name? How did he get ahold of Gulliver? Clearwater paused his thought train. Probably neither one of them were supposed to know his name.

"He met the Ghost," Taula explained as she sat beside him on the table.

"The Ghost?" Clearwater turned to her. "And, what? She had Gulliver?"

"That's right," she answered, briefly raising Gulliver to her face to coo softly at him. "Weird stuff."

ND-31. Sarge. They executed him. Lieutenant Brower was covered in burning fluids, flailing as they scorched him. Sergeant ahn Culan, he died with his sword in his hand. Clearwater could not listen to the secondhand story Taula was telling. He could feel the tremors of the wall coming down. He could see the image of the Ghost bent over the Vaar they had captured. Clearwater shook his head as if trying to sling the memories out through his ears.

"How do you feel?" Taula asked, seizing his attention with a hand on his shoulder.

He was not expecting the contact and flinched when her thigh rubbed his.

"I, I'm okay," he answered, taking deep breaths to calm himself. "Just . . . tired. Very tired."

"I'm sure. Are you sure you're okay?"

Words were failing so he nodded.

"Do you want me to leave you alone? Let you sleep?"

That was enough to put words in him. "No. No, you can stay," he said aloud while calling himself an idiot. Did he even ask how she was? "What about you? Were you hurt getting out?"

"Nothing that wasn't fixable," Taula answered before leaning her head closer to his and letting out a little growl. "Besides, I'm a tough girl."

He did not feel it, but he humored her with a chuckle. "Andira said Imperial Rose is on the ship."

"She is," Taula answered, giving Gulliver a swat on the head with one finger. He released her fingernail. "I got to spend some time with her earlier. Just before the colonel got back. I didn't get the full story, but I think the Vaar tried to assassinate her."

Clearwater stared at her. Assassinate the Imperial Rose? Of all the members of the family, she was the one they tried to kill? What good would that do? It would just make everyone at home angry.

"Wow," he finally said. "I guess it's good the colonel brought her here."

Clearwater almost smiled. There was one good thing about being a nobody. No one tried to kill you just for existing.

"I'm bored," Taula announced. "If you don't want to sleep, we should find something to do."

Clearwater closed his eyes. The images trying to invade his mind were becoming more difficult to force back out.

"I . . . think I just want to sit here. For a while."

"Oh, that's no fun," she answered. "We should cheer you up."

Her hand moved from his shoulder to his thigh, eliciting a fresh startle.

"Easy," she whispered. "I don't bite."

She also said she wouldn't scream, but that was really more his fault.

"Do you want to play *Warmetal?*" she asked.

Clearwater shook his head.

"Any other games?"

His left hand moved to grasp his right forearm as he shook his head again.

"I could print a Chongo deck."

"I don't want to play," Clearwater whispered.

"Strip-Chongo then?"

His eyes widened and he faced her. The grin on her face, he was pretty sure it meant she was expecting him to laugh. Even returning the smile was difficult, but she had taken his words for the moment. He looked down at Gulliver as Taula gave him another swat on the head. In the dim light of the infirmary, the bioluminescence glowed in her eyes. Perhaps it was keeping her from seeing his face clearly.

"Another time?" he whispered.

What he truly wanted to do was cry. To sob like a baby for a little while and feel sorry for himself. But he could not do that while she was here.

"All right," Taula whispered. She pressed down on his shoulder again, urging him to his back. "Come on, you need to lie down."

"Taula, I—"

"Shh." She pushed more insistently while lowering her other hand to send Gulliver to the floor. His pulse was quickening as she turned back to him.

"Just lay back. Relax," she said softly now with both hands on him.

His breaths became short as she tried to guide him onto his back.

"Everyone is safe here," Taula continued. "Just relax."

He did not think about what he did next. His hands shot up to wrap around her forearms. Taula's face twisted in a jolt of pain, followed by fear. Clearwater forced her hands back against her chest before pushing her away from him.

"Johnny?" she whispered. "You're hurting me."

Clearwater threw his hands open as if he had been grasping scorching steel. An instant later he was on his feet, stumbling for the infirmary door to get away. It seemed as if sounds were following him. A series of growls and hisses spun into a horrific song, a loud mechanical whine.

He was fighting both the sounds and disorientation as he spilled into the hall. He had to go. He had to be somewhere else. Anywhere but in that room. Disorientation landed one punch after another, but he stayed on his feet.

His shoulder met the wall, which he used to keep himself upright as he continued to walk. He grabbed his right arm, as if to confirm the limb was still there. He could almost feel it again—the metal probes that lanced his abs to take samples of his organs. He squeezed his arm harder as the pain of the saw tried to return, and he cradled the scream he knew was coming. Then more pain, and that strange double vision just before she took his eye.

His strength failed and he slid down the wall.

"No." He gripped his arm tighter. He squeezed until his nails started to break his flesh. Until he felt enough new pain to be certain his arm was attached and that what he felt wasn't real.

His mouth worked on long gasps, and his heart seemed to take mercy on him. His heart's pulse began to slow. Clearwater managed to open his eyes and simply sit against the wall. The air on the ship was cool, and his skin seemed to magnify the chill.

After a time, a shadow passed over him. Taula looked down at him. She did not say anything at first and merely offered her hand. He was too heavy for her to pull up, so while he took her hand, he had to rise on his own.

"I'm sorry," she whispered. "I didn't mean to upset you."

"I . . ." Clearwater shook his head. "I just want to rest."

"Okay. Come on, let's get you back to bed."

CHAPTER
15D

A PRINCE ENJOYED MANY PRIVILEGES, an emperor even more. In the years ahead, Steven intended to take full advantage of all of them. He savored one he knew would be his favorite. In one of the Cathedral's many meeting rooms, forty-nine men had gathered from each of the pillar nations, and several more from the larger duchies. Masters of the astranet, then men who ran the various companies and organizations responsible for its upkeep.

These were wealthy men, powerful compared to most. The kind of men who had every hour, perhaps every minute of every day, planned out years in advance. Men with vast legions of employees who answered their beck and call. Men who often fancied themselves masters of their domains and destinies.

Even as a Solar Prince, it would have taken Steven weeks at a minimum to arrange a meeting with all these men. When a Solar Prince asked, they would work it into their schedule. But when summoned by the emperor, one dropped what they were doing to heed the call. Steven made them wait. It was petty, he knew, and he intended to enjoy it. Besides, the lantai servitor manicuring his nails was an artist. No need to rush her.

Forty-seven minutes after the meeting was scheduled, Steven finally entered the room. A mix of veiled anger and relief greeted him as he followed his guards into the Dolcen Room. Seventeen lantai servitors followed him. Each carried refreshments for the guests and, more important, security tablets that they distributed as Steven sat at the head of the jade table.[21]

He silently counted to seven before speaking.

"Be seated, please."

The men who had stood at his entry returned to their chairs, and a couple were already examining their tablets.

"I've brought you here on a strategic initiative," Steven began. "In the

---

21 Security tablets are small computing devices meant for use specifically by Solars. These devices are designed to prevent their data from being copied, even to another Solar's nanite network or their personal memory index. As their name implies, they are often used for sensitive information that needs to remain off a network.

Combine, we face a vast and technologically sophisticated foe. You are here because I am concerned about the security of the astranet. I do not intend to wait for there to be a problem before addressing it. By this evening, I will have issued an edict mandating new regulations on the astranet and its upkeep. In these tablets, you will find a list of modifications to be made. I expect work to begin immediately."

Holy hell, this will cost billions.
Who is going to pay for this?
This could bankrupt us.
What the hell will this even do?
Going to have to negotiate a support agreement.
His Excellency isn't going to be pleased.

Steven did not even try to read their minds; the thoughts simply came to him.

This doesn't make any sense.
Who came up with this?
This, this will mean rebuilding the entire network.

All these masters of the astranet, and not even half a dozen could make out the technical specifications. Not a surprise to Steven. So rarely did those who ran the major companies actually understand the work. They were men who made deals, negotiated, and finagled finances. One of life's little oddities. One of the few who did have relevant technical expertise was the first to speak. Steven faced him.

"Majesty, may I ask—who defined these specifications?"

Martel Baan, a cudan kid. The child of narcissistic, wretched parents who were so self-absorbed, they saw their children's genetic profiles as a way to express their creativity. Mr. Baan had two hair colors, black and orange, which became asymmetrical at his face with each eyebrow in its own color. His eyes, while not absurd in size, were larger than a man's should be, and his nose was almost nonexistent. But Steven had a fondness for cudans who had made it to high positions and overcome the extra handicaps imposed on them by their parents, who made them stand out in ways that were unproductive at best and harmful at worst. The result was almost always an odd-looking child, often saddled with a strange name to add insult to the injury.

"I did," Steven answered.

Both of Mr. Baan's eyes, one yellow and one green, opened a bit wider.

"I was not aware Your Majesty was an expert on multispatial networking," Mr. Baan replied in genuine surprise, albeit with that annoying upward inflection at the end of every sentence that Elysians insisted on speaking with.

"Well." Steven rapped his fingers gently on the table. "Between politicking and diplomacy, I do occasionally find time to study. I drew up the specifications, with help on some of the more advanced technical aspects from a source I am not prepared to disclose."

"Majesty." Yanee Serba, a man so generic in appearance that it was annoyingly difficult to try to describe him. He was not technically inept but remained one of those far more focused on the financial enterprises of business. "Looking at this, I'm not even sure what this is going to do. But this will affect every multispatial system in the astranet. This work could result in temporary blackouts for a number of worlds. Probably enough to exceed our service allowance."

Steven swiveled in his chair, putting the crowd to his side, and rapped his fingers on the table again. "I am aware, Mr. Serba," he answered. "It will be your jobs to notify world governments before interruptions so that they can prepare."

Mr. Serba was about to reply, but Steven held up his hand.

"If the planetary governments or nobility give you any trouble about it, tell them to speak to me. I will tell them to shut up and do what they're told. Good enough?"

Mr. Serba looked back down at his security tablet. "Yes, Majesty."

Ha. A young emperor aching to flex his muscles.

Steven missed which of them the thought came from, but he did not let it bother him. Another man wished for his attention—Simon Loden, one of those men fate just could not keep down. Born to noble parents who were removed by their superiors for incompetence, he then lost his father to suicide. Cheated on by his first wife, survivor of an attempted murder by the second. But he persevered to eventually become head of Allied Communications, the largest astranet provider in the Republic of Andromeda.

"Majesty." Loden hesitated. He was not a technical mind; his was a mind of money. Steven knew the question before it left Loden's lips. "The sheer scope of this work, and the timetable for it—this could bankrupt several of us. Even then, I'm not sure we can meet this deadline. I will have to give this to my people to be certain, but the cost of this is certain to be crippling."

Steven offered a deliberate smile as he leaned back in his chair. He let Mr. Loden hang for a few seconds before he answered. It was not just Loden. Every man in the room had a knot in his stomach as he contemplated the cost. For if Allied could not bear the cost, how many of them could?

"The Empire considers these new regulations a strategic concern," Steven answered. "You will do the work, you will present the Empire with a bill, and I will pay it."

The sheer amount of relief in the room was practically a tranquilizer, and Steven had to pull back from it.

"As for the deadline," Steven continued, "my advisers assure me that four years is more than reasonable, and it's more than I would like. This is the new regulation, and I am covering the cost so that you need not. Any company that has *not* completed the work in the allotted time will be held in violation."

The money-grubbers were relieved but not pacified. Many contemplated their cash flow while the work was ongoing. But the technical minds—they were the ones who were truly confused.

Gannan Shoku, one of the few who was truly a master of both the technical and financial realms, prepared to speak. The only one in the group who concerned Steven at all. This Ori had a reputation for cheating, under-cutting, backstabbing, and bullying his way to the top of his field. He was an opportunist who never stopped pursuing those opportunities or seeking them out. He was the kind of businessman who upheld the negative stereotype—the result of true brilliance combining with raw ambition.

"Forgive me, Majesty," Shoku began, still looking down at the tablet. "I'm still not entirely sure what we're trying to achieve here."

"We're hardening the astranet, Mr. Shoku," Steven answered. "Simple as that."

"Yes, Majesty," Shoku answered, still looking at the tablet. "I can see that. But, to what end exactly?"

Steven showed the entire room an annoyed smile and rapped his fingers a bit louder on the table. "In case anyone did not notice, we have a very *big* war on our hands. Certainly they are not as advanced as us, but it would be a mistake to consider them primitive. The Vaar have to know that they cannot defeat us in open war. Our victory is only a matter of time. So I expect asymmetric attacks. The astranet is the biggest, and most important, target. So we will harden it."

Even now Shoku had not looked up from his tablet, and it was beginning to annoy Steven. Ori fashion sense was so ghastly. A shirt white on one side, black on the other. A jacket over it in a mirror of the shirt's patterns. Large earrings that would have looked more appropriate on a woman's ears. Quantum stars lined the lobes of the ear above the dangling tassels. A small ruffle worn from the collar of the shirt in silver. Even his eyes were decorated to reshape the irises into diamonds.

"Again, please forgive me, Majesty," Shoku replied, "but there are already many regulations hardening the astranet against attack. I'm not sure of any vulnerabilities the Combine could realistically exploit. And no one here is in violation of SEANS."[22]

Steven rapped his fingers again. "Then perhaps you should examine that document a bit closer. I have highlighted several potential vulnerabilities."

"I see those, Majesty," Shoku returned. "However, most all of these would require architectural knowledge of the astranet. Would the Combine even have anyone with that knowledge?"

---

22 SEANS is short for Solar Edict on Astranet Networking Security. Passed after the Solar Eclipse, this edict established DARM, the Department of Astranet Regulation and Management. This government agency identifies potential weaknesses in the astranet and mandates regulations to address them under SEANS authority. SEANS is often used as a catchall term referring to security regulations affecting the astranet. SEANS's first act was to break up Astranet Technologies into smaller companies to prevent any one nation from having near total control of the astranet.

This time Steven held his tongue, waiting until Mr. Shoku looked up from his tablet to seek a reply. Only when he was able to look into the man's diamond eyes did he answer.

"If the astranet were to be disrupted, it would strand unfathomable numbers of people from their homes or trap them there. Logistics, both civilian and military, would be disrupted, and people *would* die. I'm not going to leave that to chance."

Steven paused to look around the room.

"These are the new regulations," Steven said. "I brought you here to give you notice before I pass the edict. I understand it will be difficult. I understand it will be costly. I understand you will all likely have people working around the clock. But this is the way it is. Come to peace with it. The Empire will cover the cost, and I think it is reasonable that a special something could be allotted to everyone who meets their timetable."

Steven finished with a smile and knew before feeling it that he had won over the bulk of the room. Life was so dreadfully simple sometimes. The promise of financial consideration was a practical hack to reality. A lesson his father taught him well. If you surround yourself with greedy people, you'll have to tolerate their greed, but you'll always know how to keep them happy.

Shoku was not convinced, but he did not need to be. A man like him did not even need an implicit threat uttered. He already knew the consequences: meet the deadline and be rewarded, or fail and face the supernova of government sanction. That was one nice thing about a bullying backstabber—they rarely needed to be threatened. They always knew what tactics could be used against them.

"Well, gentlemen." Steven stood, prompting those in the room to do the same. "I have other matters to attend to. If you have any other questions or concerns, address them to the DARM Council. They have already been provided with this information."

Steven held out his arm toward the door, and the men filed out. Many were happy to leave, ready to get out of the room and return to the domains where they were emperors.

The Vaar couldn't possibly do anything with this. He's worried about domestic threats.

Steven heard the thoughts in Shoku's mind as the man followed the rest out. So close, but not quite there. It did not matter. They would all take the information back to their companies and their people. They would study it but not for too long. Four years did not leave them much time to spare. As the orders filtered down the line, many of the workers would question what they were doing and why. Eventually they would simply be told.

"You are certain none of them will figure it out?"

"Each has been in these halls before. Each a mind I have touched. Some will harbor suspicions and curiosities. But none have enough information to realize the truth."

"I suppose not," Steven said more to himself. They had not been given identical tablets or data either.

Steven looked down at his freshly manicured nails. That servitor was cute. Perhaps he would find out what noises she could make. It was good to be a prince. Better to be an emperor.

CHAPTER
15E

FROM THE FIRST TIME the Vaar had entered the Time-Lost Galaxy, the Great Anomaly had been its defining feature. Once more Oul'sor stood on the hull of a ship, his body bared but unharmed by the void of space. Instead of the hull of a mighty warship like the *Caustic Reverie*, he stood on the hull of a transport. It was one of many that had formed a ring around the Anomaly.

To species with lesser eyes, the Great Anomaly appeared only as a black circle, a strange emptiness that should be alight with the multitude of stars that formed the galactic core. But to Vaar eyes, the Great Anomaly had a unique beauty.

The Vaar eye could perceive the spectrum from radio waves to gamma rays. But only in the right conditions. Rarely did most Vaar or Viss actually see radio waves, X-rays, or gamma rays. The Vaar eye was most sensitive to colors from infrared to blue. On the average planet or ship, these primary colors created a pollution of light that kept the far edges of the spectrum out of view. To see the edge colors required wearing a filter to block out the primaries. The nose was often in the same handicap. Modern technology often had so many chemicals that everything blended together.

It was different in space. An ancient and distant quasar pulsed brilliantly to his left. But the greatest beauty was directly ahead. The Great Anomaly looked like a ball of fluid beset by countless ripples, all filled with color. Shades of infrared blended into gamma rays. Ultraviolet swirled with waves of X-rays amid a background of microwave radiation. Not even the most precious gemstones held such colorful luster.

Though the Great Anomaly was spherical, he could not perceive that. This close to something so enormous, light-years across, it seemed only like a wall. A wall with height and width that appeared to expand infinitely.

If there were air, he would have drawn a deep breath for a contented sigh. It was a privilege to see it, while it was here. New eras began when things ancient and enduring passed away. That time was almost here. Soon the Great Anomaly would exist only in old images, bequeathed to posterity as a reminder of something that had once been.

Indorai stepped out from behind him. The creature walked toward the sloping nose of the transport as his tendrils uncoiled around him. Oul'sor watched as those tendrils kept moving, restlessly swaying their tips from side to side.

He hoped that Indorai would not feel the need to talk, but those hopes were in vain.

"Almost time now."

Perhaps not answering would encourage him not to continue.

"Everything will change, Oul'sor. You will have to redefine reality itself. With all the awe, the terror, and potential."

Oul'sor wished for atmosphere just to sigh in annoyance. He glared down at his hand, coiling it into a fist. For a moment he was on Origin again, driving that fist into the Crykeeper's faceplate. He had won the fight but had never experienced a victory so hollow.

Indorai's words were an invasion that could not be stopped. Oul'sor knew his reality had already changed, but while recognition of that fact had brought many questions, it had offered few answers.

"When you were six hundred, you thought yourself old, Oul'sor. At twelve hundred, you thought your six-hundred-year self a fool. But mortality no longer binds you. When you have lived a million years, you might understand how long I have waited for this."

Oul'sor flinched and reflexively blinked as a pulse of color washed over him.

"It has begun!" Indorai's voices boomed.

Indorai raised his arms over his head. Another incredible flash of light poured out of the Anomaly in all directions. All motion was relative, and standing on the hull of a ship brought that reality into relief. If it were not for the absence of a feeling of motion, Oul'sor would have thought he was moving away. But it was the Great Anomaly that was moving. Blues, ultraviolets, and gamma rays came to dominate the colored field as it receded away.

Indorai's voice intensified as if he were addressing a great mass and projecting for them to hear.

"Today marks the end of the beginning! The Walls of Eternity begin to crumble. The broken time of this galaxy will be shattered! The mouths of traitors will be shut! Deception and disorder shall bend to order and truth! And that which should be, will be!

"First, the Zal will fall! Then the Empire! Then the Praetheen and the Assembly! All the worthless shall be purged! And a new reality, bounded only by eternity, shall come to pass! Revel in this moment! For it stands before the greatest of them that this universe will see!"

As Indorai bellowed to his invisible audience, the Great Anomaly contracted. Oul'sor watched as the dazzling wall began to move away from him.

"The Crossroads returns!"

In seconds the sphere had contracted to the point that Oul'sor could see it all in such impossible speed. Then, before Oul'sor had processed where it might be leading, the Anomaly exploded.

Even the brightest of the stars disappeared in the tidal wave of color. Within him something seemed to shift, and he glanced down at himself. Memories flooded through him. Memories of childhood, of young adulthood—in the moment they seemed no further away than yesterday. With Hahk'xess, Dolum, and Don Don, they sat eating the flesh of a fresh korzenk. The prey everyone told them was too much for four children to hunt.

When he blinked, he saw Vil'sor, months old in the palm of his hand. Oul'sor fed him strips of meat. That image dissolved into another as the plates of his hand aged, and Vil'na took Vil'sor's place. Then there were memories he did not recognize. Memories of his feet on a metal floor with no seams, in a hall where all metal was silver.

As the wave of color passed him, the memories left with it. His sight cleared, and he stood on the same transport.

The Great Anomaly was gone.

The signal had gone out. The hundreds of thousands of transports— packed with infantry, tanks, artillery, and equipment—were gearing up. A rattle through the transport found his feet. The stars around him seemed to stretch, and then they were also gone. There was nothing to see at warp as the light of the universe was blue-shifted into a featureless glow.

Indorai faced Oul'sor. *"Now everything hinges on what happens there."* The creature walked forward. *"Your friend and mine will attempt to interfere. They must find only failure."*

Oul'sor sneered as he glared down at his fist.

"I know, Oul'sor. But sometimes we must give up what we wanted for something better."

Oul'sor glared at Indorai with bared teeth.

"I need no lecture from you." Indorai turned back toward the nose of the ship. *"There are other preparations to make. I must divide myself elsewhere. Be visible. Keep the morale of your warriors raised. And I will come for you, when it is time."*

Indorai seemed to step out of reality as he disappeared. Oul'sor felt no sadness in seeing him go. His head rolled and he looked around the blue-shift of space. There was something sad about it. Such a funny thing that he should care. But to a Vaar's eyes, the Great Anomaly was a beautiful wonder of the universe that was taken away. No Vaar or Viss would look upon it again. The sight was lost now to all future generations.

His head dipped and he stared down at the hull of the ship.

Something lost.

CHAPTER 16A

OR THE FIRST TIME in over a hundred years, Robert Panzer opened his eyes from a full night's sleep. Only on those nights in the deep-fryer, when things in his head were not functioning correctly, did he dream. But last night, he dreamed. As the hub for their minds, his memories had taken them over the green sand beaches of Nova Calais. Over the mountains of Mars, to the ancient forests of Cano Made, and into the crystal caves of Unterbass. But that journey was at its end. Morning had come, and he awoke to the sensation of three warm bodies pressed against his. A moment later there was a sensation against his lips.

He opened his eyes to see Simmonne as she moved from his mouth to his ear.

"Good morning, Master."

"Good sleep?" he asked, raising a hand to rub his eyes.

"Yes, *Master.*"

He observed her with one eye open. "Like saying that, do you?"

She giggled and moved to kiss him again. "I like how you feel when I say it. So maybe I'll keep saying it. Master."

He flicked one of her bangs before entwining Julie with his arm. Simmonne returned her head to rest on his chest. Somehow, she got to him. She had found a way to sense him clearly, where no one ever had. How?

She was special.

"I suppose we should get up."

"*No,*" all three girls whined at once.

He drew in a relaxing breath. Life had become a *lot* more complicated. His days as a commando were over. The only real regret was the satisfaction he would give the commandant with his resignation. Oh well, couldn't win everything. He couldn't walk away from the military completely, not with a war just starting. Whatever he did, the three of them now factored into that decision. But he had options and time to think on it. Andira's latest status report waited for him in his NOD, and he opened the file. It would be another seventy-five hours before the ship was ready to go. There was time. Time for them, and time to plan for the storm. He pulled the Twins up more firmly to his chest so he could embrace all three.

The time read 08:17. He had slept six whole hours? He could not remember the last time he slept so long outside the deep-fryer. He only needed an hour every few days. Anything more than that was simply a break.

"Master?"

Was that Jennifer? No, that was Julie. He turned to her. Her eyes were still closed.

"Where will we live?"

"Not the Cathedral," Jennifer spoke up, drawing his gaze. Her eyes were barely open. "Please? I don't want to go back."

"I'd prefer to live among other Sylvanni," he thought aloud, "but the Dominion is not an option. Maybe somewhere in the Iron Stars."

"I had some thoughts on that," Simmonne offered.

"Did you?"

She nodded. "I could give you my accounts. It's enough to colonize a star system. You'd be entitled to the rank of viscount."

"Viscount Panzer?" he said. "Not sure how that sounds. I'll think about it. Probably have to change my name again once I leave the Corps anyway."

He rested his head back on the pillow. A lot of this would depend on the emperor and just how the old man reacted to this development. He wouldn't like it, but if he could accept it, that was one thing. If not, there were still options. He had been a commando for over a hundred years. One of the things the Corps did was pay lucratively. If you gave someone great power, access to secrets, and enormous autonomy, you better pay them well. He had saved his money and invested it wisely. The three of them would probably be surprised just how much he had. He was a Rhinegrave for better or worse. He was studying investing and finance before he had mastered the spelling of either word.

The four lay together in silence while he listened to their thoughts. In their minds, still dancing between lucidity and sleep, the Twins were trying to balance it all. How little they really knew about him, versus what they were feeling. He was beyond questioning whatever had happened here. Whatever brought the three of them to him, they belonged to him now, and it was time to plan a new life. He had known more than a few identical twins, triplets, quadruplets, and more. It was not encouraged but not uncommon in the Dominion. Couples anxious for a son would sometimes "batch" daughters to avoid running afoul of law and tradition.

There were always similarities in how they thought. But in his experience, it was not all that different from any given siblings. But with Jennifer and Julie? One mind seemed to share two bodies.

Their thoughts went through the same processes at the same rate. They came to the same conclusions and asked the same questions at almost precisely the same time. He had always assumed they had played up the identical twins persona for their image. Perhaps it was more real than he thought. That or they had worn the mask so long that they had trouble taking it off.

"My favorite color is gold," he answered the unspoken inquiry in their minds.

Are you always reading our minds?

"You never know."

Both nuzzled tighter to him, letting their minds wander as they prepared to return to sleep.

Simmonne's thoughts were bouncing between last night and their evening on Reichsylvannia. If he had taken her then . . . But he had waited, and his patience had been rewarded.

All three protested when he drew the Twins fully up onto his chest, turned, and deposited the three of them on the bed.

"Shower time," he announced as he rose to his feet.

"Me next," Simmonne said, moving her head to a pillow between the Twins. What a beautiful picture. He contemplated leaving them that way.

"Next?" he said with a scoff. "You're part of a portfolio now. These things are done together."

He took the leash from the headboard and tugged at it. The priceless expression from the Twins almost brought a laugh. The are-you-serious glare. But with another tug, the three filed out of the bed to follow. If they were still tired after they were clean and fed, then he would let them go back to sleep.

Time management could be an issue with one, but it was essential with three. Too much could be tedious, but a person was their routine. Now he had to set their routine to maximize everyone's time. To keep them accustomed to the new life they had started. They followed him to the washroom. Panzer stifled a grin as he watched all three walking with a limp.

When he removed the leash, each one reached for their collar but found no mechanism to release them. While the Twins were indifferent, he noticed a certain satisfaction from Simmonne. He carefully removed their collars and their manacles, resting them on the sink. Once the morning's first business was done, he held the shower door open and marshaled them inside.

His eyes twitched, and warm water rained down on them from above. From the bath-care printer, he withdrew products and set them on the small shelf nearby. Simmonne held out her hands expectantly and looked a bit confused when he took her by the arm.

"When one grows up expecting to have a portfolio, he learns a bit about how women take care of themselves."

She nodded as he turned her back to him. He reached back to the shelf to bring down a bottle of nanogel and squirt it onto her scalp.

"You have a *lot* of hair," he remarked as he worked the gel into the platinum fibers.

"Five hundred twenty thousand," she answered. "Most people have a little over a hundred thousand." He sensed the spike. She paused before offering up her question. "So." She hesitated. "We have to be naked and call you Master. Are there any more rules we need to know?"

"Several," he answered.

"Will you tell me?" She glanced over her shoulder at him. "I can't follow rules I don't know."

He had planned to go over it during breakfast, but now was as good a time as any. The gel would need time to do its work. He took her arm again and moved her back against the wall of the shower. He did the same with the Twins, placing them on either side of her. Simmonne spent half her time reading body language, so he needed to be conscious of his. He pressed his hands against the wall, putting all three of them within the enclosure of his arms.

Almost immediately he sensed Simmonne probing him, grasping hold of his feelings.

"Rule one." He checked their eyes to make sure he had their full attention. "*Never* lie to me. Never try to deceive me or hide something from me. I am your master. You have no secrets from me. I can read your minds whenever it suits me, so don't even try to hide something. It will only insult me and make me very angry."

His tone was calm, and he articulated each word carefully. That put more of a chill in their blood than any growling, any shouting, or any threat ever could. All three nodded slowly. They grew up around telepaths and knew how hard it was to deceive one. But that also meant that they knew it was not completely impossible. Especially true when most telepaths followed the etiquettes and principles. Those did not apply here, and hopefully they understood that he was on a different level than anyone in their family.

"Rule two. You are not my partners in this relationship. You are my property. You have no rights. You do not make demands of me. You do not give me ultimatums. You do not negotiate with me. Because I care for you, I will consider requests. But you are entitled to nothing."

The *p*-word stung all three a bit, but it was what they needed to hear.

I am not property!

Parallel thoughts from parallel girls. But with the use of *I*, he knew he was getting through to them. Which one? Which one felt more rebellious?

He lowered his right arm and leaned away from Jennifer.

"Then leave," he said aloud, "and don't come back."

Water cascaded over the embers, and her expression became one of shock.

"You heard me," he said as Jennifer looked at the others. "Leave." She jumped as he raised his volume.

Jennifer, you idiot! came the thought in Simmonne's mind.

Jennifer took a step forward, imagining, hoping his arm would come down to stop her. When he didn't, she took another step and put her arm on the shower door. Her thoughts raced, and he turned his back to her to look at Simmonne and Julie. The draining resolve sapped Jennifer's strength as she pressed on the door. He heard the tiny sigh as she lowered her hand.

"Are you still here?" he asked, turning again.

She tried to retake her previous position. He stopped her and pushed the shower door open. She stiffened but could hardly fight him as he forced her to step out into the colder air.

"Please?" Jennifer whispered, a lick of shame coating her eyes. Rather than give her the triumphant grin he felt, he regarded her with a curious expression. Gently this time, he pulled her back into the shower and closed the door.

"Please what?"

"I'll be good," she answered, beginning to pout.

"No," he answered coldly.

If growing up as a high prince had taught him anything, it was to be the prize of the relationship. If one was the prize, they set the terms. If he was the prize, then being his property was a privilege. If it was a privilege, they would fight to keep it and fight anyone who tried to separate them from it.

"No," he repeated. "You don't get to defy me and then pretend you didn't."

He pushed the door open again.

"I'm sorry," she mumbled.

"Sorry?" he answered. "Now you must ask to stay."

"Please?" She looked up at him.

"That's how you ask?" He began to push her back out the door.

"Please, Master?" She spoke with much more feeling in her words. "Let me stay?"

People may not remember exact words, but they would remember how they felt. She would remember this moment forever. How defying him had left her humiliated and vulnerable. The sense of loss when she tried to walk away. The fear of being invisible once again. He let the seconds pass, drawing out the tension. Finally he closed the door and guided her back against the wall.

What he found as he turned back to Simmonne and Julie surprised him. Simmonne could read him now. He half-expected a look of amusement, but Simmonne's look was one of anger, eyes like disrupters aimed at Jennifer's head. He glanced at Julie. Relief, both at the conflict ending and that she had not been the one to be humiliated.

You idiot.

She was no telepath, but Simmonne was doing her best to project that thought at Jennifer. Julie meanwhile hoped to shrink into the wall, hoped he had not heard the same thought in her mind. He turned his attention back to Jennifer. He held a single finger to her face, a silent warning that she heeded with a nod.

He took a relaxing breath, loud enough for them to hear, and placed his hands on the wall again.

"Rule three. You belong to me, and only me. I am the only man who touches you. I do not share my women. Dishonor me at your peril."

So you get all the women you want, but we only get you.

There was no defiance in the thought. Neither had the courage for that now. But he heard the thoughts in unison again, from the same source he expected.

"That's right," he answered them.

Not very fair.

"It's completely fair," he corrected them. *"I am your master."*

The Twins nodded, and he eyed Simmonne.

Only you.

She was smiling. If he declared himself a god, she would fight to be the high priestess of his temple. Such was how she had built him up in her mind. But it was more than adulation. The possessiveness meant something to her, made her feel valued. So many men could not understand what went on in a woman's head. That the difference between whether she treasured a man's possessiveness or found it oppressive, hinged entirely on her respect for him.

"Rule four. I am not your boyfriend, husband, sweetie, honey, or some other diminutive. You refer to me only as Master."

From Simmonne, this time, he felt some discomfort.

"Um." She hesitated and was met with a glare. "Master? What about in front of other people? I mean, that might be awkward in front of family. Or in public."

He couldn't grin. This was a serious matter. "Am I *not* your master in public? Does having other people around change who I am to you?"

How am I going to explain this to Daddy?

"If it makes you uncomfortable, learn to think it before you speak. I will hear it."

That relaxed the Twins a bit, but not Simmonne. She knew better. Knew how easy it would be for other telepaths to pick up on such a practiced, habitual thought without even meaning to. The Twins may have been more mature than her, but she was definitely the sharpest of the three.

"Rule five is dress code. You will be naked. Do not clothe yourself without permission."

"But," Simmonne spoke again, "you said I could wear a pahri in public? Right?"

"I said I *might* allow you one," he corrected. No rights, only privileges. He could not let any of them think they were entitled to something. That would only encourage eventual demands for more.

"Master." She spoke low. "I'm a member of the Solar Family. I can't humiliate them. Or in public? I'd be so embarrassed, I'd die."

He broadened his mind to the Twins. Both contemplated themselves nude in front of strangers—the eyes of countless men and women, laughing, leering, and more. The thought bothered them far less.

"You'll do it if I require it," he said to Simmonne.

Her expression became pleading. "Please don't."

He leaned in closer until she could feel his breath on her forehead. "You'll do it if I require it."

She squirmed and drew a breath as she weighed it in her mind. Which did she find more objectionable? The humiliation to herself or to the image of her family, or displeasing him. He already knew which would win. But it was not enough for him to know. She had to know.

He would not actually do what they were fearing. A pahri showed more than enough, and some things were not for public view. But they did not need to know that. In their minds, even dressing had to be a privilege.

I'll do it for you. She thought the words she couldn't find the strength to speak.

He stood up straighter. "Rule six is your collars. Only I know how to open them. They had better not come off unless I remove them. If they ever come off and I haven't, I will know. I will assume you are with another man, or that your kidnapper has cut them off to keep me from tracking you. For your sake, it had better be the latter. When we get home, I will have nicer collars made. The rule will continue to apply."

None of them found much objection to that one. All three had welded their hearts to their collars as engagement tokens.

"Rule seven. It is *not* easier to obtain forgiveness than permission. If you think I wouldn't like it, don't do it."

No real reaction from any of them to that one.

"Finally, rule eight." He smiled. "I like you the way you are. Do not make major changes to your appearance or attempt personality modification without my permission."

He lowered his arms and turned Simmonne back to him.

"Is . . ." She hesitated. "Is that all?"

"Those are the big ones," he answered. "The little ones, you can learn as you go along."

The gel had plenty of time by now, and he began scrubbing her hair. He recalled hearing her answer questions once about how much time went into her hair. No surprise. Julie moved from the wall, and a moment later she was gently dragging her nails over his back, feeling left out. He'd tend to her next. Jennifer kept her back to the wall, unsure if she should even move from where he had put her. She could wait there. Each needed some individual attention. As he finished with Simmonne, he took a handful of bodywash from the printer and placed it in her hands before giving her a gentle push forward. He grinned, sensing a trace of disappointment. She had been expecting the shower to progress to something more. Plenty of time in the day for that.

He tended to Julie. She had less hair than Simmonne but still more than most were entitled to. But there was no rush. The ship wouldn't be ready to move any faster. He peeked into Julie's mind. She had made a list and was repeating the rules in her mind, making sure she had each memorized. Determined to be on her best behavior. He scoffed under his breath. They'd see how long that lasted. When he was finished, he gave her the bodywash and turned to Jennifer. With a hand on her arm, he peeled her off the wall.

Her mind was reliving what had just happened. With a handful of her hair in one hand, he slid the other under her arm and closed it on her breast. That snapped her back to the present.

"Relax," he whispered into her mind while closing his eyes. He concentrated on warmth. The sensation and the comfort. He pushed it into her mind, and she let out a gasp, feeling the warmth he imagined on every nerve of her skin. *"Your master is not your master simply because you have to obey him. It is because he is master of your world. He can take you from the heights of pride and sensation, only to drag you down and put you in your place. Or he can raise you out of despair into a place of comfort and warmth."*

He felt her exhale, like an extension of his body, as she relaxed into him. He let her focus on those words and bask in the preternatural sensation while he returned to cleaning her hair. By the time he finished, her mood had improved. He waited until he saw a smile before putting the bodywash in her hands.

With more of the gel, he attended to his hair with much greater haste, though it startled him a bit when he felt an unexpected chill on his back. Simmonne grinned at him as she lathered him from behind. Julie quickly followed her lead and soaped his lower back.

"Your muscles are really hard," Julie remarked, poking two fingers into his side.

"I'm sure they are, but you're feeling my dermal armor," he answered as he folded an ear over to scrub behind.

"Oh." Julie poked him again. "So that's metal?"

"Five-millimeter endoplate."[23]

"How many cybernetics do you have?" Julie asked, giving him another poke.

"More than some, less than others. Compared to most of the Corps, I'm a fleshie."

Another poke, and he glared down at her. It was then that Julie realized she had provoked him. She began to step back, but he was on her before her foot landed. The sound of giggling filled the room as his fingers attacked.

"She's most ticklish under her arms." Simmonne snickered behind him.

"Traitor!" Julie screamed as Panzer wrapped an arm around her, lifting her off her feet and pressing her against him. "Stop! Stop! Please!"

"Are you going to stop poking me?" he asked while she writhed.

"Yes! Please stop!"

He continued for a few more seconds before stopping and leaving her to pant. Her hands came to rest on his shoulders as she caught her breath. Pressing her against the wall, he found her lips.

There was no more mischief when he finally set her down and finished washing.

When content with his cleanliness, he toggled his NOD. The falling water ceased, replaced with currents of hot air. Finally he opened the door and led them out. The first thing they did was reclaim their collars from the sink. Simmonne pulled at hers, but apparently saying twice that only he could open them had not quite sunk in. He took it from her.

"Only I can open it," he told her, drawing a nod before she raised her chin. He closed it around her neck before doing the same to Julie. With Jennifer

---

23   Endoplate is a trademark name for a specific brand of bond-forged titanium scales directly beneath the skin. Though not a standard part of military cyber-ization, it is commonly purchased by soldiers who want additional protection above and beyond what military cyberization grants.

he closed it tighter, just enough that it would be harder for her to forget it was there. With all three collars back where they belonged, new screens opened in his NOD.

SIMMONNE—ACTIVE
DISTANCE: <1 METER
STATUS: HEALTHY
MOOD: HUNGRY
RESTRAINT TENSION: RELAXED
JENNIFER—ACTIVE
DISTANCE: <1 METER
STATUS: HEALTHY
MOOD: HUNGRY / FATIGUED
RESTRAINT TENSION: TIGHT (COLLAR) / RELAXED
JULIE—ACTIVE
DISTANCE: <1 METER
STATUS: HEALTHY
MOOD: HUNGRY / FATIGUED
RESTRAINT TENSION: RELAXED

He minimized the screens and pushed them to the periphery of his sight. A finger directed them to the toiletries printer while he took his from the sink. A blast of plaquehammer, and he was finished. He passed the plaquehammer to each before toggling his NOD. The tethers in the restraints activated, and he picked up the leash and printed a brush. For now he draped the leash over his shoulder before grinning as he toggled an option in his NOD. All three glanced down as the manacles around their ankles formed chains into hobbles. A second later, chains formed for their wrists as well. He motioned for them to follow, amused by their efforts to stride.

Back in the quarters, they watched silently as he opened his drawers and began to dress. Nothing too fancy—pants and vest. But when he turned back to them, they stared enviously. He slipped the brush into his pocket.

"Master?" Julie asked.

"Yes?"

"May we get dressed?"

"No," he said with a scoff. "Why would I allow that?"

"Because." She hesitated. "Because I want to get dressed."

To be a man in a relationship with a woman was to be tested. Tested constantly, tested ceaselessly. Tested on the same material, over and over again. Tested for weakness. Tested for indecision. Tested for stability. Tested for patience. Tested most strongly when he did not realize it. Tested even when she was not aware she was doing it. Panzer knew this for what it was. He took a step toward her, hooking one finger around the chain binding her wrists. He pulled her closer, drawing the chain to his chest.

"And *I* want you naked. One of us is going to be disappointed." He offered her the most smug smile he could manage to answer the petulant pout she was giving him.

"That's not fair," she mewed, tugging gently.

"*I* decide what is fair."

She looked at his hand before looking back at him. "Maybe I'll get dressed when you're not looking."

He raised an eyebrow at her before shaking his head. "If you did that, I'd have to punish you. So we won't do that. Andira?"

"Yes sir?" she answered.

"Modify printer permissions on the ship. Do not allow Julie, Jennifer, or Simmonne to print anything that could be considered clothing without my authorization."

"Acknowledged. Should I expand that to include blankets as well?"

Andira, how well she knew him. "No. I'll allow them *a* blanket if they want one."

"Understood."

"You're so generous," Julie muttered. She yelped when his left hand met her rump. Little more than a tap, but enough of a sting to get her attention. He gave her another.

"Don't sass your master."

Both of the Twins were pouting now. But that would pass. Giving in to whining or complaining wouldn't do anything but degrade their respect for him. He called the leash back to his hand before attaching Julie to it. Simmonne and Jennifer were added as he led them to the couch. There he positioned Simmonne on his knees as he took the brush from his pocket.

Not as good as Jenna, but not bad, Simmonne thought as he finished.

"Been a while since I've groomed someone else."

She nodded, and her hair moved through her fingers.

"Leave it." He put a hand on her shoulder. "You look good with your hair down."

She smiled, and her hair fell. With a wave of his hand, he urged her off to the side and sat Julie in his lap. As he brought the brush to her hair, he stopped.

In Jennifer's mind she was bent over the couch and biting her lip. He might make that happen later. But in Julie's mind, something else entirely. She was reflecting on the threat of punishment, debating with herself if she wanted to provoke him. The identical minds had gone in very different directions.

How interesting.

He completed his work, and Jennifer took her turn. He made a note in his NOD of the order. The next day he would change it, rotating who went first.

"So what now, *Master?*" Simmonne asked as he finished with Jennifer.

"Now breakfast," he answered, tracing his thumb over her lips. "Then, practice."

CHAPTER
16B

THE SOUNDS OF POPPING grease and the scent of cooking meat filled the quarters. Master had raided his private larder and converted the printer into a cooking apparatus. Simmonne sat on the couch, taking in one of the universe's rarest sights. Rhinegraves had servants for their servants' servants. More prestigious that way. Anyone could have an automatech to do menial things for them. Only a somebody had another living being to do it. To actually see a Rhinegrave, a male of the family, no less, cooking his meal? Few people would ever witness such a spectacle.

She smiled. She doubted she would see it often in the future. Her smile briefly turned into a frown. He probably learned to do it himself after his first wife died.

You idiot! she screamed in her mind before looking at him. If he had been reading her thoughts there, she would have just dredged up some painful memories. She needed to get her mind on something else, quickly. Fortunately the Twins seemed to have him distracted. They sat together on the left side of the couch, huddled together as they hounded him with questions about what he was cooking.

Her eyes wandered across the room. The drawer with the forbidden box. The model ships. She continued to scan until her eyes came to rest near the door where the shreds of her clothes and the fragments of her tiara still lay. She brought her eyes back to the very real chain at her wrists and ankles and sighed. This was her life now, chained up and naked for his amusement. She had been born a princess, and he made her a slave.

She told herself she wouldn't let it happen this way. That if they had a relationship, this was not going to be it. She even went so far as to tell herself that if it came down to it, he might be the one in chains. What an idiot she was. She deserved this. If she let him do this to her, she deserved it. For thinking she could do it to him, she deserved it. Or, was it more that he deserved it? Simmonne shook her head. She was doing it again. It was what he wanted, so she was rationalizing it. It didn't matter now. It was too late to dip a toe. She had already jumped in.

The moments to simply sit and think gave her mind time to dredge up questions. Questions she would have preferred not occur to her. Did he know? When he offered her the badge, did he know what her answer would be? Did he foresee it? If he did, did he know he would be cured? Did he let her think he was going to die just to manipulate her feelings?

She tugged at the chain linking her wrists. The links seemed to weigh nothing but had no give. Would he really do that to her? If last night taught her anything, it was that he relished having control. Would he resort to something like that to get it? If only she could get in *his* head for a while rather than the reverse.

Simmonne looked to him at the printer, standing tall with a subdued grin as he eyed the Twins. As she looked at his face, she could not help but smile as the worry melted away. That sort of manipulation was beneath him.

The couch was way too big, made for the giant at the printer. She scooted back and brought her legs up onto the cushion, reclining into the corner. She would never be the one holding the chains. But maybe . . .

Her eyes flew open and she looked back at Master. Her heart raced, and every muscle was taut as she waited for a reaction. Thankfully, the Twins seemed to still have his attention. If he had spied that thought in her mind, knew what she was thinking on the *Hurricane*, she wasn't sure how he would react, and she didn't want to know. She had to keep the thought buried. It would be impossible to hide it completely against a telepath as strong as him, but she could at least put it where he wouldn't find it, unless he went looking for it.

Stop thinking about it, idiot!

This was going to be hard. She was from a family of telepaths. She knew how to bury her thoughts, but most of them could not read through a 4CM field. Others were wise enough to know that sometimes you really didn't want to know what someone else was thinking. At least that was what they told her. She was never sure she would have the same restraint if she had been fortunate enough to be more than an empath.

Distraction, find a distraction. She focused on the feelings in the room.

Fatigue, hunger, concupiscence—that would be the Twins. Both still very tired even after sleep. Were it not Master's conversation and the promise of food, they'd already be drifting away. Amusement and concentration, Master. She managed to read him last night, as if she never had a problem. Now it was not as easy. He was still there, but she had to focus. As she managed to clear the picture, she almost laughed. The intense, ruthless focus . . . on cooking breakfast. If she did not know better, she would think he was planning a mission. Was that how everything was for him? Ruthless determination and insistence on perfection? Methodical planning of every single step? But there was more.

A hint of worry. He had it buried, but it was there. As if something in the back of his mind refused to be completely ignored. She wanted to ask what it was, but that would be futile. That Sylvanni pride. He would not burden his woman with a problem unless he had no choice. Besides he was Master. If he wanted to keep something to himself, that was his privilege. She counted herself lucky that he didn't react poorly to the fact that she could sense him now. It had to be a shock to him. Part of her had worried that if she found the path, he might be displeased. But he seemed at least to be willing to tolerate it.

She heard a dull thump and looked over to see him shoveling the food onto a large platter. As he approached the couch, she rose a bit higher to peek. She had not seen any vegetables in the larder, and only a few fruits. Neither of which were on the platter he held. Maybe he was going to make them wait while he ate. Another way to emphasize his control. Four glasses of juice hovered over his left hand in a psionic grip. He summoned a table from the floor for the glasses. Simmonne moved her legs from the center of the couch. He sat, and she grinned when he pulled her against him.

"So tell me something," he began, drawing her gaze. "Why are you three vegetarians?"

She opened her mouth before realizing that she did not have a good answer. "That's . . . just . . . what we've always eaten."

"Thank Jenna," Jennifer answered. "She makes our diet plans."

"But you've had meat at some point?" he asked.

Simmonne shook her head. Fruits, vegetables, sweets. If she had ever had meat, she was too young to remember it.

"I sneak some from time to time," Julie answered.

The sensations from him contained bitterness and annoyance. It was subtle, but it angered him, too.

"You know," he said with a sigh, "somewhere, long ago on ancient Earth, a man watched a troop of mammoth crossing the plains. I imagine he said something to his friends along the lines of, 'You know what I'm going to do? I'm going to take this here long stick. I'm tying this here sharp rock to it. Then I'm going to go stab one of those big things to death with it.' Somehow, I doubt he picked a fight with a creature more than ten times his size so that the women and children of the tribe could eat vegetables. It's time you three eat real food."

He took a piece of bacon from the tray and brought it to Simmonne's lips. She was about to protest, but she already knew the look he gave her. The one that warned her not to argue. She opened her lips and took a nibble of the crunchy treat. It was seasoned with his smugness, and she smiled, pulling his hand closer to take the rest.

Master turned to the Twins and motioned toward the platter. Neither hesitated to grab what they wanted. While Simmonne tried to maintain some dignity in the meal, they had no such concern, practically inhaling the meat. Simmonne took another piece of bacon from the platter and nibbled. She had heard once that obesity was a huge problem for humans back before the nanites. Small wonder if food could taste this good. She might never eat a vegetable again. She was on her fourth piece of the wonder-meat when she realized he was not eating.

Oh, there was a term for this. A Reichsylvannian tradition. He wouldn't eat until his women were fed. What was it called?

"It's called sitting patri," he answered.

That was it. Interesting that he practiced the tradition even in private. Not many still did from what she knew.

"Some believe that a man is what he does. If this is true, our rituals, customs, and

traditions—are these not what color our identities?"

"So why the tradition?" she asked the question while reaching for more bacon, only to be stopped. He placed something else in her hand.

"Variety is the spice of life. Fried steak."

She bit into a new slice of heaven. *So why the tradition?*

"It's an old one. It traces back to Manfred himself, in the Conquest Wars and the Rhinevolk. Manfred was just starting to build our culture. The Therican War wasn't so long ago. One of the things Manfred did to structure society was give men full authority over their families. He also figured it could be a good way to test their character when he was considering them for an important position. He would get himself invited to dine with the man and his family."

Simmonne took another piece of meat, unsure of what it was beyond delicious, and listened carefully. She did her best to sample it all, finding new joy in each.

"Food was hard to come by in those days, sometimes even for his family. The Thericans had destroyed all the farm worlds. He knew that if he sometimes had trouble feeding his family, other men certainly were. So when they ate, he'd watch the man. If he ate first, or with his family, he failed that test. If he waited to be sure they had enough before he ate, then he passed and went on to the next.

"Eventually it leaked out that it was one of his tests, and other men in the chain started using the same test. The tradition grew from there. Not so much an issue these days. All you need is a food printer, and you can eat yourself stupid. But I think the lesson is worth keeping."

She nodded, returning to the bacon.

"All you like, but not too much. I have plans for you today." He emphasized the message by squeezing her.

A sort of contented silence followed, save for the occasional crunch or tear of meat. Simmonne broke it with another question. One she was hesitant to ask but too curious to ignore. Now seemed as good a time as any.

"Master?" She pointed to the cabinet across the room. "What's in the box? Your AI was very angry when I tried to look at it."

Her regret for the query was immediate as she felt the change in him. He took his arm from around her and held his hand toward the dresser. Across the room, the drawer opened, and Simmonne watched the box rise out of it. He handed the platter to the Twins so he could hold the box with both hands. It opened with a hiss, and Simmonne hesitated to look inside. A golden collar and a metal disc, an echo.

He took the echo in hand, and it came to life with a small hologram.

"She's beautiful," Simmonne whispered sadly. The young blonde in a red pahri stood with a smile. Simmonne noted the collar integrated into her pahri, almost certainly the same one in the box.

"Who's that?" Jennifer asked.

"That's Elsa," Master answered. "My first wife."

"Your wife?" Julie asked. Simmonne shot her a glare.

Julie, he's holding an echo, you idiot! Julie's face betrayed the realization almost as soon as Simmonne thought it.

"She died 163 years ago," Master said, deactivating the echo and placing it back in the box.

"I'm sorry," Simmonne whispered. "I didn't mean to—"

He waved his hand to silence her. "It's all right." He sent the box back to its drawer. "You're part of my life now. No reason you can't know."

All those years. Several times her life and the Twins combined. He still missed her. There was something, some small part of her that was reassured by that. It wasn't all control, passion, and status for him. Something was caring within him.

"Happier thoughts now," he said, taking the tray and motioning the three to it.

Simmonne was well on her way to satisfying her hunger. But it was so good, and Master did just instruct her to keep eating. She took more, and the contented silence returned. There were thousands more questions. But there was time.

"I can't eat anymore," Jennifer said before letting out a contented sigh. Simmonne watched her lean back against Julie, the latter's head slumped over. She was already asleep? That didn't take long.

"They need more rest. I put blue goo in their juice."

"Oh," Simmonne remarked. His words came as she was reaching for her glass. She had not been planning on going back to sleep.

"I put red in yours." She caught the wink. *"You have to keep me entertained while they rest."*

She grinned before taking a drink. "How will I do that, Master?"

He shot her a sideways glance. "Practice. Finished?"

Simmonne nodded, closing her eyes as he began his meal. The thought of returning to sleep was not the most terrible in the universe—but not her destiny today. So she simply rested while he ate. The questions lingered. She accepted the badge, but how would they do it? She had always assumed when her day came, it would be huge. Any royal wedding was. But Sylvanni disdained that sort of thing, something about big weddings feeding female narcissism. Would they at least have a ceremony? One or three?

"You're not Sylvanni. Yet," he answered. *"If you want a ceremony, we'll have one. Big or small, one or three, I'll let you three decide that."*

Three. She wanted that much to herself.

"You know, a lot of people won't like the idea of a Rhinegrave and a Mandrake together."

"Screw 'em."

She smiled. If it could be that simple. There was still something bothering him, and he was dedicating most of his attention to it. Part of her wanted to ask him what it was. She did not, certain he would not share. She had not noticed it yet, but the red goo was beginning to take effect. Her hands began unconsciously playing with the chain that linked her wrists. If he wouldn't share what was bothering him, she would share what troubled her.

She had to avoid an argument at all costs. If he felt she was trying to argue, he might interpret it as her challenging his authority. Then she would leave him with no choice but to deny her. So she spoke with her most demure tone, even as she realized she had almost certainly telegraphed everything to him by thinking about it.

"Master?"

His eyes remained ahead.

"Do I really have to be naked, all the time?"

"Yes," he answered as if the question carried no more weight than had she asked the time.

"But, *all* the time?" She let her voice whine as she watched and felt for his reaction.

"All the time," he said in a low, almost sinister whisper.

There had to be some wiggle room somewhere. She chose her next words carefully. *Play into the role. Don't challenge it.*

"Could I maybe earn clothes?" The question earned her more than an eye, and he turned his head toward her. "If I'm a good girl, follow all the rules, and do everything you tell me?"

He finally looked down. His left hand came over, tracing a line down from her forehead until he gently tapped her nose.

"No. You'll be a good girl, and you'll follow all the rules regardless."

She wasn't going to win this fight. She knew it, but she was not ready to give up yet.

"What about when you're not home? Could I wear clothes then? Just until you get home?"

He shook his head as he took a large bite of meat. Not even bothering with a verbal answer this time.

"But why?" she whined, pushing at him with both hands. Her efforts bore the same fruit as if she had tried to push a mountain. His enormous bulk did not move at all. There was a kernel of anger that she tried quickly to suppress in the hope that he would not sense it. "You're not even there to see me."

He was looking forward again, as if the conversation itself were beneath him. *"Irrelevant. My rules do not change just because I am out of the house. Besides, I want to think of you waiting for me to return looking just as you do now."*

"But what if I want to have friends over?" she whined a bit more loudly.

"Then your friends will see you naked."

She managed to quash the anger, which left her only with frustration as she began to pout.

"What about when I'm old and not pretty anymore?" she asked in a deliberately petulant tone.

"Then you'll be old and naked."

Sometimes something was funny, and one wasn't sure why. But there was something humorous in that to her, and she emitted a quiet snicker.

She noticed an uptick in her pulse when he set the platter down. That was quick. He shifted, taking hold of her and transferring her to his lap to face him. His sheer size made it easier to kneel on his thighs than straddle him, and for now he let her. But he took her arms in his hands. The chain binding her wrists split before reconnecting as he guided her hands behind her back. Quickly she realized that her wrists and ankles now shared a binding. Her pulse began to pick up its pace.

"Nooo," Simmonne whined. "You can't fill me full of stimulants, then chain me up!"

His answer was a whisper. "Yes. I can."

He made a subtle motion that she was not ready for. There was a small glint as he reached into the pocket of his vest. Before she could react, something metal was in her mouth. Hard and rigid, she flinched at the sudden invasion. But she could not lift her lips off the intruder, much less free her mouth of it. The gag—or was this a bit?—was the final piece of his vision. She had wondered when it would make an appearance. She tested it by trying to speak. The bit vibrated in reply, but there was no sound. She gave it a further test with a scream. Only silence.

"Now that looks nice."

She knew how to handle this, how to talk to telepaths. She focused on the words in her mind, directing them at him. No chance of error that the thoughts were meant for him.

You know, I'll be quiet if you tell me to be.

"This is a training tool."

Training? She opened her eyes wider to invite an answer.

He brought a finger up, tracing from her lips, up her nose, to her forehead.

"You have no filter. You have no power to choose what you do and do not communicate with me. I am in your mind. If you say it, I will hear it. If you think it but do not say it, I will still hear it. You cannot lie to me. You cannot hide or withhold from me. When I say I own you, do you think I mean only your body? No. Everything within is mine now. Every hope, every dream. Every aspiration, and every secret. Every fantasy you would never voice. Every shame you would wish to hide. Every point of pride and every insecurity."

He brought his finger down to tap the bit.

"This is to remind you. To help you internalize this reality. If all I wanted was quiet"—he flicked her collar—*"this can do that."*

I knew it! She would have blurted out the words if she were able. *These collars do more than you told us.*

He did not answer. Not even a change in his expression.

But you won't tell me, will you?

He grinned. *"You figured that out quicker than I expected."*

In some parts of her, the comment hurt. Did he think so little of her? *I know you don't think I'm very smart. Compared to you, I guess I'm not. But I know how strong you are. I knew it the first time you touched my mind. No one in my family is that strong. A T-13.*

She sensed a bit of surprise in him, and it turned into curiosity as he waited to see where she was going. He nodded, both to answer and to encourage her to go on.

I know you can control my mind. If you want me to love something, you can make me. If you want me to hate it, you can do that, too. And I'd never even know you did it unless you told me. Right?

He cocked his head slightly, shrugging a shoulder. *"It's not as simple as you think it is, but yes, I can."*

She took a deep breath and gave a short tug against her chains. *Simple or not, you can do it. That terrified me. It still does. Maybe you have been all along. But, when I thought you were dead . . .*

A tear formed in her eye.

"Calm down."

Whether she wanted to calm down or not did not matter. The wave of preternatural stillness swept through her and brought her composure back. *I realized that if you came back, I only had two choices. Two real choices. Accept that you have the power and be with you or stay far away from you.*

She pushed against his legs with her fingertips while walking on her knees, up his lap, until she could press her body into his.

I don't want to stay away.

Simmonne gorged on the feelings she felt coming out of him. The smug sense of triumph. But much more. Intense possessiveness, yet warmth, and a certain tenderness. It washed over her like a warm breeze. This was her life now, in Master's arms. She would never be the one holding the chains, and that was fine. It took a little bit to understand, but she didn't mind it.

Her eyes flew open as she felt the shift in him. All those sensations in which she had been immersed were blown away by her dread as she realized what she had done.

"Well, well. What have we here?"

Before she could react, the memory was pulled up from within her, and she relived it in her mind.

Who does he think he is? As if I would let you. Tie me up? Put me on a leash like some kind of pet? I am an Imperial princess. Not just any princess, I'm the Imperial Rose! If either of us is going to be a plaything for the other's amusement, it will be you! You will be the one tied up and helpless for my amusement. Not sitting there with that smug look on your face like some kind of, of . . . something!

The reverie faded, and there was silence. Painful, dreadful silence. Though it could not have been more than a few seconds, it felt to her like hours. It broke her. Now he knew.

"I already knew."

She flinched. He already knew? How?

"You thought about it while I was cooking."

Of course. It was stupid of her to think she could keep it to herself while he stood so close. *You're going to punish me for it, aren't you? For daring to think it?*

Her entire body tensed as she waited for the answer.

"Yes."

Just for thinking it? She lowered her chin, peeking up at him through her lashes.

"Yes," he answered aloud.

One small mercy of the bit was that it saved her from babbling as her heart raced. *But, just for thinking something?*

He pushed her back so he could lean down, and she turned her head away to avoid his gaze. His breath was hot on her cheek.

"Let's say you were the master."

But I'm not! The proposition filled her with panic.

"No," he answered with an extra dose of smug. *"You're not. But it can be fun to pretend. So let's pretend for a moment that you were. Would you punish that kind of thinking?"*

Her hair whipped around her as she shook her head. *No! I wouldn't punish someone just for thinking something! I—*

"Liar," he hissed into her mind, disrupting her thoughts as effectively as a slap across the face. *"Never lie to your master."*

But I wouldn't! I couldn't, just for—

"Do not. Lie to me. Simmonne."

She huffed, cringing as he hooked a finger under her chin and forced her to face him. With her eyes dangerously close to looking into his, he asked again. *"Would you punish for it?"*

There was no way out. She couldn't talk her way around this. *Yes.* She sighed through her nose.

"Yes what?"

She gave a frustrated, silent growl and spat the answer in her thoughts. *Yes. I would punish for it.*

"Harshly?"

She nodded.

"Why?"

He could not simply punish or admonish her for it. She had to be humiliated as well. *I don't know.*

"Liar."

She tried again to look away, but he would not allow it. Annoyed with her attempts, he took hold of her hair to keep her still.

"Why?"

Because everyone has to know their place.

His mouth opened in a menacing grin. "My, my. Quite the little totalitarian you are."

She began to pout. It was so unfair. They were not even together yet when she thought it. They had spent only an evening together, and not even a full evening. They had only shared a meal. She took a breath. That did not matter. Her universe no longer operated on that kind of logic. He was Master. She belonged to him the moment he decided he wanted her. That was how her universe worked now.

"Come to think of it," he said as he tapped his chin. "There are some other things I really should punish you for."

Other things? Her heart redoubled its efforts to beat out of her chest. What other things? She had done everything he wanted. What could she possibly have done?

He brushed the back of his fingers over her breast. *"You tried to negotiate with me over your clothes."*

The answer hit like a punch to the gut. He was right; she did try to negotiate. Twice. Not that it did any good. She took a breath. The first time, she even told him to his face that she wouldn't do it.

"But worst of all," he whispered, "you tried to hide your defiant little thoughts from me. You told yourself you could hide it and deceive me. What is the first rule, Simmonne?"

She sniffed and tried to look down. His grip on her hair kept her in place.

Never lie to you. Never try to deceive you or hide something from you. You are my master. I have no secrets from you.

"Correct. Now what kind of master would I be if I didn't punish you for that?"

She closed her eyes. *You wouldn't deserve to be master.*

"Are you ready?" he asked.

Her hands moved protectively to her rump, but she nodded slowly.

"It wouldn't be punishment if you enjoyed it."

I wouldn't enjoy that!

"Liar. Trying to get yourself in more trouble?"

She quickly shook her head.

"Your punishment. Is cold."

Cold? What did that mean? Her bewilderment did not last long. She sucked at the bit as she tried to gasp. Her head whipped around to look at her feet. Everything looked as it should. But the cold, the intense cold now biting at her toes, was unreal. Thousands of tiny needles on her skin, and they were climbing. Over the soles of her feet, they came to her ankles and continued up.

Simmonne shivered, her teeth trying to clatter as she looked back at Master. The cold had reached her knees and was still rising, a second front climbing up her fingers. The creeping ice reached her back. Her body was trembling so hard now that her vision began to blur.

This was her punishment. For a moment she told herself that she would take it. She would not complain or ask for mercy. She had erred and deserved to be punished. But that resolve drained quickly. She felt the cold creeping over the lobes of her ears and offered up a scream. The bit devoured it, and she was silent.

Mercy!

As cold as the ice, he shook his head. The only sound was the rattling of the chains as her body quaked. The icy needles reached her scalp, fully enveloping her in a chill nature could never offer. Every part of her body was subject to the piercing needles.

No more! Please no more! I'm sorry, Master!

She managed to make out that he had raised his hand, showing all five fingers. The first finger curled. She had never focused on anything quite so hard as she waited an eternity for the second finger to coil. Enough time for a star to die before he coiled the third. Another scream was futile, and he coiled the fourth. Her eyes were closed when the fifth finally coiled. The snap of his fingers was an explosion in her ears. She collapsed into him as a new sensation of warmth washed over her, sweeping the piercing cold away.

His arms enfolded her as she panted, her body still shivering as if waiting for the cold to return. *That . . . was . . . horrible.*

"It wouldn't be punishment if you enjoyed it."

She nodded, catching her breath. It was over, and the warmth of his body was all she felt now. She opened one eye, peeking over at the Twins. If Simmonne knew them, then the moment he warned of punishment earlier, they were thinking of provoking him. *Don't do it, girls. It's not a game to him.*

She nuzzled tighter into Master. Even as unpleasant as it was, there was something cathartic. A tiny part of her had feared that some of him was bluster. When he laid down his rules and threatened punishment, she worried he might not follow through. But he did. Everyone had to know their place, and he kept his. She tried to push even more firmly into him.

Tighter? Please?

His arms constricted more firmly around her.

Can still breathe. Tighter?

He obliged, securing the embrace as her body finally let the shivers go. Eventually she had the strength to rise back to her previous position and perch on his thighs. The chill was gone, and her energy returned.

So. I've been punished. What now, Master?

He pulled the bit from her mouth. Simmonne took a moment to work her lips and jaw, enjoying the simple pleasure of *not* having a hard object stuck between her teeth.

"Better things now." He smiled.

"Practice?" She slowly returned his grin.

"Practice." His grin widened. *"Last night was a simple introduction. There is so much to teach you."*

CHAPTER 16C

ELEVEN-THIRTY HOURS. MIDDAY approached as Clearwater walked silently through the corridors of the ship. He had nowhere particular to go. For two days he'd done almost nothing but sleep. The body simply needed something to do while the mind worked. If only he could stop thinking for a while.

He had screwed up with Taula again. How pathetic she had to think he was. Did she actually feel something for him? Or was it just the equivalent on her part of giving him mood elevators and a glass of water? It didn't matter. The moment she touched him, all he could hear was the saw.

He heard voices as he approached the open door. He did not feel the need to pay attention until he passed the doors and peeked inside. In a large armory, the colonel stood with the Imperial Rose, and the Katyusha Twins were with him. His eyebrows rose. The Twins and the princess, too—all three were dressed in pink pahri. Pahri had become skimpier in recent years. The three of them were certainly in style. Twin-veil bottoms had a long train that started narrow and widened on its path to the ankles. A small veil at the front stopped well before the knees. The three wore what Clearwater would call minimalist tops, with both top and bottom held together by thin chains. Gold for the Rose, silver for the Twins. All three wore detached sleeves with cuffs that belled at the wrists. In lieu of stockings, each wore wide-bell leggings as sheer as the Twins' shawls. The Imperial Rose's outfit was the most different. Rather than a shawl, she wore a blue cape suspended from tiny shoulder pads.

It was a bit strange to see the Rose without her famous hairstyle. Any time he ever saw her online, she had her cruciform arrangement. But now she simply wore it in a thick tail that fanned out on its way to her ankles. Was that how she wore it when she wasn't in public?

One of the Twins stood at the rear of the room where the walls had parted to reveal a small shooting range. She held a pistol. He could barely see the other Twin, her figure blocked by the colonel's body. The Imperial Rose stood nearest, with the colonel's arm wrapped around her.

Clearwater's eye followed the colonel's left arm, where his hand disappeared into the princess's top. He looked lower to her garters, which were silver with metal bands of gold. Those were engagement garters. The Twin at the counter wore the same. Clearwater realized he was lingering in the doorway and took a step back.

"I want to shoot a Vaar," the Twin holding the pistol said.

"Not like that you're not," the colonel answered. He extricated his arms from the women before taking a step forward to the armed Twin. The second Twin also wore engagement garters.

The Imperial Rose *and* the Katyusha Twins? Clearwater looked back at the colonel, now with his arms around the armed Twin.

"Don't lean away from it," the colonel directed her. "Lean into it. Hold it tighter. *Tighter.* Think of how I hold you. You're not trying to crush it, but you're keeping it tight. It can't do anything but what you let it do. The gunware is already on your nanites."

A hologram of a Vaar illuminated downrange. Clearwater knew it was a hologram, and knew it was going to pop up. Even so, the appearance of the armed Vaar caused him to flinch.

"Now point the pistol at it. The AI in the gun can tell where you want to shoot by where your eyes are looking. If you feel your arms want to move, let them. The gun is working with your muscles to correct imperfections in your aim. Now, the trigger is just a manual safety. Squeeze it, and let the gun do the rest. But concentrate on squeezing without moving the pistol."

The gun emitted the familiar *snap-whirr* of a pulse pistol, but subdued. A training round. The hologram flickered for a moment, and a red circle over its eye indicated her hit.

"This is easy," the Twin remarked as the colonel stepped away.

"Well, there's no jamming. This guy isn't shooting back, and no one's giving suppressing fire. But sure, pretty easy."

"I hope this isn't the only kind of practice we're doing today," the Imperial Rose remarked as the colonel took her in his arm again.

"Well, you three need a little rest. Don't want to tear up my new toys."

What little doubt remained, that killed. The Rose and the Twins. The colonel had all three of them. This had to be recent, very recent. The Imperial Rose getting engaged? That couldn't stay out of the news for very long. But the colonel was a commando. Maybe that's why it was secret. Clearwater sighed. He couldn't even get past second play with Taula without humiliating himself.

"There's a fine line between curiosity and eavesdropping, Lieutenant."

Clearwater nearly hit the ceiling when he heard the voice in his mind.

"If you have something to say, I'd appreciate it if you announced yourself."

Stupid! A commando probably sensed him before he even reached the doors. Clearwater cleared his throat and stepped into the armory. The colonel turned to face him, the princess and the Twin in his arm moving along with him.

The princess suddenly seemed to have a bit of a fit. She tried to move, only for the colonel to pull her tighter against him. Why was she standing weird? Her knees were pressed together, and her hands rose to her face to cover her mouth. Was she trying not to laugh? Bashful about being seen in a pahri? She was definitely blushing. Or was she shy about the colonel's hand in her top?

Clearwater brought his eyes up to the colonel's. This made things a bit easier, if the four of them were together. Sylvanni to Sylvanni, Clearwater could not speak to Her Majesty or the Twins. Not without the colonel's permission, or until the man brought them into the conversation. So much the better. Hopefully if he did not seek permission to speak to them, it would not be offered. Less opportunity for him to embarrass himself in front of royalty.

"I'm sorry to bother you, Colonel," Clearwater said with a quick bow of his head. "I'll be going."

"Just a moment, Lieutenant."

The colonel looked down at the Twin in his right arm. She glanced back up at him and nodded. The colonel turned to the princess, and her face remained red as she nodded. Telepathy. How nice that had to be. Clearwater could surmise that he might actually have some success with women, too, if he could read their minds.

Clearwater noticed the metal chain connecting the neck of the princess and the one Twin to the colonel's belt. He had detached it and was curling it around the princess's shoulders while she stood with her arms crossed over her chest. Keeping his women on a leash? That was a bit garish. That thought he pushed right out of his head. How another man treated his women was definitely none of his business.

"Let's talk in my second office." The colonel gestured for Clearwater to follow as he exited the armory.

"Yes sir," Clearwater answered, casting another glance at the princess who now had her back to him. Farther down the corridor, they entered another, smaller room. A metal desk lay in the center. The walls bore many decorations: A framed paper document. A large, toothy animal skull. A few weapons mounted on plaques.

The colonel rounded the desk to open a drawer. Out came a large wooden box. Next came a metal case and a pair of glasses. The colonel opened the metal case and took out a bottle.

Hemmeltonec. Clearwater read the label silently with a double take. Back home, rich people drank Hemmeltonec. Just one of those things rich people did to show everyone how rich they were. The colonel popped the cork before filling both glasses.

"When you're a telepath," the colonel began, reaching over the desk to offer Clearwater one of the glasses, "you can always tell when someone needs to talk."

Clearwater hesitated before taking the glass. He held it as carefully as he ever held anything in his life. At five hundred troys a bottle, he was not about to spill a single drop. Not sure what to say, Clearwater took a drink. He had never had Hemmeltonec before. To hear people talk about it, it was perfection in a bottle. Indeed it was pleasing as he sipped, and he could taste the honey used to make it, but Clearwater was not sure if it was five-hundred-troys good.

The colonel had opened the wood case and withdrawn a thick pair of metal tubes. He opened the first to reveal a thick cigar that the colonel then held toward him. Clearwater had no real desire to accept the cigar, but he didn't want to be rude. So he took it and opened his jaw uncomfortably far before pulling the lighting tab.

A single huff, and Clearwater had no doubt the Imperial Rose and the Twins could hear him hacking down the corridor. He snapped the cigar out from between his lips, quickly covering the mouth of the glass with his hand as his lungs tried to escape. His eyes blurred, and he must have coughed for over a minute.

Finally he was able to take a drink, the taste of Hemmeltonec far more pleasant.

"Father never teach you to smoke a cigar?" the colonel remarked, lighting his.

Trying not to choke, Clearwater shook his head and could only make out a raspy whisper. "No sir."

No wonder the colonel was still alive. If these things hadn't killed him already, what chance did the Vaar have? The colonel held out his cigar and brought one finger close to the ember.

"First third is the starter. The second third is the best part. The final third, some like it—some don't. You puff. Don't inhale. It absorbs through your mouth."

The colonel came back around the desk, took a sip from his glass, and sat on the edge.

"What's bothering you, Lieutenant?"

Clearwater stared into the golden liquid in his glass. His lungs were calming. If the cigar was as expensive as the brandy, he didn't want to waste it either. So he took a puff, careful to let none into his lungs.

"It's not really your problem, sir," Clearwater said.

"Look. I'm not a counselor. And you should probably talk to one. I'm not actively reading your mind." The colonel paused, glancing away a moment. "But, when you're a telepath, you can't help but pick up on certain things."

He pushed one of the two chairs in front of the desk out. Clearwater took the invitation to sit. Still looking into the glass and unsure of what to say, he simply opened his mouth and let the words fall out.

"I've never wanted to be anything but a legionnaire, sir. It's kind of the family business. My father, my brother, my grandfather, his father and brothers. Every man in my family. Except for the weirdo uncle who joined the army. Even as a kid, I, I knew it could get me killed one day. Really, I did understand that. I didn't think it would happen to me, but I knew it might."

His eyes narrowed, and he began to cringe as he saw the gleam in the Hemmeltonec, the light reflecting like it did on the metal of the saw.

"But to have someone . . . bolt me to a table and start . . . cutting pieces off me. Pulling them out. Just to see what would happen? I, I wasn't prepared for that, sir." Clearwater took another drink, followed by another careful puff on the cigar. Whatever comfort either could offer, he was not prepared to turn away. "I, I don't know how I'm supposed to feel about it."

When he looked up, the colonel was nodding.

"I don't know," Clearwater continued. "I know traumatic stress is a thing. But how do I know if I'm having it? Is it still coming? Am I going to start dreaming about it every night? Is it going to show up at random? Am I supposed to be angry? Am I supposed to cry? What am I supposed to do? How am I supposed to feel?"

"I don't know that anyone can tell you how you *should* feel about this."

Clearwater looked back down at the glass. "I think about my men, on ND-31. I didn't know them long enough to, you know, really get to know any of them. And I feel . . . *bad* about it. Like, I didn't get to know any of them well enough that I can grieve for them as I should. I feel like I let them down, but I don't know what I could have done." Clearwater threw up a hand and shrugged. "I don't know if that makes any sense, sir." Clearwater peeked up at him. "Have you lost men before, Colonel?"

He was answered with a slow nod. "Can't talk about it. But yes."

Clearwater gave the glass a swirl before drinking the last of its contents. The colonel quickly refilled it. "I keep thinking of my section. When I was assigned to them, I didn't feel like I was worthy. Those guys had seen action across the universe. I wasn't ready to lead that kind of unit. Did I get them killed? I keep asking, if they had a different officer, would they be alive?"

"You don't ask the blind to lead the blind," the colonel remarked, ashing his cigar. "There's a reason they put new officers with veteran units. Who was your sergeant?"

Clearwater saw him in his mind, kneeling on the ground just before he was executed. "Dolph. He was the big delta who obviously liked his scars. Kind of felt like a stray cat around him. How do you order a guy around who's already done everything?"

The colonel smiled around his cigar. "That's why they put him with you. So he could use his experience to help you, and you could learn that it's okay to do your job and give an enlisted man an order. Even if he's more experienced than you. No one expects you to come into the job already knowing everything. During the battle, who was really leading the unit? You or him?"

Clearwater closed his eyes as memories of the battle tried to invade his mind and he strained to push them out. "He was. I was just kind of there."

"Then your sergeant did his job," the colonel answered. "If he, with all that experience, couldn't get your unit through, what makes you think a different officer could? Some battles just aren't winnable. That's just good tactics. When you do it right, the fight is unwinnable for the enemy. When he does it right, it's unwinnable for you."

Ash had fallen on his pants. Clearwater flicked it aside before taking another drink.

"On the Vaar ship, Jaegda forced me to deactivate my pain inhibitors. Told me if I turned them on, she'd torture Taula instead. So I turned them off. I came so close to turning them on again. But I didn't. Some part of me feels like I should tell her. But then, that'd be stupid, wouldn't it? What would that accomplish?"

The colonel glanced up, his lips pursing around the cigar. "You ever notice how often women are scheming against each other, Lieutenant?"

A bit flanked by the question, Clearwater shook his head. "Not really, sir, no."

"Oh," the colonel answered, his eyes open in what seemed like shock. "Well, a lot of them do. Thing is, they also tend to assume men are doing it. Women project, you see. Men do it, too, but women tend to be worse about it. Left to their devices, they'll try to become the man they want, rather than become the woman that kind of man wants. They'll do something they shouldn't and justify it by telling themselves you *must* be doing it, too. And men, they tend to treat women the way they would want to be treated, rather than the way the women respond to being treated."

The colonel caught himself digressing and motioned to Clearwater.

"The point being, you go and tell her what you just told me, she may well see it as you trying to manipulate her feelings toward you. Or, she's just going to end up feeling responsible for what happened to you. I don't see either of those working well for you."

It made sense. Either the Hemmeltonec or the cigar had brought a slight buzz. Clearwater decided he wanted more and sampled both again.

"You ever been tortured, sir?" Clearwater finally asked. "Does it ever get better?"

"No," the colonel answered, setting his glass down. "No, I've never been captured by the enemy. I've been through some things. Maybe as bad, maybe not. Hard to compare traumas objectively."

Just as bad? Clearwater tried to hide the doubt in his expression. "Like what, sir?"

The colonel took a deep breath and leaned to gaze down the corridor, ensuring it was empty. Something seemed to drain from the colonel's face. He wasn't sure what it was. But it was something, like a dozen lights flickered behind his eyes and one had just gone out.

"The girls don't know this story," the colonel began, "and I'd prefer it stays that way."

Clearwater scoffed. Was the colonel worried he was going to tell them? No, he wasn't about to start a conversation with the Rose or the Twins. The colonel took a deep breath, refilled his glass for another drink, and took another puff on his cigar.

"It was one of my first missions with the Corps. I can't tell you the particulars. But basically, we had to destroy a ship and its cargo. Problem was, we couldn't find the ship and didn't know its destination. But we did manage to learn where it was going to refuel."

The colonel paused, shifted his weight, and took another drink.

"You do enough operations, eventually you have that one. That one where everything that could go wrong does, horribly. My mission was just to destroy the ship. But I took the initiative to make it look like an accident. We snuck aboard and planted charges in their transpatial drive. When the ship made its next jump, it would come out the other end and blow up. Look like a catastrophic drive failure. We were leaving the ship when it happened. I guess they realized something was going on. They jumped. The warp field ripped our shuttle in half. My team was in front—they got away. I was in the back and went through with the ship."

Clearwater's eyebrows arched. He was no expert on warp physics, but he didn't need to be to realize how astronomically small the chances were that he should have survived.

"The charges did what they were supposed to do," the colonel continued. "The ship exploded as soon as it came out on the other end. Sent my half of the shuttle careening. The crew had been planning to hide their cargo on a failed colony. After about a week in space, I managed to use my thrusters to make it to the planet. I was the only sapient there."

The colonel gazed down the hall. The man was still talking, but Clearwater could tell that he was somewhere else.

"We were beyond the astranet, too far to get a message to anyone. They say the most important thing to do in that situation is keep your head. For a while, I did. I had Andira to keep me company, and I was strong. I knew my team would come looking for me. But I also knew they had no idea where I ended up. My armor had taken a lot of damage, and it started to die. Until then, I wasn't really alone. But once it did, it was just me."

Clearwater leaned back in his chair. "How long?"

The colonel seemed to return to the present. "Five years, 109 days," the colonel answered. "That place . . . At first, nothing bothered me too much. At least until my nanites started to go. You remember in survival training, when they have you deactivate them?"

Clearwater cringed and shuddered at the same time as he recalled the event. "Yes sir."

The colonel stared at him. "The reality is so much worse," the colonel assured him. "There they just have you turn them off. But with no goo, they start to go offline. They start doing things to your body, getting it ready to survive without them. Your immune system changes, your body starts storing more fat. You feel so . . . sick. You don't just feel weak, you become weak.

"When I first landed, if I needed wood, I could rip a tree out of the ground. Then suddenly, I couldn't. If I needed wood, I had to cut the tree down. Then I had to cut it apart and carry it back in dozens of trips. Lose an arm or a leg, it would no longer grow back on its own. Get an infection, and your immune system can't handle it, you die."

The colonel paused to refill his glass and take a drink. "And that place was no picnic. Huge animals, many of them predators. While I had ammo, they weren't much of an issue. Once I ran out? With my nanites gone, even my psionics went. Just my knife and a human body with all its frailty."

The colonel shook his head.

"I couldn't fight them off with my hands. I had to sleep in the treetops."

The colonel pointed to the skull Clearwater had eyed earlier. It was long with four eye sockets and a mouth full of cruelly hooked teeth.

"That guy and his brother decided to join me in my tree one night. If eating me would have made them as sick as eating them made me, I'm not sure who really won that exchange. None of the edibles agreed with me. I was sick more often than well."

"Sounds rough, sir," Clearwater remarked. With how far away the colonel's eyes were again, Clearwater wasn't sure if the man even heard him.

"But the worst part was the solitude. Growing up, well, I used to be somebody. I was never really alone. Never had a moment to myself. Sure, I could tell people to go away, but all I ever had to do was raise my voice, and people would be there. Even as a legionnaire, there was always the unit. Go on a mission solo, I'd always be coming back. There was never a time that I thought I'd never see another person again. Not until that planet. It took a toll.

"I started talking to my rifle. Even when she ran out of ammo. She was an R-steel club, an unbreakable pry bar, and a walking stick. She felt like the one thing I could depend on. I was there so long. By the time Jorri started answering me, I didn't realize what a problem that was."

Clearwater's eyebrows rose.

"Yeah," the colonel answered his expression. "More than five years, and each day a little piece of my sanity went with it. Contemplated suicide a few times. No nanites, a person can only live so long. And the idea of spending the decades alone . . . I had a preexisting condition from a battle in the Outlands War, and the time without the machines only made it worse. The easy way out started to look very tempting."

The colonel had instructed him not to inhale the cigar, but for several long puffs, the colonel seemed to be doing exactly that.

"You tell yourself all kinds of things, trying to bargain with fate. That if you can just see another person, you'll never be mean to them again. That you'll make amends for everything you've ever done wrong. That you'll forgive all your enemies if you can just hear another person's voice."

The colonel offered the ashtray, and Clearwater tapped his cigar over it.

"Obviously they found you," Clearwater remarked.

The colonel nodded. "My team went rogue. Took my ship and came looking. I've always assumed the emperor was the only reason the Corps didn't hunt them down to take the ship back. It took them five years, plotting every possible place the ship could have jumped. Then, going there and scanning until they found me. By the time they did find me, I, I was gone."

The colonel took a longer drink this time, emptying his freshly filled glass.

"I nearly killed Novin when they landed to pick me up. Took a piece out of him with my knife. They've always assumed isolation drove me so mad, I didn't recognize them. But that's not the truth." The colonel let out a long sigh. "Truth is, I'd given up. I'd accepted my fate. I was going to spend what was left of my life on that planet. If the predators or disease didn't get me, something else would. Even convinced myself I deserved it for the mistakes in life I'd made. I knew who they were, but I'd lost hope. I didn't think I could go back and ever again be the man I was. And I didn't want to live as what I became. When I attacked them, I was hoping they would kill me."

The colonel shrugged. "Once I lost the element of surprise, it was easy for them to subdue me. But it was years before I was ready to return to duty." The colonel rolled his cigar, tapping away the ash.

"You asked if it gets better. It does. Eventually, I relearned my social skills. Got used to sleeping in a real bed again. Stopped interpreting every animal sound as something about to attack me. I stopped talking to Jorri, and she stopped talking to me. It gets better, but it's always a part of you. I never got over calling Jorri by name. And sometimes when I sleep, I'll wake up, think I'm still on that planet, and have to remind myself that I'm not. It's always a part of you. But it does get better."

Clearwater looked down at the floor, hearing the saw again. "How long did it take you, sir?"

"Longer than it should have. I made some decisions in my life. They cost me a lot, and some good people just as much. Being on that planet felt like a punishment. I had to realize that the universe doesn't work that way. It doesn't punish or reward—a deserve has very little to do with anything." The colonel leaned forward. "Why do you feel so guilty?"

"Sir?" Clearwater asked, sitting up straighter.

The colonel tapped his temple. "You can't hide strong feelings from a telepath. It's like . . ." The colonel paused. "Parading a gorgeous naked woman past an adolescent boy. He *will* notice. I'm not going to take it from your mind, but you feel real guilty about something."

Despite how hard he tried not to think it, it didn't matter. Clearwater should have figured he couldn't hide something like that from a commando. The shame he had locked up began to slither out. He looked back up at the colonel. He never intended to confess it to anyone, especially not another Sylvanni. Family was everything. But if the colonel really was that strong, he might already know and was simply pretending he didn't.

"The guilt can do worse to you than anything the trauma could dream," the colonel said. "Because you start to justify it, think you deserve it. So that guilt starts to eat you. What's eating you, Jonathan?"

He continued to stare at the glass. "Do you have any siblings, Colonel?"

"A few." He nodded. "A brother who was a child when I left home, and several sisters I never got to know. You? How many?"

"Two brothers. Two sisters. Sir," Clearwater admitted. "I had an older brother, but he died. Our father died just a few years ago, and Mom disappeared."

"I see," the colonel answered as he returned to the desk.

"Sir. I love my family. I'd do anything for them. But, I just wanted a couple of years. Just a couple. To be a free adult before I had to be a parent. Was that too much to ask?"

"So, you feel you deserve what happened for running away?"

Clearwater nodded. "Maybe I do, sir. By now, they've gotten word I died.

I know Melanie, my oldest sister, hates me because I left. I keep wondering if maybe I shouldn't tell them that I'm alive again."

"They're going to need someone to set an example for them," the colonel said. "Show them how to be a man. Your sister can't do that. Young boys who grow up without a man in their life tend to end up in prison."

Clearwater sighed.

"I haven't set much of an example for them so far."

"So start setting a better one," the colonel answered. "You still have time to do that. And what about your sisters? It won't be long until men start trying to court them. You have a responsibility to be there. They'll need your permission to marry. You owe it to them to vet any man who shows interest. Make sure he's someone who will take care of them. I don't believe you can wear that uniform if you're the kind of man who would run from that responsibility."

Clearwater looked down at himself. "Maybe I shouldn't wear the brown. If my dad wasn't a Solar Cross recipient, they'd have never let me into Hell's Gate. If it weren't for that, they wouldn't have even let me pass."

"No." The colonel held up a finger. "Your dad could get you into the program. But if you made it through, you did that on your own. How many tries did it take you? One? Two?"

Clearwater hung his head. "Four," he whispered.

"You went through Hell's Gate *four* times?"

"Yeah. Pretty pathetic, I know." Clearwater uttered a sad laugh. "I wouldn't have even got through the fourth time if they hadn't graded me on a curve."

The colonel held up a hand. He began to say something before stopping. He needed another try before words came out. "Pathetic? I never met a man who would subject himself to that hell *four times*. I wouldn't do Hell's Gate four times if I was one of the instructors. That's something special right there."

Special? Special kind of failure maybe. He doubted the colonel could understand. Special forces, apparently able to charm a princess and her handmaidens into ownership and apparently respected by everyone who knew him. How could he understand? Probably never failed anything in his life. He would have probably passed Hell's Gate on his first try.

"I did," the colonel answered. "When the thought is about you, it's particularly hard not to notice it. But you can't go through life comparing yourself to other people. They're not living your life. *You* are. You think they finally let you through because of your father. Has it occurred to you that maybe they let you through because you wouldn't give up?"

Clearwater looked up at him.

"Hell's Gate is there to find men based on ability and *dedication*. To go through four times is pretty damn dedicated. Maybe they let you through because they saw something special in you. Maybe they saw a man who would keep going after everyone else had given up. Someone who could be counted on *because* he would keep going. Had that occurred to you?"

Clearwater took another drink and shook his head. The colonel reached over to refill his glass again. "Think you're father got his cross by quitting?"

Clearwater smiled. "I don't know." He forced a chuckle. "They never even told us what he did."

"What?" the colonel asked, a hint of anger creeping into his tone.

"They never told us." Clearwater shrugged. "Just gave us his medal, a flag, and the emperor's thanks. The rest was classified."

The colonel sat up straight. "Let's find out."

"Sir?"

"When you're awarded the cross, you join the Order. When a new member joins the Order, each living brother receives a notice. So we know of our new brother and what they did. As a commando, I have absolute secret clearance. So my versions have no redactions. What was your father's name?"

Clearwater sat up straight in the chair. "Walter Clearwater."

"Andira?" The colonel glanced upward.

"Found it," she answered.

The colonel stared into his NOD. "Oh," he remarked. "I see why you weren't told. Still not right. But I understand."

"Sir?" Clearwater urged, moving to the edge of his chair.

The colonel held up a finger as he continued reading. Finally his attention returned to the room, and he looked at Clearwater. "What I'm about to tell you is classified absolute secret. If you go around blabbing, you could get us both in a lot of trouble. But you deserve to know. You weren't told the details because your father died assisting the Corps."

"Dad was helping the Corps?" Clearwater asked, not quite believing the statement.

"During the Tethren Incident, one of our operatives was trapped behind enemy lines. I can't tell you what he was doing, but your father's unit was the closest that could assist him. So when asked, your father volunteered to take a section of his men and get him out. Our guy was hiding in a small Tethren city. When they couldn't find him, the Tethren started leveling the city. Killing their people just to make sure they got him.

"I guess your father couldn't just watch innocent people dying. Even if they were the enemy's people. He attacked the force demolishing the city. Your father and some of his men ended up cut off and surrounded. He broke a hole and held the position while his men escaped. Wounded several times before he succumbed."

Clearwater hung on every word as he imagined the scene unfolding before him. Dad in his *Brutus* against a tide of the enemy.

"Your father died saving his men, our operative, and hundreds of thousands of innocent people. People who would never know his name or what he did for them. But he did it because it was the right thing to do."

The colonel went to take a drink before realizing his glass was empty, and he refilled it.

"It's not right that you weren't told," the colonel said with a sigh. "But now you know. Your father left you one hell of a legacy. Four runs at Hell's Gate tells me you're capable of living up to it. If you choose to."

The colonel took a final drink and rose to his feet. Clearwater did the same.

"I need to get back to the girls now," the colonel said, laying a hand on Clearwater's shoulder. "I'm not a counselor, and you should speak to one when we get home."

Clearwater saw a number light up in his NOD.

"If you need someone to talk to, you can call that number. It may take me time to get in touch. But I will."

Clearwater nodded. "Thank you, sir."

"It gets better, Lieutenant. The rest is up to you."

CHAPTER
17A

As Clearwater left the office, Panzer stepped out to see Rhoxx coming toward him. Panzer watched the two meet, and they pressed themselves against the wall to pass the kodaz. A tremble rattled through the deck as Rhoxx covered the distance.

"Bosss."

"Something to report?" Panzer asked.

Rhoxx nodded. "Andeera finisssh repair, compresssssion drive. Calibratin' sssstealt' sssssysstem now."

"You came all the way here to tell me that?" Panzer asked, not buying it for a second.

"No. Come checkin' on you, and new lway."

He might have suspected. Panzer crossed his arms and leaned back against the wall, puffing deep on the cigar.

"I'd say we're doing fine."

"But?" Rhoxx pressed.

Rhoxx was no telepath. He lacked the combination of senses that allowed kurai to mimic metapsionic empathy. But he didn't miss anything. Panzer sighed and peered down the corridor, ensuring none of the girls had popped out of the armory. Not that he expected any of them would.

"Here I just gave that kid a lecture like I've got life all figured out while wondering if I've made a mistake."

Rhoxx's eyes opened wider, and he turned his head toward the armory. The kodaz quickly brought his gaze back. "What t'e problem? It bein' ssso long ssssince you do t'e horizontal happy, you forgettin' where you pork sssword be goin' in?"

Panzer rolled his eyes. "No." He stopped before angling his head toward Rhoxx. "Pork sword?"

"What?" Rhoxx shrugged his big shoulders. "Don't be lookin' me like t'at. Not bein' my fault you humans wantin' call you gentles any'tin' but 'em actual name."

Panzer brought his hand up to rub his eyes.

"Sssso. What wron'?"

"After pork sword? Forget it."

"You not brin' it up, not wantin' talk about it," Rhoxx pressed. "Come on."

Panzer reached out to their minds. The three of them had already developed a new insecurity—being away from him. Simmonne would especially be clingy. Very clingy. That did not bother him. In truth he found it endearing, but it added fuel to what did bother him.

"Rhoxx, when we get back to the fleet, we're going to have to launch a major operation. I think I have everything we need to do worked out. But it will be big, and it's going to be so quick that it's going to be sloppy. We will lose a lot of people. And if half the things Anagram told me are true, there are going to be some pretty damn dark days ahead."

Panzer turned back to Rhoxx before continuing, "If I walked in there right now and asked any one of those girls for her soul, I'm pretty sure she'd find a way to pluck it out and put it in a box for me. What's going to happen to them if I get killed?"

The shift in Rhoxx's feelings caused Panzer's eyes to narrow, and he spoke before Rhoxx could answer. "What the hell about that makes you so happy?"

Rhoxx's eyes turned upward as he shook his head. "You know, sssimple sssolution, be not get killed."

"Well, I don't exactly plan on it. But the possibility does exist."

Rhoxx compacted himself like a dog in a box, hooking his head around and bending his spine so he could gaze toward the armory. "Ever sssoldier, live wit' it," Rhoxx said once he had turned and sat. "May not come home, leave loved ones wit'out him. Alwayss been, lways be. Every sssoldier bride live wit' it, too. Ever sssoldier child. But you waitin' life be perfect, you never goin' live."

Panzer glared before nodding. Rhoxx was right. He usually was.

"You knowin'. Commandant not lettin' you be commando, anymore."

"Yeah, I know. Not all that broken up about it either. Just not sure where to go from here."

"You alway wantin' you own ssship. Go Armadas?"

Panzer shrugged. "Don't know if my rank would transfer for that. They'd have to put me in as a captain. I don't think they're going to give a battleship, or even a cruiser, to someone who's never commanded anything larger than this picket."

Panzer glanced down, finding the source of the audible clacking as Rhoxx tapped a claw on the deck. "Maybe emperor help wit' it."

Panzer let out a loud scoff, using it to stifle a laugh. "Assuming his head doesn't explode at me having his daughter. Don't know that I'm going to have any capital with him. Besides, a command like that should be earned. Not given."

"Maybe, time ssstop be sssoldier," Rhoxx offered. "Go home, be family man. You havin' plenty money, be livin' on."

"I can't do that," Panzer answered. "You know that."

Rhoxx sighed. "I can be hopin'."

"In the meantime, think I'm going to buy a planet in the Iron Stars, terraform it and build a nice big house on it."

Rhoxx's neck lowered, dragging his head down with it as he peered up at Panzer. "Becomin', baron?"

"No," Panzer answered. "No, don't think I want anyone else living there. Build a swamp room for you, couple of domiciles for the brothers. Have the rest for the girls and me. Maybe a hive satellite—more secure."

"Ssssoundin' good," Rhoxx answered, rising back up. "And t'en?"

"I don't know what then."

Rhoxx drew in closer, turning a single big eye to him. Panzer stuck out his neck in response, glaring right back into it. "Where be Colonel Panssser, and what you be doin' wit' him?"

Panzer leaned back against the wall, waving a hand. "Yeah I know. I'm sorry to say I don't have a fully detailed plan for this. Not yet. Still working on it. But, we're going to have to get everyone home first."

Panzer gave Rhoxx time to say anything else, and he did. "You t'inkin' 'bout Elsssa?"

It was somewhat disturbing sometimes how someone who wasn't a telepath could be that intuitive. Panzer smiled, scratching an itch at his brow. "Yes. I keep wondering what she would think of them. If they'd get along."

"Elsssa never did be meetin' a ssstranger. I believe ssshe be watchin' you from sssomewhere. I bettin' ssshe very happy for you. And one day, bein' t'oussandss year from now, when ssshe sssee you again, ssshe be happy meetin' 'em."

The thought was enough for a smile. There weren't many believers left among the kodaz. Most of them gave up worship of Avun long ago to worship his family. Once they were ready for the idea that the Rhinegraves were not gods, most of them seemed to lose interest in gods at all. But Rhoxx believed. Avun Who Is Many, the one god with many faces, who had revealed himself to all peoples in the way he meant them to know him.

"Was there anything else?" As soon as Panzer asked the question, he sensed mischief.

"I ju' be t'inkin'."

"That can't be good," Panzer said, firing the preemptive shot. Rhoxx let out a snort. "I know I'm going to regret this, but what are you thinking?"

"The Rosssse. Ssshe you property now, right?"

Panzer gave a single nod. "Yes."

"Sssso." Rhoxx held up a claw. "Mean, ever'tin' ssshe havin' now belongin' you."

"Yes." Panzer gave another nod.

Rhoxx wiggled his claw. "Ssso. You ownin' her title too?"

"Oh no." Panzer held his breath, leaning against the wall.

"We callin' you Prinsssess Panssser now?"

"I hate you so much." Panzer shook his head, though he tried not to laugh.

Deep, reverberating chortles escaped Rhoxx's jaw while Panzer rolled his eyes. "I knew something like that was coming, and I still walked into it."

"It okay, be laughin'."

"I am laughing. This is me laughing," Panzer remarked without expression on his face.

Rhoxx's smile slowly faded before he asked the question. "You bein' in armory again tonight?"

Panzer glanced toward the armory before nodding. "Yes. Once they're asleep. Still have to figure out what Anagram did to my Hellbore. And if I think about the mission in bed, I'm liable to wake Simmonne. The three of them don't need to worry about this."

"Well." Rhoxx tilted his head. "Be tryin' get sssome sleep, 'fore mission. Be givin' you privasssy now. Just be remember, what plug into what."

"Thanks, Rhoxx," Panzer quipped. "I'll do that."

Panzer did not move immediately from the wall. Rhoxx had a point. The responsible thing to do would be to stay home. Simmonne, Jennifer, and Julie, they needed him now. He indulged in the fantasy. Build that house, spend the days pursuing entertainment, live easy, wake up in the morning and not have to be somewhere. Take a weapon out of his vault and shoot it just for fun. Just to practice, competing with himself rather than someone shooting back. The war with the Vaar would be the largest in history. Maybe he'd had enough small pies that he could pass on the big one.

With a breath he shook his head. That wasn't the man he was. That wasn't the man the three of them had fallen for. If he ever had children, that wasn't the example he would set for them. Life had to be more than existing another day. Nowhere in his character was the ability to sit home while others went to war. But now he had an obligation to live through it.

A broken sword slipped into his mind. Nuset said he would know when it was time to mend it. Was this it? The old kurai only ever did things like that for a reason. It was a riddle, challenge, problem, whatever. He did it for a reason, and figuring out why was the lesson.

He could feel Simmonne wishing for him to come back, Julie beginning to wonder where he went, Jennifer wishing he would come and teach her some more.

Whatever he did, he had to live. He took his time walking back to the armory. Let the girls anticipate his return a bit longer. He was not used to having other people on the ship. This time he'd remember to close the doors.

CHAPTER
17B

SIMMONNE LOOKED DOWN AT herself. That lieutenant just got an eyeful. She was still blushing as she recalled his quizzical look. What was his name? Cleanwater? She caught that his first name was Jonathan. The moment he announced himself, she tried to hide behind Master, only for his grip to keep her in place.

She was a naive girl, and she knew she was naive. But she was not stupid. She knew the reputation of nobility and the throes of excess to which they were sometimes disposed. She had heard the stories, even managed to see some of the astranet videos of those parties that had leaked out. Wild festivities of sex, drugs, memory sharing, and other indulgences. So much of the titled aristocracy considered the Mandrakes the paternal prudes for just how little they indulged. At least the lieutenant was a nobleman. Nobles had a sense of discretion.

Her eyes opened a bit wider as she stood upright. He *was* a nobleman, wasn't he? Oh, of course he was nobility. The titled aristocracy gave their children ancient names. It hinted at their long lineages and the endurance of their dynasties through the ages. Surely no subject parents would be pretentious enough to give their son an ancient name like Jonathan.

She looked down at herself again, to her shoes. She and the Twins had to beg for this much just to keep their feet off the cold metal floors. She was accustomed to high heels, but not this high or with such high arches. The chain linking her ankles was the clue. The shoes were an additional hobble. It was hard enough to walk in these, let alone try to run. Like the hobble itself, they were locked to her. She begged for them and now she had them, until he decided she could take them off.

Simmonne jumped as her chains contracted. Her ankles snapped together as her wrists met behind her. Robbed of her balance, she fell, but someone caught her. Her shocked cry was devoured by the bit firmly between her lips. Her heels slid on the floor, and turning her head aside, she saw Julie in the same condition as both moved back to Master's embrace. His hand reclaimed her breast as the other uncoiled the leash from her shoulders to reattach to his belt.

She tried to speak, only for the vibration between her lips to remind her that he had denied the privilege when he left the room. So instead she concentrated.

Master, I know I have to be naked. But did you have to expose me to a stranger?

Couldn't I have just stood behind you?

She sensed that predatory mirth and lack of sympathy for her humiliation. *"He didn't know."*

Her head twitched. How could he not? He looked right at her. Master's finger tapped gently at her temple.

"He saw you in a pahri. Besides, he doesn't have the security clearance to be on this ship. He'll be subject to SMP before he's allowed to leave."[24]

So he didn't see and would never know what he didn't see.

"He'll remember that he met you. I won't take that from him, and he'll remember the conversation we just had. But that's it."

Simmonne relaxed her muscles, and Julie reclaimed her place under his right arm. There was something titillating about what just happened but nothing she actually wanted to explore.

Assuming she had any choice in the matter.

Barely aware anything had happened at all, Jennifer was still shooting holograms. Simmonne eyed her with a bit of curiosity. The handling of weapons was pretty high on the Sylvanni list of unladylike behavior. Simmonne was surprised Master had allowed it. He did not like it, not even a little. But he did allow it.

"No. I don't like it. But they've been through a lot. If shooting imaginary Vaar helps her cope, I'll tolerate it. For now."

So, he was helping her cope. Simmonne grinned around the bit.

What if I want to cope by wearing clothes once in a while?

"Nice try."

Simmonne looked over at Julie, who dragged her nails gently back and forth over the arm around her. Simmonne had become one of them. The very moment she let her mind wander, she was back in the bedroom. Did he do this to her? Was he why she couldn't stop thinking of sex? Or was it her? It was easier to assume he was putting things in her head. He had the power, so why wouldn't he use it? She would in his position.

"Colonel," Andira interrupted, prompting Simmonne to look up as Master did the same. "Jenna Prideaux has left the infirmary and is approaching your position. She managed to deactivate my peripheral body. Without it, I can only stop her by engaging the ship's internal defenses."

Jenna. The air fled Simmonne's lungs as she pushed herself back harder against Master. Jenna would lose her mind. She had hoped for a little more time before breaking the news to her.

---

24 SMP is short for Secure Memory Protocols, a catchall term for a variety of systems used to prevent soldiers and other personnel from retaining knowledge that is above their security clearance. SMPs delete selected information from the host's mind, memory index, and instructs their NCP (if applicable) to delete the same information. All soldiers are required to submit to SMP as needed.

"I told you to keep her in suspension," Master grumbled.

"I'm sorry, sir. She has a nanotech modification I did not detect that prevented me from maintaining her suspension."

Simmonne was not the only one with an icy grip on her heart. She felt it from the Twins now. Julie shook, and Jennifer's hand trembled as she laid her pistol on the counter.

"I'll get rid of her."

Simmonne felt the Twins' fear. But where it might have added to hers, it triggered something else. The three of them lived in constant fear of that woman. Lived under her tyranny. Not today. Not any other day. Not anymore.

Master? She drew his gaze. *Please? I need to do this.*

He did not like that at all. But of course he didn't. He was Master. To speak for her, to protect her, that was his place. But with a sigh, he uncoiled his arm from around her, deactivated her restraints, and plucked the bit from between her lips.

Now Simmonne could sense the storm of anger drawing toward the armory. Jennifer moved behind Master, grabbing her leash as if to tie herself down against a terrible wind. Simmonne watched Jennifer's hands shake, causing the metal links to rattle.

Be strong, girls.

For an instant, Simmonne thought of seeking permission to dress. Or at least to deactivate the chains. But she dismissed both ideas. This was her life now. If Jenna wanted to be a part of it, she would have to make peace with it.

But as the storm drew closer and Simmonne's heart raced faster, her confidence waned. Her hands were shaking now. Maybe it would be better if Master handled it. She stilled her hands and focused on the doors. No. She could do this.

Jenna never called for the doors to open. She never activated the chime. The heavy doors let out a groan, and Simmonne felt the psionic ripples as Jenna pried them apart. The moment there was space enough between the metal hulks, Jenna darted into the room. Simmonne was not even a T-1. Under ordinary circumstances, she would not feel a telepathic intrusion into her mind. But Jenna's sudden assault was so tactless, so overwhelming, that Simmonne's knees buckled, and she fell into Master as the information was ripped out of her mind through her eyes. The events of the day and the previous night. It flashed through faster than she could parse it. The ripping fabric of her dress, the jingling of chains, the touch on her flesh, and the bite of cold. Jenna had seized it all in a moment.

Dizzy now, Simmonne blinked, only barely registering the fury in Jenna's eyes.

"You son of a bitch!"

Jenna held out her hand. The pistol with which Jennifer had been blasting hologram Vaar flew across the room to find her grip.

"Jenna, no!"

By the time Simmonne got the shout out, Master had acted. He threw off the leash and charged. His left hand clamped down on Jenna's arm, forcing the weapon to the ceiling. His right hand clapped audibly around her neck. A second later, a tremor ripped through the room as Jenna's back was slammed into the doors of the armory. Jenna's feet dangled a meter from the floor. But she did not endure the counterattack unanswered. Jenna swung a fist at Master's elbow. When that did not work, she brought her leg up, kicking at the joint in the hopes of breaking his grip.

As Simmonne recovered from the mental assault, she watched Jenna's futile attempt to fight. Jenna was tough; Simmonne knew that. She knew how to fight, but Master would squish her like an angry, tiny insect. A sudden wave of nausea washed over Simmonne. When physical means did not work, Jenna tried to use her mind, only for Master to clamp down on her with the same. Jenna was even further out of her league there. She was far from being in the league of the strongest. She would have better odds fist-fighting him.

Simmonne thought briefly about saying something. About shouting at them to stop. But she didn't. The more she thought about it, the more she realized she didn't want to. Especially not after having Jenna simply rip the intimate moments out of her mind. The fear she had felt—the fear she had felt in the Twins. All the things they never got to do because Jenna wouldn't allow it. All the things they never got to experience because Jenna said no. The fear the three of them had of the universe because of her. Simmonne was not alone in feeling satisfaction as Master showed Jenna who the stronger of the two was.

"So, that might have been a bit of an overreaction," Master commented as Jenna writhed. Jenna's hate only intensified, but her struggles were weakening. She knew she had lost but wasn't yet prepared to accept it. "With your augments, you can hold your breath for, what, an hour? Maybe two?" Master asked. "There are two ways this can end. Option one, you release the sidearm. I'll let you breathe, and we can talk like civilized people. Option two, I stand here and strangle you to death, throw you *back* in the deep-fryer, and we try this again when you get out."

Jenna was still fighting, each strike of her fist or foot creating audible claps in the room, but she wasn't going anywhere. Simmonne felt the resolve drain. Jenna's legs stopped kicking and dangled beneath her. Her hand opened so the pistol hung from a single finger. Master seized it, taking it apart and letting the pieces fall to the floor. The mesh bag that had caught Jennifer's spent cores spilled open, and the small cylinders rolled through the room.

He drew Jenna back from the wall but did not release her immediately. Perhaps saying something telepathically, perhaps letting his action speak for itself. Jenna's face had turned red, but only when her arms dangled at her side did Master set her back down.

Jenna gasped for air as her hand moved up to her throat. Master returned to Simmonne and the Twins, holding out a hand to call the leash from the floor.

"Try it," Master taunted, turning back to Jenna. "See what happens."

"Simmonne." Jenna's voice was gravelly now. "Come with me. We're leaving."

Simmonne did not answer.

"Simmonne?" Jenna asked. She stepped forward. "Come on. We'll get you out of here. Take you home. Your father will deal with him."

"I'm not going anywhere," Simmonne finally answered.

Jenna came closer, now in control of her breathing. "Simmonne, he's just done something to your mind. I'm not sure what yet, but I can fix it. Just come with me."

Jenna reached toward her, and Simmonne stepped back.

"I think you have your answer," Master said.

"You stay out of this!" Jenna snapped at him. "They're coming with me, Colonel. Right now! And whatever you've done to them, the emperor will know."

"My mind has never been more clear," Simmonne rebutted her.

Jenna's expression softened as she turned back to Simmonne. "Oh, honey, it could be very subtle. You wouldn't even know he did it. I'll need time to find it and fix it. But I will. Just come with me."

Simmonne sighed. She was a fool to think there was even the slightest possibility Jenna might accept it. She could not be reasoned with. "Jenna, I think you should go."

"I'm not leaving you with this monster."

Simmonne did not think about what happened next. Jenna could have easily dodged, blocked, or otherwise avoided it. But she seemed too shocked to do anything when a loud clap sounded in the room.

From her heart, to her mind, to her hand. The palm of Simmonne's hand likely hurt more now than did Jenna's face. But Jenna slowly touched her cheek with a dumbfounded look in her eyes.

Simmonne had never before felt such *hate* as she glared at Jenna and the stupid look on her face.

"Master killed the ones who murdered my guards," Simmonne began at a whisper, but became louder with each word. "He fought a Vaar warlord while all I could do was cower. He risked his life to save *you* and the Twins from that ship and nearly died doing it. And so help me, Jenna, you *will not* talk about him like that."

Simmonne's pulse raced in her ears. She wanted to strike again, but the admonishment she received days ago resonated as clearly as the pain in her hand. Another strike like that, and Simmonne was likely to break her hand.

"Master?" Jenna whispered the word in disbelief as the anger returned to her eyes. She faced the Twins. "Girls, you're coming with me."

They said nothing and hid completely behind Master, clutching his vest. They were still afraid of her, but they had their giant shield to protect them now. Simmonne was not afraid. She stepped around him to look face to face with Jenna.

"You should go," Simmonne said, pointing at the doors.

Jenna glared up at Master. "You are going to pay for this, Colonel. Release them. Now."

He crossed his arms. "You know, you're not just upset to find them here," Master answered. "Since we've met, I've sensed some kind of deep, personal animosity from you. Of course it only got worse after the *Rothburg*, but you hated me well before that. Have I wronged you in some way I don't know about? Where did this deep-seated hatred for me come from?"

A vein bulged in Jenna's forehead. "I know who you are. Victor von Rhinegrave."

Simmonne's eyes lit up. Even Jenna knew? Were she and the Twins the only people in the Empire who didn't know who he was?

"Your family." Jenna pointed at him. "Your family reduced me to a slave before I was even born. Men of your family who treat women like cattle and think only of themselves. I left your realm to make my own life. I have served the Mandrakes my entire adult life. I've watched your family hoard all the wealth and all the power they could get their bloody hands on. All of the Rhinegraves have conspired for years against the Mandrakes, hungry to take a throne they don't deserve. All to fuel their greed. And now, after His Majesty trusted me with his daughters, you came along. And now I find them like *this*." Jenna gestured to Simmonne's neck and the leash dangling from her collar. "Hatred doesn't begin to describe it," Jenna spat.

This was the first time Simmonne had ever felt him angry, and it caused her to tremble as Master took a step closer to Jenna. "You don't like me because of my family? Fine. You don't like how I live my life? I don't care. You don't like how I treat women? Relax, girl, you're not my type. But you're going to stand there and accuse *me* of being a monster? You have regulated every day of their lives. But you never let them live. How would it hurt anyone for them to have a drink? Or to eat a piece of bacon in the morning?"

Master angled his chin as he glared down at Jenna.

"You didn't like it at home, so you left because you wanted to make your own life. You were allowed to leave and make that choice, yet you've spent their whole lives taking choices away from them. You've robbed them of any confidence they may have ever had and given all three of them more insecurities than should ever be found in one person. Oh yes, there's a monster here. But it's not me."

Undaunted, Jenna took a step closer to him, matching his glare. "I chased after them when they were toddlers. I wiped their tears when they bumped their knees or broke their toys. I have bathed them, groomed them, and protected them every day of their lives. I kept them from making decisions they couldn't make for themselves. Kept them from making decisions they'd regret by keeping men like you away from them. I did not do all of that just to hand them over to the likes of *you*."

"It's not your decision, Jenna!" Simmonne screamed, stamping her foot. Anger came at her from two directions, overpowering anything she may have been feeling inside. "This is *my* choice. *Our* choice. Not my father's, and not yours. And you will not take this from me."

"This isn't your choice!" Jenna spat, reaching for the leash. Her other hand pointed up at Master. "He is giving you no choices, Simmonne. *None.* A man isn't supposed to treat you like this. I know I've taught you better than that. He's in your mind, honey. He did this to you. You have to fight it."

Simmonne pulled back slowly until Jenna let go. She briefly closed her eyes and took a breath. Jenna couldn't understand because she didn't want to. All the pathetic men Jenna had tried to push her toward. Supposed men who were scared little boys wearing the skin of adults. Men who asked her leading questions to figure out what she liked because they were too scared to say what they wanted. Men who would only flirt in the most painfully careful ways because she might not be receptive. Men who made only the most careful first moves so they could pretend it was nothing if she did not reciprocate. Cowards afraid that she might reject them.

It was so pathetic when men were intimidated by her. Made all the worse by her ability to feel it. She was not big, or strong, or mean. Nothing was intimidating about her, yet they were afraid of her. That was the kind of man Jenna wanted for her. A man who could never hurt her because he was too weak to hurt anything. A bitter part of her wished some of those men could see her now, and what they could have had if they had been man enough.

She saw the light of understanding trying to peek through the haze in her former handmaiden's bloodshot eyes as she read every thought.

"Simmonne." Jenna's tone became more conciliatory. "I know something about this appeals to you. I don't understand it, but I know. But Simmonne, he'll never love you. Men like him don't know how. You're nothing to him. Just a new toy to play with until you break or grow old and he tosses you aside for another. This is my fault. You're too young. I've sheltered you too much."

Simmonne shook her head slowly. To argue this any further was pointless.

"Simmonne. Your father—"

"Will not be emperor forever." Simmonne's efforts to be calm did not hold, and her voice gradually rose to a shout. "Do you think Steven will keep you around if I complain? Do you think Raymond will care? You are *my* servant. I am not yours, and it's time you acted like it. If you can't do that, then *get out of my life!*"

Jenna seemed to shrink and lowered her arms to her sides. The hate quickly returned as she glared at Master. "This isn't over."

Jenna turned and left, and Simmonne let out a quiet exhale, rubbing her fingers against her aching palm as both hands trembled. She felt the Twins' arms wrap around her before Master took hold of her wrist. In an instant, the pain was gone.

"I know that was hard for you."

"No, Master," Simmonne answered, standing straight. She would not let it be difficult. "If she can't handle it, that's her problem."

Master reached past her, pointing two fingers at the ajar doors and drawing them closed. "Andira, send a couple of bots down to fix my doors."

"Already dispatched, sir."

A strange calm came over her as the gentle tug on her leash drew her against him. Approval. Wonderful, delicious approval radiated over her like a warm blanket. She turned to wrap her arms around Master and press her face into him. She belonged to him now, and no one would take her away. *No one.*

CHAPTER
17C

ONCE LEAVING THE COLONEL'S office, Clearwater headed back toward the infirmary. There were no guest quarters on this ship. The closest thing were holding cells, and he was not about to use one of them. The walk gave him time, and his mind ran through what he had learned.

The things the colonel told him were classified. Absolute secret. There was no higher clearance.[25] Only agents of the emperor could obtain information that secret, or judge if someone else required access to it. Unauthorized possession of that information was bad. If it came out that he knew, it could cause problems. Should he tell the family what he learned?

He stopped. How could he *not* tell them? What Dad did, the answers to why he never came home—how could Clearwater possibly withhold that from them? He resumed his walk, unconsciously rubbing his left arm. Back home, a common warning was that the quickest way to kill a secret was to tell a woman. That would advise against telling Melanie or Froggy. But what about his brothers? They might be legionnaires one day, too. Did they not deserve to know what Dad did?

Maybe he could tell Melanie. She was mature, and it would mean the world to her to know. The rest were too young. Too young to really understand what the consequences could be. He would have to wait until they were older.

He stopped again.

He would tell them when they were older. If he saw them again. Just because he was alive now, didn't mean he'd live to see home. The Vaar had already killed him once. They could certainly do it again. By now, they had received word he died on ND-31. Poor Melanie, having to console them once again. He should send them a message as soon as they were among friendlies again.

He continued on. Froggy would have been the most devastated. She always did like him best.

He entered the infirmary to find that the lights had been dimmed. His first impulse was to look for Taula, and he found her lying on her table. She

---

25 The hierarchy of the Empire's security clearance ratings progresses from secret, restricted secret, high secret, most secret, to absolute secret.

was on her side with one arm curled under a small pillow. Her eyes were closed, and she breathed in a slow rhythm. Asleep.

Lantai could sleep like cats, better even, especially lantai of pet blood-lines. They could will themselves to sleep effectively on command. Pets, as far as he knew, would do so any time they had downtime to ensure they could spring back up with plenty of energy whenever their master called. Yet at the same time, lantai could go much longer without sleep than an un-augmented human. Funny, alike in so many ways, yet different in so many others.

Clearwater watched her, wincing as he recalled the previous night. Maybe it was because he wasn't that smart, but he could not figure her out. She was easily the prettiest girl who had ever shown interest in him—the only one for that matter. She had been the one to initiate, well, everything.

His eyes roamed the blue streaks in her hair. Her mother was a lantai. The blue streaks in her hair, the points in her ears, and the glow of her eyes. Except for those superficial things, he'd seen none of that heritage come through. Except just now finding that she had her mother's ability to sleep at will. She had her career, dressed like a professional, and she was assertive. If it weren't for the blatant markers of her lineage, one would never guess she was from the Dominion. There were definitely no lantai who would do what she did to Jaegda.

He may not have known all that much, but he did know a few things. Lantai did not put the same price on physical relations as humans. It was less an act of intimacy to them, and more a way of simply finding some joy. Which was it when she tried to initiate? Was the first time just her trying to have a good evening? Was last night her just trying to cheer him up? Or, did she actually see something in him?

If she were to wake up right now and see him looming over her, she might find that creepy. Quietly he backed away until sitting down at his table. Maybe he should have asked the colonel for some advice about women. He obviously knew what he was doing. Clearwater smiled at the thought of trying to put Taula on a leash. She'd probably slap him if he dared suggest it. Slap him with something heavy.

He swung his legs over the table to face away from Taula and looked into his NOD. Should he send a message home? What if he did, then died again? If they couldn't bring him back the second time, they would have lost him twice.

Deep breaths. He had to call. By now HECS or DOMR were already involved.[26] He needed to get proof of life to them yesterday.

---

26 HECS is an acronym for His Excellency's Child Service, the department of the Dominion government responsible for handling matters pertaining to orphaned children. The Department of Marital Records handles primarily matters pertaining to marriage. The organization maintains a department responsible for adult and near-adult women and girls with no SMA to claim ownership of them. Given

>>COMPOSE MESSAGE / SIMULATE VISUAL
CHOOSE DESTINATION FROM CONTACTS?
>>HOME
READY FOR RECORDING.

He wasn't sure how to begin, so he said the first thing that came to mind.

"Hi everyone. It's me."

It was a start. What did he say next? Oh yeah, probably should tell them he was actually alive.

"By now, they've told you I was killed in action. I was. The Vaar managed to collect my corpse and reanimate me. You all wouldn't believe what's happened since then or where I am now. Ryan. David."

His NOD was monitoring his face to create a video of him for the message, so he smiled.

"I'm on a commando's ship. That's how I escaped. He wasn't there to rescue me, but now I'm here. I wish I could show you some of it. But, I think that would get me in trouble. They'll probably wipe it all from my memory. This message may even get censored before it leaves the military network. But I had to tell you. Or try to. There's more. Froggy. Guess who's on the ship with me?"

He paused to give her time to guess.

"The Imperial Rose is on the ship! And the Katyusha Twins." He stopped as he thought of the four in the armory. "The commando who rescued me is taking care of them. Keeping them safe while the Vaar are marauding."

His fists clenched. He was the worst big brother in the Empire. How did the idea only now occur to him? "I'll try to get you a corpograph from the Imperial Rose and the Twins while we're still on the same ship. I'll try."

It was becoming harder to hold the smile, and he let it fade.

"Guys, I don't know when I'll be able to come home. I've . . . learned some things since the last time I saw you. I can't talk about them like this. But when I see you again, I'll tell you. If I get home, there's going to be some changes. Melanie, I know this has probably been especially hard on you. If HECS and DOMR are there, be sure to show them this message. I know the rest of you are being good for her. I promise, I'll see you as soon as I can. I love you all."

>>END RECORDING
>>SET AUTO-SEND
SPECIFY AUTO-SEND CONDITION.
>>AVAILABLE CARRIER
MESSAGE WILL BE SENT ONCE CARRIER IS AVAILABLE.

It was a short message, but what else was he supposed to say? So much

---

that both often deal with broken families, the two agencies often work together.

of what he wanted to say had to be said in person. He had to say it to them. They all had to know. He had a lot to fix.

With a sigh he turned back to Taula. He didn't mention her, but what would he say? What were they?

His stomach rumbled, and a moment later he was on his feet. At the printer he stood with his hand on the wall, leaning in. What sounded good? Clearwater let out a shocked cry when he felt tiny claws scaling his pant leg, and in a moment Gulliver was on his shoulder. Clearwater looked down at the tiny rodent squeaking at him.

Gulliver knew what a printer was, didn't he? Probably not. He just knew that food came out of it, so here he was. Clearwater scanned the printer's optical port.

>>*CHEESE*
SPECIFY TYPE AND QUANTITY.

Clearwater threw up his hands. What was he, a cheese monger?

"I don't know," he whispered. "Cheddar? A hundred grams."

The printer growled and produced the block of requested cheese. Gulliver's eyes followed the block as Clearwater pinched it between his fingers. Side to side, he waved the block in a line, watching the rodent's pink nose and red eyes follow.

"You want it? Want it?" he asked.

Clearwater drew back his arm and shot it forward as if to throw the cheese. But he did not let go. Gulliver looked in the direction of the lie for a moment before turning back to Clearwater. Never had he seen a more unamused face than on that rodent.

"Oh, you're no fun," Clearwater grumbled, handing over the cheese.

Gulliver squeaked happily, grabbing the block with both hands and assailing the cheese. Clearwater turned his attention back to the printer.

Now for his meal. He was hungry, but nothing sounded good. Steak. Steak was always good.

>>*STEAK—3,000 GRAMS*
ERROR—SELECTED STEAK IS TOO LARGE FOR PRINT TERMINAL.

Clearwater rolled his eyes.

>>*SIX STEAKS—500 GRAMS EACH*
SELECT COOK . . .
>>*MEDIUM RARE*
PRINTING . . .

"What are you having?"

"Gah!" Jumping closer to the printer, he startled Gulliver, who emitted a high-pitched shriek. Taula let out a startled cry of her own before jumping back.

Clearwater spun to face her, quickly regaining his calm. Gulliver soon found his, while Taula glared at them both like they were a pair of idiots.

"You scared me," Clearwater said, catching his breath.

"You scared *me!*"

With a deep breath, he turned to motion to the stack of steaks on the printer.

"That's . . ." Taula made a face. "A *lot* of steak."

"Well . . ." He curled his arm.

"Have to feed the muscles," she said with him. "Are you sure you're not using that as an excuse to overeat?"

"Your dad's a soldier," he countered as the machine continued stacking steaks. "He must eat a lot."

"Not as much as you."

Clearwater shrugged. "Well, he's not a legionnaire."

The printer dinged to indicate its task was complete, and he took the steaks out of the machine.

"Besides, I haven't—" He did not get to finish the rest of the statement before Gulliver decided a block of cheese was insufficient. The rodent leaped from his shoulder, only to let out an angry shriek as Clearwater's hand wrapped around him.

"Ha-ha! Soldier's reflexes," Clearwater taunted as he caught Gulliver before he could land on the top steak. He held his fist to force Gulliver to look at him. "This is *my* food."

Taula wrapped her hands around his and took Gulliver. "He's a big meanie, isn't he, Gulliver?" she cooed, bringing the rodent nose to nose with her. Almost as if understanding her, Gulliver answered with a soft growl. "Oh, don't feel bad. He didn't offer to share with me either."

"Did you want something?" Clearwater quickly motioned to the printer.

"I don't know, are you going to pull me away when I try to get it?"

"Um, no." He tried to control his stammer. "I, what did you want?" Trying to balance the stack of steaks with one hand, he pointed to the printer again.

She walked past him and placed her order. Two plates, each with their steak, were made for her. Both were covered in mounds of sugar. She took the first plate and set it on the deck before placing Gulliver down beside it.

"*Eeeeee!*"

Clearwater smiled. If there were a sound for maximum happiness, that was it. While Gulliver attacked the steak, Taula took the second plate, and Clearwater followed her back to her table. He set the stack of steaks beside him while Taula set hers down before walking away.

She returned to the printer before grabbing some kind of cart from the corner of the room. When she returned, she positioned the cart between them before handing him a knife and fork.

"You might need these."

He smiled as he took them and transferred the steaks to the cart.

"So," Taula began, "how are you doing?"

"I'm okay," he answered, keeping his eye on the meat. "Trying not to think about it."

"Is it working?"

Her eyes were on her plate when he looked up. Thinking about her helped. He bit his lip. He couldn't say that. It sounded corny. "Yeah, I think it is."

The steak was as pleasing to his tongue as he expected. It was not the best—not coming from a restaurant printer—but it was good.

"So what happens to you next?" he asked after swallowing. "Now that the colony is gone."

Taula rolled a cut of the steak in the sugar before biting into it. She took her time to chew and answer. "I don't know. My contract was only half-year probationary. After what happened, they'll probably just pay me out. My dad didn't want me to take a job with them to begin with. After this, I doubt he'll renew my contract with them."

Clearwater's eyebrows peaked, and he sat up a bit straighter. He would have thought she was auctor se. Was she not? "So your dad lets you work. He lets you keep the money, doesn't he?"

"Yes." She chuckled softly at the question. "Said if I didn't have a husband by the time I graduated, I'd have to get a job, or it was a waste to send me to school. That and he said I should work for a while so I know what it's like to have a job. I think part of him thought I wouldn't like it."

So she wasn't auctor se. Her father was a lot more permissive than most back home. Let her go to school, let her have a job, and she can decide for herself what to do with the money. Maybe he might not be a nightmare if Clearwater ever met him. He managed to keep his lips together as his jaw dropped. They were on their way to the *Hurricane*. He *was* going to meet the man.

"I suppose they'll send you somewhere to keep fighting," Taula said. "Or maybe you'll get lucky and end up somewhere else."

"Probably not. They'll roll me into another unit, and then, back out there."

Taula had cut her steak into many pieces and was now eating with one hand. Her other hand rested on the bench. In his mind he reached across the table to take her hand and simply hold it as they ate. His hand crept a bit closer to hers. What would her bride price be? She was more than pretty; that would raise it. Education tended to lower it. Attitude could send it either way. Could he afford it?

His hand began to move forward before snapping back as she stood quickly.

"Sorry," she whispered, seeing him jump. "Need more sugar."

Clearwater sighed before looking down at his steak. She came on to him. In the cell she held him, comforted him as a blanket and pillow.

>>*ACTIVATE NERVE HEIGHTENERS*
NERVE HEIGHTENERS ENGAGED
NOMINAL SENSITIVITY

Taula sat back down with a vial of sugar and poured it onto her steak. When she set it down, his hand slid forward to capture hers. His heart was ice as he watched her look down at his hand. She squeezed and used the other to reclaim her fork.

CHAPTER
18A

PLAYTIME WAS OVER. WHILE the girls slept, Panzer did what he could to plan for the task ahead. Six days had passed since he returned from ND-31. After a number of unexpected delays, the ship was ready to go. Andira had announced as much during the morning shower. While he dressed in the uniform of an Armadas officer, he had Andira send probes out of the Basin. Those probes found no Vaar waiting for them. The Basin may have been an obvious hiding spot, but even with millions of them in the galaxy, the Vaar did not have ships to spare. Not while they were dealing with Aetius, who had managed to slow them down for longer than Panzer had expected.

The ship was underway now. He had done what he could, but it did not feel like enough. Each night after the first, he worked while the girls slept, careful to return before they awoke in the morning. He did not actually need to sleep every night, or even every other night, but he could only do so much planning on his own. The flag officers would have to do the rest. Another problem weighed on his mind, and he had no solution for it. The time to find it was slipping away.

Panzer had summoned everyone on the ship to the CIC. Rhoxx held his familiar place on the left side of the center platform with Kassar and Novin on the right. Lieutenant Clearwater and Dr. Gilyard had acknowledged the summons. Miss Prideaux had not. Apparently the common courtesy of answering a message was too much. Panzer had met plagues with more charm than that woman. Per Andira, she had spent the days grumbling in the cargo bay.

"Twenty minutes to safe transmission," Andira announced.

Panzer doubted the Vaar could pick up a transmission from his ship, let alone fix and fire on it. But after the experience with the *Itinerant Hunter*, he was not about to take the risk. Not while the girls were still aboard. Once they were out of weapons range, then they could make a call.

Panzer stood at the center console of the CIC with the girls in front of him. Simmonne had seemed to develop a bit of territoriality about being on his left side. Thus his left arm was around her, while his right bound Jennifer and Julie to him. Sadly, he had to clothe the three of them in preparation. As they were meant to, their collars and manacles blended in as innocuous parts of their pahris. For now he had deactivated the chains, but each remained on their leash attached to his belt. For the old man's sake, Panzer would cloak the chain in public, but that was as far as he was willing to go.

He had never found pretty girls and clothes a worthwhile combination, but it provided some amusement. Amazing the new appreciation one had for basic dignity once it became a privilege. Jennifer and Julie happily seized that privilege while they could. But not Simmonne.

At first she, too, was quite thrilled about the idea of wearing clothes. Panzer easily sensed the part of her that felt so *good* to wear something for the first time in days. But it did not last, and that joy was replaced by a sense of unease. Rather adorably to Panzer, it manifested as Simmonne compulsively stroked the edge of her new cape, her body finding a way to burn off the emotional energy roiling in her head.

In her mind, Simmonne blamed him for her inability to enjoy it. But of course she did. Anytime she did not understand her thoughts and feelings, anytime she found something objectionable in them, she would assume it was his doing. So be it. One could not have all the power without having all the responsibility. All three of them knew, on some level, that he could manipulate their minds. Simmonne was the only one who had truly internalized the possibilities of that truth.

Much more was going on in her head than Simmonne realized. The mind was a thought engine with multiple processing chambers—the subconscious and the conscious chief among them. Most people lacked the self-awareness to have more than a passing acquaintance with what went on in their conscious mind, let alone the subconscious.

More than once, Panzer had contemplated this as a consequence rather than a failing. Sight, smell, hearing—the body's most powerful sensors were all designed to look outward. Taste occupied a middle ground, while touch, alone and outnumbered, was the only one dedicated to looking within.

The part of Simmonne that drank greedily from his feelings—that fed off his energy and wanted so desperately to please him—would not allow her to enjoy it. That part felt guilt. She even went so far as to tell herself that she did not deserve the privilege. But beneath that, in her subconscious, was the real culprit. A taint of fear. That somehow, being allowed to dress meant that the experience was over, and the adventure was ending.

To Jennifer and Julie, it was what it was. But to Simmonne, the dress code was the one rule she took issue with. The one too degrading, too inconvenient, too humiliating. Too much. For Panzer this was neither unacceptable, nor undesirable. It robbed them both of something if acclimating to her new life was too easy for her. But he could not miss the frustrated question she asked in her mind. Never directed at him, yet asked over and over.

Why doesn't he just make me like it?

Panzer smiled sadly as he heard the thought again. Poor Simmonne. It would be easy to feel sorry for her. Raised in a family of fairly strong telepaths, yet limited to empathy, the firsthand knowledge and secondhand experiences must have made life frustrating for her. In her mind, it was a sort of magic she could never learn, only envy. To simply make her like the rule would defeat the point, and she vastly overestimated the ease of changing such a strongly-held opinion.

He had not let go of their minds since denuding them. With that control, he had done a great deal. He had kept their spirits high by ensuring certain recent events did not enter their thoughts. Jennifer in particular seemed to need help with that one. He controlled how or if their bodies reacted to stimuli. He controlled when they felt pain or pleasure and how much of either. He had even gone so far as to begin training their minds and bodies to react in specific ways to his voice. But Simmonne was contemplating something on a different level.

A strong telepath could use many techniques to change a person's opinions and their ways of feeling. Zanga's Impresence, Holder's Debate, and Symon's Directive were but three within his power even when he was diminished. Anagram had promised to make him stronger, and it seemed she had kept her word. Each day he felt a little stronger, and each mind around him felt a little more malleable. But even if he wished to, Panzer could not do what Simmonne was asking. Not in the sweeping, immediate way she imagined. Not now.

Panzer pulled Simmonne a little tighter against him and poured a touch of pleasure into her subconsciousness. He felt her tremble a little. One could not simply throw thoughts into another person's mind and expect them to stick. The thought engine would process and then dismiss it. Just like countless other random, and ultimately meaningless, thoughts that went through on any given day. To give a sensation was easy. To permanently change an opinion, or the emotion tied to an idea, required technique and skill.

Panzer forced a frown off his face. Miner-9 had cut fingers off his telepathic hand. It did not matter how strong the arm was; the hand was still crippled. Anagram may have been able to put the fingers back on the hand, but she could not give back the mastery. Skills required practice, and for over a century, he had been unable to practice many.

Telepaths had their own schools for a reason. A nonlethal punch could still kill a man if he split his skull in the fall. Reckless or poorly controlled telepathy could be just as dangerous. Panzer could not—would not—risk it. He could not do more than he had already done. Nothing that required substantially more than imagination and then projection into their subconscious minds. Simmonne did not realize it, but her belief in his power had done as much to shape her thinking as anything else.

Panzer's head perked up as he caught Jennifer thinking about the *Caustic Reverie*. His left eye closed briefly, and he punted that thought out of her head. He replaced it with a memory of her underneath him. Once sure her mind had grabbed the memory he offered, he backed off. Simmonne had her question, while Julie was making a mental inventory of the things she wanted to take with her when she moved out of the Cathedral. Memory alteration was not something he took lightly. He would have to consider whether or not it was best to take certain memories from them entirely.

A rumble to his left broke his concentration. A belch. A loud, thundering, hot belch that seemed to raise the room's temperature.

"'Ssscusin' me," Rhoxx said ten seconds later after it ended.

All three of the girls made a sound before covering their noses. Panzer chuckled, and Andira worked to exchange the CIC's air.

Skills were fickle things. Panzer needed a test to gauge exactly where those skills stood. That was the problem for which he currently had no solution.

He needed to know before he encountered Indorai or Oul'sor again. Telepathy might be his best, or even his only, weapon. But there was no good test available. The girls would make poor test subjects even if he were willing to risk it. All three were young, naive, and eager to please him. The most difficult thing he had done since ND-31 should have been Miss Prideaux. It should have been at least a little difficult to smash through her mind and disrupt her own metapsionics. But in her blind rage, she had made the task easy. Even so, the physical disparity between them was dwarfed by the telepathic. She was strong, strong enough to pry the doors of his armory despite certainly being on the tail-end of a deep-fryer hangover. But he was a T-13.

That left the illusions he had created for Lieutenant Clearwater. Not trivial but not enough. The kid was young and recently traumatized. He had only his cybernetics and the modicum of telepathic defense training acquired from Hell's Gate. That gave him some protection, but even that was practically none to anyone above T-6. He needed something that involved both the inputs and the outputs of the thought engine, yet he was at a loss to find such a test.

Miss Prideaux *could* make an effective test if he tried it when she was not in a blind rage. Yet, somehow, their dislike for one another did not seem to justify subjecting her to that kind of risk.

Panzer took a deep breath as he felt the stress building within. Simmonne's ability to read him had improved recently, and she did not need his worries. Fortunately, her thoughts would keep her distracted so long as he controlled himself. He needed a break and opened his mind to the room.

His team's attitudes had changed. Kassar, who at first did not care for Simmonne, had adopted a quiet reverence appropriate to his lord's bride. Novin was Novin. Now he would find more excuses not to speak to them unless they spoke to him first. But Panzer could not miss Rhoxx. Were Simmonne not so distracted, she would sense it, too. Most people were ignorant of how many people cared about them—ignorant of how much they cared. For an empath, or a telepath, such ignorance was inexcusable, and Rhoxx had grown very fond of the princess.

Panzer looked down at Simmonne. *"Why are you so determined to be on my left side?"*

Simmonne turned in his grasp. She gently dragged one of her long nails down the left side of his chest. *The heart points to the left, Master.*

Panzer could not help but grin at that one. He returned her to her previous position, sliding his hand beneath one of the cups of her top and giving a gentle squeeze.

He turned to look behind him as the CIC doors opened. Lieutenant Clearwater entered the room with Dr. Gilyard just behind. According to Andira, the lieutenant had spent most of the last several days sleeping. It had done him well, and he looked decisively less corpse-like. Color had worked its way back into his face, and his eyes had lost some of the thousand-meter stare. The doors were closing when Miss Prideaux stepped through them. She did not follow the lieutenant and the doctor as they advanced on the platform. Instead she shot Panzer a fresh, hateful glare, crossed her arms, and leaned against the doorframe.

Panzer had turned forward again when he sensed a rush of nervousness. It came on like freezing rain. Simmonne felt it as well, her entire body going rigid as if someone had just poured ice water down her back.

"Excuse me, Colonel?"

Panzer looked over his shoulder to see Lieutenant Clearwater standing behind him. He held a small object.

"Yes, Lieutenant?"

"Sir, may I address Her Majesty—and Ladies?"

Panzer raised an eyebrow. What did he want? It was prominent in the lieutenant's surface thoughts. Besides, with manners that sharp, how could he say no?

"Very well."

Panzer slid his hand to Simmonne's belly before drawing the girls around him to face the lieutenant. Clearwater eyed the leash before bowing his head.

"Majesty," he began. "My s-s-sister is . . . my sister admires you, Majesty. I was hoping for a corpograph? If, um, if you wouldn't mind?"

I hope you're braver to the Vaar than you are to me.

Panzer frowned when he heard the comment in Simmonne's mind. His reprimand was wrapped in ice. *"Simmonne, he is a man and a combat veteran. Be more respectful."*

The chill sent a visible shudder through her. *I'm sorry, Master.*

"What's her name?" Simmonne asked, taking the slate once she had composed herself.

"Stephanie, but we call her Froggy, Majesty."

Simmonne cocked her head curiously. "Why do you call her that?"

Panzer rolled his eyes when the lieutenant began to stammer. "Well, see, I, uh, she . . . she tends to bounce when she's excited. Uh, Majesty."

"How old is she?"

"Nine, Majesty."

Simmonne held the slate so she and the Twins could lay fingers on it. Together they molded the image of the three standing together, much as they were now. Minus the leash, Panzer noted.

What should I say?

The question had been rhetorical, but Panzer offered a suggestion as he heard the forming thought in her mind.

"He and his siblings are orphans."

She took a breath and nodded. She dismissed the idea of noting how proud the girl's parents must be of her.

For Froggy,
Life is a wonderful thing. Treasure it and everyone who shares it with you.
—Twenty-seventh Princess of the Solar Empire, Simmonne Mandrake
—The Katyusha Twins

Simmonne deactivated the holo and offered the slate back to Clearwater.

"Thank you, Majesty," he answered with his head bowed so low, it took him two tries to grab the slate.

Without needing to be urged, Clearwater retreated, and Panzer turned back to the console.

Funny little man.

The thought came in unison from Jennifer and Julie as they leaned into Panzer once again. Simmonne had already forgotten about him, back to her previous thoughts. Panzer smiled. A signed artifact. If the little girl was indeed a big fan of theirs, it would make her day. If not, Simmonne had just cut the resale value in half by personalizing it.

"We're clear," Andira announced. "We are no longer in the fleet's weapon's range."

"Switch to rotary propulsion and get us to the *Hurricane* as quickly as possible," Panzer answered. "Then open a channel to Aetius."

"Establishing link," Andira answered. "Call is being routed."

The seconds passed as Aetius was no doubt excusing himself from a hectic duty station to take the call. A screen illuminated over the console, and the admiral's red eyes stared back at him.

"Colonel," Aetius greeted with an expected urgency in his tone. "Good to see you are still alive. Is the Imperial Rose with you?"

Panzer took control of the connection in his NOD, expanding the feed so Aetius could see everyone in the CIC. "Safe and sound with me, Admiral."

Despite the good news, Aetius's countenance did not lighten in the slightest. Instead his red eyes contracted until the pupils had practically vanished. "Colonel, you must place her under arrest immediately."

"What?"

"*What?*" The girls echoed Panzer's response as he pulled them closer.

"Colonel." Aetius took a breath. "I have very bad news. Emperor Mason, Empress Marianne, and the rest of the Solar Family—they've been assassinated. Emperor Steven was the only survivor. He has ordered Princess Simmonne's arrest as a conspirator to the assassination."

Sharp hooks sank into his heart and pulled down. Simmonne.

"They're . . . dead?" Simmonne whispered as her hands rose to her face.

"Conspirator?" Panzer spat. "That's insane."

Aetius shook his head. "That's all the information I have, Colonel. She must be placed under arrest immediately."

"They're all gone?" Simmonne croaked as the first tears ran down her cheeks. "Why? How? I—" Simmonne turned to look up at Panzer before throwing herself into him, then she lost control.

"No," Julie whispered.

"They . . . can't be," Jennifer whispered. "All of them?"

The two embraced Simmonne, and Panzer squeezed all three as tightly as he dared while they erupted into sobs. The emperor. Empress Marianne. The rest of the family. Everyone but Steven? Panzer hung his head. Surely Steven wouldn't go that far.

"They, they—" Simmonne blubbered as she clawed at him, her wails turning into high-pitched shrieks as she tried to speak.

The emperor, dead. Panzer took a deep breath through his nose. He could grieve them later. The three in his arms needed his strength right now. Every thread of his character ached to blast the anguish out of their minds, but he couldn't do that. They had to grieve, and he had to help them.

He felt Simmonne's mind falling and caught it with his. This was too much. The engineering that helped to cope with grief was never meant for a situation like this. The weight was heavy as her mind tried to rip its way out of reality to retreat from the horror. But he couldn't let her detach and go over that precipice. There was no coming back.

Jennifer and Julie began to fall, and he had not been ready for it. As if by his fingernails, he pulled their minds up as well. His eyes closed as he concentrated. Away from the abyss. Catatonia would not have them as noble grief ramrodded an entire family's tragedy through them. He had to shift the burden, and his heart slowed as he put more and more of his mind into holding them up.

Even as hard as he tried to concentrate, the question popped into his head. Simmonne was royalty. That was why she had noble grief. Why did Jennifer and Julie have it?

"Do you need help?"

Panzer turned to the source of the voice to find Miss Prideaux standing behind him. Her expression showed resolve and focus. But behind her eyes, she wanted to throw in and cry with them. But she wouldn't. She knew as well as he did that some had to keep their eyes dry so others were free to cry.

"I've got them," he answered. *"Keep a neuron on them in case one starts to slip."*

Miss Prideaux sniffed and nodded slowly. She reached into her left sleeve. There was a look of discomfort before she withdrew a silver disc. Panzer recognized it immediately. One very much like it was in a drawer in his quarters.

"Can it wait?" he asked.

Miss Prideaux shook her head. *"His Majesty's orders were very specific."*

Panzer gritted his teeth. They belonged to him. He had every right to say they were not ready. But if that was indeed what he thought it was, he would not interfere.

CHAPTER 18B

THE UNIVERSE HAD FINALLY made sense. Everything seemed to be correct and in its proper place. Life was finally where it was supposed to be. But now for Simmonne, it had all been torn apart. Dead. *All of them*. Why? How? Who could have done it? She pulled more firmly at Master as if trying to slip out of the nightmare.

Daddy. Mom. Brittany. Raymond. All of them. Gone.

She felt herself being turned. She saw Jenna when she did, standing before her and holding up a silver disc. As she watched, Jenna placed her thumb on top of the disc. It spoke.

"Recognize Jenna Prideaux, Vi-Baroness of New Bengal."

Jenna removed her thumb and offered the disc to Simmonne. The capacity to think about what was going on had dried up. She simply looked at the disc, neither comprehending what it was or why Jenna offered it to her. Master gently guided Simmonne's thumb down on it. There was a small throb in the digit as the disc analyzed her.

"Recognize Simmonne Elisabeth Mandrake, 27th Princess of the Solar Empire."

Jenna withdrew the disc before holding it to the Twins. Master had to do the same for them, guiding their thumbs one at a time to it as the device identified them. But when Jenna drew the disc back to herself, nothing happened. After a moment Jenna held it out again, and Master pressed his thumb down on it.

"Recognize name redacted, Solar Commando Corps. Please present witnesses."

Jenna turned and motioned with her hand. Lieutenant Cleanwater and the doctor—Simmonne could not remember her name. The two of them came to her.

"Name and affiliation," Jenna directed them.

"Uh, maybe someone else?" Cleanwater began to protest.

"Just do it."

He placed his thumb on the disc.

"State name and relevant affiliations," the disc ordered.

"Third Lieutenant Jonathan Clearwater, Solar Legionnaires. Service identity number, 3411-2101-6907-5510-5050."

He raised his thumb and backed off at Jenna's urging. The doctor put her thumb on the device next.

"Dr. Taula Gilyard. Expeditionary Sciences Verification Agent, currently employed by New Horizons Exploration."

"Conditions accomplished," the disc announced. Sections around its perimeter rotated, and light spilled out into a hologram as the echo came to life. Through blurred eyes, Simmonne saw the sad smile in the face staring back at her.

"Daddy."

"Simmonne." His voice was calm. With a sniff, Simmonne blinked some clarity into her sight. "Vi-Baroness Prideaux has orders to show this to you immediately in the event of my death. If you're interacting with this echo, then I am gone."

He glanced down at his hand before rubbing them together slowly.

"I know you're certainly upset and will need time to come to terms. But things will move quickly now. They always do when an emperor dies. Large or small, an emperor's death always brings about political change, and the opportunistic will move quickly to take advantage of it."

He folded his hands together and smiled once again.

"The week you were born was chaotic. Every week is. The Empire is an enormous place. There is always a war, an insurrection, terrorists, trade disputes, economic crises, or any number of other things. But your week was particularly chaotic." He seemed to chuckle for a moment. "Your mother's always been a bit bitter that when you came out of the tank, they handed you to me first. But I got to spend less than an hour with you before I had to get back to work. Next thing I knew, a week had gone by, and I'd not held you since. So, I scheduled some time for myself to do nothing but sit and hold you. My last beautiful daughter."

His faint smile faded slowly. Simmonne carefully unwrapped her arms from Master and turned to face Daddy more fully.

"I was so tired," he lamented. "I couldn't keep my eyes open. So while you slept in my arms, I started to fade. Providence is a funny thing. Your mother and I have always tried to shield you and your siblings from the full extent of our gift. To give you the bliss of not knowing how much we know. It can be hard to let a child venture out of the nest. To learn to trust their judgment and make their decisions. How much harder must that be when parents can see the future?"

He curled his arms as if holding her in them again. "I had a vision as I held you. Of all those I've had, I've never had one more clear than this."

Simmonne sniffled again when she saw a tear in his eye.

"I saw you grow up. In a flash, I saw you much as you are now. Young, beautiful, and full of life. It was hard for a father." He composed himself. "Here you were not even ten days old, and you grew up in moments. I saw many things. I saw you grieving my death, and I've known ever since then that when my time came, you would be away from the Cathedral. So any time you've left, I've entrusted Jenna with an echo like this one. I saw so many things. Among them, I saw your husband. I was a little surprised that I already knew him."

Daddy's eyes turned to look at Master.

"I won't say I was happy about it. I wasn't. And for a time, I didn't know what to do about it. I entertained some thoughts that I am not proud to admit I had. I even considered making him disappear."

Unconsciously Simmonne took a step back toward Master, putting herself more directly between him and the hologram.

"But . . ." he went on, "you seemed . . . happy. That's all a parent really wants for their child. And sometimes, as parents, we must accept that we won't like what makes our child happy. Simmonne, I know you've felt like I've been sabotaging you. That I've deliberately prevented you from having a love life, or building relationships. I should have known better. A child will always hyper-focus on what you won't let them have. The truth is I did."

His posture seemed to shrink, and a frown crept into his face.

"I won't ask for your forgiveness, as I'm not sure I should have it. But you deserve to know why. We Mandrakes are a line of incredible people. For a hundred thousand years, our family has kept humanity under a single flag. Our family has united many disparate races into a single body. The countless trillions the Empire has lifted out of poverty. For whom we have established justice, banished disease, and fed. The countless souls who never died in wars we did not allow to happen all speak for our legacy."

He rubbed his hands again, breaking eye contact briefly to gaze at the floor.

"But we have our weaknesses. We Mandrakes have never handled heartache well. It has destroyed many of us in the past. In my children, I saw what it did to Steven. To Brittany. It changed them both, and not for the better. I know what it would have done to me, if not for your mother. I don't know if you'll ever be able to understand. But I knew, Simmonne."

He brought his eyes back up to hers.

"I *knew* who the love of your life was. That meant I knew any relationship you found beforehand could only end in heartache. So, I kept you apart until you were an adult. I never told you so you wouldn't feel pressured into it."

Simmonne watched his weight shift as he nervously rubbed his hands again.

"I know I had no right. I hope you don't hate me for it."

"Daddy," Simmonne whispered, shaking her head. "Never." It may have only been an echo, but she would never forget the smile and the look of relief on his face as if he'd heard her response.

"There is another confession that needs to be made." Daddy turned, now gazing at the Twins. His hand rose, and he gently motioned them closer. With some hesitation, both lowered their arms from Master and faced the echo. "Jennifer. Julie. I'm afraid your lives are not what you think they are. The lie you were told was meant to protect you while I looked for a solution."

"Lie?" they whispered together.

"You believe you are the orphaned children of Kyle and Anne

Katyusha. That I adopted you after their deaths. You're not. Those people never existed. The truth is . . . more complicated. You're not actually twins or technically even sisters."

"*What?*" they asked together, each wiping an eye as they tried to hold their tears awhile.

Simmonne pressed her lips together. What dark secret was this? Why did he seem so ashamed?

"When I sat down to write Simmonne's genetic profile, I had . . ." He paused. "A flash of inspiration. It simply flowed out of me. But when I gave it to the geneticists, they weren't certain they could meet the specifications. So they asked for time to do some experimentation. After waiting longer than I thought was reasonable, I paid them a surprise visit. And there you were.

"The geneticists had created you both to test whether or not they could meet my specifications. They were planning to terminate you both now that they had their data. But when I saw the two of you floating in your tanks, I couldn't let that happen. You didn't deserve to be wiped out of existence before you even knew you existed.

"You were not made from my DNA, or any other. You were synthesized from base chemicals. I could not claim you directly as my daughters so I adopted you and created the fiction of your parents. I never told you, to protect you. You could not have an indiscretion or accidentally reveal information you did not have. But therein lies the problem."

His eyes crinkled as he cringed, searching for the right words.

"In the eyes of the law, neither of you is human. The law considers you arens. You are not part of the Chain of Life and have no Right of Birth. You are property of the state. Of me. I never wanted that for either of you. So, you were adopted children."

Daddy brought a finger up and took turns pointing at both of them.

"Make no mistake. The law is not the end of all things. You are as human as I am. You are sisters. You're even more identical than true identical twins. But you are each your own human person." He lowered his arm and let out a sigh. "The law may not be the end, but it's always there. For years, I tried to find an exception in the ancient doctrines or a loophole in the law I could use for the two of you. There isn't one. My only choice would be to pass a new law, specifically for the two of you. I didn't."

He crossed his arms before looking at them with a sad gaze. "There are still well-intentioned idiots who demand we free the lantai. Never mind that they kill themselves with no master. Others demand we 'free' the arens, even though they don't *want* anything but to serve the Empire. If I wrote an edict just for the two of you, I'd be sowing seeds of chaos in the realm where it's my duty to maintain order. I should have. And I intended to once I had exhausted all other possibilities. But if you're interacting with this echo, it's too late. Every emperor is sovereign, and beyond naming my successor, I have no power beyond the grave."

His eyes narrowed with disgust. "If I don't . . . *will* you . . . to someone, then you remain property of the state, under the auspices of my successor."

Simmonne held her breath, and she began to shake her head as his eyes returned to her.

"You were my first thought, Simmonne. I have never seen a group of siblings who had such affection for each other. But, I think you worry too much for them already and not enough for yourself. I can't do that to you." He took two steps back and looked at Jenna. "You were my next thought, Vi-Baroness. You've often been the parent to them when Marianne and I could not be. I regret that I never told you before now how pleased we have been. But there comes a time every child must find their place in the universe. Sometimes the child is ready for that before we are, and I know you're not."

Daddy turned back, looking at the floor. When his gaze rose, he focused on Master.

"*Three* of my daughters, Colonel," he said. "There are very few in my court who trust you. Even fewer who like you. The fact that no one can read your mind immediately makes you untrustworthy to many of them. But, I am old, and supposedly that makes me wise. I have learned that a man is not his thoughts. For even a good man can indulge his mind in wicked fancy. It is a man's actions, not his thoughts, by which he is judged. And I've been sitting in judgment of you for a while now."

Simmonne studied his face closely. His eyes were narrow, his nose raised, and the skin of his neck was taut. "I've often been disturbed by the sheer joy you take in bloodshed, but I've never known of you to kill someone just to satisfy that bloodlust. I've never seen you shy away from doing the dirty work that has to be done. But I've never known you to get any dirtier than you have to. And I believe that you truly understand what the Empire is."

Daddy's expression softened, and he leveled a finger at Master.

"It wasn't right what your father did to you. I will never understand how any father could do that to his son. Some in my court think I put you in the Corps because I got some cheap thrill out of making a Rhinegrave do my bidding. Idiots. I don't particularly like your family, Colonel. I don't approve of your totalitarian view of government. I don't care for the way you treat women and aliens. I don't care for your exhausting militarism or endless greed.

"But on Miner-9, you were a young man who had lost everything. My grievances with your father and your forefathers were not with you. If a man loses everything, the only thing that can keep him going is a sense of purpose. So I put you in the Corps to give you one. In the . . . limited . . . time we've spent together, I've tried to set a better example for you. But since I cannot read your mind, I can only hope that you took some of it to heart.

"You're not the first man I'd pick for one of my daughters—or even the tenth. But it's not my choice to make. You have a sense of duty, and family means as much to you as it does to me. So, you have my blessing, and this shall be the official record that I have willed Jennifer and Julie to you."

He turned back to Simmonne. "The final matter is who will succeed me."

Simmonne nodded. Raymond or Steven. Now she would know. Finally, there would be an answer. It was Steven, wasn't it?

"Simmonne, you and Steven have always had a special relationship. He warmed to you in a way he never did any of his brothers, or his other sisters. I would never want to damage that connection the two of you have." Daddy shook his head slowly. "But there are things you don't know about him, Simmonne. I cannot make him emperor."

Raymond then. Steven would be crushed. Simmonne already felt bad for him. It was all he wanted in life. "I offered it to Raymond, and he declined," Daddy said. "He doesn't want this life, and I don't blame him."

Neither Raymond nor Steven? As the light of understanding began to open her eyes, Simmonne shook her head.

"Daddy. No."

He took a breath. "Very often in life, lies masquerade as wisdom, and we embrace them because they are warmer than the truth. There is a very old lie about power. That idea is that power corrupts, and absolute power corrupts absolutely. It's easy to see why people love this lie. It allows those who gain the power and do horrible things to blame their actions on some mystical force of corruption the power blighted them with. When we put someone in power and they do horrible things, we say the power corrupted them so that we don't have to acknowledge our failure to see who they really were.

"Power does not corrupt, Simmonne. It reveals who we truly are. A hard lesson in life is that most people are neither good nor evil. They're simply people. They'll do what they are allowed to do and what they won't be punished for. They'll do the right thing because they're required to, not because it's actually right. When they do bad things, they do it because they feel they can. Those who are truly virtuous, and those who are truly wicked, are both minorities."

He extended two fingers of his right hand, while raising his thumb to make the image of a gun. "Every person is born with a gun to their head. That gun is authority, and the hand that wields it is power. Most will live their entire lives with that gun to their head. But when you have the power, now you're holding the gun. And you experience a freedom you never knew before. There are very few who are actually responsible enough to hold it."

"Daddy, please no." She shook her head again, backpedaling until she pressed against Master.

"A father knows his children," he answered. "I know their strengths, their flaws, and I love them all. But I have only two who can be that hand. Raymond and you."

Simmonne shook her head faster. "Daddy. I can't do this."

"Yes you can," he answered, stepping forward to her. "You *can*. But you're going to have to change. You're going to have to grow up. You're going to have to get over your allergy to responsibility. You'll have to learn to shoulder it rather than run from it. You'll have to learn to give people orders and bad news. Even when you can sense how disappointed or unhappy they might be with it."

Simmonne would have turned away if the large hand on her shoulder did not keep her in place.

"You're a Mandrake. A hundred thousand years of success is in your blood. I had hoped to begin grooming you for the role. To coach you for the days ahead. I sent you to the Hourglass so you could see a universe without the Empire. So you could see the darkness. The Empire is the light. Simmonne, there is no justice in the universe. There is no peace. There is no law or charity. These things do not exist naturally. They only exist when people with the *strength* to create them make the *choice* to do so. You can be that person. If you want to be." He swallowed and took a deep breath. "I have two children to whom I could leave the throne, and neither wants it. There is another reason I chose you, Simmonne."

Unsure she wanted to hear it, she brought her hands up to her temples, still shaking her head.

"You have a choice Raymond doesn't. As empress, you can rule the Empire to the best of your ability or you can name your husband your emperor and elevate him to rule instead."

Simmonne dropped her hands, looked back at Master, and then back. He nodded.

"I know that will be your first instinct. Look at me." She brought her eyes up to his. "If you choose to do that, know that I won't be disappointed in you. I won't feel like you let me down." The smile crept slowly back to his face. "A father wants his child to be happy. And I don't want to force this on you any more than Raymond. But I believe you can do it if you choose to."

Daddy looked at Master. "Colonel, I know my daughter well enough to know she may well name you emperor. You may not be my first choice to marry into my family, but the Empire could do much worse. You have a sense of duty, you understand just how important the Empire is, and you have the only pedigree with a history of success as long as my own. But if you will be emperor one day, you, too, will have to change.

"You will have to put aside the commando. Put aside the Sylvan-ni prince and embrace a larger universe. For the emperor cannot serve only one nation or one people. The emperor must be *everyone's* emperor. People sometimes look at me funny when I say there's never been a rebellion against the Mandrakes. They ask, 'What about the Eclipse?' or 'What about the Collapse?' They don't understand. Neither of those happened because someone rejected us. It happened because we rejected them, and then refused to allow them to leave. My family made those mistakes. The Empire may not survive it again."

Daddy stopped for a breath, his eyes darting between Simmonne and Master before settling again on the latter.

"Your family is going to be a problem, Colonel. She will need your help. I don't think they've ever forgiven us for the Eclipse. You were so young when you left, I doubt you know much of anything about your father's intrigues. But someone once said, it matters not so much who is king, as who controls the money. Your family has spent the last few generations trying to amass enough wealth to make that true. They're almost there. If she chooses to rule, Simmonne will need your help. If she chooses you, then you will deal with that in your own way."

Daddy waved his hand dismissively before closing his fist to point again. This time he brought his finger right to Master's face. "But remember. I left the throne to Simmonne, *not* to you. Only she can decide if you should be emperor. When you needed a purpose, I gave you one. I have always tried to show you the respect of a peer rather than a subordinate. And *three* of my daughters are yours now. If anything I've done for you has meant anything, I have one final order for you."

Simmonne felt Master's legs come together as he stood at attention.

"My visions have not shown me my death. Though I hope I am not so naive as to assume that I simply die in my sleep. I name you Executor of Succession. I order you to prosecute Simmonne's claim to the throne, and to ensure her rightful installation by any, and *all*, means at your disposal. This echo, and the sample of my brain tissue within, shall serve as her legal right of inheritance and verification of her claim."

"I understand," Master answered.

With eyes closed, Daddy nodded and took a step back. "You need time to grieve, so for a while, this echo will deactivate while you come to terms with my death. Jennifer, Julie, Simmonne." He waited for all three to clear their eyes. "You will live long lives. In the years ahead, you may forget certain things. If you remember nothing else about your father, remember how special you were to him, and all the potential he saw in you. I love you all."

"We love you," they answered as the tears they'd held back flowed once more.

He bowed his head, the hologram faded, and the echo was quiet, but the room filled with the sounds of grief.

CHAPTER
18C

C LEARWATER STOOD IN ABJECT silence, unsure how to process what he had just seen. He kept his head down and a hand above his eyes for good measure. As the Imperial Rose and the Twins cried, he did not watch. He did not want to see it or have it in his memory. If he were an immoral man, he could watch closely. He could pull the sights and sounds out of his memory index later and sell it for an untold fortune to the media outlets. If he were the kind of man who could look at himself afterward. Beside him, Taula was doing much the same. Her hand had found his as she began to choke up during the event. Now she faced him.

The emperor, the Solar Family. At least the Imperial Rose was here, safe. That poor girl. To lose her family like that. To lose them all at once. How could something like this happen? The Mandrakes kept themselves at least as well-guarded as the Rhinegraves.

Did he hear the echo correctly? Was the colonel Prince Victor? But he died over a hundred years ago, almost two hundred. Clearwater had seen videos of the memorial held for him in the capital. This was impossible, wasn't it? Some things made more sense now. Some made a lot less. If he was Prince Victor, what was he doing with the Rose and the Twins? The Mandrakes and the Rhinegraves weren't exactly friends.

Taula squeezed his hand tighter to get his attention, then motioned with her eyes. Clearwater lowered his hand to peek over it. The colonel had guided the Imperial Rose and the Twins to embrace each other, detached himself, and was walking toward him and Taula. Taula let go of Clearwater's hand.

"My Prince," she whispered, descending to her knees, lowering herself until her forehead met the back of her hands on the floor.

She drew the same conclusion Clearwater had. He followed her lead, dropping to one knee. His right elbow rested on his leg, his left fist on the floor as he bowed his head.

"Stand up!" The colonel's whisper was harsh. In his peripheral vision, he saw the colonel motioning for them to rise. "Up!"

Clearwater returned to his feet. The colonel's mouth opened as if about to speak before rolling his eyes.

"*All* rise."

Clearwater took Taula's arm and helped her expedite the return to her feet, but she kept her head bowed.

"Obviously I don't have a lot of time," the colonel began. "You both know what you saw. On my authority as an agent of the emperor, I am classifying this matter absolute secret. You will not be allowed to discuss it with anyone, including each other."

"Yes, My Prince," Taula answered.

The colonel's eyes nearly crossed. "Don't call me that," he directed. "Since neither of you has absolute clearance, I'm going to have to affect your minds. I'm going to take control and encrypt this portion of your memory index. You won't be able to access it. You will only know it is highly classified data, access to which will find you if and when you need it. Understand?"

"Yes, My Prince." The words fell out before Taula could stop them, and Clearwater saw her tense up.

The colonel closed his eyes in frustration. "I am *not* a prince. I haven't been one for a lot longer than either of you have been alive. I'm an officer in the Commando Corps. That's all. Now, once again, I am going to bury your memory of this event away from your conscious mind. I am going to encrypt the relevant portions of your memory index so you can't access them. Do you understand?"

"Yes, My, um, Colonel." Taula caught herself this time.

Clearwater leaned a bit closer as he eyed Taula. She was . . . shaking. He had seen her panicked when the machines on the planet grabbed her. But not like this. She was so nervous, she'd catch fire if she trembled any harder. Clearwater cursed under his breath. Great. First he rescues them, then he turns out to be a high prince. Wait a few minutes, and the colonel would probably have her on a leash, too.

"Don't read into it."

Clearwater heard his words in time to see that his mouth was not moving. Telepathy. But there was something distinctly different about the words. Something intangible he could not name.

"Every little girl back home wants to marry the high prince when they grow up. It's just a childhood fancy. It's the fantasy of the prince, not the person. Lantai part of her probably adds something to it. Besides, she and I are pretty far off from being each other's type. And I'm not going to let her remember who I was. Once I take that away, I'll go back to being that huge scary man."

Clearwater let out a shallow breath and nodded. "Thank you, sir." Clearwater looked past the colonel toward the Imperial Rose. "Sir? We're witnesses to the emperor's will. Shouldn't we keep it?"

"You will. You just won't know it," the colonel explained. "Look, I'm going to make this simple. Steven is already emperor. If he's been confirmed by the Senate, it's no longer a simple matter of showing up with the will anymore. With a war on, the Senate may decide it's in the Empire's best interest to keep him on the throne, despite the previous emperor's will. And . . ." The colonel paused, taking a breath and shaking his head. "Steven and I go back a ways. I have . . . concerns. This information endangers you and Simmonne. To protect her, I cannot risk either of you letting what you know slip, or it coming out of your minds in other ways. If and when the time comes that you're needed, I will find you."

The colonel paused again, staring straight at Clearwater. "Though it is outside of your security clearance, I will allow *you* to retain what you've learned about me. You'll remember being present for the echo, but you will retain none of the knowledge about who the emperor chose as his successor. My only other alternative to affecting your minds is to lock you both in cells back on Acheron until you're needed. I think you'll both agree that this is the preferable option."

"Yes sir."

"Yes." Taula caught herself again. "Colonel."

"Just take a deep breath and relax." The colonel brought his hands up. Clearwater could do anything but relax as a Solar Commando prepared to take hold of his mind. His left arm began to tremble as the colonel's hand settled over his face. "Don't be afraid."

Clearwater sucked in a deep breath and concentrated on remaining perfectly still. With eyes closed, he could only see his NOD. He did not will it, but he saw screens opening. Commands were being entered into the screens more quickly than he could read them.

Taula's hand found his again, and her grip was surprisingly strong. Clearwater felt a tingle in his scalp. His vision cleared as the colonel lifted his hands away and returned them to his sides.

"When the information is needed, I'll be in touch."

Information? What information? Clearwater opened his eyes. That's right. The colonel said he was taking something from their minds. What was it? There was something almost sad in the colonel's expression, and his lips formed a frown. The colonel looked to Taula, then back to Clearwater.

"You can do better."

Clearwater shook as the words entered his mind. "Sir?"

"I need to get back to the girls now," the colonel said, dodging the question. "If you'll excuse us."

Before Clearwater could answer, Taula did. "Yes, Colonel."

She held his hand and led them both out of the CIC.

Act—IV: The Long Road

CHAPTER
19A

H IS SHIP WAS APPROACHING the *Hurricane*, and Panzer stood in the loading bay. Simmonne stood at his side. She held her cape closed around her, and her head was down. The Twins were gathered with her, while Miss Prideaux loitered at the rear of the bay. Rhoxx was ahead, Kassar on the right, and Novin on the left, all in full kit. Lieutenant Clearwater and Dr. Gilyard hung back near Jenna.

"Approaching hangar now," Andira announced.

Panzer laid his hand on Simmonne's shoulder. She forced a smile before leaning against him.

"Stay behind me," he projected to Simmonne, Jennifer, and Julie. *"No matter what happens. Be silent. Do not speak, even if spoken to. You can't be incriminated by words you don't say."*

Yes, Master.

He knew they understood, but he did not leave it to chance. A switch in his NOD toggled another in their collars. For now, their speaking privileges were revoked.

"Initiating docking procedures," Andira relayed.

Panzer gently guided Simmonne to stand straight before stepping ahead of her and the Twins and behind Rhoxx. They were in the *Hurricane*'s hangar now, and he could hear the reverberation as the docking claws seized hold of the ship. They were being drawn inward now, into the citadel, toward a VIP hangar. Moments later he felt the shimmy in the deck as the ship was set on its landing skids.

Andira opened a screen in his NOD to display what waited for them. It was exactly as he expected. A gross of Legionnaire infantry, armored and light. But Panzer's eyes were drawn to what waited by the lone door to the private hangar. Four metal pods with transparent faces—incarceration pods. High-value and high-risk prisoners were rendered unto chemical stasis for transport in these machines. As they slept, the pods would pull the memories from their brains to be copied and recorded to collect evidence of their guilt. It could prove innocence or, in the face of conspiracy and a skilled programmer, it was not impossible to fabricate evidence.

Four pods. They did not just intend to arrest Simmonne. They intended to arrest the Twins and Miss Prideaux as well. The legionnaires crossed the hangar's blue floor to close the distance. Panzer took a final look around.

"Rhoxx, Kassar, Novin—these girls are my property. They are not to be separated from me."

Kassar and Novin turned on their heels to face him before bowing and then facing forward again. Rhoxx's tail flicked.

"Andira, lower the ramp," Panzer ordered.

A loud hiss filled the loading bay as the pressure to the hangar equalized, and the ramp lowered as it extended out. Rhoxx led the way as the entourage descended into the hangar. The legionnaires did not snap to attention. There was no trumpet or blast—not even the most minor of fanfare intended for royalty. At the head of the legionnaires, Panzer found the red uniform he expected. Admiral Aetius may have commanded the fleet from this ship, but it was Admiral Gilyard that was her captain.[27]

"Dad!" Dr. Gilyard exclaimed, darting past the entourage to meet her father in an embrace. Admiral Gilyard met her with open arms, hugging so tight that he took her feet off the deck. Panzer felt the warmth of family reunited, but behind him came the chill as Simmonne, Jennifer, and Julie watched something they would never experience again. He wanted to turn back, to offer his arms as comfort. But he could not. Of all the times he had ever played the scary commando, he had never needed that intimidation factor more than he did now.

"I was so worried," Admiral Gilyard whispered as he set his daughter back on her feet. "Thank you, Colonel."

Panzer answered with a respectful nod.

The admiral ushered his daughter behind him and out of the path of the coming confrontation. Panzer walked forward to stand beside Rhoxx.

"Colonel," Admiral Gilyard began, stepping forward, "my crew is ready to take Princess Simmonne and her entourage into custody."

"I don't think so, Admiral."

"Pardon?" The admiral's eyes widened.

"Princess Simmonne and her entourage are in my custody, Admiral."

The admiral waved his hand dismissively. "Oh, don't worry, Colonel. It's your arrest, your custody—we'll just store them until we get home." Admiral Gilyard waved a hand, prompting the legionnaires to move forward.

"Stand fast," Panzer growled, prompting those same legionnaires to halt.

"Colonel?" Admiral Gilyard forced a smile. "I must insist. His Majesty has given explicit orders she be detained."

"She's already detained, Admiral."

The admiral made a point of leaning to the side to look past Panzer at Simmonne.

---

27   Armadas supercruisers are always assigned an admiral as their captain, as they
     are deemed too valuable to entrust to any but a flag officer.

"Neither restrained nor ringed? Come, Colonel, you are aware of what she's been accused."

Panzer nodded slowly. The legionnaires had formed a ring around them and were slowly creeping in. Kassar and Novin stood at the ready but, for now, had the muzzles of their weapons down. The admiral moved in closer, speaking in a whisper.

"Colonel, I assure you, you'll have full credit for detaining her and delivering her to the Cathedral. But I think it would be best for everyone involved if she were sedated and kept in the brig."

The legionnaires wondered what was about to happen. Gilyard had brought only deltas. Trying to intimidate them was pointless.

"Let me be clear, Admiral. We won't be doing that."

The friendly demeanor drained from the admiral's face, and his cheek twitched. "Colonel, I'm trying to be nice about this. But this is my ship, and—"

"*My* prisoner, Admiral."

Why are they in pahri? the admiral thought. *Them and this guy? Surely not.*

A rather disrespectful thought. To Panzer it had always seemed so odd how easily people could sometimes forget they were talking to a telepath. The more familiar with them, the worse it became, and so often the more poorly they guarded their thoughts. Panzer held his tongue, waiting for the admiral to speak solely to interrupt him.

"Colonel—"

"She is a member of the Solar Family, Admiral. I do not care what she has been accused of. She is not going to be arrested, carted around, and stored in pods or in a prison like a common criminal."

Admiral Gilyard pursed his lips while shaking his head in annoyance. "Colonel." Gilyard hesitated. "I can't order you to hand her over to me."

"No, you can't."

"Colonel, I—"

"Admiral," Panzer projected, reminding the admiral who and what he was speaking to. *"There is more going on here than you know. You don't know what you're getting yourself and your family into. For your own good, drop it."*

Panzer watched the admiral's eyes light up. For several seconds the man was quiet, and again looked at Simmonne. It was a tactic he did not prefer, but men with families were often easy to intimidate. Finally the admiral straightened.

What are you up to? Gilyard's eyes returned to Panzer. *Do you know what you're doing?*

"Then she's your responsibility while she's here, Colonel. And if she, or her entourage, are seen without you or your team, then I *will* take custody."

His words carried a harsh tone, but the admiral's thoughts were more restrained as he stepped in closer.

ADM GILYARD: You saved my daughter. I owe you for that. But I can only do so much. Make sure you or one of your men is with her.

Panzer nodded, and the admiral took a step back.

"I will have to insist you have a legionnaire escort while on the ship," Gilyard said aloud. "That is not negotiable."

"As you wish, Admiral."

The admiral gazed upward as he worked in his NOD. Twelve legionnaires remained, while the rest began to fall out.

"Now that, that's handled, I need to speak with Aetius immediately."

"He's on his bridge," the admiral answered. "I'm sure he's anxious to speak with you."

CHAPTER
19B

SIMMONNE HAD NEVER FELT anything quite like the sensations crawling over her as she moved through the *Hurricane*. Every eye felt like a dagger through her flesh. Some glared at her with fear. Others stared at her with anger, or even hatred. The most inoffensive were stares of confusion. She could not read their minds and did not have to. Their faces said it all.

Murderer.

Traitor.

How could you?

Why?

Jenna was gone. Master walked ahead, with Kassar and Novin to her right and left. The Twins walked behind her, with Rhoxx at the rear. A ring of delta legionnaires surrounded them. Simmonne held her cape tightly closed, kept her eyes down, and walked as close to Master as she could. For one of so few instances, she was glad that she had not been born a telepath. Simply feeling thoughts was bad enough.

Mercifully their walk was a short one to a router, and from there to the ship's bridge. Though here she attracted a few hateful stares—mostly from gamma arens in their pits—most of the staff were too busy to throw much hate her way. Master led the way along the back wall of the chamber and past a pair of delta sentries through a doorway. After a small corridor, they entered another vast chamber, the admiral's bridge.

Workstations existed on each level, and the people here were even busier than those on the ship's bridge. A guardrail on the lowest level formed a perimeter around a giant holoscreen. On the third level, a small platform extended into an overhang where Admiral Aetius stood. The aged aren seemed to stare off into nothing, no doubt brain-deep in the fleet's network. Eleven more spokes seemed to protrude out from the top deck, all pointing to the center.

The entourage proceeded up wide ramps through the levels. A pair of gamma arens paused to give Simmonne hateful glares as they pressed their backs to the guardrails to give Rhoxx room to continue his ascent. Finally they reached the highest level and approached Aetius's platform. Simmonne looked over the guardrail at the projector on the first level.

A map of the galaxy filled with many icons stared back at her. She tried to look closer.

H.M.S. HURRICANE: ACCESS DENIED

Simmonne frowned as the message lit up in her NOD with an angry red. The projector left only the map with icons she could not translate. The Twins looked over the side as well, more out of curiosity than anything else.

Anxiety and fatigue filled this room. There were perhaps a hundred people here on the various levels. The war could not be going well if the room felt this way. There was no optimism, no excitement. Eyes human and aren looked weary, struggling to maintain focus on their work. On the top level, Simmonne could see twelve workstations ringing the pit. While Aetius stood at one, a mix of human officers and gamma arens sat in pods spread among the eleven remaining positions.

The holograms that hovered around Aetius winked out of existence, and the admiral turned to face Master.

"Colonel, I don't think she should be here."

"I need to speak to you," Master answered him. "*Now.*"

Aetius was the only one who did not have the countenance of an exhausted man. He crossed his arms. "I am a little busy at the moment, Colonel."

Two very deep voices tried to out-assert the other while keeping the conversation calm.

"I'm sure you are. But this can't wait."

Aetius took a long breath before looking to the back of the room. "Muvar!"

Simmonne turned to see another admiral look up from a workstation. The aged man did a double take at Simmonne, apparently only now noticing her presence. He rose from the workstation and approached Aetius. A single galaxy rested on each of this officer's shoulders, a rear admiral.

"I need a few minutes," Aetius spoke low.

The rear admiral simply nodded, taking the overlooking platform as Aetius vacated it. Aetius motioned for them to follow to the rear. After descending ramps, they entered a small office. Rhoxx, Kassar, and Novin waited outside while Simmonne and the Twins followed Master in.

A round desk sat in the small room's center, and the admiral rounded it to take his chair. Master guided her to one of the two guest chairs. The Twins had to share the second.

"The three of them should be in custody." Aetius leveled a finger at Simmonne.

"They are in custody," Master answered. "My custody. And that's not why I'm here."

Aetius began to retort before Master interrupted, "Admiral, I've read every thought in her head. She did not even know about the assassinations until you told her. And there has been no memory tampering."

Aetius turned his hands up and gave a small shrug. "If that's true, that will be for a formal inquest. If they're not the reason you're here, what is?"

Master took a breath. "You have to prepare an offensive. Right now."

Aetius's red eyes widened, and for a second, the admiral simply stared up at him. "I know you wouldn't ask me for something like that without a compelling reason." The admiral leaned back in his chair. Now that he was sitting down, and even only slightly relaxed, Simmonne saw it. Like an enemy who had just been waiting for a breach in the defenses, fatigue invaded his face. The lids tried to close around his red eyes.

"But no matter how compelling it is . . ." Aetius paused to flick his hand. "I doubt it matters. If it takes more than one or two ships, I don't have the numbers to attack anything. I have less than a hundred thousand ships. More than ten thousand of them are so damaged, I've had to restrict them to logistics work. At last count, the Vaar are up to six million. Besides, Emperor Steven has ordered me to abandon this galaxy to the Vaar. I couldn't attack a buffet at the moment, not in this galaxy."

Simmonne sensed the surprise in Master, but also a grim determination that sent a chill down the back of her neck.

"I didn't realize they were up to so many," Master answered. "Regardless, we have to attack, and we have less than a hundred hours to prepare."

Aetius shook his head slowly before rubbing his eyes. "What do you want to attack?"

Master motioned the admiral toward him, and Aetius rose to his feet. A moment later Master offered his hand as if to shake. When Aetius took it, the admiral's pupils contracted to fine points before exploding out until almost no iris remained. The color seemed to drain from his skin, and he was pale when Master let go.

Aetius returned slowly to his chair, the look on his face one of constrained horror. When he spoke, it was a whisper. "If the Vaar take that station, they can put the whole Empire under threat. Even the Great Fortresses."

Simmonne closed her eyes and frowned. Her family never had been able to understand how envious she was of their telepathy. It was so mundane to them. They could never truly understand why she felt so cheated by life to be born an empath. Psionics were powerful, but they were nothing compared to telepathy. All of the arguing. All of the explaining. All of the convincing, debating, and reasoning. With just ten seconds of telepathy, Master bypassed it all.

Color slowly returned to Aetius's face. "Have you independently confirmed *any* of this? Any of it at all?"

"Not that specific information," Master answered, "but the source gave me other info that has checked out."

Aetius shook his head slowly. "I can't launch this without some confirmation."

"Then send a *Rook* to the center of the galaxy. The Vaar will already be there, making themselves at home. But we have to start preparations immediately. We have to capture that station."

"Capture it?" Aetius exclaimed. "No. No that's not possible. We can try to destroy it. If it is there, I can order every ship in the galaxy to launch long-range strikes. If I have every ship fire at once on a hammer trajectory, the Vaar won't be able to stop them all."

Master leaned forward, resting his fists on the admiral's desk. "That won't do it. You could fire every missile you have, generate more, and do it again. The station will still be there. The warp field it's sustaining, you need days to bombard it into rubble. The Vaar aren't going to give you that kind of time."

Aetius leaned back in his chair once more, his expression became vacant, and silence fell over the room. Was he in the network again? What was he doing? Simmonne glanced at Master, who had crossed his arms, and waited.

What is he doing?

"You're watching him work. Right now he's contemplating every scenario of how to attack."

You can read his thoughts as he does that?

"No. I'm not wading into the maelstrom. When he phases out like that, he'll have thought a hundred or more scenarios in the time it takes me to communicate this sentence to you."

Simmonne's eyes darted between the admiral in his trance and Master patiently waiting. *He can think that fast?*

"He can run the permutations as fast as a soldier in battle-mind can think. The fact that he can work through complexities that quickly—well, he's Aetius."

Simmonne leaned back in her chair while Aetius continued to work. She jumped when Master snapped his fingers. One of the Twins started to say something, but he silenced her.

Did you tell him about the alien? Everything she said?

"No," Master responded. *"That will just distract him."*

It probably felt like more time passed than she thought, but Simmonne began to wonder if Aetius had broken when he finally returned to reality. "There is no scenario where we win this battle," the admiral said with a sigh, "and I have an obligation to protect the civilians. This would involve leaving them undefended while my forces assault the target."

"We don't have to take the field." Master leaned one hand on the desk again. "We just have to hold the Crossroads for a few hours. Enough time for the legionnaires to seize the control points and plant demolitions."

Aetius retreated into his mind, regaining his vacant expression. He stayed in his trance for a much shorter time before coming out.

"I can't do it," Aetius answered. "I just don't have the forces. Currently we've achieved a nine-to-one kill to death ratio against the Vaar. It's not nearly enough. The moment they realize what we're doing, they'll jump their fleets back to engage us. I won't even hold an hour. Not enough time for the legionnaires to do anything. You can try talking to the emperor—convince him to send reinforcements. But, by the time they get here, it will be too late."

Master stood up straight and crossed his arms. Simmonne sensed something in him then. A certain reluctance. It was something he did not want to do, but she felt the circuits firing as he willed himself.

"You get me in control of that station, and I'll get you reinforcements."

"You can guarantee that?" Aetius's gaze hardened.

Master nodded. Despite his outward confidence, Simmonne sensed his discomfort. Whatever he had in mind, he was not looking forward to it.

Aetius looked down at his desk, where he tapped the simulation wood. *Adapters* were certain behaviors people performed that helped them react to stress. Some people would pop their knuckles. Some men would stroke their beards. The action varied, but arens generally didn't have adapters. Aetius was an alpha, more human than the other breeds, but even alphas did not usually have them.

Finally the admiral looked up, reluctance and resignation swirling together. "Central?"

"Central," a feminine voice, probably a gamma, answered.

"Send to all ships." Aetius hesitated, taking a deep breath. "Broken sword."

"Yes sir."

The admiral turned back to Master. "I'll start briefing the other admirals, pull in the marshals. Assuming they don't think I've gone neuro and relieve me of duty, we'll get started on the preparations. Upload *everything* you have about that place so the tac-brains can get to work on it."

"Good," Master answered. "I'll need to use your spanner."

"Get me everyone you can," Aetius answered, rising to his feet. "*Everyone*. We'll need them."

"I'll let you know how many within the hour. Before you go . . ." He reached into his pocket and removed two items that he divided among his hands. She spied a security tablet and a crisp one hundredtroy bill. Master handed the tablet over first.

"What is this?" Aetius asked.

"My trip to the embassy wasn't wasted," Master answered him. "The Vaar's new cipher. Assuming my intrusion wasn't enough for them to change it again."

Simmonne felt a sense of cautious elation from the admiral, hidden by a lack of facial response. "They did," Aetius answered, "but this could still be useful." His eyebrows rose, and he stood a bit taller. "I'll get this to the right place immediately." Aetius slid the tablet into a terminal on his desk. "What was the other thing?"

"I believe I owe you this." Master handed the bill to the admiral. His glare moved to the Twins before he looked back at the admiral. "Aetius and I had a bet going. See, we were the only two who truly believed this was coming. But even we didn't agree. Aetius was confident they would hit us with everything they could before we could bring the local astranet online. I didn't think they'd be able to concentrate enough force to do it until after. Looks like I lost."

Aetius opened a drawer in his desk before dropping the note into it.

"You know, I've never asked," Master remarked. "What do you *do* with the money when you win these bets?"

"I put it in the WOC,"[28] Aetius replied.

Simmonne felt a small sting in Master. "And here I've just been using mine to buy cigars."

"Everyone, Colonel," Aetius pressed. "As many as possible."

Aetius left, on his way back to his command center. Master bent over the desk and punched a few buttons into a small console. A blue field lit the surface.

PRIORITY BLACK ENCRYPTION

ESTABLISHING NETWORK BOUNCE . . .

QUERYING TARGET . . .

NOTICE, THERE WILL BE A MULTI-SECOND COMMUNICA-TIONS DELAY.

QUERYING TARGET . . .

He wasn't calling Steven, was he? She wasn't ready for that. She wasn't ready to face him, so she began to rise out of the chair. Master gripped the invisible chain where it met her collar and guided her to stand at his side.

CONNECTION ESTABLISHED.

ROUTING TRANSMISSION . . .

RINGING TARGET . . .

RINGING TARGET . . .

RINGING TARGET . . .

The projected screen collapsed on itself. The image of a woman coalesced above the desk. She wore a red corissè, and an eight-point crown rested on her brow. A smile lit up her face as the connection cleared.

"Victor."

"Mother, I need a favor." Master paused to look down at Simmonne, then to the Twins, who were on their feet before he looked back at the high queen. "Actually, I need two."

---

28   WOC is an acronym for Widows and Orphans Charity, a charity that supplements the benefits received by the families of soldiers killed in action.

CHAPTER
19C

CLEARWATER STOOD IN SILENCE while the colonel faced the admiral. Now the colonel, the Rose, and the rest of that entourage were gone, though Clearwater noticed that Lady Prideaux did not go with them. Instead she made her way over to a different router.

Clearwater turned in a slow circle to take in his surroundings. Grav lines and claws on the ceiling moved ships and cargo. Refueling hoses supplied xenomatter to the smaller ships. Various automatech carried out their duties. It looked like any other hangar, and a small one at that. But it wasn't just any other hangar. It was a hangar of the *Hurricane*.

He smiled. It was one thing to be in the service. It was another to see the Imperial flagship in person. Another still to actually stand on its deck. He had to get videos and pictures, as many as he could. David and Ryan would love it. He rotated his gaze until it fell to the legionnaires loading the holding pods they had deployed.

His smile faded. They were going to put Imperial Rose and the Twins in those pods. The Imperial Rose an assassin of her family? What madness was this? How could anyone think *she* was an assassin? Clearwater frowned as he took another look around the hangar. The emperor, the empress, all but two of them gone.

Eventually his eyes fell on Taula, once more embracing the admiral that the colonel had been arguing with, her father. Clearwater had not been certain he would ever actually meet the man. Now he was about to, and the old man wouldn't be in all that good a mood given what had just happened.

Clearwater stood at attention as the two approached him. Should he salute? There were protocols about where and when to salute while aboard a ship, but he didn't have time to scan the regulations. Better to be too respectful than not enough. Clearwater brought his heels together and hand up, fingertips at his brow. His palm faced outward in the salute shared by the Legionnaires and the army.

Whether his salute was appropriate or not, regulations required all salutes to be reciprocated. So one way or another, the admiral had to return the gesture. With a smile he did, his palm down in the Armadas' version of the salute. Clearwater did not lower his hand until after the admiral had done so.

The older man stood more than a full head taller than Clearwater, easily looking down on him. If Clearwater remembered correctly, Taula said he was the captain of this ship.

"Dad, this is Jonathan," Taula introduced him. "Jonathan, this is my father, Terrance Gilyard."

"At ease, Lieutenant," Admiral Gilyard bid, almost laughing and in a better mood than Clearwater had expected. "Taula tells me you took care of her while the Vaar had you." The admiral's face became more serious. "I thank you for that."

Clearwater's eyes darted to Taula before returning to the admiral. "She's generous, sir," he answered. "I'd say she was the one taking care of me."

Though he looked the admiral in the eye, Clearwater caught the frustrated look Taula gave him.

"So where you from, Lieutenant?"

"Weiss hive, Kresser County. Sir."

The admiral's face took on a curious expression as he looked Clearwater up and down. "Immigrant?"

"No sir." Clearwater shook his head. "Born and raised on Weiss."

The admiral eyed Taula. Clearwater did not need to be a telepath to know what the older man was thinking. He sent her a message, then realized that his NOD was still using his gamer alias.

CLEAR-J: He's complaining that I'm short, isn't he?

Taula's face betrayed the truth.

DR. RHOMBUS: Not exactly.

Sure he wasn't. At least among non-Sylvanni, he wasn't considered short. But certainly the old man was thinking the same thing all the girls back home did. *If you're that short, what other genetic defects are hiding in your blood?*

"Well," the admiral started, "as much as I want to talk, duty calls. Taula will need to be debriefed, and I'm sure you'll need some rest. I'll call down to the snake pit, see to it they put some good quarters aside for you."

"Thank you, Admiral," Clearwater answered with an appreciative smile.

"This way." The admiral directed Taula to walk with him.

DR. RHOMBUS: I'll call you later.

Clearwater smiled as she fired off a wink at him before walking with her father toward the nearest router. When they were gone, Clearwater allowed himself a breath to relax. That went a lot better than it could have.

Debriefing! Taula may not have had the military cyberware for this process to be automated. But he did, and regulations had a lot to say about it. Clearwater snapped straighter before looking deep into his NOD to touch the *Hurricane*'s network.

AUTOMATED DEBRIEFING STARTED . . .

UPLOADING DATA . . .

Clearwater waited while the progress bar filled. His time on ND-31. The battle. His time on the Vaar ship. His rescue. The *Hurricane*'s computers took it all. The AIs would parse the data and scrub things not of military relevance. Anything that needed an organic officer's attention would be brought to them, and recommendations would be made based on it.

AUTOMATED PERSONNEL MANAGEMENT

THIRD LIEUTENANT JONATHAN CLEARWATER
REPORT TO LEGIONNAIRE BARRACKS.
AWAIT FURTHER ORDERS.

Simple enough. They'd have to find a new unit to put him in.

Clearwater's shoulders sank. A new unit. At least he made it here and made debriefing. Now they'd know. His section and the rest of the Iron Brows. The rest of the service would know how they fought. Maybe the Board of Commendation could do them some justice.

Before he could cover the distance to the router, a new message stopped him.

MESSAGE DELIVERY FAILURE

YOUR MESSAGE HAS BEEN FLAGGED FOR REVIEW BY ARMADAS INTELLIGENCE.

YOU WILL BE NOTIFIED WHEN YOUR MESSAGE HAS BEEN APPROVED OR DENIED.

The message to his family. He figured simply saying the word *commando* might be enough to get it flagged. That was probably it then. By mentioning the Corps, he had ensured that an organic officer would have to review it along with the security AIs. He doubted the message would be sent soon, even if it was not censored.

>>CHANGE TRANSMISSION CONDITION
SPECIFY CONDITION.
>>MANUAL SEND

It was probably for the best. If he died in whatever was coming, at least they wouldn't be given false hope from the message. A personnel router recessed into the wall waited for him, and he unconsciously returned the salute of the delta nearby as he stepped into it.

DESTINATION?
>>SNAKE PIT

CHAPTER
20A

NINETY HOURS TO ZERO. In a large conference room, Panzer sat at the foot of a long table. Aetius sat at the head. Flag officers had been filtering in for the last twenty minutes. Admirals in their red uniforms and captains in their whites sat on the right of the table; marshals in black and colonels in brown uniforms sat on the left. Aetius had managed to pull a few more ships through the gateways, but very few, as civilian evacuation took priority. All told, fifty-six thousand ships, a little more than half of a sector fleet. Aetius had pulled the heaviest ships he could in the small gaps: eight battleships, two surplus battlecruisers, and fifteen surplus heavy cruisers. All combined to face a force of Vaar warships that had numbered over seven million at last count.

Five fleets, five vice admirals—each with a rear admiral as an assistant—and fifty task forces—each led by its own rear admiral with a senior captain as adjutant—filled the room. But by comparison, there was a dearth of Legionnaires officers. It was not uncommon for Armadas ships to have more legionnaires aboard than actual crew. The *Hurricane* could bear one hundred million without making special accommodations for more. The other battlecruisers had similar capacity, plus the capacity of many other ships. But not here. The late emperor had never intended to contest the Hourglass, so the ships had carried reduced compliments of ground forces. That left Aetius with no choice but to call broken sword.

The moment Aetius gave the order, a flurry of activity had overtaken the fleet. Broken sword could only be issued by the most senior officer in a region. The order was relayed to all ships, initiating a major offensive operation. The foundries and breeding centers in each ship were working in overdrive now. Automatech, tanks, warmechs, artillery, small arms—all were rolling off the assembly lines. None knew why they were gathered, and none of them were going to like it.

The fact that Panzer had checked thirty seconds ago did not matter. While awaiting the stragglers, he closed his eyes and stretched his mind. He had left the girls and his team in an adjacent room. All but Rhoxx, who was off handling a matter. The kilosteel bulkhead between them should have made it difficult to sense, but they were clear. All three looked at the food he had told them to eat, but none were eating. With a quiet exhale he sent the message.

"You need your strength."

He sensed their mild surprise and saw through their eyes as they briefly scanned the room for him.

"Eat," he projected more firmly.

I'm not hungry. The thought came from Jennifer and Julie. But Simmonne had been down this road before. It occurred to her that he could put the hunger into her if she did not comply. She took her fork, and faintly he could taste the butter in the mashed potatoes.

"I won't take no for an answer."

The Twins claimed their forks and did as he bid.

The last straggler finally made it into the room, a muscular kurai in a marshal's uniform. A pair of colonels on the left of the table scooted farther apart to give the kurai more room to sit. Panzer had noted a particular absence at the table. As Aetius gathered himself to begin the presentation, Panzer realized that absence was not going to be filled.

"Where is Marshal Skaal?"

Aetius looked up from the security tablet that had been holding his attention. *Dead.*

Panzer eyed him.

He was inspecting the defenses on Avalon when it began. Killed in the bombardment.

With a frown Panzer bowed his head. That was a major loss. Marshal Skaal, Old Iron Scales as some called him. The most aggressive marshal the Legionnaires had. Exactly the kind they could have used here.

"Now that everyone is here," Aetius started, "I will begin the briefing for what I've dubbed Operation Fourth Wind." Aetius projected his voice loudly, hushing the other conversations. A hologram of the Crossroads lit over the table, and all eyes turned to the great silver sphere.

"The Corps has brought to my attention a critical threat to the Empire," Aetius continued. "This threat must be neutralized before we leave this galaxy. Colonel?"

With his hands on the table, Panzer rose to his feet. Some familiar faces greeted him with friendly expressions. Others received him with more hostile gazes. Panzer took a breath. "This device is known as the Crossroads. It is an alien megastructure situated at the center of this galaxy. This device was responsible for the Void Zone, the dilation waves, and much of the odd behavior of celestial bodies in this galaxy."

Panzer paused, running his mind over the room to ensure he had undivided attention before continuing.

"This is also why the Vaar are determined to have full control of this galaxy. The timing of their invasion was deliberately planned to push us away as the Void Zone evaporated and the facility became accessible."

He paused again to let them assimilate the words. Just a handful of seconds. Any longer invited questions before the due time.

"Information on the creators of this device is limited at best. It measures approximately 244,000 kilometers in external diameter. However, through advanced spatial technology that is, I'm sorry to say, far more advanced than ours, it is many orders of magnitude larger on the inside. This device contains the supermassive black hole natural to this galaxy."

Shock, disbelief, incredulity—Panzer felt it all and pushed it all away from his mind to continue the briefing. The disdainful stares had become all the more hostile.

"The Crossroads is a giant transpatial network. It is capable of opening gateways over incredible distances. Perhaps anywhere in this universe. If the Vaar manage to seize control of the facility, they will put the entire Empire under threat. We must seize it and destroy it."

"*Seize* it?" said one of the marshals. Panzer turned to him. Marshal Dousan, an old Republican counting days to retirement. One of those pairs of eyes that had greeted him with hostility.

"Seize it," Panzer answered.

Dousan scoffed. "How are we supposed to land on it?" The marshal narrowed his brown eyes at Panzer while angling his head forward. "If there's a black hole *inside*, I don't think that's going to work."

Panzer looked at the image of the Crossroads. Through his NOD he split the sphere in two, separating the halves to show the black sphere within.

"The space inside of the facility is a pocket dimension. So long as it is intact, the gravity of the singularity does not interact with the facility itself." Panzer zoomed the image out, allowing a red disc to illuminate the station. "There is an effective gray zone of approximately two hundred light-years where the effects of the singularity's gravity are nullified before returning to its appropriate strength beyond that region. Don't ask me how that works. I don't fully understand it myself."

Panzer waited as a series of murmurs circulated through the room.

"In short, on the surface we'll experience the station's artificial gravity, approximately 1.33 standard. A little less in the internal chambers. Time dilation is similar. So long as we are in the safe zone, it will pass close to the galactic standard."

"Why don't we just launch every missile we can at it?" an admiral spoke up. Only by the recognition systems in his NOD did Panzer identify this man. Rear Admiral Lok Chambler. Ori, twice decorated for conspicuous leadership.

"Our weapons won't do the job. The Crossroads has no shields or conventional defenses. But the field stabilization of the facility is immense. It would be equivalent to bombarding a major hive. The Vaar won't give us that kind of time."

Even the eyes that had been friendly started to harden with accusations. Some of the officers shook their heads. Others muttered to themselves as they glared down at the table.

"Our only option is invasion," Panzer said a bit more firmly. "We land legionnaires at selected points and seize control of vital sectors, plant demolitions in the equipment helping to maintain the facility, then we get the hell out before it blows. With its internal infrastructure compromised, the Crossroad's pocket dimension will collapse. The singularity will spill back into our normal space-time, and the facility will be consumed."

The muscular kurai, Vice Marshal Veth, raised his hand.

"Marshal?" Panzer asked.

"Just how many localities are we talking to plant these demolitions?" A strangely soft-spoken question from a kurai known both for his temper and his volume.

Panzer turned his gaze back to the Crossroads. He brought the two halves of the sphere back together before a grid illuminated on the station's surface. "The Crossroads is composed of thirty-two thousand sub-segments. They were designed to interlock but be capable of being removed and replaced on an individual basis in the event of damage or wear. Best estimate is that no less than five thousand will need to be compromised to ensure the facility's complete destruction."

The kurai's eyes darted between Panzer and the Crossroads. Panzer took the marshal's silence as an opportunity.

"There's more." He took a breath. "The creators of this facility mastered wireless routing."

That drew every eye in the room.

"Colonel?" another admiral asked. "Is that what you meant to say? I'm pretty sure that's not possible."

Panzer looked at Admiral Stuuz, a fellow Sylvanni. Also an expert well-educated in routing technologies. "From the information I have, the people who built this place were colonizing other galaxies before humanity existed. I'm not sure any of us are qualified to judge what someone that ancient can or can't do."

Panzer sensed the rising doubt, even levels of disconnect. He was losing the room. Vice Marshal Veth spoke again. "How exactly did you obtain this information, Colonel?"

Panzer frowned. "From one of its builders. The short version is that they don't want the Vaar to have it any more than we would. But they're not in a position to do anything about it. The Corps is not prepared to divulge more at this time. I have been given the necessary information to take control of the facility. While the Armadas maintain a perimeter, your legionnaires must seize the objectives. If they can help me slave control of enough of the facility before destroying it, I can use the Crossroads to open a wormhole powerful enough to send all of our ships through together. We hold the place long enough, we can get everyone out. Otherwise, you'll never get everyone out through the gates in time."

"Do we have *any* proof of wireless astranet capability?" The question came from Rear Admiral Yu Zhen, a man Panzer had a long, positive history with. The air of disbelief in the admiral's skull was not encouraging.

"The Vaar used it to seize ND-31," Panzer answered. "The planet is linked to the Crossroads' network. Though the Crossroads itself was inaccessible, the linkages on ND-31 were enough for them to bypass the planetary shield."

Many looks were exchanged, to him, across the table, and throughout the crowd. It was not the exact truth. Non-localized astranet was not the same as wireless astranet, but it was close enough. It was enough to show them something tangible in the threat.

"And when are we supposed to land this assault?" another marshal asked.

"Ninety hours from now."

The silence shattered. Every voice tried to speak at once. A few threw comments at him. Most spoke to others in the crowd. With a sigh Panzer returned to his chair. This was exactly what he hated about dealing with flag officers. There was an informality among the senior ranks one did not find lower down. A certain lack of discipline about things like not interrupting, or letting a room devolve into the exact kind of arguing happening now. All behaviors none of them would tolerate from their junior officers.

"An operation like this takes months to plan."

"The Armadas will never be able to maintain the perimeter long enough."

"We already have ships chewed up from fighting."

"Just how credible is this information? Is there any source but the Corps?"

The torrent of comments and protests continued, half of them asking questions without bothering to wait for the answers.

"We'll have to abandon the gates and the civilians to make it work."

"I still say we try bombardment."

A new sound entered the room, a firm knock. Panzer looked up at Aetius slowly rapping his knuckles on the table. The voices yielded, quieting to the rhythmic sound. Only when he had all eyes and complete silence did Aetius speak.

"When presented with this information, I dispatched a *Rook* to confirm the presence of the facility. That mission was successful. It *is* there. The Vaar *are* in the process of landing forces on the facility. We have to come up with a plan now. The tactical AIs have given their best suggestions, but they're not encouraging. So let's see if we can improve on them."

Aetius took control of the central hologram, which morphed as he spoke, bringing icons to represent warships and landing craft.

"Step one will be for the Armadas to secure a perimeter. Step two will be to land legionnaires. Step three, Armadas maintains the perimeter while legionnaires seize the ground objectives and plant their demolitions. Step four, with control of the facility, the Corps transplants stranded civilians to our ships. Step five, with demolitions planted, we evacuate the ground forces. Automatech are left behind to delay the Vaar from recapturing the vital points. Step six, the Corps opens the way and we leave."

The moment Aetius stopped talking, the room began. Aetius did not raise his voice; he simply projected. "We are *not* here to debate the operation." The room quieted again. "I am the senior officer in the region. It is my decision. I've made it. Yes, it will be difficult. Yes, it will be costly. But I think each of you needs to consider the implications."

Aetius paused to look around the room.

"If the Vaar gain control of this facility, they'll put the entire Empire under threat. Nowhere will be safe. Not the Cathedral. Not your homes. We are *all* expendable to prevent that outcome. So, no more arguing. Let's make the plan. Your security tablets have the relevant information. Let's get to work."

The tension drained like cooling water poured on a heated brow. Panzer leaned back into his chair. Aetius had it under control.

"I have engineered a preliminary plan for the fleet." Aetius manipulated the hologram again to a map of the galaxy. A sphere in the center for the Crossroads, and blue projections in the shape of deltas for his ships. "Fleet, or snake. If anyone sees a problem with this, tell me now. The fleet will be broken into three groups. Force Alpha will consist of the bulk of our combat-capable ships. Force Beta will consist of those ships too damaged to take part in the fight, but with working logistics facilities. Force Gamma will be made up of the *Hurricane*, a handful of destroyer escorts, and the civilian ships."

Panzer listened as the master worked. The longer he listened to the admiral speak, the more sense the decision made.

"Force Alpha will conduct the assault." Aetius eyed an admiral. "Admiral Muvar, you will have point control aboard the *Rowen Jereko*. Force Beta will take a position in the Entholes Cluster. There they will dedicate themselves to passing munitions to forces on the front. I will retain operational control on the *Hurricane* with the civilian fleet.

"We can't risk any of the civilians panicking and doing something stupid. So I will have technicians dispatched to slave all of their nav systems to the *Hurricane*. We don't have much time for scouting. The *Rook* established that there is a Vaar fleet of approximately thirty thousand ships currently protecting the station. Force Alpha will jump in and engage them. They should be dispatched relatively quickly. The action phrase for Force Alpha will be 'Go to town.'"

Aetius adjusted the hologram to zoom in on the Crossroads, where the icons of Armadas ships moved around the facility.

"Force Alpha will globe around the Crossroads for all-aspect defense and begin deploying legionnaires. The Vaar will respond quickly, so we must get into our defensive position as quickly as possible. We'll give what bombardment support we can to the ground forces, but we won't have a lot of time before our hands are full. Once the legionnaires have accomplished their work and the Corps is in control of the facility, the action phrase 'Walk left' will be issued."

Aetius zoomed in until a cubical grid of narrow lines became visible in the display. The admiral pushed a finger into one cube, turning it blue. "This will be the exit corridor. Once *walk left* has been called, *Hurricane* will open a wormhole for the civilian ships and send them through. The fleet's number one priority will be to keep this lane sanitized of Vaar aggression while the civilians enter the wormhole provided by the Corps. The Corps has suggested opening the point into Republic territory, and I have agreed.

Once the *Hurricane* is through, Force Beta will be next while the legionnaires are evacuated. The action phrase for this stage will be 'Drop it.'"

Aetius stopped to make eye contact with each of the marshals in the room.

"It must be impressed upon all ground forces. Once *drop it* is called, they must drop what they are doing and proceed to extraction. The battlefield will be destroyed. Anyone who doesn't get out is dead. Please ensure all of your men understand this. Once Force Beta is out, action phrase 'Out to lunch' will be for Force Alpha to begin its extraction. *Hurricane* will be the last ship out."

Aetius took a drink of ice water before clearing his throat, then he looked at Panzer.

"It is imperative that the Corps understand. The civilian ships will be slaved together. Once *walk left* is called, it is an all-or-nothing. We won't be able to call them back. So be certain the lane is clear."

Panzer nodded. "Understood, Admiral."

"That's my plan, men," Aetius said before taking another drink. "If you see a problem, say so now. Otherwise, it's time for the snakes to plan out their work."

CHAPTER
20B

I N THE SMALL CONFERENCE room, Simmonne stared at the small plate of food. Master said eat, so she ate. But there was no taste to the food or hunger for it to satisfy. The Twins pecked at their dishes in silence. She sensed Kassar and Novin outside the circular room. Both had their minds on high alert. How did they do that? Surely it had to be exhausting to remain that alert, that focused on everything for so long. Even her guards never had *that* level of ruthless focus on everything around them.

A tear slipped down her cheek as she stirred the buttered potatoes. She couldn't go home. She had not planned to spend her whole life in the Cathedral, but she had never contemplated not being able to go back. Her hand trembled, and she set the fork on the plate. How could Steven think she had anything to do with it? Maybe it was something else. But, what kind of subterfuge could he be playing at?

She looked up at the Twins. Their lives had been a lie. Their relation to each other, the parents they were told they had lost, even the name Katyusha—it was all a lie. It was a lie for their good, but it was still a lie. How much else was a lie? She shifted in the chair, trying to find a comfortable position.

Daddy knew about her and Master. How much did he know? Some of the implications were uncomfortable. But, he knew they would come together. How did he manage to keep that a secret? To never let it slip? She could have never kept a secret like that. But keeping secrets, that was part of sitting on the throne.

Empress.

Daddy had NNED for as long as she could remember, possibly before she was born. But she did not think he had it long enough for his judgment to be impacted. It had to be impaired. She could not think of any other reason he would name her.

Maybe what he said was another lie to spare her feelings. Maybe he only left it to her so she could give it to Master. But, why? Did he know what was going to happen? If he did, why didn't he stop it? If he didn't know, why would he want a Rhinegrave to be emperor? It didn't make sense. It could start another Eclipse.

A biting chill clung to her heart. Did Daddy know they would end up together and named her his successor to drive the two of them apart? Did he do it to force her to choose between Master and the dynasty? Master and the Empire? No. Daddy wouldn't do that to her. He wouldn't have said what he said if he had a problem. At least she didn't think so.

There was a time she didn't think he would lie to her or the Twins about something so important. Simmonne shifted in the chair again before reaching down to grab the front veil of her bottoms. She raised it, opening the hidden pocket within to remove the echo.

SYSTEM OFFLINE

He said it would power down to give her time to cope, but how was she supposed to cope with this? She didn't want the throne; she never did. The sleepless nights. The missed birthdays and holidays. The relationships that were often superficial because there was no time to make them something more. A husband who resented her for never having time for him. Children who grew up knowing their mother's name but barely her company. The knowledge that people were dead because she had to order it. The stress that never went away because there was always more to do. She never wanted any of that.

She laid the echo on the table, tracing her nail around the perimeter of the disc. Steven wanted it. Most of her brothers wanted it. But they were men. Men wanted power. Brittany wanted it but knew she would never get it. Several of her other sisters would have been delighted to have it. Why couldn't he just give it to Steven?

Her finger stopped its circuit as her arm began to tremble.

Did Steven know Daddy picked her? What if Steven knew, and he killed Daddy because of it? But then, why kill Mom and the rest? The line of succession was vertical. Absent a chosen successor, he'd only have to kill Daddy. As the firstborn son, he would inherit it by default. If Mom knew, it would make sense to kill them both. But why everyone else? Did they all know? Did Daddy tell everyone else, and no one tell her? That wasn't possible. Some of her brothers and none of her sisters could keep a secret. So if Steven was behind it, why them? He didn't get along with most of them, but that didn't mean he'd kill them all. Simmonne's lip trembled, and she rested her elbow on the table, shrouding her eyes with her hand. If the Twins saw or heard her crying, it would only get them started as well.

Steven. Why? She mouthed the words as the muscles in her face tightened.

Even if he didn't do it, why did he blame her? How could he or anyone think she was responsible? Daddy said there were things she didn't know about him, but he couldn't be a murderer. Not Steven. Her brother had a powerful temper, he was a womanizer, and he was convinced that he was smarter than everyone else. But he was no murderer. He did not have it in him. Did he?

Simmonne jumped when she felt hands on her shoulders. She sat up, lowering her hand and looking down. She knew those hands. In a bout of confusion, she looked ahead. There was only one door into this room, and no one had come through it.

Master? You're not actually there, are you?

"My mind is here. My body is waiting for the marshals to stop arguing."

She wiped her eye and leaned back as she relaxed into the sensation of the illusory hands massaging her shoulders.

Shouldn't you be paying attention to the meeting?

"I'll decide where my attention needs to be."

The Twins slumped back in their chairs, their heads rolling softly about their shoulders. Was he doing the same for them? Something about that sent a chill down her spine. A flawless illusion for *three*? From as far away as he was, and through the walls? Even for him, that had to be a strain.

"Don't worry about me."

Simmonne bit her lip. She was not sure she wanted to ask the question. But she thought it, and that was enough. *Master. Did Steven kill my family?*

The illusory hands rubbed a bit more firmly into her shoulders.

"I don't know."

Simmonne sniffed, looking back down at her plate. *You've known him longer than I have. Do you think he is capable of it?*

She reached up to her shoulder, knowing his hand was not actually there, but feeling it all the same. He was silent for longer than she expected.

"The Steven I knew couldn't do it, but that was a century ago."

Did she ever really know him? Was she just too stupid to see what was in front of her?

"He's your brother. You wouldn't have been a very good sister if you didn't see the best in him."

Simmonne supposed she'd have to find some comfort in that notion. *Master?*

"Yes?"

She shifted again, relaxing into his grip. She couldn't ask him to do it. She couldn't ask him to take the pain away, no matter how much she did not want to feel this way. She grieved for her guards. How could she do less for her family? He did not mention it, but she knew he heard the thought when he massaged more firmly.

Master, I don't want to be—

"Shh." His thought pushed it right out of her head. *"This is a time to grieve. Not to worry."*

Her eyes returned to Jennifer and Julie relaxed in their chairs. Her racing thoughts began to calm, and she shifted once again to find greater comfort in the seat.

"I have to turn my focus back to the meeting now. I will come and get you as soon as I can."

I understand.

She brought her hand up again, feeling his illusory fingers until they slipped away. She wanted to call out, to ask him to stay. But he had work to do, and no one else could do it. Ahead of her the Twins had reclaimed their forks and were actually eating. Simmonne focused on the empty chair at the foot of the table. The place where Jenna should be. Was this it then? After her whole life, was Jenna simply gone now? Gone because she couldn't handle the choice that they made? Simmonne looked into her NOD, intent on sending a message.

ERROR

CRIMINAL CONTROL PROTOCOLS ACTIVE.

YOU DO NOT HAVE PERMISSION TO ACCESS THIS NETWORK.

Criminal controls. That's what she was to everyone now. A criminal.

CHAPTER
20C

O
N ANY ARMADAS SHIP, army and Legionnaire personnel were snakes, down in the dirt while the oh-so-glorious Armadas did their thing in space. Anything that had to do with ground forces often had "snake" in front of it. The legionnaire barracks was no exception, known as the snake pit. When Clearwater found the *Hurricane*'s snake pit, he found that Admiral Gilyard had been generous. The quarters assigned to him were those he would expect of a colonel, or perhaps even a marshal. But he did not inspect it for long. Perhaps it was leftover fatigue from what he had endured, or perhaps it was just being safer here than he had been anywhere for some time, but not long after he entered, Clearwater was in bed. The urge to explore as much of the *Hurricane* as possible would just have to wait.

His sleep was comfortable but—as so often is the case—shorter than ideal. Staffing needs throughout the military were handled primarily by AIs. They examined the available personnel and made deployments where needed. Even now they evaluated those already aboard and those filtering in from the retreating front. The AIs had taken notice of him, sending a message barging into his NOD with a priority tag that awoke him from his sleep.

COMMAND CONDITION—BROKEN SWORD
Remain on alert. Await further orders.
Office of Marshal Veth; acting CO of Legionnaires, Hourglass Flotilla
To: Third Lieutenant Jonathan Clearwater

Jonathan Clearwater, congratulations. You have been accorded a field promotion to the rank of captain. You are hereby ordered to transfer to H.M.S. Donetter Keems to take command of the Third Company under supervision of Major Iwan Rozcheko, Seventh Battalion, Third Cohort. Please report to your new duty station no later than 2200 hours on the day of receipt of this message.
You are hereby informed that this promotion is temporary. Faithful discharge of your duties may see you reduced to your original rank once the current operation is completed. Or your new rank may be made permanent, pursuant to the needs of the Solar Legionnaires at the discretion of the Officer Corps Oversight Board. Good luck in your new command.

Mouth agape, Clearwater stood with a vacant gaze at the message. Broken sword. All hell was breaking loose. But he did not dwell on that long before the remainder of the message consumed his focus.

A promotion to *captain*? Sweat formed on his brow as he reread the message twice. This was a mistake. It had to be. Captain? That rank required at least four centuries of service. It demanded commendations he had yet to earn, training he'd yet to have. He closed his mouth as he felt the recent grilled cheese trying to reverse course through his gullet. Lead a company? Ten thousand souls? He couldn't do that. In a flash he was in uniform and on his way through the door.

He had to talk to someone *now* and get this straightened out. Who was the battalion commander? Major Rozcheko? Yes, he'd talk to him and explain a mistake had been made. No, that wasn't enough. The major would have to put in a request and wait for it to filter up the chain of command. The same was true if he went over the major to the cohort's colonel. He needed a flag officer to do an immediate override.

A hand waved in front of his face.

"You all right there, Lieutenant?"

Clearwater blinked, shut his mouth, and faced the Armadas officer addressing him. The blue-haired gamma wore the insignia of a fleet lieutenant. What was she doing down here in the snake pit?

"I'm fine," Clearwater answered, standing up straight. "Just received some unexpected news."

"Very well," she answered before continuing on her way.

A flag officer. He needed a flag officer. He continued to reread the message, as if that would change its words, and shambled to a router. From snake pit to snake den, where the bulk of the Legionnaires senior staff was officed.

The thought of walking up to a marshal and asking him for reassignment was not especially palatable. But this was urgent. Hopefully they would understand. He couldn't lead a company. Not if the marshals wanted any of those men back.

The exit router brought him into the company of chaos. Gammas raced between terminals. Arens, kurai, kodaz, and officers of other flavors stood in growing lines to pick up their command kits. Clearwater went past them. The farther back into the den, the higher the ranking officers. He could already hear angry shouting from one of the offices and began to plead inside that was not the office he needed. As he approached a narrowing hall, he was stopped by another legionnaire, a kurai holding out his hand. To his right a green-haired gamma sat in a rounded cubicle.

"Are you lost, sir?" the sergeant asked.

"No. I need to speak to Marshal Veth."

The kurai made a face, glanced aside, and pointed down the corridor with his thumb. "Are you sure you want to do that, sir?"

By now, Clearwater could make out the shouting pouring through the open door, working its way toward a scream.

"Let me tell you something, you little fink. This isn't a peacetime service anymore. Piss on the safety latches. I'm pretty sure our guys will be a bit more worried *about the Vaar shooting at them!*"

Clearwater cringed so hard, the muscles in his face ached.

"Do you have an appointment?" the gamma asked from her cubicle.

Clearwater was about to answer when a fresh shout drowned him out. "Piss on Marshal Braxter too! That miniature bastard's never fought anything more aggressive than diarrhea! And you can tell him I said that! Override! Take the number fourteens out of the deck and put in the model twelves!"

"No," Clearwater answered when there was a break in the shouting, "but it's urgent."

"What is the purpose of your visit?"

"A mistake in auto-assignment. I need the marshal's authorization to change it."

The gamma looked ahead, no doubt sending a message to the marshal. Clearwater's heart pumped as he waited for her to say something.

"The marshal will see you," the gamma announced.

"Good luck, sir," the kurai remarked before stepping out of his path. Clearwater hesitated, tapping his fingers nervously against his leg before proceeding forward.

"Maybe I'm just not being clear!" A fresh shout as Clearwater came to the door. "I'm going to call down to your techs in about five minutes. If the model twelves aren't rolling off the line when I do, I'm coming down there. When I do, I'm going to find you, take my pipe, hollow your head out with it, and shit in your skull! *Maybe then you'll have the brains to do your damn job!*"

Clearwater swallowed nervously. The most muscular kurai he had ever seen sat behind the desk. Security tablets covered the surface. Violet eyes darted around while the marshal smoked on an ivory pipe. Two golden stars flanked crossed batons on his shoulders.

Clearwater knocked gently on the doorframe, drawing the marshal's eyes.

"You do understand how doors work?" the marshal quipped, the not-quite-friendly but not-overly-hostile tone catching Clearwater off guard. "If it's already open, you can just come in."

"I, I, I . . ." Clearwater grimaced to force himself to stop stammering. "I'm sorry to disturb you, sir."

"Kid, you don't know what disturbed is." The marshal pointed to one of the two chairs in front of his desk. "What do you need?"

Clearwater slid into the chair. "Sir. There's been a serious mistake with my orders. I would bring it up with my new CO, but seeing as time is a thing, I thought I better come to you."

The marshal motioned toward himself. "Let me see."

Clearwater forwarded the message and was silent as the marshal read it. There were precious few flag officers who weren't human or aren. Most aliens simply didn't live the two or more thousand years required to get there. Fewer still had the physical and mental capacity left to do the job if they did. Even though it was synth-muscle, the fact that his aged body could support that much mass was impressive.

"I'm not seeing the problem, Captain," the marshal said as he returned eyes to Clearwater. "Congratulations on the promotion. Even if it is temporary."

The old kurai could do a lot more than shout at him. Clearwater found it hard to summon his words.

"Do you need to go back outside for your tongue?" the marshal prodded.

"Sorry, sir," he answered. "Sir, I, that's why I'm here. That promotion has to be a mistake."

"Really?" the marshal asked, throwing out his arms in an annoyed shrug.

Clearwater pressed his back into the chair as his hands coiled tightly on the armrests.

"No, you keribro palindrome! If the model thirteens were acceptable, I wouldn't have told you to put the twelves in the deck! You have three minutes before you become *literal* shit for brains!"

The marshal was ten words into the sentence before Clearwater realized he was not the target.

Keribro? Clearwater was not as familiar with kurai slurs as perhaps he should have been.[29] But palindrome, he knew. Was that really the one the marshal meant to say? He would look *keribro* up later. The marshal looked back at him.

"Sorry about that, Captain," the marshal said, rising to his feet. Clearwater began to do the same before the marshal motioned for him to remain. The muscle-bound kurai rounded the desk before sitting on the front of it. "Are you refusing promotion? It's quite an honor to get that kind of advancement with not even six months in service."

By now the marshal had his personnel file open. Clearwater was sure that was all it would take for the marshal to see this change needed to happen.

"Sir, I'm not qualified to lead a unit that size. I've only led a section, and sir, well, I'm all that's left. The men in that company need someone competent."

"I understand." The kurai nodded.

"So, you'll change the orders, sir?" Clearwater perked up.

The kurai frowned, shaking his head quickly. "No. No, I don't think I will."

"Sir, but, I—"

"I'm going to do you a favor, Captain. Promotions boards look unfavorably on people who decline promotion. They're liable to think you're not willing to step up when you're needed. When the service asks more of you.

---

29   In Errdir, *keribro* means "one who has excessively elaborate sex with themselves."

For your own sake, your orders stand."

"Sir." Clearwater hesitated, beginning to rise before the marshal motioned him back down. "Please. I can't lead a unit that size."

The marshal crossed his arms and puffed deeply on his pipe. A pair of acrid clouds steamed out seconds later from his nasal slits. The marshal stepped off his desk and approached the wall-mount printer on the side of the office. When he returned, it was with a box that he set on the desk and opened. Inside were two pairs of silver swords crossed on a matching shield: the Solar Legionnaires captain insignia.

The marshal's beefy hand closed on Clearwater's collar and drew him to his feet with ease.

"Sir," Clearwater began before he was silenced by a glare. The marshal plucked the insignia from Clearwater's collar before grabbing the first of the captain's icons to pin the insignia in place.

"When you put on this uniform, you agreed that you would meet the needs of the service above and beyond our own. Because there were people at home who needed you to do it. Every ship in the fleet is printing arens and automatech for the operation, but I can't print experience. Every officer in this flotilla is getting kicked upstairs, including you. You've fought the Vaar—you've seen them in action—so you're getting kicked a little higher."

The marshal paused to straighten Clearwater's collar.

"So. When you leave, you're going to go back to your quarters, find your balls, and put them on. Then, you're going to report to your new CO and begin your new assignment. When you're done with that, you're going to go on your mission and kill yourself a whole mess of Vaar. Then, you're going to go home awhile. Find some pretty girl, lantai, or whatever you're into. Regale them with stories of your valor, and have them show you a good evening. Understand, Captain?"

"Sir—"

"Understand, Captain?" the marshal repeated.

"Marshal, I'm not qualified. My men—" Clearwater fell silent as the marshal's forced smile faded and the pipe sagged in his mouth. But he did not yell or scream. Instead the old kurai reached to his shoulders and removed his insignia. He took Clearwater by the wrist and slapped the insignia into his hand. He did not let go.

"I've met a lot of officers in my time," the marshal said, looking into his eyes. "A lot of them weren't qualified to do what they were asked to do. But I've met far too many more concerned with their career more than their legionnaires."

The marshal pushed Clearwater's hand until it was against his chest.

"I want you to keep these," the marshal explained. "Keep them because I want you to be able to wear them someday. In the meantime, just hang on to them. And if you're having doubts, I want you to look at them. And I want you to remember that the good ones have felt what you're feeling now. Your first job is the mission. Your second is to get as many of your legionnaires home as you can. And remember, we're all doing the best we can."

"Yes sir," Clearwater whispered, looking down slowly to his hand.

"Now go, and you bring back as many as you can."

"Yes sir," Clearwater answered with a sigh. A second later, he flirted with the ceiling.

"What? Who the hell are you?" the marshal shouted. "No! I said the model twelve! Where is Colonel Shehs? No. You tell him wait right where he is. I'll be right down."

The marshal clapped him on the back before the kurai sprinted out of the office. Somehow, he had a feeling that someone was about to have a very bad day. Clearwater took one more look at the insignia. He put them in his pocket.

He walked back into the heart of the snake pit and got in line. After several minutes, he stood in front of an aged alpha, who looked at him long enough to scan his face.

"Captain Clearwater—third, seventh, third," the aren said before handing him a large metal box. Within was a stack of security tablets for him and his subordinate officers. "Here is your kit. Report immediately to your CO."

"Yes sir." He slung the shoulder strap of the case on and made for the exit. Captain Clearwater, whether he liked it or not.

CHAPTER
21A

I N A CARGO BAY of the *Hurricane*, the chamber had been locked down for a gathering. Panzer stood at the front of the assembled formation, staring into a hologram. The perpetually angry face of Nicolae Espada, Commandant of the Corps, glared back at him. His albino skin contrasted poorly against the background in the grainy connection. The details of his mask blended together to bathe the bottom of his face in black. With no functioning astranet, it was fortune to get any connection back to the Solar Galaxy. A clear connection—that was too much to ask for.

The commandant's beady eyes glared over his breath mask. He was busy in his NOD.

"My resignation," Panzer said as he transmitted the file. "Effective immediately upon my return from the Hourglass."

Within himself, he could feel the new strength Anagram had promised. As if a foundation of mud at his core had transmuted into stone. He wondered how well he might withstand the commandant's room-shaking telepathy. His own telepathy was still well away from the level of the commandant.

"As much joy as this gives me," the commandant began, leaning back in his chair, "I am tempted not to accept it. If you were another man, some might call it cowardice to resign at the start of a major war."

There was no need to respond to that comment. So Panzer did not.

"Where do you intend to go?" the commandant asked.

Panzer was not about to offer the old man an idea to ridicule. He shrugged and offered the best answer he was willing to give. "Where there's a war, there's a fight. I'm sure I'll find one."

The commandant looked down. A loud sucking sound made it through the transmission as the old man drew a deep breath from his mask. "I will accept your resignation," the commandant began, raising a finger, "but until then, I expect you to fulfill your duty."

"Of course," Panzer answered. "Perhaps, since I'm leaving, you'll tell me what your problem has been with me all these years. Is it because the emperor forced you to bring me aboard? Or was it something personal?

The commandant indulged in a rare blink.

"Are you certain you wish to have this conversation with an audience?"

Panzer scoffed. "You've never made your dislike of me a secret matter. Why should your reasons be?"

A second blink. The old man must have been tired to give himself permission for two blinks in a single day.

"You're not one of us," the commandant answered. "You never have been. Your recent debacle on the *Caustic Reverie* is one more in a long line of proof. Your responsibility was to rescue the handmaidens and get out. Yet you decided to risk their lives, your life, and that of your team to evacuate the civilians as well."

The old man sat up straighter in his chair before he went on.

"You've always had to be some kind of hero." There was a faint hiss in the words. "Perhaps it's just bred too deeply into you. It was a *noble* thing, but the Corps doesn't exist to be noble. We're not here to be heroes. We do dirty work, and we do it quietly. The work that has to be done—that noble people can't bring themselves to do. The kind of things that will hurt their little feelings and haunt their fragile consciences. We do it because it has to be done, and we're happiest when no one knows we're involved. You don't belong here. You never did."

Panzer crossed his arms. "Well. Never thought words like *heroic* or *noble* would be used to disparage me. I suppose we'll be just as happy to be rid of each other."

"Perhaps," the commandant answered. "In the meantime, you have a mission. As much as I dislike the prospect. You have the most experience with the Vaar, and yours is the critical action. So you shall have command with Fulcrum as your second. Do not end your . . . interesting . . . career with failure, Colonel."

The hologram faded as the commandant broke the link.

"Screw you, too," Panzer whispered before turning to the formation behind him.

A handful of those present, he had worked with before. One or two, in an alcohol-elevated mood, he might even call friends. But even to them, he could not share everything. Never in his whole life had he been so grateful for the sovereignty of his mind. He was perhaps the one person who could hold something back from this crowd. The Encephalon, an invasion from another universe, unbelievable on their own, let alone collectively. They were taking too much on faith already. No reason to share what they would not believe. Not when he did not know who could be trusted and who could not.

"You've all reviewed your mission kit," Panzer began, removing a small projector from his pocket to bring out a hologram of the Crossroads. "I know you probably don't need it, but let's go over the plan one more time."

An image of ND-31, dwarfed by the Crossroads, appeared beside it.

"We travel to ND-31. I will use my connection to the planet's astranet to transport us to the Crossroads." He paused to zoom in on the dome straddling the structure's northern pole. "We keep our schedule, we will arrive at zero hour minus two. That gives us all time to get into correct position and get a lay of the land."

He drew the image of the Crossroads back out before zooming in again near the center of a trench that descended from the command dome to a matching dome in the south.

"The Vaar are using the generator they pilfered from Avalon as an auxiliary power supply. They're using it to bring systems online, and soon, they'll kick-start the generators that power the station. That job will fall to Fulcrum."

Panzer drew the image back out, allowing dozens of tiny pyramids to be highlighted on the station's surface.

"The rest of you will be hitting auxiliary control points. Polon and Umbra will hit the southern command center. The Vaar fleet will respond *massively* to this incursion, and the Vaar have put at least a flagship's worth of marines down there. Probably a lot more. We're already asking the fleet and the legionnaires for a lot, and they won't be able to hold for long. Everyone must be in position no later than zero plus two. All objectives must be secured no later than zero plus four. Once *walk left* is called, the legionnaires will begin extraction. Whether or not we will extract with them will depend on mission status. Withdraw is at your own discretion."

Panzer's eyes fell on Fulcrum, front and center. Like so many of them, the commandant's golden child did battle in a custom warbody. Unlike most of them, he rarely bothered to leave it. At close to three meters in that body, perhaps he simply enjoyed being the largest in the room. The man was practically a warmech with a brain. The triangular wedge that made up his head jutted forward even as it dipped downward. Slits in the perimeter of the triangle housed the sensors that were his eyes. A rotary cannon was perched beneath each forearm, currently withdrawn and compact. Six pylons on his back coiled over his shoulders to carry many weapons or share the burden of heavy ordnance. Beneath those pylons, four tentacle-like arms coiled around him, ready to grasp whatever he might need. The question Panzer pondered briefly was whether the man in the machine was still the second strongest metapsion in the Corps.

"Fulcrum, you're our backup plan. If I can't seize control of the command center, you must destroy the Avalon generator before the Vaar can use it to bring the station's generators online. You'll have to make a judgment call when you're in position. But remember, we have to try to get the civilians out. It's also the only way we'll get whatever's left of Aetius's fleet out of here."

Fulcrum brought his arms up, the enormous square fingers of his mechanical hands clacking together. He balled one hand into a fist before laying the other over it, as if cracking his knuckles.

"But in the end"—Panzer turned his attention to the rest—"we must deny the Vaar this station by any means necessary. If they manage to gain control of this station and bring it online, they win. All other concerns are secondary; all personnel are expendable."

The daunting reality was sinking in. This was the Corps, the best the Empire had. Yet for many, this was likely their last mission. Joint operations among Corps personnel almost always took high casualties. For multiple commandos only came together for the difficult of the difficult. If they were being sent to their deaths, even they might need some encouragement.

"We've all been here for years now. We've worked on the same goal. Up until now, the Vaar believed I was doing the work of nearly all of you. It's worked. I've tasted their fear when I've fought them. I've felt them trembling in their plates as they tried to fight a nightmare."

Panzer did not feel it, but he forced a large grin.

"Imagine their horror when they learn four hundred commandos are coming for them."

A few, almost sinister, laughs reverberated through the formation.

"The Vaar haven't had a lot of time to fortify. But resistance will be fierce. They know this station may be their only chance at victory. The legionnaires should tie up most of their marines. I know some of us may be tempted to help them, but keep your focus. The quants, the nakori, and the evulta can speak to the mercy of the Vaar. The Empire does not die today. So we *will* destroy the Crossroads."

He took a final look around the formation.

"That's it. Fall out."

No more was said. He would never trade away his telepathy, but in moments like this, he wished that it did not come with empathy. Suspicion shrouded the crowd. Many were always suspicious of him. Like the commandant, they were suspicious of the mind they could not read. But it was stronger now. He should have known that some would see through him and know he was holding something back. But he had sold the commandant on the importance. That was enough.

If only he could tell them. But if they knew what Anagram had done to his mind, that mind would be under a scope without the benefit of his skull. Without proof beyond "an alien told me," they would never believe the threat he'd revealed.

The time was fourteen hundred. Simmonne and the Twins had been sitting in the conference room for many hours now. The Corps would leave first to be in position. But there was still time. He turned to find the nearest router to reclaim what was his.

CHAPTER
21B

THOUGH NOT QUITE TO the degree of Combine ships, those of the Armadas were heavily compartmentalized. They had to be as a result of their sheer size. The *Hurricane* was broken up into many districts. Crews had their bunks, galleys, recreation areas, and more within sprinting distance of their watch stations. If a ship was so damaged that its internal mininet could not transport the crew around, there probably was not enough ship left for the need to exist. Even so, this compartmentalization ensured battle damage did not cut personnel off from where they were needed most.

For those instances where something had to move and the net was unavailable, Armadas ships housed their internal tram systems. Few in number, they were mostly quiet, empty corridors no one thought about unless they were needed. It was the one place Jenna Prideaux could go and be confident that no one might disturb her.

She had walked a distance from the terminal before sitting down. She dangled her legs over the edge as she stared down at the guide rail for the trams. Her hand went into her dress, and out came a pistol. She laid the weapon in her lap and, for a time, simply looked at the characters etched into it.

FOR HONOR AND DUTY

SHAPPO ZIRI—234

Her hand came up in a fist, as if ready to strike something. But she laid it in her lap by the pistol. She should have killed the bastard before this could happen. The high prince, the colonel, the *Master*. Whatever he was calling himself now. She should have killed him in the emperor's office when he touched Simmonne. Ended him then and there. The high king wouldn't have cared. The bastard was in exile. The emperor would have been upset. Very upset. Simmonne would have been horrified to see someone die right in front of her. But she had seen that now, several times. If she had killed him, it all might have been prevented. With the vanguard he'd chosen dead, maybe the emperor wouldn't have sent her here. The emperor would have been furious, but it would have been worth it.

That's if she could have killed him. Her lips trembled as she recalled the events in the armory. When she saw Simmonne on a leash like some slave. Not even a slave. Few kept a lantai on a leash. Like an animal. All paled compared to the thoughts she drew out of Simmonne. Jenna had sensed the cold moving through the princess's body, heard Simmonne's voice as she pleaded for him to stop. And she still tried to defend him!

Her hands came up to her head as she tried to fill it with other images. Of Simmonne in her arms, nursing from her bottle. Her parents were too busy to feed her. The times that the mischief the three of them found became their little secret. No need to involve parents with larger concerns.

Perhaps some of this really was her fault. Maybe she sheltered them too much. Certainly, the emperor gave her orders to the effect. But she might have interpreted them more broadly. It was just an excuse to blame His Majesty. It was her fault.

She looked at the pistol again.

She couldn't let them do it. She couldn't let them throw their lives away for him. She had to kill him. It was the only way. Even if the three of them never forgave her, it would be a small price.

She would have to be precise. She did not know exactly what augmentations he had. A commando had cybernetics well above what most soldiers possessed. An attack from the front was stupid. She would have to come from behind, put the muzzle to the back of his head—careful not to touch and give herself away—then pull the trigger. His skull was no doubt bond-forged titanium, corrugated at the atomic level to provide every bit of defense it could against disrupter fire. Mere centimeters way, it probably wouldn't matter. Once he was down, she could put more into his head. Five or six at a minimum to make sure there wasn't enough brain left for him to come back.

If she was careful, she might take him by surprise. The problem was his guards. The Vorhan Tohl's approach to a threat was to shoot first, ask questions maybe. If they didn't consider her a threat before, losing her temper in the armory meant they certainly did now. They would never relax while she was around. The moment she drew, they would gun her down from three directions.

Could she get him alone somehow? No, that wouldn't work. He'd be suspicious, and she couldn't hide her thoughts from a T-13. It would take a distraction. Even with that, she'd probably be killed shortly after. She couldn't do it in front of Simmonne or the Twins. They didn't need to see it. But what could be an appropriate distraction?

Her lips trembled as she gripped the pistol. What if they actually were happy? What if they actually did want this? No. She could not believe that. He did not assault the Cathedral with an army and carry them off, but he stole them all the same. He was much more insidious. Who knew what kind of secret training commandos had in mind control. They were his victims, of that Jenna was certain.

The emperor foresaw this, so why didn't he say anything? Why did the old man let that monster anywhere near them? Could it have been fake? Could a T-13 control her mind cleanly enough to make her *think* the emperor said that as the echo spoke? The bastard didn't deserve them.

What if Simmonne made him emperor? Why would the emperor even consider such an idea? Had he and his sanity parted company, and she just did not notice? What could the old man have been thinking? If she were to kill him, she just might be doing the entire Empire a favor. In different circumstances, she might have expected the Corps to intervene. But the bastard was one of them. Was there a conspiracy here?

Jenna perked up as she felt tremors in the deck and turned back toward the router. In the dim light, she made out a massive hulk coming toward her. A kodaz. A maintenance tech? No, roliams did that work. Kodaz were too big. She reached out with her mind to touch the approaching consciousness.

A strong 4CM field kept her from finding any thoughts within. She caught only a glimpse of herself. A moment later she could make out the red crest on the kodaz's head and the eyes that matched it. Rhoxx.

Her pulse raced, and Jenna was on her feet in a moment with her pistol ready. The captain of the prince's guards was coming to kill her. She had done half the work for him. She was in a deserted place. Her body wouldn't be found until someone went looking for it. He had commando tech, so the ship's security sensors couldn't track him. He could kill her, leave her body, and no one would be able to prove it.

Jenna took aim. Through the crest, just above the eyes. It was her only hope of putting him down quickly. Through the brain and its connection to the spinal column. If he didn't have enough dermal armor to stop the pulse, that would paralyze him and buy her the time to finish the job. As he drew closer, she switched the safety off. In an instant her pistol scanned the target and guided her aim to the sweet spot. The reticle rested just above his eyes.

"I not lookin' for a fight," Rhoxx said. "But you wantin' one, be makin' firssst ssshot count. Not givin' you a sssecond."

"What do you want?" Jenna asked, shifting her weight, ready to spring away.

"I comin' talk."

Jenna employed every scan her optical nanites could perform. He did not appear to be carrying a weapon, but he did not need one. All he had to do was get a little closer. Claws and teeth would be sufficient.

"I have nothing to say to you."

"I understandin'." The kodaz nodded. "Not likin' my lord, figure you not able, be likin' me."

She closed an eye, trying again to read his mind. Kodaz were as hard to read as delta arens, and his 4CM was too strong. But his feelings were there. She did not even sense the tension one would expect from someone with a gun pointed at them. But neither could she sense any duplicity or hostility. With some reluctance, she thumbed the safety back on and lowered the pistol. Perhaps she should have known better. She had a lot more respect for the reputation of the Vorhan Tohl, than their masters.

Jenna returned to her seat with her legs over the side, but she kept her heels firmly against the metal, ready to propel herself into the tram pit. She set the pistol aside but did not let go. Rhoxx took it as an invitation to come closer, and in a moment, the big kodaz sat beside her. He looked into the tram pit with her, staring at nothing in particular.

"It bein' hard," he said. "Ssso hard, sssometime. Tryin' protect 'em we charged wit'. Not jussst keepin' 'em sssafe. Seein' 'em potential. Givin' all we havin', pusshin' 'em to it. Hardessst when we have to know. Can't protect 'em from 'em ssselves. Ssssometime we ssso clossse to 'em. When 'em hurt, we be hurtin'. Seein' family in pain."

Jenna sighed, throwing out an arm as if she could dismiss it all. "She's the most good-natured person I ever met. I don't know how her brothers and sisters aren't that way. She can do so much more than she thinks. And now she's tied herself to a man who will only keep her down." Jenna gazed at her feet and shook her head. "Rhoxx, his first wife—what was her name? Ella?"

"Elssssa."

"Elsa. Did he treat *her* well?" Jenna threw a sideways glare at the kodaz when she sensed annoyance.

"I not really be bessst perssson be asskin'."

"Why not?" Jenna pushed at him. What was he hiding? What did the bastard do to the last pretty girl who fell in his grip?

"You humansss," Rhoxx growled. "Can't get ten of you in a room, 'fore you no longer agreein' on any'tin'. Not even how you ssssuposssed treat each ot'er. Ssso how I sssupposed be trussst' what right and wrong, when you can't agree? What be good, what be bad?"

His long claws clacked on the edge.

"All I be able tell you, 'em bot' be happy. Never him more, not hissself, t'en after ssshe dyin'. 'Em lovin' each ot'er."

Jenna sighed again, eyeing her pistol.

She could no longer read Simmonne's mind or the Twins'. She tried when they got the news and later when they boarded the *Hurricane*. But the bastard had some kind of mental wall around them now. She couldn't hope to penetrate any barrier of a T-13. Not while he was alive. Did it even matter if Simmonne loved him? He could have written that into her like anything else.

"I knew this would happen." Jenna sighed. "If the two of them were together. She feeds on other people's approval, their happiness. I knew when she met him and couldn't sense him that it would become an obsession. And he'd use it against her. I knew it. I told the emperor. He told me not to worry. Now I know he planned it all along and didn't tell me. I served that man for over two hundred years, and he didn't tell me."

Rhoxx took his time before saying anything more. "I never be one, try ssspeakin' for ot'er. Rhoxx born good-lookin', not telepat'. Not able know what really goin' on, in ano'ter mind. Maybe him t'inkin' you underssstand if you sssee. Or maybe, him bein' emperor, hope you trussst him judgment."

She shuddered before sighing. "I don't think I can anymore."

Rhoxx scratched behind his crest. "When I just becomin' grown. Takin' oat' to Rhinegraves. Take anot'er one to Prinss. You must been takin' oat'. To t'e emperor. To him daughter. Your oat' not sssame, mine. But it alike more t'an not. We not takin' oat' for easssy time, when quiet and comfortable. We take 'em for when it bein' hard. For when we musst be endurin'. For when we not knowin' t'e dessstination. But must be followin'. To remind usss. Sssacred duty, sssacred trussst."

Jenna looked at his big eye. "Did you ever think of breaking your oath?"

Rhoxx nodded slowly. "I t'ink of it. But never do it. Even when My Prinsss offer releassse me from it."

Jenna sniffed, shaking her head before hanging it to look at her feet again. "You were Vorhan Tohl to a high prince. Not even a high prince. The first prince. You had to live like a prince yourself. Keeping your oath cost you everything."

She heard the whistle between his teeth as he drew in a long breath. "Evertin'," he agreed. The hot air of his exhale hit her face and neck as he turned to her. "But my honor."

Jenna slid the pistol back into her dress and carefully returned to her feet. "You have more honor than me," she said before beginning to walk away.

"Vi-Baronesss," she heard him call from behind. "Out o' ressspect, fellow guardian, I undersssstand. But be knowin' t'is. If not for him order, you never leavin' our ssship alive. But you ever pullin' a weapon, My Prinsss again. Be prayin' he get you, before we do."

Jenna turned back for a moment. In silence they exchanged nods before walking opposite ways.

CHAPTER
21C

H.M.S. *Donetter Keems*. The only battleship in the Armadas named for someone from one of the other services. Clearwater wore his new insignia to the ship. The fleet had a semblance of mininet online now, and thus the trip was little more than a step into one of *Hurricane*'s routers. He had hoped to say something to Taula before coming over but had been unable to reach her.

He stood on an overhang in one of the battleship's hangars, looking down on the vast arsenal under his command. An entire company. This catwalk was where he would brief the lieutenants and sergeants. They would then move on to brief their units. He still had time before the meeting.

Ten platoons in a company. Ten sections in a platoon. Ten squads in a section. That was the arrangement for infantry, at least. Vehicular and artillery units never operated below the section level in any meaningful way. Closest to his vantage point were the automatech, visible through sheer numbers. The selection here was a sign of what was to come.

On ND-31, the platoon used the *Spartoi*-class light automatech. The somewhat skeletal machines had been optimized for urban combat. Legs walked on sidewalks, ran on streets, and had no concern for stairs. Their light design was meant to deal with a variety of structures, handle stairs of questionable strength, and go into spaces that weren't necessarily designed with large species in mind. But those were not the machines his new company was taking to battle.

The *Aggressor*-class automatech waiting to be loaded into the drop ships were something else. Big, hulking machines, they were not very pretty. But then, they were not meant to do pretty things. Each machine stood two and a half meters on a spherical wheel. When necessary that wheel could transform into legs, tracks, or even hover pads. Their upper body was vaguely cruciform. The machines had no real head. Their chests jutted out to a single point, ensuring that fire from the front did not engage with a flat surface. Broad shoulders formed the top of their body to house a pair of missile launchers. Two long arms, each bearing a rotary disrupter, drooped from each shoulder. The final armament was a pair of 55mm ordnance guns, one jutting forward over each shoulder. All guided by AI targeting that could hit a gnat on the wing, while the machine rolled along at two hundred kilometers per hour.

Virgin brown paint jobs revealed their new construction. No one had the chance or inclination to paint fancy designs or stencil witticisms onto their bodies. Clearwater had never really understood the mono-wheel design. It seemed too unstable. Someone once explained that controlled instability made for good agility. It still didn't make sense to him, but they were probably in trouble if they didn't have smarter men than him designing the things.

The companies' tanks were the next column. They, too, were automatech. Each had a compartment for an operator. But that was solely so that if one of the pilots lost his warmech, he could transfer to one of his tanks. Three out of four among the tanks were *Lae*-class, large machines with tall profiles. The turret of each tank was so far forward, it seemed as if it wanted to slide down the sloping nose. The 220mm pulse cannon looked a little too large for the spherical turret.

Behind the turret lay a pair of missile launchers recessed vertically into the hull. At the rear was the cage, an armored housing for drones and other small automatech to be deployed for scouting functions.

One out of every four tanks was a *Jai*-class armor-hunter. The specialist to the *Lae*'s generalist.

Armor-hunters were there specifically to kill enemy armored vehicles and bust up fortifications too heavy for the *Lae*'s arsenal. The *Jai* had the appearance of a stretched *Lae* but lacked a turret. Instead a large hump rose near the center of its hull to form a casemate bearing a pair of fire-linked 250mm rotor cannons. What they could not pierce in one hit, they just might drill through with rapid-fire.

The casemate had always seemed like a dumb idea to Clearwater, requiring the vehicle to physically point at whatever it wanted to shoot. But then he knew how agile they could be when the AI within wanted to put those guns on something. The stretched body allowed for larger missile launchers behind that casemate.

The *Brutus*-class warmechs stood beyond the tanks, and they drew most of Clearwater's attention. If he had come up the ranks the normal way, he would have attended armor school before making second lieutenant. There he would have learned the best way to use all this heavy equipment. Now he would have to wing it. Half of his mouth grinned, while the other tried to grimace. Hopefully all the time playing *Warmetal* taught him something.

The artillery was arrayed behind the warmechs with a mix of direct-fire pulse cannons and ordnance guns up to 400mm for indirect fire. All sported healthy supplements of missile launchers. All of this equipment had been positioned for loading into the *Munro*-class drop ships at the end of the bay.

The *Munro* looked like a giant egg standing upright on a black pad. Depending on how primitive a world was, that giant egg could be the tallest structure on the planet. Each *Munro* was meant to support a platoon indefinitely. Ten stories and ten decks included a garage for the vehicles, a galley for the organics, an infirmary, and even a small foundry to fabricate equipment from local resources. All with a suitable armament to protect itself on the way down.

He was a captain now. The same rank as Dad. Hopefully that wasn't an omen. The metal tin in his mission kit held a collection of security tablets. One in yellow for him, the rest in brown and black for his lieutenants and sergeants. He had already been through it once, and then again. He withdrew the yellow tablet as if reviewing the information a third time would change it.

The tablet sampled his fingers, and the data opened to him. Clearwater ran through it before slipping the tablet back into the kit. No recon data. No information on how much or what resistance to expect. Minimal orbital support from the fleet, if there was any at all. If this was a suicide mission, he didn't have enough information to know it.

Clearwater turned, realizing he was no longer alone on the catwalk. A kurai wearing the chevrons of a master sergeant had joined him on the overhang. The kurai's red skin darkened to black around a dermal patch worn on his cheek. Personnel identification registered in Clearwater's NOD. This was his company sergeant.

"Master Sergeant ahn Qopas, I presume?"

"Yes sir," the kurai answered.

Clearwater tapped his cheek. "Looks like you've seen some action."

The sergeant nodded, a tired look in his eyes. "Yes sir. I was on Avalon."

"How bad was it?" Clearwater asked.

The kurai made a face, staring briefly out into the bay. "If it could have gone worse, I'm not sure how, sir. Stations weapons failed, interceptors, orbital defenses, theater shielding . . . nothing worked. It's like everything just broke down at once. Then when the Vaar came, we couldn't mount an effective defense while trying to corral the civilians. Spent most of the time getting them on ships to get them out of there. Until Commodore Garren ordered us out. What about you, sir?"

Clearwater frowned, suppressing the shudder that tried to move through him as he thought back. "I was on ND-31."

His response drew a confused look from the kurai. "I didn't think anyone from that unit made it out of there."

"Pretty sure it was just me."

The sergeant frowned before nodding. "You wouldn't happen to know anything about all the colonists that mysteriously routed here? Would you, sir?"

Clearwater was about to answer before catching himself. "If I did, I'm pretty sure it be above both of our security clearances."

A knowing look in the kurai's eyes came before he cleared his throat. "Well, sir. I know I'm a little early, but I thought you might appreciate a heads-up on your new unit."

"Yeah. Haven't had a chance to meet any of them yet. Only skimmed through the personnel files."

"How do you want it, sir?"

Clearwater waited until he realized what the sergeant meant. "Straight and blunt."

The sergeant nodded but frowned. "Sir. None of your officers have any real experience. Your section leads are all fresh fourths. Most of your platoon leads are freshly promoted seconds—no real combat experience among them. Things are slightly better with your NCOs. About half of them have some real combat experience. All in all, it's about the least experienced unit I've ever been part of. Sir."

How did this happen? He had gone from being the new guy surrounded by experienced legionnaires to being the veteran surrounded by new guys. Wasn't it supposed to take more than one battle to be in this situation?

"Well . . ." Clearwater groaned. "Maybe that means command doesn't expect a lot of action in our zone."

"Maybe. Sir."

Both of them knew that was a lie. That wasn't how things worked. The new guys couldn't gain experience without being subjected to the fighting. Further, it was an old strategy, older than the Empire. Put the new guys out front; it didn't just let them get experience. It also encouraged the enemy to wear out their troops and supply on the expendable before the Empire sent in the more experienced, and thus more valuable veterans. If there was an omen here, it wasn't a good one. But even then, it was typical to at least have an experienced commander over those junior troops. By some cruel twist of fate, that was him.

"Any good news?" Clearwater asked.

Sergeant Qopas shook his head.

"Well, maybe we'll get lucky."

"Captain." Qopas took a breath. "We're going in with no recon. No idea of the strength of the enemy force. Questionable orbital assistance. We're probably going to need more than luck."

Clearwater glanced back toward the arsenal waiting in the bay.

"If I may make an observation, Captain?"

Clearwater turned back to him. "Of course, Sergeant."

"You're looking a little . . . mopey right now, sir. That's not what they need to see when they get here."

Clearwater noticed the deep lines around the kurai's eyes. That comment may have been a bit inappropriate, but the sergeant was right. Clearwater was an officer and—whether he should have been or not—a captain. With a deep breath, he brought his shoulders back, stood erect, and relaxed his eyes.

"Better?"

"Yes sir."

He had no safety net now. As a third lieutenant in command of a section, Sarge was there. If he was screwing it up, Sarge had the power as first sergeant to intervene. Even if it meant taking command of the unit.

Both of them turned as the router came to life in the corner. An alpha aren came out first. More arens followed him onto the catwalk. Shortly thereafter, the NCOs filed in. A mix of deltas, kurai, and even an ingridi. Clearwater watched them form ranks ahead of him. Each officer, and the appropriate enlisted men—more than two hundred filled the space in front of him. The officers formed the front row, each of them alphas.

Clearwater looked over the arens who stood at attention, their eyes directed straight ahead. He allowed his NOD to identify each of them. Every single one was fewer than ten days out of their tank. A certain unease crept into his bones. They came out of the tank knowing everything they needed to take these low offices. The knowledge of basic tactics and the manuals of arms were imprinted on their brains before consciousness had fully formed inside of them. They weren't children. They never had an innocence to lose about life and war. But even so, something felt so very wrong about what they were about to be subjected to.

It was the same story in the deltas making up a plurality of his sergeants. Fresh production, some barely a day old. They told him at Hell's Gate that they were not children. But how else was he supposed to look at a sentient being who had yet to live double-digit days, let alone years.

"At ease," Clearwater directed when it dawned on him that they were waiting for the command. He began at one end, handing out the security tablets to the officers. In turn, each alpha split the device into two and handed one-half to the sergeant who had accompanied him. From his tin, Master Sergeant Qopas handed out tablets to the remaining sergeants.

"There's a lot to do," Clearwater began. "We're not going to get much time to know each other going in. So let's make this quick. Interface, now."

He held the yellow tablet in one hand, engaging with it as each man in the unit did the same. A private network formed, and each saw the same thing. The chamber, the overhang, and all the equipment faded away to be replaced by a new landscape.

In their new surroundings, there was no soil or vegetation. Silver-colored metal formed a seamless floor. If one looked at the north, a terrain feature lay a few kilometers ahead. Many rows of small pyramids jutted up, ending in flat tops rather than points. Each was perhaps two stories tall, two and a half at most. To the east, larger pyramids towered so high, they were practically artificial mountains. But flatland took up the south and west.

The tactical AIs had drawn up a battle plan so simple that even he could follow it. He simply had to go over the plan with them and confirm he was not making any changes to the machines' recommendations.

"We're not going to do anything fancy," Clearwater said as the legionnaires looked around. "We're going in as part of the landing force. Our job is to get on the ground and set up a routing point for additional legionnaires to route in. This will be our landing zone. We'll land the drop ships here, cross-link their power, and get our theater shield up. That's priority one. We have to do that quickly, or Vaar artillery will tear us apart.

"Priority two will be securing our perimeter while getting our artillery deployed. Next, we get the routing terminal up so that our friends can come through. They're the ones who will be going forward to seize the objectives. So once the gateway is up, our job is to hold that location against a counterattack and provide fire support as needed."

A hand rose in the formation, and Clearwater looked at the ingridi sergeant. His NOD illuminated the name, but Clearwater was not prepared to parse the long line of consonants, let alone try to pronounce it.

"Yes, Sergeant?" he asked.

"Sir. Any more information about what opposition to expect?"

Clearwater shook his head. "No," he answered before realizing he could not leave it at that. "But. This place is too damn big for the Vaar to have every square kilometer covered. They couldn't have brought that many people in the time available. Fleet is going to scan the surface and give us what bombardment they can to break any initial formations they see. Once the Combine fleet reacts, don't expect any more support. They'll probably need every interceptor they have. So, all the more important we get our artillery ready.

"The Vaar will try to respond quickly to any landing, but with luck, we'll get our guys on the offensive before they can mass a counterattack against us. That's it. That's the mission. Command isn't asking much of us, so let's not disappoint them. We must hold our gate, no matter what they throw at us.

"If, for any reason, we have to leave our landing zone, keep an ear open. Command will issue the Legionnaire-specific action phrase, *dinner bell.* We hear *dinner bell,* it means one of two things. Either we've succeeded and can withdraw or the mission has failed, and it's time to save as many as we can. *Dinner bell* will be followed by *drop it.* Once *drop it* is called, we do that. We drop what we're doing, and we go through the routers."

Clearwater tried not to let his mind run away as implications raced through his thoughts. He swallowed before clearing his throat.

"One thing the briefing is *very* clear about—if the operation is successful, the battlefield will be destroyed. Anyone still there isn't coming home. One thing they aren't clear on is how long that will take. You hear *dinner bell,* don't wait for orders from me. Get your unit squared up for departure. If we have to leave LZ, fast-track your unit to the closest one with a functioning router."

A new alpha raised his hand, perhaps to ask the first real question of his life. Clearwater's NOD identified him as Fourth Lieutenant Andellus.

"What can you tell us about the Vaar, sir? The way they fight?"

"Well . . ." Clearwater hesitated as he returned once more to ND-31. "When I fought them, they filled the entire valley until they stretched past the horizon. I think maybe they were trying to make sure that if nothing else worked, we'd run out of ammo before we could kill them all."

He paused, trying to collect his thoughts and speak rather than relive. His eyes closed, and for a moment, his mouth worked silently.

"I think the Vaar know their guys can't take ours without a numeric advantage. But they don't just throw bodies at the guns. They used effective counter-battery fire to destroy the artillery we had positioned away from the colony. They probed our defenses with enspa, then used their colossi to draw the fire of the local artillery and breach the colony shield. Only then did they bring their guys in to flood us."

Clearwater opened his eyes.

"The Vaar need their numbers. They'll try to separate you. So don't let them. Tell your people. Don't let legionnaires get separated from their squad. Don't let squads get separated from their section. Don't let sections get separated from their platoon. We have a finite area to hold, and that's what we're going to do. Everyone needs to be close enough to help anyone else who they might try to pinch off.

"Also—they drilled this into my head while I was training, so I'm telling you—tell your legionnaires. If you haven't put at least one through their head, don't assume they're out of the fight. If I understand the map correctly, then if we face a counterattack, it will come from the south. So that's where we'll plan on meeting it. If we get further orders once we're down there, we'll deal with that then."

With a breath, Clearwater shrugged.

"That's all I've got for you. Fall out and brief your units. Then get your equipment on the drop ships." Clearwater paused, speaking up again as they began to turn and leave. "One more thing. Let the bots do most of the fighting. Let's try to bring this company home. Dismissed."

Clearwater turned back to the rail as the officers and sergeants filed out. He had that feeling of being watched. When he turned, he saw who remained.

"Something else, Sergeant Qopas?" he asked.

"Yes sir," the kurai answered. "With your permission, I'd like to reorganize the NCOs through the units."

"Why?"

"Those with experience are too heavily concentrated in first platoon," Qopas replied. "If you want those other units back, we need to spread the experience."

Clearwater winced at the realization that this issue should have occurred to him. "You're right. You have my authorization. See to it now. I want the legionnaires receiving the briefings from the ones who'll lead them in."

"Yes sir," Qopas answered before bringing his heels together and offering a salute.

With the same form, Clearwater returned the gesture before watching the sergeant leave. Now that was done, and he had one more thing to do. The router took him to his new destination, the snake jaw, otherwise known as the legionnaires' armory. He was routed to the officer's segment and exited the routing booth into a relatively small room.

A gamma aren sat in a cubicle defined by a cage that separated anyone not on armory staff from the armory itself. A large armored door to the gamma's side looked locked. Clearwater approached the cage, drawing the gamma's eyes.

"What can I do for you, Captain?" she asked, sizing him up with eyes as green as her hair.

"My AICES was lost in combat. I need a new one issued to me."

"Right away, sir." She looked down at her console and stared for more than a minute before speaking again. "What suit would you like, sir?"

The question gave him pause. He had not thought on it. As a new lieutenant, he had no say in the AICES he was issued. But rank had privileges, and as a captain, he had some say in the matter.

"Well, what are my options?"

The gamma's face betrayed a hint of confusion. "Whichever one you'd like, sir."

Clearwater's head bowed as he contemplated the options. If he stuck with the Myrmidon, he wouldn't have to worry about running out of ammo. The twin disrupters—its primary armament—drew directly from the reactor. If that ran out, it was all over anyway. But then, they would have a mininet connection. If that was lost, the unit was probably lost as well.

Sergeant Dolph. Clearwater recalled him in the *Longrunner*'s belly. Not a terrible example to follow.

"Give me a Grenadier."

"Yes sir."

The gamma's right eye twitched, machinery whirred, and the armored door to her side opened. The machine he requested waited for him. The Grenadier was the bulkiest of the AICES series: Wide four-toed clover feet, wide legs, an almost portly torso with a sloping chest. Its shoulders were practically spherical with wide arms ending in three-digit hands. The primary armament, a rapid-fire, 55mm grenade launcher, bulged from the forearm of each of these limbs. Recessed behind each shoulder was a 75mm mortar. Plunging fire was the name of this machine's game. It was harder to take cover against fire coming down from above.

The Grenadier had a distinct head, practically a pyramid on its side clutching an angry red sensor. Once inside, that head would look wherever he looked. Clearwater started to climb into the machine when he noticed the pair of globes. On each shoulder, a narrow post rose to a sphere that seemed to be made of triangles welded together. He held up a finger, pointing to one of them as he turned to the gamma.

"Interceptors?" he asked.

"Yes sir," she replied. "Marshal Veth ordered the field kits installed on every AICES we deploy."

About time. Clearwater was smart enough to know it should have never required a field upgrade to give the thing an interceptor array.

The rear of the machine opened, allowing him to bring his legs up to plunge into the suit. Inside he waited for the hand and foot interfaces to find his limbs, and the machine came online.

RUNNING FIRST-TIME INTEGRATION . . .

CAPTAIN JONATHAN CLEARWATER—IDENTIFIED

CONFORMING TO USER . . .

PLEASE RAISE THE RIGHT ARM.

He started to raise the left before catching himself and raising the right.

MAN-MACHINE INTERFACE . . . CALIBRATING . . .

PLEASE RAISE THE LEFT FOOT.

The machine carried out the second command, obeying like his flesh.

INTERFACE CALIBRATION—COMPLETE

ALL SYSTEMS WITHIN STANDARD OPERATING PARAME-TERS.

SECONDARY SYSTEM DETECTED

INTERCEPTOR FIELD KIT

INTEGRATION COMPLETE

MININET CONNECTION DETECTED

PRIMARY MASTER—H.M.S. DONETTER KEEMS

SECONDARY MASTER—H.M.S. CORADO

ALL SYSTEMS NOMINAL.

READY FOR WAR.

CHAPTER
22A

K ASSAR AND NOVIN FOLLOWED Panzer and the girls back to his ship. Accommodations on the *Hurricane* would have been more comfortable, but his ship was in a restricted, secure hangar. It was difficult to access and a smaller space for his team to secure. Beyond that, to all three of them, his bed was their bed.

Metallic noises occasionally radiated through the hull. His ship did not have the means to fabricate a new transpatial drive for itself. To do the job for a ship so much smaller, however, was a simple task for the *Hurricane*. The automatech systems of the hangar were installing that drive in preparation for zero hour.

The girls remained quiet. He no longer needed to buttress their mind with his, and the initial shock had passed. The mourning had not. All three dwelled on their father, their mother, and the siblings they lost. Kassar and Novin followed him to his quarters before he sent them to posts outside the ship.

"You'll feel better after some sleep," Panzer said to them once inside.

While all three prepared for bed, he called their dream regulators to his hand.

???: Andira, I could use some help programming these.

ANDIRA: Yes sir. What do you want them to dream about?

???: Their family. Suppress all negative memories, Bring out the happiest ones.

ANDIRA: Understood. Programming now.

???: Make sure they stay asleep until I wake them. They need the rest.

ANDIRA: Understood. I will program the devices to block visual and audio stimuli once they're asleep so it cannot wake them.

He turned down the bed and guided them into it. When the three were settled, he placed a dream regulator on each one.

"What about you?" Simmonne whispered.

"I have to prepare for the mission," he answered. "I won't be far."

He flipped the switch on her dream regulator before reaching for her leash. In some ways a leash worked both ways. Simmonne latched onto it and glared at his hand.

Please don't leave.

She clutched the chain as if it were part of him—so hard her knuckles were turning pale. Panzer killed the lights in the room.

Don't go.

"All right."

All three lay on their sides, keeping their weight off their hair. Panzer used his fight hand to pry Simmonne's hand off the chain, then he engulfed it in his. He drew a chair out of the floor to sit. To keep the embrace, he leaned over Julie, resting his elbow between her and Simmonne. The dream regulators had already put Jennifer and Julie to sleep, but Simmonne fought the machine.

"I won't go anywhere. I promise."

Despite the reassurance, he had to apply a bit of pressure on her mind before she surrendered. Her eyes fluttered briefly before closing. Soon the only sounds in the room came from their breathing, almost in perfect sync as the dream regulators carried them to slumber. It took time for a brain to reach the appropriate stages for sleep, and for now their minds were quiet.

"All three are now in the sleep cycle," Andira confirmed.

Panzer was about to snap at her for the noise but managed to catch himself. With the regulators' current settings, he could have a gunfight in this room, and they would never wake up.

"Andira. Get me Fulcrum."

"Yes sir."

Panzer brushed a rogue strand of hair behind Simmonne's ear.

"Fulcrum here."

Panzer sighed. "Fulcrum, I need you to meet with the marshals and finalize the objective points based on the recon sweep."

"There a problem?"

Panzer nodded. "I'm needed on my ship."

He had never cared for Fulcrum, and the feeling was plenty mutual. But at least one of them was still a professional commando.

"I see. I'll take care of it."

"Thank you."

The channel closed. Panzer rubbed his thumb gently over Simmonne's fingers. He had deliberately positioned himself as the center of their universe, but he had never meant to be the only thing in it.

"I have to survive," he whispered.

"Sir," Andira spoke up. "Since they are asleep, how are you coping with the emperor's death?"

Panzer frowned as he shifted in the chair to keep his comfort. "Well, I've never been part of the hive. I've never been one of these people who gets shaken when a leader dies, or some big event happens. I never had an illusion of security to shatter. I've never been rudderless because I relied on someone else to do my thinking for me. But, it won't be the same without him. The old man did a lot for me. He was the only important person who threw me a line when everyone else had forgotten or turned their backs on me. He wasn't the best emperor or even second best. But he was good. The Empire is worse without him."

"Sir?"

Panzer rolled his eyes. He knew that tone. He knew what she was going to say. "Yes?"

"Sir, you may well be the next emperor. It is inappropriate now for you to risk yourself in combat."

Andira and Rhoxx. Neither ever missed an excuse to try to keep him away from the fighting. Both doing their job, and then some.

"They may not claim me anymore, but I am a Rhinegrave. We've never asked anyone to fight for us. Only with us." He lowered his head, shaking it as he contemplated the insanity. "Besides, I seriously doubt I'll ever be emperor. We've seen a version of that man that he'd never show his children. We've been doing that man's dirty work for a long time. He's trying to pull strings beyond the grave."

"I don't understand."

He was about to answer before looking back at Simmonne. "Andira, I don't buy for a second that the emperor thought she was capable of ruling the Empire. She's sweet, good-natured, kind, and very easygoing. But she's too timid. *Too* easygoing. Too submissive. Too innocent. And worst of all, she just doesn't have the ego for it. To say nothing of the fact that she doesn't want it."

"Some people believe those who don't want the power are the best-suited to having it," Andira countered.

"Those people are idiots," Panzer rebutted. "History is full of people who didn't seek power but did horrible things once had it. All while feeling justified since they never asked for it."

Though the conversation was not in text, he could practically see the line of dots as Andira formulated her next statement. "Why would he say what he did if he did not intend her to be empress?"

"He's her father." Panzer shrugged. "Maybe he just wanted to build her confidence one last time. But why he'd name her empress, I don't know."

"Perhaps His Majesty intended all along for you to be emperor. Perhaps he said what he did so she would not feel she had something to prove, and could comfortably hand the leadership to you."

Only the current mood prevented him from laughing, but it was an AI's assessment. Option one, option two. Option one invalid; the correct answer must be option two. Simple as that, even if both options were ridiculous.

"I wouldn't mind being emperor. I'd be a hell of a lot more deserving than most of his children. But, I'm afraid I find it even less likely the old man wanted me to succeed him. I haven't always known what the old man was up to when he started, but when I figured it out, it always made ridiculously good sense. This makes none.

"The man had close to thirty children. Instead of any of them, his master plan is to end his dynasty and hand the throne to an exile from his rival family? I don't buy that for a second. Exile or not. Even if he felt none of his children measured up, the Empire has survived bad rulers before. I don't know. Maybe the old man foresaw my death and her remarrying, and that's who he's really trying to pass the throne to. But, even that doesn't track. Providents rarely see much beyond their death. He's gone and we're still here."

The dots filled the air again. "The dynasty will continue through her blood. You would not be the first man to take the Mandrake name when marrying into it."

Panzer glared up at the ceiling. He uttered one scoff. But that idea deserved a second. "Sure. Because *I'm* going to do that."

He brought his eyes back down to Simmonne as she brought her knees up toward her chest.

"Sir, if the emperor did not actually intend either of you to rule, what were his intentions?"

"I don't know, but you don't spend thousands of years on the throne without being able to think *many* moves ahead. I don't know what he's up to, but I don't think it matters anymore."

"Sir?"

Unconsciously he reached toward his shirt pocket for his cigarette wallet. He did not notice until realizing the wallet was not there. There was no pain and no real need for a cigarette. Only a hundred-year-old habit not yet broken.

"Well, it's a good thing she doesn't want to rule. Because she never will. It's like I told the others. Steven has already been confirmed. In peacetime, there may have been a chance. Clear her name through inquest and present the echo. But now? She has no military background. No experience in political leadership. Only charity. Steven is a combat veteran with many political accolades. In peace it'd be a hard sell. In war, they're not about to pull him off the throne to put her on it. They'd laugh me out of the Cathedral for even suggesting it."

Andira took a stern tone this time when she answered. Not by much, but it was enough to catch him off guard. "His Majesty named you her Executor of Succession. You have a legal and moral obligation to prosecute her claim."

His head shot up as a deep ring of metal echoed through the walls of the ship. "What the hell was that?"

"The new drive being seated, sir. Nothing to worry about."

"You certain the ship is secure?"

"Yes sir."

Despite her warning, he expanded his mind out. Kassar and Novin remained outside the door. Rhoxx was back, patrolling a perimeter around the ship. No one else in the hangar. Panzer relaxed back into the chair and turned his gaze back to Simmonne.

"Sir. You have—"

"An obligation, yes," Panzer interrupted. "Just what the hell do you want me to do about it, Andira? At this point, the only chance I'd have to put her on the throne would be to kill Steven. Then the Senate would have no other heir to vote on. Of course, the high king is liable to make his bid on the throne at that point. Besides, I doubt the old man meant for me to kill his firstborn. Nor do I think she would appreciate it if I murdered her favorite and last sibling to get her a job she doesn't want."

"Sir."

Panzer's eyes narrowed. He knew that tone, too. The one warning him that he wasn't going to like what he was about to hear.

"Are you certain you are not looking for excuses because you don't want to lose power over her?"

Panzer's gaze rose to the ceiling as his jaw flexed. Even Rhoxx wouldn't dare say something *that* bold to him. If he did, he would find a much less accusatory way of saying it.

"Andira, you're not organic or telepathic, so you may not be able to understand it. But think of it like a programmer having access to your quantum box and your source code. She's mine. She always will be. I have all the power over her I could ever want. With time and inclination, if I didn't like who she was, I could rewrite her entire personality. Her being empress would change very little."

"Sir, what if that was what His Majesty intended?"

He cocked his head before looking up. "I don't follow."

"His Majesty said none of his children were suitable. What if he intended you to solve that problem? What if he saw her as a blank slate and meant for you to change her into an effective ruler? As you said, you have the power."

His gaze snapped back to Simmonne. He wanted to scoff, to lay into Andira and tell her exactly why she was wrong. But was she? The horror played on his face as his jaw dropped.

"That's exactly the kind of thing the old man would do," he whispered. "He has just enough dirty in him to do that. It's exactly how he likes to handle dirty work. Show the problem to someone who would care and can fix it. Then, watch while they do it. The job gets done, and his hands stay clean."

This was it, wasn't it? This was what the old man wanted. It solved all his problems. To turn her into that person, he would have to change nearly everything about her. If he did that and turned her into that person, that would be the end for the two of them. Neither would have much use for the other. He would keep Jennifer and Julie, one a consolation, the other a thanks for service. She would go on to rule and either find a more demure man to help provide heirs or resort to other means of genetic engineering. A Rhinegrave would still be kept away from the throne, and it would be business as usual.

"That son of a bitch," Panzer whispered. "Even when I was diminished. With the equipment in the darkroom, I could do it in a few hours. Program the new personality into the machines, use telepathy to clean up the mess. Another telepath would never notice without performing a deep scan. She's young enough, the personality change wouldn't raise many eyebrows. They'd figure she just finally grew up."

Panzer hung his head.

"Those things he said about me being emperor. They were so garbage, he knew I'd see right through them." He paused, emitting a frustrated chuckle.

"If he were here now, he'd be disappointed it took me this long to figure all this out. That was for her benefit, not mine. To put her at ease by thinking she had an out. All those things he said I'd have to put aside, he was telling me why I was unfit—and couching it in a way she wouldn't catch. He—" Panzer brought his gaze back up to Simmonne's face. "He wasn't just saying goodbye because he was dead. He was saying goodbye to the person she is now. It's why he emphasized three. *Three daughters.* As in, one too many."

"What about the things he said, about you being the love of her life?"

His throat was dry, and he swallowed as he tried to correct it. "He never actually said he was talking about me. But maybe he still wanted me to get to know her. Intimately. So I would see what needs to be done. Or maybe he was just warning that it couldn't last."

He cradled both of her hands in one of his.

"Something I don't understand, sir. If he is willing to go to this extreme, why not simply appoint Prince Raymond over his objections?"

"Because Raymond is a saint." He stroked both of her thumbs. "Saints make a lot of enemies in politics. But like you said, she's a blank slate. She'd come to the throne with no allies, but no enemies either. And . . ." His head sank again. "I don't know how much the old man saw. Couldn't have been too much or he wouldn't be dead. But, what if he knew he didn't go in his sleep? He even implied it. If he even suspected he might be assassinated, he'd wonder about the rest of his children. But he knew she'd be far away when it happened. He knew she'd survive. This plan works even if all the rest are dead. It's the politician's bet. The safest one."

The dots filled the air for a time before Andira spoke again. "It should be done before you go on this mission. I can begin preparing the darkroom."

"No," Panzer whispered.

"Sir?"

"I won't do it."

"Sir. As Executor of Succession, you have a duty—"

"I said no." He shook his head slowly. His eyes remained locked on Simmonne's sleeping face. "He's asking me to sacrifice her and build a new heir out of her parts. I won't do it."

"Sir."

"No," he repeated, his voice growing louder. "I will not let her be empress. I will not see this innocent, happy girl transformed into a bitter, world-weary shrew carrying a burden she can't handle. And I will not make fundamental changes to who she is just because the old man couldn't be bothered to better groom one of his other children for the role. If that was his hope, then his hopes were in *vain!*"

The final words came out as a snarl as he stood and brought his left hand to her cheek.

"Sir. You are allowing your personal feelings for her to influence your judgment."

The dam broke, and as his mouth opened, the room shook. "Of *course they're affecting my judgment!*"

His empty hand shot up to his mouth when he realized how loud he had bellowed. Panzer held his breath and looked down at the three. The dream regulators were doing their job, and all three remained sound asleep. Even with his nerve heighteners active, he realized he was squeezing Simmonne's hand too hard. Her fingers were turning blue. He eased his grip and rubbed gently to encourage the blood to flow again.

"Andira, I won't do it. They're mine. I'm all they have left now. If I don't look out for them, who the hell will? The man is asking me to murder the person she is and create a new one."

"I'm not sure His Majesty would see it that way—"

"I do. And I won't do it. Not for him. Not for the Empire. Not for anyone." He gently stroked her cheek. "I should destroy that echo. Purge the memory from everyone who was there. Make Miss Prideaux think the Vaar found and confiscated it."

"Sir," Andira spoke softly but deliberately. Careful articulation went into every word. "Those were her father's last words to her, sir."

"I know," he whispered, "but they're also a threat to her. I've been asking myself since I saw it. Have Steven and I been friends for a long time? Or were we friends a long time ago? A person can change a lot in a hundred years. But even then, I knew how much the throne meant to him. As long as they're both alive and she has a claim to the throne, she's in danger."

It was worse than that. Telepathic inquest could easily prove she had no involvement or even knowledge of what happened. But there were a thousand ways she could die on the way to such an inquest. Many of those methods he had used. Many of them he could protect her from. But for others? The only way to defend against them was to deny the opportunity to use them.

Even if he got her to the inquest safely, if an emperor wanted to frame someone, they would be framed. There were ways to corrupt the truth. Not all telepaths were morally upright people. Memory-scanning computers could be programmed and reprogrammed. With the right telepaths, the people operating those computers could also be reprogrammed. The emperor could turn the entire system against someone. If people wanted quick satisfaction over methodical justice, few would look too deeply into the results.

This time Andira was careful with her words and took plenty of time to formulate them.

"If you will not let her be empress, at least let her keep her father's blessing. I believe you would regret it at some point if you took that from her."

Panzer smiled sadly, drawing his fingertip over the lobe of Simmonne's ear. There were many things Andira could never understand. But that ignorance, that detachment, every now and then it provided a special perspective.

"I'll do everything I can to clear her name," he whispered as the sense of resignation set in. "I'll let her keep the echo. You're right. That's not something I should take from her. But she will never be empress."

"Yes sir."

Panzer sighed quietly as he returned to his seat. It may not be that simple. He could only hope Steven was not behind this. The Empire needed its monarch. If Steven could not stay on the throne, there was only one heir left.

"Steven," he whispered, "please don't be behind this."

Simmonne had entered a dream state. With a sad smile, he looked into her mind to see the blooming memory. She was six years old in one of the Cathedral's parks. He heard her giggling, and the voice of her father.

Oh no! I can't find her. But the tickle monster always finds his victim!

Her giggling was becoming less controlled as she pressed herself harder against the tree.

There has to be a little girl around here somewhere! Where could she be?

With a sad smile, Panzer withdrew from her mind to peek into Jennifer's and Julie's. Both were sitting together in the emperor's lap. Three years old at the most. He was holding a holoslate, telling them a story while they stared in wonderment at the images.

"Andira?" Panzer whispered as he withdrew from their minds.

"Yes sir?"

"In all the time I spent with the emperor, I never caught any of this in his mind. He wasn't an especially strong telepath, but he was skilled. He knew how to protect his thoughts. But I'd think I would have sensed something about this. Is it possible, just *possible*, that we've been doing dirty work so long, we're seeing it where it doesn't exist?"

The dots passed and Andira answered, "It is possible, sir, but this idea does fit his pattern of behavior. It also fits that he may have predicted your unwillingness and initiated a contingency."

He sat up straighter as his skin began to crawl under his uniform.

"Team. Now."

"Yes sir?"

"Yes sir?"

"Bossss?"

"Listen carefully," Panzer began. "Until further notice, none of you are to leave the ship without full combat kit and maximum 4CM. All other members of the Corps are now to be considered hostile to Simmonne, Jennifer, and Julie. If any attempt to approach, give them a single verbal warning. If the warning is ignored, terminate with extreme prejudice. And make sure they stay dead."

Without delay. Without hesitation. They answered.

"Yes sir."

"Yes sir."

"Yesss sssir."

No matter what happened next, when he did not deliver her to the Cathedral, the Corps would hunt them. Sooner or later. He had hoped not to show his hand too soon, but the risk was too great. He rose again from the chair, this time bending down to Simmonne. She was dreaming about her sister Brittany. The latter had helped her circumvent the parental controls that kept innocent young eyes from parts of the astranet where they did not belong.

All three were asleep now, with no chance of waking up. He could leave and return later. They would never know. But he told Simmonne he would stay, and he would keep his word. While they slept, he would do what he could in the fleet's network. Fulcrum would have to handle the rest.

CHAPTER 22B

WITH THE WAKING HOUR came the realization that it had not been a dream. They were in her thoughts before Simmonne had opened her eyes. There was a firm pressure on her hand. When she opened her eyes to the dim light, Master was there. His eyes were closed, and for a moment she thought he might have somehow fallen asleep sitting up.

"Zero hour is coming." His voice broke softly into her thoughts.

You have to go now. Don't you?

His eyes opened, and Simmonne felt the Twins stirring at her sides.

"Soon. I can't take you with me. Rhoxx will remain on the Hurricane *with you three."*

Simmonne gripped his hand more firmly.

What if they arrest us while you're gone?

His thumb rubbed the back of her hand gently. *"Trust me."*

Simmonne looked at his hand closed around hers. Such an enormous hand. Julie looked up at him and nodded as Master sent something into her mind. Simmonne had no desire to leave the bed, but she did not protest as she and the Twins were gathered to their feet and led to the washroom. Silently she held out her wrists, and once freed of her restraints and collar, she followed his urging into the shower.

Still wary, she turned back, expecting him to join.

"I have things to take care of. I'll be back for you in a few minutes."

Don't go.

He closed the door to the stall. *"I'll return soon."*

The warmth of the raining water offered little comfort as he left the room. Simmonne took a quiet breath and turned her attention to the bath-care printer, which distributed nanogel into her hands. She was about to apply it to her hair when she turned her head to see the Twins sitting on the shower floor, each holding the other's hand.

Simmonne felt herself tearing up all over again. She had been so consumed by her grief that she had been blinded to theirs. Their heads leaned against each other, and both were silent.

"Get up, girls," Simmonne whispered.

Both looked up at her, but neither moved. Simmonne bent, taking hold of their joined hands and pulling. The Twins continued to sit limply. Simmonne knew very little about grief, but she knew that it made people stop eating, bathing, and grooming. Overpowered by the despair, they could no longer see the point. She would make them see a point.

"Get up, girls," Simmonne repeated, pulling more firmly. "Master wants us to clean up."

The pair wore identical expressions before pushing their backs to the wall and returning to their feet. Simmonne continued to pull, dragging them away from the wall. Jennifer's mouth opened. She spoke gently, but Simmonne cut her off all the same.

"We're part of a portfolio now. We do things together."

They nodded but remained in place. Simmonne held a hand back to the printer, drawing more gel before firmly tugging Julie toward her. She was about to brush the gel into Julie's hand before she felt herself drawn forward as the pair of arms wrapped around her. In her ear Simmonne heard the sobs. For a moment, Simmonne almost joined her.

No.

With a sniffle she brought her hands up and began working the gel into Julie's hair.

"We're going to be all right," Simmonne whispered.

They needed him right now. Whatever Master was doing had better be damned important. Simmonne's hands paused the moment she had parsed her own thought. With a deep exhale she forced the anger to leave with her breath. She knew where he was going, so she returned her focus to Julie's hair.

The Twins' sources of sorrow tried to overpower her control. Together they threatened to plunge her over the edge. She focused her efforts more intently. "We do things together," Simmonne whispered. "We always have. We'll get through this together, too."

Julie nodded quietly as Simmonne reached over to the printer for more gel. Her mind wandered as she continued to work. Steven. Did he really cause this and kill Daddy? And could Daddy really have given her the throne so she could give it to Master? If Daddy knew all along who she'd choose for a husband, despite knowing who Master really was, maybe she should just give it to him.

Why did this have to happen? Raymond. Why wouldn't he just take it? For an instant she was angry at Raymond for rejecting the throne. Even furious for helping to put her in this situation. But that anger quickly turned to guilt. He was gone, too.

Simmonne felt the embrace break and let Julie step away. As Julie began to attend herself, Simmonne turned to Jennifer, who still stood against the wall. Her eyes were on the floor. Simmonne took her arm and pulled her forward. With more gel she attended Jennifer's hair as well. Jennifer simply stood in place, neither moving nor speaking.

"We do things together," Simmonne whispered to her. "We'll be all right. Together."

Jennifer did not respond. Simmonne pulled her into an embrace, but Jennifer did not return it. Simmonne pushed her back a step, bringing her hand up to tilt Jennifer's chin until they made eye contact.

"We're going to be all right," Simmonne repeated.

Jennifer nodded, and this time Simmonne was pulled into her arms.

"It's okay to be sad," Simmonne whispered. "It just means you loved them."

She concentrated on getting the gel into Jennifer's hair. She took a bit longer to let go, then began tending to herself. She tried to work quickly, unsure how much time they had. The time in her NOD read 01:31. By 01:44, she asked Andira for the heat, and the warm flow of air replaced the water. They were dry soon enough, but he had yet to return.

Simmonne began to reach for the door, but there was no strength in her hand to open it. Master did not say they could get out. Did he need to? Or was it implied? She withdrew her hand from the door. He put them here. They would wait here until he returned.

At 02:00 the door opened, and he returned. His hands were full of cloth that he set on the sink. After opening the door, he motioned them out. Simmonne led the way, holding out her wrists expectantly. Wrist pieces, ankle pieces, and finally her collar. Only after that did Master hand her the clothes.

The cape brought a welcome warmth as she pulled it tighter around herself. Behind her she felt the small comfort of each Twin amid the metallic clasping.

"Let's go," Master whispered.

He guided all three in his arms toward the door. As soon as it opened, she found Rhoxx, Kassar, and Novin all waiting. Simmonne's lip began to tremble. Why should seeing the three of them make her sad? Of all things? Rhoxx in his restored lobster armor. The kurai in his people's bladed armor.

She leaned back into Master for only a moment before he ushered them toward his armory.

"Stand here," he directed as they entered the door.

She and the Twins stood together at the doorway as Master moved to the pit at the room's center.

"Andira. AMAC, configuration three."

"Yes sir."

He held out his arms as he was encased in the black film from the pit. Simmonne watched him reach toward his mouth. He seemed to pause for a moment before extending his arm back out and stepping up onto the pair of foot pads offered to him. As his armor came together, Simmonne's eyes wandered over the armory. The big golden gun lay on the bench at the room's front.

She turned her eyes back to see Master step up into a larger set of foot pads, assembling the multi-piece feet of the large suit being erected around him. A second, larger suit was being constructed around it. A skeleton of metal formed around his limbs and torso before metal plates were attached. The finished suit was much bulkier than any she had seen him in before. The torso jutted well past his chin into a wedge that spanned from neck to groin. The armor over the legs mimicked the wedge-like shape, offering only angled surfaces from the front.

"Excuse me, Majesty."

Simmonne shuffled aside as Andira entered the room. She followed Master as he stepped out of the pit, once again helping to hoist the large backpack of ammunition on his back. Once he had claimed his golden cannon, he compacted it to his back and turned to Andira.

"I'll equip the rest when I get back. Have the ship ready to go."

"Yes sir."

He gathered her and the Twins. As they came to the ship's exit ramp, the rest of the team rejoined them. A short trip off the ship and through a router, and they were on the admiral's bridge of the *Hurricane* once more.

With more haste than before, bridge personnel cleared their path as they ascended to the highest level. Admiral Aetius was on his perch, addressing hundreds of screens showing the faces of other officers. Master had led the way but paused at the top of the highest ramp. Only when Aetius had closed the screens of the conference did the entourage proceed up to the final level.

Aetius had an argumentative look on his face as he approached. But he stopped cold. For many seconds no words were spoken, but Simmonne was confident a brisk exchange was underway. She could feel Aetius's growing consternation and saw him sigh before he pointed toward a large chair some meters behind his perch.

Master nodded to him before leading the way to that chair.

"Sit."

Simmonne did as she was told and soon found the Twins sharing the large seat with her.

"Rhoxx will remain here with you. Do not leave the bridge. Do not separate. There is a lounge through the back door if you're hungry or need a drink. Rest facilities there as well. Rhoxx can only be in one place at a time. So if one of you goes, all three of you go. Understand?"

Yes, Master.

She nodded as the Twins did the same.

"I'll return when it's all over."

Master? Simmonne stood as he began to turn away. She waited until he faced her again.

I love you.

His faceplate was up, so she could see his face, and she saw the smile. Not the predatory or smug grin she had seen on his face so many times before. Not the half smile of amusement. Just a simple, understated smile and a sensation of warmth before he lowered his faceplate. Simmonne returned to the chair.

Nothing more was said. Master nodded to Rhoxx before motioning with his hand. Kassar and Novin followed him back toward the ramp on their way out of the bridge. Behind their chair Rhoxx had taken his seat, coiling his long tail around the chair.

"Come back to us," Simmonne whispered.

CHAPTER
22C

IN ONE OF THE *Donetter Keems* hangars, Clearwater stood on the boarding ramp of a *Munro*-class drop ship. There he supervised the loading of the platoon he would accompany on the ride down to the surface. The *Munro* was the largest and toughest drop ship used by the Empire. In Legionnaire brown, the ship had the shape of a massive egg standing upright on a small boot. Four corners were created in the otherwise round silhouette by the weapons pods ready to sterilize their landing zone.

A single *Munro* could support an entire platoon. A thousand legionnaires with their tanks, warmechs, artillery, and automatech could fit within. Ten of these ships would bear the entirety of Clearwater's company to the surface. The innards were mostly hollow, with stacked decks ringing the walls. Soon he would take his place on the uppermost deck, with a clear view down through the ship.

His AICES stood behind him on the ramp. There was something cleaner, richer about the air of the battleship. Something about it seemed closer to the air of a world, so he breathed it while he could.

On the *Munro* it was last in, first out. The artillery went in first, followed by the warmechs and tanks. The light infantry loaded in behind them, and the heavy infantry last. The true first-in were the automatech, loaded into the nose of the ship to be fired out at the ground just prior to landing. The tanks were loading now, gliding up the ramps to their secure stations on the lowest level. Four doors, one to a side, accepted the ship's passengers aboard.

"Johnny!"

Clearwater turned to the sound of the voice and did a double take when he saw Taula coming toward him. "Taula?" She came to the foot of the ramp and he descended to meet her. "Taula, what are you doing here? Civilians aren't allowed in here."

"Oh." She smiled, reaching down to jiggle the large tag hanging from a band around her neck. "Admiral's daughter, remember? I know how to get around a fleet."

"Uhm." He paused. "Yeah, but . . . you're still not supposed to be here."

Her eyes opened wider before she gave him an annoyed glare. "Well fine. I'll just go."

"No. Wait." He chased after her until she turned back to him. "I didn't mean anything. Why are you here?"

"I came to see you off, silly," she answered.

"Oh," he said, beginning to stammer. "Well. Uh. Thanks."

He was not sure what else he was supposed to say. Taula reached out, gently taking his hands and bringing them together.

"Johnny." She paused when he winced.

"Taula." He hesitated. "Please don't call me Johnny."

"But why?" she asked. "I like Johnny."

Avoiding her eyes, he grit his teeth for a moment. "The only person who calls me Johnny is my mother."

Her posture shifted. "Oh," she answered. "Well. Jonathan? Are you sure you can do this?"

He had to stop himself from laughing at her. The look on her face was one of concern, and she gripped his hands a bit tighter as she asked the question.

"I don't really have a choice. The brown says I go, I go."

"Yes you do," she insisted, squeezing his hands a bit more firmly. "I talked to my dad. I told him what you went through. He spoke to Marshal Veth. He said if you request suspended duty, they'll give it to you. But you have to do it now. You don't have to go down there. You can stay up here."

He didn't have to go? He turned his head aside and guided Taula closer to the edge of the ramp as a tank ascended into the *Munro*. The air disturbed by its magnetic drive blew a breeze past their legs. Clearwater's eyes saw the tank, but his mind saw the Vaar colossus as it came down on Twilight's wall. The brilliant light of nuclear detonations flashed behind his eyes, and the sound of a saw was distant in his ears.

"Call him," Taula urged. "Call the marshal right now and request suspended duty."

Clearwater closed his eyes, pushing the sights and sounds away. When he opened them, he saw the light infantry ascending the ramp. With a frown he turned back to Taula.

"I can't," he whispered.

"No." She jerked at his hands. "You don't have to go."

"Yeah I do," he whispered. "I can't just sit up here and watch while all of them go down."

"Yes you can," Taula insisted.

With a frown, Clearwater returned the firm squeeze to her hands. "I can't." He tried to pull his hands back but instead ended up pulling her closer when she refused to let go.

"Jonathan—"

"I'm a legionnaire," Clearwater answered.

With a frown, Taula nodded.

"Jonathan." She waited for him to look at her. "Don't be a hero down there. Keep your head down. Just stay alive. Promise me."

Promise what? Promise he wouldn't be a hero? Whatever that meant. Promise he'd come back alive? How could he promise that?

"Promise me," she repeated, moving with him as he tried to look away from her.

"Taula, I can't promise that."

"Promise *me*," she insisted. "Promise you won't do anything you don't have to. Promise you'll stay down."

Clearwater nodded slowly. "I promise."

She took him by surprise, coming in to find his lips. The kiss was brief before she stepped away. Her hands slipped out of his.

"Good luck."

With a silent nod, Clearwater watched her make her way out. A small router on the perimeter of the room was her exit. He turned, startling as he realized Sergeant Qopas was standing directly behind him.

"Sergeant?" Clearwater asked. "How long have you been there?"

"Me, sir? Oh I just popped up here at this exact moment. Sir. All are aboard."

"Right."

Clearwater rounded his AICES to climb in from the rear.

"What about the rest of the company?" he asked as the sergeant followed him into the ship.

"All armor is loaded, ready for the infantry."

Clearwater scrolled through the communication options in his NOD, selecting to broadcast to his officers and NCOs. "Company, double-check all assignments. Have all legionnaires double-check their equipment."

Unnecessary orders. His unit mostly consisted of arens and kurai. Not the kind of personnel apt to carelessly leave something behind. But, it did help him feel he was doing something other than just waiting. His eyes sought Taula again as she walked beneath the wing of a large shuttle toward the nearest router. On the routing terminal, she turned back to face him and raised her hand. On reflex Clearwater did the same, and in a flash she was gone.

He stared at the empty router for a time before his eyes moved to the ship she had walked under to get there. A variation on the *Longrunner*-class, fitted with larger-than-standard wings, and four canting stabilizers on its tail. The ship bore a prominent symbol, a silhouette. The upper body of a hooded figure had its head bowed, and its hands were clasped together as if in prayer. From behind its shoulders, a pair of feathery wings stretched widely. The initials *S.A.R.C.* were stenciled beneath the image.

A pair of deltas stood beneath the ship's wing in the armor of field medics, denoted by the white crosses on their arms. A legionnaire with a cigarette was speaking to them. No doubt the Search and Rescue Contingents would have their hands busy very soon.

Each *Munro* had four loading doors and four ramps. Heavy infantry ascended on three, with the light infantry on the fourth. Clearwater stepped up the ramp to enter his AICES from behind. As he turned toward the ship, his NOD opened a screen.

FROM: *HOMEBOUND SECURITY*

TO: CAPTAIN JONATHAN CLEARWATER
YOUR MESSAGE HAS BEEN REVIEWED AND CENSORED.
THE CENSORED MESSAGE HAS BEEN APPROVED FOR FINAL
TRANSMISSION. DO YOU WISH TO REVIEW BEFORE THE
MESSAGE IS SENT?

Clearwater eyed the words for a minute. Part of him had expected the battle to begin before it could pass review. So now he had the question. Send the message home, or cancel it? If he died, it might do more harm than good.

"Are you all right, sir?" Qopas asked.

Clearwater looked through the message at him.

"Yeah. I was just having a debate with myself. Pretty sure my family thinks I died on ND-31. Just wondering if I should send them a message."

"Understood."

Clearwater frowned in his AICES. He'd only mentioned it with the hope that the kurai might offer a suggestion. But none was forthcoming. His fingers wrapped against the inner sleeve of the AICES as he reread the notice. His eyes moved to the side for a moment and pulled an image of Dad. What if he could have sent something before he took the mission?

Clearwater took a breath.

>>SEND

Act—V: The Battle of the Crossroads

CHAPTER
23A

THE FOREMOST CARGO BAY of Panzer's ship had often served as the team's staging area, a function it carried out even now. Still in his armor, he stood at a large workbench with the Hellbore lying before him. To carry his full arsenal around the *Hurricane* may not have been prudent, so he had Novin bring the rest of his weapons here for mounting. Now Novin and Kassar sat on the floor in battle meditation.

The ships of the Corps had made the jump to the Basin's edge. There the spatial disturbances of the singularities would help to conceal their movement. The Vaar would almost certainly detect that something had jumped in, but they would have no idea how many. To help with that, a single *Rook* accompanied them. When they came out, the *Rook* went its own way. If any Vaar came looking, they would spot the *Rook* and likely not even bother to chase it. The small fleet of commando ships, meanwhile, made a dash for ND-31.

While Panzer's mind worked, his hands attended to their own tasks. The first of the additional weapons was a CF-606 progo-flamer.[30] The weapon's three barrels, arrayed in a triangle, made it one of the most visually intimidating in his arsenal. When he had completed a physical inspection, he held the weapon up and released it to his mind. From there it clamped to the left side of the hump at the back of his armor.

He had to tell more lies to get here than he would have liked. Even to Aetius, he had not been completely honest. He couldn't be. Too many of the flag officers had bad experiences—with him or with other members of the Corps. The Corps was perhaps the most feared, but it was also the bastard child of the Empire's defense. Regarded as the intelligence community by the military, and as military by the intelligence community, it was fully

---

30 Programmable matter flamers (also known as progo-flamers) are an incendiary weapon utilized by Imperial ground forces. These weapons project a stream of incendiary gelatin engineered to behave as programmable matter even as it combusts. The innate behavior of the gel makes it proficient in finding gaps such as microscopic holes in environmental seals or cracks in armor. Progo-flamers are often used in closer quarters where use of apollium could present potential hazards to the operator.

accepted and trusted by neither.

The second weapon was a GML-3660, a boxy missile launcher with twelve tubes, each loaded with its own warhead. Panzer floated it up to clamp onto the right side of the hump. Both it and the flamer retracted behind him as they went into standby.

It was a strange quirk of human nature. When one was considered untrustworthy, telling the truth would see it dismissed as a lie. Then when lies were offered in frustration, they would be seen as reluctant admissions of the truth. If he told the marshals how many Vaar waited for them, they would have been more obstinate. It would be worse if he mentioned that they were only a diversion.

Panzer turned his attention to the Hellbore, inspecting it one more time. The legionnaires' objectives weren't pointless. If he was understanding the knowledge Anagram gave him correctly, the station *could* be destroyed by what they were sent to do. But they would never be able to do enough. They were going down there to soak up Vaar and draw the defenders away from Corps objectives. The Corps would hit the command infrastructure that would keep the Vaar from shunting control away from the main command center. When the time came, Panzer would destroy the station. The attrition for the legionnaires would be brutal. But when it was over, they would believe it was their victory. No one outside the Corps, save perhaps the emperor, would ever know the truth.

No matter how much he concentrated, Panzer found his mind wandering. His blood pressure rose when someone else distracted his thoughts. Simmonne. She was the Imperial Rose, and now she was his. Her worries were supposed to revolve around what piece of gossip she had missed. What another girl had said about her. What she was going to wear to the next big event. What new thing had captured her fancy—and she could not get enough until suddenly she did. At worst, she should be worrying about what people said about her on the astranet. Those were supposed to be her concerns, those of an innocent. Not the horrors of a commando. Nor those that her father tried to shuffle onto her.

I love you.

His blood pressure began to calm, and he allowed himself a quiet chuckle. She thought she gave herself to him in the bedroom. So naive. It was when she said those words, and she'd left herself vulnerable in a way few people found easy. She did it without expectation, or disappointment, when he did not say it back. One of the few pieces of advice the high king ever bothered to give him.

Make a woman work for your affection. Never work for hers. She will not respect it. Never be the first to say the L-word. She will not respect it. No woman loves a man she doesn't respect.

What she was feeling was infatuation, not love. Love was built over time. Infatuation was what gave two people the time and motivation to do it. She may not have known the difference, but he did. Yet it felt like love when she said it.

Panzer took the Hellbore by the handle.
HELLBORE MK. II MASTER CONTROL
THREE, DEVICES INSTALLED.
SYSTEMS CHECK . . . NOMINAL . . .
ALL SYSTEMS READY FOR ACTION.

There was a strange sensation when he picked the weapon up, as if a third lung within him had just inhaled. Something had happened, but he was not sure what. He allowed himself only one full night with the girls. While they slept on the second night, he went to the armory. With Andira at his side, he tore the weapon down to its pins, and every component was scanned. Yet hours of investigation found nothing changed in hardware or software. The weapon was convinced otherwise. But even its update log could not find the changes. When he function tested it, everything worked as it should.

Why, when he considered taking a different weapon, did he feel so strongly that he *needed* this one?

Panzer set the weapon back on the bench. Jennifer and Julie. Everyone had misjudged them, even Simmonne. The fact that Simmonne had was both surprising and not. How often did one examine, in exhausting detail, something that was mundane in their lives? He should have known better. In an environment like the Solar Court, gossip was rampant, and exaggeration with it. Indeed their geneticist seemed to have set their libidos a bit too high, their impulse control a little too low, and their intelligence lower than it could have been, but it was not why they acted the way they did.

All they needed was some attention—to be treated like they were more than Simmonne's jewelry. He would give them that attention. Not so much that they did not feel like they had to work for it. Not so much that they could take it for granted. But he would give it.

If he survived.

Panzer shook his head to clear his mind. He picked the Hellbore back up. The weapon had three magazine ports. The main was located on the underside. Two recessed ports normally covered by hatches were on each side of the receiver. Panzer packed a drum into the bottom port. The left port became the plug for a magazine hose connected to the ammunition pack on his back. In the right port, he inserted a magazine of nanocendiaries.

The mind had an odd propensity for dredging up random memories and ideas. Now when his mind did so, it drew from memories that were not his own. A marker lying on the bench caught his eye, and he laid the weapon back down. The marker was meant for highlighting points on the weapon that needed inspection. Panzer took it, and a button deployed the tip.

Somewhat haphazardly, he drew a line on the bench. His thoughts transitioned to ND-31 as he and Oul'sor fell through the sky. Yet he remembered more, something that had not been there before. He moved the marker to the beginning of the line and drew a curve above it. He brought it back down near the middle.

"But time as well," Panzer whispered as he drew a second curve, this time beneath the line and terminating at its end. A series of dots joined the doodle as his thoughts worked. His mind stabilized and the tapping stopped.

"When he steps off the line . . ." A long road and a short road could lead to the same destination. All things took time. No time, no actions, and no reactions.

Panzer redrew the curves, thickening both of them.

"You're going the same place. You're just taking another route."

He clicked the marker to withdraw the tip.

"You can't touch me while you're out there," he whispered as his mouth moved into what Simmonne would call a predatory grin. "But I know what can."

Panzer glanced over his shoulder as Kassar and Novin rose from the floor. With battle meditation complete, they gathered their gear. An old piece of warrior's wisdom was that one should have as many hands on a weapon as one had hands. The pair had deduced that they needed more hands. Each wore a pair of cyberlimbs mounted on their waists, adding another pair of hands for their work.

Kassar normally spurned heavy weapons, but for this mission he had forgone his prized flakker. Instead, while his organic arms checked over it, his cyberlimbs bore a Clockwork Arms Number 990 Flak Projector.[31] An old but viciously violent weapon. One pull of its trigger could send a hundred micro charges through its 52mm smart bore—all fed from an ammo hose connecting to its own armored back unit. A disembodied disrupter coil hung under the pack as Kassar collapsed the large weapon and adhered it to his back. His wireframe wings sported eight of the compacted killer drones. A sidearm on his right thigh and grenades on his left rounded out the arsenal. He carried an armored can in his left hand, a refill for his back unit.

Novin looked like a walking gadget boutique. A pylon with an aimed pod rose over each of his shoulders. Larger, more powerful iterations of a jamming/counter-jamming duo. They were separated by a pair of tall antennae reaching beyond the kurai's head. Both of his cyberlimbs sported a pair of SMGs. He held a 30mm grenade launcher in his left hand. When both had donned all of their gear, they stood at ease with their cyberlimbs folded behind them.

Panzer hadn't seen either of them so heavily equipped in some time. They may have never called him Overkill, but neither had they hid their amusement when others in the Corps did. Kassar raised his arms, testing

---

31 Often conflated, flakkers and flak projectors are two distinct categories of weapon. Flakkers utilize multiple barrels fired simultaneously to launch projectiles. A flak projector utilizes a single barrel from which multiple munitions are launched at once. In either case submunitions may or may not be involved.

that the barrels of his weapons extended and retracted on command. "It's time," Panzer said, looking at the clock. "Final checks."

Panzer ran his hand over his chest, finding all of the magazines adhering in their proper place. The drum in the Hellbore was seated, and the weapon showed green in his NOD. The twin-linked disrupters in his forearms answered his command. The heavy weapons on his back vibrated to acknowledge his query. His knife was secure in its sheath, everything ready in its proper place.

Kassar and Novin took turns raising their thumbs before donning their helmets.

"Arrival in approximately five minutes," Andira announced.

Panzer felt the gentle rattle in the hull as the MID disengaged. All the gathered ships of the Corps advanced as one on ND-31. In moments they had formed a line with his ship at the lead. Through the ship's sensors, he saw the planet closing and the path Andira had set to move them into orbit.

"Ready, Andira?"

"The ship will return to the *Hurricane* once you depart," Andira reiterated the plan.

"Kassar. Novin. Andira. I still have my doubts about some of the things Anagram told me. But if any of it is true, this is probably our most important mission. Show no quarter. We have to get this done. Even if it means all four of our lives."

He paused, giving a deliberate look to each of them.

"All four," he reiterated. "Is that understood?"

"*Yes sir.*" The answer came in unison.

Panzer gave a nod to Andira and turned as the cargo bay opened. The bay was cast in blue from the light of the planet ahead. Unsure of where exactly to direct the message, Panzer closed his eyes and projected the thoughts toward the planet.

"Anagram. We're here."

"I see you," the answer came back. *"When you are ready."*

"Moving into orbital track now," Andira advised as the ship turned, orienting its belly toward the planet. Each of the other ships followed until all followed on his trajectory.

"All ships in position," Andira reported. "All signal ready."

"All units switch to operational callsigns," Panzer said, taking a step toward the open doors. There he kneeled and slowly dragged his fingers over the smooth deck.

Panzer grabbed the edge and hurtled himself through the door. Kassar and Novin were behind him in only a second, all three thrusting down to plow through the atmosphere. He glanced behind him, spotting the other members of the Corps. Some were alone, and others were with their teams. All fell together.

"Tick-Tock-One to all clocks. Prepare for transit," Panzer commed before concentrating. *"Anytime now, Anagram."*

As the first tongues of plasma began to lick at his armor, a wave of white washed through his sight. The sights of ND-31 faded away. For several seconds he seemed to fall through an endless void of light. In a flash it was gone, and the silver landscape of the Crossroads lay below. The gentle blue of a world with vast oceans was replaced by the almost acrid yellow of a thin atmosphere.

"Tick-Tock-1 to all clocks. Disperse and engage on objectives. Good luck."

From the facility's high orbit, they descended toward its northern pole. The stupendous size of the station, larger than any planet, seemed to expand without limit. The command center existed as a dome more than a kilometer wide at the pole. The atmosphere was thin and provided little braking as they fell. The other members in the Corps spread out, angling to descend on their objectives.

"Oh hell," Panzer whispered as his sensors swept the expanding landscape. The surface of the station was anything but a smooth sphere. Pyramids rose from the deck like great forests separated by domes far larger than the command center. All brilliant silver as if the silver had been made from millions of worlds and all cast into this station.

The Vaar below were not on alert yet. The massive jamming systems their occupation force had brought with them were not yet online. Thus his sensors saw them. But it was the number of orbital defenses he saw that troubled him most. Whether they thought it likely or not, the Vaar had prepared themselves for what was about to happen.

The moment they detected the approaching fleet, they would activate the tens of thousands of jamming systems mounted on erected towers, and carried on dedicated vehicles. The fleet might be able to see through it, but on landing, the legionnaires would be blinded. Panzer briefly contemplated redirecting some of the Corps to the jamming facilities. A lot of legionnaires were going to die on the way down.

He couldn't do it. In any other operation, the jamming systems would be exactly the kind of target he would prioritize. But there wasn't time. The plan could brook no deviation. The legionnaires would have to handle it themselves. Panzer glanced back to ensure Kassar and Novin were still behind him before moving into position for their final descent.

The command center had only one entrance from the surface. To enter through unconventional means would take more time than they had. Given the choice, the Vaar would try to fight the legionnaires away from what they were protecting. That was, if enough legionnaires made it down for them to feel threatened.

A pair of meridian trenches ran from the northern to southern domes, dividing the station into two distinct hemispheres. The closer to the command center, the thicker the forest of pyramids became. As they descended, Andira had surveyed the Vaar below and mapped out a descent course for them to land with the lowest risk of detection. His target lay in one of those trenches but more than twenty kilometers south of the command dome. In the envelope, Panzer flipped to bring his feet toward the deck for the final leg of the descent.

Many Vaar were waiting. The command dome was just over a meter across, and around its perimeter, marines had gathered. Innermost were batteries of artillery and beyond them tanks and walkers. Infantry mixed between the open terrain and the pyramids. By Andira's count, fifty thousand in plain view. No doubt many more unseen in the subterranean layers.

A kilometer from the dome, there was a ring in his armor as his feet met the deck. Kassar and Novin were on the ground with him less than a second later. All three took turns glancing at each other, providing an outside observer to confirm the landing had not disrupted their cloaks. The trench was deep, more than ten meters from top to bottom and perhaps nine meters across. It would help provide concealment. With a signal to the brothers, Panzer tapped his thrusters, bounding ahead toward the goal.

CHAPTER
23B

O<small>N THE ADMIRAL'S BRIDGE</small> of the *Hurricane*, Simmonne sat in the wide-back chair behind Aetius's command station. He stood on his pedestal overlooking the large projector on the chamber's bottom floor. So many holograms were mixed around them that Simmonne had difficulty telling them apart. But the chamber, so full of noise previously, was becoming increasingly quiet as zero hour approached.

The Twins occupied the chair with her, and each of her hands was interlaced with one of theirs. Rhoxx sat behind them while his tail curled around the chair, marking a perimeter none could cross. For now the Twins were calm, but there was a knot in each of their stomachs.

Rhoxx held a sort of intense focus, and Simmonne knew it well. She had sensed it from her guards when they were in a crowd.

Simmonne's eyes darted to the left side of the platform and the ramp that led up from the previous floor. There Jenna quickly averted eye contact with her. With no word spoken or telepathy, Jenna walked farther on the floor. She took a seat at an empty console, her back to Simmonne.

YOU HAVE BEEN INVITED TO //CODED SERVER\\. DO YOU WISH TO ACCEPT?

Simmonne glared at the message for a moment. But when she turned back, she saw Aetius glancing over his shoulder at her.

>>YES

NOW CONNECTED TO MININET TERMINAL 243.

SPECTATOR MODE

YOU MAY NOT SEND MESSAGES IN THIS SERVER.

YOU MAY NOT EXERCISE COMMAND FUNCTIONS IN THIS SERVER.

YOU MAY NOT RECEIVE MESSAGES IN THIS SERVER.

The list went on and Simmonne scrolled past it. Confused for a moment, she realized that the admiral had given her a spectator link to the fleet's mininet. She could see ships now in her NOD. The closer she looked, the more numerous they were, glowing silhouettes with their names hovering above. She chose one at random, a battleship, according to the display.

FEED: H.M.S. DONETTER KEEMS

CLASS: SCARBOROUGH

TYPE: BATTLESHIP

CMD: CAPTAIN DARRON BALEN

The ship expanded in her view until Simmonne saw the *Hurricane*'s bridge dissolve to be replaced by that of another ship. The view revealed various officers at their stations and projections around a command chair and back. Simmonne realized she was seeing through the eyes of the captain.

"Waveheads are fully charged," someone said from out of view. "All field stabilizers check out. Shield systems nominal. All interceptors check out. No faults detected in outer hull."

"Weapons?"

Simmonne practically felt that voice, as if it had come from her own throat. Captain Balen.

"Missile batteries verify clean systems." A man. He sat at a console down a short ramp from the captain. "Pulse batteries verify clean systems. Guns verify clean systems."

As the captain continued through the systems check, Simmonne backed out. She chose another ship at random, a smaller vessel this time.

FEED: H.M.S. GRAY FALLS
CLASS: DEIMOS
TYPE: DESTROYER
CMD: PLT NELA PALATEEN

Simmonne heard a new voice, deep for a woman's as it commanded the crew. They ran through the same systems checklist as the previous ship. Simmonne was about to move on when the view turned down. Through Prime Lieutenant Palateen's eyes, Simmonne saw the woman's hand. There she held a crude drawing. A stick figure with long hair stood on a flying wing ship with a big smile on its face. Simmonne could barely make out the word *Mom* above the figure's head.

"Battleships." Aetius's voice drew Simmonne out of Palateen's vision and back to the *Hurricane*'s bridge. "Report ready status."

His answers came in one by one.

"*Rowen Jereko*, crew and ship ready."

"*Antess Kellmer*, crew and ship ready."

"*Jonah Wallex*, ship and crew ready."

"*Hygelleon*, ship and crew ready."

"*Ress ahn Kannor*, crew and ship ready."

"*Donnetter Keems*, ship and crew ready."

When all the battleships had answered, Aetius made the second roll call.

"Force-Com Battlecruisers. Report ready status."

"*Kondon*, ship and fleet ready."

"*Warsprite*, ship and fleet ready."

"*Enda Sortha*, ship and fleet ready."

"*Acklo*, ship and fleet ready."

"*Troder*, ship and fleet ready."

Simmonne felt the descending weight of resolution as Aetius spoke again. "*Hurricane* to all ships. All report ready. Switch to battle coms. *Rowen Jereko*, confirm point control and initiate when ready."

In Simmonne's NOD, the time reported 04:00.

"*Rowen Jereko* acknowledges positive point control. All ships transfix on our navigation. Prepare to jump on our initiative."

The *Rowen Jereko*'s captain spoke calmly, with no tension in his voice. Something about it touched Simmonne, causing her to shudder. To be so calm, knowing what they were about to get into. Courage. There was no better word for it.

"Navigation point set," the calm voice proceeded. "All ships confirm jump pairings."

In the fleet display, Simmonne watched as the ships of Force Alpha quickly paired up. In each pairing one ship took position behind the other.

NETWORK SWITCH—THOUGHT ACCELERATION . . .

YOU HAVE NOT BEEN CONFIGURED FOR THOUGHT ACCELERATION.

INSTALL EMULATOR?

Simmonne needed a moment to realize what the *Hurricane* was asking. Thought acceleration. That was what soldiers used to think faster in a fight. At least she thought that's what it was. Still not completely sure what the machine was asking, she gave her answer.

>>*YES*

Simmonne leaned back as a moment of disorientation made her feel off-kilter. It passed quickly.

"*Rowen Jereko* to fleet. All ships have confirmed jump pairings. Prepare for jump in one-zero seconds."

Aetius answered. "Go to town."

This was it. She held her breath as the *Rowen Jereko*'s captain counted down. "Six. Five. Four. Three. Two. One. Commit!"

The images of the ships were replaced by a galactic map. Tens of thousands of ships made the jump in less than a second. The map zoomed in on the galactic core, and the voices came through while the display was still populating.

"Mines! Mines!"

Simmonne sat up in the chair as she heard the cry.

"We've jumped into a damn minefield!"

"*Rowen Jereko* to *Hurricane*. We've got mines. Many mines."

The map had populated. A black sphere in the center represented the Crossroads, with the Armadas on the 180-degree angle from the station. On the perimeter of the image, she could make out the icons for the shell of stars around the galactic center. A wreath of red icons had formed a broader globe of the Crossroads. If there were a dozen of them, there had to be millions. Simmonne focused on one of the red icons. There she saw the mine, a long cylinder bearing three rings. Each of those rings spun as the cylinder threw a cluster of missiles out of its nose.

The stars of the galactic core would serve as an audience for the battle. It seemed as if this great arena had been prepared just for this battle. An unnatural void five hundred light-years in radius separated the Crossroads from the nearest stars of the galactic nucleus. Those stars would be the mute audience for the battle that had begun.

Simmonne backed out of the close-up to return to the map. There she could see the triangular icons representing the missiles that the fleet, and the mines were now throwing at each other.

"Vaar ships sighted," *Rowen Jereko* reported.

"*Hurricane* to all commands." Simmonne heard Aetius's voice, but even with his head turned, she could tell his mouth was not moving. Verbal speech was too slow now. His thoughts were going across the mininet. "All ships adopt sphere formation," Aetius ordered. "All tec fighters on intercept duty. All frigates, target the mines. *Kondon* fleet, assist with mines. All other ships target pulse cannons on the mines, and prepare to engage the Vaar with missiles."

The second fleet had populated on the display to the right of the station, relative to the Armadas. Simmonne felt a new shudder when she saw their numbers. So many. The Vaar *always* seemed to have more. Was it good leadership? Or were the Vaar just that numerous?

Both fleets were moving. Orange triangles radiated from the mines toward the Armadas as the fleet shaped itself into a sphere. The smaller ships took formation on the outer perimeter with the larger ships inside. Opposite them the Vaar fleet was moving into a vertical sheet.

Lines flashed between the Armadas and the mines, as well as between the Armadas and the Vaar ships. She managed to catch and read two of them. Five light-years to the Crossroads and fifty-three to the Vaar fleet. The mines were being destroyed quickly. It was not a matter of if the Armadas would clear the field—only how many ships would be lost in the time it took.

"The Vaar are walling up," Aetius called. "*Kondon* fleet, act with independence until task completion. All other ships, let's try to tie up their interceptors. Set ordnance guns for proximity detonation, and target the center of their formation. Key missiles on the perimeter with independent target selection. Key weapons for simultaneous intercept. Stand by. *Shoot!*"

Simmonne watched the massive wave of yellow triangles spill out of the Armadas. Their numbers were so great, she could only make out the individual shapes with focus. Otherwise they simply seemed to merge into a tidal wave of yellow. As that wave began to move on the Vaar, a second, smaller wave moved toward the Crossroads.

Simmonne heard a gamma's voice. "Time to intercept, two-one-two seconds."

"All ships," Aetius continued, "prepare to shoot again on my mark. Three . . . two . . . one . . . shoot!"

Simmonne kept her eyes on the first wave of missiles. She knew how fast those weapons moved. But over the distance, they seemed so slow. A bitter torture to watch them, seeming to belly-crawl their way to the target. But if it was torture to her just to watch from this place of safety, she could only imagine how it felt to the Vaar watching them approach.

"The Vaar are shooting." Another gamma's voice entered her head.

Orange triangles couched in a red border indicated the Vaar's formation. Perhaps not as coordinated, the Vaar weapons began as a mist. But in short order, the Vaar missiles had formed a wave of their own. Now the two waves approached each other.

"All ships, stand by guns," Aetius sounded. "Shoot!"

Yellow bullets flowed out of the Armadas into their own wave, moving much faster than the missiles.

"Shoot!" Aetius barked again, sending a third wave of missiles on its journey.

The first missile waves were preparing to meet. Simmonne's eyes darted briefly back to the Armadas. Orange icons from the mines were making it to the fleet's spherical formation. But her eyes quickly returned to the waves. Orange and yellow met with orange seeming to compress just before the waves merged into a single red sheet.

"The Vaar are using their missiles as interceptors," a gamma advised. "Thirty-five percent of Arc Fives destroyed."

Red split back to orange and yellow, both waves visibly smaller now. The Armadas weapons continued on their course. The Vaar missiles that had not successfully intercepted returned to their formation and continued toward the Armadas.

"Wave one, time to target, sixty seconds," another gamma announced. "Ordnance wave time to target, eighty seconds."

"*Kondon* to *Hurricane*, thirty-five percent of mines destroyed. Tec fighters taking heavy losses."

Simmonne focused on the first of the yellow waves drawing closer to the Vaar. But now the wave of shells threatened to overtake the missiles on the journey. As the distance shrank, the shells indeed overtook the missiles. They would arrive first.

Mere seconds after the shells had passed by, the wave of missiles ballooned in the display. The weapons were deploying their submunitions. Aetius continued to call for new missile waves, new shell waves. The Vaar were reciprocating. But the Armadas was about to draw first blood.

Not so long ago, Simmonne had watched a demonstration of what these weapons could do. Now she watched the real thing. The shells made it to the target first. She saw a handful vanish, snuffed out by massed interceptor fire. Of those that survived, only a few found targets. The shark-like ships of the Vaar struck by the weapons simply vanished from the display. But the real assault had come from the missiles. The entire Vaar formation seemed to shrink as ships on their outer perimeter vanished.

This is fleet combat? Simmonne mouthed the words. Just two sides forming up and shooting at each other until one died? Unconsciously she gripped the Twins more firmly, trying to imagine herself on one of the ships in the formation. Sitting and watching as the missiles came in. She sagged back into the chair. She was such a coward. She couldn't do it.

"Wave one terminated," one of the gammas in her head announced. "Forty percent of submunitions intercepted. Thirty-eight percent of weapons on target successfully."

Faster than the Vaar weapons, the Armadas' second strike reached the target. As before, the wave of ordnance shells overtook the missiles. The Vaar formation thinned again. But now the first wave of Vaar missiles was moving in on the Armadas formation.

>>*SEARCH—GRAY FALLS*

...

FEED: H.M.S. GRAY FALLS
CLASS: DEIMOS
TYPE: DESTROYER
CMD: PLT NELA PALATEEN

Her NOD zoomed in on the Armadas' sphere, highlighting one of the ships in the outer perimeter.

"Twenty, repeat two-zero! Locked on us! Locked on us!" Simmonne heard the warning as she once more saw through Palateen's eyes.

"Interceptors keyed," another officer sounded. "Engaging!"

Simmonne watched the interceptor systems lash out to protect Palateen's ship. Tiny green icons raced from slots in the ship's wings to meet the incoming bouquet of warheads. Fourteen of the twenty were smote by *Gray Falls* or the ships surrounding her in the formation. Six of the weapons continued to barrel down on the destroyer.

"Pulse interceptors engaging!"

A smaller screen in the corner of Simmonne's NOD focused on the ship and showed the burst-pipe effect of Palateen's interceptors spewing into space. *Gray Falls* was on the edge of the formation, and the missiles targeting her were splitting off from the wave to come in from the side. Simmonne felt the captain's body tense up, and the feed from *Gray Falls* went blank.

"No," Simmonne whispered before taking a breath.

"Two hits! Two hits!" Simmonne heard the cry before the images returned to the sound of a thunderclap. "Damage to compartments thirty-two, thirty-three. Compression manifold four is damaged. We're losing speed."

"Increase power to drive systems," Palateen shouted over the many reports flowing to her. "Maintain formation! More missiles!"

The feed blinked again.

"Damage to compartments fourteen, fifteen, sixteen. Fires reported on deck sixteen."

"Fire containment procedures," Palateen answered. "Ninety-degree X-rotation, now."

The missiles coming in for *Gray Falls* were striking the formation from the side. On Palateen's order the ship turned over, moving the undamaged wing of the ship to face out of the formation.

"Brace detonation!"

SIGNAL LOST . . . REACQUIRING . . .

"Ow!"

Simmonne flinched as both of the Twins jerked against her grip.

Sorry, she mouthed to both before releasing their hands. But she did not let them go, quickly looping an arm around each and pulling them into her.

Aetius was still ordering barrages, and Simmonne watched the next wave of weapons slam into the shrinking Vaar formation.

"This is taking too long," someone muttered out loud, the only voice on the bridge.

"Admiral." The voice of a previously quiet gamma. "Supervisor reports Vaar main fleet is buddying up for transpatial jump."

"*Kondon*, status of minefield?" Aetius barked.

"*Kondon* to *Hurricane*, twenty-six percent of mines remain."

Aetius took a breath before nodding. "*Acklo* fleet. *Warsprite* fleet. Maintain aggression. All other ships, clear out the last of those mines. Marshal Veth, prepare to deploy legionnaires. Move quickly. Company inbound."

The Armadas formation began to shift. Two groups of ships led by the large *Acklo* and *Warsprite* continued toward the Vaar, throwing more weapons all the while. The rest of the Armadas sphere was expanding, pivoting toward the Crossroads.

Simmonne looked back into the network.

FEED: H.M.S. GRAY FALLS
CLASS: DEIMOS
TYPE: DESTROYER
CMD: PLT NELA PALATEEN
SIGNAL LOST . . . ATTEMPTING TO REACQUIRE . . .

CHAPTER
23C

O N THE HIGHEST DECK of the *Munro*, Clearwater's feet were locked to the floor. Zero hour had come. Within the drop ship he could not track the progress of the fleet battle. But the word had come through; the fleet was moving into deployment position. Clearwater looked down through the ship, where his legionnaires were posted on each layer. All in position.

How many of them would make it back? They did not know how many Vaar were waiting for them. They did not know the disposition of the defenses. They did not know the nature of the fortifications. Nearly everything the Legionnaires had taught him that one needed to know before an invasion, they did not know. Would he lose them all like he did on ND-31?

No. This time would be different. It had to be different. He had to keep his focus whether he was ready for it or not. Whether he wanted it or not. He was the leader of this unit. He withdrew his arm from the machine's left to reach into his pocket and handle the marshal's insignia. *We're all doing the best we can.* That was what he had to do. It was all he could do.

The white light in the ship faded, replaced by violet. The signal that launch was imminent. Clearwater replaced his arm as a window opened in his NOD.

FINAL UPLOAD TO BACKNET COMMENCING . . .
MEMORY UPLOAD COMPLETE . . .
PERSONALITY MATRIX . . . COMPLETE . . .
MOTOR LEARNING MAPPING . . . COMPLETE . . .
BACKNET UPLOAD COMPLETE.

There it went. Everything in his brain was stored in a data file in case he died but they managed to recover his brain.

"Pilot here. Please confirm final ready status."

Clearwater realized after a moment that he needed to answer. He was the senior legionnaire on this ship. He had to give the word.

"Confirm."

"Roger. Moving to launch position."

With its own artificial gravity, the ship transferred none of the sensation to them. But in the hangar of the *Donetter Keems*, the large egg of a ship was raised from the deck, hefted onto its side, and inserted into a great hatch in the bulkheads. From there it began its trip to the launch tube to be fired out of the ship like an ordnance shell. The vibrations jarred him, then again when another was launched. The ship's nose met the ship ahead, and the next in line met behind. Tandem-loading.

"This is Captain Balen to all legionnaires."

Clearwater perked up when he heard the captain of the *Donetter Keems*.

"I just want to say good luck down there. Blood and stars."

"*Blood and stars!*" the reply echoed within the ship.

"T-minus thirty seconds to launch," the pilot said as the violet lights turned to blue.

A cold sweat on his brow, a tremor in his leg. Clearwater deployed the small hose and took a drink from the AICES's canteen.

"Ten seconds."

Clearwater counted down silently with the pilot. *Three. Two. One.*

He felt the lurch as the ship accelerated, and the MID whined as it was forced into high gear.

"We kick in the door!" Sergeant Kopas shouted over the com from his position on the next level. "If it's Vaar, you kill it! If it's in your way, you blow it up! We will get our router up!"

"Ninety seconds to descent," the pilot reported.

Clearwater reached back into his mind, pulling the memory and bringing it up on his NOD. He sat at the head of the table, and the cake Nana made for his graduation sat before him. Melanie smiled across from him, Froggy on the right, and Ryan and David on his left.

"I'll come home," he whispered. "I *will* come home."

He repeated the quiet refrain until he heard the pilot's voice again and proceeded to push the memory back into his head.

"Holy shit." Something about the calm in the pilot's voice was more terrifying than any scream. Now outside of the battleship, Clearwater could see through the *Munro*'s sensors. Ahead he saw rows of drop ships and the silver sphere of the Crossroads beyond. From the silver sphere, he saw what looked like millions of disrupter pulses fired out to meet them.

"Heavy ground fire," someone on the network warned. "All ships, stay in descent envelope. We're going in."

The drop ships descended on the Crossroads from the north. An entire hemisphere of orbital guns seemed to be firing up at them. Clearwater winced as he saw two missiles slam into a *Munro* from its sides. The ship did not survive. The ship directly ahead of them met a similar fate moments later. Clearwater felt the hull buck as they passed through the outer web of the inflation wave.

Barely sublight, they descended nose-first toward the Crossroads, and the fire only seemed to intensify. Mesmerized by the sight, Clearwater did not realize the panting sound he heard was his own breath. He tried to look directly ahead, as it seemed that each time he turned, he saw more drop ships exploding.

The deck trembled beneath him. They'd taken a hit from a large disrupter. The image began to rotate as the pilot spun the ship like a top, keeping the shield arcs rotating. As attacks came up from the surface, others came from behind the drop ships to descend on the station. The fleet laid into the Vaar with their interceptors, trying to annihilate every weapon that revealed itself by firing on the drop ships. More exploded.

"The missiles," Clearwater whispered through gnashed teeth. "Hit the missile launchers."

Thousands were already dead in destroyed drop ships. But the plunge continued. Clearwater tried to focus more intently on the Crossroads, but the further in he zoomed, the blurrier the image became. Holoflage to block visual observation and tremendous jamming to block everything else. Just how many Vaar were down there? Where were they? How hot was their landing zone going to be?

The questions in his mind stalled when Clearwater heard the familiar words within his ship on the lips of each kurai aboard. He took a calming breath. He doubted anyone existed who did not know them. Used so often in fiction, people would make inappropriate jokes about them. Clearwater had said them before as a boy fighting imaginary wars. But he clung to them now amid the lancing fingers of death and the dying blasts around him. He found some comfort in the words. Under his breath, he said it with them.

"I see now the faces of my forefathers who died before me.

"I see now the face of my mother who gave life to me.

"I see now the faces of all those who have trained me.

"I see now the faces of all those who are depending on me.

"And they all see me.

"For victory my mother will be proud of me.

"For valor, my forefathers will welcome me.

"Amen," Clearwater finished.

The moment he took a breath, the blue light vanished. An explosion tore through the center of the ship. It came in from the front, ripping through the decks on its way out of the hull. Men, tanks, and artillery, all gone in nanoseconds. Another blast followed an instant later, and Clearwater felt the concussion of displaced air as the disrupter charge tore a hole in the ship's side.

"We're hit! We're hit!"

No shit! Clearwater stopped himself from saying it in reply to the pilot's cry. He had no time to think before another blast ripped through the ship. Clearwater caught sight of a tank disintegrating as the large disrupter pulse tore through it on its way through the *Munro*.

"Main power offline!" the pilot shouted over the cacophony.

Clearwater made the mistake of looking through the gaping hole ahead of him to realize that the drop ship was tumbling over its nose.

"Attitude control is shot, and secondary propulsion offline," the pilot continued before momentarily going quiet. "Opening doors! Abandon ship! All passengers, abandon ship!"

The clamps securing the feet of his AICES released, and Clearwater was flung into the rail ahead as another attack slammed into the crippled drop ship.

"You heard him!" Clearwater shouted. "Everyone out. Out! Out!"

Like ants spilling out of the mound, his legionnaires freed themselves from their mounts and began to escape.

>>*ACTIVATE CONTACT ADHESION*

With the feet of his AICES now adhering to the deck, Clearwater was able to right himself. The doors of the drop ship were opening. Some of the legionnaires scrambled toward them. Others were already on their way out through the holes torn in the hull. He had his foot up on the rail, ready to bound over it when another hit threw Clearwater to the side, and the deck crinkled like paper beneath him and began to collapse. The *Munro* was coming apart.

The deck gave way as the artificial gravity failed. Clearwater found the drop ship spinning around him as the now-free deck rotated at a different speed. A tap of his thrusters separated him from the rogue deck, and Clearwater eyed the nearest hole in the hull. But as he sped toward it, thoughts of escape were slapped aside with one word: Captain.

He was the highest-ranking officer on this ship. That meant he was the last to leave. Clearwater flipped over, letting his feet find the wall near the hole. From there he turned to look back into the ship. His eyes raced through the collapsing decks and breaking walls. The warmechs had made it out through the main doors. The automatech tanks were still driving themselves out. The infantry scrambled out through hatches or holes.

Clearwater saw the AICES on the lowest level where a damaged tank had broken free of its mounts and pinned a legionnaire to the wall. Another hit ripping through the hull made him second-guess his decision, but Clearwater hit his thrusters, moving through the spinning ship to the pinned legionnaire.

With no artificial gravity, there was no true orientation. Clearwater used the wall as a floor for his feet as he made contact above the legionnaire's head. Only now did he notice the identification tag in his NOD. Sergeant Kopas.

"Sergeant!" Clearwater shouted, with no response coming in. "Sergeant!"

He was unconscious.

With no idea how much time he had until the ship met the ground, Clearwater walked until he was on the same footing as the wrecked tank. With a tuck of the AICES's shoulder, he paused against the tank's hull. It did not budge. The AICES had the strength to push the 120-ton mass aside, but he lacked the traction. His AICES's feet slid on the smooth metal as he tried to push.

"Sergeant! Wake up!" Clearwater screamed as he dropped lower, trying to exert as much friction on the floor as he could to push the broken mass of metal aside.

"Here!"

Clearwater turned to see a pair of light infantry join him. The two betas pressed their shoulders at the tank's rear and began to push.

"Use thrusters!"

That would be the smart thing to do. For more leverage, Clearwater moved down closer to the pair of betas. With the three in concert, a short tap on their thrusters was all it took to push the stricken vehicle aside. Sergeant Kopas's AICES slumped to the deck as the pressure was removed. With the betas on his heels, Clearwater scrambled to him, wrapping the arms of his own AICES around the sergeant's.

"I've got him!" Clearwater shouted, hefting the sergeant and turning for the nearest hole in the hull. "Is everyone else off?"

"Yes sir."

Clearwater eyed the hole and hit his thrusters again. The entire hull of the drop ship seemed to ripple, and a flash entered his peripheral. On reflex he turned away from it, altering his course in the process so that he slammed into the wall by the hole he had targeted. When he looked back his mouth hung open. The only sound was the shuddering in the deck that traveled from the floor through his AICES. But ahead of him the bisected drop ship was splitting in two.

Clearwater's eyes raced for the pair of betas who had helped him. He did not find them. The distant half of the drop ship peeled away. Sergeant Kopas was still in his grasp, and seeing no one else, Clearwater went out the hole. His thrusters carried him away from the drop ship's remains.

Debris filled the space around him. Intact drop ships continued to race toward the surface. Stricken vessels tumbled, or fragmented, creating a rain of debris that would soon find the ground below. His NOD meanwhile filled with the tracer images, marking for him the passage of disrupter pulses rising from the surface. As if rain were falling in reverse, the sky was filled with them. One hit from the orbital guns, and there would not be enough left of him to see without a microscope.

He had to get to ground. Clearwater angled his head toward the Crossroads and opened the thrusters. As he fell he sorted through his NOD for Sergeant Kopas's life signs. Unconscious, wounded, but alive.

His head turned as he saw another *Munro*. The ship was below them, damaged, but still on its way down. Holding tighter to Sergeant Kopas, Clearwater thrust toward it. If he could contact the hull, they could ride it down. If not, it put something between them and the guns waiting for them. As he closed on the ship, it began to dominate his view until, in a spray of color, the drop ship exploded.

Clearwater cried out, turning his face and Sergeant Kopas away as the expanding plasma slammed into him, pushing him away. The argument in momentum and the g-forces that came with them pulled at his joints. His arms clamped tighter around Sergeant Kopas as he was left spinning once more.

MAIN THRUSTERS DAMAGED

FORWARD SHIELDING OFFLINE

MAIN E-GRID DAMAGED . . . SWITCHING TO SECOND-ARY . . .

Had the drop ship not been in the way, the surface-to-space missile would have annihilated him and Sergeant Kopas both. But now Clearwater fought with his damaged thrusters, trying to regain control as the pair careened through the station's orbit.

CHAPTER
24A

ZERO HOUR PLUS FORTY-FIVE. Panzer, Kassar, and Novin had run their course to their standby point. The meridian trench had led them north until they stood two kilometers south of the command dome. Whereas most of the segments of the station were roughly rectangular, the northern and southern caps were bowls capping the station. The control room, their objective, lay 2.7 kilometers beneath the dome. The only way to access it from the surface was through the dome and down.

The moment the fleet arrived, the Vaar had protected themselves with theater shielding, jamming arrays, and holoflage generators to hide in phantom terrain. With jamming of this intensity, Panzer and the brothers could only read traces of the Vaar they passed on the surfaces flanking the trench. But there were many, probably a thousand for each they detected. Maybe more. A lot of sensors compacted densely, a lot of potential to see through stealth screening.

The sky above had become a fireworks display for most of their trip, and Panzer tried not to focus on it. He knew the legionnaires were going to take heavy casualties on the landing, but not *this* heavy. Solely by the flashes he had seen, he knew hundreds of thousands died on the descent. The true number had to be in the millions, dead before even reaching their fight.

They had followed the meridian trench to its end. A steep ramp led up to the flatlands on which the command dome was built. The sight of a Vaar tank sitting at the base of the ramp was neither unexpected nor welcome. Much more disturbing than the presence of the Vaar tank was that Panzer did not recognize the model. The vehicle was big, larger than either the spherical urban tanks or the larger multi-turret field tanks. Its rectangular body rounded at each corner with obvious dual-purpose disrupter mounts to serve both as point defenses and anti-infantry devices. The asymmetric turret sprouted from the rear third and bundled two cannons. Both weapons were housed in a single shroud projecting from the right side. Closer inspection revealed the outlines of hatches on the left upper face of its body. Missile tubes.

Panzer permitted himself a frustrated sigh. Another Vaar weapon they didn't know about until encountering it. The fact that Andira's analysis had plugged the words *UNKNOWN MODEL* into his NOD simply added insult to injury.

The large force of Vaar positioned around the command dome had yet to move. Jamming or not, moving hundreds of thousands if not millions of infantry and tanks would be detectable. By now they should be on their way south, ready to meet the Sixth Cohort of Second Brigade as it advanced north. If the explosions in the sky were not the clue, the Vaar's continued presence was. The Sixth Cohort was meant to advance on and destroy an auxiliary control center thirty-two kilometers south. But to the Vaar it would seem they were advancing on the command center. The fact that the Vaar were still here meant that the Sixth Cohort failed to secure their landing zone. But so, too, had the Eighth Cohort been tasked with inheriting the objective in such an event.

If either unit had managed to get a single router up, the marshals were supposed to task other units to fill the gap. If that was happening, it was taking too long. Andira had done what she could. Above the ramp seemed to be a clear and unobstructed shot to the base of the command dome. A holoflage waited. The Vaar were there, and through passive scanning, she had managed to pick out a few.

There were at least two juggernauts at the dome's entry door. Jugs operated in groups of ninety-eight. She had picked out at least two tanks, along with four jamming towers and six holoflage generators. The two-kilometer flatland around the dome left a lot of space for many more. All secure in the knowledge that their holoflage and jamming would obstruct the fleet's view of their presence.

"Sir," Kassar began.

"I know."

"The legionnaires aren't going to be able to hold," Kassar continued. "We have to go now."

"Give them a little more time."

"Sir," Novin chimed in. The pods over his shoulders followed his gaze upward. "Fleet isn't doing so well up there."

If the legionnaires could not draw the Vaar away, their only choices were to fight through or sneak past potentially tens of thousands of sensors. All before they even managed to get inside the dome and fight their way through whatever was in there.

"Sir?"

Kassar did not finish the question. He didn't have to.

"Looks like we may not have a choice," Panzer muttered before turning to Novin. "Ready the bluestreak. Then—"

All three turned toward a sudden roar. An unknown Vaar tank had engaged its engine.

"Up!" Panzer barked before tapping his thrusters. The two kurai followed him up to perch on the left side of the ramp. The tank veered slightly to the right before correcting and proceeding forward. The vehicle picked up speed quickly and was not alone. Another tank seemed to appear from nothing at the top of the ramp. It descended the decline so quickly, it left a metallic *clang* as it flattened out and followed the first.

At the top of the trench, Panzer motioned the brothers to back away with him before all three dropped to a knee. The deck was vibrating now, and the noise of more engines came online like thunder rolling through open plains.

"They're moving," Novin commented as sensor echoes came and went in Panzer's NOD. "One of the cohorts must have made it."

In moments the trench sounded like an erupting volcano. As seconds passed to minutes, more tanks appeared out of the holoflage and descended the ramp. Once in the trench, they retracted their wheels. They were moving too fast to use anything but their hover systems. The trench was just wide enough for two tanks to move through abreast. As the procession continued, other vehicles interspersed themselves. Armored infantry carriers and mobile artillery moved with the tanks. Some of the vehicles dragged trailers. In some trailers were holoflage and jamming equipment. In others, juggernauts were secured in metal frames. Yet more infantry flowed with them. Viss marines lay on the tanks, keeping low to avoid being blown off. Vaar infantry rode their thrusters, keeping the pace in long jumps that led them to briefly pop above the trench before descending back into it.

There was an almost odd humor about the fact that so many could whip themselves into a stampede and move out so quickly. Panzer might have been able to find humor in it were it not for the fact that these Vaar were on their way to kill legionnaires. The armored infantry transports could use their hover systems to move a maximum of 221 kilometers per hour on flat terrain like the trench. That gave some framework from which to estimate their travel.

Panzer watched two of the tanks slam into each other as they descended the ramp together. They simply bounced off one another, going on to strike the wall of the trench before righting themselves and continuing on.

"Novin, be ready," Panzer said with an aside glance.

Andira was keeping a count as the Vaar proceeded. Analysis of the ground tremors suggested many more were moving on the open terrain to the east and west of the trench. But they remained unseen in the shroud.

"Come on, come on," Panzer whispered as the clock continued ticking.

By the sixty-minute mark, the procession had begun to thin. The new tanks were slowly replaced by the bubble tanks, and the artillery pieces were becoming a rare sight. At the seventy-minute mark, what appeared to be the last vehicle came down the trench. A long, heavy but lightly armed truck. A mobile command center.

Tens of thousands, maybe even hundreds of thousands, flooded out of the holoflage. They stormed through the trench and over the flatlands. If there was a positive thing he could say about Vaar marines, they knew how to move quickly. Panzer had not seen any warmechs, but a unit this size certainly had them. That meant they had either been part of those unseen units moving in the east and west, or they had been left behind to help protect the dome.

"Sir?" Kassar asked. His impatience was gone as the flow into the trench finally halted. The multitude of Vaar were gaining distance, and the audible cacophony was fading.

"We don't want them to just turn around," Panzer answered. "Give them ten minutes."

Zero hour plus seventy-four minutes. Well behind schedule, but no more Vaar had come down the ramp.

Panzer turned to Novin. "Once we go forward . . ." Panzer paused to wait until Kassar and Novin both looked at him. "We don't stop until we get to the command center. Novin. Send it."

With a nod, Novin gazed upward, and the antennae on his back extended more fully. In moments they became incandescent, glowing red as they built up for a single pulse of data. Enough for mere milliseconds to punch through the Vaar jamming.

"Tick-Tock-One Gamma to Toolshed. Strike on snapshot coordinates. Effect fire. Now. Now. Now."

There was an audible thump as Novin's suit compressed the message and blasted it into space. His antennae began to retract.

"I suggest we duck," Kassar said, jamming himself against a pyramid and compacting his body.

It was an incredibly good suggestion that Panzer and Novin followed. Behind the holoflage there was no doubt a sudden startle among the Vaar. The interception of a coded and obviously enemy message. But they had little time to decide what to do about it. Within thirty seconds, the message had been received, decompressed, decoded, and acted upon.

The sky filled with thick arcs of lightning as disrupter pulses funneled down from the heavens. The ground quaked, and the yellow sky became red. The plasma-fied air expanded in a terrific thunder that would roll on for hundreds of kilometers across the surface of the Crossroads. The pulse interceptors of warships were rated in millions of rounds per minute of fire. Several such guns now targeted on the region Novin had specified.

"They've got a hell of a theater shield!" Panzer exclaimed.

The shield protecting the Vaar was gaining a sun-like brilliance, adding to the red glow now powerful enough to boil any unshielded eye. The three crowded closer to each other as more ships joined in, and their pulses fell. But the rain of disrupter pulses were merely the jab to soften the target. The star bombs coming in would deliver the knockout. They burst in high orbit, raining submunitions down on the weakened theater shield.

Panzer, Kassar, and Novin were thrown into a pile with each other as the deck beneath them quaked. With so much jamming, the Vaar had nullified their own point defenses. There was nothing to contest the sky falling on them. Plasma ribbons arced through the sky in long tongues. Tens of thousands of the munitions fell. They ranged from grenade-sized to fifty-ton vortex charges, five hundredliter apollium incendiaries, and clouds of meter-long kilosteel rods.

The fire mission lasted only thirty seconds. It was all the time that could be spared by a fleet that needed more interceptors than it had. For minutes after the last bomb fell, Panzer and the brothers remained on the deck. Short-lived tornadoes of electric arcs and plasma swirled across the landscape as the Crossroads tried to sort out the trauma inflicted on its atmosphere. Panzer climbed over Novin to crawl to the edge of the pyramid that had been their shelter and peered around it.

The holoflage was still there.

"Damn it," he whispered.

If the holoflage was still there, its projectors and generators had not been destroyed.

"Jamming intensity is down forty percent," Novin announced, placing one hand on Panzer's shoulder to climb atop him and gain his own view around the corner.

"Well, that means some of it got through," Panzer muttered.

"What's the order, sir?" Kassar asked, raising his weapon.

"Could call the fleet for another," Novin offered.

With a dry swallow, Panzer shook his head. "No. Fleet has enough of its own problems. We're going in. Novin, send the signal."

"Yes sir."

Novin climbed off him and stood. The cyberlimb holding his grenade launcher was lifted to the sky and fired. The small projectile flashed into the sky, and a kilometer up, it detonated. It released a brilliant, violet flare, supposedly invisible to any sensor not calibrated to it. In any case, the signal had been sent. Rend, Marrow, and Umbra would respond.

Panzer raised the Hellbore.

"Let's go."

He sprang from behind the pyramid and rode his thrusters. Kassar and Novin followed as his toes occasionally skidded on the deck. Kassar's wings expanded, and he dropped his drones in his wake. The small bots made their morph from spheres to pyramids and gave chase. As the perimeter of the holoflage approached, Panzer cut the thrust. He made no effort to brake and allowed his feet to slide on the smooth deck as he pierced the barrier.

More than a few of the star bombs had made it through. He emerged into a wall of smoke, and fires lit up in his sensors. Tanks, warmechs, and artillery pieces had been shredded like paper. Prefab bunkers lay smoldering. Body parts too mangled to know what they had been were strewn to all corners of sight.

"Looks like the fleet hit harder than we thought," Kassar commented as the three skidded to a halt.

"Many hostiles remain," Andira warned. Markers lit up in Panzer's NOD. "At least twelve thousand in a ten-kilometer radius."

"Novin, give us some glitter," Panzer ordered.

"Yes sir."

The kurai made an adjustment to his grenade launcher before aiming above the dome and letting off a magazine of rounds. Twenty meters up, they detonated, blanketing the terrain in sensor-reflective particles. Muck for the Vaar's sensors.

"Move."

The sounds of fighting were beginning to carry through the smoke. A particularly loud explosion clued Panzer that Marrow was pressing his assault in earnest.

"Projector," Novin indicated, pointing ahead.

It seemed impossible. There were no craters in the deck. If anything, it had been polished and made more lustrous by the assault. The command dome showed no scoring, pitting, or other damage. Panzer followed the dome's curve to a tower that had been erected at its summit. With the Hellbore at the ready, Panzer took aim.

HELLBORE MK-II MASTER CONTROL
MASTER ARM—ON
>>10 ROUNDS

Panzer marked the tower in his NOD and let the Hellbore speak. The jamming tower was unmade in a satisfying blast that left its wreckage to slide down the dome.

"Jamming now down six-six percent," Novin advised.

"Going hot—look," Panzer announced.

The brothers quickly thrust away from him as Panzer elevated the Hellbore. The counter-jamming pod came online, and almost immediately, disrupter pulses came back.

"Juggernauts," Panzer warned. "Dead ahead."

Fourteen of the machines stood ahead of the dome's entrance. The great posture, flaring pauldrons, and cobra-like heads were clearly visible. The OCM pod had exposed them through the smoke and jamming. But it did so in the same way as shining a light in a dark room. Lit up by the pod, the jugs fired toward the proverbial light. Panzer returned the welcome before quickly disengaging the pod.

With the Hellbore in full auto, he swept the muzzle. Four pulses struck his forward shields. The first ten shells to detonate in the jug's proximity claimed a few kills. The 190 that followed claimed more.

"Minor damage, right shoulder," Andira advised. With a motion of his arm, Panzer indicated the brothers to follow as he sprinted for the door. All three were suddenly struck by a wall of concussed wind and white light. The nuclear blast pushed the smoke toward the east and hurtled the remains of previously destroyed matériel into the air like confetti.

"Damn it, Marrow," Panzer grumbled as he righted himself and made for the door.

Panzer motioned the brothers to the sides as he walked to the doors of the dome, which were more than five meters vertical. He moved the Hellbore to his back as Kassar and Novin readied their weapons.

For a moment Panzer stared at his hands.

"All right, Anagram," he whispered. "You said you made me stronger. Let's see."

His hands closed and his eyes followed. He focused on the seam where the two doors met. He turned his fingers outward and extended them as if to slide them between the seam. With a long breath, he touched the doors.

He felt the strain of his mind as he pushed them away from each other, but the doors were not moving.

Panzer grunted as the strain mounted, and he tried to narrow his focus. The sounds of Marrow's nuke-happy campaign, he pushed away. The sound of Vaar artillery, he pushed away. The doors were not moving.

I was the strongest ever born.

There was pain in his fingertips now, creeping up his arms toward his head.

I was a P-10 at seven.

The pain was creeping up the back of his neck, ready to encircle his skull.

I was a P-13 at fifteen.

His skull felt as if it were swelling under his skin and his helmet were compressing to meet it.

You gave me new nanites.

His fingers curled by millimeters, and his mind's eye saw the smallest part between the doors. Kassar and Novin were shooting. The sounds of their weapons seemed distant.

Someone was shouting.

You said you fixed my mind.

Something popped in the back of his neck.

You said I'd be stronger than before.

Blood from his nose invaded his open mouth.

Well, I need it now.

His fingers coiled further, and he saw the doors move. But his concentration broke first. His empty lungs drew a gasp as he fell on his hands.

"*Sir?*" Kassar and Novin shouted together.

On his knuckles he panted, now fully realizing the pain in his head. Each throb was a knife-edge carving through his scalp.

"Sir, talk to us!" Kassar shouted. "Grenade!"

Panzer was tackled into the wall and saw the flare of his and Kassar's shields. A second later he heard the pained wail as Novin's disrupters sawed the offender in two.

"I'm all right," Panzer gasped, pushing himself off the wall.

"Plan Beta, sir?" Kassar asked.

Panzer shook his head. It would never work. If the fleet's star bombs couldn't crater the metal of this station, breaching charges would do nothing. The pain was receding, and Panzer could again make out the screen for the Hellbore in the side of his NOD.

HELLBORE MK-II MASTER CONTROL
MASTER ARM—OFF
SHELL CONFIGURATION—HE
CYCLIC SELECT—500RPM
AMMUNITION
50,000 DP-BU
500 DP-DM

800 DP-BM
100 NC
CURRENT FEED: O6400 M-I DRUM
Fifty-one thousand four hundred.
What?

That was the number he had when he left the ship.

No longer hovering over him, Kassar had returned to the firefight and was shouting. "Orders, sir? We stay here, we'll be overwhelmed!"

With one arm on the wall, Panzer pushed to help himself back to his feet.

>>QUERY, REMOTE AMMUNITION FEED
MININET AMMUNITION FEED UNAVAILABLE.
JAMMING TOO HIGH.
NO VIABLE CARRIER FOR TELEPORT COMMAND.

The teleport markers in his magazines could not reach the fleet. So where the hell did his extra ammunition come from? He'd screwed up. He had told the weapon to feed from the drum, rather than the magazine on his back. But the drum could hold a maximum of five hundred. He had fired more than half that on the juggernauts.

Anagram had not just modified him. She had modified the weapon. There was a hunch that he had to answer. Panzer took the weapon from his back. Still drawing fast breaths, Panzer aimed the weapon at the doors. If the Armadas' bombardment could not damage the metal of this place, he could not rationalize how the Hellbore would. But the hunch was there and would not be ignored.

HELLBORE MK-II MASTER CONTROL
MASTER ARM—OFF
SHELL CONFIGURATION—HE
>>SHELL CONFIGURATION—PN

With the shells set to penetrator mode, Panzer focused through the optical sight. In his mind's eye, he saw them ripping through the door. He thumbed the safety switch.

HELLBORE MK-II MASTER CONTROL
MASTER ARM—ON

When he pulled the trigger, something seemed to flow out of him. As if a third lung in his body had exhaled. First a dip, then he raised the muzzle, letting off rounds through the movement. He dragged his line of fire to the top of the doors, and when he let off the trigger, he saw holes staring back at him.

"What the hell?" he whispered as he beheld the holes cleanly punched through the silver metal.

Anagram. What did you do to us?

Panzer returned the weapon to his back and shot his hands forward. With their locks annihilated, the doors yielded to his effort.

"Entry!" Panzer shouted. "Red flare!"

Novin fired his launcher into the air. It was on Marrow, Rend, and Umbra now to ensure that none of the Vaar outside followed them in. To hold the position until the legionnaires fought their way far enough north to tie the Vaar down or secure this area.

As soon as the brothers were through the door, Panzer followed. The doors gave much less resistance as he bid them to close. But when he brought the doors back together, Panzer saw the movement.

The holes in the door were healing.

By the time he had the doors touching each other again, the holes had closed completely.

"Dead ahead!" Kassar shouted before firing.

The Hellbore was loud. But there was no sound like a CA-990 flak projector. Like thousands of neglected infants screaming for their parents, the weapon's roar filled the hall ahead. The six-meter breadth of the corridor filled with a sheet of the weapon's shells. Panzer turned to look downrange. By the time he had, there was nothing left. Whatever Kassar was shooting at no longer existed as more than pulp and metal splinters.

"Go! Go!" Panzer shouted, sprinting ahead of them.

The corridor extended into the dome, branching off into separate corridors along the way. Panzer knew the way and took the lead. There were many doors, all shut, but one ahead suddenly opened.

Kassar was a bit faster on the trigger. The CA-990's horrific howl echoed through the hall, and the Vaar that attempted to spill out into the corridor were shredded by his fire. A juggernaut had to crouch to move through the door. Its shields resisted the incoming storm. Panzer handled it with a burst from the Hellbore.

Panzer saw the numbers. The five hundred for his drum briefly ticked down to 499 before promptly returning to five hundred. He set a travel line in his NOD up through the corridor before arcing to go through the open door. He held down the trigger again. As the Hellbore growled, the numbers dipped by one. Ten seconds later, the number dipped to 498. He let off the trigger. Back to five hundred.

The drum was refilling itself. How? Where was it getting the shells? Panzer toggled the magazine to nanocendiaries plugged into the side of the weapon. He sent a burst into the open door. Ten rounds. But according to the Hellbore, there were still a hundred in the magazine.

No more Vaar were coming, and flames now lapped in the doorway. Panzer proceeded forward with the brothers in tow. The corridor split. One ramp led up. The other led down. A left turn led them to ascend.

Where are you, Oul'sor?

CHAPTER 24B

THROUGH SUPERIOR FIREPOWER, THE Armadas laid ruin to the Vaar fleet defending the Crossroads. Soon after, the Armadas had broken from their sphere to begin forming a new one around the station. Simmonne watched in her NOD as the tiny icons representing drop ships continued to pour out of the fleet.

"Legionnaires continue to report heavy ground fire," a gamma advised. "Admiral."

Simmonne followed the spoken word to see another admiral. Simmonne had heard his name, but it escaped her in the moment. She watched the officer advance on Aetius from behind.

"Sir," the admiral continued as he reached Aetius. "Star bombs aren't doing the job. We should consider turning our pulse cannons on them."

Simmonne sensed the transition in Aetius as a flash from indecision, to introspection, to determination before he answered. "No. If we manage to damage the station, we might end up killing all our legionnaires down there."

"According to Crykeeper, that won't happen," the second admiral whispered, prompting Aetius to turn back to him.

"And what if he's wrong?"

"Sir, we're not going to be able to keep our bombardment up once the Vaar get here. We should—"

"Your objection is noted," Aetius interrupted. "We don't know what the Vaar have done down there and how our bombardment may effect it. We'll keep the bombardment up as long as we can. The legionnaires will have to make do."

"Yes sir."

"Admiral!" a gamma called. "Supervisor reports transpatial spikes. The main fleet is jumping!"

"That was quicker than expected," the second admiral whispered.

"*Hurricane* to all ships. Hostile arrival imminent. We cannot allow the Vaar to bombard the legionnaires through us. Prioritize interceptors on any weapon targeting the Crossroads. Cease bombardment—contract formation to five light-years."

Per his command, Simmonne watched the shell of ships around the Crossroads draw inward.

"Transpatial spike detected! Here they come!"

Simmonne had thought there were many before. Only now did she realize that she did not know what many was. Twice she had to zoom out in her NOD to capture the full breadth of the Vaar formation. Sixty-six light-years away, the Vaar main fleet arrived. At first there was simply a cloud of green in the image. It grew as more and more ships poured in. The glow split at the center before receding toward its edges. Where the glow departed, the warships were now visible.

"Count at six million," a gamma sounded. "Repeat, six million contacts. Distance, six-six-point-five light-years."

"All ships fire at will!" Aetius bellowed. "Hit them while their formation is merging! Put all monitors and tec fighters between the formations. Set for interception."

Simmonne's arms remained around the Twins, and she pulled them tighter to herself as she panned over the Vaar formation. More ships were still arriving. The Vaar were coming in a dense formation. Together they formed a square, dominating the lower quadrant of her sight. Even with a void a thousand light-years in diameter, they were forced to crowd together. The Vaar fleet emerged as a cube, a hundred light-years to a side.

>>*SEARCH—H.M.S. GRAY FALLS*

FEED: H.M.S. GRAY FALLS

CLASS: DEIMOS

TYPE: DESTROYER

CMD: PLT NELA PALATEEN

"Here they come."

Simmonne took a breath, hearing Palateen's voice. But that moment of respite was lost as the enormity of the situation set in. Simmonne heard Aetius's voice next, both in her own ears and in Palateen's.

"*Hurricane* to all ships. Maintain coordination on your command ships. Maintain unified fire."

Simmonne watched Aetius draw a holographic screen to his hand, displaying the Vaar fleet. There he used a finger to trace a box around the center of their formation.

"Concentrate aggression on the ships in this grid. Try to split their formation. Ready organized salvo on my command—"

"They're firing, sir!"

"All ships!" Aetius barked. "Use your odd-number missile projectors on defense. Evens on target. Stand by."

Simmonne glanced back at the *Gray Falls*, hearing Prime Lieutenant Palateen relay the command to her staff.

"Shoot!" Aetius bellowed.

Simmonne zeroed in on the Vaar missiles approaching from their cuboid formation. What else could she call it but a blanket of death? She was not sure how to ask the *Hurricane* how many missiles were in that wave. She could only guess. Tens of millions? Hundreds of millions? More than a thousand missiles for each Armadas ship. How many would it take to kill one? She did not know. But she did pick up one thing very quickly. The Vaar had more ships to fire their missiles, but the Armadas could fire its own more quickly. A wave of nearly identical size raced toward the Vaar. The first missiles out stalled briefly, giving those fired after them a chance to catch up before they advanced together.

Aetius continued projecting his orders.

"All ships free-use on CASRADs. Light cruisers, give me all the blinding you have. Heavy cruisers, switch task. All missiles on defense. Shoot!"

The wave of Vaar missiles was compacting down into its own cube as it approached the Armadas. The fleet's missiles, meanwhile, expanded on the way to the Vaar. A sort of shape had formed in the Armadas' missile wave, a sphere of weapons surrounded by an outer halo of more. Simmonne watched them closely as one of the bridge's gammas counted off the time until the weapons met.

She sat up a bit straighter as she watched the sphere of Armadas missiles suddenly blossom. Aetius was using the same trick as the Vaar. The number of icons suddenly multiplied as they dispensed their submunitions. In a moment, the seemingly diminutive sphere had exploded in size to challenge the cube of Vaar weapons. When the two met, the outer halo of Armadas weapons continued past the collision.

Five submunitions per Arc-5, five chances to intercept a Vaar warhead. All the while many of the Vaar weapons attempted the same. The image in Simmonne's NOD rippled as the weapons met, the sheer number of new warp fields briefly distorting the sensors. The supremacy of Armadas firepower in action.

When the image stabilized, the cube of death had seemingly been vaporized, with only the fine particulates of surviving weapons continuing to advance on the Armadas. Meanwhile the halo of Armadas missiles that had surrounded the original sphere drew into a new ball that continued toward the Vaar.

Simmonne's arms tightened on the Twins as the first wave of Armadas weapons drew in on their targets. It was an ache in the pit of her stomach as she longed to see Vaar ships vanishing from the display. But as the weapons came in, a short-lived wall of green icons rose to meet them. With millions of ships overlapping their coverage, the Arc-5s and their submunitions met an impregnable wall of interceptors.

"No hits." A gamma confirmed Simmonne's observation. "First salvo ineffective."

"That was just the first poke," Aetius said. "All frigates and destroyers, use your missiles for active interception."

"Enemy is firing," a gamma announced. "Missile density has increased by three hundred fifty percent."

Aetius was undeterred. "All ships, three, two, one. Shoot!"

Simmonne watched as once again two waves of missiles raced toward each other and the fleets behind. So this was fleet combat. She had expected something more . . . *hectic*. It took the Armadas' missiles more than four minutes to cross the threshold, longer for the Vaar weapons. Was this all there was? Launching waves of missiles back and forth until someone gave up?

"All ships prepare next salvo," Aetius sounded. "Three, two, one. Shoot!"
The second wave of Armadas weapons left the fleet.

"Enemy is firing again!" the familiar gamma spoke up. "Missile density
has increased a *thousand* percent!"

For every second of coordinated burst fire, Aetius's fleet could put over
two million missiles into space. But the Vaar were beginning to show their
weight in numbers as even more missiles came streaming out of their fleet.
The most recent wave did not compact like the one before it. Instead it
expanded out into a wall, following the wave ahead.

"Reorder the fleet," Aetius ordered. "All battleships to the facing hemisphere. *Rowen Jereko*, assume the polar point. Re-task warhead projectors
from one-point-five to five-second burst."

Simmonne turned her attention to the display of the Armadas ships
coiled around the Crossroads. There she saw the image of the battleships
moving to concentrate themselves between the station and the Vaar. One of
the ships ascended, taking a position above the station's northern pole. The
remaining ships continued their slow circle around the station.

"Status of legionnaire deployment?" Aetius asked.

"Thirty-five percent of ground forces deployed, sir," a gamma answered.

"Too slow," Aetius muttered. "Pass to Marshal Veth. We have to accelerate deployment."

The next waves of missiles were meeting. The two concentrated waves
of Armadas and Vaar weapons met. Each was reduced to a shadow of itself
left to move forward. The second wave of Armadas weapons spread out to
match the next wave of Vaar missiles. Simmonne continued to watch the
remnants of the depleted wave as it met the Vaar.

"No hits. Second salvo ineffective."

The other admiral approached Aetius from behind. What was his name?
Gilyard? No, he wouldn't be on this bridge. Coren—that was his name.

"Admiral," Coren began. "At this rate, we're going to tank on ordnance."

Aetius did not answer him. The wide waves met, but this time far fewer
missiles found each other. When the Vaar missiles passed by those of the
Armadas, they began to draw back together. Some of the Armadas weapons
turned to give chase. Others continued toward the Vaar fleet.

"All ships, torpedoes free. Shoot on intercept!" Aetius barked.

The Vaar warheads had formed into cone. Like a thrusting dagger, they
were bearing down on the Armadas. New waves came out of the fleet as the
ships launched their torpedoes.

FEED: H.M.S. GRAY FALLS
CLASS: DEIMOS
TYPE: DESTROYER
CMD: PLT NELA PALATEEN

"Enemy warheads dispensing submunitions!"

"Detecting twelve—repeat one-two locked on us!"

"Missile projectors loading; interceptors on task!"

At first Simmonne thought the heavy breathing she heard was her own.

But it was Prime Lieutenant Palateen's breath. Through the woman's sight, Simmonne saw *Gray Falls* on the outer perimeter of the fleet. In the display of her NOD, Simmonne zoomed in on the ship. The tip of the left wing was gone, taken in the prior engagement.

"Projectors loaded!"

"Fire torpedoes!" Palateen shouted.

"Too late!"

The weapons were coming in from the right of *Gray Falls*. Four expanding spheres in her NOD showed Simmonne the detonation of the warheads that made it through the interlocking array of interceptors to strike their target.

FEED LOST . . . RECONNECTING . . .

Simmonne's arms coiled tighter around the Twins, and she failed to notice them squirming.

CONNECTION REESTABLISHED . . .

"Direct hits. Heavy damage to starboard shield projectors. Interceptor array one is offline. Array three damaged."

"Ninety-degree axis rotation!" Palateen shouted over the noise filling her bridge. "Belly out!"

"We have casualties on decks seven, nine, ten, eleven, twelve, and thirteen. Fire suppression systems activated."

"Weapons?" Palateen asked, rising slightly out of her chair to look at the young man down the ramp from her command chair.

"All weapons functional, sir," he answered. "Projectors are loaded."

"Pull the torpedoes, load the missiles, be ready for the admiral's next launch order," Palateen replied. "Damage control, deploy emergency stabilizers to deck ten."

Simmonne pulled out of the *Gray Falls* just in time to hear Aetius.

"Shoot!"

"Admiral," one of the gammas called out. "*Kondon* reports damage. Six ships destroyed."

"Move ships with critical damage to our inner perimeter," Aetius answered. "Keep everyone in tight formation."

The largest wave yet poured out of the Vaar fleet.

"Reading, seven-two million weapons inbound," a gamma warned. "Repeat, seven-two million."

"All ships, task all missiles to intercept. Five-second salvo. Fire in three. Two. One. Shoot!"

The supremacy of Armadas firepower was confirmed once again as an even larger wave of 128 million poured out of Aetius's fleet.

"Sir." Coren tried unsuccessfully to get Aetius's attention.

"Do you dare come closer, Kreth'nell?" Aetius muttered. "Where is your supercruiser? What are you up to?"

A minute later the wave of Vaar missiles broke against that of the Armadas. The Vaar wave became nothing but scattered remnants. The Imperial wave, reduced by about half, continued on.

"He's testing us," Coren offered. "Seeing how quick we can pump them out."

Aetius shook his head. "I don't think so."

A minute later the Imperial weapons arrived at the Vaar fleet. More than fifty million warheads. But dozens of interceptors per ship waited to meet them. Simmonne saw only a scattering of detonation spheres as weapons found their targets.

"Two-seven-six, repeat, two-seven-six Vaar ships destroyed."

Simmonne wanted to cheer, but what was a few hundred out of millions? If the attack had any effect, it seemed only to make the Vaar angry.

"Now reading, two hundred million inbound." The gamma paused. "Correction, two-four-zero million inbound."

"He's trying to tank our supply," Aetius said, seemingly more to himself than Coren. "Send to Force Beta. We need all the ordnance they can route us. All ships, seven-second salvo. Ready in three, two, one, shoot! Prepare next salvo, ten seconds."

Aetius's fist was raised, twitching as he counted off the seconds.

"Shoot."

"Legionnaire deployment, fifty percent, Admiral."

"Admiral, the Vaar are accelerating, on bearing to intercept us."

Simmonne watched Aetius glare back at the gamma who made the announcement. He seemed to sneer before looking back to his screens.

"So that's it, Kreth'nell?" Aetius whispered. "Close in and slug it out? That's all you have?"

Simmonne watched as the largest wave of missiles yet closed in on the Vaar. She was about to cheer as she saw masses of their ships vanishing from the display.

"Transpatial spikes detected!"

The Vaar fleet thinned, most of it vanished, and then they promptly reemerged. Where there had been one formation, now there were six, four to surround them from the sides, one above, and one below.

"They're firing!"

"Point-to-point maneuvering," Aetius said to himself. "I underestimated you, Kreth'nell."

A bubble of missiles had been created by the six formations, and it was closing in on the Armadas from all sides.

"Transition to zone defense," Aetius ordered, using two fingers to draw a new hologram screen in front of him. In it Simmonne saw the fleet arrayed. "Fleet battlecruisers, take salvo control for your zones. *Rowen Jereko*, take salvo control for the battleships. Concentrate fire here."

Simmonne watched as he reached out to another display, highlighting what she could only think to call the eastern formation. Simmonne's heel began tapping on the metal floor. She could sense it, and she did not want to. Aetius was nervous.

Missiles were coming from all directions now, and the Vaar were sending the waves more quickly. Their ships were less than fifty light-years away, with around five minutes for each wave to reach its target.

"*Hurricane* to all ships, prepare for new deployment position. Execute immediately," Aetius bellowed and raised his hands to the new screen he had drawn. His movements were slow at first, but they began to accelerate as the waves of missiles poured in.

When sending everything from one direction did not work, the Vaar had spread out to attack from all angles. Simmonne was forced to admit it was working as she saw more and more missiles from each wave make it into the Armadas' formation. Most of the big ships were near the core of the formation, but one continued to loom in on the northern point. She focused on it.

H.M.S. ROWEN JEREKO
CLASS: SCARBOROUGH
TYPE: BATTLESHIP
CMD: F-CPT JOGEN DEMER
ATTACHED: R.ADM DELLON MUVAR

She heard a voice almost as deep as Master's as the feed opened.

"Set all interceptors to free-fire. Focus all jamming on our zero vector."

"Captain, battlecruiser *Warsprite* asks us to relinquish the polar point to her destroyers."

"Negative, our orders are to hold this point. Continue fire on target."

Simmonne backed out to go to the next feed. *H.M.S. Gray Falls* was still on the perimeter of the sphere, in the upper half. She cringed when she saw the ship, its left wing now split in two.

H.M.S. GRAY FALLS
CLASS: DEIMOS
TYPE: DESTROYER
CMD: PLT NELA PALATEEN

"Port waveheads have collapsed. Ventral and port shield projectors offline. Starboard interceptor array down to ten percent!"

When Palateen's eyes opened, Simmonne was greeted by a wall of smoke.

"Fire-suppression failures on decks twenty, twenty-two, twenty-six."

Simmonne realized she was holding her breath and forced herself to exhale. There was no smoke here.

"Evacuate those decks and depressurize," Palateen answered. "Damage control, get our port waveheads back online."

"More missiles locked on us!"

"Axis rotation!" Palateen shouted. "Bring starboard interceptors to bear. Launch CASRADs!"

"CASRADs not responding!"

"Shoot them down," Simmonne whispered in a quiet, frantic plea. "Shoot them down!"

In the periphery of her vision, Simmonne saw Palateen's fist clench just before the image stuttered.

Simmonne made out a flash of light and heard a roar. Arms flailed as the image went dark.

FEED LOST...

"No," Simmonne whispered. She had flinched hard enough to throw herself back in the chair. In an instant she was on the edge of the seat.

>>SEARCH—H.M.S. GRAY FALLS

FEED LOST...

ATTEMPTING TO RECONNECT...

Simmonne wanted to hope. She wanted to believe *Gray Falls*, her captain, and her crew were still alive. Maybe even still in the fight. But the sinking sensation in the pit of her stomach told her that she knew better.

"Send to Marshal Veth," Aetius called. "He has five minutes, then I'm reorganizing the formation whether he's ready or not."

CHAPTER
24C

FROM SUCH GREAT ALTITUDE, it took time to fall, but it did not seem all that long to Clearwater. In his attempts to hit their landing zone, he had gone nose-in, thrusting toward the station. But by doing so, he had traded one peril for another.

MAIN THRUSTERS DAMAGED . . .
DESCENT SPEED CRITICAL . . .
SHED WEIGHT . . . SHED WEIGHT . . . SHED WEIGHT . . .

Only the thrusters on the back of his left foot were firing. They sputtered in short bursts as he tried to open the throttle to full. Clearwater glared down at the landing zone, at a clearing among the forests of flat-top pyramids. The five-kilometer square was a small but growing target.

DESCENT SPEED CRITICAL . . .
HARD DROP LIMIT EXCEEDED . . .
SHED WEIGHT . . . SHED WEIGHT . . . SHED WEIGHT . . .

Shed weight? What was he supposed to shed? Drop his ammo and be defenseless until the routers were up? There was only one other thing he could shed.

He looked at Sergeant Qopas's AICES, still cradled in the arms of his own.

"Sergeant, I need you to wake up!" Clearwater shouted. The landing zone was getting bigger, a seamless plate of silver waiting for them to become a smear on its surface.

"Sergeant, wake up!" Clearwater shouted again, directing his leg down. The thrusters continued to sputter, doing little to slow their fall.

DESCENT VELOCITY—526 m/s
ALTITUDE—11,000

The AICES was proofed to hard landings, but not at this weight with this much speed. The thin atmosphere did little to offer a resisting force. He had to shed weight. He had no choice. He was not going to surrender his ammo. That just left Qopas.

Clearwater looked again at the inactive AICES. He had to let go.

DESCENT VELOCITY—522 m/s
ALTITUDE—10,000

The AICES was proofed to hard impacts. Qopas might survive.

ALTITUDE—9,000

Not at this speed with this much weight. Four hundred meters per second was the hard drop limit for his current load..

"*Sergeant*! Wake up!" Clearwater screamed, stuttering his fall with another spurt from his remaining thrusters.

ALTITUDE—8,000

They were both going to die. The impact would overwhelm their inertial dampers and turn their brains to jelly.

ALTITUDE—7,000

"I'm sorry, Sergeant," Clearwater croaked.

He released the limp AICES. The machine and its unconscious operator began to drift away, but as the distance increased, Clearwater saw many faces. Dolph, Brower, ahn Culan, and more. Their voices seemed to carry on the winds whipping past.

ALTITUDE—5000

Clearwater turned, tapping the thrusters. A loud ring flared through the armor as the two AICESes slammed into each other and Clearwater wrapped his arms around the Qopas again.

"Wake up. *Wake up!*"

Clearwater drew him in, aiming his leg once more at the expanding square.

"Work!" he shouted at the thrusters. "Work, damn it! Work!"

ALTITUDE—3000

The silver pyramids were like trees reaching toward them, seeming to spread apart as the landing zone drew ever nearer.

"What the? Ah!"

Clearwater's chest thumped when he heard the words, and the AICES in his grasp came alive.

"Brake! Brake!" Clearwater shouted a moment before feeling the jolt.

"Who is that?" Qopas demanded as he edged his own thrusters higher.

"Clearwater."

"Brace for impact!" Qopas warned.

DESCENT VELOCITY—446 m/s

Clearwater caught the number a second before the hit. The panicked attempt to slow threw them off course. They struck the angled surface of a pyramid, tumbling down the slope and away from each other. The world spun around him, and he continued to roll when he struck flat ground. Finally Clearwater came to a stop on his back, looking up into the star field above.

A long groan escaped his mouth as he stared blankly. Strange. Some of the stars simply disappeared.

He drew in a deep breath and let out a sigh when he realized that the vanishing stars were exploding drop ships.

"Captain?"

"Yeah?" Clearwater let out another groan, raising the AICES onto its feet. He had come to rest on the edge of the landing zone where the flat met the pyramids. He glanced at the strange metal ground. There was no soil. It was all so smooth. Even the pyramids lacked brick lines, seams, or lines of any kind. It was as if the landscape and everything on it were cast from a single piece of metal.

Qopas was on his feet, approaching Clearwater.

"You okay, Sergeant?" Clearwater asked.

"Hurting all over, sir," the kurai answered, coming to stand next to him. "But alive. Think my g-collar is malfunctioning."

Clearwater's eyebrows went up. The g-collar was the head's last-ditch defense against jarring impact. That would explain how he lost consciousness when the tank hit him, though it raised more questions about the impact they just took. Good thing he was kurai—a human might not have fared so well without a g-collar.

"Sergeant," Clearwater asked, turning in a circle to survey the square. "I tried to bring us down in the landing zone, but I think I might have blown it. Any idea where we are?"

"I can't reach the network," Qopas answered. "Too much jamming. I'd say we're definitely in the engagement zone. Give me a moment, sir, I'll starplot it."

Clearwater continued scanning the surroundings as the sergeant gazed upward. He waited while the sergeant's AICES mapped the stars above them, calculating their exact place on the station's surface.

"Well, sir," Qopas said after a minute, "the good news is you hit our landing zone. The bad news is no one else is here."

Clearwater hung his head. Did they get all his drop ships? Again? His whole unit. He'd lost them again?

"Look out!"

Clearwater was swept to the ground. Explosions followed them as the sergeant plowed between two of the pyramids and dumped them into the trench that separated the structures.

"The hell was that?" Clearwater asked, rolling to his front as Qopas separated from him.

"Growler," Qopas answered. "Across the clearing, zero-three-five. If there's a heavy weapons team, then there's more nearby."

Clearwater angled the arm of his AICES over the edge of the trench. "Yeah? I've got something for them."

A bass thrum sounded as he sent a five count of 60mm mortars into the air. In all the jamming and hologram camouflage, the mortars might not have seen them, but the growler team made the mistake of firing again. The mortars saw the trace of their rounds and angled down.

Through his gun camera, Clearwater saw the rippling blast, and the growler went silent. But where one rock may kill a bee, it would also disturb the nest. The pyramids across the clearing seemed to come alive as the sound of growlers filled the air. Clearwater quickly drew his arm down, pressing his body firmly into the ground.

Ten seconds later, and Clearwater was alive longer than he expected. Disrupter pulses and explosives came in. He expected the trench's wall to disintegrate behind him, and that would be that. But the silvery metal assailed by the disrupters did not seem to care. As he realized what was happening, part of him wondered what the silvery metal could be. The other part of him was glad to have it between him and the Vaar.

The flash of a large shell striking one of the pyramids drew Clearwater's eyes upward.

"Sir, we can't stay here! We'll be overrun!"

"I'm open to suggestions," Clearwater answered, trying in vain to compress the AICES further behind the wall.

"We try for Seventh Company's landing zone." Qopas raised his volume as more fire came in. "Some of them might have made it down!"

Clearwater was about to answer when his eyes were drawn to the end of their trench. Four kilometers away, just narrow enough to fit, a Vaar tank had situated itself.

"Look out!" Clearwater pointed, springing onto his arms and knees before hitting his thrusters.

He and the sergeant had the same idea, and they thrusted toward the tank until they were able to peel apart, each moving into the gap between pyramids. An electric crackle notified him that the interceptors on his shoulders were firing. Now separated on opposite sides of the trench, the blast that followed was assurance that they had made the right move. When Clearwater cut thrust, he found himself in a narrowing gap. The space between pyramids was too small for the AICES's foot to go through it and reach the deck.

"Looks like we're already surrounded," Clearwater answered.

The Vaar that had been shooting at them did not fail to follow through in the moment they were visible. Clearwater was informed of this fact by the notice in his NOD, relating the depleted status of his rear shield arc.

Clearwater pressed himself tighter to the slope as another blast from the tank filled the trench with short-lived flame and longer-lived electric arcs. But again, only the thin air was disrupted.

"Looks like we're going to have to fight our way out, sir," Qopas called.

Clearwater edged his arm far enough around the pyramid's corner to glare into the trench with the gun sensor. Viss infantry moved into the trench from behind the pyramids. They kept in a crouch with their weapons ready, advancing on him and the sergeant. Others were ducking into the trenches between the structures, spreading out to come at them from multiple directions.

The decision to go no deeper into the forest of pyramids had saved their lives. The rain of fire from above washed through the pyramids, creating geysers of electric plumes. The destruction started inward and rolled out, and Clearwater found himself in the eye of the storm as lightning arced around him. He slid deeper into the wedge between pyramids as everything shook.

Clearwater looked back toward the clearing, angling his eyes up. Plasma trails followed automatech that landed hard in the clearing. Kilometers up but descending fast were three *Munro*s. On the deck, the T-shaped automatech stood upright and added their weapons to the bombardment coming from the sky. Clearwater edged away from the trench as a torrent of missiles and disrupter pulses howled through.

The firestorm ended with a final, concussive blast as the drop ships braked for landing. Arrayed in a triangle, they gently set themselves down in the clearing. With a look to Qopas he turned, and both engaged their thrusters to bound into the field. The automatech forming the perimeter quickly took notice, identified them as friendly, then continued on their course into the pyramid forest.

As soon as the drop ships were on the ground, the legionnaires poured out. Clearwater and Qopas continued toward them. The infantry were filing out, and Clearwater scanned the ID plaques over their heads in his NOD to find one of his lieutenants. He found one as a pair bounded into the shadows of the towering ships.

"Lieutenant Endas!" Clearwater called to the alpha.

"Captain!"

Clearwater and Qopas landed ahead of them. "Thanks for the rescue," Clearwater began. "But what took so long?"

"Sir. We were taking such heavy ground fire, the pilot chose to disengage and reattempt entry at a more oblique angle." The aren paused to turn back toward the ship towering over him. "Worked for us three."

"Did any of the heavy artillery make it, sir?" Qopas asked.

"Some of it," the lieutenant answered before turning back to Clearwater. "We still have three functional routers."

"Then get them up. Quickly," Clearwater ordered. "They can send us more once we open the door."

"Already working on it, sir."

Indeed they were. The moment the ships landed, black cables had snaked out of each one of them. Those cables met at the center of the triangle and drew taut, raising the unified cable halfway up the ships' height. Now that they shared power, the three vessels projected a small theater shield to cover the landing zone. Beneath that cable, rows of light infantry carried the metal frameworks on their shoulder. There they prepared to erect them beneath the shared cables.

"So, this all that made it?" Clearwater asked as he took in the scene.

"Yes sir," Lieutenant Endas answered. "Probably several that made it to ground on their own like you did, but we'll never find them through all this jamming."

"No." Clearwater hesitated. "Maybe once the gates are open and we get more people in here, we can send out someone to find them. But mission first."

Clearwater switched to broadcast.

"Company, I want all automatech positioned in these pyramids to give us a defensive perimeter. All heavy infantry on standby to assist them."

Everything turned white. The world around him seemed to take on the imagery of a black-and-white sketch. The outlines of the AICES, the hull of the nearest drop ship, even the pyramids beyond the clearing. All the contours and corners looked like nothing more than lines of ink. The Vaar artillery fell into a 3-1 pattern: three disrupter shells to break shields and crack armor, followed by one thermonuclear to exploit breached defenses.

Color returned as the nuclear flash faded. Clearwater glanced up to see the theater shield rippling like water, but it held.

"Well the rest of the Vaar definitely know we're here," Qopas remarked.

"Yeah," Clearwater answered. "They'll be coming soon. Get the router up. Artillery, get in the game. Triangulate that fire and shoot back!"

CHAPTER
25A

THE CURIOUS CONSTRUCTION OF the Crossroads required them to go up before they could go down. In a place he had never been, Panzer remembered the layout as though he had moved through these corridors thousands of times. This should have been a familiar feeling to him, having taken information like this from the minds of others so many times before. Still, there was a knot in his stomach, and a part of him questioned the reality of his surroundings.

Kassar had taken point, as he had so often insisted on doing. Panzer was in the center with Novin bringing up the rear. Kassar's drones trailed them, covering their rear against any Vaar. The group followed a spiraling ramp upward in a corridor no more than six meters wide. In such a confined space, stealth was far less valuable. There were only so many places the enemy could be, and the opposition could tightly focus their sensors for maximum effect.

Every few steps, Kassar's CA-990 would scream. The ramp was becoming a waterfall supplied by the blood of Viss marines. A severed hand let out a metallic wail as it was compressed beneath his foot. Kassar held his flak projector with his left hand, and the left cyberlimb reached up to hold it by the stock for extra support.

Truly this place was not built with defense in mind. An Imperial warship or space station would have security doors, retractable barricades and embattlements, and other defensive aids in such a critical area. But the Crossroads had none. The trio passed through what seemed to be damage-control bulkheads, but all were retracted. No embattlements and no barricades but those the Vaar had brought with them.

The upright units were effectively stationary power shields, each wide enough to block half the corridor. They had been stationed on opposite sides so that one had to zigzag through. Kassar skirted around every barricade, Panzer followed, and Novin brought up the rear before they pinned themselves back against the wall. Kassar halted and knife-handed his right arm toward the wall.

Panzer remained where he was as Novin moved up. The kurai's right cyberlimb rose as the hand morphed into an umbrella-like dome. The retreating marines had left a number of these behind them—smart mines. But not smart enough. The rectangular device clamped to the wall, where it mimicked the silver surrounding it until it was barely noticeable. Novin moved quickly, but deliberately, keeping the opening of the umbrella toward the mine. In the last second, he skipped forward and placed the dome over the mine. The limb contracted like an empty sleeve, and with a loud *pop*, the mine came loose from the wall.

A portion of the material pinched off, still cocooning the trap. Novin turned and tossed the now-inactive mine behind them. After he resumed his position at the rear, the three continued forward.

It was only a bit farther now. The ramp would terminate at a landing, and there would be the path down into the control room. The rule in this kind of movement was five men's worth of space between each man in the line. Despite that distance, Panzer still caught Kassar when the latter suddenly leaped backward.

"Heavy weapons," Kassar announced as he regained some separation. "Looks like two growler emplacements."

A screen opened in Panzer's NOD as Kassar shared what he had seen. The ramp flattened to a large disc in a dome-shaped chamber. The Vaar defending this corridor were prepared to make their final stand. Their size barely allowed them to fit in the room. Ahead of them were twelve Viss marines, each on a knee with their weapons held forward. But the larger concern were the two ring formations front and center. Turrets.

One ring lay flat on the deck to form the base of each turret. Another ring stood upright. A Viss lay in each ring, controlling the turrets with foot pedals. Each Viss held the controls of a growler over their chests, inserted through the upright ring. He could not actually see the operators—obscured behind armor plating mounted on the top and flanks of the gun—but what he could see were the long tubes mounted under the barrel of each of the two autocannons.

"Looks like Type-9 targeting pods." Novin had noticed the same. This close and in this confined space, those pods would need around four seconds to see through his team's stealth.

Several large cylinders connected by wires to the turrets—generators for their shield systems—formed a ring around the room. Kassar glanced back at Panzer.

"Hellbore should be able to break through."

"Probably," Panzer agreed, "but we're getting close to the control room. Getting a bit worried about collateral damage."

"So what's the plan, sir?" Kassar asked as he turned ahead.

Panzer reached out, taking Kassar's shoulder and guiding him back as he interposed their positions.

"Sir?"

Panzer slung the Hellbore. With his back to the wall, he began to move forward, following the curvature until he was just out of view of the Vaar. Panzer edged his right hand out, closing his eyes.

All right, Anagram, let's see.

Sixteen minds. There was a prickly texture in two, the heavily cyberized brains of the juggernauts. That left fourteen to filter through. He almost did not sense the powerful 4CM systems protecting all their minds. Only his failure to notice it led him to look harder. It was there, yet not. There was no static in the thoughts—no disorientation in the interaction.

With careful control of his breath, Panzer pierced each mind to find their eyesight. He sought a particular pair. Since Miner-9, his ability to exert remote control had died almost completely. Telepathy was already more difficult across species lines. But he was a new mind now or, perhaps, something closer to what he had been.

Sweat beaded on his brow. He found the first mind. Through it, he could almost feel himself reclining as he saw through the eyes of one of the Viss sitting in her turret. In his mind Panzer constructed a box around her sight, then set it aside. A few seconds later, he found the second mind in a turret, which he gave its own box. Panzer brought them together. There was a wiggle in his fingers as he focused more intently.

The human brain was surprisingly quick to accept new limbs. That was what he had to make of the two Viss. He had to wear their limbs like sleeves, drawing them closer to his brain than theirs. Slowly he began to feel the pressure of the new hands, and their grips on the growlers. His new feet felt the pressure of the footplates. Panzer opened his eyes and saw through the eyes of each gunner.

His new legs hit the pedals. The turrets spun, and when he saw the juggernauts, he let up while he forced the Viss to squeeze the triggers. Like the growl of angry dogs, magnified a hundred times over, the growlers came to life. The juggernauts staggered as they were hosed with explosive shells and driven back into the wall.

"No, you don't," Panzer murmured as the pair of Viss struggled to release the controls. His concentration slipped for an instant, and one of the Viss rotated her turret. Panzer ordered the other foot to counteract the command, locking the turret in place. The juggernaut on the right came apart, and Panzer pressed down with the Viss's other foot. The turret spun, still firing and drawing its line of death through the generators at the rear of the room. When electricity spilled through the Viss's eyes, Panzer let go.

"Kassar! Now!"

Kassar skipped past Panzer, rounded the corner, and let his flak projector speak for him. For five seconds, Kassar held the trigger down. Thousands of tiny disrupter charges pulped the Viss, shredding the unshielded turrets and their operators. When Kassar let off the trigger, the corridor fell silent but for the stray crackles of residual static.

"Let's go."

The three proceeded onto the landing. At the center, a seam formed a ring—the final door to the control room.

"Novin." Panzer motioned to the hatch. "Kassar, any action on your bots?"

"No sir." Kassar shook his head. "No one has tried to follow us up."

Novin kneeled to inspect the hatch. That didn't make sense. Certainly the legionnaires had managed to draw away most of the Vaar defending the dome. Marrow and the others had the rest occupied outside, but that was simply those on the surface. This place had millions of kilometers of internal corridors. In their place, he would have filled the nearby corridors with legionnaires. Why weren't marines converging on them?

When an attack was going better than expected, it often meant one was walking into a trap. Or had the Vaar not managed to get into the nearby catacombs? Or were they there, and biding their time? If that were the case, why allow him to get this far? Oul'sor. Indorai. Where were they?

There were two access points to the command center, one accessible from the catacombs below and this one. With the Vaar already in control of the station, how many awaited them down there?

"I can't find any kind of access point," Novin announced. "Might have to cut it."

"Cut it?" Panzer scoffed. Star bombs hadn't done a thing to the surface outside. Whatever this place was made of, only his Hellbore seemed able to damage it. "What about phase resonators?"

Novin's head ticked as he contemplated the question. "Could probably do it, sir, but it could take me hours to find the right modulation."

Well, an electron saw *was* an electron saw.

"Cut it."

Novin shrugged off his tool kit, while Kassar returned to the ramp to keep watch. After several seconds, Novin had deployed the tool. The long device unfurled in his grasp with one handle behind and another atop. A long, toothy blade projected forward. With a loud hum, the electric motor came to life, and the blade's teeth began to move along the blade's edges. Like a neon sign, they took on a bright green glow and cast it over the room.

Novin brought the blade down, and the two metals squealed on contact with one another. Novin's head tilted, and his posture shifted as he bore down more firmly. Electron saws were where sophistication and brute force met. They could cut even the majority of bond-forged metals. The teeth broke chemical bonds by ripping electrons and similar particles away from their host atoms. As the freshly ionized matter crumbled, the teeth scooped it out. But as Panzer watched Novin pushing the blade, no cuts formed.

"It's not biting!" Novin announced before switching the saw off. "It won't cut."

For a moment, Panzer contemplated his knife. If R-steel couldn't cut it, it could not be cut. But there was no time. The one thing he knew would puncture the metal of this place was his Hellbore.

"Stand back." Panzer readied the weapon. Below them was a room of sensitive equipment. He had to be mindful of where he shot—straight down or at an angle so that shells just traveled through wall rather than into the room? How far would they actually penetrate?

"Thinking can be a reasonable alternative to shooting."

Panzer stilled. *"Anagram?"*

He scanned the room, though he doubted he could miss a brightly glowing alien in their midst.

"I told you. We modified this place to respond to telepathic commands. The Cross-roads sees you as one of us. Use your thoughts."

"I tried that at the front door. It didn't work."

Anagram did not answer.

"Are you all right, sir?" Andira asked within his helmet.

With the Hellbore in his left hand, Panzer held the right toward the hatch. He gripped its borders with his mind, but he sensed only tremendous resistance as he tried to draw it up. His hand lowered.

"Telepathic command," he whispered to himself. His eyes moved to the center of the hatch and he projected the word.

"Open."

The hatch answered. Its rigid body seemed to flex, and before his eyes, it turned into fluid. That fluid flowed back into the floor around it, revealing the pit below.

"Telepathic command," Panzer muttered. "Andira, see anything down there?"

"I believe this is a grav lift," she answered. "There is a great deal of interference. I cannot be certain what is below."

"Of course," he answered, looking to Kassar and Novin. "Let's not waste any time. Check your fire. We can't damage any of the equipment, but anyone down there dies."

The kurai nodded. Panzer would not risk the Hellbore and moved it to his back. The twin-linked disrupters in the forearms of his armor deployed, and he took a step forward to descend into the pit. Novin's arm stopped him.

"I have point, sir," Kassar insisted.

Panzer motioned Kassar toward the pit, and the kurai leaped in. His fall was quickly arrested and he drifted slowly. Panzer followed, yet he felt no sudden change in his momentum. He only knew he had slowed in his descent when he saw the silver tube around him passing by more slowly.

Panzer pulled a screen to network to Kassar's view. Kassar's drones were now at the top of the lift. Two remained behind to act as sentries. The rest raced to join them at the bottom. The silver tunnel was well lit—another strange thing about this place. Nowhere on the path had he seen something clearly identifiable as a light source. Yet every area, even this descending abyss, gave nothing to darkness.

Was Oul'sor at the control center? Was Indorai? For Oul'sor he had a plan, but Indorai, he was still not certain what to do with that problem.

Where are you, Oul'sor?

Oul'sor—perhaps Indorai as well—had to be in the control room. Where else could they be? What could be more important than this? Where else would they be but here?

At the bottom of the shaft, they found another circular room and the first of six security doors. Kassar was center, Panzer was left, and Novin was right as they faced it.

"Novin, I want glitter in a full spread as soon as we're through. I'll take care of heavies. Kassar, soft targets. Ready?"

"Ready," they answered together.

Panzer focused on the door. *"Open."*

The center liquefied and receded out of their path. The next door in the line followed until all six opened to a dark chamber. The three moved as one, sprinting through the open doors.

Thump! Thump! Thump!

Novin's launcher sent the glitter bombs ahead where they burst in clouds of brilliant particles. The three emerged on a platform, and as it ended, they engaged their thrusters together, rising high into the chamber as the dancing particles fell slowly in a wide umbrella.

Panzer saw no icons in his NOD. His head moved on a swivel as Kassar and Novin did the same. But in the vast chamber, none found a Vaar or Viss to target. The three hovered in a circle, each scanning and finding nothing.

"Where are they?" The muzzle of Kassar's flak projector moved with his eyes.

"There's no one here," Panzer whispered, more to himself.

Despite "remembering" it, the vastness of the chamber struck him. Rooms typically did not need to be so large. This was a place constructed for people who no longer needed ground to walk upon. Thousands of pillars rose out of the floor of the chamber far below. Each platform was perhaps three meters square, with more than a hundred separating them from the floor.

Unlike everything before, this chamber was dim. The tops of each platform were a rich blue that reminded him of a neon light. Yet even with so many sources of this light, the chamber was dark. The bottom held its own glow, barely visible through a fog. The floor was the face of the coolant system for the many pillars.

Panzer could almost remember the sight of Ascendant standing on them, floating between them, even fighting on them so long ago. Like an empathic echo, whispers of rage and pain lingered in this place.

"They couldn't get in," Panzer said, drawing Kassar's and Novin's gazes. "Both entryways are controlled via telepathy. There's only one Vaar metapsion. Looks like he isn't here."

Panzer looked to the southern end of the room at a large, round door, the second access point. It was one of six security cordons they had to pass through to enter the command center through the subterranean layers. With the inner door shut, the odds were good that the outer doors were sealed as well.

"Then what were all those guards we cut through getting here?" Kassar asked, returning to scanning the chamber with his weapon.

The center platform was the largest, circular rather than square, and perhaps five meters in diameter. The platform's blue surface brightened as Panzer touched down on it with the brothers behind. With his presence, the platform came to life.

A cone of light projected toward the ceiling, and wide screens seemed to float in that light like bubbles in water. But as Panzer turned a full circle, he saw that all of the screens were blank. Panzer swallowed dryly. He knew what he had to do, but there was still a hint of trepidation. First, a brief scan.

TERRAMATICS . . .
ATMOSPHERE:
NITROGEN: 74%
OXYGEN: 24%
HELIUM: 1%
OTHER: 1%
PRESSURE: 107,499 Pa
AMBIENT TEMPERATURE: 10°

The air was cool but safe. Panzer slid his faceplate up and focused on the largest floating screen.

"Open."

He never felt himself exhale; it was as though the air had teleported out of his lungs. Odd tendrils of light formed in the blue and immediately found his eyes. Kassar and Novin saw them as well, both startled by the sight. They laid a hand on his shoulder as Panzer doubled over, on his knees. To him it seemed as if the entire weight of the Crossroads had become a pair of bullets, passing through his eyes on their way to his brain.

Kassar and Novin shouted, but he could not hear them. Andira added her voice, also unheard. Panzer could only glare into the all-consuming light. His vision began to pixilate as his NOD was overwhelmed by the incoming data. The pixilation worsened as his sight fogged over, and Panzer fell on his back.

As quickly as it had come, the tidal wave faded.

CROSSROADS—ONLINE

Panzer's vision cleared. Kassar and Novin kneeled over him, each holding one of his arms.

"I'm fine," he wheezed, blinking forcefully.

"Can you stand?" Kassar asked.

Panzer nodded and the pair drew him up to his feet.

"I thought something like that might happen," Panzer answered before whispering, "Anagram, we're going to have a talk about the things you didn't share."

"Thanks for warning us," Kassar quipped.

Panzer ignored the remark. "The Crossroads wasn't meant for a human mind. It had to adapt, reverse engineer how my brain works—write emulators."

"Are you all right, sir?" Novin still held his arm.

"I'm fine." Panzer nodded. "The Crossroads is linked to my NOD now. It's still adapting."

Panzer turned his head to the largest of the screens floating in the blue. Now it was full of data. The strange, Ascendant characters appeared as Solar to his mind.

"Oh no," Panzer whispered as he stepped past the brothers to the screen. "No. No. No."

"What is it, sir?" Kassar asked as both followed him. "Talk to us. What's wrong?"

Panzer glared deep into the screen. "The Vaar have already brought the station online." He reached out to the intangible display but felt substance when he closed his fingers on it. "They're ahead of schedule. They've already brought the generators online. The station's building power. The merger has resumed."

"How is that possible?" Novin inquired. "How'd they get things working if they can't get in here?"

Panzer's head dipped. His thoughts turned to the southern command center, and the information came to him like a memory. He beheld a room much like this one, filled with glowing silhouettes of Vaar and Viss. Yet each was separated. They had no link to the station.

"They're in the southern command center. But . . ." His mind raced through possibilities before settling on the obvious, and he let out a sigh. "They didn't have to get in here. They used Avalon's reactor to force start the station's. It's back online, continuing the last orders it was given. The merger. The fools, they don't know what they're doing. By the time they access the system, it will be too late."

"Can you stop it?" Kassar asked. "Sir?"

"Time," Panzer answered. "The Crossroads is still adapting to me. A little time and—"

Panzer froze as his sight took on a new texture, as if he were immersed in water. Glowing spheres emerged from that water, all in gold. They were connected to each other by a web of wire-link strands, all glowing in red.

"Andira," Panzer whispered. "Are you seeing this?"

"Negative, sir, I've been forced out of your NOD."

Panzer narrowed his eyes.

>>*LIST OPEN NODES*

OPENING NODES . . .

N/A

Every node, every connection point his NOD could make, had been subsumed by the Crossroads. That would not do.

>>*FORCE PURGE—NODE 80*

PURGING . . .

>>*LIST OPEN NODES*

OPENING NODES . . .

80

"Andira, reconnect through node 80. I'm going to need your help."

"Yes sir."

The water in Panzer's NOD turned into an angry, boiling red. He did not know the problem; he felt it.

"Crossroads, the AI in my NOD is my assistant. Grant it full access with administrator privileges."

A mind was waking from a deep and dreamless sleep. There was more

to the interface, to the station, than connections and data. There was a
sentience here, something approaching sapience. Not quite as complete as
that of an animal, yet more than the substance of a mere machine. In some
way he did not fully grasp, the Crossroads had an awareness of its own.

"Andira?"

"Stand by," she answered. "Stand by. The Crossroads architecture is
not compatible with my software. I am assisting the station in writing an
emulator."

"Incredible," Panzer whispered with a single chuckle. Normally it was
Andira reverse engineering and writing emulators for herself to control
more primitive systems. But now, the Crossroads was doing the same for
her.

"Sir?" Novin spoke up. "Do you have control of the station?"

Novin was right; he needed to get to work. The water had returned to
blue, and Panzer focused on the glowing spheres that seemed to float within
it. Lettering appeared on one sphere's surface to reveal its nature. Panzer
turned his head to see spheres in every direction, countless in number. It was
the Crossroads that seemed to *suggest* where he should look.

Four spheres formed a diamond around a fifth. More red wires connected
them all. Panzer reached up to them and felt substance when he grabbed the
bottom sphere. The five moved together as he brought them down to eye
level. One by one he looked at them so that their nature was revealed. *Spatial
Network (Local)*, *Spatial Network (Wide)*, *Linkage Control*, *Sensor Amalgam*, and
the last, *Hyper-Singularity*.

"Sir, are you in control?" Novin repeated the question.

Panzer concentrated on the sphere that revealed itself as *Hyper-Singularity*.
Plain text in his NOD answered him.

ACCESS DENIED

"No." Panzer shook his head, his eyes moving to a web of wires. Some
were changing, trading their shimmering red hue for tones of silver or gold.
"I'm in, but all the command pathways are encrypted. Encryptions on top
of encryptions. Someone didn't want someone else touching any of this. It's
decrypting now, but it's going to take time."

"How long, sir?" Kassar asked.

"I . . . don't know," Panzer answered. "It looks like some are decrypting
a lot faster than others. There might be some I can already access."

A gluttony of screens opened in his NOD as Panzer began touching
spheres with his mind. The more silver or gold threads he found, the more
screens that were opened.

"I can get a com signal. But it will have to reformat for the fleet. And . . ."
He kept the big five in the center of his vision. Two shed the red threads
for gold and silver. He focused on *Spatial Network (Wide)*, and no rejection
came to his NOD.

"Andira, how's your emulator?" Panzer asked.

"Still working, sir."

"I'll do it myself. Load the first set of coordinates into my NOD. We're too far behind already."

TRANSPATIAL COORDINATES LOADING . . .

"Crossroads, receive communication protocols from my AI."

The Crossroads had awareness. It had understanding. He had to try.

"Crossroads. Terminate the spatial merger."

The central sphere labeled *Hyper-Singularity* flared an angry red.

ACCESS DENIED

No choice. He had to wait for the decryption to finish.

"Crossroads, how long until the merger can no longer be reversed?"

Panzer felt the answer within himself, and he used it to set a timer in his NOD.

NO RETURN—3:57:35

Four hours. Four hours until it could no longer be stopped. He could not halt the merger. Not yet. But other facets were open. He turned his attention to the sphered labeled *Spatial Network (Wide)*.

"Andira, give me the first set of coordinates. I'll enter them myself."

CHAPTER
25B

THE BATTLE ABOVE THE Crossroads was entering its second hour. Simmonne strained to block out the feelings that were beginning to permeate the bridge. Officers who had been alert at their stations had begun to sag in their chairs. Those on their feet stood with slouching shoulders. The only energy in the chamber seemed to come from the gammas reporting on the unfolding disaster.

When launching all of their attacks from one angle did not work, the Vaar had spread to attack from every direction. This had thinned their interceptor coverage. But not enough. Aetius was being forced to expend his missiles on defense, with only a scant few directed toward the enemy's ships. All to soften the incoming wave of Vaar weapons, thinning their number before they met the declining number of point defenses.

"Message from *Troder*, critical damage."

"*Acklo* reports her defense perimeter is collapsing."

"*Warsprite* reports heavy damage."

"*Kondon* reporting. Their fleet is suffering critical attrition. Interceptor density failing. They cannot maintain their defense zone."

Simmonne leaned back into the chair as she felt both Twins lean into her. Her attention remained on Aetius. With his back to her, she could not see his face. But his posture was clear. His hands moved on his display as he shifted the position of ships in the fleet. For a time he had seemed like a conductor drawing music from his orchestra. But now his movements were slower, even hesitant as his hands seemed to become heavy.

The next wave of missiles came in from all sides, perfectly timed to assault the Armadas together. Each missile that had run the gauntlet of Arc-5s and point defenses detonated in the midst of the Armadas' formation. Every blast that penetrated a shield ripped at the hull of the ship beneath it, obliterating interceptors and shield projectors. Each successful hit left the fleet's defenses weakened against the next salvo.

"Message from *Troder*. They're abandoning ship."

"*Donnetter Keems* no longer has any port interceptors."

"Admiral, interceptor density across the fleet is down by sixteen percent."

"Concentrate more tec fighters into *Donnetter Keems*'s grid," Aetius ordered. "Divide *Troder*'s fleet between *Enda Sortha* and *Warsprite*. Contract our formation three-point-five light-years."

"Heavy cruiser *Athos Les* had been destroyed!"

The reports were coming in so quickly, Simmonne could not parse them all. The Vaar were concentrating their fire on the big ships and getting through. She eyed the Vaar formations. The four at the sides moved in a slow circle around the Crossroads and the Armadas. The pair above and below rotated like discs. All while the waves of missiles kept coming. One after another, faster and faster, relentless.

>>SEARCH—H.M.S. GRAY FALLS
NO FEED AVAILABLE . . .
H.M.S. GRAY FALLS—SHIP ABANDONED

Simmonne closed her eyes as she recalled the drawing and uttered a silent plea that child would see their mother again.

She opened her eyes to focus on another ship.

FEED: H.M.S. DONETTER KEEMS
CLASS: SCARBOROUGH
TYPE: BATTLESHIP
CMD: DARRON BALEN

"Heavy damage to our outer hull. Outer waveheads failing. We've lost ventral shield projectors."

"Port weapons grid has sustained heavy damage."

"Sir! Heavy cruiser *Damos Tel* is abandoning ship!" The gamma's cry brought Simmonne back to the *Hurricane*'s bridge.

Aetius's hands ceased their direction and slowly lowered to the railing of his console. The admiral's head bowed as he leaned his weight on the rails.

"That's it," Aetius spoke, barely above a whisper. "We're done. Send to all commands, begin extracting the Legionnaires. We'll get as many as we can before we jump. All ships, prepare to jump to fallback point."

"Admiral!" Simmonne bolted to her feet. "We can't leave them."

Aetius shifted to gaze back over his shoulder at her. "Once our interceptors go below critical mass, the Vaar will fold us up," he answered. "We have no choice."

"Admiral!" another gamma demanded his attention. "Transpatial gateway opening!"

The cup of despondence was beginning to overflow. Simmonne felt the Twins grasp her hands as they pulled her back into the chair.

"What were you holding back, Kreth'nell?" Aetius whispered as he turned back to his console.

In her NOD, Simmonne was the glowing sphere above them all. The enormous bubble larger than the fleet it had appeared above.

"How many?" Aetius asked.

"Many, sir," a man answered at the top level. "Thousands. Many thousands. Directly up-point of Vaar formation one."

"More?" Julie whispered in a whimpering tone.

"Sir." The same man, a lieutenant, hesitated. "Something big is with them."

Aetius stood up a bit straighter. "How big?"

"*Big.* Sir. Tensor curve suggests—" The officer's head reared back as if he could not believe his own NOD. "That can't be right."

"I need an informative answer, Lieutenant," Aetius pressed.

"I can't get an exact reading, sir." The lieutenant shook his head. "But tensor curve suggests at least sixty-four times our own mass."

Sixty-four times the mass of the Hurricane? Simmonne mouthed the words in disbelief. That couldn't be right. Who could even build a ship that big? She perceived the feelings in the room as a landslide. Disbelief, shock, fear. Further despair at her sides as both Twins began to pout.

There was a point of light.

Simmonne stared ahead at Aetius, standing straight once more.

"Tick-Tock-One to Rockhouse."

The Twins sat up straight, and Simmonne smiled when they heard the voice. The hologram of Master illuminated before the admiral.

"Tick-Tock, you have something to tell me?" Aetius asked, holding out his hand.

"I promised you reinforcements," Master answered him. "Here they come."

"It's coming through!"

The one great sphere had broken into thousands in the sensor feed. There, spheres expanded like bubbles, and when each popped, a ship was revealed. Simmonne sucked in a breath at the sudden shift in the room's energy. The crew seemed to be figuring out what was coming. Simmonne's breath suddenly quickened. The trinary eclipse on the M'gah home world, the Summer's End Twilight among the Elrua. Only in such times and places had she felt something like what she sensed now. The admiral's bridge of the *Hurricane* had fallen silent as the bubble popped around the largest ship in the new formation.

Whatever this ship was, it was not Armadas. It did not have the flying wing shape and was far too long. Two seemingly stubby wings swept back from a blunt nose, with a third descended to make an angular chin. The long bow extended back to a bulging hull with a broad belly flanked by a pair of bulges. Above the bulges was a pair of broad delta wings. Where the upper portion of the ship's neck met the body, it formed a slope to a great plateau. On that slope were four pairs of columns, and atop each, a large turret. Within each turret were eight of what Simmonne could only assume were the largest guns ever made. Each capped by a crown-like projection on its end. Three more columns and turrets were arrayed in a triangle at the base of the ship's long, flat tail.

The image began to colorize as Simmonne rotated the ship in her view. The body was painted in a rich red, with brilliant gold highlights. But the last of her possible doubts were removed when she saw the image on the ship's bow. The large icon, a three-headed eagle with wings outstretched, and feet perched atop a mythic hammer. Simmonne smiled to herself. The same people who built the *Hurricane*. That was who could build something bigger.

"Admiral, hail coming in for you."

Aetius pointed to the gamma who said it and jiggled his finger.

A new hologram lit in front of the admiral. A large man wore golden chest armor and pauldrons made of many overlapping plates. His sleeves were red fur, matching his hair and beard that were bound into many gilded braids. Atop his head rested an eight-point crown.

"This is High Prince Heinz von Rhinegrave aboard Dominion heavy battleship *Prince of Mars* to Imperial ship *Hurricane*. Admiral Aetius, mind if we attend your party?"

Simmonne could not see it from behind, but she could feel Aetius's smile as the admiral stared into the hologram.

"I." Aetius hesitated. "I am very happy to see you, Excellency. I see you finally let that monster out of its cage and pulled off quite the Hale Storm."

The high prince's head tilted, and his nose flared as if given to mild offense.

"Rhinegrave Shuffle, Admiral," the high prince corrected.

"Of course," Aetius answered. "Tell me, how many ships do you bring?"

Simmonne could see it. The family resemblance in the high prince's half-grin.

"More than you, Admiral. I have 120,000 ships ready for battle. Let us into your mininet. We'll dance with the Vaar and give you time to clean yourselves up. Then meet your ships in the middle."

"Do it!" Aetius barked to one of his officers. "Keep this com open."

"*Prince of Mars* to all Dominion ships," the high prince bellowed. "We must buy the Imperials time to regroup. Captain! We spent a long time on this ship. Let's give the Vaar a closer look."

"How close, sir?"

"Dance with them."

"Yes sir!"

"If the Imperials kill more Vaar than us, I will be very disappointed in all of you. All ships, fire at will!"

Thousands of ships had emerged around the behemoth. They formed on its flanks to paint the Dominion formation into an arrowhead. Together they plunged down on the Vaar from above. The exchange of hostilities had already begun. A funnel of warheads spread from the fleet toward the Vaar directly below and stretched out to the four formations surrounding the Crossroads.

Simmonne kept her eyes on the *Prince of Mars*.

The big turrets were moving. More movement was taking place on the plateau that formed the ship's uppermost level. There lay a wedge of twelve rectangular devices, each on its own turret. Simmonne's image blinked briefly under distortion, and each of those boxes emitted a well-defined cone. Like spotlights searching a dark sky, the cones swept out to the Vaar. Suddenly each cone narrowed into a beam, each focused on one of the larger Vaar ships. Simmonne almost didn't catch it. The ships caught in the rays suddenly stopped spewing missiles. In the gaze of the *Prince of Mars*, they had fallen silent.

Simmonne flinched as the image went black. It returned a second later.

The main guns forward on the ship had fired sixty-four shells in a single attack. Each of the hyper-luminal shells left a glowing tail of swirling vortex behind it. In each vortex was a faint curve, as the shells maneuvered on their targets. Each shell found a ship, and when it did, that ship disappeared from the display. As if there were a hacker in the system simply deleting the images, the Vaar ships vanished.

Some of the shells took more than one ship. Simmonne spied one Vaar ship as a shell not meant for that vessel passed just beyond its nose. The Vaar destroyer could not turn away before it crossed the wake. Briefly Simmonne recalled a Viss cut apart by kilowire.

As if it were a great kilowire strand of its own, the vortex of the shell's wake cut through the destroyer's hammerhead, its right wing, and the right pylons of its tail.

When the big guns fired again, more weapons across the *Prince of Mars* joined them. Those new weapons moved fast, and the shells sailed on to leave them behind, smiting down another sixty-four of the Vaar. All the while the devices on the ship's plateau kept finding new targets, silencing them in their imminent demise.

As Simmonne watched the third salvo, she could see the Vaar were all moving as one.

"The Vaar are turning away!" one of the bridge officers exclaimed. "Transpatial spikes! The Vaar are retreating! The Vaar are retreating!"

Simmonne held a hand to her chest, briefly overwhelmed as cheers erupted through Aetius's bridge. The formations of Vaar were vanishing.

"Settle down!" Aetius boomed. "They're just regrouping."

The excited shouts were silenced, and the crews quickly returned their attention to their stations.

"Get our fleet back in order!" Aetius shouted. "They won't give us long. Scuttle any ships that can't keep fighting. Damaged ships to the center. Get our formation back in order. Now!"

The Vaar ships continued to blink out, and in less than a minute, all were gone.

"All Vaar have jumped. Scanning now."

"Cancel withdraw order," Aetius continued. "That's two jumps in a little over an hour. We probably have about thirty minutes before they come back. They won't be too far. Find them."

"All ships, surround the Imperial formation," the high prince ordered. "Send to *Rowen Jereko*—ask her to surrender the polar point to us. Stand by to deploy the Könskreegar. I'm sure the Legionnaires would appreciate the assistance."

It was quick, but Simmonne caught it. Master's hologram was still alight. He and the high prince looked at each other. Nothing was said. Only a quick nod and a reciprocation before Master faded away.

Simmonne closed her eyes as she leaned back into the chair. Her racing pulse was beginning to calm. But no sooner had she caught her breath than she felt the icy chill around her heart.

Everything had gone silent.

She opened her eyes to see the Twins looking around the bridge. Jennifer rose out of the chair to glare behind it.

"Rhoxx?" Jennifer whispered.

Simmonne quickly turned to share her view. The big kodaz continued to peer over it. But he did not move. No one on the bridge was moving. Simmonne turned to Jenna, frozen as she glared toward Aetius's station. The gammas were silent, and everyone on the bridge seemed to have become statues.

"What's going on?" Simmonne whispered as she began to stand.

The scream was caught in her throat as a figure emerged from the air before her. Translucent for an instant, the silhouette filled in. Simmonne found three eyes glaring down at her. Black tendrils expanded from its back, stretching wide before contracting around her and the Twins. The air around them seemed to ripple, forming into a sphere, and the bridge of the *Hurricane* was lost as everything beyond the sphere turned to black.

CHAPTER
25C

ONLY THREE OF CLEARWATER'S drop ships had made it to ground. Three platoons out of ten. A thousand souls out of ten thousand. The ships had landed in a triangle, and a second triangle formed around them as the routers went up. Each consisted of two thick discs, separated from each other by three metal pillars. Thanks to the jamming, it took longer to contact the fleet than anyone would have liked.

The first units out of the routers were engineers and their automatech. They brought the parts to set up larger routers that would bring armored forces through. First-insertion routers were simply too small for anything larger than armored infantry.

Clearwater ordered his AICES to mute the outside world simply to hear himself think. Vaar artillery clawed at the theater shield projected by the drop ships. Every few seconds, a nuclear charge went off, casting the world in a flash of white before the sky settled to a hellish red glow. The Vaar bombardment had mutated. Now four vortex charges came in before a fifth was nuclear. His artillery responded with counter-battery fire. Clearwater took some comfort in the sight of the additional generators set up for the shield.

He sat on the boarding ramp of one of the surviving drop ships. A six-arm automatech hovered made quick repairs to his AICES behind him. Beside him, Sergeant Qopas got out of his own AICES, hastily replacing the defective g-collar that had cost him his consciousness during the landing.[32]

Clearwater had feared a moment like this at least as much as he feared facing the Vaar again. He was in command, unsure what he should be doing.

The engineers were setting up the burgeoning router farm. They did not need his help or guidance. The casualties had gutted his armored force along with the rest. With a full company, he should have had twenty armored sections, totalling two hundred warmechs, and two thousand automatech tanks and armor-hunters. Instead he had sixty warmechs and two hundred tanks. The pilots of the warmechs had arrayed the tanks in a circular perim-

---

32 While all AICES are equipped with their own concussion systems, g-collars are meant to protect the soldier's head against any shifts in momentum or inertia that overpower this system.

eter around the titanic drop ships, just within the theater shield. His similarly depleted infantry, who were not helping the engineers, had formed their own perimeter further in.

His orders were to hold the landing zone. He would not dare send any of his forces out, yet the feeling gnawed at him. He had reached the ground alive. Hopefully, so had more of his section—more than what he'd seen. Either way, he could not divide his force. If a counterattack hit this position, he would need everything he had left.

There must have been a mistake somewhere, but a glimpse of his coordinates showed that he was in the right landing zone. His map showed the pyramids on two sides of the platform, yet he was surrounded on four sides by the looming structures. If that information was wrong, what else was wrong?

Perhaps it had helped. Perhaps that was why the Vaar had fallen back, rather than be funneled through the pyramids in their pursuit.

With no resistance, Clearwater was left without anything to do. His orders were to hold the landing zone, and thus far, no one was contesting him. His lieutenants and sergeants had everything firmly in hand. To take charge just to feel like he was doing something would be childish, and he would only get in their way.

A look at the chronometer showed zero hour plus three.

"Repairs complete," the automatech announced behind him.

Clearwater guided the AICES to stand and started a systems check.

FROM: MAJ. ROZCHECKO
TO: CPT J. CLEARWATER
Coming to your LZ. Stand by for new orders.

The message overlaid his screen to assert its priority. The battalion CO? Perhaps he would soon have something to do. Clearwater gave Sergeant Qopas a meaningful stare.

"Got it, sir," Qopas answered without being asked. The kurai made a face, then slammed his fist four times into the meat locker of his AICES. After hearing an audible click, the kurai hopped inside.

Minutes passed. The largest router yet erected flashed to life at Clearwater's left. The first warmech came through, a *Brutus*-class. It had some scorching on its bullet nose and discoloration on its boxy shoulders. One of its reverse-joint legs did not move as quickly as the other.

The holographic IFF tag above the machine read *Major Rozcheko*. Clearwater descended the ramp, with Qopas in tow, to meet the major's *Brutus*. More of the machines followed the major. All but one bore IFFs identifying captains at the helm. The only exception bore the name of an alpha lieutenant, acting in his deceased CO's stead.

"Gather 'round." The major's gravelly voice came over the com. Clearwater was the only one not in a *Brutus*, which made him the runt of the forming circle. The machines towered over him and Qopas.

"All right, listen up," the major began. "We have a lot to do and not much time to do it. Jamming is much worse than anticipated, so coms should be considered unreliable at best."

The major paused as a series of white flashes lit up overhead. Clearwater counted the distinct flares of at least a dozen nuclear charges. They weren't giving up. With so much hot gas expelled into the upper atmosphere, things were getting weird above. Lightning flashed in the sky, and what seemed like a red sun hovered above them.

"And as you can see, Vaar artillery is doing its best to dislodge us," the major continued. "Clearwater."

He stood upright at the sound of his name. "Sir?"

"You did good taking the landing zone," the major answered, "but your unit is too depleted to hold it effectively. So Seventh Company of Ninth and Thirteenth will arrive shortly to relieve you."

"Understood, sir," he said. "What are my new orders?"

The major's *Brutus* twisted at the waist until one of its double-gun arms pointed toward the southern horizon.

"You're going out there. The Fourteenth Cohort was annihilated on the way down. So the rest of us will assume their missions."

Somehow, it was even worse than he thought. An *entire* cohort, wiped out. Clearwater turned his gaze south. Somehow, he knew something like that was coming.

"You're getting one of those missions," the major continued before a map appeared in Clearwater's NOD and revealed a forest of pyramids. One pyramid was perhaps twice the size of the rest and marked in red. "Your mission is to reach that objective. According to our information, all these pyramids are part of this facility's thermal management system. That pyramid is built directly over one of the couplings that help hold the pieces of this place together. When you reach the objective, you'll find an access point on the north face. It is a plasma vent that leads straight down to the coupling. You'll drop two YD-90s down that hole, then get your ass back here. Understood?"

Clearwater glanced aside at Qopas, then toward the major's opaque canopy.

"Sir," he began, "that's over two hundred kilometers from here. Can you—"

"Give you more legionnaires?" the major finished when Clearwater hesitated. "No. We all took a beating on the way down, and we already have Vaar counterattacking at over a hundred landing zones. You're all I can spare on this. Too many Vaar are advancing east and west of this position, but none are moving here that we can see. So you'll go south and hopefully not attract too much attention. Remember, your job is to drop those charges, not kill Vaar. So don't pick any fights you don't have to."

Clearwater took a deep breath. "Yes sir. Any idea what resistance we're going to run into on the way there?"

"Not exactly." The expected answer. "We're putting eyes in the sky as fast as we can, and the Vaar are knocking them down just as quickly. But from what we've managed to see in that area, you should encounter minimal resistance on your way. That's the good news. The bad news . . ."

Clearwater eyed the *Brutus*, growing more uncomfortable the longer the pause lasted.

"You'll have to leave your artillery here."

"*Sir!*" Clearwater and Qopas protested in unison.

"Orders from above," the major cut them off. "All artillery is to be tasked at the cohort level. We need every barrel and launcher we've got putting counter-battery fire on the Vaar. Otherwise their artillery will blast us out of the landing zones and nobody goes home. Your light infantry can keep their mortars, but everything else stays *here*."

The major punctuated his statement by pointing the right arm of his *Brutus* down at the deck. "You need heavy arty while you're out there. Call Toolshed. They'll give you what they can spare."

"Why don't you just cut off my organ while you're at it," Clearwater mumbled.

Every *Brutus* in the circle turned toward him, and several uneasy seconds of silence set in on the channel.

"Forget your transceiver was open, Captain?"

Clearwater's head ticked. "Yes sir," he answered. "Sorry, sir."

"I'll ascribe your insubordination to combat stress. *This* time," the major said. "Gather your legionnaires. If the Vaar to our flanks wheel this direction, I want you out there before they can block your path. Move out."

"Yes sir."

Clearwater motioned Qopas to follow as the meeting carried on without him. "Qopas, round them up."

"Yes sir!"

Clearwater returned to the drop ship's ramp, focused on the map. Vaar from the east and west. A pyramid forest in each direction—that would at least slow any Vaar trying to move in on him from the sides. But those pyramid forests would be walls, confining him to the plain of flatland between them. On this huge world, fifty kilometers was a lot less than the horizon. But his misgivings didn't matter. Orders were orders.

The replacements were already coming through the routers, and the white flashes above were becoming more numerous.

CHAPTER
26A

NO RETURN—*1:24:27*
Hours had ticked by while battle raged on the surface of the station. In the command center, Panzer watched the changing colors of the threads. Yet no matter how many times he silently urged them to mutate faster, the rate of change remained the same. By now, Rend, Marrow, and Umbra would have withdrawn. Yet the drone Kassar left behind had detected no Vaar approaching to reclaim the command center. So either the legionnaires were doing a far better job of holding the Vaar, or something else was happening.

The longer Panzer was connected with the Crossroads, the more he understood. The Crossroads did not have a personality of its own. It was controlled by telepathy and was a mirror to it. The station had created an incomplete reflection of him, a model based on his personality, used to serve as an operating system for the network.

The red threads were still turning color. Gold threads, command input pathways, carried his commands to the various systems. The silver threads were sub-processing pathways, lines for the station's systems to share data with each other. By now Panzer had control of communications, life support, and platform linkage. But in the big five of the golden spheres, those linked to *Hyper-Singularity* still had a lot of red threads. He could open new wormholes with control over the spatial network, but the door, the bridge to the next universe, that was *Hyper-Singularity*. Until its threads turned gold, he could not countermand its previous orders.

Panzer's fist opened briefly before balling up again. He had control of the platform linkage, and that was most important. The last resort. With that he could send a single command, decoupling every platform at once. That would break all connections, shut down every system, and halt the merger. But it would also destroy the station as the supermassive black hole escaped its prison and killed everyone aboard.

He would stick to the plan: give them as much time as he could. But if success proved elusive, if he still could not access the *Hyper-Singularity* control, he had only one choice left. He would decouple the station and condemn everyone aboard. Fortunately, things seemed to be progressing.

"Andira, any luck patching the rest?" Panzer asked as another red thread turned gold, this one outside of the big five spheres.

"Not yet, sir. I am still assimilating program architecture."

Panzer cursed under his breath. If they could find a way to patch both the Armadas and Legionnaires, then route them through the Crossroads coms, the Vaar's jamming would be irrelevant for communications. But that might be too much to ask. Emulator or not, the system architecture was too different. Andira could need days to process and adapt to it all. He could reach out to the Armadas light-years away, yet not down the proverbial block to the legionnaires or the commandos. He had to assure himself that the latter knew their tasks and could improvise where needed.

"Don't get distracted," Panzer whispered to himself. Mission creep cost lives.

But what if?

Panzer looked through the watery interface at the many platforms the Ascendant had once floated between as they did their work. What if he could save this place? What could it do for humanity? For all the Empire? Once he had full control, he could pull units from anywhere in the Empire. However many it took.

Panzer swallowed before clearing his throat. It would not work. Not this close to the Combine. He and Aetius tried to warn them, but they did not listen. The Empire was not ready for this war. No matter how fast he could bring forces here, choke points of supply and personnel would form back home. Even if he stopped the merger, if he tried to hold the station, he risked having it pried out of his hands by the Vaar. High risk, high reward. So much reward, yet still not worth the risk. He had to keep to the mission. This place had to go.

"Come on. Come on." His heel bounced with his impatience. "This is taking too long. Kassar, anything on your drones?"

"Negative."

Where were they? The Vaar were in the southern command center. By now they had to know something was going on here, even if none of the guards they cut through got off a message. Why weren't Vaar surrounding the area? The forces that left had plenty of time to turn around and come back. Were the legionnaires really having that much success keeping them occupied? Panzer wanted to believe that. But it was too convenient.

There was something else going on here. Something he did not see. One thing Panzer had perceived through the station's mind, as he looked to the many spheres, were silver corridors. Subterranean tunnels, sprawling through and linking the many platforms that formed the station. Many of them filled with Vaar troops and armor. They were using the subterranean networks to reposition themselves without having to fight through legionnaires on the surface to do it. That was bad. Unhindered movement would allow them to set ambushes, avoid them, and reposition to points of greatest advantage. Panzer's eyes widened. His fixation on *Hyper-Singularity* had blinded him to tools already available.

"Andira, can you upload to the station a biometric template for Imperial species? Scratch that. Just upload a biometric template for the Vaar?"

"I believe so, sir."

Panzer nodded, a smile creeping across his face.

"Then do it." He paused. *"Crossroads, my AI is uploading a biometric template. This species is called Vaar, and they are hostile."*

Panzer flinched at the sense of anger and hostility seeping from the station. With some hesitation, he finished his command.

"Lock on to all Vaar. Teleport them into deep space."

The red threads around the sphere labeled *Spatial Network (Local)* flashed, and Panzer felt a sense of rejection as the message came to his NOD.

ACCESS DENIED.

Panzer grit his teeth. If one solution didn't work, another could.

"Close all sectional interlocks. Do not allow the Vaar free movement through the subterranean layers. Grant access to any other bio-template that attempts to move through."

At first Panzer was not sure of the reaction, until he felt satisfaction. The sentiment was confirmed when he saw a vision of a silver corridor. Within it, a Vaar tank moved at flank speed before it skidded to a stop. It did not stop in time. Silver fluid rose from the deck ahead of it, flowing against gravity like an inverted waterfall until reaching the ceiling. The metal hardened again as the tank plowed into it. The vehicle was bisected, with one half falling on each side of the new barrier. Panzer felt an odd clenching sensation in his muscles. Each segment in the Crossroads was closing itself off. The Vaar beneath the surface were trapped.

"Crossroads, how many Vaar are in the subterranean layers?"

The number flashed in his NOD.

748,972,900

The Vaar had put every marine they could on the station, including hundreds of millions from the *Caustic Reverie* and more from the rest of their fleet. Yet the number in his NOD only included those beneath the surface.

Panzer's hand clenched tighter. He had to keep them there, keep them trapped until he decoupled the station. It would not cripple the Combine, but he could not pass up the opportunity to destroy such a large concentration of enemy troops.

That brought him back to his previous inquiry. The Vaar had ample numbers. Why hadn't they attempted to evict him from the command center?

Panzer stood up straight as he sensed it. As if to confirm the impossible data, three screens opened in his NOD.

SIMMONNE
DISTANCE: 42 METERS
STATUS: HEALTHY
RESTRAINT TENSION: RELAXED
MOOD: AFRAID

JENNIFER
DISTANCE: 42 METERS
STATUS: HEALTHY
RESTRAINT TENSION: RELAXED

MOOD: TERRIFIED

JULIE
DISTANCE: 42 METERS
STATUS: HEALTHY
RESTRAINT TENSION: RELAXED
MOOD: TERRIFIED

Panzer spun on his heel. Four platforms away he saw them: Indorai, Oul'sor, and between them, Simmonne, Jennifer, and Julie.

He did not think. His left hand shot out before closing in a fist. His right hand shot up to seize the Hellbore from his back. He drew the women to him so rapidly that he forced the air out of their lungs as they shrieked.

HELLBORE MASTER CONTROL
MASTER ARM ON
>>100-ROUND BURST / MAXIMUM CYCLIC

The moment the girls were behind him, Panzer pulled the trigger. Nothing happened.

His finger halted fractions of centimeters from the break, where the trigger would finally engage the firing sequence. Panzer saw then that Indorai had his hand raised, two talon-like fingers held in a pinching motion. Panzer locked his mind on his finger, trying to force it. But neither his finger nor the trigger moved.

Panzer's nostrils flared. His eyes widened. Pain shot from his fingertip through his arm like rays of fire, but his finger did not move.

"You should keep closer watch on your things," Indorai called out in that wretched voice. "Someone might take them from you."

Panzer heard a laugh from Oul'sor as the Vaar planted his hammer on the deck beside him. The two aliens looked to each other for a moment. Oul'sor nodded, and Indorai offered a grotesque smile.

"Someone wishes to speak with you," Indorai announced. *"Crossroads, security barrier on this platform. Now!"*

At his command, a golden dome formed around them from the ether. As he stared through the new field at Indorai, Panzer continued to exert his will on the Hellbore's trigger, but it still would not move.

"Kassar!" Panzer strained. "Novin. Shoot!"

Panzer turned his head to one side, and what he saw was its own punch in the gut. A golden glow formed an egg-like barrier around Kassar, who faced the wrong way. His arms were crossed at his chest and he stared down. Novin stood in the same position. A look behind showed that only he and the girls had been spared.

Panzer reached toward Kassar. The second his fingers met the glowing field, an electric shock traveled from Panzer's fingers to each of his toes, leaving him shaking the hand to flush the numbness out.

"What did you do to them?" Panzer growled at the Therican, straining with every neuron to somehow pull the Hellbore's trigger.

"The same thing you just did," Indorai answered, motioning him with his arm. *"Only, a little better. I have suspended their time. Do not worry. I have not been told to break your things. Not yet. But I thank you. I could only unlock the controls I sealed, so I appreciate you unlocking those Anagram sealed as well."*

Indorai's outer mouth opened wider in a larger smile.

SYSTEM LOCKOUT

"Agh!" Panzer exclaimed as the spheres, the watery vision of the Cross-roads, and the connecting threads vanished from his sight. The pain of thousands of volts seemed to pour out of his eyes, twitching his cheek so hard that the muscle tore, and sending pain through his ears and neck. He doubled over, holding his hand over his face.

"Master!" Simmonne cried out. She tried to move toward him, only to be stopped by his mind's grip on her hips.

"I'm all right."

"Anagram was a fool to think you could contest control of this place with me," Indorai taunted.

Indorai. Why did he bring the girls here? As Panzer stood upright again, an invisible hand on the Hellbore forced its muzzle down. He did not have the strength for both. He released the girls and redoubled his efforts on the weapon. But there was nothing he could compare to the incredible force at work. A second invisible hand seemed to take hold of his. His teeth gnashed together, he growled, but he could not stop it. One by one, the second hand pried his fingers open. Panzer tried to block the movement, only to feel a third grip on his left wrist. His right hand was forced completely open, his arm turned, then the Hellbore fell with a loud thump at his feet.

The invisible hands seemed to let go of him. Panzer tried to draw the weapon back up to him, but it did not move. A mind far stronger than his kept it pinned to the deck.

CHAPTER 26B

WHAT SIMMONNE WATCHED MADE no sense. It seemed as if Master and the creature were having a mental battle, and the creature was winning. In what universe could Master lose a metapsionic fight? She had been drawn into his mind before. How could anyone be stronger? Maybe he was just going along with it, some kind of deception to get the upper hand later. Of course, that had to be it.

She clung to the back of Master's armor. She stared through the gap between his arm and torso, through the barrier that now encircled them, to the alien that had abducted her. It glared at the four of them with three eyes. No matter how hard she stared at it, she could not believe it was what it appeared to be. She had only seen ancient images. That was all that was left to see. In none of those images did they have those tendrils. Nor did their eyes glow like molten gold. But the shape of its head, its body, the color of its carapace. What else could it be? How could a Therican be here?

The horror that was the creature's mouth opened again. Simmonne could not stop herself, nor could the Twins, from letting out a whine as it spoke. Four voices seemed to suck the air out of her lungs, speaking as one. High-pitched and inhuman tones placed inflection on each word.

"There is someone who wishes to speak with you."

Simmonne could barely sense the projection. Master arrayed a telepathic screen around them. As her mind cleared, a second entity seemed to materialize beside the Therican. A Vaar, his head and shoulders taller than the Therican's body. It held the haft of a great hammer. Wicked blades from its barbed head rested on the floor.

"The door is opening," the Therican said as he raised his arms outward.

Simmonne felt a rumble in the floor. The walls were rattling. The strange fog rippled between the platforms. The Twins each made utterances but no complete words. An impossible light seemed to come from every direction, washing out everything in the chamber.

She cried out at the searing pain it brought. Her vision went black as her optical nanites tried to protect her eyes. Even in the shade of Master's hulking stature, the scalding light seemed to touch every part of her. Her strength was fading, and numbness creeped into her flesh.

When Simmonne managed to open her eyes, she saw Jennifer and Julie flat on their backs. Their eyes were closed, and their mouths were open, sucking in large breaths of air. She clung to Master when her legs gave out, and she slid down to her knees. Her arms around his leg were all that kept her from joining the Twins on the floor. She could no longer feel her limbs. Her thoughts raced, yet her heartbeat was calm, as if the very strength needed for her body to panic had already winnowed away.

Master grunted, and something shifted. Only her eyes and mouth still seemed to respond to her command, and like the Twins, she had been reduced to gasping for air.

This was impossible. Whatever it was, it was telepathic. So blatant and so powerful, she sensed it as strongly as emotion. But that made no sense. What telepathy was so strong that she could sense it directly? What could possibly be so strong that Master could not block it? Whatever it was, it filled the air with a mist the color of fresh blood. The mist passed through the golden barrier, only halting at the ring created by Master's mind.

The mist seemed to be rising out of the Therican like a geyser, and above him, something was taking shape. Within moments, the Therican stood at the feet of a towering silhouette, a golden outline in the mist—too insubstantial for her to call it anything but a ghost. It towered over the Therican, over the Vaar, as tall as the ceiling.

When it spoke, Simmonne froze. Her heart seemed to stop as air fled from her lungs. Any sound she might have made was drowned in a sea of innumerable voices. They spoke in octaves high and low. They spoke as one, devoid of inflection—monotone. With each word, the mist seemed to come alive with arcs of gilded lightning.

"As I told you. Only at Origin would you understand."

Master gently patted Simmonne's arm before he stood taller.

"Soon, the merging of realities will be complete."

"Encephalon," Master answered.

Encephalon? Master knew what this thing was? He did. She could sense it in him, an odd cascade of realization and anger.

"So, it was you all along. You were the one inciting the Vaar against us."

"Ignorance is recursive. You know too little to understand the depths of what you do not know."

Simmonne tried to cling tighter, to stand back up, to do something—but it was in vain. Her eyes and her breath—not even enough breath to form words—were all she had left.

"All this time," Master said in a venomous tone, "we thought you were our prisoner. You played us all for fools."

"There is nothing of greater ease to exploit than hubris. I am as I have always been. I am where I have always been. Those before saw what they wished to see. You, and all those after, saw what you were told."

What was this thing? Master knew, and it horrified her. Not that he knew, not that he spoke to it—it was what she sensed in him. Nothing could have convinced her that he even knew what fear was. The coldness of his punishment was sweet ecstasy compared to this discovery: he *did* know fear.

"Perhaps it is time you correct some of that ignorance, Encephalon. Or should I call you Teacher?"

Teacher? Why would he call him that?

"More than once, our minds have touched. Your nature is known to me. Anagram told you much, but you believe little."

Simmonne tried to turn her head to check on Jennifer and Julie. Instead her head slumped forward against the metal plates of Master's armor. Each breath felt harder to draw. Second by second, weight pulled at her eyelids, and her mind drew toward an abyss.

"So tell me what she didn't. You incite the Empire and the Vaar against each other. For what? We weaken each other for you to come in and conquer us both?"

"Such are the limitations of spoken word, that you might insult me without attempt. Conquest is your domain. I have no coffers to fill with treasure. I have no temple to fill with supplicants. You have nothing that I require. I am of salvation, not of conquest."

"Salvation?" Master's voice rose with anger. "In what universe are you the savior of anything? Certainly not this one."

Simmonne's toes curled with the surge of anger from Master. She managed to grab just enough of it to fuel the movement. But it was not enough. In her mind she could only plead for the chorus of voices to be silent. Yet they grew louder, vibrating the chamber around them.

"I am nemesis to the inevitable destroyer, and guardian of the reaction. In the audience of the cosmic tragedy, I do not laugh. For eons uncountable, I have existed. In more than you can fathom, I have watched. I have seen the reaction begin, and I have seen it end.

"Countless times I have watched them come into being. I have watched the pitiless cruelty of their sagas. Their tribulations, their triumphs, and their ruin. To disaster, to war, to their own folly. I have watched the inevitable destroyer take them. I watched the wind and rain erode their monuments. I watched the deaths of stars consume their worlds. Their cries of jubilation, their tears of despair. Their songs of joy and lament. Forever lost as the reaction ended. And it became as though they never existed at all.

"Through their struggle, I learned the concept of compassion. None of them, not even the Ascendant, could ever triumph against the inevitable destroyer. I realized that only my help could save them."

"Your help?" Master spat. Simmonne managed a deeper breath and to twitch her fingers with the new surge of anger he summoned. She clung to that anger, drawing strength from it enough to breathe deeply. "Is that what you call the Thericans? Is that what you called it when they tried to destroy us? When they drove countless other sapient species to extinction?"

Master's shout echoed. The entity did not answer until that echo was silent.

"The Thericans were never anything more than the page on which a test was written."

"A test?"

Simmonne felt enough strength to rise off her knees, but it faded as curiosity polluted the anger she fed on. Master took half a step with his free leg.

"Eternity is a finite resource. One who seeks to save all may, in the end, save none. Anagram flooded the universe with weeds upon the flowers of sapience. Only the most deserving may be preserved. The Thericans were the test of their worth. A test given only to those capable of passing. Vast in its simplicity. Dispassionate in its execution. The answer simple, yet so many failed."

Still she could not move, but Simmonne found her voice, enough for a faint whisper.

"What . . . question?"

If the entity heard her, it did not respond. But Master did. He glanced down at her for a moment. "What was the question?"

"No civilization survives abundance. The most fit survive to become apex predators. Intelligent. Cunning. Ruthless. But when they achieve success, it is slain by their victory. What evolution built in billions of years, abundance slays in centuries. They adopt principles. They wallow in sentiments destructive to their success. They claim the excess of plenty as its cause. Sin is made of strength, and virtue of weakness. All that brought them success becomes scorned by the foolish who call their folly enlightenment. Demons are made of those who succeed. The parasites of civilization are elevated to its leadership. In the naivete only abundance brings, they cast aside all that made them strong.

"The Thericans presented a test. Measured and exacting. No more force. No more technology. No more strategy than necessary. All to give the pupils the opportunity to pass and earn their salvation. If only they could find the correct answer."

Simmonne could sense it in him. Master knew the answer before he asked.

"What was the answer?"

"Survival at any cost. Not of the idea, nebulous and subjective. Not of the abstracts or the principles. But of the species. The herbivore asks not the consent of the plant. Nor does the predator beg the flesh of the herbivore. The question was answered by proving the will to preserve their own existence. Every species put to the test had the opportunity to survive. If only they could abandon their principles.

"Yet there were so many. Corrupted by ease. Twisted by plenty. By hollow ideas. The formula was beyond them. Ideals and principles mean nothing if there are none left to carry them. Countless in this universe tested. Countless failed. Until humanity."

Humanity survived by abandoning its principles? How? She was no professor of history, but Simmonne knew the history of the Empire, her family. Humanity fought with everything it had. They sacrificed countless and died fighting at every step. They never gave up. How could abandoning their principles be what saved them all?

Her eyes opened wider. She felt suspicion, even impending shame. But not from herself.

"Manfred," Master whispered. "It was Manfred, wasn't it?"

"It is pleasing that the intellect granted you is not wasted. Your ancestor saw the poisons of ease and excess. He knew the principles for lies. Through my emissary Indorai, I made a pact with Manfred. That I would spare your species. That through his line, I would bring about a better humanity.

"For thousands of years, my device has sat in the halls of power, working toward that promise. Through it I have heard the thoughts of all who drive the Solar Winds, and they have heard mine. Through unknowing agents, I have guided the rise and fall of dynasties and nations. Through their history, I have taught the lessons.

"Into one family, I condensed the strengths. To breed a lineage that was the sum of human potential. When you were born, my work was complete."

Simmonne's eyes widened. It was the first thing the creature said that she was able to believe.

"I don't believe you," Master answered. His head shook, and the foot he had put forward slowly drew back to its previous place.

"You know I have spoken no lies to you. Did you never find oddity in how easy it has all been for you? Did you never have the self-awareness to reflect? As but a child, you had the strength of metapsions centuries your elder. Was it never strange the ease with which your lessons came? That even the most brilliant of your peers so often found mountains where you found hills? Did you never question the sovereignty of your mind?"

Master's upper body turned away from the entity. She did not understand everything she felt in him, but Simmonne knew denial. She wanted to squeeze him tighter, but her arms wouldn't respond.

"Eight times the natural muscle density. Eight times the bone density. Forty percent greater neuron density. Three hundred seventy-six percent faster reflexes. All above others who are pinnacles of engineered genetics. You are better. You have always been better. Because you were made to be better. I know because I made you. All four of you."

Master snapped his attention back to the silhouette. In her mind, Simmonne quietly repeated, *All four?*

"Did you notice that she cannot look you in the eye?"

"What did you say?" Master whispered.

"Mason Mandrake never understood why I called him the fool. Those who have believed themselves above my influence have always been the most susceptible to it. None believed themselves quite so far above as he."

Only force of will kept Simmonne's eyes open. She could not stand. She could not scream. Every gram of strength in her body failed to produce so much as a shudder.

"From the moment you met, you could not stop thinking of each other. Were you not surprised how quickly all three fell in love with you? Did you never question the ease with which they surrendered their destinies to you? Was there no shock that she, and only she, could sense the feelings within?"

Simmonne slid down his leg. Only her left eye was open now. Every breath was a feat of will.

"When their father wrote their genetics, he worked my design. When he gave them life, he carried out my will. When he organized their lives, it was by my plan. When he gave them to you, he had completed his use."

Master growled. His hand came back up as his volume rose. The constricting ring on their reality seemed to loosen. For a moment, Simmonne felt cool air in her lungs. Her right arm managed to rise, and she pulled herself up higher on his leg. But something seemed to snap. The ring coiled around them again, and she fell down his leg.

"Through them and others, you shall father the ruling caste of a new humanity. The pinnacle species I promised Manfred a hundred thousand years ago. As this universe merges with the next, the chosen shall be spared. You shall lead them from this cradle to the place I have prepared for you."

"Metapsions," Master muttered before yelling, "Metapisons! That's what you mean."

"Those who bear my gift may make contribution to the next humanity. They shall be your people."

"And what about the rest of humanity?" Master demanded with a step forward again. "What of the Eight? What of anyone who isn't human?"

"Your family is my chosen line, and the Eight belong to you. They may endure to serve the new humanity, if you will it."

"Everyone else?" Master asked. "What happens to them?"

"The gardener keeps not the weeds. All shall be swept clean, that the next flowers may grow."

Master shook his head and swept his arm at both the Therican and the Vaar. "I don't believe you. If I'm some kind of *chosen*, why have these two been trying to kill me?"

"Impede your hubris." The rebuke was monotone, yet somehow terrible and overwhelming. Heat passed over her skin.

"Indorai made no efforts on your life. Oul'sor has done only as was needed. In eras past, I created lieutenants to bear my will. Yet the effort was folly. If given the measure of free will to be useful, their rebellion was inevitable. And those they were meant to save from the destroyer, were damned to its grasp. Those born to immortality, to the means I offered, could not appreciate it. To save those I watched, I had to raise lieutenants from them."

Oul'sor? Simmonne glared at the Vaar. Anger brought a measure of strength, enough to grind her teeth. But it did not come from Master's energy. The tears formed in her eyes, and her grip tightened. For the first time she saw his face. His real face. The monster who murdered her guards.

"All my emissaries have tasted the end of the reaction. All have been made to face the hopeless finality and deprivation of destiny. Only confronted with the finality of their existence, could they be enlightened. The stubborn, like you, like Oul'sor, have oft needed to experience it more than once. You, better than most, have felt the grasp of the inevitable

destroyer.

"Anagram did not tell you what she did. When she invested her technology in you. She ripped you from the destroyer's grip. As though it were her gift to give. You shall not wither. But she simply played her unwitting part, and set you on the path to me. To the purpose I have created. Through you she has delivered that which she created in my opposition. Through you the Wayward, who call themselves Ascendant, authored their final failure."

Simmonne blinked. Did that mean what she thought it meant? What had the alien done to him? Yet even the hate that fueled her renewed strength was not enough. She could not muster a voice for her questions.

"Without free will, I would not be useful." Master seemed to speak more to himself than the creature. "So what happens if I say no?"

There was a new sound, as if the mist were hiding the onset of rain.

"Your reason fails you. You were not brought here to be given a choice. You are here to be told the future. Your compliance is not required. Your free will would be a liability, were it allowed to interfere. Even your death in protest would not stop what is already in motion. There are others, less deserving, but capable, who could take your place. Many, already positioned.

"I know the heart I placed within you. You were created to dominate those who would submit, and to destroy those who would not. A life of violence has primed your appetite. Dominion over an entire universe, and all those within. All to structure to your own design. It is a prize you cannot resist. Such would be inimical to your true nature."

Master? Simmonne called to him. Terror twisted her feelings as her sense of him changed and began to slip away. Was he actually considering it? These were all lies. They had to be. This monster, his allies—she did not need to understand what they were to know evil while in its presence.

Master? Please . . .

"As the door opens, my force shall sweep the stars. This shall be the port of departure for the chosen. Indorai. It is time. Open the way."

The mist seemed to thin, and at last Simmonne drew a complete breath before it turned into panting. Her body allowed no more than the easy breath she had been denied, yet she struggled to inhale it quickly.

Simmonne looked to the Therican as he raised his arms out and up. His talons moved briefly on unseen levers. A new sound filled the room like the winds of a coming storm.

On a platform ahead and to the left, the mist retracted from one of the pillars. A silver globe formed on top. It seemed to swirl in multiple directions at once as it expanded to dominate the platform.

"The new humanity can have but one leader. The same qualities that make of you an ideal choice, will bring only pain if you remain. Step beyond. Familiarize yourself with the new reality, and be ready to welcome your people."

Master drew in a deep, slow breath. He hung his head for several seconds. Simmonne could not sense him. No matter how she clawed at his feelings, she could not grasp them. He had shut her out.

He spoke just above a whisper. "If you know me that well, you know I won't let you do this."

"Every step in your life has been on a road I paved for you. Every falter, failure, and loss, an attempt to step off that road. You will do what you will because you must, and in the singularity of your destiny, there is only one destination. Thousands of years before you existed, this choice was made. You cannot stop it. Nor can you turn from what you are. Choice offers no bearing. The liquid must take the shape of its container. This is a mercy, refuge from unnecessary pain.

"In the new realm, you will be the power. Your being shall grow into the role. If you wish to be their emperor, so shall you be. If you desire to be their god, they will erect your church. Beyond the reach of the inevitable destroyer. You shall rule."

"Master?" A whisper finally escaped Simmonne's lips.

"Godhood?" Master emitted a loud exhale. "In what way are you serving godhood?"

Are you considering this? Master? You don't need him.

Her mind clawed at him, trying desperately to take back what had slipped away. When they first met, it was as if he did not exist. Now she couldn't feel him again.

Perhaps he'd heard the thoughts she could not find the strength to speak and that was why he shut her out. He looked down at her. She could not see his eyes for his helmet, but neither did she feel his gaze.

He drew her up. The red mist and the constricting ring slowly receded away. Master held her with one arm, then drew the Twins to their feet with the other. Both Twins let out quiet moans.

"Help them," Master directed as he guided Simmonne to stand. To her surprise, her legs obeyed the command to hold her weight. As Jennifer and Julie stood upright, Simmonne grabbed them both and pulled them to her.

Master? Are you considering this?

His left hand came up to cradle her chin. His cold, armored thumb rubbed gently on her cheek. *"What if I am?"*

Her eyes clouded, and she held her sisters tight against her. With all her strength, she forced a smile. She strained to focus on his faceplate, where his eyes were.

You're Master.

He nodded at her slowly before turning back to the towering silhouette. Master took an audible breath, then raised his arm.

"To this end." Master extended his middle finger and shoved it toward the Encephalon.

Simmonne sensed the immediate, overwhelming power from the mist. Hostility and disappointment. But through it, she sensed him. Resolution. The silver sphere on the nearby platform shrank away and then it was gone.

"Your answer is unfortunate. But anticipated. Too many have inter-

fered, and perhaps too much has been given. No joy is to come from it. But you must experience that which I hoped to spare you. I believe in you. That you can become more than what you are. Yet perhaps the finality of your existence is not enough. I am left with no choice but to take from you. To take until you understand. Indorai! Oul'sor! Do what must be done."

The command quaked the chamber, and the answer from Oul'sor was quick.

"Gladly."

In seconds, the red mist faded. The golden silhouette shrank back into the Therican until it, too, was gone. Simmonne clutched the Twins harder around their waists.

"Which one do you think, Oul'sor?" the four voices asked.

The many pupils of Oul'sor's eyes found Simmonne and contracted.

"No. Not that one," the quadraphonic voice mused. "Not yet. Kill one of the twins. That will leave him a spare."

Master?

The color washed out of the Therican's form, and in an instant, he was gone.

"Don't move," Master commanded.

What happened next was too quick for Simmonne to see. It had happened, and it was done before she began processing it.

Crunch!

Master had stepped out of the barrier. His left hand shot out to the side and closed on something. His arm was trembling, straining against whatever it held. It was only when she leaned slightly that she could see it from the side—the nearly transparent tendril, so thin it could not be perceived from the front. It had pierced the barrier. Its sharp point had stopped centimeters from Jennifer's forehead.

"I see you," Master whispered. "Indorai."

Simmonne planted her feet before lurching into Julie, dragging both girls with her to the ground. Simultaneously Master jerked the intercepting hand around his chest and back. His right hand balled into a fist, and the air rippled around them. The psionic presence sent a wave of nausea through her.

When Master's fist struck, glowing rings of ionized air expanded out in shockwaves. When Simmonne could see the Therican again, Master's fist was in its face. But his head did not explode into a cloud of bloody meat. His carapace did not shatter. It seemed as though when the fist struck the Therican's cheek, it simply stopped.

Sparks shot from Master's gauntlet as the tendril contracted and jerked out of his grasp. The creature's laugh rattled Simmonne to her bones. Master drew his fist back for a second blow. The Therican raised his tendrils like a spread of snakes ready to strike.

A hand landed on the Therican's shoulder.

Master startled. Indorai turned his head to the golden entity standing behind him. Its silver eyes narrowed in determination, focused on Indorai.

"Anagram," the four voices rasped.

Anagram answered in a whisper. "Come and get me."

Simmonne's eyes darted between the three of them. Master, Indorai, and Anagram. It was her. The one Master spoke of. The ancient creature.

"Oul'sor?" Indorai's four voices spoke with a high inflection, like a parent calling to a child. "Handle this. Remember what we talked about."

The black tendrils closed in. Both Indorai and Anagram seemed to turn hollow before leaving faint streaks of light that shot through the room, to the wall, and beyond. With her hands on the backs of their heads, Simmonne kept the Twins down as she turned to the remaining threat. Oul'sor.

CHAPTER
26C

ERO HOUR PLUS TWO hours, thirty-three.

Clearwater was on the move with his three platoons, less their artillery. Their path took them through a long plain of seamless metal surrounded by pyramid forests. When he looked either direction, he could see the flashes in the sky. Every artillery piece on this world was occupied trying to destroy the enemy's. If one side gained an upper hand, they would take the battle. The tanks, the warmechs, the infantry, they would just mop up.

Clearwater would have lied if he told someone that he fully understood what they were doing here. But one did not need an all-encompassing grasp of the orders to follow them. Go to a spot on the map and drop some bombs down a hole. Better to keep it nice and simple.

Barely more than five kilometers separated the eastern and western pyramids. His force moved south in column formation with the tanks abreast up front. The warmechs controlling them were arrayed behind them. Light infantry followed the warmechs while the armored infantry formed rows to fill the gaps between columns. At the middle and end of each column were tanks towing the generators for the overshield that would hopefully protect them if Vaar artillery took notice.

Clearwater walked near the front. A dwarf among giants, his AICES occupied a position that would otherwise have been filled by a warmech. He did not occupy the square alone, as his company sergeant stayed beside him.

Periodically a screen would open in his NOD, and within seconds it would close. The legionnaires still tried gain overhead views of the battlefield, but with the immense jamming, drones could provide little more than optical data. Even that could be invaluable, but no drone lasted. As soon as it had appreciable altitude, too many Vaar had a line of sight to it. In the handful of glimpses Clearwater had received of what lay ahead, none showed Vaar in his path. Thus he was more than a little surprised when the alert came.

CONTACT . . . CONTACT . . . CONTACT . . .

Clearwater held up his arm, and Sergeant Qopas bellowed for everyone to stop.

Clearwater had a dozen *Aggressor*-class automatech scouting four kilometers ahead. They relayed to him what they had found. Clearwater zoomed in on the screen that opened in his NOD. The horizon stretched far across the expansive, flat terrain. Thirty-four kilometers away, where the two forests of pyramids seemed drawn toward the horizon, Clearwater saw a roughly rectangular body, with a number of legs sprouting from its sides.

At this distance, it looked like a metallic misshapen spider. But Clearwater had seen it up close. A Vaar colossus—it was not alone, and it was heading toward them. Clearwater's cheek twitched, and a tingle ran down his back as more of the machine crossed the visual threshold.

He had to avoid any fights he could. Clearwater brought up his map. The plain extended all the way to his objective and had no branches. No roads, paths, or other plains intersected it. At least, if that information was correct. His map indicated that the landing zone would only be surrounded on two sides. So either the map was wrong, or the terrain was not consistent from day to day. Given where he was, he would believe either.

The pyramid forests to the east and west were each around five kilometers wide. Beyond them, the land alternated between plain and pyramid. He could try to go around the Vaar and move into the next plain. His infantry could pass through the east, but the pyramids here left too little space between them for the heavy armor. His tanks and his warmechs would have to float over on their thrusters.

Each pyramid here was over two hundred meters tall. Line of sight for an object floating over them would be over hundreds of kilometers. That was a lot of opportunity for Vaar to see and shoot.

Clearwater took a deep breath. They did not know whether more Vaar were advancing through those plains. He needed an answer to that question, or else he might simply trade one block of enemies for another.

"Send two bots east and west. I need to know what's in those plains."

One of his alpha lieutenants, Serrens, took the initiative. Four automatech split off from the formation, rolling away on their monowheels to pass through the forests. The eyes in the sky had all been short-lived, but this area had been observed. Where did all these Vaar come from? How did multiple *colossi* go unspotted? His questions had to be answered another time. The Vaar were coming, and he did not have long to decide. In the scouts' feed, new shapes, tanks, moved under and around the colossi.

The Vaar weren't shooting yet, so he had some confidence they did not yet know he was here. But the moment he tried to cross into another plain, they would definitely see him. Now he just needed to know if there were other Vaar nearby that would try to join the fight. Precious time was ticking by, taking the opportunity for a surprise attack with it.

"Lieutenant Serrens?" Clearwater asked.

"No contacts in the other valleys," the aren reported.

"Sir?" Qopas commed on a private channel. "We could call for artillery."

Clearwater's eyes lit up. Yes, they could try to handle this in something other than the dumbest way possible. Artillery was a good idea. He toggled his com.

"BlueCat-Two-One calling Toolshed," Clearwater called out to the Armadas. He drew a square in his NOD around the approaching Vaar. He drew another on his map to position the Vaar formation for his transmission.

But he did not receive an answer.

"BlueCat-Two-One calling Toolshed. Come in, Toolshed."

Clearwater perked up when his com came to life.

". . . shed. Reading . . . BlueCat-Two-One."

The reply was laden with static. Just how strong was the jamming that an Armadas warship with a bird's-eye view was having trouble burning through it?

"Toolshed, Vaar in the open on these coordinates." He paused to transmit the data from his map. "Request immediate fire mission."

Clearwater's foot tapped in its control sleeve as he waited. Thirty seconds passed without answer.

"Toolshed. This is BlueCat-Two-One. Vaar in the open, on these coordinates. Request immediate fire mission." He transmitted the map data again.

"Repeat . . . Two-One. Re . . . ended . . . No . . . available. Your . . . is queued."

Was it *that* bad? All the ships up there, all the artillery on the ground. They had to stick him in a line to wait for artillery?

"Looks like we might have to do this without them," Qopas remarked.

Qopas was right. The Vaar might be on top of them before support fire could come. Clearwater worked the feet of his AICES, turning a full circle as he looked around him. He needed a better view. Lieutenant Serrens's warmech was directly behind him.

"Serrens, don't move," Clearwater said before hitting his thrusters. He climbed in front of the mech before cutting thrust and setting down on the shoulders of the *Brutus*-class machine. Once he had reoriented himself to the south, he made a count. A dozen colossi. More than five hundred tanks. The small bubble tanks meant for urban work led the heavier vehicles. The Vaar had thrown everything down here.

"Hong's Phalanx." Clearwater gave the order. "Everyone."

The commands were relayed down, and his platoons shifted into the formation.

This isn't Warmetal, Clearwater mouthed. But what else did he have to work with? If command didn't want a gamer leading this unit, then they should have chosen someone who had been to armor school for this job.

There were few occasions where Hong's Phalanx was a good idea. Occasions where the enemy had no opportunity to flank the formation. Occasions where they had a durability advantage over the enemy, where their aggression could successfully be taken to the face. Occasions where the enemy did not have enough artillery to simply break through it.

The closer his units were, the better they could pool and overlap their shield coverage. But it also meant that more would be hit by any artillery that successfully made it through. Hopefully the Vaar artillery was just as busy as his. This was not his only option. It probably wasn't his best option. But it was the one he thought of.

"Everyone," Clearwater began after a swallow, "I don't see any choice but to try to push through the Vaar ahead of us. If any of you think I'm wrong about that, please say so now."

We're all doing the best we can.

He waited, but neither his lieutenants nor his sergeants spoke up.

"All right, then we go ahead," Clearwater said. "The colossi are weakest on their backs. I want all warmechs to focus them with plunging fire. Don't bother with a frontal attack. You won't break through. Keep our jamming focused on them to mitigate as much of their point defense as we can. I want our tanks to focus on their shield generators. If artillery decides to help us today, let's help it count. *Aggressors* on their tanks. Infantry and secondary weapons on their infantry."

Clearwater brought up the video memory. Everyone was gathered to share cake, celebrating his graduation from Hell's Gate.

"Sir?" Qopas came through on his private channel again. "I have two suggestions, sir."

"By all means, Sergeant."

"We put up our own holoflage, we can lure them in closer. If we wait until ten to twenty kilometers, that'll neuter a lot of their point defense."

That was the kind of thing Clearwater should have thought of. But at least someone did.

"Agreed. Get our holoflage up. Let's become the plain," Clearwater broadcast to the unit before switching back to the personal channel. He was about to ask for the second suggestion when he saw the picture Qopas had put in his NOD: a hastily drawn wireframe sketch. Points for creativity. It brought a smile to his face. "Do it, Sergeant."

"Light infantry!" Qopas bellowed. "Break out your mortars! Mortar teams, bring yourselves forward."

By now the unit had finished assembling into the phalanx. All of his tanks lined up, side by side, with less than a meter separating their hulls. The T-shaped automatech had likewise formed lines alongside the tanks. With the height to see over it all, the warmechs took the rear. Light infantry ahead, armored infantry between them and the tanks. The four tanks bearing generators for the overshield formed a line down the formation's center.

At Qopas's direction, a pair of light infantry climbed onto each tank, bearing a mortar tube. Once atop a tank's turret, a team planted and secured their mortar before doing the same with their feet. Clearwater did not envy their positions. At least they were all betas. Take away the skin and their hair, and they were basically automatech. They might survive.

"Become the plain," Clearwater whispered to himself.

The Vaar had themselves to thank when this blew up in their face. Had they not been drowning everyone in so much jamming that no one could see past their nose, this wouldn't work. The Vaar were coming into clearer view, and moving quickly. Clearwater did not recognize the heavy tanks that followed the bubble tanks.

An idea occurred to him, and he had to reference the list in the side of his NOD.

"Lieutenant Rekker, take over on coms. Provide Toolshed constant updates on the Vaar's position. If they manage to help us, let's make sure it lands on the right spot."

Clearwater had taken command of the overshield. The moment that went up, the Vaar would know they were there, with or without jamming and holoflage. The overshield would provide little help against the formation ahead—it was not a theater shield. The overshield was meant to work like spaced-armor, tricking artillery shells into detonating early so that their blasts were weaker by the time they hit his formation. In an odd way, more direct-fire weapons were too dumb to be fooled like that.

He saw no Viss in the ranks of the approaching infantry, only Vaar. They bound on their thrusters, moving in columns behind the tanks. Behind the infantry, enspa rushed to keep up. Ten kilometers. That's how close he would let them come. Any closer, and his point defenses would suffer. His eyes moved down to the formation laid out ahead of him.

I'm trying, guys. I'm trying.

Twelve colossi. Four hundred heavy tanks. Nine hundred bubble tanks. Seven thousand infantry. An undetermined number of enspa. That was the sum count that his sensors made out ahead of him.

"Rekker, any word from Toolshed?"

"We are still in queue."

Clearwater sighed. The hard way it was. The Vaar drew closer, and the colossi seemed to grow with each step until their true towering nature was apparent. When they hit ten kilometers, Clearwater's command came barely above a whisper.

"Open fire."

Thunder and fire drowned the plain. The boxy shoulder beneath Clearwater's feet rattled as missiles spewed out of it. A volcano of missiles erupted out of his tanks, the armor-hunters, his automatech, and his heavy infantry. Everyone contributed to a rain of disrupter pulses. Clearwater engaged the overshield.

Vaar interceptors came to life and managed to pluck off some of the missiles and shells, but not enough. Clearwater locked onto one of the colossi as a torrent of missiles came down on its spine. The machine's head jerked as though it were an organic lifeform suddenly drowning in pain. The attack had caught the machines with their shields offline and struck with devastating effect. The eight legs wobbled, and the machine collapsed. Its enormous body flattened an entourage of enspa beneath it.

The Vaar started with four hundred heavy tanks. Now they had twenty-one. The valley quaked nine separate times as the number of colossi fell from twelve to three. Yet despite the fury of the surprise attack, the Vaar reacted before Clearwater had a full count of the casualties. Their overshield went up, and his sensors fogged as the jamming devices in the Vaar formation focused on his unit.

When one played team battle in *Warmetal*, the winner was often the team whose leader best micromanaged the other players. Close enough to what the military called command and control.

"Mechs maintain focus on the colossi. Lieutenant Serrens has point control. Everyone else, finish off the heavy tanks, then switch to infantry!"

The Vaar were moving in reverse. The surviving colossi were walking backward now, their defenses active. Tanks moved in the same way, and even infantry ran backward. The Vaar were not retreating; they were regrouping. Their formation was contracting much like his own, bringing forces together to overlap shield coverage. The first serious counterattack came from the colossi. Hatches opened on their sides, and missile racks deployed and fired.

It was as though Clearwater were trapped in the middle of a swarm of insects with the overlapping, reverberating sound of his unit's interceptors firing. But just as the Vaar did not get all of his, he did not get all of theirs.

White flashes came from above as nuclear charges released conical detonations down on his formation. Occasionally trails of plasma shot downward like reversed geysers as disrupter shells pierced the overshield.

While regrouping, the Vaar commander sent his expendables forward. Clearwater heard the shrieking. They flailed their scythe-like limbs, and the enspa rushed toward him. On ND-31, wave guns and mines did a decent job of stemming the tide. Clearwater had neither here. In *Warmetal*, artillery was the best hard counter to masses of light infantry. But the powers that be decided his need was not sufficient. Chemical weapons were a potential hard counter. Clearwater was about to order that very thing, until he zoomed in. Unlike the enspa on ND-31, he could not see the horrid faces of these creatures. Their helmets were fully sealed spheres capping the ends of their serpentine bodies. Incendiaries worked, too. He had plenty of that.

"All units, apollium spread—begin at five kilometers. Draw it up to their formation." Clearwater paused a second for them to process the order. "Fire now!"

The light infantry took on this task. Their mortars spoke in thrumming tones, chucking the charges into the air. Vaar interceptors smashed several of them, but that did not do so much to stop them from dispensing their gelatinous payload. When the apollium ignited, Clearwater felt a slight rock as the concussion of heat met his AICES.

On ND-31, the enspa had happily charged through mines and wave guns to find meat. But no animal was dumb enough to run directly into a sea of fire. A column of red rose into the sky as the apollium ionized the air. The sea of apollium stretched over the east and west pyramids, collapsing the enspa unfortunate enough to be in the zone. Their sealed armor did not allow the steam in their bodies to escape. Those that had not yet made it to the condemned zone ground to a halt. With one look in front of them, they turned and ran.

They did not get far. Somewhere in the Vaar formation, a handler had access to the implants in their brains. He shepherded the creatures to the rear of the formation.

Now was the time. His surprise attack had shattered them before they reached formation.

Clearwater gathered himself before bellowing the order.

"All units, high shield opacity. Advance!"

In this wide space, the apollium would not last long, and nothing here could set it ablaze. The Vaar had gathered their formation into a square with a colossi at three corners. Three became two as the one front and left of Clearwater fell out of formation to land on its side.

It would work. The surprise attack had taken enough. The Vaar no longer had the weight of metal to stop him.

But Clearwater did not realize how much worse his situation had become. The first clue was when all his formation's interceptors turned toward the sky. The second sign was the multi-megaton charge that struck the overshield.

The Vaar were already surprised to find an enemy unit this far behind their lines. The result had been an overreaction. First Clearwater's opposite number reported the hostile contact. Then he reported the decimation of his unit by surprise attack. The same combination that fell on his landing zone, fell on his unit. Of each gun in the battery focused on him, three were disrupter charges, one nuclear. Arcs of lightning and jets of plasma danced in the air around them.

"All units! Full advance! Full advance!"

Clearwater stumbled as engines revved and the command was followed. The *Brutus* under his feet charged forward with the formation. He'd been killing the Vaar, and now he needed to give them a great big hug. If his formation embraced theirs like star-crossed lovers, the Vaar might not be so willing to drop artillery on him.

One of the disrupter shells made it through the overshield. Two tanks and an armor-hunter exploded directly in front of Clearwater. His formation responded quickly with the other vehicles moving in the horizontal to close the gap.

"Keep the formation tight!" Clearwater shouted. He dropped to a knee to stabilize himself on the moving machine. Unlike Lieutenant Serrens, Clearwater did not have a stabilized cockpit. Each of the *Brutus*'s thundering footfalls sent a jolt through his body.

The Vaar saw the hug coming and wanted no part of it. Infantry had turned and run. The bubble tanks not exploding had become the front of their formation and were spinning backward. Colossi and heavy tanks moved in reverse. Vaar running *away*? That wasn't supposed to happen.

"Faster!" Clearwater shouted. "Give them a kiss!"

CHAPTER
27A

O N THE CENTER PLATFORM, Panzer glared down at his right hand. He had never punched anything with remotely as much force as he used on Indorai. How? How did anything survive that punch? Let alone be unharmed by it? He felt it flowing through him—enough psionic force to act like a vortex charge, shredding matter into shrapnel. Yet it did nothing.

For now it did not matter. Indorai was gone. Hopefully Anagram knew what she was doing.

"Crossroads."

The station answered with a single message to his NOD.

ACCESS DENIED

"No," he whispered. *"Crossroads? Respond!"*

ACCESS DENIED

Indorai. The Therican had severed his connection and locked him out. The timer in his NOD, however, remained.

NO RETURN—1:14:09

Panzer looked past the numbers, his eyes falling on Oul'sor. The Vaar had not moved. His hammer still rested on his shoulder. Anagram had lured Indorai away, but was that boon or blunder? Indorai had locked him out. Could anyone but Indorai open the system back up? Had he already lost?

???: Andira. Is your emulator still connected to the station?

ANDIRA: The emulator is still intact, but I have been locked out.

Panzer took a long breath as he and Oul'sor glared at one another. The answer was looking right back at him. It had to be. Too much rode on this. What did Indorai have to do that was more important than this? Where did he need to be more than right here? What if something went wrong? What if adjustments had to be made? Surely, Indorai would not let himself be lured away unless he was leaving behind someone who could handle it. The Vaar were his tools if not his allies. There was only one Vaar telepath, and Panzer was looking at him.

Briefly, Panzer considered reactivating his cloak. No point. Panzer was not sure how, but Oul'sor had proven he could see through it. No point in dedicating power to it when it wasn't contributing.

???: Andira, I'll control my armor. Dedicate all processing power to getting me back into the Crossroads. I don't care how you do it. Just get me past the lockout.

ANDIRA: Yes sir. I'll only hold enough back to assist you.

???: All of it, Andira. Don't waste any on me. One hundred percent. Get me back into the station.

ANDIRA: Sir, you will need my help.

???: Don't argue. If I can't get back in control of this station, what's about to happen won't matter.

ANDIRA: . . .

ANDIRA: Understood. Good luck, sir.

A new screen opened in his NOD.

INITIALIZING SWEEP ATTACK . . .

Network hacking was beyond his expertise, but Panzer knew what a sweep attack was. Andira was not scanning every possible node of connection, reading every response, looking for any hole—any method of connection that had been missed. By now she had organized a list of hacks to run through. Panzer could only hope success came soon. She would prioritize the selection. The farther down the list she went, the lower their odds of success.

Only one option left. What Oul'sor was waiting for, Panzer did not know, but he would not waste the opportunity. His telepathic hand reached out to close on Oul'sor's mind.

What the hell is this?

Like smooth glass covered in grease, the Vaar's mind slipped from his grasp. He tried again with a firmer grasp, but the mind slipped all the more quickly. What was this? There was no 4CM strong enough to stop a T-13, nor did it feel like this. Panzer could sense thought, but he could not grab it. Why couldn't he read Oul'sor's thoughts?

Direction. Make the thoughts move a predictable direction. Position his grip and seize.

"This Aklonese bargain isn't going to end the way you want it to, Oul'sor."

Panzer felt the momentum shift. He had the mind in his grasp and squeezed gently. Ahead of him, the twirling of Oul'sor's hammer stopped. The Vaar sucked in a hiss of air before speaking.

"What do you know of Prosperity on the Sea?" Oul'sor bared his teeth as he stood straighter. His voice seemed to rise with every word until he was just shy of shouting. "What do you know of the Days of Zero and jungle spoken to life? What do you know of the raising of *Destiny*? What do you know of the Fourteenth Example? Tona'tass's grief? Or Von'tu's Gamble? Do not speak to me as if you understand us, Crykeeper."

In the past, making Oul'sor angry had always brought profit. But not this time. Perhaps Panzer had gone to that well too many times. His grip on the Vaar's mind was tightening. There was a thought here, yet he could not comprehend it. As if the Vaar's brain had been encrypted along with the Crossroads, there was nothing within that made sense.

SWEEP ATTACK FAILURE

INITIALIZING FLASH ATTACK . . .

One more try. Panzer called out again.

"What did they promise you, Oul'sor? Our worlds? To pilfer our technology? Have they made you nothing but goza, hungry for our scraps?"

Panzer did not find the reaction he hoped for. A loud snort blew through the Vaar's six nostrils before he smiled.

"You know, Crykeeper, I'm actually happy you're still alive."

Behind his faceplate, Panzer cocked an eyebrow. "Somehow, I question that sentiment."

The Vaar's jaw came forward as if pursing his lips, and he shook his head before his smile faded. There was a pulse in the static of the Vaar's mind. Yet static remained. As Panzer tried to grip more firmly to see through it, he was forced to back off, lest the mind slip his grasp again.

"You shouldn't," Oul'sor answered. "On Origin, I tore the limbs from your body. I crushed your head. I felt you go limp. I felt the life leave your body. Yet I felt no satisfaction. No joy in your demise. At first, I thought it was because Indorai gave me the strength to win. When your body was stolen, I knew only fury. But in the days after, I meditated. I had an epiphany."

Oul'sor took several steps to the edge of his platform. He tried to peer over or around Panzer before coming back.

"I realize that simply *killing* you could never be enough," Oul'sor said as he adjusted his grip on his hammer. "Because you did not simply kill me, and I did not hate you for it. It was what you took from me, Crykeeper. I realized I can only find satisfaction if I take from *you*."

Oul'sor pointed with his hammer as his voice became a growl.

"The Elder, I think, wishes only one, but perhaps three of your females will be enough to equal my greatest son. I will not kill you, Crykeeper. Only break you, so you may watch them die."

Perhaps it was the contact with the Encephalon. Perhaps it was the threat on what was his. Maybe it was both. The calm Panzer had worked so hard to retain shattered like glass. His breath quickened and he could not stop it. His pulse raced, and he could not stop it. His mind clamped down, and Oul'sor's thoughts shot out of his grip. Panzer aimed his palm down, intent on calling the Hellbore up from the floor. That was when it all stopped.

The fog rising from below stilled. The air circulating through the chamber stalled. Even Panzer's racing heartbeat had come to a stop. Everything was frozen. Oul'sor had stepped off the line. From the arrow of time they shared to another all his own. But Oul'sor was not unseen. A provident mind saw him move.

The Vaar bent at the knees before moving into a hop. Easily he cleared the distance to land on the platform ahead of him. Oul'sor walked casually, practically strolling, convinced that all the time in the universe was his in which to act. When Oul'sor was only one platform away, he paused. His posture shifted one way and then the next as he contemplated where he would make the final jump. But Panzer could see him, and his mental hand moved.

It was not that his body could not move. Only that its movement was limited to the prime time—so slow as to be motionless by comparison. Just like a dilation wave. Panzer would have taken a deep breath if he could and manifested a second mental hand. Were he able, he would have grinned when he felt it close on Oul'sor's hammer. He applied no pressure and simply let the hand follow what it held. With another mental hand, he reached down and felt the Hellbore's handle.

That's it Oul'sor. Come closer.

Oul'sor made his jump and landed directly beside Panzer. The Vaar turned toward him. Panzer could barely see him in his peripheral vision, but he had grip and knew where Oul'sor was. The Vaar squared himself up and made the final step. Panzer saw the bubble that was forced over him as if it were a wave of air. Oul'sor was committed to the swing.

Panzer spun on his heel and raised his left hand. A metallic crash rang through the chamber. Its echo had yet to fade when Oul'sor shouted.

"What?"

Panzer's left arm shook, but it did not yield. Two hands—one metal, one mental—caught the hammer by the haft just beneath its head. The psionics met in opposition, one waveform canceling another. Panzer turned his head to glare up at the towering Vaar.

"I'm not a cripple anymore, Oul'sor. I see *you*, too."

Panzer had a plan for this fight. It was a simple plan, but still a plan. Inflict injury on Oul'sor faster than he could regenerate it. The Hellbore leaped from the deck to the call of his right hand. Panzer sensed what he could only describe as an explosion of fear as he turned the weapon in. Oul'sor's left hand shot off the hammer, audibly clamping down on the Hellbore's muzzle. The fear compelled him to keep the assault cannon out of alignment with his body. On the *Caustic Reverie*, Oul'sor had charged through a hail of disrupter pulses and been unharmed by them. But somehow, Oul'sor knew the weapon Hellbore was a threat to him now.

Panzer seized the moment of fear. His knees bent as he angled his head forward, and his thrusters opened to full. His helmet led the way as he used his entire body to thrust an uppercut through the Vaar's jaw. The combatants bound themselves to each other with their grips on the other's weapon, and Oul'sor was dragged with him as Panzer gained altitude.

Oul'sor did not go quietly. As the Vaar twisted and jerked, Panzer lost control of his center of balance. His rapid, upward ascent was twisted, putting them on a course parallel to the tops of the pillars. It ended when they slammed into the chamber wall. They rolled around each other, taking turns scraping the wall as they followed the curve of the circular room.

Panzer managed to pull out, dragging both of them off the wall. Oul'sor was contorting, trying to get his leg high enough to deliver a kick. Panzer adjusted thrust, accelerating their spin to sling the Vaar off. But Oul'sor's thrashing made it impossible for him to control their vector. The pair slammed into one of the pillars, skipping like stones before they went over the side. Panzer cut thrust as they tumbled through the fog, descending into the abyss below. Somehow in their struggle, they found a point of equilibrium. Their feet struck the chamber's bottom almost simultaneously.

Panzer focused the full force of his mind on Oul'sor's body as if to crush him from every angle. If he was correct, it was the only way this would work. With Oul'sor's new strength, the weight of his mind had to bind the Vaar and sap that strength.

WARNING—ENVIRONMENT CRITICALITY
WARNING—CONTACT TEMPERATURE -268.15°

Oul'sor's mouth opened in a howl of pain. The air vacating his lungs froze almost as soon as it left his mouth. It fell to the dull blue of the floor.

WARNING—WARNING—WARNING—WARNING!
ENVIRONMENT CRITICALITY

"Sir! Don't stay here!" Andira warned in his helmet.

???: Focus on your work!

The three barrels of the CF-606 came over his shoulder. Oul'sor's eyes could not have opened any wider and then they filled with fire. That should have been it. The heat of the progo-flamer should have done more than simply burn the Vaar's head away. Such heat should have flash boiled the water in his tissue and detonated his head in a steam explosion. Instead the flames crawled down, finding more body to offer their heat.

The cone of fire continued on meters past Oul'sor's head. Panzer had trouble finding thought in the flame, but he sensed the momentary change from irritation to anger.

Panzer jerked back, intent on avoiding the headbutt that came down for him, but his head was not the target. Oul'sor rammed his face into the flamer's muzzles. A loud snap, and the weapon broke free. Panzer heard the impact as the flames were quenched and the weapon slid away.

FLASH ATTACK FAILURE
INITIALIZING PAC ATTACK . . .

Panzer hit his thrusters again. Ice crystals that had formed on their legs broke free as he pulled Oul'sor with him again. Even this extreme cold was not enough to break whatever Oul'sor was now. The Vaar managed to pull himself up. This time Panzer's face was the target, and the headbutt landed squarely.

CONCUSSION FIELD . . . FAULT DETECTED

Panzer might have had a sarcastic thought about that, had thought itself not been punted out of his skull. His mind did not so much as register the loud *pop* that came from his neck. Stunned by the blow, he lost control of his course. The side of the pillars were covered in a black, spongy material. They provided far less cushion than appearance would have suggested. Still bound together, the two ricocheted between the pillars.

When a measure of awareness returned, Panzer threw his shoulder to alter their course and thrust upward. The pair crested the pillars and began to turn when he cut the throttle. Together they skipped on the face of one pillar before crashing down on another. Despite being covered in a black, spongy material, the pillars provided far less cushion than appearances would have suggested.

He and the Vaar were finally freed as their grips broke, and the weapons flew from their hands. The ammunition hose linking the Hellbore to the magazine on his back was split. The shells within the hose were freed, expanding to full size and clattering around them like falling hail.

Panzer was the first on his feet. The Level-3 AMAC had the strength to lift a tank and throw it. All that strength was magnified with psionic force in a descending punch. It seemed to do little more than turn Oul'sor's head, but Panzer had hands more dangerous than the ones in his gauntlet.

Panzer thrust backward as Oul'sor exploded off his knees, trying to land a tackle. His real hands mimicked the motion. His fingers curled as Panzer closed mental hands on Oul'sor's neck. When his feet met the ground, he twisted his body, hurtling the Vaar away and down. Oul'sor was inverted when he slammed into the side of the pillar with such force that the entire edifice trembled. Panzer worked with the momentum of his bounce, hurtling the Vaar up and rocketing his skull into the ceiling.

For all his strength, Oul'sor lacked the skill. It was far easier to break a psionic gasp on one's own body than to keep that grip on a resisting psion. But only if they knew how. Only if one knew the techniques for disrupting a psionic grasp. When Oul'sor came off the ceiling, Panzer drew him down, planting his face on a platform five pillars away.

Quietly, unconsciously, Panzer chuckled. To have been so crippled, for so long—how had madness never claimed him?

The hands were still on Oul'sor's throat when Panzer pulled the Vaar toward him. Panzer's left arm went back, his palm facing the Vaar as he focused on the air between them. Oul'sor was thrashing, clawing at his neck. A sphere of fire opened like a wormhole between them before Panzer released the building force, and Oul'sor was engulfed in an explosion of plasma.

Panzer's heart raced, each breath coming fast. In his mind he saw Simmonne in his lap, Julie laughing as he tickled her. Jennifer in his arms as he taught her to shoot. Each image built on his growing fury.

PAC ATTACK FAILURE
INITIALIZING TRAP ATTACK . . .

Panzer had not let go of the Vaar. Oul'sor's body flailed like a puppet with tangled strings as the blast washed over him. The moment it subsided, Panzer slammed him down onto another pillar.

"You will not take them from me. I'm sorry you can't see a life without your son, but they are innocent. You and I are not. Nor was your son. We abandoned our innocence long ago so innocence may exist in others."

Panzer did not realize he had projected the thoughts until he saw the grin on Oul'sor's face. Fuel to the flames of rage. More mental hands converged on the Vaar. One gripped the fan of his head like it was hair to drag him up to his knees. Another took the Vaar's hand, balled it into a fist, and drove it into Oul'sor's face. Another pair of hands closed on his head. The imaginary thumbs had a very real effect as he drove them into the Vaar's eyes.

The high-pitched scream from Oul'sor sounded more like a Viss that Panzer gutted than the proper scream of a Vaar warrior. Black blood flowed out of the edges of his eyeballs as the large orbs began to collapse inward.

"I was the strongest ever born. Yet I lived as a shadow of what I could have been. I suppose I carried some anger around because of it. You'll take that off my hands for me. Won't you, Oul'sor?"

Panzer took the fresh scream as an affirmative answer when Oul'sor's eyes popped.

I want them to suffer.

Panzer saw Simmonne in the armory—heard the words as she reflected on what the Vaar took from her. He dissolved the mental hands. Almost immediately the Vaar's mouth shot open, and the sound of the wind came as he inhaled.

That's right, Oul'sor. Deep breath. It delights me to know, as tough as you are, you still feel pain. Grow them back so I can do it again!

Red mist filled Oul'sor's empty eye sockets. By the time it vanished, a fresh set of twelve pupils dilated. Oul'sor looked down and saw the Vaar's hand open. He reacted too late. The hammer flew up, emitting a loud clap as it found the Vaar's palm.

Panzer staggered backward. Every mental hand he had on the Vaar dissolved within a moment. He raised his arms to grab for Oul'sor again, then time stopped. Oul'sor rose to his feet, one hand on the hammer, the other on the side of his head. He breathed in deep, angry gasps.

Panzer could not compress his mental grasp on Oul'sor. There was no strength to the grip. Across the gulf, he could touch, yet seemed to have no power.

Oul'sor gathered himself before leaping to the next pillar. The Vaar's eyes stayed on him as he came in, and Panzer waited for the moment when he could move again.

He understood. No matter what Oul'sor was doing, everything took time—on the line or off the line. Without time, the molecules of atmosphere could not get out of his way. The force exerted by his muscles could not reach the floor for him to push off it. No time, no action. Panzer could almost see the bubble around Oul'sor, the influence of his personal time.

The Vaar joined him on his platform, adjusted his step, and came in. When movement came, Panzer lunged into the Vaar. Mental hands merged with physical as Panzer grabbed the hammer's haft, and its motion halted. The shockwave passed through him, and the pillar beneath them shook.

Just as he thought. Oul'sor *wasn't* some beast of impossible strength. Oul'sor was physically stronger now. Stronger by far than any organic being his size. But the bulk of the strength was psionic, not physical.

Both of their arms trembled as they pushed against each other. "I will kill them," Oul'sor growled, towering over him. With his height advantage, Oul'sor slid a foot forward, intent on using that leverage to push Panzer down. "But first I will break you. You will watch. As I did on Origin, I will take your limbs so you cannot fight me when I force their blood down your throat!"

TRAP ATTACK FAILURE

INITIALIZING SLAP ATTACK . . .

Anger was the eternal foe of clear thought. Panzer threw his hips to the right as he pushed the hammer left. The hammer hit the deck, and Panzer drove the uppercut. It never landed. Oul'sor caught his forearm. The Vaar's mouth opened in a wide grin.

Oul'sor wore his mental hand like a glove over his real hand. The psionic flow felt like fluid swirling about his arm. It softened the metal, working the space between atoms. Panzer did not know that technique. He did not understand it. But he knew a psionic grip when he felt it, and with his own mind, he slipped the glove off. Oul'sor could not crush bond-forged titanium without psionic help.

Oul'sor growled. Panzer could see the Vaar's forked tongue clearly and focused on it. His eyes went wide when he felt his mental hand flicked away.

"You've got him, Master!"

What was that? Panzer turned his gaze to the center of the chamber.

Simmonne stood with her left arm around Julie and the right around Jennifer. The pair stared with frightened, doe-eyed gazes. But not Simmonne.

"You've got him! Finish him!"

There was little she could do to help. Yet behind the barrier, she did the one thing for him she could. She cheered. But it was a distraction he could not afford. Panzer turned back as he felt himself jerked off the deck, and Oul'sor's face came forward.

CONCUSSION FIELD FAILURE

Panzer's eyes opened to the message, and he spat out the blood trying to drown him. He was only unconscious for a second. But it was enough for Oul'sor to stomp down, painting the inside of his helmet with more blood. The relationship between Panzer's lungs and air briefly became estranged. He tried to sit up when a punch laid him back down. More followed, alternating between his helmet and chest, shearing and deforming metal with each strike.

SINUS COLLAPSE . . .
VERTEBRAE SPLIT . . .
CONCUSSION . . .
CEREBRAL CLOT DETECTED . . .

Panzer was too dazed to read the messages. With a hand on his shoulder, Oul'sor gripped and raised him up. He couldn't breathe. The deformed plates of his armor bowed in, compressing his chest.

Panzer may not have been able to read the messages in his NOD, but he understood what he saw. Oul'sor had dropped his hammer. He reached toward the center of the room, toward the barrier. He was trying to slip a mental hand through it, trying to grab the girls.

Panzer's deep, bellowing roar frightened the three of them more than the Vaar reaching for them. When Oul'sor's head turned back to him, Panzer's mental hand shot forward, straight into the Vaar's mouth. His hand closed on the forked tongue before he jerked it past the teeth. With a quick exchange to a physical hand, Panzer drew it up, and his knife cut cleanly through Oul'sor's tongue.

Panzer fell to his feet as Oul'sor doubled over, spewing black blood onto the deck. This time nothing stopped his mental grasp from seizing the Vaar. Panzer had six of those hands holding him in place as the Vaar's plates deflected his blade. The second attack was a stab. The blade sank cleanly into the Vaar's right chest, and Panzer forced the blade down. Oul'sor's legs pushed feebly at the deck as he tried to back away. Panzer's mind jerked him back. He gloved his physical hand with a mental grasp and swung the blade again.

Oul'sor's left hand fell to the floor. The next stab was at the neck. Panzer had lost the plot as reason danced away. Oul'sor tried to protect his body with his right hand. The blade took it as well. Panzer bore down on him, stabbing with abandon. The fury had taken over. Each word of Oul'sor's threats on the girls entitled him to a hundred experiences as the blade's sheath.

His inability to breathe was catching up to him. Panzer threw the knife down as he drew his arms down and back. A short time ago, Oul'sor had the body of a warmech. With it he had delivered a kick that sent Panzer into a skyscraper. There was no less force in the psionic wave that hurtled Oul'sor across the breadth of the chamber. Pieces of the Vaar fell out of his body as he cartwheeled into the wall with a sickening impact. His blood splattered around him.

Panzer spun in a full circle until he found it. The Hellbore rocketed toward him with such speed that catching it nearly took him off his feet. Oul'sor was falling as Panzer spun. The Vaar was laid out on the pillar that caught him as the sights aligned, and Panzer toggled to the drum magazine. By the time Panzer pulled the trigger, Oul'sor had thrown himself over the edge. The third lung exhaled.

Globes of electric corona danced as the pillar that caught Oul'sor took the brunt of the assault. The alien, silvery metal turned to splinters under the detonation of the shells. By the time Panzer let off the trigger, he had shaved a full meter of height from the pillar. Electric arcs were still sparking as he lowered the weapon.

SLAP ATTACK FAILURE

INITIALIZING SWAMP ATTACK . . .

Panzer's breath came in sharp, raspy gasps as he became aware of the pounding of his heart.

What the hell am I doing?

Still panting, he lowered the Hellbore. He had become victim to his own tactic. He let anger take him and blind him to his task. How many attempts had Andira made now? Each with less chance of success than the last. He had asked too much of her. The Crossroads was too big. Too alien. She could not break back in. He needed Oul'sor alive. His only way back in was through Oul'sor's mind. The Vaar warlord would have a hard time contributing if he was rendered into bloody gruel.

Panzer lowered to a knee as he tried to force his chest out, but his armor denied him. No choice. The heavier armor had done its best for him. It was a liability now.

>>*AMAC CONTROL*
AMAC ONLINE
>>*DECOUPLE LAYER—3 / LAYER—2*

Hisses and sizzling filled his ears as the outer layers of his armor began sloughing off. The missile launcher fell off his shoulder, along with the Hellbore as his mechanical hand disintegrated. The forearm continued to fall apart until revealing his actual hand and the protective gauntlet around it.

Panzer heard the faint whisper of wind. The fog rolled as the currents of air disturbed it. Oul'sor was rebuilding his body. As the plates fell off, Panzer's eyes rested on one of the hands he had taken from Oul'sor. The orphaned appendage began to collapse, then liquefied, becoming the same black ink that seemed to be the Vaar's blood now.

Panzer sucked in a great breath as his outer chest plate finally disintegrated, and his lungs once again found volume for air. Panzer looked to the center platform. Simmonne still had her arms around Jennifer and Julie, but now she was dead silent.

He brought his eyes back down to the Hellbore. Near it, Oul'sor's hammer still lay where he had dropped it. The final plates fell away, leaving Panzer only the AMAC-1 scout suit. The same armor he so often wore. The same level of protection he had on Avalon. Somehow, Panzer doubted a hit from the hammer would be any less powerful than a certain kick. Not if Oul'sor held the hammer.

Panzer grabbed the Hellbore. Whatever Anagram did to it, it could damage the metal here when even bombardment did not. Oul'sor was afraid of it. Panzer was certain the weapon could kill him, and that was the problem. Until he could break into Oul'sor's mind and find a way back into the Crossroads, the Vaar had to be alive. But the weapon could do something else for him.

Panzer reached for Oul'sor's hammer. He did not realize the enormity of that error until his hand closed on the haft.

"What. The—" The effect was immediate. Every muscle from his scalp to his toes seized at once. What began as a tremble in his left arm graduated quickly to violent spasms. Even his eyes squinted, his jaw locked, and his tongue tried to impale the roof of his mouth.

He had not sensed it before. It was too faint, too easy to miss. Like a tiny light that sat next to one a hundred times brighter. The eye would only see the one. Beside Oul'sor's mind, it had been hidden. But it was here. A semi-sapience, not quite the equal of an animal's mind, yet there was form, awareness, direction. Consciousness, and an understanding of Panzer's ill intentions toward it.

Panzer's eyes watered. His nose bled. He looked at his left arm, expecting to see it covered in flame. Only apollium ignition came close to what he felt climbing up through his arm. There were whispers behind his eyes. Faint, loud enough to hear, too quiet to understand. They grew louder.

"Master! Help us!"

"Please no!"

"Nooo!"

"Why?"

His muscles were clenching so hard, they were beginning to tear. Panzer tore those in his neck further when he forced his head to rotate. Simmonne. Jennifer. Julie. They were still in the barrier. They were still watching him.

"Please!"

He looked back at the hammer. Whatever this thing was, if it was alive, it could die.

A ligament gave an audible pop in his knee when Panzer forced himself up. His hips turned, and he flailed as he tried to launch the hammer away. But he simply spun. He could not let go. He could not force the muscles of his hand to relax.

The whispers became screams. He heard Simmonne's voice. He heard Jennifer's and Julie's. He heard others as well. All crying out, all begging for him to save them. His focus shattered as soon as he tried to gather it. He had to get rid of the hammer.

Panzer oriented his body again and swung. He managed to squeeze out a mental hand to jerk the hammer away. His muscles relaxed, the screams were gone, and the hammer flew away. Left almost limp, Panzer struggled to bring his right arm under control.

Panzer's sensors had not picked him up. In his distraction, he had not sensed Oul'sor's mind. He did not see him clinging to the sides of the pillars, leaping from one to the next. Panzer was raising the Hellbore to fire on the hammer, but his first indication that Oul'sor was there was when he came over the edge of the pillar.

He had too little time to react. The Vaar came in, leading with his fist. The silvery sheen of R-steel was exposed in Panzer's helmet as the outer layers were ablated. Some of it crumbled. Some of it turned to liquid. Some of it even flashed to gas. All the parts tried to dissipate and vent the incredible force of the punch. Panzer's left eye could not escape its socket fast enough to avoid bursting like an overripe fruit. The blood in his mouth was filled with solid objects—teeth freed from his gums. The whiplash split soft tissues in two. Panzer would have been sent careening if not for the psionic hand that grabbed his leg and slammed him to the ground.

WARNING—MASSIVE CRANIAL TRAUMA

"Stand by, sir. I will dispense ETNs and attempt repairs."

Just because his eye was open did not mean he was conscious. The primitive side of the mind was the first to recover. On his belly, Panzer saw the Hellbore in front of him. His left arm reached out for it, but Oul'sor swung down with his reclaimed hammer. The spear-like face found Panzer's wrist and cut through it like paper.

Panzer was too dazed to feel the pain. There was not enough thought in his head to understand what just happened. He held up his left arm and glared at the appendage. Wasn't there supposed to be something at the end of the limb?

8,741 SYNAPTIC ERRORS COULD NOT BE REPAIRED.
BYPASSING . . .

Panzer was rolled onto his back. That was a *really* tall creature standing over him. It seemed angry. He should probably do something about it. His left arm probed at the knife beside him, then again, and a third time, his brain not comprehending that it took a hand to actually grab something. The big angry thing was holding something, and it began to glow. That seemed bad. He continued to slap at the knife but couldn't grasp it.

BYPASS COMPLETE

Panzer drew in a gasp and raised his right arm. The knife flew to his hand, and he swung, but Oul'sor stumbled and fell over the edge of the pillar.

By the time Panzer had the brains to roll forward onto a knee, Oul'sor was out of sight. In his life he had known many headaches, though never one as pure as this one. His head rested flat against his shoulder. Panzer guided his head upright, only for it to fall back as soon as he let go.

"Damn it!"

He forced his head upright again with his hand. His NOD told the story. The rigid parts of his cybernetic skeleton were mostly intact. The soft parts, less so. The headache worsened as he forced out a mental hand. From a compartment at the rear of his armor, he withdrew a pill tube and lifted his faceplate. He popped open the tube and downed the pills.

The pain had only begun as they came apart in his mouth. The nanites bored through flesh on their way to find more serious trauma. They found it quickly, and Panzer held his head up until they finished.

A realization came as the machines worked and his faceplate closed. He could beat, cut, burn, and bludgeon Oul'sor until Founder's Day, but that wouldn't accomplish anything. Nothing beyond giving Oul'sor a chance to return the favor. He needed information from the Vaar's brain—the rest of him was surplus to requirements—but he could not read the Vaar's thoughts.

There were techniques to scramble one's mind, but it took a telepath of great skill to block a stronger telepath. He needed time, and Oul'sor was rudely refusing to give it to him. He needed to keep the Vaar busy, distracted. Maybe in some pain to make it harder to concentrate.

Panzer couldn't read Oul'sor's mind. But just because he couldn't take something out, didn't mean he couldn't put something in.

Panzer sighed. It was too soon. He had not had his test. Whether he liked it or not, Oul'sor would have to be that test. Advanced telepathy with this headache, with this trauma. No. He needed to find the simplest thing that could do the job.

SWAMP ATTACK FAILURE
INITIALIZING FLOOD ATTACK . . .

Panzer forced himself up to his feet. He could not use the Hellbore now, so he let it lie. He saw the movement five pillars over as Oul'sor leaped onto the top. Through the forest of pain, over the fog of brain trauma,

Panzer focused on the Vaar's mind.

"You're strong, Oul'sor, but you're not trained. Those of us who are? We call this one Event Horizon."

A single telepathic suggestion. It was simple, but it was everything.

CHAPTER
27B

ABOARD THE *Hurricane*, THE red eyes glared in a look of frustration and barely restrained anger. What happened to Her Majesty? What was going on that he had not been told? No sooner had Her Majesty vanished than her handmaiden, and Colonel Panzer's man, rushed from the bridge. What had the colonel not told him?

Aetius did not have time to contemplate it. Even his segmented mind could not spare a sliver for this. He needed all his focus on the battle. The Grand Fleet's arrival forced the Vaar to fall back, but Aetius knew better than to think they would give up the battle that easily. At the center of this galaxy was an artifact of an unknown, but powerful, civilization. Enough for the two to fight over, even if they had no other reason.

"Coms, any word from Tick-Tock-One?" Aetius asked as he looked to his left across the open pit.

"Negative, sir," the gamma there answered. "Still no word."

The Armadas and the Grand Fleet had formed up together to create their own sphere around the silver globe. Aetius had given the order to contract that sphere to a diameter of barely a light-year. The tighter the sphere, the denser the ships' jamming systems and interceptors would be against incoming weapons. But the trade-off was that the Vaar had a smaller volume of space to concentrate their attacks into.

The titanic *Prince of Mars* had assumed the polar point, placing it above the Crossroads's northern pole. All ships were light-years from the station, but moved around it as if orbiting. At the polar point, the *Prince of Mars* would have the smallest ring to follow. Last Aetius heard, the ship was preparing to embark on its star trials. If it was here, the high prince had chosen to cut that venture short. Aetius could only hope the ship was ready. He hoped it was the phenom Galaxy Staryards Corporation promised the high king it would be.

"Sir?" Aetius looked at the gamma who spoke. "Transpatial signatures, they're coming back. Grid zero-one-three. Distance, five-zero light-years."

Aetius answered with a nod, looking through the ship's network, through the lieutenant's eyes, to see her display. A thousand scenarios played in his mind in the time it took him to take a breath. Angles of attack, points to intercept, focused fire, and counterfire. As he focused on the millions of bubbles forming in space, he did what he could to analyze their patterns. A finger on each of his hands followed the motion as he drew a square in his NOD, centering a cube ahead of the bubbles. He projected that cube through the network.

"All ships, ten-second burst on these coordinates. Lock after launch. Prepare to shoot." Aetius paused. He watched the bubbles growing, anticipating when they would pop.

"Shoot!"

Aetius's order was mirrored across the feed on the *Prince of Mars*. Missiles from the Armadas, heavy torpedoes from the Grand Fleet. All moved together toward the indicated coordinates.

Aetius had a decision to make. When the bubbles popped, the incoming Vaar would be positioned into a wall-up. He could meet it with his own or keep his forces in a sphere. His mouth opened, a sound came out, but he stopped himself before the words formed. He did not know the exact number of bubbles he was seeing, but he could tell that this was not all of them. Kreth'nell was trying to bait him. To lure him into walling up and leaving his forces vulnerable to more from a different direction.

The massive salvo fired by the joint fleet streaked toward the coordinates. Each warhead in the wave queried the others in their search for a target.

All answered each other when the bubbles popped. The Vaar interceptors had little time to react.

"Three hundred forty-six thousand hits," the gamma in the ten pod announced as the wave slammed into the new formation of warships. "Many destroyed."

Kreth'nell would know those losses were coming since he'd jumped directly in front of a battle-ready force. But the Vaar had the weight of numbers to absorb the blow. The Vaar fired back.

"All ships, three-second intercept burst," Aetius ordered. "Shoot."

"Dominion ships." The high prince's voice drew Aetius's attention. "Let the Armadas intercept for us. All weapons on the Vaar. Twelve-second alpha burst. Oculory, help the Armadas out."

The *Prince of Mars* rotated in place in the polar point, the Vaar were to the ship's starboard. Turrets moved on its bows. As the turrets on the starboard turned out to face the Vaar, those to port elevated on their barbettes to superfire over the port turrets. Similar motions were made by the wedge of elongated boxes atop the ship's highest levels.

"Spotlight the Vaar warheads!" the high prince barked. "Now!"

The oculi came alive and the cones returned. Each oculus was a sensor of such incredible power that other sensors off their axis saw the distortions they created. Such power that they became weapons to any sensor within their gaze. The gamma in the ten pod was calling out time to intercept when all twelve cones of the oculi focused on the cube of Vaar missiles.

The cube disintegrated.

Vaar missiles blinded by the cones attempted to switch to home-on-jam. But like the active sensors that had already suffered the fate, passive sensors burned out as they were overloaded. The weapons were blind. They continued maneuvering, a few having escaped the ravaging of their sensors. But most streamed away in odd directions, seeking targets they would never find.

Aetius briefly closed his eyes. *Majesty, please. Pay whatever they ask for it.*

When Aetius opened his eyes again, the cones parted, keeping as many of the separating missiles in their influence as they could. Those few with functioning sensors found unmolested space and snapped back to their target. Fewer spread out, vulnerable to massed interceptor fire.

"Cut blind!" the high prince called. "Target their cruisers. Blind them!"

The cones collapsed into rays once more, each targeting one of the larger Vaar ships. Aetius had not failed to see it the first time, and he saw it this time. Each Vaar ship spotlighted by the oculi fell silent. Each ship in the beams was now blind to the outside universe, yet to the sensors of Aetius's fleet, they now glowed like a mirror under a spotlight.

"All ships." Aetius raised an arm. "Ready thirty-second salvo. Three. Two. One. Shoot!"

It was the largest torrent of missiles yet to come from his fleet. But the battle was about to turn, and Aetius realized it as the warheads crossed the gulf.

"Admiral! Massive spatial disturbances! Many grid squares!"

"Is it the rest of the Vaar?" he asked.

"No sir," the five pod answered. The young lieutenant didn't look old enough to be in a uniform. Aetius saw a mix of fear and confusion in his eyes.

Aetius focused on the main display ahead of him, no surer than the lieutenant what he was seeing. Between the joint fleet and the Vaar, a cloud-like ring had formed in the sensors. Thirty-five light-years across, it looked like the roiling clouds of a thunderstorm. The ring was growing. In seconds its thickness had become five light-years. Something new was entering the battle, and Aetius caught a glimpse just before he heard the lieutenant.

"What the hell is going on?" the high prince whispered.

"New contact!" The words came simultaneously on the bridges of the *Hurricane* and the *Prince of Mars*.

"Contact—" Aetius's lieutenant hesitated. "Unclassifiable."

Aetius glared at the lieutenant. "Give me something, Rudes."

The lieutenant's large green eyes widened in disbelief. "Admiral, it *looks* like a singularity."

The answer made no sense. Aetius looked back to the ring. Something rose out of the cloud-like distortion. Ripples in the sensors surrounded an opaque core. Aetius reeled in the image, giving himself a tighter view. Primitive sensors used by less-advanced species could easily mistake an Armadas ship at sublight for a black hole. Such was the distortion of their MID and shielding. But that would not fool Imperial sensors.

The opaque sphere was perhaps a hundred kilometers across. It seemed to exert no influence on the distortion that had spawned it. It had emerged directly in the path of the missiles meant for the Vaar, and now at FTL, it was moving toward them. It could not be a singularity. Yet, after forty-two hundred years in space, Aetius knew a singularity when he saw it in warp sensors. It looked exactly like what stared him in the face: spherical, surrounded by a glowing shell of trapped particles.

A new ripple broke through the sensors. A sphere of distortion erupted from the opaque globe just in time to meet the approaching warheads. As they passed through the expanding sphere, every missile vanished from the screen. Seconds later as the globe continued to expand, he made out tiny detonations, millions in number. The tech fighters, the monitors, and all the small vessels erupted. The wave continued on until Aetius's display went black, and he flinched.

As he looked around his bridge, he saw only bewildered expressions. The hologram of the high prince was gone, as were the links to his field officers aboard the battleships and battlecruisers. Aetius drew breath to bark a command when the feed returned. The image came back to life just in time for Aetius to see the expanding wave reach his fleet. It passed them by, and he watched the wave split before it could reach the Crossroads. Like a tidal wave parted by the station's field stabilizers.

"What the hell am I looking at?" the high prince asked as his hologram returned.

"What just happened?" Aetius demanded as he looked to his coms officer.

"I don't know, sir." She paused to stare more intently at her display. "Sir, nearly all com traffic is dead. There are only a few voices."

"Get me the *Rowen Jereko*," Aetius barked as he looked to the high prince, who turned in a circle as he looked around his bridge.

"Rucker?" the high prince asked. "Stannec? Jolldring?"

With his circuit complete, the high prince looked directly at Aetius.

"Aetius, are you still reading me?"

"I read you, Excellency," Aetius answered as the high prince moved out of view.

"No response from *Rowen Jereko*, Admiral," Aetius's coms officer reported.

"Excellency, what's happening there?" Aetius bellowed. "Excellency?"

After several seconds, the high prince stepped back into view.

"My crew," the high prince began. "They're frozen. No one's moving. No one's answering. They're—I can't even sense their minds."

The high prince paused and glared up. Aetius heard an echo as the channel split, and the high prince patched him into the *Prince of Mars*'s internal network.

"This is the high prince. Any watch officer who hears me, answer."

The high prince's blue eyes widened as the responding silence stretched on.

"This is Sebenmorg," a voice finally said.

"General, what's happening in your area?" Prince Heinz asked, a twinge of fear carrying in his voice.

"I don't understand it, sir. It's just me, Colonel Kauer, and Lieutenant

Haklok. Everyone else is acting like they're dead."

"Admiral!" His coms officer called for Aetius's attention again. "Contact from Captain Balen."

"Put him through."

A new hologram came to life. An aged Tirrish man sat in his chair, his bald head turning as he scanned his bridge.

"Let me guess, Captain," Aetius began. "No one on your ship is responding?"

"Almost none of my bridge crew," the captain answered. "A few on various decks. I don't know what's going on. It's like they're all brain-dead."

Aetius would not be Aetius if he did not spot the pattern. The high prince, then the increasing number of Sylvanni answering the high prince's call on the other end. Aetius knew General Sebenmorg and the rising star that was Colonel Kauer. Known telepaths.

Aetius eyed the Vaar fleet. They had slowed their approach and did not fire at them. The Vaar had no telepaths; were they affected, too? Or did they know what was happening and were staying out of it?

Aetius turned to the high prince, ready to speak again when he saw the flash in his sensors. A quartet of beams shot out from the mysterious singularity. They crossed the distance impossibly fast—instantly to Aetius's eyes. Each beam focused on one of his ships.

As he glared closer at the display, Aetius read the names of the four ships. Destroyers all. *High Marshes*, *Blue Pastures*, *Nine Lakes*, and *R. Em Yoffe*. Aetius barely had time to see the four vessels shrinking in the sensors before the blast. From each ship, there was an explosion of gamma rays, expanding spheres, in the sensors. The spheres ballooned out, then the ships were gone.

Aetius's face worked into a sneer as he glared at his coms officer.

"Get me Tick-Tock-One. *Now!*" Aetius turned back to the display as the four beams shot out again. Three more destroyers, *Hauden ahn Rejan*, *Molten Shores*, and *Rhyme Wind*. The fourth beam chose a larger target, the battleship *Jonah Wallex*.

Aetius could only watch as the three destroyers quickly compressed before melting into gamma rays. *Jonah Wallex* lasted a time more, five or six seconds. But the mighty battleship's wings collapsed, crinkling inward as its teardrop body morphed into a sphere. Within seven seconds, it, too, had melted away.

"Get me any ship that can move."

Aetius's eyes raced over his fleet and the Dominion's as well. Each helmsman in the fleet had ordered the ship into a ring to hold their spot in the formation. With that helmsman neutralized they continued to act on those last orders. They were helpless targets now.

"You were wrong, Colonel," Aetius whispered. "This place does have defenses. And we just tripped them."

"*Prince of Mars* to anyone who can hear my voice. Target the anomaly and fire!"

The high prince gave the order, but no ship was able to obey it.

CHAPTER
27C

O NE WHO STOOD AT a distance from the silver plain would have beheld an odd sight. Two large groups were on the move, oblivious to the events in the stars above them. One group chased the other, and the pursuer gave off what could have been mistaken for a laser light show. The interceptors across Clearwater's unit were all firing high. The jamming took a bite out of their efficacy, but they were still swatting shells on the way in. Thus far none of them had inflicted substantial damage on Clearwater's phalanx.

His warmechs ran. His tanks moved in a single line of armor, guns, and ill will. His infantry bounded on their thrusters to keep up. All maintained formation as his unit continued to pursue the fleeing Vaar company. The limiting factor for both sides was their infantry, and Clearwater's was faster. The Vaar commander had realized that he could not outrun the pursuers. To buy himself and his friendly artillery more time, he sent his remaining enspa to the phalanx. Nothing pretty came out of that venture, only blood and noise. Clearwater's tanks, lined abreast, plowed the enspa underneath like stalks of vegetation. His infantry and warmechs trampled the bodies.

Target fixation had been a problem for soldiers and hunters as long as either of them existed. This mixed with a sense of elation that his plan seemed to be working. It was enough to delay how long it took Clearwater to realize he had made a mistake. His *Aggressor*-class automatech could outrun anything here. If he freed them from the formation to race ahead, he could eat whatever casualties they suffered and cut the Vaar off. He was about to order this very thing, before his situation worsened.

When the Vaar learned that a legionnaire unit had penetrated so many kilometers behind their lines, they overreacted. That came in the form of an artillery battery, desperately needed for counter-battery fire to hit Clearwater's three platoons. That one battery was not enough to overwhelm the point defenses of that platoon, but when their response failed, they fanned the flames, more so when they learned that the majority of the Vaar's occupying force was trapped in the underground. The explosive reaction that came added artillery batteries to Clearwater's unit. But a command that would have been sufficient for three batteries, was instead directed to thirty-three.

Clearwater had no inkling of any of this, not until he saw icons flare on the upper edge of his NOD. They were coming from three directions: south, east, and west. The streams of fire would come together, timed to make it to the ground within the same second. Fourteen guns per Vaar battery. Each fired in four-round bursts: three disrupter, one nuclear. Twenty-five thousand eight hundred seventy-two shells every five seconds. Clearwater saw them all converging in the sky.

"Oh shit," he whispered as the color drained from his face. Without thinking, he shouted, "Scatter! Scatter!"

Once again it may or may not have been the best solution, but it was the one that occurred to him. His T-shaped formation disintegrated as his legionnaires followed the command. Clearwater was one of the few not sprinting. He rode on the shoulder of Lieutenant Serrens's *Brutus* and fought to keep a semblance of balance as the machine charged forward.

For a time, the definitions of *landscape* and *explosion* became one. Clearwater's already muddled sensors were completely awash in static. His vision was replaced with naught but white light, and the air around him thundered as though he were underground amid an earthquake.

"Hug the Vaar! Hug the Vaar!" Clearwater screamed into his com in the hope that he would be heard. "Fix bayonets! Use the bots to cut them off!"

His message was clear enough. His legionnaires, previously scattering, raced toward the fleeing Vaar formation. The *Aggressor*s raced ahead, strafing the Vaar as they passed them by. Clearwater caught glimpses of Vaar marines falling, some on the ground, some plucked from the air.

Clearwater fell on his AICES's arms when something heavy struck it. Through the distortions and the white flash, he saw a Vaar bubble tank knocked aside like a billiard ball by one of his own. Seconds later it was a flaming billiard ball as an armor-hunter put a round through it before slamming it in a different direction.

Back on his feet, Clearwater raised his arm. The AICES thumped three times as he sent mortars into a cluster of five warriors. He never saw the impact as the static of disrupter charges and the white flash of nuclear detonation stole his sight once more. Serrens's *Brutus* stumbled, and Clearwater fell on his arms. He regained a measure of vision in time to see Lieutenant Serrens drive the *Brutus*'s leg into a kick that sent a bubble tank careening through a cluster of Vaar infantry.

The two groups were merging into a single formation fighting a war within itself. Of the thirty-three Vaar batteries ordered to plaster the area, only the first had been told about friendlies in the attack zone. Thus as the incoming barrages began to roll, they did so without exclusion zones.

A pause in the white allowed Clearwater to catch a glimpse of a lightning storm. The overshields of the two formations had met, and each unsuccessfully tried to repulse the other. The sole remaining colossus took a shell. The round pierced the machine's back, went through its body, and came out of its belly before detonating. Another shell came down on three Vaar where two tried to help a wounded friend to his feet. In the vortex blast, the three vanished into bloody dust.

"Oh no," Clearwater whispered. The plan was not going to work.

More nuclear flashes obscured his view as he looked east and then west. He filled his lungs for another shout when he was forced to steady himself as the *Brutus* beneath him lurched. He skidded to a halt on the edge of the machine's shoulder, then saw Lieutenant Lornes's *Brutus*. An artillery shell bisected the machine an instant before the detonation tore it apart.

"They're hitting their own guys!" someone shouted over the com.

As one of the heavier Vaar tanks smashed into one of his from the side, the two light infantry who had been aboard hit their thrusters to leap onto the offender. The tank they departed erupted in electric arcs behind them as the point-blank blast penetrated the turret. One of the betas grappled the turret. As the Vaar tank tried to back off its kill, the second beta tossed a grenade to the first, and that grenade went down one of the barrels.

A green mushroom cloud erupted to Clearwater's right, briefly drawing his eyes. One of his shield tanks had taken something close to a direct hit. The generator was damaged and unmade itself in the resulting overload. Clearwater looked east to west once again. They were slightly closer to the western pyramids. As his vision turned white again, he filled his lungs and began to shout.

"West—" The *Brutus* lurched. Clearwater tried to keep his balance, but he was struck by something and thrown off the machine. A trail of smoke followed him to the ground, then another white flash blew it away. Clearwater fell into a tumble just before impact.

By now he was used to seeing his NOD filled with health warnings and simply looked past them. After his head rolled around his shoulders, his focus came to a list near the top of his NOD—green squares quickly turning red. Clearwater had landed facedown. With both arms, he pushed the AICES up to its knees.

His ears rang. Blood in the back of his neck caused him to cough. His vision blurred, and smoke invaded his nostrils. When he looked up, his brain could not fully process what he was seeing. A pair of betas grappled a Vaar, one pulling the larger foe's legs out from under him. The other one held a knife and, with the other hand, grabbed at the warrior's helmet. Just beside them, two AICES fired around an overturned tank being used for cover. But none of it made sense.

Even as the two forces tried to kill one another, their interceptors had become unwilling allies. All fired into the air at the descending shells, but none of them scored enough hits to stop the falling sky. The rolling barrage had passed beyond and dropped its ordnance behind their shared formation.

SYNAPTIC REPAIR COMPLETE

Clearwater drew a deep breath as his vision and mind cleared. He found the command board at the top of his NOD listing the name of every legionnaire in his unit like a small periodic table. Many of the names had turned red.

With a dragging leg, Clearwater maneuvered his machine up and ran for the overturned tank. Between the pair of AICES, he pressed his back against the vehicle and briefly scrolled through the medical alerts in his NOD. If he wasn't going to die in the next few minutes, it didn't need his attention now.

Brought together by artillery, the two units had found themselves in a melee. Clearwater peered over the tank. The lone colossus was still up, still backing away. A kilometer south, it had removed itself from the chaos and was firing its wave cannon. A funnel of voltage poured out as the wave disrupted the atmosphere and broke apart two tanks and six AICES.

Clearwater had seen it take a hit earlier. He locked in on the hole in its belly.

>>SNAPSHOT

He sent the picture out before shouting, "Armor-hunters! Bring that damn thing down!"

The AIs driving the machines figured out exactly what he meant. They dropped their current task. Their triangular profiles spun as they oriented themselves, elevated their main cannons, and fired at the hole shown to them. The combined blast sent a tremor through the silver metal beneath Clearwater's feet. Electric arcs erupted from the colossus's belly, and its legs wobbled. The armor-hunters hit it again. Then again. The colossus took another step before its legs simply gave out. In direct contact with the ground, Clearwater felt the tremor as the machine fell backward and then simply splayed out on the silver plain.

"Captain!" Clearwater picked Qopas's voice out in his com. "More Vaar! Coming in! South! One-five kilometers!"

"What?" he whispered before peeking over the tank again.

The approaching Vaar stopped almost as soon as Clearwater had his eyes on them. The Vaar were in their own sort of phalanx, with enough of their new tanks to form a line abreast from one pyramid forest to another. Behind them were Vaar warmechs, looking much like their owners save for the tracks used in place of ambulatory legs. The infantry formed ranks between the warmechs and the eleven colossi at the rear.

"Where the hell did they come from?" Clearwater whispered. Major Rozcheko had suggested minimal resistance.

Major Rozcheko was wrong.

They couldn't have come over from another valley. There was no way they could have floated all those tanks and warmechs over the pyramids without being seen. Could the colossi even cross those forests? Did they just spring up from the ground? It did not matter. They were here, and they were his problem.

There was no path to the objective without going through them. Nearly half of the command board had turned red. They knew he was here. Even if he tried to make it to one of the other plains now, they would simply follow. Clearwater ducked behind the broken tank as it took a hit. The Vaar reinforcements had decided to join the fight. The silver plain, already so grossly violated, was subjected to another assault as the Vaar to the south opened fire.

"Cover!" Clearwater shouted as the first attacks came in.

They were in the open. The only cover came from destroyed vehicles.

Unshielded hulks would not last long against the firepower amassed to the south. At first it came in only as disrupter pulses. The Vaar to the south provided covering fire for their comrades engaged in the melee. The Vaar nearby took the opportunity and dashed toward the pyramid forests.

The interceptors on Clearwater's shoulders came to life, firing into the sky as mortars rained down on them. On his right, a beta aren stood behind a wrecked bubble tank. The robotic legionnaire fell when one blast took his arm. As he tried to climb back up, another blast took the rest.

"We can't stay here!" Sergeant Qopas shouted.

He was right, but they couldn't run either. Overshield or not, there was enough direct firepower to the south. If they tried to move through the open, they were dead.

"Reform!" Clearwater yelled. "Tanks to the front! Shield wall!"

Of the three hundred tanks he started with, he had ninety-four left. The artillery, the melee, and the Vaar had taken the rest. They were moving together now, forming up to provide a wall with their faces. The Vaar to the south seemed to be waiting for this, and their own tanks opened fire. Almost immediately, ten of the ninety-four turned red on the command board.

It was happening again.

Medics had created a triage pool in the shadow of a broken colossus to his left. Another tank exploded to his right, and its main armament was ripped out of its body and sent careening north as it skipped on the silver terrain.

He looked to a place where he might find solutions, but the red command board told him what his options were. He was the only officer left. All of his lieutenants were gone.

Not again.

This was not winnable. He would never plow through these reinforcements with what he had left. It was happening again. He was going to lose them all.

Clearwater shook his head.

No. Not this time.

He could kiss his new rank goodbye. Small matter. He would have to justify himself to Major Rozcheko, if they both survived. Perhaps to the cohort's colonel as well. Piss on them both if they didn't like it. The worst they could do was court-martial him. He refused to throw all his units away.

Clearwater drew in as deep a breath as he could manage.

"All tanks! Horizontal slide. West! West! West!" He took another breath to shout at the top of his lungs. "Retreat! Retreat! Bug out west! Get to the pyramids!"

Clearwater spun until he found what he sought.

"Sergeant Qopas! Get them out of here!"

Many of the tanks were unmanned, but not all. They could not all move into the forest. Once the rest had found their cover, the tanks would have to reverse and try to escape across the plain. Clearwater knew he was sacrificing many of them to cover the rest. But no alternative showed itself.

"Go! Go!" Clearwater shouted.

There was a nagging question. Vaar liked to fight up close when they could. Why were they loitering south? Clearwater received his answer when the interceptors on his shoulders turned spastic, and icons flared at the top of his NOD.

The overreaction was not complete. It had simply paused.

"Move!" Clearwater screamed as he bolted from behind the tank. "Move! Move! Move!"

Clearwater broke into a sprint. He ducked and scooped the wounded kurai and the beta medic up from the ground.

"Run, damn it! Run!"

The mix of disrupter and nuclear charges returned, the nukes bringing the white with them. Clearwater fired his thrusters when he saw a *Brutus* falling ahead of them. He bounded over the machine and came back to his feet, then dropped the medic still carrying the wounded legionnaire.

Plasma arcs and static were drawing together. A nearby blast caused Clearwater to stumble. He dropped the wounded legionnaire. His left leg gave out as he tried to turn back.

"Qopas! Get them out!"

A blue wave filled Clearwater's sight, and just before the next flash of white came, the arms of his AICES disintegrated in the embrace of a vortex charge.

CHAPTER
27E

THE FIGHT THUS FAR had been exercises in confusion and frustration. Oul'sor scrambled his brain trying to understand why he was weaker now. Why his blows did not hit as hard. How was the Crykeeper stronger?

One of his questions had an answer, and he hated it. An unwelcome truth was still the truth. Indorai was not here, coaching him from on high.

So be it. Without the hollow one's help, could come the satisfaction of authentic victory.

"You're strong, Oul'sor, but you're not trained. Those of us who are? We call this one Event Horizon."

Oul'sor blinked at the first of the black spots in his vision. In the time it took him to reach toward his face, they had expanded and multiplied. Dozens at first, then hundreds, until all was black and all was silent.

He found himself in a world without light. Without sound. The smells of the chamber had followed his sight on its way out of his universe. The chemical smell of the fog. The overpowering stench the females called perfume. The hot particles in the air. Even the oppressive magnetic fields felt by his tongue when he opened his mouth. All of his senses were gone.

There was no sensation of the floor nor of his feet pressing down on one. He drew a deep breath, feeling the movement of air neither in his mouth nor lungs. He could not even be sure the hammer was still in his hand.

What cowardly trick is this?

He tried to shout the words, but unable to hear them, unable to feel the shout in his throat, he did not know if he had.

"You were a fool to fight me without 4CM."

His body was in pain. He did not feel it. He simply knew it. Flesh was cut in his back, and he lurched forward. The awareness of pain was there, even if the pain itself was not. He moved in response to it, and he knew he moved.

Not all of his nerves were gone. He knew where his arms were, as well as his legs. He had something. The void had not taken it all. One hand easily found the other in darkness. Oul'sor clapped his right hand over his left before moving it up. He was still holding the hammer, and both hands were on it.

Something like steam disturbed the void, whipped about by a body's passage through it. Oul'sor stepped in and swung at it, but he felt no impact, and his arms did not slow until he slowed them. He missed. It was not fear playing tricks on his mind. Something had been there.

He saw the image of pain. A blade entered his thigh, cutting meat before leaving. Oul'sor sensed his leg wobbling a second before his ears smelled the blood exposed by a new wound in his arm. He no longer sensed the fingers of his right hand. His nose heard the rush of air through his mouth.

Multi-sense was the ability of the Vaar brain to cross-reference the data of the sensory organs. To impose one over another and reveal what neither could find separately. Viss had weak multi-sense. Their sensory organs were but a fraction of the size, and smaller brains afforded less volume for analysis. Oul'sor's multi-sense had always been weak—a private, closely guarded handicap to avoid the feminine nicknames that might have otherwise been hung on him. His multi-sense was weak, but it was there, and it was his only hope.

Why would the Crykeeper *not* block his multi-sense? Certainly one who had studied his foe so closely knew of it. Did it mean his telepathy could not do it? Or did it mean he did not know how? For multi-sense to be working, his other senses had to be working. If not, they would not have information to cross-reference. The blindness, the deafness—was it all an illusion? Or suggestion?

Oul'sor was once again aware of a right hand and fingers. What was going on here? The Crykeeper had him at his mercy. Yet he seemed only to be wounding him. Why? Why not go for the kill? Why not target his head? Why not his eyes or his neck?

He saw the shape of the wound, once again in his back. His orientation changed. The resistance his arms met told him he had fallen flat. The blade had cut his spine. His mouth was open, and soon he was able to move. He tapped around him with his hammer, using the stops of his movement to identify the ground and stand on it.

"You are even more of a coward than I thought. Is that why you fight only in shadow?"

"It's not a prizefight, Oul'sor. It's not supposed to be fair."

Oul'sor could only be certain of his own perception. Fear. He made the effort to calm lungs he could not feel working.

Are you ever afraid in battle?

Focus and confidence.

Oul'sor threw all his strength into a swing when he sensed ripples in the void once more. Yet he never sensed the motion of his arms challenged. Seconds later Oul'sor tasted the wound as a blade cut from the back of his thigh down to his knee. The limb could not support the weight while cleaved. Oul'sor used the hammer's haft to catch himself before he fell.

There were shapes in the void, objects so distant that he could barely gaze upon them. In deprivation of senses, the mind paid closer attention to what remained. Once certain his leg would bear weight, he returned to a fighting stance.

Make armor of fear.

A streak of white came toward him. He waited as long as he could, baiting it in. Then he swung. In the wide arc, Oul'sor sensed his right hand turn a few degrees. It was only hundredths of a second, but light flashed in the void before the blackness returned.

He hit something. A glancing blow. Oul'sor returned to his fighting stance. He held his guard with the hammer in front of him. He had to let go of his questions. The questions melted away as his focus turned in. It was all there. Every sense, ready to be referenced or ignored. As Oul'sor withdrew into the shelter of his mind, the void began to yield. There was no light to distract him. As if the blackness were solid, and invisible hands drew on it with chalk, white outlines formed around him. There was no scent to beguile him. The chalk was thickening. There was no sound to question him. The sketch of his world took form. There was no taste of magnetics to pester him.

As he turned his head, Oul'sor made out the dome drawn in squiggly lines, then the barrier where the females hid. Oul'sor turned toward it. Now he had a reference point in space. The farther he held the hammer, the clearer it all seemed.

Make armor of fear.

Ripples moved to his left. Oscillations of chalk came and went. Breath. Deep, gasping breath. Oul'sor did not turn to it. A prey that saw the hunter needed to believe the hunter did not see it. Oul'sor drew the head of the hammer back, raising it over his head. The ripples moved. On the edge of his vision, Oul'sor saw it. The invisible hands drew the outline, and Oul'sor cocked the hammer at his shoulder, edging his foot out. Just a little closer.

Oul'sor swung to the right, halting the follow-through halfway. His feet skipped as he hurtled himself to the right, jabbing with the bludgeon at the haft's end.

His movement was deflected. Oul'sor followed through on the motion as he turned, jamming the haft ahead. This time he felt his elbows bend. His arms absorbed impact. The armored outline faded away, but the foe staggered. With all his strength, and all his mind, Oul'sor swung the hammer across his body.

When sight and sound rushed back into his universe, Oul'sor saw first the trail of metal fragments in the air.

CHAPTER
28A

FACEDOWN ONCE AGAIN, PANZER'S mouth popped like a grounded fish as his lungs fought for air. Only now did he realize it. Oul'sor was not the one healing every wound in an instant. No Vaar could regenerate that fast. Oul'sor was not the one striking him with psionic force that even the commandant would be hard-pressed to match. No one developed that kind of force as a novice. It was the hammer. It was always the hammer.

The phantasm within it—the formless malevolence—bound to the Vaar's mind by telepathic threads. All this time, Panzer was fighting the wrong enemy. The hammer had struck squarely, embedding the R-steel trauma plate in his torso. Of his soldier's lungs, perhaps 7 percent still functioned. His right arm trembled as he tried to push himself up. His body had become a force immovable. Without enough nanites, what he had scrambled to heal even his critical wounds.

"Truly there is no end to your cowardice, Crykeeper," the Vaar taunted, standing over him. "You truly don't know how to fight, except in the shadows."

Panzer felt the Vaar's toes at his shoulder before he was rolled onto his back.

"You asked what they promised me. On Avalon, the hollow one gave me new flesh. And the Elder touched my mind."

DISPENSING FINAL ETNS . . .

LUNG REPAIR COMMENCING . . .

Panzer coughed a clot of blood as microlungs were fused back together.

Oul'sor twisted his hands around the hammer.

"He showed me the future. And how to change it."

A tremor ripped through the chamber, rocking the pillars like wind bending branches in the forest.

"Do you feel it, Crykeeper? Surely you must, if I do. Beneath our feet, space-time boils! Soon the door opens, and the merger cannot be stopped. The Elder's forces will sweep through this reality." Oul'sor's voice rose in pitch, his teeth bared in a deranged grin. "Indorai told me who you are. Your family considers themselves the guardians of your species. I can think of no revenge greater. The next universe shall become your sanctuary, and your *prison!* There, you will know they die, and you can do nothing. And every time you speak with the survivors, you will be reminded of the countless you could not save."

Panzer closed his faceplate and began to sit up when a punch laid him back down. The Vaar's fingers wrapped around Panzer's head and drew him to his knees. A shove forced him to turn until he faced the barrier with Simmonne, Jennifer, and Julie within.

"Pick which one dies first," Oul'sor whispered. "Then beg me to spare one, and I just might."

Panzer began to raise his right hand.

"Yes," Oul'sor urged. "Tell me which one."

Panzer pointed ahead, but his eyes were on his knife. The blade rocked as he tried to focus on it. His mental grasp was growing weak.

"Say the name, Crykeeper. Which one first?"

Panzer pointed low.

"Which one?"

The question was replaced with a howl as the blade leaped from the deck and found residence in the Vaar's knee. Oul'sor doubled over, and Panzer turned on his knees when he landed. He found the handle, and with a savage twist, the blade was freed.

Panzer made it upright only briefly. He stumbled and fell on his back. He had no choice but to risk it now. While Oul'sor inhaled deeply through his pain, Panzer held his hand toward the Hellbore. The gun slid on its platform. It dipped over the edge, but it did not fall. His hand-less left arm motioned to it, begging it to come faster to its master's call. Then his right hand closed on the Hellbore.

Panzer swung his weapon high, but Oul'sor swung his to aim low. The hammer struck the Hellbore, launching it from Panzer's hand with such force that his index finger went with it.

His thrusters carried him up, and with a low sweep, he tackled Oul'sor down before he groped around for his knife.

CHAPTER
28B

MASTER AND THE MONSTER moved so fast, Simmonne could barely follow them. At times they disappeared from her view completely, only to reappear somewhere else with no sign of how they got there. For a time, everything slowed down, and he seemed to attack the Vaar freely. Then he took the hammer to his chest. It seemed impossible that he could be losing, but Master did not seem to be winning either.

He fought most of the fight without his gun, and Simmonne did not understand why. When he did try to call it to him, Oul'sor knocked it away. It had landed to the right of her, on the next platform over. Simmonne did not understand why he was fighting this way. She did not understand how the vicious attacks with his knife were not killing the Vaar. But she did understand that Master needed his gun to finish the fight.

She took her eyes away to gaze at the golden weapon. Could she help? Even if she grabbed it, how would she get it to him? How could she do it without getting in the way? Or giving Oul'sor the opportunity to use her against Master? She looked back in time to see Master drive his knife into the Vaar's leg and cut a path out. Oul'sor responded with a pained howl before delivering a punch that sent Master reeling. Oul'sor should have died a dozen times now. Yet whenever Master injured him, the Vaar healed almost immediately. What could anyone do against that?

Simmonne looked back at the golden gun. Not him. If the universe planned to take everything else from her, it couldn't take him, too. If she didn't stop their stalemate, fatigue would set in. The injuries would add up. Master would die. She would be alone. Jennifer and Julie would be alone.

Her arms fell away from the Twins. On Avalon, she cowered while her guards fought. Lilac was cut in half, and she watched. Isis was impaled, and Simmonne watched. One by one she watched them die. On the eye station, she cowered while Rhoxx fought the Vaar captain. Now, from behind the safety of the barrier, she watched again.

Something in her head cleared, and she took a deep breath. Not him. She could not watch while she lost him, too.

Simmonne eyed the Twins as she backed away, checking that neither noticed her. Both were too fixated on the fight, too afraid to do more than watch and breathe. Simmonne crept right until the barrier was in reach, and hesitantly, she reached her hand out. When her fingers passed through the golden field, she flinched. But she felt no shock or resistance. It was one way.

Once her whole body passed through, there was no way back in.

Master said not to leave the barrier. He and the Vaar were grappling now. Master was on Oul'sor's back, one arm around the Vaar's neck while the other drove his knife into his shoulder. But it didn't seem to be doing anything. Master needed his gun.

Master said not to leave the barrier.

If he decided to punish her for disobeying, he had to be alive to do it. It would not be her excuse for doing nothing. Simmonne looked down at her feet. She could not run well in these shoes, but Master wasa not available to unlock them from her ankles. No choice.

"I can make it," she whispered to herself. "I *can* make it."

Simmonne backed up, stopping at the opposite end of the barrier.

"Simmonne? What are you doing?"

She did not know which Twin asked, and she did not answer. Her eyes were on the far platform. Adrenaline fueled her resolve. With rapid breaths, she took the first step.

"I can make it. I can make it." The words became her mantra as she broke into sprint and dashed out of the barrier.

"*Simmonne!*" the Twins called out together. But it was too late to go back.

Simmonne sprinted for the platform. Her feet were heavy, her steps were awkward, but she was moving. With each step, she repeated the thought.

I can make it.

Her feet left the edge in a leap over the gulf. The fog rising from the abyss seemed to call to her, inviting her down as her leap carried her. But her jump was not good enough.

She fell short of the platform but grappled for the edge, grasping it with her left hand. The rest of her body slammed into the side of the pillar. Had the impact not knocked the air out of her lungs, she would have screamed. The side of the platform seared her exposed flesh. All the willpower she ever had converged to keep her grip on the pillar's edge.

"Climb!" one of the Twins shouted. "Climb, Simmonne!"

She managed to suck in enough air for a cry of pain. Trying to add more fingers to her grip, she stretched her right arm. She ground her teeth with the effort, then kicked desperately at the side of the pillar to help her climb. Another cry of pain came when the edge scalded her knees.

The edge of the platform had a small lip, and her fingers found it. She pulled with all the might in her left arm, raising herself enough to get her right hand on the edge. She heard a sizzle from her skin pressed against the metal as she urged her palm over the edge.

She adjusted her right arm, embedding her manacle in the lip of the platform. With that anchor, she put everything she could into another pull, and she gripped the platform up to her elbow. If the fear of the fall were not motivation enough, the horrific pain of the burns were. She inched upward, dragging the rest of her body over. When she pulled her chest onto the platform, she shoved forward with a final whine of effort. As if her arms gave out, she rolled onto her back, and she writhed in pain.

The pain brought tears to her eyes as she looked down at herself. The tops of her breasts, her belly, and her thighs were burned red. But she did not have time to cry. She dragged herself to the gun. When she reached the weapon, she climbed to her feet.

She tried to pull the gun up with her, but its weight pulled her back down. The grip was much too large for her hands. She bent over and pulled with both hands, managing to slide her fingers under the handle. She cried out in defiance of the pain in her scalded palms.

Frantic now, Simmonne looked around her for anything that could help. Anything she might use to pry or leverage it off the floor. Her eyes found her only hope for help. She stared across the gulf at Jennifer and Julie.

"Help me!"

They simply stared at her. For a second, she thought she might have caught a headshake.

"Help me, please!" Simmonne cried louder. She used her legs for support and pulled with all the strength her arms and back could offer. It did no good. The weapon weighed more than she did—too much for her strength.

Simmonne glanced back at the Twins.

"Jennifer! Julie! Get over here and help me!"

Still they stared.

Damn them. She was just as afraid as they were, but Master needed his gun. His knife was not enough. Couldn't they see that?

"Help me!" she called to them again.

A loud crash echoed across the chamber, drawing her attention back to the fight. Master was facedown on the platform, and Oul'sor had driven the hammer into his side. She heard a grunt as the Vaar withdrew the hammer, drawing out red flesh like bloody string intermingled with pieces of metal. Master rolled on his side to avoid a second swing and drove his blade into Oul'sor's gut.

Simmonne turned back to the Twins. "Help me, *now*!" Her scream echoed. But the two did not move. Julie shook her head, and this time it was clear.

Simmonne released the gun, walking to the edge of the platform to face them. The fear was as much a fog between them as what was coming up from below. They held each other's hand as they glared at her. Simmonne wanted to scream, to demand they help. But their fear was a chill so strong, it seemed to alleviate the burns for a moment. Simmonne took a breath and calmed her voice.

"Jennifer? Julie?" The burns in her face hurt once again as she forced herself to smile. "We can be brave, too."

They looked at each other and then back to her. Simmonne held out her arms.

"Help me. Please?"

The pair dropped their hands, looking toward the fight and then back to her.

"Please?"

Simmonne took a breath as they backed away. They stepped to the far edge of the barrier. Their hands met between them, and Simmonne nodded. They broke into sprint together.

"Yes! Yes! Jump!"

They emerged from the barrier, and their feet left the platform in sync. Simmonne reached as far as she might when they began to fall and cried out in fresh agony as her scalded hands grabbed theirs, but she would be damned if she let go, so she clutched them tighter.

"Climb!" Simmonne strained to get the word out. The Twins screamed as their legs touched the platform's side. Putting all the leverage, all the strength she could into pulling them over the edge, Simmonne leaned back and hugged her fists against her chest. The Twins brought their feet up, pressing their shoes into the platform to walk upward. Simmonne fell on her back, still pulling them into her and ignoring the pain that ripped through her body and across her skin.

It seemed like forever, but finally she released a sigh of relief alongside the Twins' pained cries.

"Get up!" Simmonne prodded, wrapping her arms around them and sitting up with them. "Help me!"

They scrambled together for the enormous gun.

"What do we do?" Jennifer asked.

Simmonne glared at her. "Jennifer, you've shot a gun."

Jennifer's eyes could not possibly open any wider as she shook her head. "But it wasn't—I didn't . . . not this. We weren't—" Jennifer stammered.

The chill was too much. "I'll do it myself," Simmonne answered before pointing to the front. "Help me pick it up!"

The Twins scrambled toward the barrel and took hold.

"On three!" Simmonne ordered. "One. Two. Three!"

They lifted it, all three crying out in exertion as they forced the weapon off the floor. With Jennifer on the right and Julie on the left, each brought a shoulder under the gun and used their legs as support. Simmonne did the same. It was too big for her to shoulder, too heavy even if she could. She slipped her shoulder under the stock instead, and together they made it to their feet.

Simmonne clamped both hands down on the handle.

HELLBORE MK-II MASTER CONTROL
YOU ARE NOT THE AUTHORIZED USER OF THIS WEAPON.

"No," Simmonne whimpered when she saw the characters in her NOD. "No. No! You have to let me in!"

ANDIRA: Stand by, Majesty.

"Andira!" Simmonne exclaimed as the coded characters raced through her NOD.

HELLBORE MK-II MASTER CONTROL
GUNWARE INSTALLING . . .
INSTALLATION COMPLETE

The gun came alive. Simmonne's eyes moved for Oul'sor, who swung down on Master, but Master managed to roll away.

HELLBORE MK-II MASTER CONTROL

MASTER ARM—OFF

"Left!" Simmonne called to the Twins as she moved. "To the left!"

>>MASTER ARM—ON

Simmonne acted as the rudder, lining up on the Vaar.

Smart gun, smart shells.

Simmonne checked it in her mind. Everything Master said to her. Everything she heard him tell Jennifer. Her thumb found the safety, but it was already down. Her knees wobbled under the weight as she tried to line the gun up with Oul'sor's body.

The AI in the gun can tell where you want to shoot.

If you feel your arms want to move, let them.

The golden gun seemed to want to move on its own, and Simmonne let it guide her.

The gun is working with your nanites to correct imperfections in your aim.

A green ring appeared in Simmonne's eyes and surrounded her sight. It collapsed inward until it encircled Oul'sor. The ring flashed.

Squeeze it, and let the gun do the rest.

Master was too close. But her moment came as Oul'sor raised the hammer high. Master's arm shot up. Simmonne saw the explosion of air that sent the Vaar reeling. A second later, Master threw his knife, and Oul'sor screamed as it entered his left eye. Oul'sor pulled the blade out, the lights in the chamber flickered, and Simmonne pulled the trigger.

In an instant, she was assaulted by two attacks on her existence. The first came with the sensation that every organ within her body had been torn out and fired down the barrel of the weapon. The second came before the first had even finished. There was nothing behind the gun to obstruct its movement. The Hellbore launched itself straight back. It traveled unhindered until the handle caught Simmonne's shoulder. Her ears, already deafened by the shot, could not hear the shattering of bone. Her head was concussed. She saw only a flash of gold as the impact caused the muzzle to flip upward before the weapon sailed behind her.

She seemed to glide with it until it passed out of view and she came down. Twisted by the impact, she landed on her side. The Twins fell straight on their backs while she rolled. But she came to a stop. She could not move her head. She could not move at all. But she had a view of the Twins and Oul'sor.

She could not hear him screaming, but she could see it. His mouth opened in a wail of the purest agony. Oul'sor's right arm was gone just below the shoulder. What she thought were ribs protruded from the hole in his side. Black blood flowed out of three more holes in the left side of his body. Simmonne smiled as she watched him writhe in agony.

Oul'sor's mouth worked as if he were gasping for air and suffocating instead. His head dipped, and his eyes zeroed in on her. The Vaar's right arm lay on the ground beside him, still grasping his hammer. Oul'sor called the weapon up to his left. He took a step before leaping high into the air.

Ahead of her, the Twins screamed, raising their arms as the Vaar descended on them.

Simmonne smiled when he stopped in midair. Oul'sor's legs shot forward, but his body was seized. Across the chamber, Master was up on a knee, his right arm extended, and his fist closed.

CHAPTER
28C

WARNING: HIGH-RADIATION AREA
EXPOSURE RISING

Clearwater drew in a gasp as he opened his eyes and sat up, letting out a pained cry. He touched his left leg. What remained of the calf muscle hung like shredded meat from exposed bone, and his foot was nowhere to be found.

His breath came in heavy gasps as Clearwater scanned the area and found his AICES facedown behind him. With one arm still holding his leg, Clearwater used the other to drag himself toward the broken machine. The hatches lay open, and smoke wafted out. He used both hands to pull down the main hatch. What he needed was tucked under the back cushion. He ripped it away to reveal a broad box.

HESS-12

The Hostile Environment Survival Store was clamped to the hatch. One of its securing latches had broken loose, but the other two still held it shut. With some effort, Clearwater tore the box free and dropped it on the ground beside him.

He scanned the area while he pried the box open. The only sounds came from smoldering fires. There was no exploding artillery. No ongoing firefight or melee. No quaking ground from an armored force on the move. Only smoke and bodies. His last memory was calling for retreat. Where were the Vaar to the south? Did they pursue? Or did they decide they were needed elsewhere in the retreat? Wherever they were, they were not here. No one was. Except him.

The question was if Qopas managed to lead the remains of his company out.

With the box open, Clearwater grabbed the first aid kit. His cheek was already twitching as he grabbed the ELR. Somehow, he could not remember the name of the kurai commando, the one who put an ELR on him back on the Vaar ship. But he remembered the pain quite clearly. With some hesitation, Clearwater held the black disc toward his leg before slapping it against the exposed tibia. The disc quickly liquefied.

He growled, watching the metal flow over the meat at one end and extend into an artificial foot at the other. It took only a few seconds for the ELR to provide him the new leg he required. But seconds of pain were long seconds. With the metal foot formed, Clearwater rotated it briefly, ensuring his mind was in control before turning his attention elsewhere. The HESS bore an emergency communicator, and that was what he grabbed next.

"BlueCat-Two-One to any receiver, respond."

Clearwater shook his wounded leg, as if hoping to fling the lingering pain from it.

"BlueCat-Two-One to any receiver. Please respond."

Useless. The small com could not make it through the jamming.

Clearwater took another look around in the vain hope that someone friendly—or something—might still be nearby. How long was he out? He referenced his NOD for the answer to find that he had been unconscious for at least twenty minutes. They left him. Either because they thought he was dead, or they just couldn't get to him. Or there was no one left.

Either way, he was in trouble.

An RA-117 Compact was compressed into the HESS, and Clearwater grabbed it next. Only two magazines left. As he slung the rifle, he grabbed a collection of metal tubes from the first aid kit. The one he required was labeled *Hostile Environment Supplements*. Clearwater bit the cap off the vial before pouring the pills into his mouth. While they dissolved, he closed the HESS, pulled its sling, and threw it over his shoulder.

When Clearwater stood up, he felt the object hanging from his pants and twisted to look over his shoulder. A metal hand gripped his belt with scant pieces of flesh still on it. "Shit!" He grabbed frantically at the orphaned appendage to pry it loose. When he tossed it away, he realized whose it was.

They didn't just leave him behind. One of his betas must have tried to carry him out when they lost their limb. For a moment Clearwater simply stared at the hand.

"Thanks for trying," he muttered.

"Repeating message."

Clearwater's eyes snapped to the emergency com clamped to the side of his belt. He fumbled for it, then dropped it, caught it, and almost dropped it again before holding it in front of his face.

"Dinner bell. Dinner bell. Dinner bell. Repeating message. Dinner bell. Dinner bell. Dinner bell."

The device wasn't strong enough to broadcast out of the jamming, but it was picking up the message coming in.

Dinner bell.

The withdraw order. Every legionnaire on the station was falling back to the landing zones right now. How long had the command been going out? Everyone was preparing to leave, *now*. Clearwater looked north. Did he have time? Even if he sprinted the entire way, could he make it out before *drop if?*

He definitely wouldn't make it if he just stood around. Clearwater looked down at his new cyberlimb.

"Don't fail me."

He ducked low, preparing to sprint, when he saw something familiar. There on its back, thirty meters away, lay the *Brutus* of Lieutenant Serrens. Its legs were still intact. Clearwater sprinted toward the downed machine.

He climbed onto the arm and made for the cockpit. The initial sight was not encouraging. On the left side, a hole large enough for both of his fists revealed the cockpit, and the right side was painted in red with a matching hole.

Serrens's nameplate at the base of the cockpit was still readable. Clearwater had bounded over him in his attempt to get out.

The smell of smoke gave way to another as Clearwater laid his hands on the machine. He grabbed the emergency release, giving it time to identify him before pulling. With a loud hiss, the cockpit rose. Clearwater held a hand over his mouth and nose, closed his eyes, and turned away.

A shell had come through the side of the armored canopy but failed to detonate before exiting the other side. The parts of Lieutenant Serrens it did not take with it had been scattered throughout the cockpit. In a battle for control of his stomach, he forced his eyes open.

There was damage, but the main console appeared to be intact. Clearwater turned his head away again and took a deep breath before crawling in. He trembled as he felt the wetness of the seat against the back of his neck. He brushed off the center console to expose the optical port.

SYSTEM STANDBY . . .

It was alive! The machine was still alive. Clearwater pumped his fist briefly before adjusting himself to drive his feet through the sleeves of the machine's stirrups. When he met resistance, his smile faded, and Clearwater pulled his feet back out. He drove his hands through the sleeves and felt what blocked his way, then grabbed and tossed what he realized was a pair of feet out of the cockpit.

"I'm sorry, Serrens." Clearwater groaned before sticking his feet back into the sleeves. This time he found the stirrups without obstacles.

>>INITIATE STARTUP SEQUENCE
ERROR—YOU ARE NOT THE AUTHORIZED USER OF THIS
BRUTUS.

He pinched his nose as he entered the command.

>>OVERRIDE ON MY AUTHORITY
SCANNING . . .
IDENTIFY—CLEARWATER, JONATHAN, CAPTAIN
COMMAND ACCEPTED
STARTUP INITIALIZED

Clearwater allowed himself a breath as he heard the deep reverberations of the *Brutus*'s reactor spooling back into action.

"I can do this," he whispered as he took hold of the control sticks. "Just like the game. Just like the game."

ERROR—MAGNADRIVE DAMAGED
ERROR—MAIN ABR FAILURE
ERROR—SECONDARY ABR FAILURE
ERROR—TERTIARY ABR FAILURE
ERROR—PILOT STABILIZATION COMPROMISED
ERROR—PRIMARY SHIELD CAPACITANCE FAILURE

ERROR—SECONDARY SHIELD CAPACITANCE FAILURE

Clearwater cleared the errors away. Metal probes slithered out of the seat to caress his head. With the Auto-Balance Rectifier damaged, the machine could not control its balance, so the probes linked to him, using his inner ear. Now he had to get the twelve-meter *Brutus* on its feet.

He had to feel the machine—to sense the new body attached to his mind.

>>*CLOSE CANOPY*

The opaque canopy simulated transparency as it closed, the holes in its side denying the hermetic hiss he listened for. But he could see through the canopy, which meant the sensors were working. Though he was forced to pause and rub the blood away from the center.

The legs bent went he directed them, and Clearwater unconsciously threw his right shoulder forward as he commanded the *Brutus* to roll over. The machine planted its nose into the deck, jarring him in the cockpit, and he let out a fresh groan. The complex system meant to immunize the operator from shock was not functioning either. This was not going to be a smooth ride.

The arms obeyed his command as he pressed the barrels that formed each limb into the deck and pushed.

He glanced behind him when he heard something break. "Hope that wasn't important." With eyes forward, he brought the right foot under the machine, then the left, and straightened the body. Clearwater felt the entire *Brutus* leaning, ready to fall on its back. His body shot forward before he sat as straight as possible, letting the machine translate his balance to its own.

>>*SYSTEM CHECK—COMS*

COMS OPERATIONAL

That might help if he could get close enough to someone. The *dinner bell* message was blaring on nearly every channel now.

"Time to go."

Clearwater turned until the compass indicated the desired direction. He leaned forward and guided the machine into its first step, which sent a jarring sensation straight into his skull. The second was happy enough to do the same. Both of them wrenched fresh pain from his leg.

"Tsk! Damn it!" At each step, he fought the *Brutus* for control of the center of balance, zigzagging as they went too far one way and then overcompensated the next. *Warmetal* never made ABR failure seem *this* difficult.

"I can do this!" Clearwater used the stirrups to exert manual control. "I *can* do this! I'm not dying here!"

He extended the right leg, locking it as he turned the foot and brought his uncontrolled run to a skidding stop. While he gagged on the odor of death in the cockpit, the *Brutus* shuddered under his amateurish control. But the machine stopped.

"Try it again."

He was careful with his next step. The shock of each step seemed to compress his spine a little more. After several seconds, he was walking straight, but there was no time to walk. He leaned forward once again and began to run.

Clearwater kept his teeth clenched to keep them from smacking into each other with each step.

"This is ground control." Clearwater glanced at the console as a gamma's voice came through the static. "Evacuation eighty-seven percent complete."

There was still time.

Clearwater managed a smile. He just might make it back to his landing zone.

He ground the *Brutus* to a halt again. The quake did not come from the warmech, he realized. The silver ground itself rumbled beneath him.

"That can't be good," he whispered before forcing the machine back into a long stride. Clearwater toggled the com. "BlueCat-Two-One Lead to BlueCat-Two-One Beta," Clearwater called out, hoping that somehow Sergeant Qopas might answer on the other end. But no answer came.

If he could keep up his current pace, he could make it back to the landing zone in thirty minutes. The speedometer read seventy-six kilometers per second. The machine's movement was a special torture. With the cockpit stabilization broken, each thunderous impact rang his ears and sent fresh agony through his leg. No choice. He could lament the pain later. One thing upper command had been very clear about was that when *drop it* was called, whoever didn't make it would be left behind.

Every few minutes, he called again for Sergeant Qopas. He was fifteen minutes from the landing zone when the static in his sensors began to thin. Perhaps some of the Vaar jamming capability had been degraded. He was ten minutes away when a crackle caught his attention.

"Qopas?" Clearwater whispered as he adjusted the volume on the com.

"There's an artillery battery . . . top of us!"

His NOD identified the voice as Sergeant Ubel ahn Skoto, Sixty-Fourth Cohort, light infantry. Clearwater strained to process the conversation as the *Brutus* continued beating his body with heavy steps.

"We're . . . to get you!" another voice shouted.

"Negative!" Sergeant Skoto shouted. "The artillery . . . cut you . . . Take the wounded and . . . out of here!"

Where were they? Clearwater sorted through his NOD. Thirty kilometers west. Their cohort had been assigned TEOD, Termination of Enemy Orbital Defense. They were hunting for jamming sources to destroy.

"We . . . not . . . behind!" the unidentified voice protested.

Sergeant ahn Skoto's voice was calmer when it answered. "We're already dead. Can't risk . . . whole . . . us. You'll never . . . them all. Go . . . be . . . late."

A short pause followed before the unidentified voice came back.

"I'm sorry, Ubel."

"Don't . . . Tell my children . . ."

"I will."

Clearwater shuffled his NOD, bringing up eye-in-the-sky reports. He needed the most recent one, until he realized he didn't. He brought the

Brutus to a halt, raised the right arm, and loaded the drone. His right ear did not appreciate the concussion that came through the hole in the cockpit as the drone hurtled into the sky.

"Come on, show me something," Clearwater whispered as the feed came to life, showing silver plain and pyramid forest below. A warning indicator sounded as Clearwater directed the main sensor toward the source of the transmission. It arrived when the drone went dark. High above, Clearwater saw the tiny pinpoint of light as the drone was destroyed, followed by the streak of the missile that had destroyed it.

It was enough.

A still image opened in his NOD. A wide trench, practically a canyon, ran north to south. Vaar tanks took up the north and south ends of that trench, backed up by infantry. A bridge, or some kind of covering, blocked his view of the center of the trench. But the drone had captured IFFs—there were legionnaires beneath it. They were trapped.

Clearwater zoomed out. The drone barely caught them in the image. Four kilometers to the west of the trench, a small rise created a plateau where he noticed fourteen guns—an artillery battery.

"That's why they're in the trench," Clearwater whispered. "They were trying to sneak up on the arty."

That was why rescue was not coming to them. Anyone who had to reach them had to contend with that battery. If they'd taken enough casualties, that would be impossible.

How far were they? Just under thirty kilometers.

The briefing was clear. If *drop it* had been called, then this place was about to die. Anyone still here went with it. Clearwater was ascending a rise when he looked at the artillery again. Only a few infantry surrounded it. They obviously didn't know what was going on, or they wouldn't still be there. That was not a lot of guards.

He fought for balance at the top of the rise when he looked to the map again. The pyramids on this elevation were shorter. Their columns were thinner. He could probably jump them. From there, it would be a straight shot to the artillery. They probably wouldn't expect an attack from that direction.

The *Brutus* came to a halt.

In this wreck?

>>CURRENT LOADOUT
-90MM: 1400 MPTC
-MML-44: 6 ADI, 10 AV, 2 NC

Fourteen hundred rounds for the 90mm cannon, just under nine seconds of firing time. Six apollium missiles, ten anti-vehicle missiles, two nuclear. That was all Serrens had left when the machine went down. After that, he'd only have the pulse guns in the nose and the twin-linked pulse cannons that formed the left arm. When he checked if they were online, he was answered with green.

Six tanks guarded the area north of the trapped unit, and seven south of them. He couldn't clear the way completely, but he could open it. If he took the artillery and the Vaar in the north, he might be able to pin those in the south.

Many thoughts raced through Clearwater's mind as he turned east, but one of them sobered him.

Your father left you a hell of a legacy.

"Yeah," Clearwater murmured, "and it got him killed."

He turned north, but he could not push the feet forward. He did not know if there were ten legionnaires under that bridge or a hundred. But they were there, and they had been left behind.

Clearwater swallowed as he brought an image up from his memory index. Froggy's first birthday. She was in his lap, her big eyes staring in wonderment at the cake Zach had made. How they laughed about that cake. Ugly, poorly decorated, but big enough to feed fifty people.

Clearwater dismissed the image.

"I'm sorry," he whispered as he turned the machine east.

He needed as much speed as possible. He leaned as far forward as he dared. The smaller pyramids seemed to race toward him now. This was not going to be fun. The speedometer read eighty-six when he hit the thrusters.

The inertial damper had not survived the damage. Clearwater was thrown back into the seat, and the *Brutus*'s posture flowed with him. While the blast of the thrusters sent him rocketing into the sky, the mech began to lie back. Clearwater began to swear as he looked up, and saw the ground above him from the machine's inverted position.

"Shit! Shit! Shit!"

He threw his body forward in the chair, opening the thrusters wider. It was easier to go with the roll, and the moment his feet pointed at the ground, he cut thrust. His eyes seemed to dribble in their sockets when the *Brutus*'s feet met the plain. His bottom teeth went to war with those on top, filling his mouth with fresh blood. Despite the agony, Clearwater kept his left leg still so the *Brutus* would stay erect on its feet.

"Let's not do that again." He groaned as he leaned forward and resumed the run. In a new plain, he made for the next row of pyramids. Everything he did wrong in the first jump relayed through his mind as he prepared for the second.

The Sixty-Fourth Cohort had done its work. His sensors were steadily clearing as more com channels became available. All had the same thing to say.

"Dinner bell! Dinner bell! Dinner bell!"

As he approached the second row of pyramids, Clearwater growled, "Don't screw it up."

He gave the thrusters much less power this time. The feet left the deck, and Clearwater's head moved on a swivel. The higher he went, the greater the odds of being seen. In the mech's shape, he was not sure how many potshots he might survive. Everything clenched as he prepared for the second impact. It did little about the pain, but it was enough for the *Brutus* to lose its balance and fall over.

"Get up," Clearwater whispered as he rolled the machine onto its nose. "Get up. Get up."

He had the legs under the machine when the com caught his attention.

"Pilot, *dinner bell* has been called. Withdraw immediately."

Clearwater was about to dismiss it, then he saw the yellow light above the com shining through the blood crusted to the console. Somewhere, far above, someone was watching him. More than watching, they were talking to him.

"Not yet," Clearwater said as he leaned forward once again. The third try was painful, but he managed to keep the machine upright. Under ideal conditions, a *Brutus* could hit 150 kilometers per hour. Time to see what it could do under less-than-ideal conditions.

"Pilot, you are ordered to withdraw. Withdraw immediately."

Clearwater bounded up a rise and gained a view of what the eye in the sky didn't show him. Three trenches intercepted his path. A glance left and right did not show him an end to any of the trenches. More jumps it was.

As he approached the first trench, Clearwater heard a new, but familiar, voice.

"Who's piloting that mech?"

Clearwater briefly saw the mental image of a massive kurai behind a desk.

"Ident shows Captain Jonathan Clearwater, Third Cohort. Sir."

"Let me speak to him."

Clearwater hit the thrusters and began the climb over the first trench. His head swiveled once more to look for signs that someone was taking a potshot at him.

"Captain Clearwater, this is Marshal Veth. Do you read me?"

Something popped in the back of his neck, or perhaps the base of his skull. But his head was still attached, and the *Brutus* was upright. He continued forward.

"Captain Clearwater, if you can hear me, respond."

Clearwater toggled the transceiver. "Yes sir, I hear you," he answered as he crossed the second trench.

"Captain, are you aware you're going the wrong direction?" Marshal Veth asked in an especially friendly tone, as if trying to correct him without embarrassing him.

"Yes sir," Clearwater answered. He was cut off before he could finish. Again, the machine rocked unsteadily. Clearwater threw his head back and ground the machine to a halt.

"Well, don't you think maybe you should go the *right* direction?" Veth asked.

When he was sure it would not tip over, Clearwater guided the *Brutus* back into a run. "Sir, legionnaires from Sixty-Fourth Cohort are pinned down ahead of me."

"Yes, we're monitoring their situation," Veth answered but did not elaborate.

"Can you do anything for them, sir?" Clearwater asked, trying to keep his voice steady despite rocking in the cockpit. He heard the marshal sigh before answering.

"Negative. There are no units currently available to assist."

Clearwater stopped again as the *Brutus* decided to challenge him for balance while he crossed the final trench. There was no one else. "I'm here, sir."

A long pause with nothing but blips of static before the marshal came back.

"Captain, don't you think your family back home wants to see you again?"

Clearwater closed his eyes, taking in a deep breath. "Sir, I'm sure their families want to see them, too."

Clearwater called up the inventory again, checking that he had not misread.

"Captain, I want to be completely clear. If you go in there, I can't get you out."

That *was* the problem, wasn't it? Maybe this was a bad idea. Of course it was a bad idea. But he had no others. The *Brutus*'s upper body rotated as he faced north. He could still get out. There was still time.

"Marshal?" Clearwater asked.

"Yes, Captain?"

"My father once told me, living is all about making choices. So we better make choices we can live with."

On the other end, Clearwater heard a deep breath. For a moment, he thought he might have heard an argument. If so, it was resolved quickly.

"It's your call, Captain."

Clearwater frowned. His choice or not, he knew which one he could live with.

"I'm going in."

In his NOD the *Brutus* was practically wailing for mercy, but he drove the legs faster. The landscape was little more than a blur as the machine tried to take its revenge by rattling his skull. That did not stop him from seeing targeting icons in his NOD. The cohort did its work well, at least in this area.

Clearwater hit an incline. As he crested the rise, he saw the Vaar batteries twenty kilometers ahead. He could fire now, but he would wait. He needed as much surprise, and to sow as much chaos, as possible.

At fifteen kilometers, he toggled the master arm to bring the weapons to life. He pulled Sergeant Skoto's call sign from the list in his NOD.

"BlueCat-Two-One to RedBird-Three-Five, prepare to get out of that trench."

"Are you crazy?" a crystal-clear voice shot back. "They'll cut us to pieces."

"They're about to have bigger problems," Clearwater answered. No point in arguing, so he dropped the com.

At ten kilometers, he picked his targets. At five kilometers, he opened fire. He needed only to mark them and give the command. The *Brutus* did the rest in the order he had specified.

He did not know the condition of the legionnaires beneath the bridge, so he withheld the nuclear charges but let the rest of his missiles fly. By coming so close, he gave interceptors as little time as he could to react.

The battery's guns were arrayed in a semicircle with the gap facing away from him. The missiles went over their heads to plunge down into the trench. Two were shot down. Two went south, and the rest went north. As the Vaar deduced what had happened, the *Brutus* moved to the second step. With sixteen half-second bursts of ammo available, Clearwater marked the shield generator at the rear of the semicircle, then each gun, before moving back to the generator with the last mark in the sequence. The *Brutus* followed the commands. Clearwater let out a moan of pain. The hole in the cockpit left a void for the concussion of the 90mm cannon to join him inside.

The ordnance shells smashed into the battery's shielding. The first burst did not make it through to the generator. Nor did any of those that followed. But when the targeting circled back, a shell engaged the generator in dialogue. It made a strong case, and the generator disassembled.

Clearwater had hit the incline to their plateau. The Vaar guns were still turning toward him when he let the pulse cannons howl. The small guns on the chin were for the infantry. The big disrupters in the left arm were for the guns. The pulse cannons tore through the small cockpits, made for Viss, nestled by each barrel.

Disrupter pulses ground at the front of his cockpit. Twenty-eight infantry scattered as they fired at him. Even without its shields, the *Brutus* could handle that. Clearwater would not take the risk of someone else commandeering the guns. Each gun carriage was around half as tall as his mech. When they came close, he cut the speed before skidding to a stop.

This was as point-blank as it got, and Clearwater drew fire from the left arm across each of the batteries. As he did, something heavier than a pulse gun hit from behind. The *Brutus* staggered, but it did not fall. It smoked, but it did not fail. Clearwater continued the circuit, leaving the chin guns to autonomously shred infantry.

Clearwater's eyes moved to the trench.

"BlueCat-Two-One to RedBird-Three-Five. Now!"

Clearwater dashed for the trench. Disrupter fire hailed from above and legionnaires leaped out from the trench.

"Go!" Clearwater shouted. "Go now! Go now!"

Some legionnaires helped others who could not walk. Others dragged bodies. But they all took the command and made their way north. Thirty at his glimpse. Too many looked wounded; they would need more time. Clearwater did not stop until he was on the bridge and then he pivoted south. Tanks raised their guns as Clearwater lowered his.

His pulse cannon carved into a tank in front of him, and the *Brutus* lurched backward at the return fire. Clearwater could not regain balance before he went over the edge of the bridge. The mech's feet came down in the trench. As the Vaar tanks lowered their guns to reengage, Clearwater dashed forward and hit the thrusters. The *Brutus* followed his targeting priorities, drawing disrupter pulses through two of the tanks as he sailed over them. Vaar infantry saw the metal hulk coming toward them and decided they did not want to be where it landed.

Now the tanks were trapped. Three abreast, the walls and each other blocked them from turning their hulls or their turrets to face him. Behind them now, his pulse cannons happily found their weakest defenses. Beyond the tanks, he glimpsed the shelter the legionnaires had made: a bunker built from a fallen Vaar tank on one end and a wall of scrap metal and broken AICES on the other. Both were built around a shallow divot in the trench.

ALERT! CLING! CLING! CLING!

The infantry did not simply watch him take their tanks apart. Several had used their own thrusters to leap onto his mech. Six became ten as he toggled the thrusters and rocketed back out of the trench. Ten became eight as two were dislodged by either the rise or the impact with the ground. In the corner of his bouncing eye, Clearwater saw one Vaar land on his face. He would not get back up. Clearwater raised the *Brutus*'s left foot and brought it down hard to make sure of that.

Seven still clung to the back of the machine, out of range of the chin guns. This was the moment for what mech jockeys called a *break dance*. Clearwater threw out the arms, stomped the legs, hit the thrusters, and twisted to shed Vaar, while at the same time, he fought for balance. Seven became six, but he did not see where that Vaar landed.

A display opened in his NOD to show that two of the Vaar had made it up onto his shoulders. With one arm still on the controls, Clearwater's other reached for the RA-117. He brought the left arm up to smack the Vaar off. When he tried the same with the right arm, the Vaar there tapped his thrusters. The warrior bounded over the arm and came back down.

More climbed out of the trench to join the fracas, and the chin guns made them pay. But those on his machine were his immediate concern.

"Don't fall. Don't fall," Clearwater whispered as he leaned and fired his thrusters. The machine lurched to the right, skidding on the silver deck. Clearwater leaned left, and the machine reversed course. Six became four.

On reflex Clearwater looked up as a Vaar splayed out atop his canopy. While the warrior rose to his knees and positioned his rifle, Clearwater raised the right arm. The Vaar fired into the seam of the cockpit, but the mech's arm punted him away.

At first he was not certain what hit him. But seconds after he knocked off the Vaar, an explosion shattered what was left of Clearwater's hearing. He spun in another dance for control. Then he spied the Vaar on the bridge and the weapon on his shoulder. He could only watch as the top half of his cockpit was separated by the machine's spin.

Four became three and then two. Clearwater lurched and twisted, and the *Brutus* slid and jerked like an idiot on an icy floor. Two became one as he fired the thrusters, trying to gain momentum to overcome momentum. As his movement righted, Clearwater looked up. The last one hung on between the shoulders, trying to climb upright. He locked the legs.

The machine skidded to a halt, flinging the Vaar, but he clamped a hand down on the edge of the broken cockpit. As the warrior drew himself up, Clearwater brought the RA-117 around. The warrior had lost his helmet, so Clearwater saw the Vaar's face clearly as he brought his eyes over the threshold. As the Vaar's left arm came into view, Clearwater pulled the trigger.

The RA-117 barked five times. Electricity sparked between them as the Vaar let out a gurgle, then his eyes rolled back. The right hand that held the Vaar to the *Brutus* slipped, but in the same moment, the left hand fell open.

Clearwater felt the impact on his chest, then his right thigh, before the object rolled between his legs.

Grenade!

His hand shot down between his knees, the *Brutus* moved with him, and he felt the sphere roll behind his right foot. Clearwater dropped the rifle and reached down for it. With all his strength, he came up out of the chair and hurtled the grenade away.

His ears were in ruins, so he did not hear the blast. But as he fell back into the chair, he felt the drill-like flechettes enter his arm, his face, and pepper his scalp. He felt them enter his neck and chest like rays of fire. What balance he had left was lost as another charge hit the warmech from behind. Clearwater's body rocked, and the *Brutus* hit the deck.

CHAPTER
29A

FLOOD ATTACK SUCCESSFUL
ACCESS GRANTED
The watery interface had flowed back into his vision. Panzer looked through the spheres, through the watery image. He glowered at Oul'sor, writhing in his mental grip above the ground. Panzer sensed the hostility, though it was not directed at him. The Vaar raised his arm toward the girls. They had left the barrier. Panzer felt the flow of the room's energy, and the bloodhammer began to glow.

Panzer's thoughts embraced the spatial controls. *"Goodbye. Oul'sor."*

As if to hurtle a grenade as far as he could, Panzer turned and threw out his arm. Oul'sor was sent hurtling toward the far wall of the control chamber. The hammer had just begun to leave his hand when both were bathed in golden light. In but a second, he and his hammer were gone.

Panzer fell forward, his mangled lungs filling his faceplate with blood. Flood attack. He would never have put money on it. One of the oldest forms of cyberattack, it flooded the target with garbage requests. One after another, over and over, until the system failed and had to reset itself. He never should have doubted Andira. He drew his left arm up beneath him. With the threat gone, the awareness of his many pains filled the void.

"Every time I fight that guy, I lose a hand," Panzer muttered to himself.

Master!

The terrible shriek jerked him to his feet. At the edge of the center platform, Jennifer and Julie were on their knees, both holding Simmonne. With the thruster he had left, Panzer returned to the center. What remained of his heart raced, creating a disjointed pulse in his ears as he stumbled to them. He dropped his knife as he fell to his knees and slid to their sides.

Jennifer's and Julie's faces were red. Tears flowed from their eyes above quivering lips.

"Master, do something," Jennifer pleaded, hefting Simmonne higher off the deck and pushing her toward him.

Panzer supported her and raised a hand to her face. He grasped for it. He looked and listened for it. His breath came quicker as he failed to find hers. Panzer toggled his NOD.

SIMMONNE
DISTANCE: <1 METER
STATUS: DECEASED

"Simmonne?"

There was still a spark in her head. She was not gone. Not yet. But her heart did not beat, her lungs did not breathe, and her skin was cold to his touch.

"Simmonne? Can you hear me?" Panzer swallowed. "Andira, medical scan. Now! Jennifer, above the small of my back, open the compartment. Take the medkit out."

While Jennifer did as she was told, so did Andira, scanning Simmonne from scalp to toe. Burns covered much of her skin. The weeping gash in her shoulder hinted at the true extent of the trauma. It came into increasing view as layer after layer of medical warnings filled his NOD. The Titan Works Hellbore was designed for a military-grade cyborg in power armor. It was never intended for use by a fleshie. So much of her body was highlighted in his NOD that he could barely see her.

Every bone in her left arm was broken. So, too, were her left ribs. Cracked vertebrae, snapped ligaments and tendons, and a collapsed lung. Her brain was concussed, and he received the dreaded confirmation that her heart was not beating. Other organs were ruptured, with many bleeding.

Jennifer dropped the medkit when she tried to offer it to him. Quickly Panzer seized it. He raised his faceplate before using his teeth to pull the hose, then he jabbed the needle into Simmonne's neck.

MEDKIT SCANNING . . .
THIS PATIENT IS DEAD
SELECT COURSE OF ACTION:
REPAIR & RESUSCITATE
PRESERVATION PROTOCOL (NOT RECOMMENDED)
Panic started to build as Panzer made his choice.
>>REPAIR & RESUSCITATE
ACKNOWLEDGED . . . DISPENDING ETNS . . .
WARNING . . .
THIS PATIENT'S TRAUMA IS OUTSIDE OF KIT CAPACITY . . .
SEEK IMMEDIATE MEDICAL ASSISTANCE.

In his NOD, Andira gave him the sight to see the machines flowing through the hose and into Simmonne's blood. Panzer turned his head. Kassar and Novin remained encased in two barriers, both unmoving.

"Crossroads! Release them!" The moment their prisons dissolved away, he shouted, "Kassar! Get over here!"

The kurai searched around them with bewildered looks before Kassar bolted over. Novin followed soon after.

"Novin, take them." Panzer nodded to Jennifer and then to Julie.

"What?"

"No!"

Despite their protests, Novin drew them away. In an instant Kassar was kneeling on Simmonne's opposite side, ripping a larger field trauma kit from his back.

"Iden's Trust!" Kassar whispered loudly as he scanned her. "What happened here?"

"She fired my Hellbore," Panzer answered.

Kassar threw his kit open. With one hand he inserted lines into Simmonne's limbs. With the other, he held a small device and gave it a double take.

"Your gun couldn't do this." Kassar's voice broke a whisper. "All her nanites are burned out. *All of them.* Even massive electrocution wouldn't do this. They're all gone. Extensive cellular damage. How—"

"Fix now, ask later," Panzer answered. "Come on, Kassar."

"Lay her flat."

Panzer did as he was told, gently lowering Simmonne to her back.

"There's still some brain activity." Kassar's voice was loud now as he affixed leads to Simmonne's chest. "I'm taking respiratory control."

Kassar thumbed commands into his device. Simmonne's body lurched as her lungs suddenly inflated.

"I have a heartbeat," Kassar announced. But no sooner had Panzer exhaled than Simmonne's body began to convulse. "Damn! She's neurostorming!"

Simmonne almost seemed to be shaking her head as her body twitched. Her eyes had been opened in a blank stare, but neither eye moved even as her spasms threatened to dribble her head on the ground.

Panzer slid his left arm under her head. "What's happening?"

Kassar delivered an injection to her leg. "Her nanites are fried." He pulled an autosyringe. "Her body doesn't know how to operate without them. Her brain is panicking, cross-firing. I have to stop it."

Kassar reached back to his kit, removing a new autosyringe and a series of vials. He plugged the first into place and injected Simmonne in the neck.

"She still has brain activity. Talk to her, sir," Kassar urged. "Talk to her."

Panzer leaned down, staring into the lifeless eyes that looked back at him. *"We're here, Simmonne. We're here."* With his right hand, Panzer took hold of hers. *"Do you hear me? We're here."*

"Talk to her, sir!" Kassar raised his voice.

"I am," Panzer projected at him before looking back at her.

He could sense it like a thunderstorm in her skull. In all the minds he had touched—more than one as it was dying—he had never sensed something like this.

"Her brain is fighting me," Kassar hissed. "Keep talking to her. I can't stop the panic attack. I have to cut her brain off from her body."

Panzer tried to close his mind more firmly around the storm in her head. There was no reason. There was no thought. There was not even pain. There was only fear. The most primitive part of her brain, the one that only understood survival, was in a state of primal terror. Panzer glimpsed the metal rod before Kassar drove it down into her chest.

"I'm here, Simmonne. I won't let you go. Kassar is taking care of you. You'll be all right soon."

"Bypass complete," Kassar announced. "Andira, link to my kit and take control of her autonomics."

"Understood."

The tremors ripping through Simmonne's body stopped, and she went limp. Her only motion came from the forced rise and fall of her chest. The ETNs that had spread through her body were working. The burns that covered her skin were fading away.

"Attempting phantom stabilization," Kassar announced as he readied a new vial in his autosyringe. With one hand on Simmonne's forehead, he turned her gaze aside and delivered the injection behind her ear.

"We're working on it. You'll be okay."

"It's not working," Kassar murmured. He went to his kit and brought a scanner over Simmonne's head. "Even her cranial nanites are burned out. I have to try again."

Panzer was no doctor and had only a vague understanding of what Kassar was attempting: to fool her brain into thinking the body was responding properly to its commands. He delivered a second injection behind the ear.

"There's too much damage," Kassar whispered, sitting back on his heels. "I've never had to fix something like this. I don't understand how this happened."

Panzer's eyes moved briefly to the golden gun lying behind Kassar. Panzer did not know the how, but he knew the what. When he shot the Hellbore, he felt it—the energy that flowed out of him. Somehow, Anagram had linked the weapon to his metapsionics. But he was T-13—he had metapsionics to spare. What had the weapon done to her? Not even T-1.

Anagram. If what you did to my Hellbore kills her, I swear, I'll feed you to Indorai myself.

Panzer could feel it before Kassar said it.

"The neurostorm is stopping." There was no joy in Kassar's voice. "Brain activity is dropping."

"Simmonne. Can you hear me?"

Kassar sat back on his heels, his face an image of fear and reluctance. "No choice," the kurai whispered low before turning back to his kit.

The storm was passing, but nothing was coming to replace it. Panzer knew this blackness. He had seen it every time he killed someone while having a hold on their minds. The black abyss of a dead mind.

"Simmonne. Don't go." Panzer cleared his throat. "Put her in stasis. Now! Preserve her until we get to the ship."

"I can't."

"Do it now!" Panzer screamed at the kurai.

"It won't work, sir." Kassar didn't look up. "In her condition, she won't survive the process. There's only one choice now."

"I have restored communications," Andira announced moments before Panzer heard Aetius's voice. High and urgent—and for the first time to Panzer's ears—it bordered on panic.

"Rockhouse to Tick-Tock-One! Come in! We've tripped some kind of defense system! It's tearing the fleet apart! Tick-Tock-One. Come in!"

Panzer could hear the admiral's voice, but he could not process it. Kassar withdrew a red tube practically painted in warning labels. He exchanged an empty vial into his syringe before plugging the needle into the red tube.

"Nanite replacement?" Panzer whispered. "Here?"

"It's the only choice, sir." The kurai unplugged the syringe.

"You could fry her brain," Panzer protested, grabbing Kassar's arm.

"She's dead if I don't." Kassar jerked his arm away, but Panzer did not let go. "Sir. I have to do it *now*."

He did not have to be a doctor to know what Kassar wanted to do. The brain's greatest weakness was its delicate complexity. Millions of nanites moving through it—cutting, bridging, splicing neurons—could kill her just as easily as save her.

"Stasis—" Panzer began before Kassar cut him off.

"Won't. Work. Sir. Human stasis relies on her nanites to work. She doesn't have any. I do this, or she dies. Please sir. Trust me."

Panzer opened his hand. Kassar turned Simmonne's head aside and inserted the needle behind her ear. In his NOD, Panzer toggled his view so he could see through her flesh. The ETNs had dispensed earlier, and those still flowing from Kassar's kit appeared as a silver fluid across her body. Those he had injected into her skull now moved like a golden cloud, encompassing her brain before flowing into it. Some would work to repair the damage. Others would evict the destroyed nanites and take their place.

But past her eyes, he saw only the abyss.

"Sir. Rhoxx and Miss Prideaux have arrived in the ship," Andira reported, but Panzer did not answer. "Rhoxx is deploying."

The ETNs were running out of work. They had mended the organs and stopped the bleeding. They had drawn the fragments of bone back together and become an adhesive for them to regrow. Without scar or even discoloration, they had mended the burns. Her heart could beat on its own again. Her lungs were drawing breath. Yet no light broke through the abyss.

"Rockhouse to Tick-Tock-One! We're getting butchered up here! Respond!"

As the ETNs completed their work, they flowed out of her body via the hoses Kassar had inserted in her limbs. There was nothing left for them to do. Panzer squeezed Simmonne's hand as he watched the golden cloud in her head, searching frantically for light in the darkness.

"Brain activity zero," Kassar whispered. "NRNs still working."

"Come on, Simmonne. Don't go."

Panzer did not know how long he searched in the darkness. But he found no light. Soon the golden cloud began to dissipate. It flowed down her neck to find the tubes and leave her body.

"Her neural array has been restored." Kassar choked as he read from his device. "Brain activity. Still zero. I don't understand. Everything's fixed. Her neurons should be firing."

"Simmonne?"

Shame burned so intently in him that he tasted it, gagged on it, and ultimately was overwhelmed by it. His head spun, and he was forced to momentarily pull back from the abyss to clear his perceptions.

"I'm sorry, sir. There's nothing more I can do." Kassar bowed his head. "I'm sorry."

"*No!*" Jennifer and Julie wailed. Novin followed them down as both fell on their knees.

Panzer could not turn from the abyss. *"Simmonne?"* His arm trembled beneath her weight.

"Rockhouse to Tick-Tock-One! Are you at the control center? Can you help? We're losing ships! Respond! Respond!"

"Sir," Andira spoke up.

"No. Not like this."

"Sir. The fleet needs help."

Panzer shook his head, leaning down to bring his face closer to hers. Kassar had fixed the physical damage, but he could not fix the trauma to the mind.

"Not like this. You can't die to save me."

Panzer adjusted his arms, cradling her.

"You don't get to do this, Simmonne. It's a daunting thing. To make peace with death and then learn you're going to live—you don't get to do this to me. You don't get to make me look forward to days ahead and then leave."

Panzer turned to Jennifer and Julie, whose cries broke into bawling. Panzer captured that image in his mind before turning back and sending it into the abyss.

"Don't do this to them. You're the only family they have left. Don't leave them."

There was no light. There was no sensation. Only a hollow echo of his voice in the darkness.

"You told me you loved me. Do you remember when we met? How afraid of me you were? Do you remember how alive you felt the first time I put my arm around you? Remember it, Simmonne. Remember how it felt to be alive."

"*Prince of Mars* to Tick-Tock-One. Do you receive this transmission?"

The new voice went through his ears but stopped at his mind. Not again. No matter what he could do. No matter what was in his power. He could not do this again.

"On the third night, I caught you thinking of what our children might look like. You weren't ready for that. But you wanted it someday. You have to come back for it."

The abyss did not answer, and Panzer closed his eyes. A pleading, frantic, desperate man. That was not the man she fell in love with. That was never the man she needed.

"Simmonne. You always suspected I was in your mind. While I held you, I wove my voice into the pleasure centers of your brain. I coupled it to your fight-or-flight response. Verbal, or telepathic, it does not matter. You can't help but respond to it. You don't have a choice. So answer me."

"Rockhouse to Tick-Tock-One. Rockhouse to Tick-Tock-One."

"Sir?" Novin spoke up. "The fleet."

"Answer me, Simmonne. I am your master. I decide. You do not have my permission to die."

"Sir." Kassar was standing behind him now, a hand on his shoulder. "Sir, there's nothing more we can do."

"You gave me your life."

If the abyss would not answer on its own, he would make it answer. The best antidote to darkness was light. Panzer imaged brilliant light spilling into the abyss and projected the thought. Memory of waking up with her. Memory of a night in a bar. Memory of the optimism for the light ahead.

"You do not have my permission to die."

There was something in the abyss with him. Formless, featureless. Panzer gave it form with his own mind. He sculpted it, as a hand reaching into the light. He grabbed that hand.

"Answer me. Simmonne."

He drew the hand toward him.

Kassar had left his medical slate on the deck by Simmonne's head. Prompted by the sound of a beep, he nearly tripped over his feet as he raced to reclaim it.

"I—I . . ." Kassar stammered as he held the device up. "What?"

"You told me you loved me. You gave me your life. Now answer me."

"What? What the—"

Panzer opened his eyes and saw a blink.

"Brain activity is rising," Kassar whispered. "I don't understand."

"Answer me, Simmonne," Panzer spoke aloud when he saw the second blink.

Simmonne's eyes closed. Kassar's machines were still breathing for her. She had to fight them to do it, but the tiny whisper came.

"Master?"

Panzer took in a full breath. Simmonne coughed.

"*Simmonne!*" the Twins cried out to her.

"Novin, release them."

NO RETURN—56:21

Jennifer and Julie practically fell on Simmonne as they took her left hand.

"Watch the hoses!" Kassar snapped.

"Julie, kneel there." Panzer pointed above Simmonne's head as he sent the mental image. She was quick to obey, and Panzer gently positioned Simmonne to recline against Julie's legs. With a hand on her chin, Panzer drew Simmonne's gaze up.

"Rest."

His legs did not want to hold him, and Panzer stumbled as he climbed back to his feet.

"Sir, Rhoxx has entered the command dome," Andira announced. "I am directing him here."

Panzer was about to take a step when a tremor in the floor stole his balance. He fell to a knee but popped up before Novin could cross the distance to help him.

"What was that?" Novin asked.

"The merger," Panzer answered. "We're running out of time. Spatial shear is growing."

Panzer used what was left of his thrusters to return to the center platform. Somewhere between stumbling and crawling, he made his way back to the center. There the screens continued to float in the rays of blue light.

"Tick-Tock-One. Tick-Tock-One. Come in!"

At the center, Panzer faced one of the screens. *"Crossroads, show me the battle happening around the station."*

The station obeyed, bringing the image up on the screen he faced. The Crossroads understood more than he might have expected. It illuminated the Imperials in blue and the Vaar in green, but it was the object between fleets that drew his eye, colored in red. Panzer's veins knew ice as he stared at it. From the countless hosts that Anagram had showed him, an entity of malice was obscured in the clothes of a singularity.

As Panzer opened his mouth, rays projected from the sphere, a dozen in all. Each found an Armadas warship, and in seconds, the ship melted away. Panzer closed his eyes. The sphere labeled *Spatial Network (Wide)* had only gold and silver threads.

"I don't know what you are, but I know where you're going. Crossroads! Throw that thing into the hyper-singularity!"

The Crossroads understood. On the screen, a new sphere expanded to swallow the entity. The brilliant beams projecting from it were severed. Yet as the wormhole closed, the entity from beyond remained. It fired a dozen fresh beams into Aetius's fleet.

"Crossroads. Throw it into the hyper-singularity!"

Panzer felt a sense of determination. The wormhole returned to encompass the sphere. This time the wormhole's globe grew, and the lights dimmed in the chamber. The entity was fighting it, even as the Crossroads mustered all its strength to the effort. The fog began to roil, and the quaking returned.

"You can do it. Throw it in!"

A single beam pierced the globe. In less than a second, it crossed the light-years and came down on the Crossroads, targeting the command dome. Jennifer and Julie cried out as the chamber seemed to lurch to its side. The walls rattled, and the platforms began to sway. Panzer fell on his side, and Novin tried to catch him before losing his balance and falling as well.

The light in which the screen floated seemed to dim. A roar filled the air, and Panzer felt the station's pain. The beam escaping the wormhole faded, the sphere popped, and the entity was gone.

Panzer's gaze shot to Simmonne. All three girls returned to their previous position. Simmonne was coughing but also nodding at Jennifer.

"Andira, can you get me in touch with Aetius?"

"Stand by," Andira answered before pausing. "Go ahead."

"Tick-Tock-One to Rockhouse." Panzer waited several seconds. "Tick-Tock-One to Rockhouse."

"Rockhouse."

Panzer took a breath at the sound of Aetius's voice. "What is your status?"

"Bad," Aetius answered. "That thing destroyed a lot of ships, and it—did *something*. Scrambled the minds of every non-telepath in the fleet. I'm getting reports from all ships that people are coming to, but it might take some time before I have control of the fleet again."

Panzer looked back to the screen of the two fleets, noting that he saw no missiles in flight.

"Looks like the same thing might have happened to the Vaar," Panzer offered.

"I think you're right. They quit shooting the moment in showed up."

"I don't think we're going to get a better chance, Admiral. We should move the civilians now."

"Is the lane clear?"

The fight had left Panzer a bit cross-eyed. He reached out to hold the screen and draw himself closer. The field stabilization of the Crossroads was so strong, even the *Hurricane* could not open a wormhole any closer than five light-years from it. Panzer checked and rechecked the coordinates. No Vaar ships. No missiles. No mines.

"The lane is clear. Walk left. I say again. Walk left!"

"Understood. Generating now."

Panzer rested a hand on the floor as he transitioned to a seated position.

"Crossroads, take the second and third sets of coordinates. Open the wormholes between the points."

Panzer felt the acknowledgment. On a bearing of ninety degrees, activity in the designated grid cube. A glowing sphere emerged, the *Hurricane* opening the way for the civilians. A second later a new, larger sphere opened as the Crossroads opened its wormhole. Panzer's relieved breath was halted. His heart spiked when he saw a third sphere pop up in the display. One he had not called for.

In a second he was back up on a knee. The third sphere was the first to pop. When it did, Panzer's eyes were drawn to the vertical hammerhead. A whisper escaped his lips.

"Caustic Reverie."

A dozen destroyers emerged to flank the Vaar supercruiser, now less than a quarter light-year from the wormhole *Hurricane* was generating.

"Abort the jump!" Panzer shouted. "Aetius, do you read me? Abort the jump!"

No answer came.

"Crossroads. Throw the Caustic Reverie and its escorts into the hyper-singularity!"

An apologetic feeling, then a message in his NOD.

UNABLE TO COMPLY. WIDE SPATIAL NETWORK OVER-LOADED.

"Aetius!" Panzer shouted. "Abort the jump! The *Caustic Reverie* is in the lane! I repeat, the *Caustic Reverie* is in the lane! Don't let the civilians through! Abort the jump! Abort the jump!"

Panzer clawed at the screen. The entity had damaged the Crossroads.

The station couldn't manage another wormhole. At the top of his lungs, Panzer screamed, for all the good he knew it wouldn't do.

"*Aetius! Abort* the damn *jump!*"

"It's too late, sir," Andira answered. "They're coming through."

Panzer's mind raced, and this time he was caught by Novin as he began to fall. In his thoughts he saw the little girl in her cell. Emessa Sardonn from Crystal Rivers. The thousands of others who had been in their cells. Countless others about to be fed to the monster that had leaped into their path.

Panzer's mouth worked the words silently.

I'm sorry.

Flashes of missiles fell in a thick rain as the slaughter began. He closed his eyes and raised a hand to his head before he heard Rhoxx's voice.

"Bosss, look. Bein' *Hurricane.*"

Panzer's eyes flew open as he steadied himself and locked his gaze on the panel. *H.M.S. Hurricane* emerged from the wormhole into the rain of Vaar missiles and promptly answered with her own. The connection was restored, and he heard Admiral Gilyard's voice.

"Fire at will."

Panzer whispered through a bloody grin. "Aetius."

The Vaar thought they knew what a rain of warheads was. They thought wrong. The *Hurricane* took their aggression and answered with its own. The fury of their interceptors turned the space between them into static. But in the competing flows of hostility, there was only one victor. From across the ship, torpedoes leaped out of the hull. Their combined image created a spiral around the *Hurricane*, a galaxy of warheads that turned on the Vaar. The destroyers were gnats amid giants and swatted aside just as easily.

The *Caustic Reverie* tried to turn from the foe in front of her. But it was too late. The hunter had caught a prey beyond its measure. Massive hatches in the roots of the *Hurricane*'s wings were open, and her ordnance guns fired. As Panzer zoomed in, he saw the fury of the impact. The upper half of the Vaar ship's hammerhead was blown away into nothing. Space rippled around the *Caustic Reverie* as she clawed for her escape. Her efforts were in vain, and the storm of impacting torpedoes left space-time too distorted. Her transpatial drive could not build the bridge of escape. Even her MID failed, leaving her dead in space.

It lasted seconds. As the *Caustic Reverie* took the brunt of *Hurricane*'s torpedoes, the Vaar titan began to crumble. A second salvo from the ship's main guns split the front half of the Vaar supercruiser into an image of fraying rope. Torpedoes continued to rain on her, ripping her wings from her body before grinding what remained to nothing. From her nose to her tail, the ship was unmade, her outer hull ripped away in fragments. The ship's skeleton was exposed before it, too, seemed to simply blow away. Her long tail and its pylons disintegrated after.

"*Hurricane* to all ships. Get your crews back in action, and ready evac. Evacuating civilian ships now. Send to all commands. Drop it. I say again. Drop it!"

Panzer smiled. The multitude flowed out of the *Hurricane*'s wormhole. The civilian ships came in many shapes and sizes. Yet on the display, they appeared as a line of ants spilling out of one wormhole, flowing around the *Hurricane*, and pouring into the next.

NO RETURN—49:18

"Rockhouse to Tick-Tock-One."

"Tick-Tock-One, responding," Panzer answered.

Aetius's voice was reserved, his tone almost hushed. "IR-1 no longer here. Your attaché departed as well. Is IR-1 with you?"

IR-1? Panzer began to question it before blinking. He might have a bit of brain trauma.

"Affirmative, Admiral," Panzer answered.

"Understood. Rockhouse out."

He should have lied. The plan was well in motion, and Indorai had forced the next stage. But if Aetius did not know where she was, he might not let everyone leave. Two more tasks to complete now.

"Andira. Upload bio-templates for all Imperial species in this galaxy."

"Yes sir."

Panzer returned to a seated position, looking to the monitor as civilian ships continued to flow between wormholes. The *Hurricane* was perched above them, ready to intercept if the Vaar fleet managed to open fire.

"Sir. Rhoxx is approaching the command center," Andira advised.

"Crossroads, allow the kodaz approaching to access the command center."

With all the civilian ships slaved together, it would not take much longer. There was one task left to complete now. Panzer looked back to the big five, the golden spheres controlling the station's most important systems. In stress, in panic, in despair and resolution, there was something he had failed to see. Until now.

The spheres had all been connected by red threads turning gradually to silver and gold. The work was done. But now, there were threads missing. Not a single thread connected *Hyper-Singularity* and *Platform Linkage*. Not to each other, or any other sphere.

Panzer's mouth fell open in a whisper. "No."

Focused on *Hyper-Singularity*, one mental hand after another attempted to close on the spheres, yet none found substance. He shifted focus to *Platform Linkage*. The result was the same. No matter how many mental hands he tried to lay on it, no matter hard he tried to grasp, the sphere did not respond to him. His gaze turned again to *Spatial Network (Local)*. Moments ago it had been bristling with golden threads as he used it to evict Oul'sor. But no sooner had he laid eyes on it now, than the last of the golden threads faded away. Of the Big Five, only *Spatial Network (Wide)* still had gold to its name, and that too was dwindling before his eyes.

"Sir?" Novin asked from behind him. "What's going on?"

For a moment Panzer stood in silence, still trying to grab inaccessible spheres with his mind.

"Crossroads, restore the command pathways."

Panzer felt an answer. Apologetic, sorry, and certain.

NO RETURN—40:30

"Sir?" Novin laid a hand on his shoulder to get his attention. "What's wrong?"

Panzer glared at Novin before turning back to the big five.

"I failed. Indorai did something. It decrypted the command pathways, and then deleted them! I can't control the hyper-singularity. I can't control platform linkage. I can't stop the merger! I—" Panzer paused. His head and shoulders began to sag. "I failed."

Panzer turned as the door to the command center began to flow. Rhoxx barreled through and stopped, realizing the nature of the floor. The kodaz reared back, then jumped so his thrusters could carry him to the center platform in a single leap.

"There has to be something, sir," Novin answered. "Some way to restore it."

"Andira, is there anything you can do?"

Dots passed through his NOD before she answered. "Negative. I cannot access either system."

"Andira, could you insert a new command pathway?" Novin asked. Behind him Rhoxx walked toward Kassar and the girls, looking down at Simmonne.

"Negative," Andira answered. "My emulator does not allow me to exercise command functions."

"Can you walk us through it?" Panzer unconsciously held his breath as he awaited the response.

"The point of no return will be crossed in thirty-eight minutes. An attempt to manually create new pathways would take several hours given my limited knowledge of the system architecture."

Panzer's legs were failing. Thinking he was going to fall, Novin put hands on him, slowing his descent until he could sit. Panzer took a breath.

"Indorai needed me to help decrypt the controls."

A hundred thousand years. The Therican War. The War of Kings. The Kaurken War. The golden ages. The Eclipse. Every human life that has ever been lived. Every life that would be lived. Every ancestor who gave so much for humanity's future. Events throughout history flashed through him like the images of a dying life. All for nothing. He failed them all. He coughed on the bile in his throat as he looked at the clock.

NO RETURN—37:11

"Sir?" Andira spoke up. "The data you shared with me indicated that this facility was not originally built with telepathic control in mind."

Panzer shot up to his feet and clutched his helmet. Anagram gave him the knowledge. It was in his head. It was implanted memory, but still it was memory. He had to find the one he needed. He had to remember. It was there.

Panzer's head swiveled. Which one? Which edge?

Novin followed Panzer back toward Simmonne. Rhoxx was in his path, and Panzer jumped over the kodaz's long tail. He fell when he hit the deck, sliding on one knee toward the corner of the platform.

"Where is it?" he whispered. "Where is it?"

He pressed his fingertips against the metal beneath him. He had to find it. Now.

"Sir?" Novin asked.

"Bossss? Doin' what?"

He felt a lump where the silver metal stretched like carpet over a faint bulge. Panzer raised his fist and brought it down on the bulge. It did not reply.

"Sir?"

"Bosss?"

"Master?"

Panzer ignored them and struck the lump again. A third time. A fourth and fifth. Back on his feet, he raised one foot and leaned into it as he brought his heel down. There was a sound like shattering glass, and the lump seemed to melt.

Simmonne let out an unconscious moan as the entire platform began to vibrate. A noise started small and grew, as if they had found themselves at the center of a thousand waterfalls. The platforms moved. Ripples of metal moved up the pillars, slow at first, then accelerating. Some of the pillars seemed to melt away, but most remained. Tendrils of metal stretched from one pillar to the next, linking each to those around them. When the connections were made, the metal hardened, forming walkways complete with high guardrails.

Panzer faced the center of the platform. The multitude of spheres seemed to rocket out of his sight, and the watery interface flowed away. A column of metal had risen and began to expand. In seconds, it formed a console in the shape of a crescent, bearing a single holographic screen.

He dashed past Novin and leaped over Rhoxx's tail again as he rounded the edge to stand in the crescent. The device almost seemed more instrument than computer. Gold keys were shaped like those of a piano with a different Ascendant symbol carved in each. Between banks of keys, he saw long levers colored in red, yellow, and white.

"A keyboard?" Panzer asked. "How . . . odd."

He had no choice. His memory knew the characters on the keys.

"Sir?" Novin asked. "Can you do it?"

"Stand by," Panzer answered. He was not accustomed to a keyboard. He had only one hand, and it was missing a finger. He used what was left to press the keys. His hand seemed to know where to go. A muscle memory he had never developed. The clacking became the only sound as that of falling water stopped.

"No." Panzer glared at the screen. "It's too late to stop it."

"If you have control, there has to be some way," Novin insisted.

Panzer's head was shaking. "I can't just stop it. Not now. There's a maelstrom of space-time beneath our feet. It will just keep spinning. It has to be slowed down first."

Panzer rested a hand on the center of the console, the one place where there were no levers or keys.

"I wish we could find some way to save this place," he whispered. "All we could learn. But there's no choice. I think I can purge the platforms. Kassar! Get Simmonne ready to move. Jennifer, Julie, you'll piggyback."

"Yes, Master," Jennifer and Julie answered together.

Panzer went where the memories led him, repositioning the levers and hammering the keys. It would take too long to decouple every platform in the station one by one. He had to set up a cascade, dropping off certain platforms so that they would bring down the others.

NO RETURN—31:19

Minutes ticked by as he drove the commands into the console. His thoughts couldn't keep up, but when he finally reached for the yellow lever to send out the commands, he stopped. His stomach seemed to fall to his feet. Foreign memories sometimes did not come together as knowledge in the way one wanted.

"Sir?" Novin asked. "What is it?"

There had to be another way. Panzer jolted as a potential solution tapped him on the mental shoulder.

"Andira, get me Heinz."

His foot tapped as he waited. The image came to his NOD, revealing the boy he once knew now grown into a man.

"Heinz? What's your status?"

Heinz was looking away, toward his bridge.

"Crew is still coming to. We're getting them back on their stations as quickly as we can."

"Do you have any ammo left for those big guns?" Panzer asked no later than the last syllable had left Heinz's mouth. "Can you target the station?"

Heinz brought his gaze to Panzer. "I'm sorry to say, no."

Panzer's hand clenched. "Why not?"

Heinz's face carried a hint of shame, and Panzer heard him take a shallow breath.

"We should have completed our star trials. All turrets have broken down. We can't load or fire the main guns."

That was it then. The one set of weapons in the fleet that might be able to overpower the station's field stabilization was offline. Panzer nodded before breaking the connection. His choices dwindled, so he followed what was left. Panzer lowered his arm to the console once more. His mouth was dry as he whispered.

"Someone has to stay behind."

CHAPTER
29B

RHOXX STARED DOWN AT Simmonne. By the slightly stronger perfume, he was certain it was Julie cradling her head, gently stroking her cheek. Jennifer held her hand while Kassar unplugged hoses from his kit and connected them to other devices. The other end of each hose remained in her limbs. He withdrew a thermal blanket. With the devices resting on Simmonne's belly, Kassar gently took her from Julie and wrapped her in the blanket.

As he had with Elsa so long ago, the lord had shared certain data. Rhoxx looked through it.

SIMMONNE
DISTANCE: 1.5 METERS
STATUS: UNCONSCIOUS—SEDATED

Rhoxx was not certain how she got here. Now did not seem the time to be asking questions.

"Someone has to stay behind."

Rhoxx looked up when he heard the words. "Ssstayin'?" He spread his legs to keep his balance. A sharp tremor ripped through the chamber, causing the platform to sway.

Panzer turned back to the console. "Spatial sheer is getting worse. I don't think there's any other way," Panzer said, tapping several keys. "The station isn't designed to come apart like this. It has safeties, overrides, automated safeguards."

The crescent console made a thrumming, oscillating noise, like the string of a harp given a hard pluck. Panzer turned back to it. In a frenzy, he smashed keys while looking into the screen.

"We have another problem," he announced before speaking through gnashed teeth. "Indorai—he opened the doors. The Vaar are no longer trapped in the subterranean layers. There's a large contingent of them; they're at the security doors." Panzer pointed to the door at the south end, the gateway to the station's catacombs.

"Can they get in?" Kassar asked.

Panzer leaned closer to the screen. A second later there was a new image in Rhoxx's helmet, shared with him and the brothers. A circular view into a silver corridor. Many warriors crowded shoulder to shoulder as far as the image could show. There were juggernauts interspersed among them. The activity at the front drew his eye. Viss marines had set black boxes connected by cables on the circular doors. Rhoxx was about to ask what they were doing when Novin answered the question.

"Phase resonators."

"Phase resonators?" Kassar's voice was incredulous. "Will that even work? The fleet's bombardment didn't even scratch this place."

"If they know the right frequency, it will work," Novin replied, looking at Kassar. "If it's matter and they know the frequency, phase resonators can do it."

"Indorai," Panzer grumbled. "He must have told them. That's how they got into the southern command center. They know we're here, and they can't control the station while I am. They have six to go through. We have to start decoupling. But someone—"

Someone would have to stay behind. Rhoxx was about to offer an idea before his lord beat him to it.

"Andira!" Panzer exclaimed before his head dipped. "How quickly can you get your peripheral body down here?"

There was a pause before she answered. "I am sorry, sir. I do not believe I can comply."

"What?" Panzer snapped. "Why not?"

"Sir, my peripheral body was not made for hard dropping. It would not survive the drop."

"So then use the *Intruder!*"

"Sir, Rhoxx took the *Intruder* to reach you."

Rhoxx lowered his head. He brought it in anticipation of bringing the girls back to the *Hurricane.* An error. An error for which a price would be paid.

"So bring the ship down!"

"Yes sir, but Vaar are attempting to advance on the command center on the surface. I am using the ship's interceptors to suppress them. Descent will inhibit my firing arcs."

"I don't—" Panzer was about to shout before he turned toward the girls and then to the door of the command center. "Andira, stay out of the atmosphere."

Panzer looked to Rhoxx. He looked to Novin, then Kassar, and last to Simmonne. He took a breath.

"Even if she gets here, if the Vaar break in before it's done, Andira's body isn't designed for that kind of punishment. It has to be one of us. If they reach this console, or damage it, they might be able to stop it."

"So destroy the console," Kassar insisted.

"We can't," Panzer answered. "We are using the console to override the safeguards. The station will stop disassembling automatically."

He laid his hands on the console before his head lowered.

"There's no other way. Novin, carry Simmonne. Rhoxx, take Jennifer and Julie. Kassar, cover them on the way out."

"I don't *think* so," Kassar and Novin answered in unison as the former jolted to his feet.

Rhoxx's upper lip curled as Panzer shook his head.

"Follow my orders."

"*No*," Kassar and Novin answered in unison again.

"If someone is staying, it's not you." Kassar didn't break his gaze. "You're not doing that to us again."

Panzer stood upright and turned to the brothers. Rhoxx sneered.

"You three have served me better, and more loyally, than I had any right to ask you. But I'm not a prince anymore, and you're not bodyguards. We're soldiers. I am the ranking officer. If someone has to stay, it's my responsibility."

"*No!*" a pair of much higher voices spoke in shrill unison. Rhoxx watched the Twins run to Panzer, grabbing at his right arm.

"What about us?"

"You can't just leave us."

Rhoxx's teeth parted as Panzer looked down at them.

"Jennifer. Julie," he whispered. "Sometimes life—"

"I'll stay!" Kassar broke his whisper. Panzer and the girls looked to him. "Tell me what I need to do, then go."

"No," Novin interjected, drawing Kassar's angered gaze. "He'll need you. I'll stay."

"Neither of you—" Panzer began to speak. The Twins began to speak. Kassar and Novin were about to speak.

Rhoxx silenced them all.

"*Sssshuttin' up!*"

Simmonne's closed eyes were the only ones that did not turn on him as his roar echoed among the pillars. With slow, deliberate steps, Rhoxx approached his lord.

"Onssse a prinsss, alwaysss prinsss," Rhoxx growled. "You *not* stayin'."

"Rhoxx—"

"No!" He raised his voice again, drowning his prince's volume with his own. "Sssinsse Elsssa go, I watchin' you livin' wit' it. I watchin' you fightin' wit'out fear. Wit'out value of ssself. And I sssayin' not'in'. Causse I knew t'e pain you feelin'."

Rhoxx loomed over him and bent his forelimbs to bring his head lower.

"But you gotten' usssed t'e pain. You forgettin' it wasss pain. Livin' wit'out hope of tomorrow. But you not gettin' do it, anymore." Rhoxx paused to point a claw at each Twin before drawing it to point at Simmonne. "You not havin' t'at freedom anymore. 'Em givin' you 'em lives, and 'em yoursss."

Panzer shifted his posture, and his eyes widened. "Rhoxx." Panzer tried his most commanding tone. Rhoxx cared nothing for it.

"No." Rhoxx pointed straight ahead. "When you ssstill a baby, in you mot'er's grasssp, I, and we, ssswearin' an oat' to you. We leavin' 'hind all we knowin', keep t'at oat'. I misssin' bir'dayss, Founder'sss Daysss, graduations-ss, followin' you t'at oat'. Too much, lettin' t'is happen. We be Vorhan Tohl; *you* be our prinss. If sssomeone ssstay, it not be you!"

Rhoxx curled his claw in to point to himself.

"*I* be t'e captain t'esse guardss. It *my* resssponsssibility."

Panzer looked down at the teary-eyed girls still clutching his arm.

"Tellin' me, what I needin' do," Rhoxx urged.

"Sir," Andira spoke up, "the Vaar have breached the first door. Based on their rate of progress, I estimate they will breach this chamber in less than ten minutes."

Panzer gently withdrew his arm from the Twins' grasps and turned toward the console. He struck several more keys, and the lone screen turned red. A silver sphere came alive at its center—an image of the station.

Panzer swallowed. "I've set it all up." He hesitated before pointing to the yellow lever on the left. "All you'll have to do is hit that lever. But the station's safeguards will trip that lever as it tries to save itself. Each time the lever falls, you'll have to push it back up. It has to go all the way down and back. Or—"

"I understandin'." Rhoxx nodded slowly. "Better be goin' now. 'Fore Vaar getting' in here."

Panzer turned back to face him with a distant gaze. His head was shaking, twitching. Rhoxx knew that look. He saw it before when they told him that Elsa couldn't come back. His jaw was tight. He wore the look of a man who wanted to cry but didn't know how. In the seconds it took him to regain his composure, he walked to Simmonne and scooped her up.

As soon as Panzer vacated the gap between points of the crescent, Rhoxx positioned himself there. Area denial at its most basic. Panzer returned a moment later with Simmonne in his grasp. His eyes were still distant, vacant.

"Rhoxx. I—"

Rhoxx cut him off so that the girls would not hear the quavering in his voice. He lowered his head once again to look his lord eye to eye. This time he spoke softly.

"You bein' more t'an an oat' to me, My Prinsss. You alwaysss bein' like a little brot'er. Well t'is sssomet'in' you big brot'er goin' do for you. You goin' wit' em now. Gettin' back t'e life what wasss takin' from you."

He knew he had to go. But he simply stood there, his expression a mixture of emotions and pain. "Rhoxx—"

"Go," Rhoxx urged. "Before 'em meltin' t'rough."

Panzer closed his eye, and a new screen opened in Rhoxx's helmet.

NO RETURN—21:22

"It has to go by five," Panzer whispered.

Panzer shifted Simmonne so that he could lay a hand on Rhoxx's shoulder. Rhoxx nodded. His lord's jaw trembled as he said the words.

"Thank you, Rhoxx. For everything."

The Twins sniffled, holding their hands to their mouths as their eyes did what their master's could not. Rhoxx turned his gaze back to his lord and bowed his head. "It been mine honor, my lord."

A nod to Kassar and Novin. Each grabbed a Twin and guided them onto their backs. They took the lead, thrusting toward the exit.

"Hold tight," Kassar warned the Twin gripping him from behind. "We'll be going very fast."

"I'll tell them, Rhoxx," Panzer whispered. "I promise."

Rhoxx bowed his head lower, and the hand on his shoulder was removed. While his lord carried Princess across the newly formed bridge, Rhoxx bent around to face the control console, fixated on the yellow lever. He measured carefully with his tail to ensure he had the proper reach and turned back to see a final gaze from his lord between doors. With his head raised, the lone thruster on his ankle ignited and he climbed out of view.

"The Vaar have made it through the third door," Andira announced.

"Andeera." Rhoxx smiled. "T'ank you. Bein' here wit' me."

"I am sorry I could not handle this task," she answered in a sad tone.

NO RETURN—20:30

"Don't bein'," Rhoxx returned. "Lookin' after our lord. Be leanin' heavy on you now."

A screen in Rhoxx's NOD showed the progress. His lord, Rhoxx, and Novin rode their thrusters out of the station. The moment they made it to the *Intruder*, he would trip the lever.

"The Vaar have breached the fourth door."

Rhoxx did not answer. He continued to watch through their screens as they made their way out. His smile at last faded, and Rhoxx took a deep breath and murmured amid the rattling walls.

"Avun-Gor, Lord o' Warriorsss. Be hearin' my plea. My time bein' sshort, and I bein' afraid.

Ssso much I wantin' sssee, Avun-Gor. Never sssaw. Ssso much I wantin' sssay. Never sssaid. Ssso much I wantin' do. Never did. Be givin' me ssstrengt' Avun-Gor. Let 'em go."

Rhoxx watched them exit the open doors to the *Intruder*. When the door closed, Rhoxx looked back, and his tail slapped the lever.

"Station dissolution has begun," Andira announced.

"Avun-Adra, Maiden of Fate. Hearin' my prayer."

The *Intruder* blasted out of the atmosphere. Rhoxx spread his legs as the pillar beneath him began to oscillate.

"Bein' wit' 'em, I leavin' 'hind. Give 'em counsel, I not able. Be guidin' Novin to him voisse. Teachin' him itss pow'a."

A distant explosion rang through the chamber. Rhoxx glanced back to the console's screen. Thousands of squares formed a grid pattern on the silvery ball. A small number of them were turning black. Segments detached and fell toward the singularity. Only a few so far. Around them, geysers of gas squirted into space as the atmosphere began to convulse.

"Be helpin' Kassssssar, Maiden of Fate. Teachin' him, pursssuit of exss-selense, not be wort' it, if one forgettin' to live. Be wit' my lord'ss bridesss, Avun-Adra. Guide 'em t'rough 'em losss. Blesss 'em many children, and for all 'em livess, t'e love of family."

"I am about to dock with them," Andira advised. "Don't worry. I will make sure they get out."

Rhoxx nodded.

"Bein' wit' my lord, Avun-Adra. Be teachin' him. No matter how little bein' left. Life alwaysss wort' livin'."

Rhoxx heard the loud clang and looked back to see the lever had fallen. A slap of his tail sent it back up.

"The Vaar have reached the final door."

Rhoxx swallowed and said his final prayer.

"Avun-Tor, Judge of Deed. I havin' little ssayin' to you. For I livin' my life by an oat'. And I never be breakin' it. Judge me, Avun-Tor. I no reassson to fear you."

Rhoxx took a step forward before rearing up on his hind legs. In each of the cyberlimbs flanking his belly, he grasped an RA-117 compact. Six guns he pointed forward as he guided the big cannons over his shoulders. His remaining pair of cyberlimbs held magazines at the ready. The door ahead rippled as if it were water agitated by the quaking. Any moment now. There was enough black in the silver sphere now to see it, even if one had not been looking for it. The station was breaking from its equator, and segments fell away on paths leading north and south. It would take hours to decouple every segment. But he did not need to. Only enough to break the prison.

Another metallic sound. Rhoxx slapped the lever again as he drew his deepest breath and shouted, "Vaar! I be Rhoxx! Captain of t'e Vorhan Tohl! Come to my clawsss!"

The ripples thinned, and the metal of the door flowed away. Every trigger was pulled as Rhoxx opened fire. The liquefied metal had not fully dispersed before dead Vaar fell through the gaps to land on the bridge. With six automatic rifles, Rhoxx had unleashed a river of disrupter pulses at the door. Yet his heavy cannons remained silent, waiting.

Rhoxx knew the target had come when he saw the snake-like hoods of their helmets. One round of his 51mm cannons would not pierce a juggernaut. Even ten rounds might not. Rhoxx gave them more. The cannons opened to a speed where pulses practically formed beams. Eighty-five thousand pulses per second from each gun, twin-linked to the same target. Two juggernauts came through the doorway side by side. With a sweep of his shoulders, Rhoxx turned them and those behind them to fragments.

NO RETURN—15:09

Clang!

He shifted to slap the lever again. The next pair of juggernauts made it through. Rhoxx stumbled as a missile exploded against his shields. The momentum transferred from the shields to his projectors, then to his body. His mouth opened in a roar and he reared up again, then cut them both down.

The strongest tremor yet threw him forward as Vaar fell backward. Bodies tumbled off the bridge into the swirling fog below. Many scrambled to their feet just to be cut down again by the river of pulses. Rhoxx reared up a third time. He had to stay on his feet. He had to shield the console with his body.

"Andeera!" Rhoxx screamed over his weapons' firing. "Takin' armss, one. T'ree. Grenades!"

Rhoxx had called it seconds before it happened. The uppermost of his cyberlimbs came under her control as interceptors to the grenades flooding through the doorway. As his disrupters continued to fire, bodies formed a new barrier at the door. The Vaar had some semblance of what was going on. Those in front had nowhere to go but forward as they were pushed by those behind in a desperate scramble to stop the dissolution.

NO RETURN—14:20

"It's working!" Andira raised her volume. "Spatial shear is stabilizing!"

Another missile made it through. His shields failed to stop it in full. A concussive wave battered his helmet and sent him reeling. He never stopped firing. Rather than try to break his fall, he kept his body square to the door so that the river could flow. A team of Vaar down the corridor tried to set up a pair of growlers. The river took them.

Clang!

The initial slap missed. So did the second. Rhoxx turned back so that his aim was true, and his tail found the lever on the third. The lever went up and immediately fell back down. With a growl, Rhoxx looped his tail around it, pulling hard. He felt the click, and this time when he slapped the lever up, it remained there. Heat and ammo warnings flared in his sight as the RA-117s drained their capacity for both.

NO RETURN—13:40

"Forty more seconds," Andira called.

The segments broke free from north and south, each a new wave moving toward the dissolution at the equator. Thousands of black spots covered the silver sphere. The sound of his weapons began to fade. It was not gone, merely overpowered. Collapsing corridors and buckling walls all came together to create a noise that drowned out the firefight. Rhoxx righted himself. In his peripheral vision, he saw one of the pillars begin to fall. It struck another, and it, another as the quaking tore it apart. Even the domes turned black on the silver sphere.

As he made it upright again, the river began to dry up. The sensitive electronics that could not be bond-forged melted in the RA-117s. They were cutting themselves off to avoid self-destruction.

"Overridin' sssafetiess!" Rhoxx bellowed, and the river returned.

Clang!

Rhoxx turned to make sure his tail found its mark. One final trip. His tail slapped the lever.

NO RETURN—13:30
NO RETURN—13:32
NO RETURN—13:35
NO RETURN—ERROR . . .
MERGER CANNOT CONTINUE.

Rhoxx grinned, reading the characters seconds before they faded from sight.

His RA-117s had melted their circuits. His cannons were sputtering now. It was over. But no reason to leave it to chance. Rhoxx raised his forelimbs and exposed his claws. As he readied his final weapons, he was gripped by the sensation of falling. Yet everything seemed to fall with him. He just had to make sure the Vaar could not try to reverse the process. He had to stay until it was too late. The connection to the others was breaking up. As static overwhelmed the image, Rhoxx made out a final glimpse of the *Intruder* pulling into the ship's hangar.

The Greeks at Thermopylae. The Jews at Masada. The Byzantines at Constantinople. Benkei on his bridge. The Battle of Earth. William and Hale at Saturn Gate. The stories of courageous last stands had a way of surviving the forgetfulness of the ages. They endured as monuments of courage and defiance. But Corps missions were never declassified. Rhoxx versus the Vaar on the Crossroads was a story that would be known by only a few, remembered most dear by those who loved him.

Rhoxx felt a presence. An enemy had slipped behind him. He turned, raising his claws, determined to make his last fight a worthy one.

CHAPTER
29C

"ALL UNITS! ALL UNITS! Drop it! I say again. Drop it! Drop it! Drop it!" The drill-like flechettes of the grenade had ravaged Clearwater's body, and he lay on his side much like the collapsed *Brutus*. The synthetic organs of a legionnaire could withstand tremendous, but still finite, punishment. Three of the flechettes had torn his heart into as many pieces. More had shredded his compound lungs, leaving only a handful of the microlungs that composed them to continue functioning. Yet more had found his liver, his intestines, and his trachea.

His eyes never closed, but it would be a stretch to say he retained consciousness. It was his saving grace. When the Vaar found him lifeless in the cockpit, one poked him with his bayonet. It pierced his left lung, or at least what was left of it. When the Crossroads began quaking in earnest, they decided they were needed elsewhere.

Lieutenant Serrens's sudden death was Clearwater's true salvation. The round that had penetrated the cockpit killed the aren quickly. Thus none of the *Brutus*'s medical resources were expended on him. They were retained instead for the cockpit's inheritor. A series of hoses extended out of the chair and embedded their needles in Clearwater's flesh. Medical nanites and synthetic blood flowed through every vein and capillary, but they could do only so much.

Clearwater blinked as he tried to make sense of what he saw. His right eye seemed to be at the base of a pole, looking up. One of the flechettes had found the bone of his cheek, just below his eye. Before he was fully aware, he reached up and grabbed hold of the flechette. He couldn't pull it out. As awareness increased, he brought his left hand up, pushing back on his forehead while continuing to pull. But it did no good. The flechette and his skull had become one.

His face was crusty as increasing awareness brought pain with it. His head slammed into a side console as the ground beneath him seemed to leap from one place to another. A terrible roar filled the air. Something flopped on his scalp, and he straightened and reached up. A large portion of his scalp had peeled off his skull like wrapping paper on a partially opened gift. He coughed. Foaming blood spilled past his lips.

While his heart was repaired, the remains of his lungs took over the task of forcing blood through his body. He hacked and sputtered as his heart came back online, and his lungs tried to return to their primary duty.

The ground quaked again, and Clearwater let out a cry as he slammed against the console. Flechettes in his torso were forced deeper into his flesh. His eyes went wide.

The Crossroads was breaking up.

He cleared the medical notices from his NOD and looked once more to the optical port.

SYSTEM OFFLINE

Clearwater blinked. With two fingers, he pried one eye open wider and looked into the port again.

SYSTEM OFFLINE

The message seemed to sap the strength from his muscles. Flechettes were embedded all over the console. Whether it had been them or something else, the machine was offline. The *Brutus* gave all it could give. The only thing that seemed to still work was the com, loudly repeating its message.

"All units! All units! Drop it! I say again. Drop it! Drop it! Drop it!"

Another quake came with such strength that Clearwater felt the *Brutus* go airborne before crashing back down. Yet more pain for his wounds. He was too late. The station was breaking up. If the *Brutus* could go no further, he had to do it on his own.

He fumbled with the restraints and released himself from the chair. His legs seemed reluctant to obey as he began to crawl and dropped out of the cockpit. With another bloody cough, the flechettes were driven deeper. Clearwater crawled north. He had to make it to a landing zone and hope the mininet routers were still online.

He would never make it. Not like this. Weeping wounds left a trail of blood on the metal behind him. For Froggy, for David and Ryan, for Melanie. No matter how futile it was, he had to try. The flechettes merged with the bone of his right forearm and drew his gaze.

Smoke of destroyed tanks continued to pour out of the trenches, dancing to a new beat with each of the tremors. Did the legionnaires make it out? He hadn't seen their bodies.

Each time he dragged himself forward, the flechettes in his torso scraped against the ground. Only a single thought propelled him.

Home.

Clearwater paused, overtaken by a coughing fit. Once more he had to clear the medical alerts from his NOD. He did not need them to tell him what shape he was in. When he looked up, he wheezed.

Kilometers ahead, the ground rose into the sky. When he looked east, he saw the same, and the same to the west and south. No, he realized. The ground was not rising around him. The ground around him was falling.

Clearwater left the deck, and he felt weightless. What little strength he had was slipping. He managed to roll, putting his eyes to the sky.

I tried.

The quaking was replaced by the rushing wind, which forced him against the metal. This was it. There would be no coming back this time.

Clearwater scanned the distant stars. He would have thought here, at the core of the galaxy, they would seem closer. As if he could reach out and touch them. His left arm rose toward the sky as if to do that very thing.

One star in particular caught his attention, twinkling brightly as if to wave at him. He focused on that star as he waited for what came next.

The star was growing.

Clearwater sputtered as he tried to laugh. Nothing made sense here. He watched the star grow brighter. The air was becoming thin and his already shallow breath more strained with it. The star continued to grow until it seemed larger than his fist. Then it vanished. His left arm fell weakly.

What little strength Clearwater had manifested as a flinch when a gentle wave of compressed air washed over him as though he were on the edge of an explosion. When Clearwater managed to right his head and open his eyes again, he saw blue and gold.

A ship hovered above him.

Was he hallucinating? White light spilled down on him as a door in the craft's belly opened, and two figures dropped from it. Atmo-wings opened wide from their armor, leaving trails of blue plasma in their descent. The air was too thin now to hear the thump as their feet met the silver deck on either side of him.

While Clearwater tried to blink the hallucination away, a pair of metallic arms lifted him into a tight embrace. He no longer had the strength to hold his own head up, and it sagged forward onto the shoulder of the enormous creature. On the pauldron in front of his face was an emblem, a hooded figure with feathery wings, its head and arms in praying posture.

G-forces told Clearwater he was climbing, and the white light grew brighter.

"We have him!" announced the figure holding him as they touched down on another metal surface. "Go!"

The door in the drop ship's belly sealed, and Clearwater felt air in his lungs once again.

"You're all right, sir," the armored delta assured him. "Just relax."

Clearwater was laid on a soft surface. He managed to turn his head to look down the bay. Two dozen beds projected from the walls, filled with humans, kurai, alphas, and deltas. Most of their armor was piled beside them in a heap as mechanical arms sprouting from their beds attended their bodies.

"Priority," another voice called as three figures loomed over him. "We start now."

A metal gauntlet cupped his head, turning his gaze to one of the reflective faceplates looking down at him.

"Relax, sir, you're going to be fine. We're going to sedate you now."

Clearwater reached up to grab the armored delta's arm.

"My—" he strained. "Company."

"Just rest, sir." The delta produced a syringe from a finger. Clearwater snatched the syringe.

"My company!" he wheezed. "Third of Seventh, and Third? What—"

He could not manage anymore.

The reflective faceplate slid up, revealing the delta's green-eyed face. "Central, can you patch me through to Third Company, Seventh Battalion, Third Cohort?"

Clearwater didn't release his grip as a wait tone pulsed in the aren's helmet.

"Third Company, Sergeant Qopas answering."

A tear fell from Clearwater's cheek. His mouth opened in a smile. His arm fell away from the delta's hand.

"It's going!" someone shouted. "Massive tensor curve! The singularity is escaping!"

At full throttle the drop ship blasted away from the disintegrating station on its way to the *Hurricane*.

CHAPTER
30A

A HEAVY PRICE WAS PAID for victory at the Crossroads. Hundreds of Armadas ships were destroyed or so damaged that they were fated for the scrapyard. The Solar Legionnaires paid a much heavier price. Out of every four souls deployed to the station, two did not return. The final disposition of the Vaar fleet was not determined at the battle's end. The bulk of their numbers was still dead in space when *H.M.S. Hurricane* was the last ship out.

The *Prince of Mars* was the second-to-last ship out. Along with the *Hurricane*, it defended Imperial ships as they made for the wormhole the *Hurricane* held open, protecting against potshots from the handful of Vaar ships that had regained control. As the *Prince of Mars* departed, the *Hurricane* left behind a final message: 144 Arc-5 missiles. In response, they destroyed the transpatial gateways: Ralleck, Stoplen, and Haplen. The titanic rings were broken, severing the Empire's last connection to the galaxy. With that work done, the *Hurricane* took the wormhole and missed the show that followed.

For thousands of years, the destruction of the Crossroads would baffle the scientists of primitive civilizations. Those who were just beginning to gaze into the universe would see things they could not understand. In a distant spiral galaxy with six arms, the core would draw their attention. For many, their observations would serve as early proof of alien life. In the end, nothing else would explain what they would observe.

The Crossroads was the greatest prison in its universe. Platforms fell away by the dozens and hundreds. Twin waves of collapse traveled north and south from the equator. The pocket dimension they had labored to create began to fail, dumping the prisoner back into the proper space-time. The supermassive black hole's event horizon expanded at the speed of light. It escaped first between the disintegrating hemispheres ballooning out as a black disc. But as more platforms fell away, and all pretext of containment was lost, the disc expanded. It overtook the waves of falling platforms to complete the destruction of the prison that had held it for so long. The remains of the Crossroads were trapped in the black from which they would never escape.

Countless Vaar died on the station. Unable to extricate themselves, unable to secure transport in time, they had no chance. Massive bursts of radiation killed many of them, while falling walls, ceilings, and machinery killed others. Most died a death of eons that seemed like mere minutes.

Beyond the event horizon, in the dilated time, they fell toward the singularity at the monster's heart until its unimaginable gravity shred the atoms of their bodies.

The Crossroads lost control, and a spatial wave was released. The larger the object it encountered, the more strongly that object was affected. Hundreds of stars in the galactic core would undergo strange novae stretched to the point that their gravity could no longer hold them together. Planets as far as the beginning of the galaxy's arms would have their orbits disrupted. The wave went beyond them all. To those with the right sensors, it remained detectable long after it passed through stars where neither Solar nor Vaar had ever treaded.

Panzer could have sent virtually anyone, anywhere, and done it instantly. He chose to follow the plan. A wormhole opened within a wormhole. The fleet took one, and his ship took the other. For the fleet, he had stretched the wormhole to give them a two-week journey. Time enough for a head start. For the second wormhole, Panzer had set a two-day geometry. Just long enough for preparations to be completed at their destination.

Panzer spent the first few hours in the deep-fryer. He could have used more time, but he was needed outside, and he could not afford the hangover. Novin had brought a spare recliner out of storage. Panzer sat in that recliner now, with Jennifer and Julie in his lap, both deep in sleep with their heads resting on his chest.

Hoses still ran to each of Simmonne's limbs beside them. A row of probes protruded from her chest and belly. An oxygen mask covered most of her face. Total nanite replacement—a misery few would have to suffer, with many days of recovery ahead. On Simmonne's opposite side, Kassar sat on a stool. In her peripheral body, Andira stood behind him, neither willing to leave their patient.

The deep-fryer would have been quicker, but an empath was still a metapsion, and Panzer did not wish her the hangover that would come from such a long stay. Trillions of cells in her body would receive new nanites via the hoses delivering them to her blood. So many damaged cells would have to be destroyed and replaced. It could be a hundred days or more before she felt like her old self.

Panzer needed little sleep, only an hour or two every few days. It had been long enough to warrant it, but sleep did not find him. Every time he closed his eyes, every time he let his mind wander, it went to the same place. Rhoxx. He had to keep his mind occupied. If any part of Simmonne's empathy was still functioning, the last thing she needed was to feel him coming apart. There would be a time to grieve for Rhoxx, but it was not now. Rhoxx would have understood. He always did.

Panzer looked at his left hand resting on the table and holding Simmonne's. Her hand looked like a child's in his, a fact that had enamored her. Yet as he looked at it now, he felt a sense of shame that clenched his throat.

He had failed.

Panzer checked Jennifer's and Julie's collars in his NOD. Simmonne had guessed that the devices had secret functions, a revelation he had shared with the two of them. In their minds, all three attempted to guess what those hidden features may be. Of course, they only guessed those he could use to lord his power over them. Not one had thought of what he could do out of affection.

Neither Jennifer nor Julie wanted to sleep, so Panzer had to induce it. No sense letting them miserably stew over Simmonne while they could do nothing for her. Their devices kept them there, inhibiting the release of adrenaline and stress hormones to keep their pulses from racing and to keep their breathing at steady rhythms. It freed him to control their dreams. A dream regulator would have been easier, but this gave him a distraction. He wanted to give them better times and happier moments. Nightmares, traumatic stress, survivor guilt—none of these things would have them. Not while they belonged to him.

Panzer let out a sigh as he leaned his head back. Simmonne understood what she was getting into. On some level, Jennifer and Julie understood it, too. But there was much more than that. Every relationship had terms and conditions. Anyone who thought otherwise was blinded by naivete or strong emotion. When he laid out his rules to them, he actually had them convinced that he set all the terms, but they had their own. To him, at least, their terms had been crystal clear.

Take them away from the lives they hated. Give them new experiences. Make them feel things they had never felt before, things they might never feel otherwise. Do it all while keeping them safe. He'd understood it in their minds and in their sporadic imaginings. They met his terms, but he had failed to meet theirs, and he failed because he wasn't strong enough.

He watched Simmonne take a deep breath and exhale in a yawn. When she chose to intervene, the fight with Oul'sor was not going his way. In the end, he did not even defeat Oul'sor; Andira did. A hundred thousand years of controlled breeding. A childhood spent learning from the best warriors in the Empire. Enhancement by an alien capable of building something like the Crossroads. Despite all of it, he still failed. Simmonne was watching him die before her eyes, and his failure nearly cost her life. On top of all of it, instead of either of them, his failure took Rhoxx.

Some man he was.

Master?

He had to climb out of his hole of shame to answer.

"Yes?"

One of Simmonne's eyes cracked open. *I'm sorry.*

Stab wounds hurt less. *"For what?"*

She took a deep breath. Kassar was suddenly on the edge of his stool as he watched for signs of trouble.

You told me not to leave the barrier.

What was he supposed to say? His mouth worked, but her next thoughts came before he had a response.

I couldn't just watch. Not again. He killed them. Isis, Lilac, and the others. I had to do something. I had to hurt him. For them.

Panzer's eyes narrowed as he reached deep into her mind. She wasn't trying to save him but wanted to avenge her guards? Most lies tasted bitter. This one was bittersweet, the taste of a lie she told herself. The pain in Panzer's jaw made him realize he was clenching his teeth. Simmonne could lie to herself but not to him. His grip was gentle on her mind as he helped her hold the lie more tightly.

It was that simple. She had to rewrite the history of what she saw so that he could be what she needed him to be: Invincible. Indestructible. Too powerful to be challenged. Someone so strong and unassailable that not even someone like Oul'sor could beat him. An unbreakable rock in her life that could not be moved, even as everything else was taken. The unstoppable force that had swept into her life and carried her away.

She'd never had a realistic view of him. She would have to learn eventually that he did have limits, that he did have weaknesses. He could fail, and he was not perfect. But perhaps she did not have to learn it today. Like graphite on paper, Panzer rubbed at the memory of her taking the Hellbore until it was smudged. The reality she told herself was the one she would remember.

Master?

"Yes?" More to bear.

I'm sorry about Rhoxx.

Panzer gave her hand a gentle squeeze. *"Me, too."*

It was coming. Panzer had spent the first day while she was unconscious dwelling on it. But it was here now, before he found the perfect answer.

Master?

"Yes?"

An unconscious shudder moved through Simmonne's body, urging Kassar to his feet. While Kassar brought out a device to scan, Panzer listened.

That creature. It knew you. And you knew it.

Both of her eyes were open now, fluttering with the strain of the effort. *What it offered you . . . Do you think it could have . . . made good?*

Panzer shook his head slowly. *"I don't know. Maybe."*

Panzer barely felt it, but for her, it was a feat of will to squeeze his hand. *Why did you say no?*

His right arm coiled tighter around Jennifer and Julie, holding them steady as he leaned over the arm of the chair.

"I don't know how much of what he said was true. The more one knows, the better a liar they can be. But I don't care. I know who I am and what I come from."

The strength to keep her eyes open was fading, but then the real question came. *What about what he said—about us? That he made us. That has to be a lie, doesn't it?*

In a matter of days, the universe had taken a knife to her innocence. Panzer took a big piece for himself when he took her. The Vaar took one when they killed her guards. Perhaps the biggest piece had been taken with the lives of her family, possibly by her own brother. She surrendered a piece to pick up his Hellbore. Now, another piece.

Yet innocence remained. The girl didn't know the value of a troy and had never needed to. She did not understand the difference between strength and cruelty. She saw strength as something to envy, rather than the product of walking a road paved in pain. She gave herself to him completely and without reservation because she had never known an ending love. If he did not protect what was left, then what would survive?

"Simmonne."

Is it true?

This was only a difficult choice if he made it one. Damn the Encephalon. Even if what he said was true, why say it in front of them?

Master?

Either the Encephalon was lying, and letting her keep the memory would do nothing but fill her with confusion and doubt, or the Encephalon was telling the truth, and the result was the same. Every memory of the Twins' closeness, of Simmonne's touch, would be violated. Every moment of intimacy would be cast under a shadow. Every thought of a future together, poisoned by doubt. The final death of innocence came when one realized how little control they had over their life.

"I don't know."

Panzer heard her sniffle behind the mask. *You don't know? But it can't be true!*

Panzer could not prove or disprove it. He could only know what reason told him. The Encephalon was telling the truth. It explained too much and made sense of too much: why the three of them fell for him so quickly, why they were so eager to jump into a lifetime commitment, rather than waste the currency of their youth, and why his judgment seemed to change when they were near.

It explained too much. But how did he do it? Knowing the telepathic manipulation that would require, there was no way he would have missed that in Simmonne's mind. Genetics to predispose telepathy? Or a life so carefully controlled to shape the personality? Or was it actually a lie? Did the creature just see what was there and take credit for it?

Panzer slipped his hand from Simmonne's grasp to gently stroke her hair. *"Simmonne, you trust me."*

Another sniffle. *Yes.*

"Do you love me?"

A single tear ran from her eye. *Yes, Master.*

"Then that's all you need to know."

She had accepted a premise. She had no secrets from him. He was Master and had the right to keep any secret he wished. In her conscious mind, she'd resolved to play into her new role. In her innocent subconscious, she believed that if he kept a secret, it had to be for a good reason. He didn't plan to prove her wrong. If someone had to carry a burden in this, it would not be her. She gave him her life and, with it, a responsibility for her happiness.

"Look me in the eye."

The fluttering of her eyes ceased briefly, and she met his gaze. He emptied her thoughts before she had fully put together what he was about to do. Through her eyes he saw the mist. Through her mind, the words of the Encephalon. The sensation of her clinging to his leg as she fought for consciousness.

To cut the memory away risked creating a hole that she would be driven to fill. He could not remove it all. She needed to know the danger if Indorai or Oul'sor came near her. He could always modify more later if needed. The things the Encephalon said about him, about the three of them, were smudged.

Panzer withdrew from her mind. Her body, almost completely para-lyzed, still seemed relaxed. When he broke eye contact, her eyes closed, and she let out a tiny sigh. The relief he expected to feel did not come.

Was it the right choice? Her hand rose, and he realized it was seeking his. He held it firmly. At least Jennifer and Julie *had* lost consciousness, or he would have had to consider taking on their burdens as well. Maybe there was no right choice, but if he was the only person trying to protect her, then protecting her heart seemed best.

"Sir?" Andira's volume suggested it was not her first attempt to get his attention.

"Yes?"

"We will complete jump in fifteen minutes."

"Understood."

Kassar rose from the stool and began cocooning Simmonne in a blanket. Panzer turned his attention back to Jennifer and Julie, guiding them back to the waking world.

"Andira, be sure the overdrive is charged," Panzer said in a cautionary tone.

"It is, sir."

No one went where they were going unexpected or uninvited.

A gray zone surrounded their destination a hundred light-years across. It did not matter who they were or why they blundered in. Even an Armadas warship that entered unscheduled would be engaged and fired on. Of the three Great Fortresses in the Empire, it was not the Cathedral, nor Reichsyl-vannia, in which access was most tightly controlled. Their destination was where the Empire's greatest warships were designed and built, the Valhalla Shipyards.

For many Sylvanni, Valhalla served as a proof of their people's suprem-acy, one of the first great feats of stellar engineering. At Valhalla's center lay the blue hyper-giant star, named like a monarch as Asgard the Sixth. In close orbit around it, seven smaller stars were brought to heel by a colossal transpatial gateway. Each star housed its own hive—some to build the ships, others to design them. Entire nations had fewer scientists than Valhalla.

Only a ship could access it, as there was not a single astranet router in the system. No one entered without security clearance. There was nowhere else Panzer could take the girls where they could be hidden even from the

Corps.

Panzer's pulse raced as Andira counted down the seconds before they exited the wormhole. There was no such thing as a stealth ship in the gray zone. Millions of sensors stared tirelessly into it, all slaved to an arsenal ready to go toe to toe with an armada. The only way their arrival would not be seen was if someone had been told *not* to see it.

"Jump complete," Andira reported, prompting Panzer to hold his breath. "Val-Com has not acknowledged our presence."

Panzer exhaled.

"On course now," Andira continued. "ETA, thirty minutes."

They could have jumped closer, but Panzer had wanted some buffer in case someone did not get the message about what they were not supposed to see. The Twins were coming out of their sleep, and Panzer had them on their feet before they were fully ready. Kassar took that as his cue to approach with an autosyringe.

"Hold out your arms," Panzer directed.

Still groggy, each held one arm out toward Kassar.

"What is it?" Julie mumbled.

"These will cut you off from the astranet," Kassar explained as he reached for Jennifer's arm.

The level of awareness in each spiked, and both quickly withdrew.

"No astranet?" Jennifer asked.

"But—" Julie was about to ask her own question before Panzer interrupted.

"We have to cut you off. Otherwise the Marshals and the Corps will be able to find you as soon as you leave the ship."

The pair looked up at him. When he nodded, they turned back to Kassar and offered their arms again. He gave each the injection normally used on prisoners. Panzer played the role normally held by a court telepath, a function he executed by forcing their NODs to grant the new nanites access. Simmonne was spared for now, her present state rendering it a nonissue. With that done, Kassar returned to Simmonne and once more began cocooning her in a blanket. When he was finished, Panzer took her in his arms once more. Jennifer and Julie followed him down to the cargo bay.

Andira approached Asgard VI with a descent aligned to its north pole. The giant bowl they approached was the largest hive segment in Valhalla, relying on technology rather than orbital mechanics to stay in place. Atop the bowl and at its center was one of the Rhinegraves' many ancillary palaces. This one was known as the Forge Palace, one of the few places Panzer could take them where they could have luxury while they hid. He could not keep them on the ship. He would need it, and the Corps would come looking for it. They could not be on the ship if they caught him.

The Forge Palace was a massive pyramid at the center of the platform. It was made up of many layers. Andira guided them toward the highest layer, which had its own landing pad. She was on final descent as Panzer led the way into the cargo bay.

Miss Prideaux was waiting for them. The raw hate radiating from her had never been stronger. Panzer avoided her thoughts. What she so wished to attack was already broken. Panzer took a deep breath as the ship touched down and the loading door slid open.

The artificial atmosphere here normally revealed a sky of emerald green filled with puffy blue clouds. But the atmosphere simulated night now, and the only light came from flashes of lightning. As Panzer looked at the falling sheets of rain, he realized he had no umbrella. He turned only to see that Kassar held the black disc. He took a step forward and tossed it down the ramp.

"Did you—"

Novin knew the question was coming and moved to answer it. With one hand he held up the crystal board that had once been the guts of the ship's transponder. Panzer adjusted Simmonne in his grip once more and proceeded down the ramp.

A long platform of gold led to triangular doors. Above that platform was an arch, and atop it a statue of the patriarch. He stood in ruby robes, a book in one hand, and the other pointing to the stars. Panzer's eyes traced the curls of his hair and beard.

Manfred. Is it true? Is this really our legacy?

Simmonne moaned, snapping Panzer out of his fugue.

Many had gathered beneath the overhang. Towering figures in gold armor and red capes stood over three meters—members of the Vorhan Tohl's Special Assignments Contingent. The AMAC was good armor, but it was layered paper compared to the *Argos* suits in front of them. Each stood with one arm cocked, bearing the occupant's Hellbore in hand. Another thing for which Panzer would never forgive the high king—forcing Rhoxx and the brothers to give up theirs when they followed him into exile. A woman waited between the gold giants. She wore a red corissè and an eight-point crown.

"Victor!" His mother bowed her head as he joined them beneath the overhang. So much meaning in such a small gesture. The high queen was superior to her sons only before they reached adulthood. As an exile he had no status, yet she bowed her head all the same.

"Mother," he answered.

"Kassar. Novin," his mother greeted before rising on her toes. She looked to the ship, then to Panzer. "Victor? Where's Rhoxx?"

Panzer's throat tightened. "He . . . didn't make it."

A bullet did not shatter a mirror as effectively as the statement shattered her expression. With a deep frown, she nodded. "I'm sorry. He was a good man."

For a moment, he forgot how to speak. As his throat clenched again, Panzer closed his eyes.

His mother motioned when he opened his eyes. "Let's go inside."

Panzer led the way. The Vorhan Tohl formed ranks around his entourage.

"What's wrong with her?" his mother asked as they passed the first set of

security doors.

"Nanite replacement. A long story."

He had not yet worked out how much to tell her and how much not to, but whatever it was had to be minimal. He did not relish having to ask his mother for help. There was no point in endangering her any more than he already had.

"A Mandrake, Victor?"

She wanted to have this conversation now? Panzer did not hide the bite in his tone. *"Does mother dearest not approve?"*

He easily sensed her annoyance. She huffed. *"I am simply surprised. She'll need to attend integration school once she's well."*

"Mother, this is hardly the time."

"They'll all need bridal tabs as well."

"Another. Time."

That was enough for her to take the hint and steer the conversation elsewhere. *"How long can you stay?"*

"Not long."

He knew it was coming, and for this question he was ready.

"Victor, if they belong to you, I will shelter them regardless. But I have to know. Did she do it?"

Panzer brought the procession to a halt when he turned to her, raising Simmonne higher in his grasp. *"No. I have all three of their minds. They did not know about it until Aetius told them."*

Forward again, the procession fell silent. The Forge Palace had many layers of security. The final set of security doors that led to the lobby were heavy, gold, and slow to open. When the first crack revealed the inside, Panzer's pulse spiked.

"Hold your fire!"

The doors swung open. At the center of the lobby, a Vaar and a glowing silhouette stood on a risen heagle.

"Hold your fire!" His mother confirmed the order as the Vorhan Tohl blitzed forward. Together they formed a line abreast against the uninvited guests. Arms rose, and Hellbores were ready. Panzer's temper bolted for an escape. With a steady motion, he turned back. Kassar raised his arms, and Panzer gently handed Simmonne over.

"Friends of yours?" his mother asked.

"Allies of circumstance."

Anagram floated several paces forward as Panzer stepped between the Vorhan Tohl.

"Anagram," Panzer growled. "We're going to have a little dialogue about the things you chose not to tell me."

Before she could answer, Panzer's hand shot up, clenching into a fist. Anagram's entire body seemed to contract. Even the motion of her simulated clothing was halted by the psionic grip. Ullenk let out a guttural sound as his feet left the deck. He grabbed at the intangible grip around his throat.

"I knew it," Panzer hissed. "Whatever you are, you have some kind of substance. Psionics can hold you."

"Release . . . her!" Ullenk managed to choke out.

Panzer drew his fist inward. Anagram shot toward him, moving with such ease that she almost seemed without mass. When she was within arm's reach, his eyes traveled the length of her body.

"You seem . . . diminished."

"Once engaged, Indorai is not easily evaded," Anagram answered. "Had he not divided his waveform to so many tasks, it is unlikely I could have escaped him."

Panzer only partially listened to the answer. There was definitely a mind in front of him but with a strange hollowness about it. If Indorai's thoughts were trillions of tons, ready to fall on whoever tampered with them, Anagram's were vapor.

"Divided his waveform?"

"Indorai is a wave entity, as am I." Anagram's body compressed further, shrinking her stature. "As the prism splits the light, we may divide ourselves. He uses this ability often—to be in many places at once."

Panzer was about to speak again before pausing as his analytical engine worked. He rolled his eyes. He should have figured it out sooner. "That's how you found me. Just how long were you hiding in my nanites?"

Anagram nodded. "When you used my network to reach the Crossroads, I placed a frequency of myself within you. Enough for the Crossroads to respond to you. Enough to find you now. The rest of my spectrum lured Indorai away from you."

She *did* show up to help. That should probably count for something.

"Obviously you escaped. So what do you want now?"

Her orbs for eyes narrowed. "Would you kindly stop strangling my servant?"

Panzer's eyes darted to Ullenk, and he released the grip. The Vaar came down on his feet, but his legs buckled, and he fell prone, gasping for air.

"Why are you here?" Panzer presented the query with more volume.

"Because you must come with me now."

"Victor?" his mother interjected. "Who is this? Who is that Vaar? What—"

Panzer held up his hand for silence. Whether he was an exile or not, his mother would not disrespect him in front of his new brides by challenging his control of the situation. He might have smiled at that if his blood were not boiling.

"Anagram is the one who told me about the megastructure at the center of the Hourglass," he began. "She's why I knew to ask you to send Heinz with his fleet. But we took care of that problem, so I'm not sure why she thinks I'd go somewhere with her now."

Anagram's eyes flared before her entire body faded away. Panzer flinched as his psionic grasp was suddenly emptied. A second later, Anagram blinked back into existence.

"Interesting trick," Panzer remarked.

"It is one you will learn," she answered. "Once you have mastered your own wave entity."

"*My* wave entity?" Panzer scoffed. "What are you talking about?"

"That is why I am here." She raised a hand to motion toward him. "I have restored your abilities. But my technology has imbued you with much more. Abilities you cannot grasp. You do not have time to learn them on your own, so you must come with me, and learn."

Leave? Now? Out of the question. Out of any question. "If you have something to teach me, teach me here."

Her eyes shrank to points. She shook her head. "Insufficient. You cannot learn it here."

"Well then that's too bad," Panzer answered. "I can't leave. I have no time to go to *Ascendantland* for tutoring."

"Don't make the wrong choice," she warned.

Panzer gave her a dismissive wave. "I can train on my own."

"And you are the only one here who won't die of age in the time it takes you," Anagram retorted. "You know that the Crossroads was not the end. You know there is more happening than you see. You know, as you are, you cannot harm Indorai. You are not strong enough."

That's not true! Master can beat anyone!

Panzer's eyebrows went up and he twisted toward Simmonne in Kassar's arms.

"Calm down," he told her as Anagram floated closer to him.

"With his guidance, Oul'sor will eclipse you. Indorai knew you were the better telepath. So he did not give Oul'sor what you might take from his mind. He gave him only an instinctual, intrinsic awareness of his abilities. But he will learn. He will come for you. And for them." Anagram nodded toward the women. "You, your Vorhan Tohl, the walls of this palace—they will not stop him. Nor will you, if you do not learn."

Panzer's chin dipped. "Where would I be going?"

"Where my people reside. A place neither *he* nor his minions can reach."

Panzer could feel eyes boring into the back of his head.

Master?

"How long would I be gone?"

Anagram's body rippled for several seconds before she answered the question. "It would be years. How many depends on you."

"Years?" Panzer exclaimed. He shot a glance behind him. "What do you think, girls? Want to go spend a few years in Ascendantland?"

Jennifer and Julie had crept up to him, each now holding onto his belt from behind. They shook their heads.

"They cannot come."

Anger was not far from breaking free. The muscles in Panzer's face tightened as he strained to force his temper back down. "You're not exactly incentivizing me, Anagram."

A ripple spread through her eyes. "You are what puts them in danger. *He* wants what I have given you. If he believes I will give more, he will wait."

"I can't leave."

Anagram floated a meter closer. "You cannot protect them as you are."

"I sure as hell can't protect them if I leave." Panzer's voice rose.

Anagram was back within arm's reach. "Do you think they were given to you to make you happy?"

Panzer took a step closer, fighting the urge to seize her once again. "They have lost *everything*"—Panzer's voice rasped—"and you want me to just leave? For *years*? Now? No. You're a fool if you think I would do that."

"You—"

Panzer waved his hand. "I think you should go now."

Anagram tried again. "You—"

"I said *no!*" The dam broke, and his arm came up again. Ullenk had just begun to recover his breath and was plucked from the deck once again while Anagram contracted.

Panzer felt a hand on his shoulder.

"Victor, calm down."

Panzer closed his eyes. His mother had shown the respect of not treating him like an exile. So he would not disrespect her. His index finger uncoiled, and Ullenk fell back to the deck.

"I won't pretend I know what's going on, but do you need to go?"

He gave her a sideways glance. "I'm needed here more."

"If you do not come with me—"

"Anagram," Panzer interrupted, "no matter what you say, I can't protect them if I'm gone."

Anagram's gaze lowered, and the motion of her clothes was still. "If that is your answer, then there is no point in fighting. You have condemned us all."

"I think you are trying to convince me that I am more important than I am." Panzer had to force his teeth not to grind against one another. He who was in control was calm. Panzer opened his hand. "You gave me a second chance. I don't take that lightly. But if it means leaving them, I will not go. That is neither negotiable, nor debatable. If they don't go, I don't go. And I'm not inclined to take them somewhere I know nothing about."

Her colors dimmed, and Anagram opened the distance between them. "I will return," she said as she floated away. "Perhaps you will be more reasonable in time."

A globe of light encapsulated her, another ballooned out around Ullenk, and in a flash, both were gone. Kassar surrendered Simmonne as soon as Panzer turned. Her eyes moved behind closed eyelids, and she let out a tiny moan as he adjusted her in his arms.

He failed because he was not strong enough. But abandoning his responsibilities was not the answer. What was the point of titanic warships, armies of billions, and weapons of terrible power? What was the point of training and discipline? What was the point of any of that, if a man had to leave those who loved him when they needed him most? No. He had to be stronger, and he would be. But not by leaving them behind.

CHAPTER
30B

SIMMONNE'S BODY FELT MORE like an incomplete idea to her than something that actually existed. She could not feel the fabric of the blanket against her skin. She could not feel the movement of the air when she breathed. Even Master's arms around her felt as if they were thousands of meters away. Consciousness was evasive, never seeming to linger for more than a minute at a time. It was only enough for her to listen to pieces of the conversations that went on around her.

With all her will, she strained to listen. She heard Master's angry words and his refusal. She never spoke or called out to him in her mind. But silently she pleaded for him not to go. It felt selfish, but still she pleaded.

When a new bout of consciousness came, she made out voices. Master and the high queen were talking.

"You're certain you can keep this a secret?"

"I selected servitors who will not be missed," the high queen answered. "They will remain here as long as your brides do. I will attend the memory of my guards personally."

"What about *your* memory? If the high king spots this in your mind, it's going to be a problem."

Empathy was gone, but there was hurt in the tone of her answer.

"I know how to protect my thoughts. Do not worry."

"I suppose you do," Master answered.

When consciousness came again, Simmonne saw herself. The ceiling was a polished mirror. She had opened her eyes in time to see Master lay her on an enormous bed. Her eyes ached as she used the mirror to scan the room.

Jenna?

She tried to call out and only managed to mouth the words without sound. *Jenna?*

"Miss Prideaux," Master called. "She's calling you."

She struggled to follow when she caught movement. Jenna's reflection vanished. A second later, she saw Jenna standing over her.

Are you staying?

Simmonne saw a frown. "No. I'm leaving now."

Simmonne tried to bring her arms up, but what little strength she had was already expended.

Jenna, I'm sorry. I . . . Unconsciousness tried to take her once again.

Please, don't go.

Simmonne did not know if Jenna heard the thought because she saw no change in expression. As darkness began to creep into her vision, Simmonne saw days past. She sat at a table with a cup. Jenna drank imaginary tea with her. With a breath she opened her eyes again. Jenna was still looming over her.

Please stay.

Why wasn't she answering?

Jenna?

Jenna's hands came to Simmonne's face as each looked into the other's eyes.

"Goodbye, Simmonne."

Don't go!

Her former handmaiden's touch fell away as Jenna turned. Simmonne could not sit up. She could not call out. She could only watch as Jenna walked away.

"You bitch," Master growled. "You'd walk away from her now?"

She watched the scene play out overhead. Jenna spun around, walking fast to Master with her finger aimed at his face.

"I'm walking away from *you.*"

Jenna? Please?

"Stop her!" the high queen screeched. A pair of the golden guards seemed to teleport into Jenna's path. A second later, the high queen had her finger in Jenna's face.

"Who do you think you are talking to, Vi-Baroness?" the high queen growled. "You speak to him that way again, I will have my guards hang you by your ankles and—"

"Mother," Master interrupted, drawing Jenna's and the high queen's eyes. The high queen bowed her head and took a step back.

Master turned his attention to Jenna. "I'm afraid we can't just let you leave, Miss Prideaux."

"What?" Jenna snapped. She leaned away from a new death glare delivered by the high queen. It was probably a good thing that the high queen did not know about what happened in the armory.

Simmonne would have flinched if she could have, hoping for Jenna's sake that she had not just informed the high queen by thinking of it.

"You know they're here," Master explained. "We can give you a ship, and frankly, I don't care where you go or what you do. But you know they're here. I can't risk that information being taken from you."

"So? What? You'll just throw me in a cell?" Jenna said with an overdramatic scoff. "Or do you plan to kill me?"

"The thought did occur to me."

Master? Summon tried again and once more failed to muster the strength to speak.

Still facing Jenna, he reached back to take Simmonne's hand.

"Option two, you submit to memory alteration. I'm sure you don't want

, ᴊᴜ my mother can handle it. Option three, her Vorhan Tohl ᴊɪtal memory controls. Or, you can stay and be *here* for them."

For a moment Simmonne dared to hope. *Jenna, it doesn't have to be this way.*

Her hopes were dashed as Jenna turned to the high queen and bowed. "Your Excellency, I will accept digital alteration at your guards' convenience."

No! Jenna!

"I am sorry, Simmonne. But if you're going to throw your life away, I can't watch you do it."

What might have been tears turned quickly to anger. Why? Why did it have to be this way?

"You cannot reason with hate." Master's voice. *"It will be okay. I will make sure they do not do more than what is necessary."*

"Take her to my ship," the high queen ordered her guards while waving dismissively at Jenna.

Master turned back to Simmonne as the guards led Jenna away.

"I must go soon." The high queen turned to Master. "If I stay too long—"

"You will be missed," Master answered. "Thank you."

"How could I do less?" Simmonne found the high queen's green eyes looking into hers. "We will become better acquainted once you are well. Get some rest."

Weeks ago, if someone had told Simmonne she would one day find shelter among the Rhinegraves, she would never have believed it. She could have never conceived of a universe that led to such a thing. Yet here she was, in one of their palaces. She replied with the only thought she could.

Thank you, Excellency.

A certain smile ghosted her lips before the high queen embraced Master from behind. They shared a conversation Simmonne was not privy to, and after several seconds, the high queen led her remaining guards out.

Simmonne did not realize she had passed out again until she opened her eyes. Kassar loomed over her now, gently disconnecting the hoses from her limbs.

"That's it," he whispered to Master beside him. "Time is the remedy now. I'll keep a monitor on her vitals in case there's a problem. She won't be ambulatory for some time, but she'll feel like walking before she can. Don't let her unless you're there to catch her. Control her diet. Meat, cheese, butter, and violet goo. No less than five thousand calories per day to help her system. Make sure she eats it, even if she's not hungry."

"Good work," Master whispered.

Kassar turned to him. "You need rest as well. I'll come back in eight hours."

Master did not answer, and Kassar was silent as he made his way out of the room. As Kassar passed out of the reflection, movement in the other direction caught her attention. The Twins rose from a couch and approached. As both stripped out of their pahris, Master pulled the blankets down. With a surprising gentleness, Master disrobed her, yet Simmonne could not feel it. Nor did she feel the weight on the bed as the Twi... covers.

Master? You are staying, right?

He smiled. *"Of course. I'll be right back."*

She watched him in the mirror as he walked to a printer terminal and returned with a handful of dream regulators. Jennifer sat up to receive hers before Julie did the same. Gently he placed one on Simmonne's forehead before attaching his.

I am sorry, Master. I am sorry you have to see me like this.

"Shh." He wiped her thoughts away. *"No more of that."*

When he climbed into bed, she felt herself lifted again. Seconds later she was facedown with her head on his chest and the Twins crowded around them. The lights faded, and Simmonne closed her eyes.

Master?

"Yes?"

I heard what Anagram said. That you could be stronger if you went with her. Do you think it's true?

She was not sure how it possibly could be. But she had to know the answer.

"Perhaps."

She tried to look up at him, but she did not have the strength to move.

Then why did you stay?

He brushed her hair from her eyes.

"Did you want me to go?"

No! I just . . . I do not want to feel like I held you back.

"I will decide where I need to be." He took a deep breath. *"We will rest. For a while."*

Okay. She summoned every ounce of strength, every shred of will, to wrap her arms around him. At last she felt something. When she felt his warmth, it was as if her body melted into him. *Because you're here.*

She closed her eyes. Across the gulf in the dream world, she seemed to briefly awaken. She was still lying atop him but on her back. She could feel her body pressing against his. There was a warm breeze washing across an open beach. The night sky above gazed down on them with a countless multitude of distant stars. She moved briefly, rolling over to wrap her arms around him and close her eyes. Beyond the reach of the universe and its troubles, she rested her head on his chest and slept within the dream.

CHAPTER
30C

CLEARWATER HAD SLEPT THROUGH the return to the Empire. The *Hurricane* had been filled far beyond its life support capacity to transport so many refugees. All nonessential personnel were thus put into stasis. When he was brought out of the stasis, it was at the Republic Shipyards. His experiences on the *Caustic Reverie* had marked him 716.

Code 716, mandatory suspension of duty. The Empire was on WarStat 2, so he didn't need to be ready for immediate deployment.[33] A month's suspended service, mandatory visits with counselors, then a mental fitness test before it was decided whether he could return to duty. He couldn't go back to work. So there was only one place to go.

With the fleet's return, the battle in the Hourglass had come to dominate the news. Everywhere he went, it seemed every holoprojector was talking about it. It was somewhat humorous, just how little information they actually had. Yet talking heads did what talking heads did, finding as many ways as possible to repeat the same information until they had more. Though to listen to them, the Empire might as well have been outnumbered billions to one rather than thousands.

After Code 716 was declared, he had forty-eight hours of mandatory cooldown, and then he was free with a simple step onto one of the *Hurricane*'s routers. He had stepped through a *Hurricane*. The joys of being back in the astranet. But astranet or no, one did not move between nations at will. Borders mattered, and crossing one meant transit through a border station. On the small space station, Clearwater stood in a line approaching a small booth. The walls were painted in rich red, with an almost ashen floor of

---

33 WarStat is short for *War Status* and has ten levels. WarStat is determined by the emperor and has broad effects ranging from how leave for soldiers is handled to the ability of the state to confiscate civilian property for the war effort. Code 716 is mandatory for soldiers who have been tortured, have been the sole survivor of a destroyed unit, or the victim of a heinous crime while in service. Code 716 and similar personnel codes may be rescinded when WarStat is five or higher. The nearly identical Code 717 is reserved for those who are deemed a possible danger to themselves or others and require supervision.

stone. Officers in neatly pressed uniforms stood by each of the four booths where the travelers were divided.

"Jonathan?"

Clearwater turned to Taula, standing to his right. "Yeah?"

"Tell me how this reads."

As the next person was processed, Clearwater took a step forward, and a text document opened in his NOD. A cursory scan revealed that Taula had significantly overestimated his vocabulary. But with words like *resignation*, *pending*, and *compensation*, he got the message. Pay her more, or she was gone.

"What do you think?" she asked as they took another step forward.

"It's . . . a little wordy."

"Well I can't just say 'pay me more or I quit.' That would be unprofessional."

"It would get the point across," Clearwater countered while she looked ahead. It was plenty warm on the station, but she insisted on wearing a heavy coat. "Do you really want to quit?"

Her eyes moved toward the ceiling before she let out a sigh. "My father wants me to. I haven't really decided. But after putting me there to be taken prisoner by the Vaar, I think the company owes me more than what they were paying."

Clearwater said nothing as they stepped forward again, now fourth in line.

"You're thinking about them, aren't you?" Taula asked. "Your section."

"Yeah," he whispered.

"It's not your fault." She laid her hand on his shoulder.

"I know." He sniffed before glancing down. "A lot of them, I still have to record messages for their families. I still haven't figured out what I'm supposed to say."

"I'm sure you'll think of something," Taula answered. "Just tell them that they were very brave, and it was a pleasure to know them."

"That just seems so . . ." He paused. "Generic. I don't know. I'll come up with something."

A lull in the conversation took over. Clearwater reached into his uniform jacket and removed the corpograph. It was inactive now, appearing as little more than a data slate. What a trip it had been. A commando officer, the Imperial Rose, and her handmaidens, the likes of people he never dreamed he'd meet. And most importantly, Taula.

"Are you still planning on giving it to her?" Taula asked as she eyed the corpograph.

"I don't know," he answered with a shrug before slipping the device back into his pocket.

One more step forward and they were at the booth. On the other side of the transparency, an aged man flirting with the status of elder welcomed them with a smile.

"Travel cards please." The man motioned to a device mounted in the transparency.

Clearwater removed the small wafer of metal from his pocket and inserted it into the device. This place had at least a hundred ways to know exactly who he was the moment he came aboard. But it did not matter. No travel pass, no entry or exit.

The machine gave an approving buzz, and Clearwater withdrew his card.

"And your wife, sir?" the old agent asked.

"Friend," Clearwater corrected.

The old man had a bit of a disapproving look as Taula inserted her own pass into the machine. When the device gave another buzz, she withdrew her card. The old agent said nothing more and simply motioned them ahead. There a small router waited, and one after another, they stepped through.

His NOD sent the address and password. In a flash they arrived between two rows of old trees. Colored leaves and green walnuts covered a long concrete walkway. Pure air carried a slight chill on the wind, plucking more leaves from the trees. His dad had wanted something special for his family. Three square kilometers within one of Weiss's habitation satellites. A cell with a fully planetized interior, complete with functioning seasons.

Directly ahead lay a fountain where a serpentine dragon blew water rather than flame from its mouth. Behind the fountain lay the house. Three stories of white marble with an entryway deck supported by thick columns. The simulated sky was turning to evening, and lights were on in the windows.

"This is your house?" Taula asked as she looked up toward the crest of the entryway.

It had never truly dawned on him until that moment. It wasn't Dad's house anymore. It was his. His house now. Clearwater glanced down as his foot found one of the large walnuts. He bent, taking the walnut in hand before rising and holding it for Taula to see.

"When I was six, my dad gathered a couple hundred of these—made cookies with them for my birthday. I've tried a thousand different printers and never found one that could get his recipe right."

There was something in Taula's smile as she answered, "You never will."

Taula's head turned, and she nodded toward the house. When Clearwater looked, he saw her. At the top of the entryway stairs in a fancy green dress. The young girl's mouth and eyes were both open wide. Clearwater rounded the fountain, and his vision blurred as he held out his arms.

Down the stairs and into the leaves, it sounded as if a stampede of wild creatures barreled toward him. But it was only one that sprang into his arms, wrapping her own around him. Clearwater heard the sniffle and wanted to tell Froggy not to cry. But he couldn't do that when he felt a tear slip down his own cheek.

"You." Clearwater paused to clear his throat. "You must have grown ten centimeters."

Clearwater turned, looking at Taula who appeared as if she were trying to let out her own tears. For several minutes he rocked Froggy side to side in his arms.

"Are you real?" the innocent voice asked.

"I'm not a hologram," he answered, hoisting her up a bit higher. "I'm home."

"To stay?"

"For a while," Clearwater answered.

She did not fight it when he lowered her slowly to her feet. But she quickly took hold of his hand as firmly as her tiny fingers could grasp. A stray leaf had blown into her golden hair, and Clearwater plucked it away as he kneeled beside her.

"Froggy, I'd like you to meet my friend, Taula."

Taula bent at the waist to look Froggy in the eye.

"Froggy," Taula said with a smile. "I've heard a lot about you."

Froggy wiped her eyes with her free hand before returning Taula's gaze.

He noted the curious look on Froggy's face and needed no telepathy to know the thoughts in her head.

"Are you lantai?" Froggy asked.

Taula winked, raising a finger to tweak the pointed lobe of her own ear. "My mother is."

"You're pretty."

"Awww." Taula placed her hand over her mouth, looking to Clearwater, who grinned.

"Come on." Clearwater stood. "Let's go inside."

A message lit in his NOD as Clearwater led them toward the stairs.

TAULA: I thought you said she was nine.

JONATHAN: I always do that. Sorry, Froggy is six; David is nine.

Together they ascended the stairs, and the big wooden door swung open. In the entryway, Clearwater opened his mouth to call out. Froggy beat him to it with more noise than such a tiny body should be able to generate.

"Jonathan's home!"

The sound of footfalls erupted from the upper floors as David and Ryan came stomping down the stairs.

"Careful," Clearwater cautioned.

"You're back!"

"How many Vaar did you see?"

"Did you really meet a commando?"

"What was the ship like?"

The questions came in much too fast for him to answer, and he raised his hand, ineffectually signaling them to cease.

"Ryan. David."

Clearwater looked up the stairs where Melanie stood on the second floor. The front tail of her white pahri bore a small monogrammed *L* near its tip. A lot of troys for a tiny letter. Clearwater stood quietly as she descended the stairs to him. This was the moment that had given him trepidation. Melanie stared at him, and he could practically see the thoughts moving behind her eyes.

She came forward and wrapped her arms around him. "Welcome home."

Froggy was not about to give up the hand she had claimed, so with the one that was free, he returned the embrace. Melanie did not hold it long before backing away.

"Who's your friend?" she asked.

"Melanie, Ryan, David—this is Taula."

"Pleased to meet you." Taula smiled, bowing her head.

"The pleasure is ours," Melanie answered. "May I take your coat?"

"Thank you."

Clearwater's eyebrows rose when the coat came off and he saw skin. Taula's pahri sported twin tails of its own, with long tassels on the side reaching her ankles. The fabric was a checker pattern of green and white. An amber shawl descended from a thin choker. Silver garters grasped her thighs, though she spared herself stockings.

Melanie took the coat, quickly shuttling it to the closet beneath the stairs.

TAULA: What? Why are you looking at me like that?

JONATHAN: Nothing. I've just never seen you in a pahri before.

Melanie returned, but before she could speak, another feminine voice called out. The house AI, asking for attention.

"Three visitors are requesting admittance to the main router."

"Who is it?" Melanie asked.

"Three officers of the Solar Legionnaires, requesting to meet with Jonathan."

Melanie shot him a glare.

I don't know, he mouthed before answering the house. "Let them in."

Clearwater turned back to the still open door. Through it he saw the three brown uniforms emerge from the router, all three human. The family followed as Clearwater stepped back out onto the deck and walked toward the stairs. The three legionnaires moved in a march, and Clearwater spotted the colonel's insignia on the eldest man as the trio rounded the fountain. All three were in dress uniform, with a lieutenant's insignia on the remaining men.

"No," Froggy whispered as the trio ascended the stairs. "No. No. No."

With the three now on the large deck with him, Clearwater was about to raise his hand when he felt the sudden tug.

"No!" Froggy shouted. "No! You can't have him! He just got back!"

"Froggy," Clearwater whispered as she backed away, trying to drag him toward the house.

"Go away!" Froggy belted out in a shrill tone that stung his ears.

"Froggy," Clearwater whispered more firmly.

Her green eyes turned up to him.

"Stand at attention with me," he said, pulling her back to stand beside him. "Froggy? I need this hand."

With a sneering face, Froggy released his hand, allowing Clearwater to raise his salute to the colonel.

"Sorry about that, Colonel," Clearwater remarked as the salute was returned. The moment his hand was down, Froggy reclaimed it. If looks could kill, the colonel would have been a heap of ash.

"My name is Vlyr Samos," the colonel said. "Are you Jonathan Clear-water?"

"Yes sir."

The colonel turned to the lieutenant on his right. The younger officer handed over a data slate to the colonel. He held it out, looking at each member of the family before clearing his throat.

"Captain Jonathan Clearwater. It is my duty, and my privilege, to bear you this missive. On Day-204, 100,016 the Combat Conduct AIs flagged your battlefield performance for accelerated inspection by the Board of Commendations. After review of your actions in what has been deemed the Battle of the Hourglass, the board has recommended and appropriate authorities have decided."

The colonel paused to look Clearwater in the eye before returning his gaze to the slate.

"For great valor in time of war. For acts of selfless courage. For heroism in the face of the enemy. It is the decision of the Board of Commendations, with the consent of His Majesty, Emperor Steven Mandrake I, that you be awarded the Solar Cross."

Just above a wisp of wind, Clearwater heard stereo gasps from Taula and Melanie. The colonel continued.

"You and your loved ones are invited to the Solar Cathedral on a date to be determined. There His Majesty, on behalf of the citizens of the Solar Empire, shall present you with this honorable merit, the first awarded to any member of the Solar Armed Forces in the present conflict. Along with this commendation, you are inducted into the Fraternity of the Cross and shall be granted immediately all rights and privileges appropriate."

The colonel and the lieutenants still at attention raised their hands, now saluting him. Clearwater tugged with his right hand until Froggy let go. He brought his hand up and returned the salute.

"Congratulations, Captain," the colonel said, handing over the slate. "I'm sure you're eager to visit with your family. We'll show ourselves out."

Clearwater watched them go. The voices behind him, and the tugging at his hands, seemed so far away. A Solar Cross, for him? He held the slate ahead of him, reading the words the colonel had just spoken. His knees did not seem to be working, and he heard voices of concern as he sat roughly on the deck. His eyes rested on the fountain.

Well, Dad, I guess I have one, too.

With a long breath, Clearwater returned to his feet.

"Let's go inside," he said, marshaling the clan back toward the door.

"We, we have to celebrate," Melanie was stammering as they returned inside. "I'll start cooking. Ryan, David, I need your help."

Clearwater watched them leave for the kitchen. Nana had always cooked, all the way up to the point that she could no longer stand. Such a short time ago, he could hear the words, see her and Melanie together as master and apprentice. *Cooking is no less art than painting or poetry. A good artist suffers for their art. There's no suffering if you print it all.*

Clearwater looked down to Froggy, still holding so tight to his fingers that her little knuckles were turning white. His message before the Crossroads. More must have gotten through the filters than he expected. Ryan and David wanted to know about the commando and his ship. But Imperial Rose's number one fan never even mentioned her.

"Froggy, have you been watching the news?"

She nodded.

"You don't believe what they said about Imperial Rose, do you?"

"No," Froggy answered. "She's not bad."

Clearwater reached into his pocket and removed the holograph. With a curious expression, Froggy took it with her free hand. Her eyes became stars as the device illuminated the hologram, Imperial Rose together with the Twins. Somehow Froggy's eyes got even wider when she heard the Rose's voice.

"Froggy. Life is a wonderful thing. Cherish it, and everyone you share it with."

Clearwater grinned as he watched her, mouth agape, hopping on her toes.

"Oh," she managed to choke out. "Oh! Oh!"

The toe-hopping progressed to bouncing, and she tried to twirl but was not willing to release his hand to do it.

"Thank you! Thank you! Thank you!" she exclaimed, still staring at the holograph. Froggy held the device to her chest.

"You should go put it in your room," Clearwater urged. Froggy moved as if she were about to race up the stairs before stopping to look at her hand in his. "My hand will still be here when you get back."

With a grin she released his hand and thundered up the stairs.

"I think you just made her year," Taula said.

What he did next carried no forethought. He slipped his hand under the rear tail of her pahri and pinched her rump.

"Ooh!" Taula jumped away from his hand before turning to him. There was no anger in the look she gave. More a surprised shock. He reached as if he were about to do it again, and her hands shot back to protect her rump as she stepped away. But she was smiling.

Perhaps it didn't hurt to be a little assertive.

>>NERVE HEIGHTENERS / MAXIMUM SENSITIVITY

Clearwater took a step, capturing Taula's waist with his left arm while his right found the wall. A moment later he had her pinned against it.

"Jonathan." Taula giggled. She tried to say more, but he silenced her with his lips. He did not close his eyes but instead glanced down as her arms wrapped around him. He held the kiss for as long as it suited him, only letting go when he was satisfied.

"Jonathan." Taula was trying not to laugh. "Just what's gotten into you?"

"Don't worry about what's gotten into me," he answered. "Worry about what's going to get into *you*."

The stomping of fast feet on the stairs was enough for him to release

Taula from the wall. The tiny hand soon reclaimed his right. Imperial Rose was in her room now, but big brother was here.

"I think I'd like to make some cookies," Clearwater mused. "Froggy, want to collect walnuts with me?"

"Okay!"

With a smile he wrapped his left arm around Taula and led them outside.

CHAPTER
30D

D AYS SEEMED TO GO by like hours. Meeting after meeting. Briefing after briefing. Council after council. From his time in the Armadas, Steven had the augments that enabled him to stay awake for days at a time when it was necessary, but it caught up eventually. It always did. Steven's mouth hung open, and his upper eyelids drooped so far, he navigated more by memory than sight. The moment the doors of his domicile closed, his one thought was of his bed. His clothes made a trail behind him as he made for that promised land.

One of the servitors was cleaning. In another circumstance, he would have noticed she was new, and he would have soon been formulating designs on her flesh. Yet he did not notice her at all, even as she trailed behind him to pick up the attire as he shed it.

Steven paused at the door. Natalie and Jasmine were already in bed. Not unexpected at 03:00. The only illumination inside came from the room he was in. Steven was ready to climb in when he saw the glimmer near Natalie's head. The promise of sleep seemed to be sucking what little energy he still had. He could no longer manage to get his feet off the floor. He shuffled around the bed, where he saw the glass bottle still clenched in Natalie's hand.

"Natalie," Steven whispered with a frown. He took the bottle, and her hand followed, unwilling to let go. His frown deepened as he gently pried her fingers from the bottle's neck. He was about to set the bottle on the nightstand when he noticed a single drink still inside. With a shrug, he drank it.

His face twisted as the liquid went down his throat like a war between bees and hornets. The moment his throat was clear, the air fled his lungs as though his body were desperate to eject the tonic. It transitioned to gagging as Steven glared down at Natalie and tossed the bottle aside.

He had underestimated her connection to his family, but this was not the way to deal with it. In the morning, they would have to talk about it. Steven moved toward the other side of the bed. It couldn't be tomorrow. He had a meeting with the Army in the morning. Evening? No, he'd be talking to Justice about their ongoing investigation until the late hours. The day after? That was out, too. Weekend then. He could probably fit some time in there.

Rather than risk waking Natalie, he completed his trip to the opposite side, by Jasmine. Intent on climbing over her, he pulled up the blankets before pausing again. Jasmine's attire drew his eye—some kind of strappy lingerie and high stockings. What was going on here? He glared at her for more than a minute before his addled brain pieced it together. She sent him a message hours ago asking if he would be home in time for dinner. He told her he would, not intending to lie. But then news from the Hourglass came in, and his plans changed. Whatever she had planned, it wasn't going to happen tonight.

Steven climbed over her. The stench of marvat was enough for him to put his back to her as he wrapped an arm around Natalie. A happy sigh escaped him, and Steven closed his eyes.

Yet they opened again, almost immediately. There was a new energy. He no longer felt the anchors of fatigue trying to pull him down, and a new chain seemed to be drawing him. Action came before thought. He slid out of bed, realizing afterward that he moved through Jasmine rather than over her.

When Steven turned back, Jasmine and Natalie were still in bed. So was he. For a moment of bewilderment, he stared at his own back, contemplating the surreal. But the new chain was pulling, and he turned back toward the door.

The living room he expected was nowhere to be found. He could not even make out walls, only mist. The swirling vortex exposed shapes, chairs, in a circle ahead of him. He walked toward them, hearing voices as he closed in.

"He rejected your offer, Elder. Is it not now time to destroy him?"

The words were not Solar, yet he understood them. He was closer to a chair now. With the next step, a ball of light like a golden sun became visible. It sat at the circle of many chairs in a ring. It should have blinded him the moment he opened the door, but his gaze didn't waver.

"The choice is regrettable, but acceptance was desired, not expected."

The body he lacked shuddered with the chorus of voices. It could not be mistaken for any other. But the other voice, the one he somehow understood. What was it? Who was it? The nearest chair was close enough now, and Steven sat in it.

"I don't understand." The alien voice beseeched answer. "Why ask, if the answer would be no?"

Steven sat up straighter, trying to see through the mist. To see the source of the voice. But it was futile. He could only sense the presence of an alien mind.

"He was created to dominate, not submit. Long have Anagram and the Wayward sought to turn one of my lieutenants against me. In him, and his rejection, they believe they found success. But their plan spells ruin. The opening of the second door began before the first was shut."

"It was all a trick?" the alien voice seemed to cry out in despair. "A deception?"

"A trap executed in success, despite your deviation."

The mist began to move, and Steven sensed the new presence before he saw it. Flowing tendrils seemed to glow in the darkest of black. Indorai stood across the room. The mist seemed to allow Steven to see its form—a scalp with horns, and inhumanly long fingers. Indorai's tendrils were wrapped about him, all but one, which held the glowing sphere. The moment Steven noticed it, he felt a pain so sharp, so precise, that it corrected him. He had lived a life knowing the word *agony* without ever truly knowing what it was. Until now. His stomach churned as his eyes seemed to be drawn into the glow, and breath became laborious. The sensations came from that sphere.

"Fortunately, Oul'sor, your task was not the critical venture."

Steven knew that name. It passed through his ears, yet it never seemed to enter his mind. The confusion managed to break his gaze on the golden sphere, but it did not last. By the time he could think about the name, he lost track of his thoughts.

What was he trying to think of?

The sphere drew his eyes again.

"What is that?" His whisper was so low that even he did not hear it. There was a sentience before his eyes, and in gazing, he learned so much that he only thought he knew before. Steven thought he had an understanding of terror. He thought he grasped the idea of agony. The golden sapience in Indorai's tendril taught him in moments that he knew neither. The deeper he gazed into it, the more he sensed screaming he could not hear.

Back in the bed, his throat clenched, and his gut drew in as his stomach tried to empty contents it did not have. Steven pressed a hand to his face and leveraged his gaze away from the sphere. Whatever it was, there was a sapience about it. It felt pain and fear, it understood them, and it would remember them.

"She proved more elusive than anticipated." The quadraphonic voice filled the room. "But the division, less so. We have what we need."

The tendril that bound the sphere flicked away, vanishing into the mist.

A new question came from the alien voice, belonging to the entity Steven could not see.

"And what of me? Am I to remain in this place?"

"For a time."

"So, I am being punished then?"

"You are given opportunity to reflect. Twice you have indulged in defiance, and twice your defiance was accounted before it was enacted. Yet this time your defiance bore cost. Your purpose was to distract and prevent inhibition of the task. Not to kill for satisfaction of vengeance. Now a longer road must be taken. When you have reflected on the error of your ways, Indorai shall retrieve you."

"And what of the Crykeeper now?"

Crykeeper? Steven perked up. Victor? How was he involved in this?

"He takes the shape of his container and thus becomes the trap. He has many purposes to serve and will fulfill them all."

"But if he has already rejected you, how—"

"Into his line, I bred many hungers: flesh, wealth, glory, conquest. But you cannot take from one who has nothing. In deprivation, he has lived, but

soon I shall feed his hungers. Those hungers shall grow. In the embrace of feast, he will fear return to famine."

Steven did not hear it as much as he felt the pained grumble in the mist, a rage that seemed to stretch and swirl faster through the room.

"I know it hurts to see plenty heaped on your hate, but remember whom you obey. For I shall make of you a mighty people and craft within you the destiny of highest potential. They shall all reap the rewards of your suffering."

Steven flinched when the mist shifted, now rotating the opposite direction. The alien presence was gone.

"Steven."

Steven sat up straighter in the chair. "What is this? Who was that?"

"Another to whom promises are made, and in whom promise exists. But of concern that is not yours."

Having this creature dropping into his thoughts and dreams at will was becoming something of an inconvenience.

"You sit on the throne I promised you. The time to covet has ended, and to act begins. Your adversaries multiply, and the Empire must be ready. Your people still do not perceive the threat. You must act with the initiative they lack."

Steven shifted in the chair. "What about Simmonne? And what does Victor have to do with this?"

"I told you, your sister has her own destiny. So, too, does your friend. Each to play their part in the dawn of a new era. Soon Indorai shall begin to remove those who are a threat to your leadership. Marshal your strength now, Steven. The great war of your time comes."

Steven listened in silence as the days ahead were laid out before him.

CHAPTER
30E

WITHIN THE COMBINE, THE intelligence community had always been responsible for diplomatic relations. Every ambassador, counselor, and other functionary had training in both intelligence and counter-intelligence. Most who bore such titles were former agents. That was why Dolum, Warlord of the Clandestine, now stood aboard the destroyer *Patient Hunter*.

On the ship's bridge, he grumbled as he watched the timer ticking toward zero. He had objected in the most strenuous way possible to this ship being sent. Objected to the prospect of allowing a power they knew so little about seeing one of the Deep Fleet's newest and most advanced ships. To be an enemy's enemy did not make one a friend; it made one useful. But so often, useful things were disposed of when that usefulness expired. Too many of the warlords were too focused on the Empire. They were not thinking of the potential next wars or the ones after them. Yet, Hahk'xess had insisted as had several others. Enough of them that the result would not have changed had Oul'sor been there to cast his vote.

Dolum and the crew of the *Patient Hunter* had traveled deep into the local supercluster. Far beyond any point the Empire had explored with any vigor. The foundations of the coming summit had been laid more than a year before war began.

Dolum stood at the rear of the ship's bridge. He was not alone.

"Be at ease, Dolum."

The Vaar turned toward the sound of the four voices but saw no one. *Stay out of my mind.*

"Would you prefer the entire crew hear our conversation, Spymaster?" Indorai asked, and Dolum flinched when he felt the tendril on his shoulder.

Your voices do not seem as strong. Are you ill?

"You honor me with your concern. But pay no worry to me."

"Warlord?" The ship's captain swiveled in his central chair to face him. "We will arrive in five turns."

Dolum nodded and turned for the bridge's exit.

"I wish to depart as soon as we arrive." He spoke loud enough to be heard before his voice quieted. "Better to get it over quickly."

"I tried to give your people the key to victory, Dolum." The four voices followed him on his path to the primary shuttle bay. *"But with the loss of the Crossroads, that key is gone. A new one must be made."*

Dolum did not answer. Many on the Council, Hahk'xess included, had hoped that the Crossroads would be enough to deliver victory against the Empire. But Dolum knew better. He had seen the projections, the calculations. The Empire would increase its supply of personnel and war matériel in one year by more than the Combine had in five. Once committed to total war, the Empire's shipyards could turn out a dozen destroyers for each new one constructed by the Deep Fleet. With their soulless arens and AI, they could drown the Deep Fleet and the Deep Marines in a never-ending stream of reinforcements.

The war could not be won without striking deep into the Empire. Demolish their shipyards. Destroy the hub worlds of their astranet. Break their lazy decadent population of their ability to tolerate the war. The Combine could not do it alone. The losses would destroy the Deep Fleet and marines. Even if the Empire did not choose to invade, and it would, the Combine would not be able to hold itself together. But the Empire would invade, and the Vaar would share the same fate as so many other species. To be little more than slaves to the destiny authored by humanity.

That could not be allowed to happen. The species that rose from the ashes of the Return to Zero, banished the Gray Fleet, and destroyed the Rethan—that species could not be allowed to fall and have stolen from it the destiny it had so many times earned.

Dolum came to a stop. He was working himself up. Aging arteries did not contract the way they used to, and his blood pressure was rising too high. It had dilated his pupils, overloading him with light and color. Several calming breaths slowed his arteries, and he stepped onto the tram. As he sat, he looked down at himself and the silver polish of his armor. It had been so long since he had attended an occasion requiring such preening attire.

"Are you vexed, Dolum?"

Dolum turned toward the sound of the voice but still saw no one. The tram brought him to the shuttle bay where the small craft waited. Dolum ascended the boarding ramp and reached up to grab the handlebar above with one hand. Once pleasantries were exchanged with the pilot, he was silent.

"Warlord, we have completed the transpatial jump. Rendezvous partners detected on station," the ship's captain reported. "May we initiate contact protocol?"

"Initiate," Dolum answered.

"Code signals are good. You are clear for launch, Warlord."

"Pilot," Dolum barked. "Take us out."

Dolum kept his hand on the long rail above as he moved up toward the cockpit. A pair of Viss acknowledged his order and set the ship in motion. Through the transparency ahead, Dolum watched the hangar door open, and the shuttle soon plunged itself into the Empty Ocean. When the pilots turned the shuttle, Dolum saw the other two ships at this rendezvous.

One ship was almost colorless, its black hull reflecting only traces of ultraviolet. Its body was a long cylinder with a bulging nose. A pair of wings extended in a forward sweep from the rear quarter. At the tip of each wing, two large guns were bundled with one atop the other. The second ship was more appealing to his eyes. Its hull was bright, practically a rainbow to Vaar. Its hull was roughly triangular, with all three of its points canting down. Neither of them compared to the beauty of the *Patient Hunter*.

Only these three ships were present, as had been the agreement. One destroyer-type ship for each party. Together the warships had formed a triangle around a small space station built for this event, courtesy of the hosts of this summit. Protocol was to let various diplomatic staff go aboard first, just in case perfidy awaited. But Dolum had opted to go first. Despite all his misgivings, desperate times, and measures, he had been the driving force that initiated this conclave.

"We are cleared to board, Warlord," the Viss on his left announced.

"Go in."

The space station had the appearance of a giant bolt, flanged near its base. It was toward one of those flanges that the shuttle was now moving. A reception party awaited him, and Oul'sor sneered at the infantry that waited. Metal. So much metal. Spindly skeletons covered in bulky armored plate. Smooth faces that had no features.

The shuttle touched down, and Dolum wasted little time departing the shuttle. The metal creatures soon flanked him, guiding him toward a disc recessed into the floor of the shuttle bay. He stepped through.

In a flash of light, Dolum stood at a segmented door. Pieces slid up and down to grant him entry into the meeting room. A wide chamber bore a triangular chair at the center. There three beings stood, one of them Indorai.

"Ah!" Indorai proclaimed, raising one of his arms toward Dolum. "At last the final party arrives."

Dolum's fingers tapped against his thigh before he walked forward to join them at the table. One of the metal aliens stood to his left. To his right was another. Dolum could see very little of the creature on the right; its body was enclosed in armored robes. Its shape was vaguely like that of a Vaar, but he saw no flesh. The four fingers of each hand poking out of the sleeves were covered in metal. Beneath its hood was a mask with a single circular sensor in the forehead. A pair of metal wings with blade-like feathers extended from its back. The creature's metal was black, so dark, it was practically water of the Empty Ocean. Its robes by contrast practically radiated in red and infrared.

Indorai extended one arm to the robed creature.

"Warlord Dolum. May I present Gaw'zai, High Rector of the Great Assembly."

Dolum brought his fists together and nodded. Gaw'zai did the same. Dolum turned as Indorai raised his other hand to the metal alien. It lacked the armored plates of the soldiers who had escorted him, but its body was much larger, taller, in fact, than Dolum himself. Its limbs were bulkier, squared rather than rounded. Its metal hands were simply flat plates that bore no obvious digits.

"Warlord Dolum," Indorai continued. "I present the Central Coordinator of the Praetheen Unity."

Dolum brought his fists together once again and gave a second bow. He watched as metal turned to liquid and flowed. The featureless hands of the metal being formed fingers, and they, in turn, formed fists. A metallic clang echoed in the room as the machine-alien brought its fists together.

A vertical line appeared on the screen the Praetheen had deployed from its face. That line oscillated as the creature spoke. Dolum heard its words in well-articulated Ivex.

"Warlord Dolum, the Praetheen Unity welcomes you. It is significant to finally meet in physical form."

Even its voice was that of a machine, something between digital and mechanical. There was an almost strumming effect in its tones as it articulated the growls to form the words.

"Thank you for receiving me, Central Coordinator."

"Has our technology served you well, Warlord?" the Praetheen asked.

Dolum nodded. "Your aid has been quite valuable. It is my hope that our scientists might soon add their own innovations to yours."

The Praetheen extended his arm toward the table even as the metal that had formed his fingers flowed back into his arm. Indorai remained on his feet, while Dolum and the other two took their chairs.

"Remember the great import of this meeting," Indorai spoke to all three. "Two of you have traveled quite far to be here. One of you has already walked the path the others face. Let it be here that your destinies, and those of your people, are decided."

To Be Continued . . .
Solar Winds—Blood and Stars

Meet author Bryan G. Shewmaker
and get updates for forthcoming books
in the Solar Winds series!

www.TheEncephalon.com
www.Facebook.com/SolarWindsSeries

www.ingramcontent.com/pod-product-compliance
Lightning Source LLC
Chambersburg PA
CBHW030837030726
47495CB00005B/1259